THE PORTABLE FAULKNER

The Portable

FAULKNER

Edited by Malcolm Cowley

THE VIKING PRESS • NEW YORK

1954

THE PORTABLE FAULKNER

PUBLISHED BY THE VIKING PRESS IN APRIL 1946

SECOND PRINTING OCTOBER 1949

THIRD PRINTING JANUARY 1951

FOURTH PRINTING APRIL 1954

FIFTH PRINTING DECEMBER 1956

SIXTH PRINTING MARCH 1959

Part III of the Introduction originally formed part of a separate essay, "William Faulkner's Legend of the South," which appeared in the summer, 1945, issue of the Sewanee Review. It is reprinted here by permission of Prentice-Hall, Inc., which holds the book publication rights on that essay.

SET IN LYDIAN, BRUSH, AND CALEDONIA TYPES AND PRINTED IN U. S. A. BY THE COLONIAL PRESS INC.

CONTENTS

5. The End of an Order

6. Mississippi Flood

7. Modern Times

INTRODUCTION

I

WHEN the war was over—the other war—William Faulkner went back to Oxford, Mississippi. He had served in the Royal Air Force in 1918. Now he was home again and not at home, or at least not able to accept the postwar world. He was writing poems, most of them worthless, and dozens of immature but violent and effective stories, while at the same time he was brooding over his own situation and the decline of the South. Slowly the brooding thoughts arranged themselves into the whole interconnected pattern that would form the substance of his later novels.

This pattern, which almost all his critics have overlooked, was based on what he saw in Oxford or remembered from his childhood; on scraps of family tradition (the Falkners, as they spelled the name, had played their part in the history of the state); on kitchen dialogues between the black cook and her amiable husband; on Saturday-afternoon gossip in Courthouse Square; on stories told by men in overalls squatting on their heels while they passed around a fruit-jar full of white corn liquor; on all the sources familiar to a small-town Mississippi boy—but the whole of it was elaborated, transformed, given convulsive life by his emotions; until, by the simple intensity of feeling, the figures in it became a little more than human, became heroic or diabolical, became symbols of the old South, of war and reconstruction, of commerce and machinery destroying the standards of the past. There in Oxford,

1

Faulkner performed a labor of imagination that has not been equaled in our time, and a double labor: first, to invent a Mississippi county that was like a mythical kingdom, but was complete and living in all its details; second, to make his story of Yoknapatawpha County stand as a parable or legend of all the Deep South.

For this double task, Faulkner was better equipped by talent and background than he was by schooling. He was born in New Albany, Mississippi, on September 25, 1897; he was the oldest of four brothers. The family soon moved to Oxford, where he attended the public school, but without being graduated from high school. For a year after the war, he was a student at the University of Mississippi, in Oxford, where veterans could then matriculate without a high-school diploma; but he neglected his classroom work and left without taking a degree. He had less of a formal education than any other good writer of his time, except Hart Crane—less even than Hemingway, who never went to college, but who learned to speak three foreign languages and studied writing in Paris from the best masters. Faulkner taught himself, largely, as he says, by "undirected and uncorrelated reading." Among the authors either mentioned or echoed in his early stories and poems are Keats, Balzac, Flaubert, Swinburne, Mallarmé, Wilde, Housman, Joyce, Eliot, Sherwood Anderson, and E. E. Cummings, with fainter suggestions of Hemingway (in a fishing scene), Dos Passos (in the spelling of compound words), and Scott Fitzgerald. The poems he wrote in those days were wholly derivative, but his prose from the beginning was a form of poetry; and in spite of the echoes it was always his own. He traveled less than any of his writing contemporaries. After a succession of odd jobs in Oxford, there was a brief period when he lived in New

Orleans with Sherwood Anderson and met the literary crowd—he even satirized them in a very bad early novel, *Mosquitoes;* then he went to New York, where for a few unhappy months he clerked in a bookstore; in 1925 he took a long walking trip in Europe without settling on the Left Bank. Except for recent visits to Hollywood, the rest of his life has been spent in the town where he grew up, less than forty miles from his birthplace.

Although Oxford, Mississippi, is the seat of a university, it is even less of a literary center than was Salem, Massachusetts, during Hawthorne's early years as a writer; and Faulkner himself has shown an even greater dislike than Hawthorne for literary society. His novels are the books of a man who broods about literature but doesn't often discuss it with his friends; there is no ease about them, no feeling that they come from a background of taste refined by argument and of opinions held in common. They make me think of a passage from Henry James's little book on Hawthorne:

The best things come, as a general thing, from the talents that are members of a group; every man works better when he has companions working in the same line, and yielding to the stimulus of suggestion, comparison, emulation. Great things of course have been done by solitary workers; but they have usually been done with double the pains they would have cost if they had been produced in more genial circumstances. The solitary worker loses the profit of example and discussion; he is apt to make awkward experiments; he is in the nature of the case more or less of an empiric. The empiric may, as I say, be treated by the world as an expert; but the drawbacks and discomforts of empiricism remain to him, and are in fact increased by the suspicion that is mingled with his gratitude, of a want in the public taste of a sense of the proportion of things.

Like Hawthorne, Faulkner is a solitary worker by

choice, and he has done great things not only with double the pains to himself that they might have cost if produced in more genial circumstances, but sometimes also with double the pains to the reader. Two or three of his books as a whole and many of them in part are awkward experiments. All of them are full of overblown words like "imponderable," "immortal," "immutable," and "immemorial" that he would have used with more discretion, or not at all, if he had followed Hemingway's example and served an apprenticeship to an older writer. He is a most uncertain judge of his own work, and he has no reason to believe that the world's judgment of it is any more to be trusted; indeed, there is no American author who would be justified in feeling more suspicion of "a want in the public taste of a sense of the proportion of things." His early novels were overpraised, usually for the wrong reasons; his later and in many ways better novels have been obstinately condemned or simply neglected; and in 1945 all his seventeen books were out of print, with some of them unobtainable in the second-hand bookshops.

Even his warm admirers, of whom there are many— no author has a higher standing among his fellow novelists—have sometimes shown a rather vague idea of what he is trying to do; and Faulkner himself has never explained. He holds a curious attitude toward the public that appears to be lofty indifference (as in the one preface he wrote, for the Modern Library edition of *Sanctuary*), but really comes closer to being a mixture of skittery distrust and pure unconsciousness that the public exists. He doesn't furnish information or correct misstatements about himself (most of the biographical sketches that deal with him are full of preposterous errors). He doesn't care which way his name is spelled in the records, with or without the "u"—"Either way suits me," he said. Once he has finished a book, he is apparently not concerned with the question how it will be presented, to what sort of audience; and sometimes he doesn't bother to keep a private copy of it. He said in a letter, "I think I have written a lot and sent it off to print before I actually realized strangers might read it." Others might say that Faulkner, at least in those early days, was not so much composing stories for the public as telling them to himself—like a lonely child in his imaginary world, but also like a writer of genius.

II

Faulkner's mythical kingdom is a county in northern Mississippi, on the border between the sand hills covered with scrubby pine and the black earth of the river bottoms. Except for the storekeepers, mechanics, and professional men who live in Jefferson, the county seat, all the inhabitants are farmers or woodsmen. Except for a little lumber, their only product is baled cotton for the Memphis market. A few of them live in big plantation houses, the relics of another age, and more of them in substantial wooden farmhouses; but most of them are tenants, no better housed than slaves on good plantations before the Civil War. Yoknapatawpha County—"William Faulkner, sole owner and proprietor," as he inscribed on one of the maps he drew—has a population of 15,611 persons scattered over 2400 square miles. It sometimes seems to me that every house or hovel has been described in one of Faulkner's novels; and that all the people of the imaginary county, black and white, townsmen, farmers, and housewives, have played their parts in one connected story.

He has so far written nine books wholly concerned with Yoknapatawpha County and its people, who also appear in parts of three others and in thirty or more uncollected stories. *Sartoris* was the first of the books to be published, in the spring of 1929; it is a romantic and partly unconvincing novel, but with many fine scenes in it, like the hero's visit to a family of independent pine-hill farmers; and it states most of the themes that the author would later develop at length. *The Sound and the Fury* was written before *Sartoris,* but wasn't published until six months later; it describes the fall of the Compson family, and it was the first of Faulkner's novels to be widely discussed. The books that followed, in the Yoknapatawpha series, are *As I Lay Dying* (1930), about the death and burial of Addie Bundren; *Sanctuary* (1931), always the most popular of his novels; *Light in August* (1932), in many ways the best; *Absalom, Absalom!* (1936), about Colonel Sutpen and his ambition to found a family; *The Unvanquished* (1938), a book of interrelated stories about the Sartoris dynasty; *The Wild Palms* (1939), half of which deals with a convict from back in the pine hills; *The Hamlet* (1940), a novel about the Snopes clan; and *Go Down, Moses* (1942), in which Faulkner's theme is the Negroes. There are also many Yoknapatawpha stories in *These Thirteen* (1931) and *Dr. Martino* (1934), besides other stories privately printed (like "Miss Zilphia Gant") or published in magazines and still to be collected or used as episodes in novels.

Just as Balzac, who seems to have inspired the series, divided his *Comédie Humaine* into "Scenes of Parisian Life," "Scenes of Provincial Life," "Scenes of Private Life," so Faulkner might divide his work into a number of cycles: one about the planters and their descendants, one about the townspeople of Jefferson, one about the poor whites, one about the Indians (consisting of stories already written but never brought together), and one about the Negroes. Or again, if he adopted a division by families, there would be the Compson-Sartoris saga, the still unfinished Snopes saga, the McCaslin saga, dealing with the white and black descendants of Carothers McCaslin, and the Ratliff-Bundren saga, devoted to the backwoods farmers of Frenchman's Bend. All the cycles or sagas are closely interconnected; it is as if each new book was a chord or segment of a total situation always existing in the author's mind. Sometimes a short story is the sequel to an earlier novel. For example, we read in *Sartoris* that Byron Snopes stole a packet of letters from Narcissa Benbow; and in "There Was a Queen," a story published five years later, we learn how Narcissa got the letters back again. Sometimes, on the other hand, a novel contains the sequel to a story; and we discover from an incidental reference in *The Sound and the Fury* that the Negro woman whose terror of death was described in "That Evening Sun" had later been murdered by her husband, who left her body in a ditch for the vultures. Sometimes an episode has a more complicated history. Thus, in the first chapter of *Sanctuary,* we hear about the Old Frenchman place, a ruined mansion near which the people of the neighborhood had been "digging with secret and sporadic optimism for gold which the builder was reputed to have buried somewhere about the place when Grant came through the country on his Vicksburg campaign." Later this digging for gold served as the subject of a story published in the *Saturday Evening Post:* "Lizards in Jamshyd's Courtyard." Still later the story was completely rewritten and became the last chapter of *The Hamlet.*

As one book leads into another, Faulkner sometimes falls into inconsistencies of detail. There is a sewing-machine agent named V.K. Suratt who appears in *Sartoris* and some of the later stories. By the time we reach *The Hamlet,* his name has changed to Ratliff, although his character remains the same (and his age, too, for all the twenty years that separate the backgrounds of the two novels). Henry Armstid is a likable figure in *As I Lay Dying* and *Light in August;* in *The Hamlet* he is mean and half-demented. His wife, whose character remains consistent, is called Lula in one book and Martha in another; in the third she is nameless. There is an Indian chief named Doom who appears in several stories; he starts as the father of Issetibeha and ends as his grandson. The mansion called Sutpen's Hundred was built of brick at the beginning of *Absalom, Absalom!* but at the end of the novel it is all wood and inflammable except for the chimneys. But these errors are comparatively few and inconsequential, considering the scope of Faulkner's series; and I should judge that most of them are afterthoughts rather than oversights.

All his books in the Yoknapatawpha saga are part of the same living pattern. It is this pattern, and not the printed volumes in which part of it is recorded, that is Faulkner's real achievement. Its existence helps to explain one feature of his work: that each novel, each long or short story, seems to reveal more than it states explicitly and to have a subject bigger than itself. All the separate works are like blocks of marble from the same quarry: they show the veins and faults of the mother rock. Or else—to use a rather strained figure—they are like wooden planks that were cut, not from a log, but from a still living tree. The planks are planed and chiseled into their final shapes, but the tree itself heals over the wound and continues to grow. Faulkner is incapable of telling the same story twice without adding new details. In the present volume I wanted to use part of *The Sound and the Fury,* the novel that

deals with the fall of the Compson family. I thought
that the last part of the book would be most effective as
a separate episode, but still it depended too much on
what had gone before. Faulkner offered to write a very
brief introduction that would explain the relations of the
characters. What he finally sent me is the much longer
passage here printed as an appendix: a genealogy of
the Compsons from their first arrival in this country.
Whereas the novel is confined to a period of eighteen
years ending in 1928, the genealogy goes back to the
battle of Culloden in 1745, and forward to the year
1945, when Jason, last of the Compson males, has sold
the family mansion, and Sister Caddy has last been
heard of as the mistress of a German general. The
novel that Faulkner wrote about the Compsons had
long ago been given its final shape; but the pattern or
body of legend behind the novel—and behind all his
other books—was still developing.

Although the pattern is presented in terms of a single
Mississippi county, it can be extended to the Deep
South as a whole; and Faulkner always seems conscious
of its wider application. He might have been thinking
of his own novels when he described the ledgers in the
commissary of the McCaslin plantation, in *Go Down,
Moses*. They recorded, he said, "that slow trickle of
molasses and meal and meat, of shoes and straw hats
and overalls, of plowlines and collars and heelbolts
and clevises, which returned each fall as cotton"—in a
sense they were local and limited; but they were also
"the continuation of that record which two hundred
years had not been enough to complete and another
hundred would not be enough to discharge; that chronicle which was a whole land in miniature, which multiplied and compounded was the entire South."

"Tell about the South," says Quentin Compson's roommate at Harvard, a Canadian named Shreve Mc-Cannon who is curious about the unknown region beyond the Ohio. "What's it like there?" he asks. "What do they do there? Why do they live there? Why do they live at all?" And Quentin, whose background is a little like that of Faulkner himself and who sometimes seems to speak for him—Quentin answers, "You can't understand it. You would have to be born there." Nevertheless, he tells a long and violent story that he regards as the essence of the Deep South, which is not so much a mere region as it is, in Quentin's mind, an incomplete and frustrated nation trying to relive its legendary past.

The story he tells—I am trying to summarize the plot of *Absalom, Absalom!*—is that of a mountain boy named Thomas Sutpen whose family drifted into the Virginia lowlands, where his father found odd jobs on a plantation. One day the father sent him with a message to the big house, but he was turned away at the door by a black man in livery. Puzzled and humiliated, the mountain boy was seized upon by the lifelong ambition to which he would afterward refer as "the design." He too would own a plantation with slaves and a liveried butler; he would build a mansion as big as any of those in the Tidewater; and he would have a son to inherit his wealth.

A dozen years later, Sutpen appeared in the frontier town of Jefferson, where he managed to obtain a hundred square miles of land from the Chickasaws. With the help of twenty wild Negroes from the jungle and a French architect, he set about building the largest house in northern Mississippi, using timbers from the forest and bricks that his Negroes molded and baked on the spot; it was as if his mansion, Sutpen's Hundred, had been literally torn from the soil. Only one man in Jefferson—he was Quentin's grandfather, General Compson—ever learned how and where Sutpen had acquired his slaves. He had shipped to Haiti from Virginia, worked as overseer on a sugar plantation and married the rich planter's daughter, who had borne him a son. Then, finding that his wife had Negro blood, he had simply put her away, with her child and her fortune, while keeping the twenty slaves as a sort of indemnity.

In Jefferson, Sutpen married again. This time his wife belonged to a pious family of the neighborhood, and she bore him two children, Henry and Judith. He became the biggest cotton planter in Yoknapatawpha County, and it seemed that his "design" had already been fulfilled. At this moment, however, Henry came home from the University of Mississippi with an older and worldlier new friend, Charles Bon, who was in reality Sutpen's son by his first marriage. Charles became engaged to Judith. Sutpen learned his identity and, without making a sign of recognition, ordered him from the house. Henry, who refused to believe that Charles was his half-brother, renounced his birthright and followed him to New Orleans. In 1861, all the male Sutpens went off to war, and all of them survived four years of fighting. Then, in the spring of 1865, Charles suddenly decided to marry Judith, even though he was certain by now that she was his half-sister. Henry rode beside him all the way back to Sutpen's Hundred, but tried to stop him at the gate, killed him when he insisted on going ahead with his plan, told Judith what he had done, and disappeared.

But Quentin's story of the Deep South does not end with the war. Colonel Sutpen came home, he says, to find his wife dead, his son a fugitive, his slaves dispersed (they had run away even before they were freed by the Union army), and most of his land about to be seized for debt. Still determined to carry out "the design," he did not even pause for breath before undertaking to restore his house and plantation to what they had been. The effort failed and Sutpen was reduced to keeping a crossroads store. Now in his sixties, he tried again to beget a son; but his wife's younger sister, Miss Rosa Coldfield, was outraged by his proposal ("Let's try it," he had said, "and if it's a boy we'll get married"); and later poor Milly Jones, with whom he had an affair, gave birth to a baby girl. At that Sutpen abandoned hope and provoked Milly's grandfather into killing him. Judith survived her father for a time, as did the half-caste son of Charles Bon by a New Orleans octoroon. After the death of these two by yellow fever, the great house was haunted rather than inhabited by an ancient mulatto woman, Sutpen's daughter by one of his slaves. The fugitive Henry Sutpen came home to die; the townspeople heard of his illness and sent an ambulance after him; but old Clytie thought they were arresting him for murder and set fire to Sutpen's Hundred. The only survival of the conflagration was Jim Bond, a half-witted creature who was Charles Bon's grandson.

"Now I want you to tell me just one thing more," Shreve McCannon says after hearing the story. "Why do you hate the South?"—"I don't hate it," Quentin says quickly, at once. "I don't hate it," he repeats, speaking for the author as well as himself. *I don't hate it,* he thinks, panting in the cold air, the iron New England dark; *I don't. I don't hate it! I don't hate it!*

The reader cannot help wondering why this somber and, at moments, plainly incredible story had so seized upon Quentin's mind that he trembled with excitement when telling it and felt that it revealed the essence of the Deep South. It seems to belong in the realm of Gothic romances, with Sutpen's Hundred taking the place of the haunted castle on the Rhine, with Colonel Sutpen as Faust and Charles Bon as Manfred. Then slowly it dawns on you that most of the characters and incidents have a double meaning; that besides their place in the story, they also serve as symbols or metaphors with a general application. Sutpen's great design, the land he stole from the Indians, the French architect who built his house with the help of wild Negroes from the jungle, the woman of mixed blood whom he married and disowned, the unacknowledged son who ruined him, the poor white whom he wronged and who killed him in anger, the final destruction of the mansion like the downfall of a social order: all these might belong to a tragic fable of Southern history. With a little cleverness, the whole novel might be explained as a connected and logical allegory, but this, I think, would be going far beyond the author's intention. First of all he was writing a story, and one that affected him deeply, but he was also brooding over a social situation. More or less unconsciously, the incidents in the story came to represent the forces and elements in the social situation, since the mind naturally works in terms of symbols and parallels. In Faulkner's case, this form of parallelism is not confined to *Absalom, Absalom!* It can be found in the whole fictional framework that he has been elaborating in novel after novel, until his work has become a myth or legend of the South.

I call it a legend because it is obviously no more intended as a historical account of the country south of the Ohio than *The Scarlet Letter* was intended as a history of Massachusetts or *Paradise Lost* as a factual description of the Fall. Briefly stated, the legend might run something like this: The Deep South was settled partly by aristocrats like the Sartoris clan and partly by new men like Colonel Sutpen. Both types of planters were determined to establish a lasting social order on the land they had seized from the Indians (that is, to leave sons behind them). They had the virtue of living single-mindedly by a fixed code; but there was also an inherent guilt in their "design," their way of life; it was slavery that put a curse on the land and brought about the Civil War. After the War was lost, partly as a result of their own mad heroism (for who else but men as brave as Jackson and Stuart could have frightened the Yankees into standing together and fighting back?) they tried to restore "the design" by other methods. But they no longer had the strength to achieve more than a partial success, even after they had freed their land from the carpetbaggers who followed the Northern armies. As time passed, moreover, the men of the old order found that they had Southern enemies too: they had to fight against a new exploiting class descended from the landless whites of slavery days. In this struggle between the clan of Sartoris and the unscrupulous tribe of Snopes, the Sartorises were defeated in advance by a traditional code that kept them from using the weapons of the enemy. As a price of victory, however, the Snopeses had to serve the mechanized civilization of the North, which was morally impotent in itself, but which, with the aid of its Southern retainers, ended by corrupting the Southern nation.

Faulkner's novels of contemporary Southern life continue the legend into a period that he regards as one of moral confusion and social decay. He is continually seeking in them for violent images to convey his sense of despair. *Sanctuary* is the most violent of all his novels; it is also the most popular and by no means the least important (in spite of Faulkner's comment that it was "a cheap idea . . . deliberately conceived to make money"). The story of Popeye and Temple Drake has more meaning than appears on a first hasty reading— the only reading that most of the critics have been willing to grant it. Popeye himself is one of several characters in Faulkner's novels who represent the mechanical civilization that has invaded and partly conquered the South. He is always described in mechanical terms: his eyes "looked like rubber knobs"; his face "just went awry, like the face of a wax doll set too near a hot fire and forgotten"; his tight suit and stiff hat were "all angles, like a modernistic lampshade"; and in general he had "that vicious depthless quality of stamped tin." Popeye was the son of a professional strikebreaker, from whom he had inherited syphilis, and the grandson of a pyromaniac. Like two other villains in Faulkner's novels, Joe Christmas and Januarius Jones, he had spent most of his childhood in an institution. He was the man "who made money and had nothing he could do with it, spend it for, since he knew that alcohol would kill him like poison, who had no friends and had never known a woman"—in other words, he was the compendium of all the hateful qualities that Faulkner assigns to finance capitalism. *Sanctuary* is not a connected allegory, as one critic explained it, but neither is it a mere accumulation of pointless horrors. It is an example of the Freudian method turned backward, being full of sexual nightmares that are in reality social symbols. It is somehow connected in the author's mind with what he regards as the rape and corruption of the South.

In all his novels dealing with the present, Faulkner makes it clear that the descendants of the old ruling caste have the wish but not the courage or the strength to prevent this new disaster. They are defeated by Popeye (like Horace Benbow), or they run away from him (like Gowan Stevens, who had gone to school at Virginia and learned to drink like a gentleman, but not to fight for his principles), or they are robbed and replaced in their positions of influence by the Snopeses (like old Bayard Sartoris, the president of the bank), or they drug themselves with eloquence and alcohol (like Quentin Compson's father), or they retire into the illusion of being inviolable Southern ladies (like Mrs. Compson, who says, "It can't be simply to flout and hurt me. Whoever God is, He would not permit that. I'm a lady."), or they dwell so much on the past that they are incapable of facing the present (like Reverend Hightower of *Light in August*), or they run from danger to danger (like young Bayard Sartoris) frantically seeking their own destruction. Faulkner's novels are full of well-meaning and even admirable persons, not only the grandsons of the cotton aristocracy, but also pine-hill farmers and storekeepers and sewing-machine agents and Negro cooks and sharecroppers; but they are almost all of them defeated by circumstances and they carry with them a sense of their own doom.

They also carry, whether heroes or villains, a curious sense of submission to their fate. "There is not one of Faulkner's characters," says André Gide in his dialogue on "The New American Novelists," "who properly speaking, has a soul"; and I think he means that not one of them exercises the faculty of conscious choice between good and evil. They are haunted, obsessed, driven forward by some inner necessity. Like Miss Rosa Coldfield, in *Absalom, Absalom!* they exist in "that dream state in which you run without moving from a terror in which you cannot believe, toward a safety in which you have no faith." Or, like the slaves freed by

General Sherman's army, in *The Unvanquished,* they blindly follow the roads toward any river, believing that it will be their Jordan:

They were singing, walking along the road singing, not even looking to either side. The dust didn't even settle for two days, because all that night they still passed; we sat up listening to them, and the next morning every few yards along the road would be the old ones who couldn't keep up any more, sitting or lying down and even crawling along, calling to the others to help them; and the others—the young ones—not stopping, not even looking at them. "Going to Jordan," they told me. "Going to cross Jordan."

All Faulkner's characters, black and white, are a little like that. They dig for gold frenziedly after they have lost their hope of finding it (like Henry Armstid in *The Hamlet* and Lucas Beauchamp in *Go Down, Moses*); or they battle against and survive a Mississippi flood for the one privilege of returning to the state prison farm (like the tall convict in "Old Man"); or, a whole family together, they carry a body through flood and fire and corruption to bury it in the cemetery at Jefferson (like the Bundrens in *As I Lay Dying*); or they tramp the roads week after week in search of men who had promised but never intended to marry them (like Lena Grove, the pregnant woman of *Light in August*); or, pursued by a mob, they turn at the end to meet and accept death (like Joe Christmas in the same novel). Even when they seem to be guided by a conscious purpose, like Colonel Sutpen, it is not something they have chosen by an act of will, but something that has taken possession of them: Sutpen's great design was "not what he wanted to do but what he just had to do, had to do it whether he wanted to or not, because if he did not do it he knew that he could never live with himself for the rest of his life." In the same way, Faulkner himself writes, not what he wants to, but what he just has to write whether he wants to or not.

IV

He is not primarily a novelist: that is, his stories do not occur to him in book-length units of 70,000 to 150,000 words. Almost all his novels have some weakness in structure. Some of them combine two or more themes having little relation to each other, like *Light in August,* while others, like *The Hamlet,* tend to resolve themselves into a series of episodes resembling beads on a string. In *The Sound and the Fury,* which is superb as a whole, we can't be sure that the four sections of the novel are presented in the most effective order; at any rate, we can't fully understand and perhaps can't even read the first section until we have read the other three. *Absalom, Absalom!* though pitched in too high a key, is structurally the soundest of all the novels in the Yoknapatawpha series; but even here the author's attention shifts halfway through the book from the principal theme of Colonel Sutpen's ambition to the secondary theme of incest and miscegenation.

Faulkner is best and most nearly himself either in long stories like "The Bear," in *Go Down, Moses,* and "Old Man," which was published as half of *The Wild Palms,* and "Spotted Horses," which was first printed separately, then greatly expanded and fitted into the loose framework of *The Hamlet*—all three stories are included in this volume; or else in the Yoknapatawpha saga as a whole. That is, he is most effective in dealing with the total situation that is always present in his mind as a pattern of the South; or else in shorter units that can be conceived and written in a single burst of creative effort. It is by his best that we should judge him, like every other author; and Faulkner at his best—even sometimes at his worst—has a power, a richness of life, an intensity to be found in no other American novelist of our time. He has—once more I am quoting from Henry James's essay on Hawthorne—"the element of simple genius, the quality of imagination."

Moreover, he has a brooding love for the land where he was born and reared and where, unlike other writers of his generation, he has chosen to spend his life. It is ". . . this land, this South, for which God has done so much, with woods for game and streams for fish and deep rich soil for seed and lush springs to sprout it and long summers to mature it and serene falls to harvest it and short mild winters for men and animals." So far as Faulkner's country includes the Delta, it is also (in the words of old Ike McCaslin)

. . . this land which man has deswamped and denuded and deriverred in two generations so that white men can own plantations and commute every night to Memphis and black men own plantations and ride in jimcrow cars to Chicago and live in millionaires' mansions on Lake Shore Drive, where white men rent farms and live like niggers and niggers crop on shares and live like animals, where cotton is planted and grows man-tall in the very cracks of the sidewalks, and usury and mortgage and bankruptcy and measureless wealth, Chinese and African and Aryan and Jew, all breed and spawn together.

Here are the two sides of Faulkner's feeling for the South: on the one side, an admiring and possessive love; on the other, a compulsive fear lest what he loves should be destroyed by the ignorance of its native serfs and the greed of traders and absentee landlords.

No other American writer takes such delight in the weather. He speaks in various novels of "the hot still pinewiney silence of the August afternoon"; of "the moonless September dust, the trees along the road not rising soaring as trees should but squatting like huge fowl"; of "the tranquil sunset of October mazy with windless wood-smoke"; of the "slow drizzle of November rain just above the ice point"; of "those windless Mississippi December days which are a sort of Indian summer's Indian summer"; of January and February when there is "no movement anywhere save the low constant smoke . . . and no sound save the chopping of axes and the lonely whistle of the daily trains." Spring in Faulkner's country is a hurried season, "all coming at once, pell mell and disordered, fruit and bloom and leaf, pied meadow and blossoming wood and the long fields shearing dark out of winter's slumber, to the shearing plow." Summer is dust-choked and blazing, and it lasts far into what should be autumn. "That's the one trouble with this country," he says in *As I Lay Dying*. "Everything, weather, all, hangs on too long. Like our rivers, our land: opaque, slow, violent; shaping and creating the life of man in its implacable and brooding image."

And Faulkner loves these people created in the image of the land. After a second reading of his novels, you continue to be impressed by his villains, Popeye and Jason and Joe Christmas and Flem Snopes; but this time you find more place in your memory for other figures standing a little in the background yet presented by the author with quiet affection: old ladies like Miss Jenny Du Pre, with their sharp-tongued benevolence; shrewd but kindly bargainers like Ratliff, the sewing-machine agent, and Will Varner, with his cotton gin and general store; long-suffering farm wives like Mrs. Henry Armstid (whether her name is Lula or Martha); and backwoods patriarchs like Pappy MacCullum, with his six middle-aged but unmarried sons named after the generals of Lee's army. You remember the big plantation houses that collapse in flames as if a whole civilization were dying, but you also remember men in patched

and faded but quite clean overalls sitting on the gallery
—here in the North we should call it the porch—of a
crossroads store that is covered with posters advertising
soft drinks and patent medicines; and you remember
the stories they tell while chewing tobacco until the
suption is out of it (everything in their world is reduced
to anecdote, and every anecdote is based on character).
You remember Quentin Compson, not in his despairing
moments, but riding with his father behind the dogs as
they quarter a sedge-grown hillside after quail; and not
listening to his father's story, but still knowing every
word of it, because, as he thought to himself, "You had
learned, absorbed it already without the medium of
speech somehow from having been born and living beside it, with it, as children will and do: so that what
your father was saying did not tell you anything so much
as it struck, word by word, the resonant strings of remembering."

Faulkner's novels have the quality of being lived,
absorbed, remembered rather than merely observed.
And they have what is rare in the novels of our time, a
warmth of family affection, brother for brother and
sister, the father for his children—a love so warm and
proud that it tries to shut out the rest of the world.
Compared with that affection, married love is presented
as something calculating, and illicit love as a consuming
fire. And because the blood relationship is central in his
novels, Faulkner finds it hard to create sympathetic
characters between the ages of twenty and forty. He is
better with children, Negro and white, and incom-
parably good with older people who preserve the
standards that have come down to them "out of the old
time, the old days."

In his later books, which have attracted so little attention that they seem to have gone unread, there is a

quality not exactly new to Faulkner—it had appeared
already in passages of *Sartoris* and *Sanctuary*—but now
much stronger and no longer overshadowed by violence
and horror. It is a sort of homely and sober-sided
frontier humor that is seldom achieved in contemporary
writing (except by Erskine Caldwell, another Southerner). The horse-trading episodes in *The Hamlet*, and
especially the long story of the spotted ponies from
Texas, might have been inspired by the Davy Crockett
almanacs. "Old Man," the story of the convict who surmounted the greatest of all the Mississippi floods, might
almost be a continuation of *Huckleberry Finn*. It is as
if some older friend of Huck's had taken the raft and
drifted on from Aunt Sally Phelps's farm into wilder
adventures, described in a wilder style, among Chinese
and Cajuns and bayous crawling with alligators. In a
curious way, Faulkner combines two of the principal
traditions in American letters: the tradition of psychological horror, often close to symbolism, that begins
with Charles Brockden Brown, our first professional
novelist, and extends through Poe, Melville, Henry
James (in his later stories), Stephen Crane, and Hemingway; and the other tradition of frontier humor and
realism, beginning with Augustus Longstreet's *Georgia
Scenes* and having Mark Twain as its best example.

But the American author he most resembles is Hawthorne, for all their polar differences. They stand to
each other as July to December, as heat to cold, as
swamp to mountain, as the luxuriant to the meager but
perfect, as planter to Puritan; and yet Hawthorne had
much the same attitude toward New England that
Faulkner has toward the South, together with a strong
sense of regional particularity. The Civil War made
Hawthorne feel that "the North and the South were
two distinct nations in opinions and habits, and had

better not try to live under the same institutions." In the spring of 1861, he wrote to his Bowdoin classmate Horatio Bridge, "We were never one people and never really had a country."—"New England," he said a little later, "is quite as large a lump of earth as my heart can really take in." But it was more than a lump of earth for him; it was a lump of history and a permanent state of consciousness. Like Faulkner in the South, he applied himself to creating its moral fables and elaborating its legends, which existed, as it were, in his solitary heart. Pacing the hillside behind his house in Concord, he listened for a voice; you might say that he lay in wait for it, passively but expectantly, like a hunter behind a rock; then, when it had spoken, he transcribed its words —more slowly and carefully than Faulkner, it is true; with more form and less fire, but with the same essential fidelity. If the voice was silent, he had nothing to write. "I have an instinct that I had better keep quiet," he said in a letter to his publisher. "Perhaps I shall have a new spirit of vigor if I wait quietly for it; perhaps not." Faulkner is another author who has to wait for the spirit and the voice. Essentially he is not a novelist, in the sense of not being a writer who sets out to observe actions and characters, then fits them into the architectural framework of a story. For all the weakness of his own poems, he is an epic or bardic poet in prose, a creator of myths that he weaves together into a legend of the South.

v

Because of the special nature of Faulkner's achievement, the book that follows presented more of an editorial problem than other Viking Portables, like the Fitzgerald or the Hemingway, for example. It had to have some other aim than merely to select the best of

Faulkner's work: the best single novel, the best episodes from others, and a group of the best stories. Such an arrangement, which presents a fairly accurate picture of most authors, might fail to reveal what is really best in Faulkner: that is, the scope and force and interdependence of his work as a whole.

Accordingly I followed a somewhat different scheme, with the author's consent and later with his advice at doubtful points. I tried to make selections that would give a general panorama of life in Faulkner's county, decade by decade, from the days when the early settlers rode northward along the Natchez Trace. With regret for a few good stories that had to be put aside, I included nothing unless it had some bearing on the Mississippi background (or on Faulkner's Mississippi characters in other backgrounds); I therefore had twelve books from which to choose, and managed to use selections from ten of them, omitting only *Sartoris* and *As I Lay Dying*. There are no complete novels here, for reasons already suggested, but there are three stories almost of novel length: "The Bear," "Spotted Horses," and "Old Man." The passages from novels are really (and not merely in the phrase from book jackets) "complete in themselves." Thus, the book can be dipped into as if it were a Faulkner anthology; but I also hope that some readers will go through it from beginning to end, following the characters and the sequence of events as if they were reading one continued story; and I hope they will find that it retains something of the organic unity of Faulkner's legend.

MALCOLM COWLEY

1. The Old People

HERE are four of Faulkner's stories dealing with early days in Yoknapatawpha County: with the Indians, the first white settlers, and the McCaslin plantation in the time of Uncle Buck and Uncle Buddy.

The Indians in Faulkner's country were Chickasaws. He paints them as being slow, brooding, cruel, serene, like the land itself, to which they belonged as much as did the wild creatures they hunted. The settlers disturbed this natural relationship. They found it easy to buy the Chickasaws' land—even to cheat them out of a hundred square miles in one transaction, as did Thomas Sutpen—because the Indians were psychologically unable to place a cash value on it. Then, having driven the natives westward and having peopled the land with slaves—to grow more cotton to buy more Negroes to grow more cotton—the planters set about creating their own aristocratic order.

Faulkner keeps looking back nostalgically to the old

order, but he presents its virtues as being moral rather than material. There is no baronial pomp in his novels; no profusion of silk and silver, mahogany and moonlight and champagne. All the planters lived comfortably, with plenty of servants, but Faulkner never lets us forget that they were living on what had recently been the frontier. What he admires about them is not their wealth or hospitality or florid manners, but rather their unquestioning acceptance of a moral code that taught them "courage and honor and pride, and pity and love of justice and of liberty." The code was the secret lost by their heirs and successors.

"A Justice" is a story of the old days as told to Quentin Compson, the hero of *The Sound and the Fury* and the narrator of *Absalom, Absalom!* Besides describing the Compson family, it also introduces Sam Fathers, the Chickasaw hunter who lived among the Negroes. He will reappear in a later story, but with other dates assigned to his birth and death; that is one of the inconsistencies mentioned in the Introduction. "Wedding in the Rain" is the second chapter of *Absalom, Absalom!* (1936), the only chapter that stands by itself. It tells how Thomas Sutpen, the mountain boy, built his huge plantation house with the help of a French architect and twenty wild Negroes from the jungle, and how he imposed himself on Jefferson society. "Red Leaves" is another story dealing with the Chickasaws, and one of the best. Like "A Justice," it was included in *These Thirteen*, Faulkner's first volume of stories, published in 1931. "Was" appeared in *Go Down, Moses* (1942). It introduces Uncle Buck and Uncle Buddy McCaslin, the two poker-playing bachelors who lived in a cabin built with their own hands, because—although they had inherited a big plantation—they refused to profit from the fruits of slavery.

1820.   A JUSTICE

I

UNTIL Grandfather Compson died, we would go
out to the farm every Saturday afternoon. We
would leave home right after dinner in the surrey, I in
front with Roskus, and Grandfather and Candace
(Caddy, we called her) and Jason in the back. Grandfather and Roskus would talk, with the horses going fast,
because it was the best team in the county. They would
carry the surrey fast along the levels and up some of the
hills even. But this was in north Mississippi, and on
some of the hills Roskus and I could smell Grandfather's
cigar.

The farm was four miles away. There was a long, low
house in the grove, not painted but kept whole and
sound by a clever carpenter from the quarters named
Sam Fathers, and behind it the barns and smokehouses,
and further still, the quarters themselves, also kept
whole and sound by Sam Fathers. He did nothing else,
and they said he was almost a hundred years old. He
lived with the Negroes and they—the white people; the
Negroes called him a blue-gum—called him a Negro.
But he wasn't a Negro. That's what I'm going to tell
about.

When we got there, Mr. Stokes, the manager, would
send a Negro boy with Caddy and Jason to the creek
to fish, because Caddy was a girl and Jason was too
little, but I wouldn't go with them. I would go to Sam
Fathers' shop, where he would be making breast-

yokes or wagon wheels, and I would always bring him some tobacco. Then he would stop working and he would fill his pipe—he made them himself, out of creek clay with a reed stem—and he would tell me about the old days. He talked like a nigger—that is, he said his words like niggers do, but he didn't say the same words —and his hair was nigger hair. But his skin wasn't quite the color of a light nigger and his nose and his mouth and chin were not nigger nose and mouth and chin. And his shape was not like the shape of a nigger when he gets old. He was straight in the back, not tall, a little broad, and his face was still all the time, like he might be somewhere else all the while he was working or when people, even white people, talked to him, or while he talked to me. It was just the same all the time, like he might be away up on a roof by himself, driving nails. Sometimes he would quit work with something half-finished on the bench, and sit down and smoke. And he wouldn't jump up and go back to work when Mr. Stokes or even Grandfather came along.

So I would give him the tobacco and he would stop work and sit down and fill his pipe and talk to me.

"These niggers," he said. "They call me Uncle Blue-Gum. And the white folks, they call me Sam Fathers."

"Isn't that your name?" I said.

"No. Not in the old days. I remember. I remember how I never saw but one white man until I was a boy big as you are; a whiskey trader that came every summer to the Plantation. It was the Man himself that named me. He didn't name me Sam Fathers, though."

"The Man?" I said.

"He owned the Plantation, the Negroes, my mammy too. He owned all the land that I knew of until I was grown. He was a Chickasaw chief. He sold my mammy to your greatgrandpappy. He said I didn't have to go unless I wanted to, because I was a warrior too then. He was the one who named me Had-Two-Fathers."

"Had-Two-Fathers?" I said. "That's not a name. That's not anything."

"It was my name once. Listen."

II

This is how Herman Basket told it when I was big enough to hear talk. He said that when Doom came back from New Orleans, he brought this woman with him. He brought six black people, though Herman Basket said they already had more black people in the Plantation than they could find use for. Sometimes they would run the black men with dogs, like you would a fox or a cat or a coon. And then Doom brought six more when he came home from New Orleans. He said he won them on the steamboat, and so he had to take them. He got off the steamboat with the six black people, Herman Basket said, and a big box in which something was alive, and the gold box of New Orleans salt about the size of a gold watch. And Herman Basket told how Doom took a puppy out of the box in which something was alive, and how he made a bullet of bread and a pinch of the salt in the gold box, and put the bullet into the puppy and the puppy died.

That was the kind of a man that Doom was, Herman Basket said. He told how, when Doom got off the steamboat that night, he wore a coat with gold all over it, and he had three gold watches, but Herman Basket said that even after seven years, Doom's eyes had not changed. He said that Doom's eyes were just the same as before he went away, before his name was Doom, and he and Herman Basket and my pappy were sleeping on the same pallet and talking at night, as boys will.

Doom's name was Ikkemotubbe then, and he was not born to be the Man, because Doom's mother's brother was the Man, and the Man had a son of his own, as well as a brother. But even then, and Doom no bigger than you are, Herman Basket said that sometimes the Man would look at Doom and he would say: "O Sister's Son, your eye is a bad eye, like the eye of a bad horse."

So the Man was not sorry when Doom got to be a young man and said that he would go to New Orleans, Herman Basket said. The Man was getting old then. He used to like to play mumble-peg and to pitch horseshoes both, but now he just liked mumble-peg. So he was not sorry when Doom went away, though he didn't forget about Doom. Herman Basket said that each summer when the whiskey trader came, the Man would ask him about Doom. "He calls himself David Callicoat now," the Man would say. "But his name is Ikkemotubbe. You haven't heard maybe of a David Callicoat getting drowned in the Big River, or killed in the white man's fight at New Orleans?"

But Herman Basket said they didn't hear from Doom at all until he had been gone seven years. Then one day Herman Basket and my pappy got a written stick from Doom to meet him at the Big River. Because the steamboat didn't come up our river any more then. The steamboat was still in our river, but it didn't go anywhere any more. Herman Basket told how one day during the high water, about three years after Doom went away, the steamboat came and crawled up on a sand-bar and died.

That was how Doom got his second name, the one before Doom. Herman Basket told how four times a year the steamboat would come up our river, and how the People would go to the river and camp and wait to see the steamboat pass, and he said that the white man who told the steamboat where to swim was named

David Callicoat. So when Doom told Herman Basket and pappy that he was going to New Orleans, he said, "And I'll tell you something else. From now on, my name is not Ikkemotubbe. It's David Callicoat. And some day I'm going to own a steamboat, too." That was the kind of man that Doom was, Herman Basket said.

So after seven years he sent them the written stick and Herman Basket and pappy took the wagon and went to meet Doom at the Big River, and Doom got off the steamboat with the six black people. "I won them on the steamboat," Doom said. "You and Craw-ford (my pappy's name was Crawfish-ford, but usually it was Craw-ford) can divide them."

"I don't want them," Herman Basket said that pappy said.

"Then Herman can have them all," Doom said.

"I don't want them either," Herman Basket said.

"All right," Doom said. Then Herman Basket said he asked Doom if his name was still David Callicoat, but instead of answering, Doom told one of the black people something in the white man's talk, and the black man lit a pine knot. Then Herman Basket said they were watching Doom take the puppy from the box and make the bullet of bread and the New Orleans salt which Doom had in the little gold box, when he said that pappy said:

"I believe you said that Herman and I were to divide these black people."

Then Herman Basket said he saw that one of the black people was a woman.

"You and Herman don't want them," Doom said.

"I wasn't thinking when I said that," pappy said. "I will take the lot with the woman in it. Herman can have the other three."

"I don't want them," Herman Basket said.

"You can have four, then," pappy said. "I will take the woman and one other."

"I don't want them," Herman Basket said.

"I will take only the woman," pappy said. "You can have the other five."

"I don't want them," Herman Basket said.

"You don't want them, either," Doom said to pappy. "You said so yourself."

Then Herman Basket said that the puppy was dead. "You didn't tell us your new name," he said to Doom.

"My name is Doom now," Doom said. "It was given me by a French chief in New Orleans. In French talking, Doo-um; in our talking, Doom."

"What does it mean?" Herman Basket said.

He said how Doom looked at him for a while. "It means, the Man," Doom said.

Herman Basket told how they thought about that. He said they stood there in the dark, with the other puppies in the box, the ones that Doom hadn't used, whimpering and scuffing, and the light of the pine knot shining on the eyeballs of the black people and on Doom's gold coat and on the puppy that had died.

"You cannot be the Man," Herman Basket said. "You are only on the sister's side. And the Man has a brother and a son."

"That's right," Doom said. "But if I were the Man, I would give Craw-ford those black people. I would give Herman something, too. For every black man I gave Craw-ford, I would give Herman a horse, if I were Man."

"Craw-ford only wants this woman," Herman Basket said.

"I would give Herman six horses, anyway," Doom said. "But maybe the Man has already given Herman a horse."

"No," Herman Basket said. "My ghost is still walking."

It took them three days to reach the Plantation. They camped on the road at night. Herman Basket said that they did not talk.

They reached the Plantation on the third day. He said that the Man was not very glad to see Doom, even though Doom brought a present of candy for the Man's son. Doom had something for all his kinsfolk, even for the Man's brother. The Man's brother lived by himself in a cabin by the creek. His name was Sometimes-Wakeup. Sometimes the People took him food. The rest of the time they didn't see him. Herman Basket told how he and pappy went with Doom to visit Sometimes-Wakeup in his cabin. It was at night, and Doom told Herman Basket to close the door. Then Doom took the puppy from pappy and set it on the floor and made a bullet of bread and the New Orleans salt for Sometimes-Wakeup to see how it worked. When they left, Herman Basket said how Sometimes-Wakeup burned a stick and covered his head with the blanket.

That was the first night that Doom was at home. On the next day Herman Basket told how the Man began to act strange at his food, and died before the doctor could get there and burn sticks. When the Willow-Bearer went to fetch the Man's son and tell him that he was to be the Man, they found that he had acted strange and then died too.

"Now Sometimes-Wakeup will have to be the Man," pappy said.

So the Willow-Bearer went to fetch Sometimes-Wakeup to come and be the Man. The Willow-Bearer came back soon. "Sometimes-Wakeup does not want to be the Man," the Willow-Bearer said. "He is sitting in his cabin with his head in his blanket."

"Then Ikkemotubbe will have to be the Man," pappy said.

So Doom was the Man. But Herman Basket said that pappy's ghost would not be easy. Herman Basket said he told pappy to give Doom a little time. "I am still walking," Herman Basket said.

"But this is a serious matter with me," pappy said.

He said that at last pappy went to Doom, before the Man and his son had entered the earth, before the eating and the horse-racing were over. "What woman?" Doom said.

"You said that when you were the Man," pappy said. Herman Basket said that Doom looked at pappy but that pappy was not looking at Doom.

"I think you don't trust me," Doom said. Herman Basket said how pappy did not look at Doom. "I think you still believe that that puppy was sick," Doom said. "Think about it."

Herman Basket said that pappy thought.

"What do you think now?" Doom said.

But Herman Basket said that pappy still did not look at Doom. "I think it was a well dog," pappy said.

III

At last the eating and the horse-racing were over and the Man and his son had entered the earth. Then Doom said, "Tomorrow we will go and fetch the steamboat." Herman Basket told how Doom had been talking about the steamboat ever since he became Man, and about how the House was not big enough. So that evening Doom said, "Tomorrow we will go and fetch the steamboat that died in the river."

Herman Basket said how the steamboat was twelve miles away, and that it could not even swim in the

water. So the next morning there was no one in the
Plantation except Doom and the black people. He told
how it took Doom all that day to find the People. Doom
used the dogs, and he found some of the People in hollow logs in the creek bottom. That night he made all
the men sleep in the House. He kept the dogs in the
House, too.

Herman Basket told how he heard Doom and pappy
talking in the dark. "I don't think you trust me," Doom
said.

"I trust you," pappy said.

"That is what I would advise," Doom said.

"I wish you could advise that to my ghost," pappy
said.

The next morning they went to the steamboat. The
women and the black people walked. The men rode in
the wagons, with Doom following behind with the dogs.

The steamboat was lying on its side on the sand-bar.
When they came to it, there were three white men on
it. "Now we can go back home," pappy said.

But Doom talked to the white men. "Does this steamboat belong to you?" Doom said.

"It does not belong to you," the white men said. And
though they had guns, Herman Basket said they did not
look like men who would own a boat.

"Shall we kill them?" he said to Doom. But he said
that Doom was still talking to the men on the steamboat.

"What will you take for it?" Doom said.

"What will you give for it?" the white men said.

"It is dead," Doom said. "It's not worth much."

"Will you give ten black people?" the white men
said.

"All right," Doom said. "Let the black people who
came with me from the Big River come forward." They
came forward, the five men and the woman. "Let four

more black people come forward." Four more came
forward. "You are now to eat of the corn of those white
men yonder," Doom said. "May it nourish you." The
white men went away, the ten black people following
them. "Now," Doom said, "let us make the steamboat
get up and walk."

Herman Basket said that he and pappy did not go
into the river with the others, because pappy said to go
aside and talk. They went aside. Pappy talked, but
Herman Basket said that he said he did not think it was
right to kill white men, but pappy said how they could
fill the white men with rocks and sink them in the river
and nobody would find them. So Herman Basket said
they overtook the three white men and the ten black
people, then they turned back toward the boat. Just before they came to the steamboat, pappy said to the black
men: "Go on to the Man. Go and help make the steamboat get up and walk. I will take this woman on home."

"This woman is my wife," one of the black men said.
"I want her to stay with me."

"Do you want to be arranged in the river with rocks
in your inside too?" pappy said to the black man.

"Do you want to be arranged in the river yourself?"
the black man said to pappy. "There are two of you, and
nine of us."

Herman Basket said that pappy thought. Then pappy
said, "Let us go to the steamboat and help the Man."

They went to the steamboat. But Herman Basket
said that Doom did not notice the ten black people until
it was time to return to the Plantation. Herman Basket
told how Doom looked at the black people, then looked
at pappy. "It seems that the white men did not want
these black people," Doom said.

"So it seems," pappy said.

"The white men went away, did they?" Doom said.

"So it seems," pappy said.

Herman Basket told how every night Doom would make all the men sleep in the House, with the dogs in the House too, and how each morning they would return to the steamboat in the wagons. The wagons would not hold everybody, so after the second day the women stayed at home. But it was three days before Doom noticed that pappy was staying at home too. Herman Basket said that the woman's husband may have told Doom. "Craw-ford hurt his back lifting the steamboat," Herman Basket said he told Doom. "He said he would stay at the Plantation and sit with his feet in the Hot Spring so that the sickness in his back could return to the earth."

"That is a good idea," Doom said. "He has been doing this for three days, has he? Then the sickness should be down in his legs by now."

When they returned to the Plantation that night, Doom sent for pappy. He asked pappy if the sickness had moved. Pappy said how the sickness moved very slow. "You must sit in the Spring more," Doom said.

"That is what I think," pappy said.

"Suppose you sit in the Spring at night too," Doom said.

"The night air will make it worse," pappy said.

"Not with a fire there," Doom said. "I will send one of the black people with you to keep the fire burning."

"Which one of the black people?" pappy said.

"The husband of the woman which I won on the steamboat," Doom said.

"I think my back is better," pappy said.

"Let us try it," Doom said.

"I know my back is better," pappy said.

"Let us try it, anyway," Doom said. Just before dark Doom sent four of the People to fix pappy and the black man at the Spring. Herman Basket said the People returned quickly. He said that as they entered the House, pappy entered also.

"The sickness began to move suddenly," pappy said. "It has reached my feet since noon today."

"Do you think it will be gone by morning?" Doom said.

"I think so," pappy said.

"Perhaps you had better sit in the Spring tonight and make sure," Doom said.

"I know it will be gone by morning," pappy said.

IV

When it got to be summer, Herman Basket said that the steamboat was out of the river bottom. It had taken them five months to get it out of the bottom, because they had to cut down the trees to make a path for it. But now he said the steamboat could walk faster on the logs. He told how pappy helped. Pappy had a certain place on one of the ropes near the steamboat that no-body was allowed to take, Herman Basket said. It was just under the front porch of the steamboat where Doom sat in his chair, with a boy with a branch to shade him and another boy with a branch to drive away the flying beasts. The dogs rode on the boat too.

In the summer, while the steamboat was still walking, Herman Basket told how the husband of the woman came to Doom again. "I have done what I could for you," Doom said. "Why don't you go to Craw-ford and adjust this matter yourself?"

The black man said that he had done that. He said that pappy said to adjust it by a cock-fight, pappy's cock against the black man's, the winner to have the woman, the one who refused to fight to lose by default. The black man said he told pappy he did not have a cock, and that pappy said that in that case the black man lost by default and that the woman belonged to pappy. "And what am I to do?" the black man said.

Doom thought. Then Herman Basket said that Doom called to him and asked him which was pappy's best cock and Herman Basket told Doom that pappy had only one. "That black one?" Doom said. Herman Basket said he told Doom that was the one. "Ah," Doom said. Herman Basket told how Doom sat in his chair on the porch of the steamboat while it walked, looking down at the People and the black men pulling the ropes, making the steamboat walk. "Go and tell Craw-ford you have a cock," Doom said to the black man. "Just tell him you will have a cock in the pit. Let it be tomorrow morning. We will let the steamboat sit down and rest." The black man went away. Then Herman Basket said that Doom was looking at him, and that he did not look at Doom. Because he said there was but one better cock in the Plantation than pappy's, and that one belonged to Doom. "I think that that puppy was not sick," Doom said. "What do you think?"

Herman Basket said that he did not look at Doom. "That is what I think," he said.

"That is what I would advise," Doom said.

Herman Basket told how the next day the steamboat sat and rested. The pit was in the stable. The People and the black people were there. Pappy had his cock in the pit. Then the black man put his cock into the pit. Herman Basket said that pappy looked at the black man's cock.

"This cock belongs to Ikkemotubbe," pappy said.

"It is his," the People told pappy. "Ikkemotubbe gave it to him with all to witness."

Herman Basket said that pappy had already picked

up his cock. "This is not right," pappy said. "We ought not to let him risk his wife on a cock-fight."

"Then you withdraw?" the black man said.

"Let me think," pappy said. He thought. The People watched. The black man reminded pappy of what he had said about defaulting. Pappy said he did not mean to say that and that he withdrew it. The People told him that he could only withdraw by forfeiting the match. Herman Basket said that pappy thought again. The People watched. "All right," pappy said. "But I am being taken advantage of."

The cocks fought. Pappy's cock fell. Pappy took it up quickly. Herman Basket said it was like pappy had been waiting for his cock to fall so he could pick it quickly up. "Wait," he said. He looked at the People. "Now they have fought. Isn't that true?" The People said that it was true. "So that settles what I said about forfeiting."

Herman Basket said that pappy began to get out of the pit.

"Aren't you going to fight?" the black man said.

"I don't think this will settle anything," pappy said. "Do you?"

Herman Basket told how the black man looked at pappy. Then he quit looking at pappy. He was squatting. Herman Basket said the People looked at the black man looking at the earth between his feet. They watched him take up a clod of dirt, and then they watched the dust come out between the black man's fingers. "Do you think that this will settle anything?" pappy said.

"No," the black man said. Herman Basket said that the People could not hear him very good. But he said that pappy could hear him.

"Neither do I," pappy said. "It would not be right to risk your wife on a cock-fight."

Herman Basket told how the black man looked up, with the dry dust about the fingers of his hand. He said the black man's eyes looked red in the dark pit, like the eyes of a fox. "Will you let the cocks fight again?" the black man said.

"Do you agree that it doesn't settle anything?" pappy said.

"Yes," the black man said.

Pappy put his cock back into the ring. Herman Basket said that pappy's cock was dead before it had time to act strange, even. The black man's cock stood upon it and started to crow, but the black man struck the live cock away and he jumped up and down on the dead cock until it did not look like a cock at all, Herman Basket said.

Then it was fall, and Herman Basket told how the steamboat came to the Plantation and stopped beside the House and died again. He said that for two months they had been in sight of the Plantation, making the steamboat walk on the logs, but now the steamboat was beside the House and the House was big enough to please Doom. He gave an eating. It lasted a week. When it was over, Herman Basket told how the black man came to Doom a third time. Herman Basket said that the black man's eyes were red again, like those of a fox, and that they could hear his breathing in the room. "Come to my cabin," he said to Doom. "I have something to show you."

"I thought it was about that time," Doom said. He looked about the room, but Herman Basket told Doom that pappy had just stepped out. "Tell him to come also," Doom said. When they came to the black man's cabin, Doom sent two of the People to fetch pappy. Then they entered the cabin. What the black man wanted to show Doom was a new man.

"Look," the black man said. "You are the Man. You are to see justice done."

"What is wrong with this man?" Doom said.

"Look at the color of him," the black man said. He began to look around the cabin. Herman Basket said that his eyes went red and then brown and then red, like those of a fox. He said they could hear the black man's breathing. "Do I get justice?" the black man said. "You are the Man."

"You should be proud of a fine yellow man like this," Doom said. He looked at the new man. "I don't see that justice can darken him any," Doom said. He looked about the cabin also. "Come forward, Craw-ford," he said. "This is a man, not a copper snake; he will not harm you." But Herman Basket said that pappy would not come forward. He said the black man's eyes went red and then brown and then red when he breathed. "Yao," Doom said, "this is not right. Any man is entitled to have his melon patch protected from these wild bucks of the woods. But first let us name this man." Doom thought. Herman Basket said the black man's eyes went quieter now, and his breath went quieter too. "We will call him Had-Two-Fathers," Doom said.

v

Sam Fathers lit his pipe again. He did it deliberately, rising and lifting between thumb and forefinger from his forge a coal of fire. Then he came back and sat down. It was getting late. Caddy and Jason had come back from the creek, and I could see Grandfather and Mr. Stokes talking beside the carriage, and at that moment, as though he had felt my gaze, Grandfather turned and called my name.

"What did your pappy do then?" I said.

"He and Herman Basket built the fence," Sam Fathers said. "Herman Basket told how Doom made them set two posts into the ground, with a sapling across the top of them. The nigger and pappy were there. Doom had not told them about the fence then. Herman Basket said it was just like when he and pappy and Doom were boys, sleeping on the same pallet, and Doom would wake them at night and make them get up and go hunting with him, or when he would make them stand up with him and fight with their fists, just for fun, until Herman Basket and pappy would hide from Doom.

"They fixed the sapling across the two posts and Doom said to the nigger: 'This is a fence. Can you climb it?'

"Herman Basket said the nigger put his hand on the sapling and sailed over it like a bird.

"Then Doom said to pappy: 'Climb this fence.'

" 'This fence is too high to climb,' pappy said.

" 'Climb this fence, and I will give you the woman,' Doom said.

"Herman Basket said pappy looked at the fence a while. 'Let me go under this fence,' he said.

" 'No,' Doom said.

"Herman Basket told me how pappy began to sit down on the ground. 'It's not that I don't trust you,' pappy said.

" 'We will build the fence this high,' Doom said.

" 'What fence?' Herman Basket said.

" 'The fence around the cabin of this black man,' Doom said.

" 'I can't build a fence I couldn't climb,' pappy said.

" 'Herman will help you,' Doom said.

"Herman Basket said it was just like when Doom used to wake them and make them go hunting. He said the dogs found him and pappy about noon the next day, and that they began the fence that afternoon. He told me how they had to cut the saplings in the creek bottom and drag them in by hand, because Doom would not let them use the wagon. So sometimes one post would take them three or four days. 'Never mind,' Doom said. 'You have plenty of time. And the exercise will make Craw-ford sleep at night.'

"He told me how they worked on the fence all that winter and all the next summer, until after the whiskey trader had come and gone. Then it was finished. He said that on the day they set the last post, the nigger came out of the cabin and put his hand on the top of a post (it was a palisade fence, the posts set upright in the ground) and flew out like a bird. 'This is a good fence,' the nigger said. 'Wait,' he said. 'I have something to show you.' Herman Basket said he flew back over the fence again and went into the cabin and came back. Herman Basket said that he was carrying a new man and that he held the new man up so they could see it above the fence. 'What do you think about this for color?' he said."

Grandfather called me again. This time I got up. The sun was already down beyond the peach orchard. I was just twelve then, and to me the story did not seem to have got anywhere, to have had point or end. Yet I obeyed Grandfather's voice, not that I was tired of Sam Fathers' talking, but with that immediacy of children with which they flee temporarily something which they do not quite understand; that, and the instinctive promptness with which we all obeyed Grandfather, not from concern of impatience or reprimand, but because we all believed that he did fine things, that his waking life passed from one fine (if faintly grandiose) picture to another.

They were in the surrey, waiting for me. I got in; the

horses moved at once, impatient too for the stable. Caddy had one fish, about the size of a chip, and she was wet to the waist. We drove on, the team already trotting. When we passed Mr. Stokes' kitchen we could smell ham cooking. The smell followed us on to the gate. When we turned onto the road home it was almost sundown. Then we couldn't smell the cooking ham any more. "What were you and Sam talking about?" Grandfather said.

We went on, in that strange, faintly sinister suspension of twilight in which I believed that I could still see Sam Fathers back there, sitting on his wooden block, definite, immobile, and complete, like something looked upon after a long time in a preservative bath in a museum. That was it. I was just twelve then, and I would have to wait until I had passed on and through and beyond the suspension of twilight. Then I knew that I would know. But then Sam Fathers would be dead.

"Nothing, sir," I said. "We were just talking."

1833. WEDDING IN THE RAIN

IT WAS a summer of wistaria. The twilight was full of it and of the smell of his father's cigar as they sat on the front gallery after supper, while in the deep shaggy lawn below the veranda the fireflies blew and drifted in soft random. It was a day of listening too— the listening, the hearing in 1909 mostly about that which Quentin Compson already knew, since he had been born in and still breathed the same air in which the church bells had rung on that Sunday morning in 1833 and, on Sundays, heard even one of the original three bells in the same steeple, where descendants of the same pigeons strutted and crooned or wheeled in short courses resembling soft fluid paint-smears on the soft summer sky.

That Sunday morning in June long ago, with the bells ringing peaceful and peremptory and a little cacophonous—the denominations in concord though not in tune —and the ladies and children, and house Negroes to carry the parasols and flywhisks, and even a few men (the ladies moving in hoops among the miniature broadcloth of little boys and the pantalettes of little girls, in the skirts of the time when ladies did not walk but floated), when the other men sitting with their feet on the railing of the Holston House gallery looked up, and there the stranger was. He was already halfway across the Square when they saw him, on a big hard-ridden roan horse, man and beast looking as though they had been created out of thin air and set down in the bright summer sabbath sunshine in the middle of a tired foxtrot—face and horse that none of them had ever seen before, name that none of them had ever heard, and origin and purpose which some of them were never to learn. So that in the next four weeks (Jefferson was a village then: the Holston House, the courthouse, six stores, a blacksmith and livery stable, a saloon frequented by drovers and peddlers, three churches and perhaps thirty residences) the stranger's name went back and forth among the places of business and of idleness and among the residences in steady strophe and antistrophe: *Sutpen. Sutpen. Sutpen. Sutpen.*

That was all that the town was to know about him for almost a month. He had apparently come into town from the south—a man of about twenty-five as the town learned later, because at the time his age could not have been guessed because he looked like a man who had been sick. Not like a man who had been peacefully ill in bed and had recovered to move with a sort of diffident and tentative amazement in a world which he had believed himself on the point of surrendering, but like a man who had been through some solitary furnace experience which was more than just fever, like an explorer say, who not only had to face the normal hardship of the pursuit which he chose but was overtaken by the added and unforeseen handicap of the fever also, and fought through it at enormous cost not so much physical as mental, alone and unaided and not through blind instinctive will to endure and survive, but to gain and keep to enjoy it, the material prize for which he accepted the original gambit. A man with a big frame but gaunt now almost to emaciation, with a short reddish beard which resembled a disguise and

above which his pale eyes had a quality at once vision-
ary and alert, ruthless and reposed, in a face whose flesh
had the appearance of pottery, of having been colored
by that oven's fever either of soul or environment,
deeper than sun alone beneath a dead impervious surface as of glazed clay.

That was what they saw, though it was years before
the town learned that that was all which he possessed
at the time—the strong spent horse and the clothes on
his back and a small saddlebag scarcely large enough to
contain the spare linen and the razors, and the two
pistols with the butts worn smooth as pickhandles,
which he used with the precision of knitting needles;
later Quentin's grandfather saw him ride at a canter
around a sapling at twenty feet and put both bullets
into a playing card fastened to the tree. He had a room
in the Holston House but he carried the key with him,
and each morning he fed and saddled the horse and rode
away before daylight, where to the town likewise failed
to learn, probably due to the fact that he gave the
pistol demonstration on the third day after his arrival.
So they had to depend on inquiry to find out what they
could about him, which would of necessity be at night,
at the supper table in the Holston House dining-room
or in the lounge which he would have to cross to gain
his room and lock the door again, which he would do as
soon as he finished eating. The bar opened into the
lounge too, and that would or should have been the
place to accost him and even inquire, except for the
fact that he did not use the bar. He did not drink at
all, he told them. He did not say that he used to drink
and had quit, nor that he had never used alcohol. He
just said that he would not care for a drink; it was years
later before even Quentin's grandfather (he was a young
man too then; it would be years yet before he would

become General Compson) learned that the reason Sutpen did not drink was that he did not have the money with which to pay his share or return the courtesy; it was General Compson who first realized that at this time Sutpen lacked not only the money to spend for drink and conviviality, but the time and inclination as well: that he was at this time completely the slave of his secret and furious impatience, his conviction gained from whatever that recent experience had been—that fever mental or physical—of a need for haste, of time fleeing beneath him, which was to drive him for the next five years—as General Compson computed it, roughly until about nine months before his son was born.

So they would catch him, run him to earth, in the lounge between the supper table and his locked door to give him the opportunity to tell them who he was and where he came from and what he was up to, whereupon he would move gradually and steadily until his back came in contact with something—a post or a wall —and then stand there and tell them nothing whatever as pleasantly and courteously as a hotel clerk. It was the Chickasaw Indian agent with or through whom he dealt, and so it was not until he waked the County Recorder that Saturday night with the deed, patent, to the land and the gold Spanish coin, that the town learned that he now owned a hundred square miles of some of the best virgin bottom land in the country, though even that knowledge came too late because Sutpen himself was gone, where to again they did not know. But he owned land among them now and some of them began to suspect what General Compson apparently knew: that the Spanish coin with which he had paid to have his patent recorded was the last one of any kind which he possessed. So they were certain now that he had departed

to get more; there were several who even anticipated
in believing (and even in saying aloud, now that he
was not present) that he had found some unique and
practical way of hiding loot and that he had returned to
the cache to replenish his pockets, even if he had not
actually ridden with the two pistols back to the River
and the steamboats full of gamblers and cotton- and
slavedealers to replenish the cache. At least some of
them were telling one another that when two months
later he returned, again without warning and accompanied this time by the covered wagon with a Negro
driving it and on the seat with the Negro a small,
alertly resigned man with a grim, harried, Latin face,
in a frock coat and a flowered waistcoat and a hat which
would have created no furore on a Paris boulevard, all
of which he was to wear constantly for the next two
years—the somberly theatric clothing and the expression of fatalistic and amazed determination—while his
white client and the Negro crew which he was to advise
though not direct went stark naked save for a coating of
dried mud. This was the French architect. Years later
the town learned that he had come all the way from
Martinique on Sutpen's bare promise and lived for two
years on venison cooked over a campfire, in an unfloored
tent made of the wagon hood, before he so much as
saw any color or shape of pay. And until he passed
through town on his way back to New Orleans two
years later, he was not even to see Jefferson again; he
would not come, or Sutpen would not bring him, to
town even on the few occasions when Sutpen would be
seen there, and he did not have much chance to look
at Jefferson on that first day because the wagon did
not stop. Apparently it was only by sheer geographical
hap that Sutpen passed through town at all, pausing
only long enough for someone (not General Compson)

to look beneath the wagon hood and into a black tunnel filled with still eyeballs and smelling like a wolfden.

But the legend of Sutpen's wild Negroes was not to begin at once, because the wagon went on as though even the wood and iron which composed it, as well as the mules which drew it, had become imbued, by sheer association with him, with that quality of gaunt and tireless driving, that conviction of haste and of fleeing time; later Sutpen told Quentin's grandfather that on that afternoon when the wagon passed through Jefferson they had been without food since the previous night and that he was trying to reach Sutpen's Hundred and the river bottom to try to kill a deer before dark, so he and the architect and the Negroes would not have to spend another night without food. So the legend of the wild men came gradually back to town, brought by the men who would ride out to watch what was going on, who began to tell how Sutpen would take stand beside a game trail with the pistols and send the Negroes in to drive the swamp like a pack of hounds; it was they who told how during that first summer and fall the Negroes did not even have (or did not use) blankets to sleep in, even before the coon-hunter Akers claimed to have walked one of them out of the absolute mud like a sleeping alligator and screamed just in time. The Negroes could speak no English yet and doubtless there were more than Akers who did not know that the language in which they and Sutpen communicated was a sort of French and not some dark and fatal tongue of their own.

There were many more than Akers, though the others were responsible citizens and landowners and so did not have to lurk about the camp at night. In fact, they would make up parties to meet at the Holston House and go out horseback, often carrying lunch. Sutpen had

built a brick kiln and he had set up the saw and planer
which he had brought in the wagon—a capstan with a
long sapling walking-beam, with the wagon team and
the Negroes in shifts and himself too when necessary,
when the machinery slowed, hitched to it—as if the
Negroes actually were wild men; as General Compson
told his son, Quentin's father, while the Negroes were
working Sutpen never raised his voice at them, that
instead he led them, caught them at the psychological
instant by example, by some ascendancy of forbearance
rather than by brute fear.

Without dismounting (usually Sutpen did not even
greet them with as much as a nod, apparently as unaware of their presence as if they had been idle shades)
they would sit in a curious quiet clump as though for
mutual protection and watch his mansion rise, carried
plank by plank and brick by brick out of the swamp
where the clay and timber waited—the bearded white
man and the twenty black ones and all stark naked beneath the encroaching and pervading mud. Being men,
these spectators did not realize that the garments which
Sutpen had worn when he first rode into Jefferson were
the only ones in which they had ever seen him, and few
of the women in the county had seen him at all. Otherwise, some of them would have divined that he was
saving his clothes, since decorum even if not elegance
of appearance would be the only weapon (or rather,
ladder) with which he could conduct the last assault
upon what they believed to be respectability—that
respectability which, according to General Compson,
consisted in Sutpen's secret mind of a great deal more
than the mere acquisition of a chatelaine for his house.
So he and the twenty Negroes worked together, plastered over with mud against the mosquitoes and
distinguishable one from another by his beard and eyes

alone, and only the architect resembling a human creature because of the French clothes which he wore
constantly with a sort of invincible fatality until the day
after the house was completed save for the windowglass
and the ironware which they could not make by hand,
and the architect departed—working in the sun and
heat of summer and the mud and ice of winter, with
quiet and unflagging fury.

It took him two years, he and his crew of imported
slaves which his adopted fellow citizens still looked on
as being a good deal more deadly than any beast he
could have started and slain in that country. They
worked from sunup to sundown while parties of horsemen rode up and sat their horses quietly and watched,
and the architect in his formal coat and his Paris hat
and his expression of grim and embittered amazement
lurked about the environs of the scene with his air
something between a casual and bitterly disinterested
spectator and a condemned and conscientious ghost—
amazement, General Compson said, not at the others
and what they were doing so much as at himself, at the
inexplicable and incredible fact of his own·presence.
But he was a good architect; Quentin knew the house,
twelve miles from Jefferson, in its grove of cedar and
oak, seventy-five years after it was finished. And not
only an architect, as General Compson said, but an
artist, since only an artist could have borne those two
years in order to build a house which he doubtless not
only expected but firmly intended never to see again.
Not, General Compson said, the hardship to sense and
the outrage to sensibility of the two years' sojourn, but
Sutpen: that only an artist could have borne Sutpen's
ruthlessness and hurry and still manage to curb the
dream of grim and castlelike magnificence at which
Sutpen obviously aimed, since the place as Sutpen

planned it would have been almost as large as Jefferson itself at the time; that the little grim, harried foreigner had singlehanded given battle to and vanquished Sutpen's fierce and overweening vanity or desire for magnificence or for vindication or whatever it was (even General Compson did not know yet) and so created of Sutpen's very defeat the victory which, in conquering, Sutpen himself would have failed to gain.

So it was finished then, down to the last plank and brick and wooden pin which they could make themselves. Unpainted and unfurnished, without a pane of glass or a doorknob or hinge in it, twelve miles from town and almost that far from any neighbor, it stood for three years more surrounded by its formal gardens and promenades, its slave quarters and stables and smokehouses; wild turkey ranged within a mile of the house and deer came light and colored like smoke and left delicate prints in the formal beds where there would be no flowers for four years yet. Now there began a period, a phase, during which the town and the county watched him with more puzzlement yet. Perhaps it was because the next step toward that secret end which General Compson claimed to have known but which the town and the county comprehended but dimly or not at all, now required patience or passive time instead of that driving fury to which he had accustomed them; now it was the women who first suspected what he wanted, what the next step would be. None of the men, certainly not those who knew him well enough to call him by name, suspected that he wanted a wife. Doubtless there were some of them, husbands and bachelors both, who not only would have refused to entertain the idea but would even have protested against it, because for the next three years he led what must have been to them a perfect existence. He lived out there, eight miles from any neighbor, in masculine solitude in what might be called the half-acre gunroom of a baronial splendor. He lived in the Spartan shell of the largest edifice in the county, not excepting the courthouse itself, whose threshold no woman had so much as seen, without any feminized softness of window-pane or door or mattress; where there was not only no woman to object if he should elect to have his dogs in to sleep on the pallet bed with him, he did not even need dogs to kill the game which left footprints within sight of the kitchen door but hunted it instead with human beings who belonged to him body and soul and of whom it was believed (or said) that they could creep up to a bedded buck and cut its throat before it could move.

It was at this time that he began to invite parties of men out to Sutpen's Hundred, to camp in blankets in the naked rooms of his embryonic formal opulence; they hunted, and at night played cards and drank, and on occasion he doubtless pitted his Negroes against one another and perhaps even at this time participated now and then himself. Sutpen drank now, though there were probably others besides Quentin's grandfather who remarked that he drank very sparingly save when he himself had managed to supply some of the liquor. His guests would bring whiskey out with them, but he drank of this with a sort of sparing calculation as though keeping mentally, General Compson said, a sort of balance of spiritual solvency between the amount of whiskey he accepted and the amount of running meat which he supplied to the guns.

He lived like that for three years. He now had a plantation; inside of two years he had dragged house and gardens out of virgin swamp, and plowed and planted his land with seed cotton which General Compson loaned him. Then he seemed to quit. He seemed to just sit down in the middle of what he had almost finished, and to remain so for three years during which he did not even appear to intend or want anything more. Perhaps it is not to be wondered at that the men in the county came to believe that the life he now led had been his aim all the time; it was only General Compson, who seemed to have known him well enough to offer to lend him seed cotton for his start, to whom Sutpen ever told anything about his past. It was General Compson who knew first about the Spanish coin being his last one, as it was Compson (so the town learned later) who offered to lend Sutpen the money to finish and furnish his house, and was refused. So doubtless General Compson was the first man in the county to tell himself that Sutpen did not need to borrow money with which to complete the house, supply what it yet lacked, because he intended to marry it. Not the first person to know: rather the first man, since the women in the county had been telling one another and their husbands as well that Sutpen did not intend to quit there, that he had already gone to too much trouble, gone through too much privation and hardship, to settle down and live exactly as he had lived while the house was being built, save that now he had a roof to sleep under in place of an unfloored wagon hood. Probably the women had already cast about among the families of the men who might now be called his friends, for that prospective bride whose dowry might complete the shape and substance of that something more than respectability that General Compson anyway believed to be his aim. So when, at the expiration of this second phase, three years after the house was finished and the architect departed, and again on Sunday morning and again without warning, the town saw him cross the square, on foot now, but in the same garments in which he had ridden into town five years ago and which no one had seen since (he or one of the Negroes had ironed the coat with heated bricks, General Compson told Quentin's father) and enter the Methodist church, only some of the men were surprised. The women merely said that he had exhausted the possibilities of the families of the men with whom he had hunted and gambled and that he had now come to town to find a wife exactly as he would have gone to the Memphis market to buy livestock or slaves. But when they comprehended who it was that he had apparently come to town and into church to invest with his choice, the assurance of the women became one with the men's surprise, and then even more than that: amazement.

Because the town now believed that it knew him. For two years it had watched him as with that grim and unflagging fury he had erected that shell of a house and laid out his fields, then for three years he had remained completely static, as if he were run by electricity and someone had come along and removed, dismantled the wiring or the dynamo. So that when he entered the Methodist church that Sunday morning in his ironed coat, there were men as well as women who believed that they had only to look around the congregation in order to anticipate the direction his feet would take him, until they became aware that he had apparently marked down Miss Coldfield's father with the same cold and ruthless deliberation with which he had probably marked down the French architect. They watched in shocked amazement while he laid deliberate siege to the one man in the town with whom he could have had nothing in common, least of all, money—a man who obviously could do nothing under the sun for him save give him credit at a little cross-roads store or cast a vote in his favor if he should ever seek ordination as a

Methodist minister—a Methodist steward, a merchant not only of modest position and circumstances but who already had a wife and family of his own, let alone a dependent mother and sister, to support out of the proceeds of a business which he had brought to Jefferson ten years ago in a single wagon—a man with a name for absolute and undeviating and even Puritan uprightness in a country and time of lawless opportunity, who neither drank nor gambled nor even hunted. In their surprise they forgot that Mr. Coldfield had a marriageable daughter. They did not consider the daughter at all. They did not think of love in connection with Sutpen. They thought of ruthlessness rather than justice and of fear rather than respect, but not of pity or love: besides being too lost in amazed speculation as to just how Sutpen intended or could contrive to use Mr. Coldfield to further whatever secret ends he still had. They were never to know. Because from that day there were no more hunting parties out at Sutpen's Hundred, and when they saw him now it would be in town. But not loafing, idling. The men who had slept and matched glasses with him under his roof (some of them had even come to call him Sutpen without the formal Mister) watched him pass along the street before the Holston House with a single formal gesture to his hat and go on and enter Mr. Coldfield's store, and that was all.

"Then one day he quitted Jefferson for the second time," Mr. Compson told Quentin. "The town should have been accustomed to that by now. Nevertheless, his position had subtly changed, as you will see by the town's reaction to this second return. Because when he came back this time, he was in a sense a public enemy. Perhaps this was because of what he brought back with him this time: the material he brought back this time, as compared to the simple wagonload of wild

Negroes which he had brought back before. But I don't think so. That is, I think it was a little more involved than the sheer value of his chandeliers and mahogany and rugs. I think that the affront was born of the town's realization that he was getting it involved with himself; that whatever the felony which produced the mahogany and crystal, he was forcing the town to compound it. Heretofore, until that Sunday when he came to church, if he had misused or injured anybody, it was only old Ikkemotubbe, from whom he got his land—a matter between his conscience and Uncle Sam and God. But now his position had changed, because when, about three months after he departed, four wagons left Jefferson to go to the River and meet him, it was known that Mr. Coldfield was the man who hired and dispatched them. They were big wagons, drawn by oxen, and when they returned the town looked at them and knew, no matter what they might have contained, that Mr. Coldfield could not have mortgaged everything that he owned for enough to fill them; doubtless this time there were more men than women even who pictured him during this absence with a handkerchief over his face and the two pistol barrels glinting beneath the candelabra of a steamboat's saloon, even if no worse: if not something performed in the lurking dark of a muddy landing and with a knife from behind. They saw him pass, on the roan horse beside his four wagons; it seems that even the ones who had eaten his food and shot his game and even called him 'Sutpen' without the 'Mister,' didn't accost him now. They just waited while reports and rumors came back to town of how he and his now somewhat tamed Negroes had installed the windows and doors and the spits and pots in the kitchen and the crystal chandeliers in the parlors and the furniture and the curtains and the rugs; it was that same Akers who had blundered onto the mudcouched Negro five years ago who came, a little wild-eyed and considerably slack-mouthed, into the Holston House bar one evening and said, 'Boys, this time he stole the whole durn steam-boat!'

"So at last civic virtue came to a boil. One day and with the sheriff of the county among them, a party of eight or ten took the road out to Sutpen's Hundred. They did not go all the way because about six miles from town they met Sutpen himself. He was riding the roan horse, in the frock coat and the beaver hat which they knew and with his legs wrapped in a piece of tarpaulin; he had a portmanteau on his pommel and he was carrying a small woven basket on his arm. He stopped the roan (it was April then, and the road was still a quag-mire) and sat there in his splashed tarpaulin and looked from one face to the next; your grandfather said that his eyes looked like pieces of a broken plate and that his beard was strong as a curry-comb. That was how he put it: strong as a curry-comb. 'Good morning, gentlemen,' he said. 'Were you looking for me?'

"Doubtless something more than this transpired at the time, though none of the vigilance committee ever told it that I know of. All I ever heard is how the town, the men on the gallery of the Holston House saw Sutpen and the committee ride onto the square together, Sutpen a little in front and the others bunched behind him— Sutpen with his legs and feet wrapped neatly in his tarpaulin and his shoulders squared inside the worn broadcloth coat and that worn brushed beaver cocked a little, talking to them over his shoulder and those eyes hard and pale and reckless and probably quizzical and maybe contemptuous even then. He pulled up at the door and the Negro hostler ducked out and took the roan's head and Sutpen got down, with his portmanteau

and the basket and mounted the steps, and I heard how
he turned there and looked at them again where they
huddled on their horses, not knowing what to do exactly. And it might have been a good thing that he had
that beard and they could not see his mouth. Then he
turned, and he looked at the other men sitting with their
feet on the railing and watching him too, men who
used to come out to his place and sleep on the floor and
hunt with him, and he saluted them with that florid,
swaggering gesture to the hat (yes, he was underbred.
It showed like this always, your grandfather said, in all
his formal contacts with people. He was like John L.
Sullivan having taught himself painfully and tediously
to do the schottische, having drilled himself and drilled
himself in secret until he now believed it no longer
necessary to count the music's beat, say. He may have
believed that your grandfather or Judge Benbow might
have done it a little more effortlessly than he, but he
would not have believed that anyone could have beat
him in knowing when to do it and how. And besides,
it was in his face; that was where his power lay, your
grandfather said: that anyone could look at him and say,
*Given the occasion and the need, this man can and will
do anything*). Then he went on into the house and commanded a chamber.

"So they sat on their horses and waited for him. I suppose they knew that he would have to come out some
time: I suppose they sat there and thought about those
two pistols. Because there was still no warrant for him,
you see: it was just public opinion in an acute state of
indigestion; and now other horsemen rode into the
square and became aware of the situation, so that there
was quite a posse waiting when he walked out onto the
gallery. He wore a new hat now, and a new broadcloth
coat, so they knew what the portmanteau had contained.

They even knew now what the basket had contained because he did not have that with him now either. Doubtless at the time it merely puzzled them more than ever, because, you see, they had been too busy speculating on just how he was planning to use Mr. Coldfield and, since his return, too completely outraged by the belief that they now saw the results even if the means were still an enigma, to remember about Miss Ellen at all.

"So he stopped again doubtless and looked from face to face again, doubtless memorizing the new faces, without any haste, with still the beard to hide whatever his mouth might have shown. But he seems to have said nothing at all this time. He just descended the steps and walked on across the square, the committee (your grandfather said it had grown to almost fifty by now) moving too, following him across the square. They say he did not even look back. He just walked on, erect, with the new hat cocked and carrying in his hand now that which must have seemed to them the final gratuitous insult, with the committee riding along in the street beside him and not quite parallel, and others who did not happen to have horses at the moment joining in and following the committee in the road, and ladies and children and women slaves coming to the doors and windows of the homes as they passed to watch as they went on in grim tableau, and Sutpen, still without once looking back, entered Mr. Coldfield's gate and strode on up the brick walk to the door, carrying his newspaper cornucopia of flowers.

"They waited for him again. The crowd was growing fast now—other men and a few boys and even some Negroes from the adjacent houses, clotting behind the eight original members of the committee who sat watching Mr. Coldfield's door until he emerged. It was a good while and he no longer carried the flowers, and when

he returned to the gate, he was engaged to be married.
But they did not know this, and as soon as he reached
the gate, they arrested him. They took him back to
town, with the ladies and children and house niggers
watching from behind curtains and behind the shrub-
bery in the yards and the corners of the houses, the
kitchens where doubtless food was already beginning to
scorch, and so back to the square where the rest of the
able-bodied men left their offices and stores to follow,
so that when he reached the courthouse, Sutpen had a
larger following than if he actually had been the runaway slave. They arraigned him before a justice, but
by that time your grandfather and Mr. Coldfield had got
there. They signed his bond and late that afternoon he
returned home with Mr. Coldfield, walking along the
same street as of the forenoon, with doubtless the same
faces watching him from behind the window curtains,
to the betrothal supper with no wine at table and no
whiskey before or after. During none of his three passages that day through that street did his bearing alter
—the same unhurried stride to which that new frock
coat swung, the same angle to the new hat above the
eyes and the beard. Your grandfather said that some of
the faïence appearance which the flesh of his face had
had when he came to town five years ago was gone now
and that his face had an honest sunburn. And he was
not fleshier either; your grandfather said that was not it:
it was just that the flesh on his bones had become
quieter, as though passive after some actual breasting
of atmosphere like in running, so that he actually filled
his clothes now, with that quality still swaggering but
without braggadocio or belligerence, though according
to your grandfather the quality had never been belligerence, only watchfulness. And now that was gone, as
though after the three years he could trust his eyes alone

to do the watching, without the flesh on his bones standing sentry also. Two months later, he and Miss Ellen were married.

"It was in June of 1838, almost five years to the day from that Sunday morning when he rode into town on the roan horse. It (the wedding) was in the same Methodist church where he saw Ellen for the first time. The aunt had even forced or nagged (not cajoled: that would not have done it) Mr. Coldfield into allowing Ellen to wear powder on her face for the occasion. The powder was to hide the marks of tears. But before the wedding was over the powder was streaked, caked and channelled. Ellen seems to have entered the church that night out of weeping as though out of rain, gone through the ceremony and then walked back out of the church and into the weeping again, the tears again, the same tears even, the same rain. She got into the carriage and departed in it (the rain) for Sutpen's Hundred.

"It was the wedding which caused the tears: not marrying Sutpen. Whatever tears there were for that, granted there were tears, came later. It was not intended to be a big wedding. That is, Mr. Coldfield seems not to have intended it to be. You will notice that most divorces occur with women who were married by tobacco-chewing j.p.'s in country courthouses or by ministers waked after midnight, with their suspenders showing beneath their coattails and no collar on and a wife or spinster sister in curl papers for witness. So is it too much to believe that these women come to long for divorce from a sense not of incompleteness but of actual frustration and betrayal? that regardless of the breathing evidence of children and all else, they still have in their minds the image of themselves walking to music and turning heads, in all the symbolical trappings and circumstances of ceremonial surrender of that which they no longer possess? and why not, since to them the actual and authentic surrender can only be (and has been) a ceremony like the breaking of a banknote to buy a ticket for the train.

"Of the two men, it was Sutpen who desired the big wedding, the full church and all the ritual. I have this from something your grandfather let drop one day and which he doubtless had from Sutpen himself in the same accidental fashion, since Sutpen never even told Ellen that he wanted it, and the fact that at the last minute he refused to support her in her desire and insistence upon it accounts partly for the tears. Mr. Coldfield apparently intended to use the church into which he had invested a certain amount of sacrifice and doubtless self-denial and certainly actual labor and money for the sake of what might be called a demand balance of spiritual solvency, exactly as he would have used a cotton gin in which he considered himself to have incurred either interest or responsibility, for the ginning of any cotton which he or any member of his family, by blood or by marriage, had raised—that, and no more. Perhaps his wanting a small wedding was due to the same tedious and unremitting husbandry which had enabled him to support mother and sister and marry and raise a family on the proceeds of that store which ten years ago had fitted into a single wagon; or perhaps it was some innate sense of delicacy and fitness (which his sister and daughter did not seem to possess, by the way) regarding the prospective son-in-law whom just two months ago he had been instrumental in getting out of jail. But it was not due to any lack of courage regarding the son-in-law's still anomalous position in the town. Regardless of what their relations before that had been and of what their future relations might be, if Mr.

Coldfield had believed Sutpen guilty at the time of any crime, he would not have raised a finger to take Sutpen out. He might not have gone out of his way to keep Sutpen in jail, but doubtless the best possible moral fumigation which Sutpen could have received at the time in the eyes of his fellow citizens was the fact that Mr. Coldfield signed his bond.

"When they were married, there were just ten people in the church, including the wedding party, of the hundred who had been invited; though when they emerged from the church (it was at night: Sutpen had brought in a half-dozen of his wild Negroes to wait at the door with burning pine knots) the rest of the hundred were there in the persons of boys and youths and men from the drovers' tavern on the edge of town—stock traders and hostlers and such who had not been invited. That was the other half of the reason for Ellen's tears. It was the aunt who persuaded or cajoled Mr. Coldfield into the big wedding. But Sutpen wanted it. He wanted, not the anonymous wife and the anonymous children, but the two names, the stainless wife and the unimpeachable father-in-law, on the license, the patent. Yes, patent, with a gold seal and red ribbons too if that had been practicable. But not for himself. Others might have called the gold seal and the ribbons vanity. But then, so had vanity conceived that house and built it in a strange place and with little else but his bare hands and further handicapped by the chance and probability of meddling interference arising out of the disapprobation of all communities of men toward any situation which they do not understand. And pride: the same pride which wanted such a house, which would accept nothing less, and drove through to get it at whatever cost. And then he lived in it, alone, on a

pallet on the floor for three years until he could furnish
it as it should be furnished—not the least of which furniture was that wedding license. It was not just shelter,
just anonymous wife and children that he wanted, just
as he did not want just wedding.

"But when the female crisis came, when Ellen and the
aunt tried to enlist him on their side to persuade Mr.
Coldfield to the big wedding, he refused to support
them. He doubtless remembered even better than Mr.
Coldfield that two months ago he had been in jail; that
public opinion which at some moment during the five
preceding years had swallowed him even though he
never had quite lain quiet on its stomach, had performed one of mankind's natural and violent and inexplicable volte-faces and regurgitated him. And it did not
help him any that at least two of the citizens who should
have made two of the teeth in the outraged jaw served
instead as props to hold the jaw open and impotent
while he walked out of it unharmed.

"Ellen and the aunt remembered this too. The aunt
did. Being a woman, she was doubtless one of that
league of Jefferson women who, on the second day after
the town saw him five years ago, had agreed never to
forgive him for not having any past, and who had remained consistent. Since the marriage was now a closed
incident, she probably looked upon it as the one chance
not only to secure her niece's future as his wife, but to
justify the action of her brother in getting him out of
jail and her own position as having apparently sanc-
tioned and permitted the wedding which in reality she
could not have prevented. It may have been for the
sake of that big house and the position and state which
the women realized long before the men did that he not
only aimed at but was going to attain. Or maybe women

are even less complex than that and to them any wedding is better than no wedding and a big wedding with a villain preferable to a small one with a saint.

"So the aunt even used Ellen's tears; and Sutpen, who probably knew about what was going to happen, as the time drew near became graver and graver. Not concerned: just watchful, like he must have been from the day when he turned his back upon all that he knew —the faces and the customs—and (he was just fourteen then, he told your grandfather) set out into a world which even in theory he knew nothing about, and with a fixed goal in his mind which most men do not set up until the blood begins to slow at thirty or more and then only because the image represents peace and indolence or at least a crowning of vanity. Even then he had that same alertness which he had to wear later day and night without changing or laying aside, like the clothing which he had to sleep in as well as live in, and in a country and among a people whose very language he had to learn—that unsleeping care which must have known that it could permit itself but one mistake; that alertness for measuring and weighing event against eventuality, circumstance against human nature, his own fallible judgment and mortal clay against not only human but natural forces, choosing and discarding, compromising with his dream and his ambition like you must with the horse which you take across country, over timber, which you control only through your ability to keep the animal from realizing that actually you cannot, that actually it is the stronger.

"His was the curious position now. He was the solitary one. Not Ellen. She not only had the aunt to support her, but the fact that women never plead nor claim loneliness until impenetrable and insurmountable circumstance forces them to give up all hope of attaining

the particular bauble which at the moment they happen
to want. And not Mr. Coldfield. He had not only
public opinion but his own disinclination for the big
wedding to support it without incongruity or paradox.
Then (the tears won; Ellen and the aunt wrote out
a hundred invitations—Sutpen brought in one of the
wild Negroes, who carried them from door to door by
hand—and even sent out a dozen more personal ones
for the dress rehearsal) when they reached the church
for the rehearsal on the night before the wedding and
found the church itself empty and a handful of men
from the town's purlieus (including two of old Ikkemotubbe's Chickasaws) standing in the shadows outside
the door, the tears came down again. Ellen went
through the rehearsal, but afterward the aunt took her
home in a state very near hysteria, though by the next
day it had become just quiet intermittent weeping again.

"There was some talk even of putting the wedding
off. I don't know who it came from, perhaps from Sutpen. But I know who vetoed it. It was as though the
aunt were now bent, no longer on merely thrusting Sutpen down the town's throat, but thrusting the wedding
itself. She spent all the next day going from house to
house, the invitation list in her hand, in a house dress
and a shawl and one of the Coldfield Negroes (they
were both women) following her, perhaps for protection, perhaps just sucked along like a leaf in the wake
of that grim virago fury of female affront; yes, she
came to our house too, though your grandfather had
never intended anything else but to attend the wedding:
the aunt must have had no doubts about Father since
Father had helped take Sutpen out of jail, though she
was probably past all ratiocination by then. Father and
your grandmother were just married then and Mother
was a stranger in Jefferson and I don't know what she

thought except that she would never talk about what happened: about the mad woman whom she had never seen before, who came bursting into the house, not to invite her to a wedding but to dare her not to come, and then rushed out again. Mother could not even tell what wedding she meant at first, and when Father came home he found Mother in hysterics too, and even twenty years later Mother could not tell what actually happened. There was nothing comic in it to her. Father used to tease her about it, but even twenty years after that day, when he would tease her I have seen her begin to raise her hand (perhaps with the thimble on one finger) as though to protect herself and the same look come into her face that must have been there when Ellen's aunt departed.

"The aunt covered the town that morning. It did not take her long and it was complete; by nightfall the circumstances of the situation had spread not only beyond the town but beneath it, penetrating the livery stable and the drovers' tavern which was to supply the guests who did attend. Ellen of course was not aware of this, any more than the aunt herself was, or would have believed what was going to happen even if she had been clairvoyant and could actually have seen the rehearsal of events before time produced them. Not that the aunt would have considered herself insulated against being thus affronted, she simply could not have believed that her intentions and actions of the day could have any result other than the one for which she had surrendered for the time not only all Coldfield dignity but all female modesty as well. Sutpen I suppose could have told her, but doubtless he knew that the aunt would not have believed him. Probably he did not even try: he just did the only thing he could do, which was to send out to Sutpen's Hundred and bring in six or seven

more of his Negroes, men on whom he could depend,
the only men on whom he could depend, and arm them
with the lighted pine knots which they were holding at
the door when the carriage came up and the wedding
party got out. And this is where the tears stopped, because now the street before the church was lined with
carriages and buggies, though only Sutpen and possibly
Mr. Coldfield remarked that instead of being drawn up
before the door and empty, they were halted across the
street and still occupied, and that now the banquette
before the church door was a sort of arena lighted by
the smoking torches which the Negroes held above
their heads, the light of which wavered and gleamed
upon the two lines of faces between which the party
would have to pass to enter the church. There were no
catcalls yet, no jeering; evidently neither Ellen nor the
aunt suspected that anything was wrong.

"For a time Ellen walked out of the weeping, the
tears, and so into the church. It was empty yet save
for your grandfather and grandmother and perhaps a
half dozen more who might have come out of loyalty
to the Coldfields or perhaps to be close and so miss
nothing of that which the town, as represented by the
waiting carriages, seemed to have anticipated as well
as Sutpen did. It was still empty even after the ceremony started and concluded. Ellen had something of
pride too, or at least that vanity which at times can
assume the office of pride and fortitude; besides, nothing
had happened yet. The crowd outside was quiet yet,
perhaps out of respect for the church, out of that apti-
tude and eagerness of the Anglo-Saxon for complete
mystical acceptance of immolated sticks and stones.

"She seems to have walked out of the church and so
into it without any warning whatever. Perhaps she was
still moving beneath that pride which would not allow

the people inside the church to see her weep. She just walked into it, probably hurrying toward the seclusion of the carriage where she could weep; perhaps her first intimation was the voice shouting, 'Look out! Don't hit her now!' and then the object—dirt, filth, whatever it was—passing her, or perhaps the changing light itself as she turned and saw one of the Negroes, his torch raised and in the act of springing toward the crowd, the faces, when Sutpen spoke to him in that tongue which even now a good part of the county did not know was a civilized language. That was what she saw, what the others saw from the halted carriages across the street—the bride shrinking into the shelter of his arm as he drew her behind him and he standing there, not moving even after another object (they threw nothing which could actually injure: it was only clods of dirt and vegetable refuse) struck the hat from his head, and a third struck him full in the chest—standing there motionless, with an expression almost of smiling where his teeth showed through the beard, holding his wild Negroes with that one word (there were doubtless pistols in the crowd; certainly knives: the Negro would not have lived ten seconds if he had sprung) while about the wedding party the circle of faces with open mouths and torch-reflecting eyes seemed to advance and waver and shift and vanish in the smoky glare of the burning pine. He retreated to the carriage, shielding the two women with his body, ordering the Negroes to follow with another word. But they threw nothing else. Apparently it was that first spontaneous outburst, though they had come armed and prepared with the ones they did throw. In fact, that seemed to have been the entire business which had come to a head when the vigilance committee followed him to Mr. Coldfield's gate that day two months before. Because the men who had composed the mob, the traders and drovers and teamsters, returned, vanished back into the region from which they had emerged for this one occasion like rats; scattered, departed about the country—faces which even Ellen was not to remember, seen for the night or the meal or just the drink at other taverns twenty and fifty and a hundred miles further on along nameless roads and then gone from there too; and those who had come in the carriages and buggies to see a Roman holiday, driving out to Sutpen's Hundred to call and (the men) to hunt his game and eat his food again and on occasion gathering at night in his stable while he matched two of his wild Negroes against one another as men match game cocks or perhaps even entered the ring himself. It blew away, though not out of memory. He did not forget that night, even though Ellen, I think, did, since she washed it out of her remembering with tears. Yes, she was weeping again now; it did, indeed, rain on that marriage."

I

THE two Indians crossed the plantation toward the slave quarters. Neat with whitewash, of baked soft brick, the two rows of houses in which lived the slaves belonging to the clan, faced one another across the mild shade of the lane marked and scored with naked feet and with a few homemade toys mute in the dust. There was no sign of life.

"I know what we will find," the first Indian said.

"What we will not find," the second said. Although it was noon, the lane was vacant, the doors of the cabins empty and quiet; no cooking smoke rose from any of the chinked and plastered chimneys.

"Yes. It happened like this when the father of him who is now the Man died."

"You mean, of him who was the Man."

"Yao."

The first Indian's name was Three Basket. He was perhaps sixty. They were both squat men, a little solid, burgherlike; paunchy, with big heads, big, broad, dust-colored faces of a certain blurred serenity like carved heads on a ruined wall in Siam or Sumatra, looming out of a mist. The sun had done it, the violent sun, the violent shade. Their hair looked like sedge grass on burnt-over land. Clamped through one ear Three Basket wore an enameled snuffbox.

"I have said all the time that this is not the good way. In the old days there were no quarters, no Negroes. A man's time was his own then. He had time. Now he must spend most of it finding work for them who prefer sweating to do."

"They are like horses and dogs."

"They are like nothing in this sensible world. Nothing contents them save sweat. They are worse than the white people."

"It is not as though the Man himself had to find work for them to do."

"You said it. I do not like slavery. It is not the good way. In the old days, there was the good way. But not now."

"You do not remember the old way either."

"I have listened to them who do. And I have tried this way. Man was not made to sweat."

"That's so. See what it has done to their flesh."

"Yes. Black. It has a bitter taste, too."

"You have eaten of it?"

"Once. I was young then, and more hardy in the appetite than now. Now it is different with me."

"Yes. They are too valuable to eat now."

"There is a bitter taste to the flesh which I do not like."

"They are too valuable to eat, anyway, when the white men will give horses for them."

They entered the lane. The mute, meager toys—the fetish-shaped objects made of wood and rags and feathers—lay in the dust about the patinaed doorsteps, among bones and broken gourd dishes. But there was no sound from any cabin, no face in any door; had not been since yesterday, when Issetibbeha died. But they already knew what they would find.

It was in the central cabin, a house a little larger than the others, where at certain phases of the moon the Negroes would gather to begin their ceremonies before removing after nightfall to the creek bottom, where they kept the drums. In this room they kept the minor accessories, the cryptic ornaments, the ceremonial records which consisted of sticks daubed with red clay in symbols. It had a hearth in the center of the floor, beneath a hole in the roof, with a few cold wood ashes and a suspended iron pot. The window shutters were closed; when the two Indians entered, after the abashless sunlight they could distinguish nothing with the eyes save a movement, shadow, out of which eyeballs rolled, so that the place appeared to be full of Negroes. The two Indians stood in the door.

"Yao," Basket said. "I said this is not the good way."

"I don't think I want to be here," the second said.

"That is black man's fear which you smell. It does not smell as ours does."

"I don't think I want to be here."

"Your fear has an odor too."

"Maybe it is Issetibbeha which we smell."

"Yao. He knows. He knows what we will find here. He knew when he died what we should find here today." Out of the rank twilight of the room the eyes, the smell, of Negroes rolled about them. "I am Three Basket, whom you know," Basket said into the room. "We are come from the Man. He whom we seek is gone?" The Negroes said nothing. The smell of them, of their bodies, seemed to ebb and flux in the still hot air. They seemed to be musing as one upon something remote, inscrutable. They were like a single octopus. They were like the roots of a huge tree uncovered, the earth broken momentarily upon the writhen, thick, fetid tangle of its lightless and outraged life. "Come," Basket said. "You know our errand. Is he whom we seek gone?"

"They are thinking something," the second said. "I do not want to be here."

"They are knowing something," Basket said.

"They are hiding him, you think?"

"No. He is gone. He has been gone since last night. It happened like this before, when the grandfather of him who is now the Man died. It took us three days to catch him. For three days Doom lay above the ground, saying, 'I see my horse and my dog. But I do not see my slave. What have you done with him that you will not permit me to lie quiet?'"

"They do not like to die."

"Yao. They cling. It makes trouble for us, always. A people without honor and without decorum. Always a trouble."

"I do not like it here."

"Nor do I. But then, they are savages; they cannot be expected to regard usage. That is why I say that this way is a bad way."

"Yao. They cling. They would even rather work in the sun than to enter the earth with a chief. But he is gone."

The Negroes had said nothing, made no sound. The white eyeballs rolled, wild, subdued; the smell was rank, violent. "Yes, they fear," the second said. "What shall we do now?"

"Let us go and talk with the Man."

"Will Moketubbe listen?"

"What can he do? He will not like to. But he is the Man now."

"Yao. He is the Man. He can wear the shoes with the red heels all the time now." They turned and went out. There was no door in the door frame. There were no doors in any of the cabins.

"He did that anyway," Basket said.

"Behind Issetibbeha's back. But now they are his shoes, since he is the Man."

"Yao. Issetibbeha did not like it. I have heard. I know that he said to Moketubbe: 'When you are the Man, the shoes will be yours. But until then, they are my shoes.' But now Moketubbe is the Man; he can wear them."

"Yao," the second said. "He is the Man now. He used to wear the shoes behind Issetibbeha's back, and it was not known if Issetibbeha knew this or not. And then Issetibbeha became dead, who was not old, and the shoes are Moketubbe's, since he is the Man now. What do you think of that?"

"I don't think about it," Basket said. "Do you?"

"No," the second said.

"Good," Basket said. "You are wise."

II

The house sat on a knoll, surrounded by oak trees. The front of it was one story in height, composed of the deck house of a steamboat which had gone ashore and which Doom, Issetibbeha's father, had dismantled with his slaves and hauled on cypress rollers twelve miles home overland. It took them five months. His house consisted at the time of one brick wall. He set the steamboat broadside on to the wall, where now the chipped and flaked gliding of the rococo cornices arched in faint splendor above the gilt lettering of the stateroom names above the jalousied doors.

Doom had been born merely a subchief, a Mingo, one of three children on the mother's side of the family. He made a journey—he was a young man then and New Orleans was a European city—from north Mississippi to New Orleans by keel boat, where he met the Chevalier Sœur Blonde de Vitry, a man whose social position, on its face, was as equivocal as Doom's

own. In New Orleans, among the gamblers and cut-
throats of the river front, Doom, under the tutelage
of his patron, passed as the chief, the Man, the hereditary owner of that land which belonged to the male
side of the family; it was the Chevalier de Vitry who
spoke of him as *l'Homme* or *de l'Homme*, and hence
Doom.

They were seen everywhere together—the Indian,
the squat man with a bold, inscrutable, underbred
face, and the Parisian, the expatriate, the friend, it was
said, of Carondelet and the intimate of General Wilkinson. Then they disappeared, the two of them, vanishing from their old equivocal haunts and leaving behind
them the legend of the sums which Doom was believed
to have won, and some tale about a young woman,
daughter of a fairly well-to-do West Indian family,
the son and brother of whom sought Doom with a
pistol about his old haunts for some time after his
disappearance.

Six months later the young woman herself disappeared, boarding the Saint Louis packet, which put in
one night at a wood landing on the north Mississippi
side, where the woman, accompanied by a Negro maid,
got off. Four Indians met her with a horse and wagon,
and they traveled for three days, slowly, since she was
already big with child, to the plantation, where she
found that Doom was now chief. He never told her
how he accomplished it, save that his uncle and his
cousin had died suddenly. Before that time the house
had consisted of a brick wall built by shiftless slaves,
against which was propped a thatched lean-to divided
into rooms and littered with bones and refuse, set in
the center of ten thousand acres of matchless parklike
forest where deer grazed like domestic cattle. Doom
and the woman were married there a short time before

Issetibbeha was born, by a combination itinerant minister and slave trader who arrived on a mule, to the saddle of which was lashed a cotton umbrella and a three-gallon demijohn of whiskey. After that, Doom began to acquire more slaves and to cultivate some of his land, as the white people did. But he never had enough for them to do. In utter idleness the majority of them led lives transplanted whole out of African jungles, save on the occasions when, entertaining guests, Doom coursed them with dogs.

When Doom died, Issetibbeha, his son, was nineteen. He became proprietor of the land and of the quintupled herd of blacks for which he had no use at all. Though the title of Man rested with him, there was a hierarchy of cousins and uncles who ruled the clan and who finally gathered in squatting conclave over the Negro question, squatting profoundly beneath the golden names above the doors of the steamboat.

"We cannot eat them," one said.

"Why not?"

"There are too many of them."

"That's true," a third said. "Once we started, we should have to eat them all. And that much flesh diet is not good for man."

"Perhaps they will be like deer flesh. That cannot hurt you."

"We might kill a few of them and not eat them," Issetibbeha said.

They looked at him for a while. "What for?" one said.

"That is true," a second said. "We cannot do that. They are too valuable; remember all the bother they have caused us, finding things for them to do. We must do as the white men do."

"How is that?" Issetibbeha said.

"Raise more Negroes by clearing more land to make

corn to feed them, then sell them. We will clear the land and plant it with food and raise Negroes and sell them to the white men for money."

"But what will we do with this money?" a third said.

They thought for a while.

"We will see," the first said. They squatted, profound, grave.

"It means work," the third said.

"Let the Negroes do it," the first said.

"Yao. Let them. To sweat is bad. It is damp. It opens the pores."

"And then the night air enters."

"Yao. Let the Negroes do it. They appear to like sweating."

So they cleared the land with the Negroes and planted it in grain. Up to that time the slaves had lived in a huge pen with a lean-to roof over one corner, like a pen for pigs. But now they began to build quarters, cabins, putting the young Negroes in the cabins in pairs to mate; five years later Issetibbeha sold forty head to a Memphis trader, and he took the money and went abroad upon it, his maternal uncle from New Orleans conducting the trip. At that time the Chevalier Sœur Blonde de Vitry was an old man in Paris, in a toupee and a corset and a careful, toothless old face fixed in a grimace quizzical and profoundly tragic. He borrowed three hundred dollars from Issetibbeha and in return he introduced him into certain circles; a year later Issetibbeha returned home with a gilt bed, a pair of girandoles by whose light it was said that Pompadour arranged her hair while Louis smirked at his mirrored face across her powdered shoulder, and a pair of slippers with red heels. They were too small for him, since he had not worn shoes at all until he reached New Orleans on his way abroad.

He brought the slippers home in tissue paper and kept them in the remaining pocket of a pair of saddle-bags filled with cedar shavings, save when he took them out on occasion for his son, Moketubbe, to play with. At three years of age Moketubbe had a broad, flat, Mongolian face that appeared to exist in a complete and unfathomable lethargy, until confronted by the slippers.

Moketubbe's mother was a comely girl whom Isse-tibbeha had seen one day working in her shift in a melon patch. He stopped and watched her for a while —the broad, solid thighs, the sound back, the serene face. He was on his way to the creek to fish that day, but he didn't go any farther; perhaps while he stood there watching the unaware girl he may have remembered his own mother, the city woman, the fugitive with her fans and laces and her Negro blood, and all the tawdry shabbiness of that sorry affair. Within the year Moketubbe was born; even at three he could not get his feet into the slippers. Watching him in the still, hot afternoons as he struggled with the slippers with a certain monstrous repudiation of fact, Isse-tibbeha laughed quietly to himself. He laughed at Moketubbe's antics with the shoes for several years, because Moketubbe did not give up trying to put them on until he was sixteen. Then he quit. Or Issetibbeha thought he had. But he had merely quit trying in Isse-tibbeha's presence. Issetibbeha's newest wife told him that Moketubbe had stolen and hidden the shoes. Isse-tibbeha quit laughing then, and he sent the woman away, so that he was alone. "Yao," he said. "I too like being alive, it seems." He sent for Moketubbe. "I give them to you," he said.

Moketubbe was twenty-five then, unmarried. Isse-tibbeha was not tall, but he was taller by six inches than his son and almost a hundred pounds lighter. Moketubbe was already diseased with flesh, with a pale, broad, inert face and dropsical hands and feet. "They are yours now," Issetibbeha said, watching him. Moketubbe had looked at him once when he entered, a glance brief, discreet, veiled.

"Thanks," he said.

Issetibbeha looked at him. He could never tell if Moketubbe saw anything, looked at anything. "Why will it not be the same if I give the slippers to you?"

"Thanks," Moketubbe said. Issetibbeha was using snuff at the time; a white man had shown him how to put the powder into his lip and scour it against his teeth with a twig of gum or of alphea.

"Well," he said, "a man cannot live forever." He looked at his son, then his gaze went blank in turn, unseeing, and he mused for an instant. You could not tell what he was thinking, save that he said half aloud: "Yao. But Doom's uncle had no shoes with red heels." He looked at his son again, fat, inert. "Beneath all that, a man might think of doing anything and it not be known until too late." He sat in a splint chair hammocked with deer thongs. "He cannot even get them on; he and I are both frustrated by the same gross meat which he wears. He cannot even get them on. But is that my fault?"

He lived for five years longer, then he died. He was sick one night, and though the doctor came in a skunk-skin vest and burned sticks, Issetibbeha died before noon.

That was yesterday; the grave was dug, and for twelve hours now the People had been coming in wagons and carriages and on horseback and afoot, to eat the baked dog and the succotash and the yams cooked in ashes and to attend the funeral.

III

"It will be three days," Basket said, as he and the other Indian returned to the house. "It will be three days and the food will not be enough; I have seen it before."

The second Indian's name was Louis Berry. "He will smell too, in this weather."

"Yao. They are nothing but a trouble and a care."

"Maybe it will not take three days."

"They run far. Yao. We will smell this Man before he enters the earth. You watch and see if I am not right."

They approached the house.

"He can wear the shoes now," Berry said. "He can wear them now in man's sight."

"He cannot wear them for a while yet," Basket said. Berry looked at him. "He will lead the hunt."

"Moketubbe?" Berry said. "Do you think he will? A man to whom even talking is travail?"

"What else can he do? It is his own father who will soon begin to smell."

"That is true," Berry said. "There is even yet a price he must pay for the shoes. Yao. He has truly bought them. What do you think?"

"What do you think?"

"What do you think?"

"I think nothing."

"Nor do I. Issetibbeha will not need the shoes now. Let Moketubbe have them; Issetibbeha will not care."

"Yao. Man must die."

"Yao. Let him; there is still the Man."

The bark roof of the porch was supported by peeled cypress poles, high above the texas of the steamboat, shading an unfloored banquette where on the trodden earth mules and horses were tethered in bad weather. On the forward end of the steamboat's deck sat an old man and two women. One of the women was dressing a fowl, the other was shelling corn. The old man was talking. He was barefoot, in a long linen frock coat and a beaver hat.

"This world is going to the dogs," he said. "It is being ruined by white men. We got along fine for years and years, before the white men foisted their Negroes upon us. In the old days the old men sat in the shade and ate stewed deer's flesh and corn and smoked tobacco and talked of honor and grave affairs; now what do we do? Even the old wear themselves into the grave taking care of them that like sweating." When Basket and Berry crossed the deck he ceased and looked up at them. His eyes were querulous, bleared; his face was myriad with tiny wrinkles. "He is fled also," he said.

"Yes," Berry said, "he is gone."

"I knew it. I told them so. It will take three weeks, like when Doom died. You watch and see."

"It was three days, not three weeks," Berry said.

"Were you there?"

"No," Berry said. "But I have heard."

"Well, I was there," the old man said. "For three whole weeks, through the swamps and the briers——" They went on and left him talking.

What had been the saloon of the steamboat was now a shell, rotting slowly; the polished mahogany, the carving glinting momentarily and fading through the mold in figures cabalistic and profound; the gutted windows were like cataracted eyes. It contained a few sacks of seed or grain, and the fore part of the running gear of a barouche, to the axle of which two C-springs rusted in graceful curves, supporting nothing. In one corner a fox cub ran steadily and soundlessly up and down a willow cage; three scrawny gamecocks moved in the dust, and the place was pocked and marked with their dried droppings.

They passed through the brick wall and entered a big room of chinked logs. It contained the hinder part of the barouche, and the dismantled body lying on its side, the window slatted over with willow withes, through which protruded the heads, the still, beady, outraged eyes and frayed combs of still more game chickens. It was floored with packed clay; in one corner leaned a crude plow and two hand-hewn boat paddles. From the ceiling, suspended by four deer thongs, hung the gilt bed which Issetibbeha had fetched from Paris. It had neither mattress nor springs, the frame crisscrossed now by a neat hammocking of thongs.

Issetibbeha had tried to have his newest wife, the young one, sleep in the bed. He was congenitally short of breath himself, and he passed the nights half reclining in his splint chair. He would see her to bed and, later, wakeful, sleeping as he did but three or four hours a night, he would sit in the darkness and simulate slumber and listen to her sneak infinitesimally from the gilt and ribboned bed, to lie on a quilt pallet on the floor until just before daylight. Then she would enter the bed quietly again and in turn simulate slumber, while in the darkness beside her Issetibbeha quietly laughed and laughed.

The girandoles were lashed by thongs to two sticks propped in a corner where a ten-gallon whiskey keg lay also. There was a clay hearth; facing it, in the splint chair, Moketubbe sat. He was maybe an inch better than five feet tall, and he weighed two hundred and fifty pounds. He wore a broadcloth coat and no shirt, his round, smooth copper balloon of belly swelling above the bottom piece of a suit of linen underwear. On his feet were the slippers with the red heels. Behind his chair stood a stripling with a punkah-like fan made of fringed paper. Moketubbe sat motionless, with his broad, yellow face with its closed eyes and flat nostrils, his flipperlike arms extended. On his face was an expression profound, tragic, and inert. He did not open his eyes when Basket and Berry came in.

"He has worn them since daylight?" Basket said.

"Since daylight," the stripling said. The fan did not cease. "You can see."

"Yao," Basket said. "We can see." Moketubbe did not move. He looked like an effigy, like a Malay god in frock coat, drawers, naked chest, the trivial scarlet-heeled shoes.

"I wouldn't disturb him, if I were you," the stripling said.

"Not if I were you," Basket said. He and Berry squatted. The stripling moved the fan steadily. "O Man," Basket said, "listen." Moketubbe did not move. "He is gone," Basket said.

"I told you so," the stripling said. "I knew he would flee. I told you."

"Yao," Basket said. "You are not the first to tell us afterward what we should have known before. Why is it that some of you wise men took no steps yesterday to prevent this?"

"He does not wish to die," Berry said.

"Why should he not wish it?" Basket said.

"Because he must die some day is no reason," the stripling said. "That would not convince me either, old man."

"Hold your tongue," Berry said.

"For twenty years," Basket said, "while others of his

race sweat in the fields, he served the Man in the shade. Why should he not wish to die, since he did not wish to sweat?"

"And it will be quick," Berry said. "It will not take long."

"Catch him and tell him that," the stripling said.

"Hush," Berry said. They squatted, watching Moketubbe's face. He might have been dead himself. It was as though he were cased so in flesh that even breathing took place too deep within him to show.

"Listen, O Man," Basket said. "Issetibbeha is dead. He waits. His dog and his horse we have. But his slave has fled. The one who held the pot for him, who ate of his food, from his dish, is fled. Issetibbeha waits."

"Yao," Berry said.

"This is not the first time," Basket said. "This happened when Doom, thy grandfather, lay waiting at the door of the earth. He lay waiting three days, saying, 'Where is my Negro?' And Issetibbeha, thy father, answered, 'I will find him. Rest; I will bring him to you so that you may begin the journey.'"

"Yao," Berry said.

Moketubbe had not moved, had not opened his eyes.

"For three days Issetibbeha hunted in the bottom," Basket said. "He did not even return home for food, until the Negro was with him; then he said to Doom, his father, 'Here is thy dog, thy horse, thy Negro; rest.' Issetibbeha, who is dead since yesterday, said it. And now Issetibbeha's Negro is fled. His horse and his dog wait with him, but his Negro is fled."

"Yao," Berry said.

Moketubbe had not moved. His eyes were closed; upon his supine monstrous shape there was a colossal inertia, something profoundly immobile, beyond and impervious to flesh. They watched his face, squatting.

"When thy father was newly the Man, this happened," Basket said. "And it was Issetibbeha who brought back the slave to where his father waited to enter the earth." Moketubbe's face had not moved, his eyes had not moved. After a while Basket said, "Remove the shoes."

The stripling removed the shoes. Moketubbe began to pant, his bare chest moving deep, as though he were rising from beyond his unfathomed flesh back into life, like up from the water, the sea. But his eyes had not opened yet.

Berry said, "He will lead the hunt."

"Yao," Basket said. "He is the Man. He will lead the hunt."

IV

All that day the Negro, Issetibbeha's body servant, hidden in the barn, watched Issetibbeha's dying. He was forty, a Guinea man. He had a flat nose, a close, small head; the inside corners of his eyes showed red a little, and his prominent gums were a pale bluish red above his square, broad teeth. He had been taken at fourteen by a trader off Kamerun, before his teeth had been filed. He had been Issetibbeha's body servant for twenty-three years.

On the day before, the day on which Issetibbeha lay sick, he returned to the quarters at dusk. In that unhurried hour the smoke of the cooking fires blew slowly across the street from door to door, carrying into the opposite one the smell of the identical meat and bread. The women tended them; the men were gathered at the head of the lane, watching him as he came down the slope from the house, putting his naked feet down carefully in a strange dusk. To the waiting men his eyeballs were a little luminous.

"Issetibbeha is not dead yet," the headman said.

"Not dead," the body servant said. "Who not dead?"

In the dusk they had faces like his, the different ages, the thoughts sealed inscrutable behind faces like the death masks of apes. The smell of the fires, the cooking, blew sharp and slow across the strange dusk, as from another world, above the lane and the pickaninnies naked in the dust.

"If he lives past sundown, he will live until daybreak," one said.

"Who says?"

"Talk says."

"Yao. Talk says. We know but one thing." They looked at the body servant as he stood among them, his eyeballs a little luminous. He was breathing slow and deep. His chest was bare; he was sweating a little. "He knows. He knows it."

"Let us let the drums talk."

"Yao. Let the drums tell it."

The drums began after dark. They kept them hidden in the creek bottom. They were made of hollowed cypress knees, and the Negroes kept them hidden; why, none knew. They were buried in the mud on the bank of a slough; a lad of fourteen guarded them. He was undersized, and a mute; he squatted in the mud there all day, clouded over with mosquitoes, naked save for the mud with which he coated himself against the mosquitoes, and about his neck a fiber bag containing a pig's rib to which black shreds of flesh still adhered, and two scaly barks on a wire. He slobbered onto his clutched knees, drooling; now and then Indians came noiselessly out of the bushes behind him and stood there and contemplated him for a while and went away, and he never knew it.

From the loft of the stable where he lay hidden until

dark and after, the Negro could hear the drums. They were three miles away, but he could hear them as though they were in the barn itself below him, thudding and thudding. It was as though he could see the fire too, and the black limbs turning into and out of the flames in copper gleams. Only there would be no fire. There would be no more light there than where he lay in the dusty loft, with the whispering arpeggios of rat feet along the warm and immemorial ax-squared rafters. The only fire there would be the smudge against mosquitoes where the women with nursing children crouched, their heavy, sluggish breasts nippled full and smooth into the mouths of men children; contemplative, oblivious of the drumming, since a fire would signify life.

There was a fire in the steamboat, where Issetibbeha lay dying among his wives, beneath the lashed girandoles and the suspended bed. He could see the smoke, and just before sunset he saw the doctor come out, in a waistcoat made of skunk skins, and set fire to two clay-daubed sticks at the bows of the boat deck. "So he is not dead yet," the Negro said into the whispering gloom of the loft, answering himself; he could hear the two voices, himself and himself:

"Who not dead?"

"You are dead."

"Yao, I am dead," he said quietly. He wished to be where the drums were. He imagined himself springing out of the bushes, leaping among the drums on his bare, lean, greasy, invisible limbs. But he could not do that, because man leaped past life, into where death was; he dashed into death and did not die because when death took a man, it took him just this side of the end of living. It was when death overran him from behind, still in life. The thin whisper of rat feet died in fainting gusts along the rafters. Once he had eaten rat. He was a boy then, but just come to America. They had lived ninety days in a three-foot-high 'tween deck in tropic latitudes, hearing from topside the drunken New England captain intoning aloud from a book which he did not recognize for ten years afterward to be the Bible. Squatting in the stable so, he had watched the rat, civilized, by association with man reft of its inherent cunning of limb and eye; he had caught it without difficulty, with scarce a movement of his hand, and he ate it slowly, wondering how any of the rats had escaped so long. At that time he was still wearing the single white garment which the trader, a deacon in the Unitarian church, had given him, and he spoke then only his native tongue.

He was naked now, save for a pair of dungaree pants bought by Indians from white men, and an amulet slung on a thong about his hips. The amulet consisted of one half of a mother-of-pearl lorgnon which Issetibbeha had brought back from Paris, and the skull of a cottonmouth moccasin. He had killed the snake himself and eaten it, save the poison head. He lay in the loft, watching the house, the steamboat, listening to the drums, thinking of himself among the drums.

He lay there all night. The next morning he saw the doctor come out, in his skunk vest, and get on his mule and ride away, and he became quite still and watched the final dust from beneath the mule's delicate feet die away, and then he found that he was still breathing and it seemed strange to him that he still breathed air, still needed air. Then he lay and watched quietly, waiting to move, his eyeballs a little luminous, but with a quiet light, and his breathing light and regular, and saw Louis Berry come out and look at the sky. It was good light then, and already five Indians squatted in their

Sunday clothes along the steamboat deck; by noon there were twenty-five there. That afternoon they dug the trench in which the meat would be baked, and the yams; by that time there were almost a hundred guests —decorous, quiet, patient in their stiff European finery —and he watched Berry lead Issetibbeha's mare from the stable and tie her to a tree, and then he watched Berry emerge from the house with the old hound which lay beside Issetibbeha's chair. He tied the hound to the tree too, and it sat there, looking gravely about at the faces. Then it began to howl. It was still howling at sundown, when the Negro climbed down the back wall of the barn and entered the spring branch, where it was already dusk. He began to run then. He could hear the hound howling behind him, and near the spring, already running, he passed another Negro. The two men, the one motionless and the other running, looked for an instant at each other as though across an actual boundary between two different worlds. He ran on into full darkness, mouth closed, fists doubled, his broad nostrils bellowing steadily.

He ran on in the darkness. He knew the country well, because he had hunted it often with Issetibbeha, following on his mule the course of the fox or the cat beside Issetibbeha's mare; he knew it as well as did the men who would pursue him. He saw them for the first time shortly before sunset of the second day. He had run thirty miles then, up the creek bottom, before doubling back; lying in a pawpaw thicket he saw the pursuit for the first time. There were two of them, in shirts and straw hats, carrying their neatly rolled trousers under their arms, and they had no weapons. They were middle-aged, paunchy, and they could not have moved very fast anyway; it would be twelve hours before they could return to where he lay watching them. "So I will have until midnight to rest," he said. He was near enough to the plantation to smell the cooking fires, and he thought how he ought to be hungry, since he had not eaten in thirty hours. "But it is more important to rest," he told himself. He continued to tell himself that, lying in the pawpaw thicket, because the effort of resting, the need and the haste to rest, made his heart thud the same as the running had done. It was as though he had forgot how to rest, as though the six hours were not long enough to do it in, to remember again how to do it.

As soon as dark came he moved again. He had thought to keep going steadily and quietly through the night, since there was nowhere for him to go, but as soon as he moved he began to run at top speed, breasting his panting chest, his broad-flaring nostrils through the choked and whipping darkness. He ran for an hour, lost by then, without direction, when suddenly he stopped, and after a time his thudding heart unraveled from the sound of the drums. By the sound they were not two miles away; he followed the sound until he could smell the smudge fire and taste the acrid smoke. When he stood among them the drums did not cease; only the headman came to him where he stood in the drifting smudge, panting, his nostrils flaring and pulsing, the hushed glare of his ceaseless eyeballs in his mud-daubed face as though they were worked from lungs.

"We have expected thee," the headman said. "Go, now."

"Go?"

"Eat, and go. The dead may not consort with the living; thou knowest that."

"Yao. I know that." They did not look at one another. The drums had not ceased.

"Wilt thou eat?" the headman said.

"I am not hungry. I caught a rabbit this afternoon, and ate while I lay hidden."

"Take some cooked meat with thee, then."

He accepted the cooked meat, wrapped in leaves, and entered the creek bottom again; after a while the sound of the drums ceased. He walked steadily until daybreak. "I have twelve hours," he said. "Maybe more, since the trail was followed by night." He squatted and ate the meat and wiped his hands on his thighs. Then he rose and removed the dungaree pants and squatted again beside a slough and coated himself with mud— face, arms, body and legs—and squatted again, clasping his knees, his head bowed. When it was light enough to see, he moved back into the swamp and squatted again and went to sleep so. He did not dream at all. It was well that he moved, for, waking suddenly in broad daylight and the high sun, he saw the two Indians. They still carried their neatly rolled trousers; they stood opposite the place where he lay hidden, paunchy, thick, soft-looking, a little ludicrous in their straw hats and shirt tails.

"This is wearying work," one said.

"I'd rather be at home in the shade myself," the other said. "But there is the Man waiting at the door to the earth."

"Yao." They looked quietly about; stooping, one of them removed from his shirt tail a clot of cockle-burs. "Damn that Negro," he said.

"Yao. When have they ever been anything but a trial and a care to us?"

In the early afternoon, from the top of a tree, the Negro looked down into the plantation. He could see Issetibbeha's body in a hammock between the two trees where the horse and the dog were tethered, and the concourse about the steamboat was filled with wagons and horses and mules, with carts and saddle-horses, while in bright clumps the women and the smaller children and the old men squatted about the long trench where the smoke from the barbecuing meat blew slow and thick. The men and the big boys would all be down there in the creek bottom behind him, on the trail, their Sunday clothes rolled carefully up and wedged into tree crotches. There was a clump of men near the door to the house, to the saloon of the steamboat, though, and he watched them, and after a while he saw them bring Moketubbe out in a litter made of buckskin and persimmon poles; high hidden in his leafed nook the Negro, the quarry, looked quietly down upon his irrevocable doom with an expression as profound as Moketubbe's own. "Yao," he said quietly. "He will go then. That man whose body has been dead for fifteen years, he will go also."

In the middle of the afternoon he came face to face with an Indian. They were both on a footlog across a slough—the Negro gaunt, lean, hard, tireless and desperate; the Indian thick, soft-looking, the apparent embodiment of the ultimate and the supreme reluctance and inertia. The Indian made no move, no sound; he stood on the log and watched the Negro plunge into the slough and swim ashore and crash away into the undergrowth.

Just before sunset he lay behind a down log. Up the log in slow procession moved a line of ants. He caught them and ate them slowly, with a kind of detachment, like that of a dinner guest eating salted nuts from a dish. They too had a salt taste, engendering a salivary reaction out of all proportion. He ate them slowly, watching the unbroken line move up the log and into oblivious doom with a steady and terrific undeviation. He had eaten nothing else all day; in his caked mud mask his eyes rolled in reddened rims. At sunset, creeping along the creek bank toward where he had spotted a frog, a cottonmouth moccasin slashed him suddenly across the forearm with a thick, sluggish blow. It struck clumsily, leaving two long slashes across his arm like two razor slashes, and half sprawled with its own momentum and rage, it appeared for the moment utterly helpless with its own awkwardness and choleric anger. "Olé, Grandfather," the Negro said. He touched its head and watched it slash him again across his arm, and again, with thick, raking, awkward blows. "It's that I do not wish to die," he said. Then he said it again— "It's that I do not wish to die"—in a quiet tone, of slow and low amaze, as though it were something that, until the words had said themselves, he found that he had not known, or had not known the depth and extent of his desire.

V

Moketubbe took the slippers with him. He could not wear them very long while in motion, not even in the litter where he was slung reclining, so they rested upon a square of fawnskin upon his lap—the cracked, frail slippers a little shapeless now, with their scaled patent-leather surface and buckleless tongues and scarlet heels, lying upon the supine, obese shape just barely alive, carried through swamp and brier by swinging relays of men who bore steadily all day long the crime and its object, on the business of the slain. To Moketubbe it must have been as though, himself immortal, he were being carried rapidly through hell by doomed spirits which, alive, had contemplated his disaster, and, dead, were oblivious partners to his damnation.

After resting for a while, the litter propped in the center of the squatting circle and Moketubbe motion-

less in it, with closed eyes and his face at once peaceful
for the instant and filled with inescapable foreknowledge, he could wear the slippers for a while. The
stripling put them on him, forcing his big, tender,
dropsical feet into them; whereupon into his face came
again that expression, tragic, passive, and profoundly
attentive, which dyspeptics wear. Then they went on.
He made no move, no sound, inert in the rhythmic litter
out of some reserve of inertia, or maybe of some kingly
virtue such as courage or fortitude. After a time they
set the litter down and looked at him, at the yellow face
like that of an idol, beaded over with sweat. Then Three
Basket or Louis Berry would say: "Take them off.
Honor has been served." They would remove the shoes.
Moketubbe's face would not alter, but only then would
his breathing become perceptible, going in and out of
his pale lips with a faint ah-ah-ah sound, and they
would squat again while the couriers and the runners
came up.

"Not yet?"

"Not yet. He is going east. By sunset he will reach
Mouth of Tippah. Then he will turn back. We may
take him tomorrow."

"Let us hope so. It will not be too soon."

"Yao. It has been three days now."

"When Doom died, it took only three days."

"But that was an old man. This one is young."

"Yao. A good race. If he is taken tomorrow, I will win
a horse."

"May you win it."

"Yao. This work is not pleasant."

That was the day on which the food gave out at the
plantation. The guests returned home and came back
the next day with more food, enough for a week longer.
On that day Issetibbeha began to smell; they could

smell him for a long way up and down the bottom when it got hot toward noon and the wind blew. But they didn't capture the Negro on that day, nor on the next. It was about dusk on the sixth day when the couriers came up to the litter; they had found blood. "He has injured himself."

"Not bad, I hope," Basket said. "We cannot send with Issetibbeha one who will be of no service to him."

"Nor whom Issetibbeha himself will have to nurse and care for," Berry said.

"We do not know," the courier said. "He has hidden himself. He has crept back into the swamp. We have left pickets."

They trotted with the litter now. The place where the Negro had crept into the swamp was an hour away. In the hurry and excitement they had forgotten that Moketubbe still wore the slippers; when they reached the place Moketubbe had fainted. They removed the slippers and brought him to.

With dark, they formed a circle about the swamp. They squatted, clouded over with gnats and mosquitoes; the evening star burned low and close down the west, and the constellations began to wheel overhead. "We will give him time," they said. "Tomorrow is just another name for today."

"Yao. Let him have time." Then they ceased, and gazed as one into the darkness where the swamp lay. After a while the noise ceased, and soon the courier came out of the darkness.

"He tried to break out."

"But you turned him back?"

"He turned back. We feared for a moment, the three of us. We could smell him creeping in the darkness, and we could smell something else, which we did not know. That was why we feared, until he told us.

He said to slay him there, since it would be dark and he would not have to see the face when it came. But it was not that which we smelled; he told us what it was. A snake had struck him. That was two days ago. The arm swelled, and it smelled bad. But it was not that which we smelled then, because the swelling had gone down and his arm was no larger than that of a child. He showed us. We felt the arm, all of us did; it was no larger than that of a child. He said to give him a hatchet so he could chop the arm off. But tomorrow is today also."

"Yao. Tomorrow is today."

"We feared for a while. Then he went back into the swamp."

"That is good."

"Yao. We feared. Shall I tell the Man?"

"I will see," Basket said. He went away. The courier squatted, telling again about the Negro. Basket returned. "The Man says that it is good. Return to your post."

The courier crept away. They squatted about the litter; now and then they slept. Sometime after midnight the Negro waked them. He began to shout and talk to himself, his voice coming sharp and sudden out of the darkness, then he fell silent. Dawn came; a white crane flapped slowly across the jonquil sky. Basket was awake. "Let us go now," he said. "It is today."

Two Indians entered the swamp, their movements noisy. Before they reached the Negro they stopped, because he began to sing. They could see him, naked and mud-caked, sitting on a log, singing. They squatted silently a short distance away, until he finished. He was chanting something in his own language, his face lifted to the rising sun. His voice was clear, full, with a quality wild and sad. "Let him have time," the Indians said, squatting, patient, waiting. He ceased and they approached. He looked back and up at them through the cracked mud mask. His eyes were bloodshot, his lips cracked upon his square short teeth. The mask of mud appeared to be loose on his face, as if he might have lost flesh since he put it there; he held his left arm close to his breast. From the elbow down it was caked and shapeless with black mud. They could smell him, a rank smell. He watched them quietly until one touched him on the arm. "Come," the Indian said. "You ran well. Do not be ashamed."

VI

As they neared the plantation in the tainted bright morning, the Negro's eyes began to roll a little, like those of a horse. The smoke from the cooking pit blew low along the earth and upon the squatting and waiting guests about the yard and upon the steamboat deck, in their bright, stiff, harsh finery; the women, the children, the old men. They had sent couriers along the bottom, and another on ahead, and Issetibbeha's body had already been removed to where the grave waited, along with the horse and the dog, though they could still smell him in death about the house where he had lived in life. The guests were beginning to move toward the grave when the bearers of Moketubbe's litter mounted the slope.

The Negro was the tallest there, his high, close, mud-caked head looming above them all. He was breathing hard, as though the desperate effort of the six suspended and desperate days had capitulated upon him at once; although they walked slowly, his naked scarred chest rose and fell above the close-clutched left arm. He looked this way and that continuously, as if he were not seeing, as though sight never quite caught up with the looking. His mouth was open a little upon his big white teeth; he began to pant. The already moving guests halted, pausing, looking back, some with pieces of meat in their hands, as the Negro looked about at their faces with his wild, restrained, unceasing eyes.

"Will you eat first?" Basket said. He had to say it twice.

"Yes," the Negro said. "That's it. I want to eat."

The throng had begun to press back toward the center; the word passed to the outermost: "He will eat first."

They reached the steamboat. "Sit down," Basket said. The Negro sat on the edge of the deck. He was still panting, his chest rising and falling, his head ceaseless with its white eyeballs, turning from side to side. It was as if the inability to see came from within, from hopelessness, not from absence of vision. They brought food and watched quietly as he tried to eat it. He put the food into his mouth and chewed it, but chewing, the half-masticated matter began to emerge from the corners of his mouth and to drool down his chin, onto his chest, and after a while he stopped chewing and sat there, naked, covered with dried mud, the plate on his knees, and his mouth filled with a mass of chewed food, open, his eyes wide and unceasing, panting and panting. They watched him, patient, implacable, waiting.

"Come," Basket said at last.

"It's water I want," the Negro said. "I want water."

The well was a little way down the slope toward the quarters. The slope lay dappled with the shadows of noon, of that peaceful hour when, Issetibbeha napping in his chair and waiting for the noon meal and the long afternoon to sleep in, the Negro, the body servant, would be free. He would sit in the kitchen door then, talking with the women that prepared the food. Beyond the kitchen the lane between the quarters would be quiet, peaceful, with the women talking to one another across the lane and the smoke of the dinner fires blowing upon the pickaninnies like ebony toys in the dust.

"Come," Basket said.

The Negro walked among them, taller than any. The guests were moving on toward where Issetibbeha and the horse and the dog waited. The Negro walked with his high ceaseless head, his panting chest. "Come," Basket said. "You wanted water."

"Yes," the Negro said. "Yes." He looked back at the house, then down to the quarters, where today no fire burned, no face showed in any door, no pickaninny in the dust, panting. "It struck me here, raking me across this arm; once, twice, three times. I said, 'Olé, Grandfather.'"

"Come now," Basket said. The Negro was still going through the motion of walking, his knee action high, his head high, as though he were on a treadmill. His eyeballs had a wild, restrained glare, like those of a horse. "You wanted water," Basket said. "Here it is."

There was a gourd in the well. They dipped it full and gave it to the Negro, and they watched him try to drink. His eyes had not ceased rolling as he tilted the gourd slowly against his caked face. They could watch his throat working and the bright water cascading from either side of the gourd, down his chin and breast. Then the water stopped. "Come," Basket said.

"Wait," the Negro said. He dipped the gourd again and tilted it against his face, beneath his ceaseless eyes. Again they watched his throat working and the unswallowed water sheathing broken and myriad down his chin, channeling his caked chest. They waited, patient, grave, decorous, implacable; clansman and guest and kin. Then the water ceased, though still the empty gourd tilted higher and higher, and still his black throat aped the vain motion of his frustrated swallowing. A piece of water-loosened mud carried away from his chest and broke at his muddy feet, and in the empty gourd they could hear his breath: ah-ah-ah.

"Come," Basket said, taking the gourd from the Negro and hanging it back in the well.

I

WHEN Cass Edmonds and Uncle Buck ran back to the house from discovering that Tomey's Turl had run again, they heard Uncle Buddy cursing and bellowing in the kitchen, then the fox and the dogs came out of the kitchen and crossed the hall into the dogs' room and they heard them run through the dogs' room into his and Uncle Buck's room, then they saw them cross the hall again into Uncle Buddy's room and heard them run through Uncle Buddy's room into the kitchen again and this time it sounded like the whole kitchen chimney had come down and Uncle Buddy bellowing like a steamboat blowing, and this time the fox and the dogs and five or six sticks of firewood all came out of the kitchen together with Uncle Buddy in the middle of them hitting at everything in sight with another stick. It was a good race.

When Cass and Uncle Buck ran into their room to get Uncle Buck's necktie, the fox had treed behind the clock on the mantel. Uncle Buck got the necktie from the drawer and kicked the dogs off and lifted the fox down by the scruff of the neck and shoved it back into the crate under the bed and they went to the kitchen, where Uncle Buddy was picking the breakfast up out of the ashes and wiping it off with his apron. "What in damn's hell do you mean," he said, "turning that damn fox out with the dogs all loose in the house?"

"Damn the fox," Uncle Buck said. "Tomey's Turl has

105

broke out again. Give me and Cass some breakfast quick. We might just barely catch him before he gets there."

Because they knew exactly where Tomey's Turl had gone, he went there every time he could slip off, which was about twice a year. He was heading for Mr. Hubert Beauchamp's place just over the edge of the next county, that Mr. Hubert's sister, Miss Sophonsiba (Mr. Hubert was a bachelor too, like Uncle Buck and Uncle Buddy) was still trying to make people call Warwick after the place in England that she said Mr. Hubert was probably the true earl of only he never even had enough pride, not to mention energy, to take the trouble to establish his just rights. Tomey's Turl would go there to hang around Mr. Hubert's girl Tennie, until somebody came and got him. They couldn't keep him at home by buying Tennie from Mr. Hubert because Uncle Buck said he and Uncle Buddy had so many niggers already that they could hardly walk around on their own land for them, and they couldn't sell Tomey's Turl to Mr. Hubert because Mr. Hubert said he not only wouldn't buy Tomey's Turl, he wouldn't have that damn white half-McCaslin on his place even as a free gift, not even if Uncle Buck and Uncle Buddy were to pay board and keep for him. And if somebody didn't go and get Tomey's Turl right away, Mr. Hubert would fetch him back himself, bringing Miss Sophonsiba, and they would stay for a week or longer, Miss Sophonsiba living in Uncle Buddy's room and Uncle Buddy moved clean out of the house, sleeping in one of the cabins in the quarters where the niggers used to live in his great-grandfather's time until his great-grandfather died and Uncle Buck and Uncle Buddy moved all the niggers into the big house which his great-grandfather had not had time to finish, and not even doing the cooking while they were there and not even coming to the house any more except to sit on the front gallery after supper, sitting in the darkness between Mr. Hubert and Uncle Buck until after a while even Mr. Hubert would give up telling how many more head of niggers and acres of land he would add to what he would give Miss Sophonsiba when she married, and go to bed. And one midnight last summer Uncle Buddy just happened by accident to be awake and hear Mr. Hubert drive out of the lot and by the time he waked them and they got Miss Sophonsiba up and dressed and the team put to the wagon and caught Mr. Hubert, it was almost daylight. So it was always he and Uncle Buck who went to fetch Tomey's Turl because Uncle Buddy never went anywhere, not even to town and not even to fetch Tomey's Turl from Mr. Hubert's, even though they all knew that Uncle Buddy could have risked it ten times as much as Uncle Buck could have dared.

They ate breakfast fast. Uncle Buck put on his necktie while they were running toward the lot to catch the horses. The only time he wore the necktie was on Tomey's Turl's account and he hadn't even had it out of the drawer since that night last summer when Uncle Buddy had waked them in the dark and said, "Get up out of that bed and damn quick." Uncle Buddy didn't own a necktie at all; Uncle Buck said Uncle Buddy wouldn't take that chance even in a section like theirs, where ladies were so damn seldom thank God that a man could ride for days in a straight line without having to dodge a single one. His grandmother (she was Uncle Buck's and Uncle Buddy's sister; she had raised him following his mother's death. That was where he had got his christian name: McCaslin, Carothers McCaslin Edmonds) said that Uncle Buck and Uncle Buddy both used the necktie just as another way or daring people to say they looked like twins, because even at sixty they would still fight anyone who claimed he could not tell them apart; whereupon his father had answered that any man who ever played poker once with Uncle Buddy would never mistake him again for Uncle Buck or anybody else.

Jonas had the two horses saddled and waiting. Uncle Buck didn't mount a horse like he was any sixty years old either, lean and active as a cat, with his round, close-cropped white head and his hard little gray eyes and his white-stubbled jaw, his foot in the iron and the horse already moving, already running at the open gate when Uncle Buck came into the seat. He scrabbled up too, onto the shorter pony, before Jonas could boost him up, clapping the pony with his heels into its own stiff, short-coupled canter, out the gate after Uncle Buck, when Uncle Buddy (he hadn't even noticed him) stepped out from the gate and caught the bit. "Watch him," Uncle Buddy said. "Watch Theophilus. The minute anything begins to look wrong, you ride to hell back here and get me. You hear?"

"Yes, sir," he said. "Lemme go now. I won't even ketch Uncle Buck, let alone Tomey's Turl——"

Uncle Buck was riding Black John, because if they could just catch sight of Tomey's Turl at least one mile from Mr. Hubert's gate, Black John would ride him down in two minutes. So when they came out on the long flat about three miles from Mr. Hubert's, sure enough, there was Tomey's Turl on the Jake mule about a mile ahead. Uncle Buck flung his arm out and back, reining in, crouched on the big horse, his little round head and his gnarled neck thrust forward like a cooter's. "Stole away!" he whispered. "You stay back where he won't see you and flush. I'll circle him through the woods and we will bay him at the creek ford."

He waited until Uncle Buck had vanished into the
woods. Then he went on. But Tomey's Turl saw him.
He closed in too fast; maybe he was afraid he wouldn't
be there in time to see him when he treed. It was the
best race he had ever seen. He had never seen old Jake
go that fast, and nobody had ever known Tomey's Turl
to go faster than his natural walk, even riding a mule.
Uncle Buck whooped once from the woods, running on
sight, then Black John came out of the trees, driving,
soupled out flat and level as a hawk, with Uncle Buck
right up behind his ears now and yelling so that they
looked exactly like a big black hawk with a sparrow
riding it, across the field and over the ditch and across
the next field, and he was running too; the mare went
out before he even knew she was ready, and he was
yelling too. Because, being a nigger, Tomey's Turl
should have jumped down and run for it afoot as soon
as he saw them. But he didn't; maybe Tomey's Turl
had been running off from Uncle Buck for so long that
he had even got used to running away like a white man
would do it. And it was like he and old Jake had added
Tomey's Turl's natural walking speed to the best that
old Jake had ever done in his life, and it was just
exactly enough to beat Uncle Buck to the ford. Because
when he and the pony arrived, Black John was blown
and lathered and Uncle Buck was down, leading him
around in a circle to slow him down, and they could
already hear Mr. Hubert's dinner horn a mile away.

Only, for a while Tomey's Turl didn't seem to be at
Mr. Hubert's either. The boy was still sitting on the
gatepost, blowing the horn—there was no gate there;
just two posts and a nigger boy about his size sitting on
one of them, blowing a fox-horn; this was what Miss
Sophonsiba was still reminding people was named Warwick even when they had already known for a long

time that's what she aimed to have it called, until when
they wouldn't call it Warwick she wouldn't even seem
to know what they were talking about and it would
sound as if she and Mr. Hubert owned two separate
plantations covering the same area of ground, one on
top of the other. Mr. Hubert was sitting in the spring-
house with his boots off and his feet in the water,
drinking a toddy. But nobody there had seen Tomey's
Turl; for a time it looked like Mr. Hubert couldn't
even place who Uncle Buck was talking about. "Oh,
that nigger," he said at last. "We'll find him after dinner."

Only it didn't seem as if they were going to eat either.
Mr. Hubert and Uncle Buck had a toddy, then Mr.
Hubert finally sent to tell the boy on the gatepost he
could quit blowing, and he and Uncle Buck had another
toddy and Uncle Buck still saying, "I just want my
nigger. Then we got to get on back toward home."

"After dinner," Mr. Hubert said. "If we don't start
him somewhere around the kitchen, we'll put the dogs
on him. They'll find him if it's in the power of mortal
Walker dogs to do it."

But at last a hand began waving a handkerchief or
something white through the broken place in an upstairs shutter. They went to the house, crossing the back
gallery, Mr. Hubert warning them again, as he always
did, to watch out for the rotted floor-board he hadn't
got around to having fixed yet. Then they stood in the
hall, until presently there was a jangling and swishing
noise and they began to smell the perfume, and Miss
Sophonsiba came down the stairs. Her hair was roached
under a lace cap; she had on her Sunday dress and
beads and a red ribbon around her throat and a little
nigger girl carrying her fan and he stood quietly a step

behind Uncle Buck, watching her lips until they opened
and he could see the roan tooth. He had never known
anyone before with a roan tooth and he remembered
how one time his grandmother and his father were
talking about Uncle Buddy and Uncle Buck and his
grandmother said that Miss Sophonsiba had matured
into a fine-looking woman once. Maybe she had. He
didn't know. He wasn't but nine.

"Why, Mister Theophilus," she said. "And McCaslin,"
she said. She had never looked at him and she wasn't
talking to him and he knew it, although he was prepared and balanced to drag his foot when Uncle Buck
did. "Welcome to Warwick."

He and Uncle Buck dragged their foot. "I just come
to get my nigger," Uncle Buck said. "Then we got to
get on back home."

Then Miss Sophonsiba said something about a
bumblebee, but he couldn't remember that. It was too
fast and there was too much of it, the earrings and
beads clashing and jingling like little trace chains on a
toy mule trotting and the perfume stronger too, like the
earrings and beads sprayed it out each time they moved
and he watched the roan-colored tooth flick and glint
between her lips; something about Uncle Buck was a
bee sipping from flower to flower and not staying long
anywhere and all that stored sweetness to be wasted on
Uncle Buddy's desert air, calling Uncle Buddy Mister
Amodeus like she called Uncle Buck Mister Theophilus,
or maybe the honey was being stored up against the
advent of a queen and who was the lucky queen and
when? "Ma'am?" Uncle Buck said. Then Mr. Hubert
said:

"Hah. A buck bee. I reckon that nigger's going to
think he's a buck hornet, once he lays hands on him.

But I reckon what Buck's thinking about sipping right now is some meat gravy and biscuit and a cup of coffee. And so am I."

They went into the dining room and ate and Miss Sophonsiba said how seriously now neighbors just a half day's ride apart ought not to go so long as Uncle Buck did, and Uncle Buck said Yessum, and Miss Sophonsiba said Uncle Buck was just a confirmed roving bachelor from the cradle born and this time Uncle Buck even quit chewing and looked and said, Yes, ma'am, he sure was, and born too late at it to ever change now but at least he could thank God no lady would ever have to suffer the misery of living with him and Uncle Buddy, and Miss Sophonsiba said Ah, that maybe Uncle Buck just ain't met the woman yet who would not only accept what Uncle Buck was pleased to call misery, but who would make Uncle Buck consider even his freedom a small price to pay, and Uncle Buck said, "Nome. Not yet."

Then he and Mr. Hubert and Uncle Buck went out to the front gallery and sat down. Mr. Hubert hadn't even got done taking his shoes off again and inviting Uncle Buck to take his off, when Miss Sophonsiba came out the door carrying a tray with another toddy on it. "Damnit, Sibbey," Mr. Hubert said. "He's just et. He don't want to drink that now." But Miss Sophonsiba didn't seem to hear him at all. She stood there, the roan tooth not flicking now but fixed because she wasn't talking now, handing the toddy to Uncle Buck until after a while she said how her papa always said nothing sweetened a Missippi toddy like the hand of a Missippi lady and would Uncle Buck like to see how she use to sweeten her papa's toddy for him? She lifted the toddy and took a sip of it and handed it again to Uncle Buck and this time Uncle Buck took it. He dragged his foot

again and drank the toddy and said if Mr. Hubert was
going to lay down, he would lay down a while too,
since from the way things looked Tomey's Turl was
fixing to give them a long hard race unless Mr. Hubert's
dogs were a considerable better than they used to be.

Mr. Hubert and Uncle Buck went into the house.
After a while he got up too and went around to the
back yard to wait for them. The first thing he saw was
Tomey's Turl's head slipping along above the lane
fence. But when he cut across the yard to turn him,
Tomey's Turl wasn't even running. He was squatting
behind a bush, watching the house, peering around the
bush at the back door and the upstairs windows, not
whispering exactly but not talking loud either: "Whut
they doing now?"

"They're taking a nap now," he said. "But never
mind that; they're going to put the dogs on you when
they get up."

"Hah," Tomey's Turl said. "And nem you mind that
neither. I got protection now. All I needs to do is to
keep Old Buck from ketching me unto I gets the word."

"What word?" he said. "Word from who? Is Mr.
Hubert going to buy you from Uncle Buck?"

"Huh," Tomey's Turl said again. "I got more protection than whut Mr. Hubert got even." He rose to his
feet. "I gonter tell you something to remember: anytime you wants to git something done, from hoeing out
a crop to getting married, just get the womenfolks to
working at it. Then all you needs to do is set down and
wait. You member that."

Then Tomey's Turl was gone. And after a while he
went back to the house. But there wasn't anything but
the snoring coming out of the room where Uncle Buck
and Mr. Hubert were, and some more light-sounding
snoring coming from upstairs. He went to the spring-

house and sat with his feet in the water as Mr. Hubert
had been doing, because soon now it would be cool
enough for a race. And sure enough, after a while Mr.
Hubert and Uncle Buck came out onto the back gallery, with Miss Sophonsiba right behind them with the
toddy tray only this time Uncle Buck drank his before
Miss Sophonsiba had time to sweeten it, and Miss
Sophonsiba told them to get back early, that all Uncle
Buck knew of Warwick was just dogs and niggers and
now that she had him, she wanted to show him her
garden that Mr. Hubert and nobody else had any sayso
in. "Yessum," Uncle Buck said. "I just want to catch
my nigger. Then we got to get on back home."

Four or five niggers brought up the three horses.
They could already hear the dogs waiting still coupled
in the lane, and they mounted and went on down the
lane, toward the quarters, with Uncle Buck already out
in front of even the dogs. So he never did know just
when and where they jumped Tomey's Turl, whether
he flushed out of one of the cabins or not. Uncle Buck
was away out in front on Black John and they hadn't
even cast the dogs yet when Uncle Buck roared, "Gone
away! I godfrey, he broke cover then!" and Black John's
feet clapped four times like pistol shots while he was
gathering to go out, then he and Uncle Buck vanished
over the hill like they had run at the blank edge of the
world itself. Mr. Hubert was roaring too: "Gone away!
Cast them!" and they all piled over the crest of the hill
just in time to see Tomey's Turl away out across the
flat, almost to the woods, and the dogs streaking down
the hill and out onto the flat. They just tongued once
and when they came boiling up around Tomey's Turl
it looked like they were trying to jump up and lick him
in the face until even Tomey's Turl slowed down and
he and the dogs all went into the woods together, walk-

ing, like they were going home from a rabbit hunt. And
when they caught up with Uncle Buck in the woods,
there was no Tomey's Turl and no dogs either, nothing
but old Jake about a half an hour later, hitched in a
clump of bushes with Tomey's Turl's coat tied on him
for a saddle and near a half bushel of Mr. Hubert's
oats scattered around on the ground that old Jake never
even had enough appetite left to nuzzle up and spit
back out again. It wasn't any race at all.

"We'll get him tonight though," Mr. Hubert said.
"We'll bait for him. We'll throw a picquet of niggers
and dogs around Tennie's house about midnight, and
we'll get him."

"Tonight, hell," Uncle Buck said. "Me and Cass and
that nigger all three are going to be half way home by
dark. Ain't one of your niggers got a fyce or something
that will trail them hounds?"

"And fool around here in the woods for half the night
too?" Mr. Hubert said. "When I'll bet you five hundred
dollars that all you got to do to catch that nigger is to
walk up to Tennie's cabin after dark and call him?"

"Five hundred dollars?" Uncle Buck said. "Done! Because me and him neither one are going to be anywhere
near Tennie's house by dark. Five hundred dollars!"
He and Mr. Hubert glared at one another.

"Done!" Mr. Hubert said.

So they waited while Mr. Hubert sent one of the
niggers back to the house on old Jake and in about a half
an hour the nigger came back with a little bob-tailed
black fyce and a new bottle of whiskey. Then he rode
up to Uncle Buck and held something out to him
wrapped in a piece of paper. "What?" Uncle Buck said.

"It's for you," the nigger said. Then Uncle Buck took
it and unwrapped it. It was the piece of red ribbon that
had been on Miss Sophonsiba's neck and Uncle Buck

sat there on Black John, holding the ribbon like it was a little water moccasin only he wasn't going to let anybody see he was afraid of it, batting his eyes fast at the nigger. Then he stopped batting his eyes.

"What for?" he said.

"She just sont hit to you," the nigger said. "She say to tell you 'success.'"

"She said what?" Uncle Buck said.

"I don't know, sir," the nigger said. "She just say 'success.'"

"Oh," Uncle Buck said. And the fyce found the hounds. They heard them first, from a considerable distance. It was just before sundown and they were not trailing, they were making the noise dogs make when they want to get out of something. They found what that was too. It was a ten-foot-square cotton-house in a field about two miles from Mr. Hubert's house and all eleven of the dogs were inside it and the door wedged with a chunk of wood. They watched the dogs come boiling out when the nigger opened the door, Mr. Hubert sitting his horse and looking at the back of Uncle Buck's neck.

"Well, well," Mr. Hubert said. "That's something, anyway. You can use them again now. They don't seem to have no more trouble with your nigger than he seems to have with them."

"Not enough," Uncle Buck said. "That means both of them. I'll stick to the fyce."

"All right," Mr. Hubert said. Then he said, "Hell, 'Filus, come on. Let's go eat supper. I tell you, all you got to do to catch that nigger is——"

"Five hundred dollars," Uncle Buck said.

"What?" Mr. Hubert said. He and Uncle Buck looked at each other. They were not glaring now. They were not joking each other either. They sat there in the be-

ginning of twilight, looking at each other, just blinking
a little. "What five hundred dollars?" Mr. Hubert said.
"That you won't catch that nigger in Tennie's cabin at
midnight tonight?"

"That me or that nigger neither ain't going to be
near nobody's house but mine at midnight tonight."
Now they did glare at each other.

"Five hundred dollars," Mr. Hubert said. "Done."

"Done," Uncle Buck said.

"Done," Mr. Hubert said.

"Done," Uncle Buck said.

So Mr. Hubert took the dogs and some of the niggers
and went back to the house. Then he and Uncle Buck
and the nigger with the fyce went on, the nigger leading
old Jake with one hand and holding the fyce's leash (it
was a piece of gnawed plowline) with the other. Now
Uncle Buck let the fyce smell Tomey's Turl's coat; it
was like for the first time now the fyce found out what
they were after and they would have let him off the
leash and kept up with him on the horses, only about
that time the nigger boy began blowing the fox-horn
for supper at the house and they didn't dare risk it.

Then it was full dark. And then—he didn't know how
much later nor where they were, how far from the
house, except that it was a good piece and it had been
dark for good while and they were still going on, with
Uncle Buck leaning down from time to time to let the
fyce have another smell of Tomey's Turl's coat while
Uncle Buck took another drink from the whiskey bottle
—they found that Tomey's Turl had doubled and was
making a long swing back toward the house. "I godfrey,
we've got him," Uncle Buck said. "He's going to earth.
We'll cut back to the house and head him before he
can den." So they left the nigger to cast the fyce and
follow him on old Jake, and he and Uncle Buck rode

for Mr. Hubert's, stopping on the hills to blow the horses and listen to the fyce down in the creek bottom where Tomey's Turl was still making his swing.

But they never caught him. They reached the dark quarters; they could see lights still burning in Mr. Hubert's house and somebody was blowing the fox-horn again and it wasn't any boy and he had never heard a fox-horn sound mad before either, and he and Uncle Buck scattered out on the slope below Tennie's cabin. Then they heard the fyce, not trailing now but yapping, about a mile away, then the nigger whooped and they knew the fyce had faulted. It was at the creek. They hunted the banks both ways for more than an hour, but they couldn't straighten Tomey's Turl out. At last even Uncle Buck gave up and they started back toward the house, the fyce riding too now, in front of the nigger on the mule. They were just coming up the lane to the quarters; they could see on along the ridge to where Mr. Hubert's house was all dark now, when all of a sudden the fyce gave a yelp and jumped down from old Jake and hit the ground running and yelling every jump, and Uncle Buck was down too and had snatched him off the pony almost before he could clear his feet from the irons, and they ran too, on past the dark cabins toward the one where the fyce had treed. "We got him!" Uncle Buck said. "Run around to the back. Don't holler; just grab up a stick and knock on the back door, loud."

Afterward, Uncle Buck admitted that it was his own mistake, that he had forgotten when even a little child should have known: not ever to stand right in front of or right behind a nigger when you scare him; but always to stand to one side of him. Uncle Buck forgot that. He was standing facing the front door and right in front of it, with the fyce right in front of him yelling fire and murder every time it could draw a new breath; he said the first he knew was when the fyce gave a shriek and whirled and Tomey's Turl was right behind it. Uncle Buck said he never even saw the door open; that the fyce just screamed once and ran between his legs and then Tomey's Turl ran right clean over him. He never even bobbled; he knocked Uncle Buck down and then caught him before he fell without even stopping, snatched him up under one arm, still running, and carried him along for about ten feet, saying, "Look out of here, old Buck. Look out of here, old Buck," before he threw him away and went on. By that time they couldn't even hear the fyce any more at all.

Uncle Buck wasn't hurt; it was only the wind knocked out of him where Tomey's Turl had thrown him down on his back. But he had been carrying the whiskey bottle in his back pocket, saving the last drink until Tomey's Turl was captured, and he refused to move until he knew for certain if it was just whiskey and not blood. So Uncle Buck laid over on his side easy, and he knelt behind him and raked the broken glass out of his pocket. Then they went on to the house. They walked. The nigger came up with the horses, but nobody said anything to Uncle Buck about riding again. They couldn't hear the fyce at all now. "He was going fast, all right," Uncle Buck said. "But I don't believe that even he will catch that fyce, I godfrey, what a night."

"We'll catch him tomorrow," he said.

"Tomorrow, hell," Uncle Buck said. "We'll be at home tomorrow. And the first time Hubert Beauchamp or that nigger either one set foot on my land, I'm going to have them arrested for trespass and vagrancy."

The house was dark. They could hear Mr. Hubert snoring good now, as if he had settled down to road-gaiting at it. But they couldn't hear anything from upstairs, even when they were inside the dark hall, at the foot of the stairs. "Likely hers will be at the back," Uncle Buck said. "Where she can holler down to the kitchen without having to get up. Besides, an unmarried lady will sholy have her door locked with strangers in the house." So Uncle Buck eased himself down onto the bottom step, and he knelt and drew Uncle Buck's boots off. Then he removed his own and set them against the wall, and he and Uncle Buck mounted the stairs, feeling their way up and into the upper hall. It was dark too, and still there was no sound anywhere except Mr. Hubert snoring below, so they felt their way along the hall toward the front of the house, until they felt a door. They could hear nothing beyond the door, and when Uncle Buck tried the knob, it opened. "All right," Uncle Buck whispered. "Be quiet." They could see a little now, enough to see the shape of the bed and the mosquito-bar. Uncle Buck threw down his suspenders and unbuttoned his trousers and went to the bed and eased himself carefully down onto the edge of it, and he knelt again and drew Uncle Buck's trousers off and he was just removing his own when Uncle Buck lifted the mosquito-bar and raised his feet and rolled into the bed. That was when Miss Sophonsiba sat up on the other side of Uncle Buck and gave the first scream.

II

When he reached home just before dinner time the next day, he was just about worn out. He was too tired to eat, even if Uncle Buddy had waited to eat dinner first; he couldn't have stayed on the pony another mile without going to sleep. In fact, he must have gone to sleep while he was telling Uncle Buddy, because the next thing he knew it was late afternoon and he was lying on some hay in the jolting wagon-bed, with Uncle Buddy sitting on the seat above him exactly the same way he sat a horse or sat in his rocking chair before the kitchen hearth while he was cooking, holding the whip exactly as he held the spoon or fork he stirred and tasted with. Uncle Buddy had some cold bread and meat and a jug of buttermilk wrapped in damp towsacks waiting when he waked up. He ate, sitting in the wagon in almost the last of the afternoon. They must have come fast, because they were not more than two miles from Mr. Hubert's. Uncle Buddy waited for him to eat. Then he said, "Tell me again," and he told it again: how he and Uncle Buck finally found a room without anybody in it, and Uncle Buck sitting on the side of the bed saying, "O godfrey, Cass. O godfrey, Cass," and then they heard Mr. Hubert's feet on the stairs and watched the light come down the hall and Mr. Hubert came in, in his nightshirt, and walked over and set the candle on the table and stood looking at Uncle Buck.

"Well, 'Filus," he said. "She's got you at last."

"It was an accident," Uncle Buck said. "I swear to godfrey——"

"Hah," Mr. Hubert said. "Don't tell me. Tell her that."

"I did," Uncle Buck said. "I did tell her. I swear to God——"

"Sholy," Mr. Hubert said. "And just listen." They listened a minute. He had been hearing her all the time. She was nowhere near as loud as at first; she was just steady. "Don't you want to go back in there and tell her again it was an accident, that you never meant nothing and to just excuse you and forget about it? All right."

"All right what?" Uncle Buck said.

"Go back in there and tell her again," Mr. Hubert

said. Uncle Buck looked at Mr. Hubert for a minute. He batted his eyes fast.

"Then what will I come back and tell you?" he said.

"To me?" Mr. Hubert said. "I would call that a horse of another color. Wouldn't you?"

Uncle Buck looked at Mr. Hubert. He batted his eyes fast again. Then he stopped again. "Wait," he said. "Be reasonable. Say I did walk into a lady's bedroom, even Miss Sophonsiba's; say, just for the sake of the argument, there wasn't no other lady in the world but her and so I walked into hers and tried to get in bed with her, would I have took a nine-year-old boy with me?"

"Reasonable is just what I'm being," Mr. Hubert said. "You come into bear-country of your own free will and accord. All right; you were a grown man and you knew it was bear-country and you knew the way back out like you knew the way in and you had your chance to take it. But no. You had to crawl into the den and lay down by the bear. And whether you did or didn't know the bear was in it don't make any difference. So if you got back out of that den without even a claw-mark on you, I would not only be unreasonable, I'd be a damned fool. After all, I'd like a little peace and quiet and freedom myself, now I got a chance for it. Yes, sir. She's got you, 'Filus, and you know it. You run a hard race and you run a good one, but you skun the hen-house one time too many."

"Yes," Uncle Buck said. He drew his breath in and let it out again, slow and not loud. But you could hear it. "Well," he said. "So I reckon I'll have to take the chance then."

"You already took it," Mr. Hubert said. "You did that when you came back here." Then he stopped too. Then he batted his eyes, but only about six times. Then he stopped and looked at Uncle Buck for more than a minute. "What chance?" he said.

"That five hundred dollars," Uncle Buck said.

"What five hundred dollars?" Mr. Hubert said. He and Uncle Buck looked at one another. Now it was Mr. Hubert that batted his eyes again and then stopped again. "I thought you said you found him in Tennie's cabin."

"I did," Uncle Buck said. "What you bet me was I would catch him there. If there had been ten of me standing in front of that door, we wouldn't have caught him." Mr. Hubert blinked at Uncle Buck, slow and steady.

"So you aim to hold me to that fool bet," he said.

"You took your chance too," Uncle Buck said. Mr. Hubert blinked at Uncle Buck. Then he stopped. Then he went and took the candle from the table and went out. They sat on the edge of the bed and watched the light go down the hall and heard Mr. Hubert's feet on the stairs. After a while they began to see the light again and they heard Mr. Hubert's feet coming back up the stairs. Then Mr. Hubert entered and went to the table and set the candle down and laid a deck of cards by it.

"One hand," he said. "Draw. You shuffle, I cut, this boy deals. Five hundred dollars against Sibbey. And we'll settle this nigger business once and for all too. If you win, you buy Tennie; if I win, I buy that boy of yours. The price will be the same for each one: three hundred dollars."

"Win?" Uncle Buck said. "The one that wins buys the niggers?"

"Wins Sibbey, damn it!" Mr. Hubert said. "Wins

Sibbey! What the hell else are we setting up till midnight arguing about? The lowest hand wins Sibbey and buys the niggers."

"All right," Uncle Buck said. "I'll buy the damn girl then and we'll call the rest of this foolishness off."

"Hah," Mr. Hubert said again. "This is the most serious foolishness you ever took part in in your life. No. You said you wanted your chance, and now you've got it. Here it is, right here on this table, waiting on you."

So Uncle Buck shuffled the cards and Mr. Hubert cut them. Then he took up the deck and dealt in turn until Uncle Buck and Mr. Hubert had five. And Uncle Buck looked at his hand a long time and then said two cards and he gave them to him, and Mr. Hubert looked at his hand quick and said one card and he gave it to him and Mr. Hubert flipped his discard onto the two which Uncle Buck had discarded and slid the new card into his hand and opened it out and looked at it quick again and closed it and looked at Uncle Buck and said, "Well? Did you help them threes?"

"No," Uncle Buck said.

"Well I did," Mr. Hubert said. He shot his hand across the table so that the cards fell face-up in front of Uncle Buck and they were three kings and two fives, and said, "By God, Buck McCaslin, you have met your match at last."

"And that was all?" Uncle Buddy said. It was late then, near sunset; they would be at Mr. Hubert's in another fifteen minutes.

"Yes, sir," he said, telling that too: how Uncle Buck waked him at daylight and he climbed out a window and got the pony and left, and how Uncle Buck said that if they pushed him too close in the meantime, he would climb down the gutter too and hide in the woods until Uncle Buddy arrived.

"Hah," Uncle Buddy said. "Was Tomey's Turl there?"

"Yes, sir," he said. "He was waiting in the stable when I got the pony. He said, 'Ain't they settled it yet?' "

"And what did you say?" Uncle Buddy said.

"I said, 'Uncle Buck looks like he's settled. But Uncle Buddy ain't got here yet.' "

"Hah," Uncle Buddy said.

And that was about all. They reached the house. Maybe Uncle Buck was watching them, but if he was, he never showed himself, never came out of the woods. Miss Sophonsiba was nowhere in sight either, so at least Uncle Buck hadn't quite given up; at least he hadn't asked her yet. And he and Uncle Buddy and Mr. Hubert ate supper and they came in from the kitchen and cleared the table, leaving only the lamp on it and the deck of cards.

Then it was just like it was the night before, except that Uncle Buddy had no necktie and Mr. Hubert wore clothes now instead of a nightshirt and it was a shaded lamp on the table instead of a candle, and Mr. Hubert sitting at his end of the table with the deck in his hands, riffling the edges with his thumb and looking at Uncle Buddy. Then he tapped the edges even and set the deck out in the middle of the table, under the lamp, and folded his arms on the edge of the table and leaned forward a little on the table, looking at Uncle Buddy, who was sitting at his end of the table with his hands in his lap, all one gray color, like an old gray rock or a stump with gray moss on it, that still, with his round white head like Uncle Buck's but he didn't blink like Uncle Buck and he was a little thicker than Uncle Buck, as if from sitting down so much watching food cook, as if the things he cooked had made him a little thicker than he would have been and the things he cooked with, the flour and such, had made him all one same quiet color.

"Little toddy before we start?" Mr. Hubert said.

"I don't drink," Uncle Buddy said.

"That's right," Mr. Hubert said. "I knew there was something else besides just being woman-weak that makes 'Filus seem human. But no matter." He batted his eyes twice at Uncle Buddy. "Buck McCaslin against the land and niggers you have heard me promise as Sophonsiba's dowry on the day she marries. If I beat you, 'Filus marries Sibbey without any dowry. If you beat me, you get 'Filus. But I still get the three hundred dollars 'Filus owes me for Tennie. Is that correct?"

"That's correct," Uncle Buddy said.

"Stud," Mr. Hubert said. "One hand. You to shuffle, me to cut, this boy to deal."

"No," Uncle Buddy said. "Not Cass. He's too young. I don't want him mixed up in any gambling."

"Hah," Mr. Hubert said. "It's said that a man playing cards with Amodeus McCaslin ain't gambling. But no matter." But he was still looking at Uncle Buddy; he never even turned his head when he spoke: "Go to the back door and holler. Bring the first creature that answers, animal mule or human, that can deal ten cards."

So he went to the back door. But he didn't have to call because Tomey's Turl was squatting against the wall just outside the door, and they returned to the dining-room where Mr. Hubert still sat with his arms folded on his side of the table and Uncle Buddy sat with his hands in his lap on his side and the deck of cards face-down under the lamp between them. Neither of them even looked up when he and Tomey's Turl entered. "Shuffle," Mr. Hubert said. Uncle Buddy shuffled and set the cards back under the lamp and put his hands back into his lap and Mr. Hubert cut the deck and folded his arms back onto the table-edge. "Deal," he said. Still neither he nor Uncle Buddy looked up. They just sat there while Tomey's Turl's saddle-colored hands came into the light and took up the deck and dealt, one card face-down to Mr. Hubert and one face-down to Uncle Buddy, and one face-up to Mr. Hubert and it was a king, and one face-up to Uncle Buddy and it was a six.

"Buck McCaslin against Sibbey's dowry," Mr. Hubert said. "Deal." And the hand dealt Mr. Hubert a card and it was a three, and Uncle Buddy a card and it was a two. Mr. Hubert looked at Uncle Buddy. Uncle Buddy rapped once with his knuckles on the table.

"Deal," Mr. Hubert said. And the hand dealt Mr. Hubert a card and it was another three, and Uncle Buddy a card and it was a four. Mr. Hubert looked at Uncle Buddy's cards. Then he looked at Uncle Buddy and Uncle Buddy rapped on the table again with his knuckles.

"Deal," Mr. Hubert said, and the hand dealt him an ace and Uncle Buddy a five and now Mr. Hubert just sat still. He didn't look at anything or move for a whole minute; he just sat there and watched Uncle Buddy put one hand onto the table for the first time since he shuffled and pinch up one corner of his face-down card and look at it and then put his hand back into his lap. "Check," Mr. Hubert said.

"I'll bet you them two niggers," Uncle Buddy said. He didn't move either. He sat there just like he sat in the wagon or on a horse or in the rocking chair he cooked from.

"Against what?" Mr. Hubert said.

"Against the three hundred dollars Theophilus owes you for Tennie, and the three hundred you and Theophilus agreed on for Tomey's Turl," Uncle Buddy said.

"Hah," Mr. Hubert said, only it wasn't loud at all this time, nor even short. Then he said "Hah. Hah. Hah" and not loud either. Then he said, "Well." Then he said, "Well, well." Then he said: "We'll check up for a minute. If I win, you take Sibbey without dowry and the two niggers, and I don't owe 'Filus anything. If you win——"

"—Theophilus is free. And you owe him the three hundred dollars for Tomey's Turl," Uncle Buddy said.

"That's just if I call you," Mr. Hubert said. "If I don't call you, 'Filus won't owe me nothing and I won't owe 'Filus nothing, unless I take that nigger which I have been trying to explain to you and him both for years that I won't have on my place. We will be right back where all this foolishness started from, except for that. So what it comes down to is, I either got to give a nigger away, or risk buying one that you done already admitted you can't keep at home." Then he stopped talking. For about a minute it was like he and Uncle Buddy had both gone to sleep. Then Mr. Hubert picked up his face-down card and turned it over. It was another three, and Mr. Hubert sat there without looking at anything at all, his fingers beating a tattoo, slow and steady and not very loud, on the table. "H'm," he said. "And you need a trey and there ain't but four of them and I already got three. And you just shuffled. And I cut afterward. And if I call you, I will have to buy that nigger. Who dealt these cards, Amodeus?" Only he didn't wait to be answered. He reached out and tilted the lamp-shade, the light moving up Tomey's Turl's arms that were supposed to be black but were not quite white, up his Sunday shirt that was supposed to be white but wasn't quite either, that he put on every time he ran away just as Uncle Buck put on the necktie each time he went to bring him back, and on to his face; and Mr. Hubert sat there, holding the lamp-shade and looking at Tomey's Turl. Then he tilted the shade back down and took up his cards and turned them face-down and pushed them toward the middle of the table. "I pass, Amodeus," he said.

III

He was still too worn out for sleep to sit on a horse, so this time he and Uncle Buddy and Tennie all three rode in the wagon, while Tomey's Turl led the pony from old Jake. And when they got home just after daylight, this time Uncle Buddy never even had time to get breakfast started and the fox never even got out of the crate, because the dogs were right there in the room. Old Moses went right into the crate with the fox, so that both of them went right on through the back end of it. That is, the fox went through, because when Uncle Buddy opened the door to come in, old Moses was still wearing most of the crate around his neck until Uncle Buddy kicked it off of him. So they just made one run, across the front gallery and around the house and they could hear the fox's claws when he went scrabbling up the lean-pole, onto the roof—a fine race while it lasted, but the tree was too quick.

"What in damn's hell do you mean," Uncle Buddy said, "casting that damn thing with all the dogs right in the same room?"

"Damn the fox," Uncle Buck said. "Go on and start breakfast. It seems to me I've been away from home a whole damn month."

2. The Unvanquished

EDITOR'S NOTE

THE Chickasaws moved westward to Oklahoma in President Jackson's time. Only a few of them adopted the white man's ways and stayed behind, as dependents of a half-French chieftain named François Vidal (or Frank Weddel), who turned the last of their land into a rich plantation. The Man remained with this branch of the tribe, losing his theocratic honors and becoming a sort of plantation overseer. There was only Sam Fathers—Had-Two-Fathers—living in the slave quarters, who was faithful to the old customs of the tribe.

Uncle Buck McCaslin married Miss Sophonsiba. When the war came, Uncle Buck and Uncle Buddy played three hands of poker to see which of them would enlist. Uncle Buck lost and stayed at home with his wife, while Uncle Buddy went off to Virginia, as a sergeant in the regiment raised and commanded by

Colonel John Sartoris. In Virginia, the regiment held a new election of officers, and Colonel Sartoris was demoted to major; Thomas Sutpen took over his command. Sartoris resigned from the regiment and came home to lead an irregular troop of cavalry attached to General Forrest's highly irregular army.

Of the three stories in this section, "Raid" and "An Odor of Verbena" are both taken from *The Unvanquished* (1938), the novel or connected series of stories that Faulkner devotes to the Sartoris clan in the Civil War and reconstruction. Faulkner always turns romantic when writing about the Sartorises. He says of the family name, in one of his most overwritten sentences, "There is death in the sound of it, and a glamorous fatality, like silver pennons downrushing at sunset or a dying fall of horns along the road to Roncevaux." And yet, in "An Odor of Verbena," he is pretty hard and unsentimental about the character of Colonel John Sartoris, who happens to be one of the few figures in his novels copied from a historical person. His prototype was Colonel William Falkner, the author's great-grandfather, who organized and for a time commanded the Second Mississippi Infantry, who built the first railroad in his section, who wrote several books (including one successful novel, *The White Rose of Memphis*), and who was killed in a duel.

"Wash," the second story in this section, describes the death of Colonel Sutpen. Its first book publication was in *Doctor Martino and Other Stories* (1934). At that time Faulkner was working on a whole cycle of stories about poor whites and backwoods farmers, in preparation for writing his novel *The Hamlet;* but he found that "Wash" didn't belong in the cycle. It seems to have been the germ out of which developed another novel, *Absalom, Absalom!*

1864. RAID

I

GRANNY MILLARD wrote the note with poke-berry juice. "Take it straight to Mrs. Compson and come straight back," she said to me and Ringo. "Don't you-all stop anywhere."

"You mean we got to walk?" Ringo said. "You gonter make us walk all them four miles to Jefferson and back, with them two horses standing in the lot doing nothing?"

"They are borrowed horses," Granny said. "I'm going to take care of them until I can return them."

"I reckon you calls starting out to be gone you don't know where and you don't know how long taking care of——" Ringo said.

Louvinia was standing there; she was Joby's wife and Ringo's grandmother. "Do you want me to whup you?" she said.

"Nome," Ringo said.

We walked to Jefferson and gave Mrs. Compson the note, and got the hat and the parasol and the hand mirror, and walked back home. That afternoon we greased the wagon, and that night after supper Granny got the pokeberry juice again and wrote on a scrap of paper, "Colonel Nathaniel G. Dick, ——th Ohio Cavalry," and folded it and pinned it inside her dress. "Now I won't forget it," she said.

"If you was to, I reckon these hellion boys can re-mind you," Louvinia said. "I reckon they ain't forgot

133

him. Walking in that door just in time to keep them others from snatching them out from under your dress and nailing them to the barn door like two coon hides."

"Yes," Granny said. "Now we'll go to bed."

Now that the house was burned, we lived in Joby's cabin, with a red quilt nailed by one edge to a rafter and hanging down to make two rooms. Joby was waiting with the wagon when Granny came out with Mrs. Compson's hat on, and got into the wagon and told Ringo to open the parasol and took up the reins. Then we all stopped and watched Joby stick something into the wagon beneath the quilts; it was the barrel and the iron parts of the musket that Ringo and I found in the ashes of the house.

"What's that?" Granny said. Joby didn't look at her.

"Maybe if they just seed the end of hit they mought think hit was the whole gun," he said.

"Then what?" Granny said. Joby didn't look at anybody now.

"I was just doing what I could to help git the silver and the mules back," he said.

Louvinia didn't say anything either. She and Granny just looked at Joby. After a while he dug beneath the quilts again and took the musket barrel out of the wagon. Granny gathered up the reins.

"Take him with you," Louvinia said. "Leastways he can tend the horses."

"No," Granny said. "Don't you see I have got about all I can look after now?"

"Then you stay here and lemme go," Louvinia said. "I'll git um back."

"No," Granny said. "I'll be all right. I shall inquire until I find Colonel Dick, and then we will load the chest in the wagon and Loosh can lead the mules and we will come back home."

Louvinia stood there holding to the wagon wheel and looked at Granny from under Father's old hat, and began to holler.

"Don't you waste no time on colonels or nothing!" she hollered. "You tell them niggers to send Loosh to you, and you tell him to get that chest and them mules, and then you whup him!" The wagon was moving now; she had turned loose the wheel, and she walked along beside it, hollering at Granny: "Take that pairsawl and wear hit out on him!"

"All right," Granny said. The wagon went on; we passed the ash pile and the chimneys standing up out of it; Ringo and I found the insides of the big clock too. The sun was just coming up, shining back on the chimneys; I could still see Louvinia between them, standing in front of the cabin, shading her eyes with her hand to watch us. Joby was still standing behind her, holding the musket barrel. They had broken the gates clean off; and then we were in the road.

"Don't you want me to drive?" I said.

"I'll drive," Granny said. "These are borrowed horses."

"Case even Yankee could look at um and tell they couldn't keep up with even a walking army," Ringo said. "And I like to know how anybody can hurt this team lessen he ain't got strength enough to keep um from laying down in the road and getting run over with they own wagon."

We drove until dark, and camped. By sunup we were on the road again. "You better let me drive a while," I said.

"I'll drive," Granny said. "I was the one who borrowed them."

"You can tote this pairsawl a while, if you want something to do," Ringo said. "And give my arm a rest." I took the parasol and he laid down in the wagon and put his hat over his eyes. "Call me when we git-ting nigh to Hawkhurst," he said, "so I can commence to look out for that railroad you tells about."

That was how he travelled for the next six days—lying on his back in the wagon bed with his hat over his eyes, sleeping, or taking his turn holding the parasol over Granny and keeping me awake by talking of the railroad which he had never seen though I had seen it that Christmas we spent at Hawkhurst. That's how Ringo and I were. We were almost the same age, and Father always said that Ringo was a little smarter than I was, but that didn't count with us, any more than the difference in the color of our skins counted. What counted was, what one of us had done or seen that the other had not, and ever since that Christmas I had been ahead of Ringo because I had seen a rail-road, a locomotive. Only I know now it was more than that with Ringo, though neither of us were to see the proof of my belief for some time yet and we were not to recognize it as such even then. It was as if Ringo felt it too and that the railroad, the rushing locomotive which he hoped to see symbolized it—the motion, the impulse to move which had already seethed to a head among his people, darker than themselves, reasonless, following and seeking a delusion, a dream, a bright shape which they could not know since there was nothing in their heritage, nothing in the memory even of the old men to tell the others, "This is what we will find"; he nor they could not have known what it was yet it was there—one of those impulses inexplicable yet invincible which appear among races of people at in-tervals and drive them to pick up and leave all security and familiarity of earth and home and start out, they don't know where, emptyhanded, blind to everything but a hope and a doom.

We went on; we didn't go fast. Or maybe it seemed slow because we had got into a country where nobody seemed to live at all; all that day we didn't even see a house. I didn't ask and Granny didn't say; she just sat there under the parasol, with Mrs. Compson's hat on and the horses walking and even our own dust moving ahead of us; after a while even Ringo sat up and looked around.

"We on the wrong road," he said. "Ain't even nobody live here, let alone pass here."

But after a while the hills stopped, the road ran out flat and straight; and all of a sudden Ringo hollered, "Look out! Here they come again to git these uns!" We saw it, too, then—a cloud of dust away to the west, moving slow—too slow for men riding—and then the road we were on ran square into a big broad one running straight on into the east, as the railroad at Hawkhurst did when Granny and I were there that Christmas before the war; all of a sudden I remembered it.

"This is the road to Hawkhurst," I said. But Ringo was not listening; he was looking at the dust, and the wagon stopped now with the horses' heads hanging and our dust overtaking us again and the big dust cloud coming slow up in the west.

"Can't you see um coming?" Ringo hollered. "Git on away from here!"

"They ain't Yankees," Granny said. "The Yankees have already been here." Then we saw it, too—a burned house like ours, three chimneys standing above a mound of ashes, and then we saw a white woman and a child looking at us from a cabin behind them.

Granny looked at the dust cloud, then she looked at the empty broad road going on into the east. "This is the way," she said.

We went on. It seemed like we went slower than ever now, with the dust cloud behind us and the burned houses and gins and thrown-down fences on either side, and the white women and children—we never saw a nigger at all—watching us from the nigger cabins where they lived now like we lived at home; we didn't stop. "Poor folks," Granny said. "I wish we had enough to share with them."

At sunset we drew off the road and camped; Ringo was looking back. "Whatever hit is, we done went off and left hit," he said. "I don't see no dust." We slept in the wagon this time, all three of us. I don't know what time it was, only that all of a sudden I was awake. Granny was already sitting up in the wagon. I could see her head against the branches and the stars. All of a sudden all three of us were sitting up in the wagon, listening. They were coming up the road. It sounded like about fifty of them; we could hear the feet hurrying, and a kind of panting murmur. It was not singing exactly; it was not that loud. It was just a sound, a breathing, a kind of gasping, murmuring chant and the feet whispering fast in the deep dust. I could hear women, too, and then all of a sudden I began to smell them.

"Niggers," I whispered. "Sh-h-h-h," I whispered.

We couldn't see them and they did not see us; maybe they didn't even look, just walking fast in the dark with that panting, hurrying murmuring, going on. And then the sun rose and we went on, too, along that big broad empty road between the burned houses and gins and fences. Before, it had been like passing through a country where nobody had ever lived; now it was like passing through one where everybody had died at the same moment. That night we waked up three times and sat up in the wagon in the dark and heard niggers pass in the road. The last time it was after dawn and we had already fed the horses. It was a big crowd of them this time, and they sounded like they were running, like they had to run to keep ahead of daylight. Then they were gone. Ringo and I had taken up the harness again when Granny said, "Wait. Hush." It was just one, we could hear her panting and sobbing, and then we heard another sound. Granny began to get down from the wagon. "She fell," she said. "You-all hitch up and come on."

When we turned into the road, the woman was kind of crouched beside it, holding something in her arms, and Granny standing beside her. It was a baby, a few months old; she held it like she thought maybe Granny was going to take it away from her. "I been sick and I couldn't keep up," she said. "They went off and left me."

"Is your husband with them?" Granny said.

"Yessum," the woman said. "They's all there."

"Who do you belong to?" Granny said. Then she didn't answer. She squatted there in the dust, crouched over the baby. "If I give you something to eat, will you turn around and go back home?" Granny said. Still she didn't answer. She just squatted there. "You see you can't keep up with them and they ain't going to wait for you," Granny said. "Do you want to die here in the road for buzzards to eat?" But she didn't even look at Granny; she just squatted there.

"Hit's Jordan we coming to," she said. "Jesus gonter see me that far."

"Get in the wagon," Granny said. She got in; she squatted again just like she had in the road, holding the baby and not looking at anything—just hunkered

down and swaying on her hams as the wagon rocked
and jolted. The sun was up; we went down a long
hill and began to cross a creek bottom.

"I'll get out here," she said. Granny stopped the
wagon and she got out. There was nothing at all but
the thick gum and cypress and thick underbrush still
full of shadow.

"You go back home, girl," Granny said. She just
stood there. "Hand me the basket," Granny said. I
handed it to her and she opened it and gave the woman
a piece of bread and meat. We went on; we began to
mount the hill. When I looked back she was still standing there, holding the baby and the bread and meat
Granny had given her. She was not looking at us. "Were
the others there in that bottom?" Granny asked Ringo.

"Yessum," Ringo said. "She done found um. Reckon
she gonter lose um again tonight though."

We went on; we mounted the hill and crossed the
crest of it. When I looked back this time the road was
empty. That was the morning of the sixth day.

11

Late that afternoon we were descending again; we
came around a curve in the late level shadows and our
own quiet dust and I saw the graveyard on the knoll
and the marble shaft at Uncle Dennison's grave; there
was a dove somewhere in the cedars. Ringo was asleep
again under his hat in the wagon bed but he waked
as soon as I spoke, even though I didn't speak loud and
didn't speak to him. "There's Hawkhurst," I said.

"Hawkhurst?" he said, sitting up. "Where's that railroad?" on his knees now and looking for something
which he would have to find in order to catch up with

me and which he would have to recognize only through
hearsay when he saw it: "Where is it? Where?"

"You'll have to wait for it," I said.

"Seem like I been waiting on hit all my life," he said.
"I reckon you'll tell me next the Yankees done moved
hit too."

The sun was going down. Because suddenly I saw
it shining level across the place where the house should
have been and there was no house there. And I was
not surprised; I remember that; I was just feeling sorry
for Ringo, since (I was just fourteen then) if the house
was gone, they would have taken the railroad too,
since anybody would rather have a railroad than a
house. We didn't stop; we just looked quietly at the
same mound of ashes, the same four chimneys standing
gaunt and blackened in the sun like the chimneys at
home. When we reached the gate Cousin Denny was
running down the drive toward us. He was ten; he ran
up to the wagon with his eyes round and his mouth
already open for hollering.

"Denny," Granny said, "do you know us?"

"Yessum," Cousin Denny said. He looked at me,
hollering, "Come see——"

"Where's your mother?" Granny said.

"In Jingus' cabin," Cousin Denny said; he didn't
even look at Granny. "They burnt the house!" he hollered. "Come see what they done to the railroad!"

We ran, all three of us. Granny hollered something
and I turned and put the parasol back into the wagon
and hollered "Yessum!" back at her, and ran on and
caught up with Cousin Denny and Ringo in the road,
and we ran on over the hill, and then it came in sight.
When Granny and I were here before, Cousin Denny
showed me the railroad, but he was so little then that

Jingus had to carry him. It was the straightest thing I ever saw, running straight and empty and quiet through a long empty gash cut through the trees, and the ground, too, and full of sunlight like water in a river, only straighter than any river, with the crossties cut off even and smooth and neat, and the light shining on the rails like on two spider threads, running straight on to where you couldn't even see that far. It looked clean and neat, like the yard behind Louvinia's cabin after she had swept it on Saturday morning, with those two little threads that didn't look strong enough for anything to run on running straight and fast and light, like they were getting up speed to jump clean off the world.

Jingus knew when the train would come; he held my hand and carried Cousin Denny, and we stood between the rails and he showed us where it would come from, and then he showed us where the shadow of a dead pine would come to a stob he had driven in the ground, and then you would hear the whistle. And we got back and watched the shadow, and then we heard it; it whistled and then it got louder and louder fast, and Jingus went to the track and took his hat off and held it out with his face turned back toward us and his mouth hollering, "Watch now! Watch!" even after we couldn't hear him for the train; and then it passed. It came roaring up and went past; the river they had cut through the trees was all full of smoke and noise and sparks and jumping brass, and then empty again, and just Jingus' old hat bouncing and jumping along the empty track behind it like the hat was alive.

But this time what I saw was something that looked like piles of black straws heaped up every few yards, and we ran into the cut and we could see where they had dug the ties up and piled them and set them on fire. But Cousin Denny was still hollering, "Come see what they done to the rails!" he said.

They were back in the trees; it looked like four or five men had taken each rail and tied it around a tree like you knot a green cornstalk around a wagon stake, and Ringo was hollering, too, now.

"What's them?" he hollered. "What's them?"

"That's what it runs on!" Cousin Denny hollered.

"You mean hit have to come in here and run up and down around these here trees like a squirrel?" Ringo hollered. Then we all heard the horse at once; we just had time to look when Bobolink came up the road out of the trees and went across the railroad and into the trees again like a bird, with Cousin Drusilla riding astride like a man and sitting straight and light as a willow branch in the wind. They said she was the best woman rider in the country.

"There's Dru!" Cousin Denny hollered. "Come on! She's been up to the river to see them niggers! Come on!" He and Ringo ran again. When I passed the chimneys, they were just running into the stable. Cousin Drusilla had already unsaddled Bobolink, and she was rubbing him down with a crokersack when I came in. Cousin Denny was still hollering, "What did you see? What are they doing?"

"I'll tell about it at the house," Cousin Drusilla said. Then she saw me. She was not tall; it was the way she stood and walked. She had on pants, like a man. She was the best woman rider in the country. When Granny and I were here that Christmas before the war and Gavin Breckbridge had just given Bobolink to her, they looked fine together; it didn't need Jingus to say that they were the finest-looking couple in Alabama or Mississippi either. But Gavin was killed at Shiloh and so they didn't marry. She came and put her hand on my shoulder.

"Hello," she said. "Hello, John Sartoris." She looked at Ringo. "Is this Ringo?" she said.

"That's what they tells me," Ringo said. "What about that railroad?"

"How are you?" Cousin Drusilla said.

"I manages to stand hit," Ringo said. "What about that railroad?"

"I'll tell you about that tonight too," Drusilla said.

"I'll finish Bobolink for you," I said.

"Will you?" she said. She went to Bobolink's head. "Will you stand for Cousin Bayard, lad?" she said. "I'll see you-all at the house, then," she said. She went out.

"Yawl sho must 'a' had this horse hid good when the Yankees come," Ringo said.

"This horse?" Cousin Denny said. "Ain't no damn Yankee going to fool with Dru's horse no more." He didn't holler now, but pretty soon he began again: "When they come to burn the house, Dru grabbed the pistol and run out here—she had on her Sunday dress—and them right behind her. She run in here and she jumped on Bobolink bareback, without even waiting for the bridle, and one of them right there in the door hollering, 'Stop,' and Dru said, 'Get away, or I'll ride you down,' and him hollering, 'Stop! Stop!' with his pistol out too"—Cousin Denny was hollering good now—"and Dru leaned down to Bobolink's ear and said, 'Kill him, Bob,' and the Yankee jumped back just in time. The lot was full of them, too, and Dru stopped Bobolink and jumped down in her Sunday dress and put the pistol to Bobolink's ear and said, 'I can't shoot you all, because I haven't enough bullets, and it wouldn't do any good anyway; but I won't need but one shot for the horse, and which shall it be?' So they burned the house and went away!" He was hollering good now, with Ringo staring at him so you could have raked Ringo's eyes off his face with a stick. "Come on!" Cousin Denny hollered. "Le's go hear about them niggers at the river!"

"I been having to hear about niggers all my life," Ringo said. "I got to hear about that railroad."

When we reached the house Cousin Drusilla was already talking, telling Granny mostly, though it was not about the railroad. Her hair was cut short; it looked like Father's would when he would tell Granny about him and the men cutting each other's hair with a bayonet. She was sunburned and her hands were hard and scratched like a man's that works. She was telling Granny mostly: "They began to pass in the road yonder while the house was still burning. We couldn't count them; men and women carrying children who couldn't walk and carrying old men and women who should have been at home waiting to die. They were singing, walking along the road singing, not even looking to either side. The dust didn't even settle for two days, because all that night they still passed; we sat up listening to them, and the next morning every few yards along the road would be the old ones who couldn't keep up any more, sitting or lying down and even crawling along, calling to the others to help them; and the others—the young strong ones—not stopping, not even looking at them. I don't think they even heard or saw them. 'Going to Jordan,' they told me. 'Going to cross Jordan.'"

"That was what Loosh said," Granny said. "That General Sherman was leading them all to Jordan."

"Yes," Cousin Drusilla said. "The river. They have stopped there; it's like a river itself, dammed up. The Yankees have thrown out a brigade of cavalry to hold them back while they build the bridge to cross the infantry and artillery; they are all right until they get up there and see or smell the water. That's when they go mad. Not fighting; it's like they can't even see the horses shoving them back and the scabbards beating them; it's like they can't see anything but the water and the other bank. They aren't angry, aren't fighting; just men, women and children singing and chanting and trying to get to that unfinished bridge or even down into the water itself, and the cavalry beating them back with sword scabbards. I don't know when they have eaten; nobody knows just how far some of them have come. They just pass here without food or anything, exactly as they rose up from whatever they were doing when the spirit or the voice or whatever it was told them to go. They stop during the day and rest in the woods; then, at night, they move again. We will hear them later—I'll wake you—marching on up the road until the cavalry stops them. There was an officer, a major, who finally took time to see I wasn't one of his men; he said, 'Can't you do anything with them? Promise them anything to go back home?' But it was like they couldn't see me or hear me speaking; it was only that water and that bank on the other side. But you will see for yourself tomorrow, when we go back."

"Drusilla," Aunt Louise said, "you're not going back tomorrow or any other time."

"They are going to mine the bridge and blow it up when the army has crossed," Cousin Drusilla said. "Nobody knows what they will do then."

"But we cannot be responsible," Aunt Louise said. "The Yankees brought it on themselves; let them pay the price."

"Those Negroes are not Yankees, Mother," Cousin

Drusilla said. "At least there will be one person there who is not a Yankee either." She looked at Granny. "Four, counting Bayard and Ringo."

Aunt Louise looked at Granny. "Rosa, you shan't go. I forbid it. Brother John will thank me to do so."

"I reckon I will," Granny said. "I've got to get the silver anyway."

"And the mules," Ringo said; "don't forget them. And don't yawl worry about Granny. She 'cide what she want and then she kneel down about ten seconds and tell God what she aim to do, and then she git up and do hit. And them that don't like hit can git outen the way or git trompled. But that railroad——"

"And now I reckon we better go to bed," Granny said. But we didn't go to bed then. I had to hear about the railroad too; possibly it was more the need to keep even with Ringo (or even ahead of him, since I had seen the railroad when it was a railroad, which he had not) than a boy's affinity for smoke and fury and thunder and speed. We sat there in that slave cabin partitioned, like Louvinia's cabin at home, into two rooms by that suspended quilt beyond which Aunt Louisa and Granny were already in bed and where Cousin Denny should have been too except for the evening's dispensation he had received, listening too who did not need to hear it again since he had been there to see it when it happened;——we sat there, Ringo and I, listening to Cousin Drusilla and staring at each other with the same amazed and incredulous question: *Where could we have been at that moment? What could we have been doing, even a hundred miles away, not to have sensed, felt this, paused to look at one another, aghast and uplifted, while it was happening?* Because this, to us, was it. Ringo and I had seen Yankees; we had shot at one; we had crouched like two rats and heard Granny, unarmed and not even rising from her chair, rout a whole regiment of them from the library. And we had heard about battles and fighting and seen those who had taken part in them, not only in the person of Father when once or twice each year and without warning he would appear on the strong gaunt horse, arrived from beyond that cloudbank region which Ringo believed was Tennessee, but in the persons of other men who returned home with actual arms and legs missing. But that was it: men had lost arms and legs in sawmills; old men had been telling young men and boys about wars and fighting before they discovered how to write it down: and what petty precisian to quibble about locations in space or in chronology, who to care or insist *Now come, old man, tell the truth: did you see this? were you really there?* Because wars are wars: the same exploding powder when there was powder, the same thrust and parry of iron when there was not—one tale, one telling, the same as the next or the one before. So we knew a war existed; we had to believe that, just as we had to believe that the name for the sort of life we had led for the last three years was hardship and suffering. Yet we had no proof of it. In fact, we had even less than no proof; we had had thrust into our faces the very shabby and unavoidable obverse of proof, who had seen Father (and the other men too) return home, afoot like tramps or on crowbait horses, in faded and patched (and at times obviously stolen) clothing, preceded by no flags nor drums and followed not even by two men to keep step with one another, in coats bearing no glitter of golden braid and with scabbards in which no sword reposed, actually almost sneaking home to spend two or three or seven days performing actions not only without glory (plowing land, repairing fences, killing meat for the smoke house) and in which they had no skill but the very necessity for which was the fruit of the absent occupations from which, returning, they bore no proof—actions in the clumsy performance of which Father's whole presence seemed (to us, Ringo and me) to emanate a kind of humility and apology, as if he were saying, "Believe me, boys; take my word for it: there's more to it than this, no matter what it looks like. I can't prove it, so you'll just have to believe me." And then to have it happen, where we could have been there to see it, and were not: and this no poste and riposte of sweat-reeking cavalry which all war-telling is full of, no galloping thunder of guns to wheel up and unlimber and crash and crash into the lurid grime-glare of their own demon-served inferno which even children would recognize, no ragged lines of gaunt and shrill-yelling infantry beneath a tattered flag which is a very part of that child's make-believe. Because this was it: an interval, a space, in which the toad-squatting guns, the panting men and the trembling horses paused, amphitheatric about the embattled land, beneath the fading fury of the smoke and the puny yelling, and permitted the sorry business which had dragged on for three years now to be congealed into an irrevocable instant and put to an irrevocable gambit, not by two regiments or two batteries or even two generals, but by two locomotives.

Cousin Drusilla told it while we sat there in the cabin which smelled of new whitewash and even (still faintly) of Negroes. She probably told us the reason for it (she must have known)—what point of strategy, what desperate gamble not for preservation, since hope of that was gone, but at least for prolongation, which it served. But that meant nothing to us. We didn't hear, we didn't even listen; we sat there in that cabin and waited and watched that railroad which no longer existed, which was now a few piles of charred ties among which green grass was already growing, a few threads of steel knotted and twisted about the trunks of trees and already annealing into the living bark, becoming one and indistinguishable with the jungle growth which had now accepted it, but which for us ran still pristine and intact and straight and narrow as the path to glory itself, as it ran for all of them who were there and saw when Ringo and I were not. Drusilla told about that too; "Atlanta" and "Chattanooga" were in it—the names, the beginning and the end—but they meant no more to us than they did to the other watchers —the black and the white, the old men, the children, the women who would not know for months yet if they were widows or childless or not—gathered, warned by grapevine, to see the momentary flash and glare of indomitable spirit starved by three years free of the impeding flesh. She told it (and now Ringo and I began to see it; we were there too)—the roundhouse in Atlanta where the engine waited; we were there, we were of them who (they must have) would slip into the roundhouse in the dark, to caress the wheels and pistons and iron flanks, to whisper to it in the darkness like lover to mistress or rider to horse, cajoling ruthlessly of her or it one supreme effort in return for making which she or it would receive annihilation (and who would not pay that price), cajoling, whispering, caressing her or it toward the one moment; we were of them—the old men, the children, the women—gathered to watch, drawn and warned by that grapevine of the oppressed, deprived of everything now save the will and the ability to deceive, turning inscrutable and impassive secret faces to the blue enemies who lived among them. Because they knew it was going to happen; Drusilla told that too: how they seemed to know somehow the very moment when the engine left Atlanta; it was as if the gray generals themselves had sent the word, had told them, "You have suffered for three years; now we will give to you and your children a glimpse of that for which you have suffered and been denied." Because that's all it was. I know that now. Even the successful passage of a hundred engines with trains of cars could not have changed the situation or its outcome; certainly not two free engines shrieking along a hundred yards apart up that drowsing solitude of track which had seen no smoke and heard no bell in more than a year. I don't think it was intended to do that. It was like a meeting between two iron knights of the old time, not for material gain but for principle—honor denied with honor, courage denied with courage—the deed done not for the end but for the sake of the doing—put to the ultimate test and proving nothing save the finality of death and the vanity of all endeavor. We saw it, we were there, as if Drusilla's voice had transported us to the wandering light-ray in space in which was still held the furious shadow—the brief section of track which existed inside the scope of a single pair of eyes and nowhere else, coming from nowhere and having, needing, no destination, the engine not coming into view but arrested in human sight in thunderous yet dreamy fury, lonely, inviolate and forlorn, wailing through its whistle precious steam which could have meant seconds at the instant of passing and miles at the end of its journey (and cheap at ten times this price)—the flaring and streaming smoke stack, the tossing bell, the starred Saint Andrew's cross nailed to the cab roof, the wheels and the flashing driving rods on which the brass fittings glinted like the golden spurs themselves—then gone, vanished. Only not gone or

vanished either, so long as there should be defeated or
the descendants of defeated to tell it or listen to the
telling.

"The other one, the Yankee one, was right behind
it," Drusilla said. "But they never caught it. Then
the next day they came and tore the track up. They
tore the track up so we couldn't do it again; they
could tear the track up but they couldn't take back
the fact that we had done it. They couldn't take that
from us."

We—Ringo and I—knew what she meant; we stood
together just outside the door before Ringo went on
to Missy Lena's cabin, where he was to sleep. "I know
what you thinking," Ringo said. Father was right; he
was smarter than me. "But I heard good as you did.
I heard every word you heard."

"Only I saw the track before they tore it up. I saw
where it was going to happen."

"But you didn't know hit was fixing to happen
when you seed the track. So nemmine that. I heard
And I reckon they ain't gonter git that away from me,
neither."

He went on, then I went back into the house and
behind the quilt where Denny was already asleep on
the pallet. Drusilla was not there only I didn't have
time to wonder where she was because I was thinking how I probably wouldn't be able to go to sleep
at all now though it was late. Then it was later still and
Denny was shaking me and I remember how I thought
then that he did not seem to need sleep either, that
just by having been exposed for three or four seconds
to war he had even at just ten acquired that quality
which Father and the other men brought back from
the front—the power to do without sleep and food
both, needing only the opportunity to endure. "Dru

says to come on out doors if you want to hear them passing," he whispered.

She was outside the cabin; she hadn't undressed even. I could see her in the starlight—her short jagged hair and the man's shirt and pants. "Hear them?" she said. We could hear it again, like we had in the wagon— the hurrying feet, the sound like they were singing in panting whispers, hurrying on past the gate and dying away up the road. "That's the third tonight," Cousin Drusilla said. "Two passed while I was down at the gate. You were tired, and so I didn't wake you before."

"I thought it was late," I said. "You haven't been to bed even. Have you?"

"No," she said. "I've quit sleeping."

"Quit sleeping?" I said. "Why?"

She looked at me. I was as tall as she was; we couldn't see each other's faces; it was just her head with the short jagged hair like she had cut it herself without bothering about a mirror, and her neck that had got thin and hard like her hands since Granny and I were here before. "I'm keeping a dog quiet," she said.

"A dog?" I said. "I haven't seen any dog."

"No. It's quiet now," she said. "It doesn't bother anybody any more now. I just have to show it the stick now and then." She was looking at me. "Why not stay awake now? Who wants to sleep now, with so much happening, so much to see? Living used to be dull, you see. Stupid. You lived in the same house your father was born in, and your father's sons and daughters had the sons and daughters of the same Negro slaves to nurse and coddle; and then you grew up and you fell in love with your acceptable young man, and in time you would marry him, in your mother's wedding gown, perhaps, and with the same silver for presents she had received; and then you settled down forevermore while you got children to feed and bathe and dress until they grew up, too; and then you and your husband died quietly and were buried together maybe on a summer afternoon just before suppertime. Stupid, you see. But now you can see for yourself how it is; it's fine now; you don't have to worry now about the house and the silver, because they get burned up and carried away; and you don't have to worry about the Negroes, because they tramp the roads all night waiting for a chance to drown in homemade Jordan; and you don't have to worry about getting children to bathe and feed and change, because the young men can ride away and get killed in the fine battles; and you don't even have to sleep alone, you don't even have to sleep at all; and so, all you have to do is show the stick to the dog now and then and say, 'Thank God for nothing.' You see? There. They've gone now. And you'd better get back to bed, so we can get an early start in the morning. It will take a long time to get through them."

"You're not coming in now?" I said.

"Not yet," she said. But we didn't move. And then she put her hand on my shoulder. "Listen," she said. "When you go back home and see Uncle John, ask him to let me come there and ride with his troop. Tell him I can ride, and maybe I can learn to shoot. Will you?"

"Yes," I said. "I'll tell him you are not afraid too."

"Aren't I?" she said. "I hadn't thought about it. It doesn't matter anyway. Just tell him I can ride and that I don't get tired." Her hand was on my shoulder; it felt thin and hard. "Will you do that for me? Ask him to let me come, Bayard."

"All right," I said. Then I said, "I hope he will let you."

"So do I," she said. "Now you go back to bed. Good night."

I went back to the pallet and then to sleep; again it was Denny shaking me awake; by sunup we were on the road again, Drusilla on Bobolink riding beside the wagon. But not for long.

We began to see the dust almost at once and I even believed that I could already smell them though the distance between us did not appreciably decrease, since they were travelling almost as fast as we were. We never did overtake them, just as you do not overtake a tide. You just keep moving, then suddenly you know that the set is about you, beneath you, overtaking you, as if the slow and ruthless power, become aware of your presence at last, had dropped back a tentacle, a feeler, to gather you in and sweep you remorselessly on. Singly, in couples, in groups and families they began to appear from the woods, ahead of us, alongside of us and behind; they covered and hid from sight the road exactly as an infiltration of flood water would have, hiding the road from sight and then the very wheels of the wagon in which we rode, our two horses as well as Bobolink breasting slowly on, enclosed by a mass of heads and shoulders—men and women carrying babies and dragging older children by the hand, old men and women on improvised sticks and crutches, and very old ones sitting beside the road and even calling to us when we passed; there was one old woman who even walked along beside the wagon, holding to the bed and begging Granny to at least let her see the river before she died.

But mostly they did not look at us. We might not have even been there. We did not even ask them to let us through because we could look at their faces and know they couldn't have heard us. They were not singing yet, they were just hurrying, while our horses pushed slow through them, among the blank eyes not looking at anything out of faces caked with dust and sweat, breasting slowly and terrifically through them as if we were driving in midstream up a creek full of floating logs and the dust and the smell of them everywhere and Granny in Mrs. Compson's hat sitting bolt upright under the parasol which Ringo held and looking sicker and sicker, and it already afternoon though we didn't know it anymore than we knew how many miles we had come. Then all of a sudden we reached the river, where the cavalry was holding them back from the bridge. It was just a sound at first, like wind, like it might be in the dust itself. We didn't even know what it was until we saw Drusilla holding Bobolink reined back, her face turned toward us wan and small above the dust and her mouth open and crying thinly: "Look out, Aunt Rosa! Oh, look out!"

It was like we all heard it at the same time—we in the wagon and on the horse, they all around us in the sweat-caking dust. They made a kind of long wailing sound, and then I felt the whole wagon lift clear of the ground and begin to rush forward. I saw our old rib-gaunted horses standing on their hind feet one minute and then turned sideways in the traces the next, and Drusilla leaning forward a little and taut as a pistol hammer holding Bobolink, and I saw men and women and children going down under the horses and we could feel the wagon going over them and we could hear them screaming. And we couldn't stop anymore than if the earth had tilted up and was sliding us all down toward the river.

It went fast, like that, like it did every time anybody named Sartoris or Millard came within sight, hearing or smell of Yankees, as if Yankees were not a people

nor a belief nor even a form of behavior, but instead
were a kind of gully, precipice, into which Granny and
Ringo and I were sucked pell-mell every time we got
close to them. It was sunset; now there was a high
bright rosy glow quiet beyond the trees and shining on
the river, and now we could see it plain—the tide of
niggers dammed back from the entrance to the bridge
by a detachment of cavalry, the river like a sheet of
rosy glass beneath the delicate arch of the bridge which
the tail of the Yankee column was just crossing. They
were in silhouette, running tiny and high above the
placid water; I remember the horses' and mules' heads
all mixed up among the bayonets, and the barrels of
cannon tilted up and kind of rushing slow across the
high peaceful rosy air like split-cane clothespins being
jerked along a clothesline, and the singing everywhere
up and down the river bank, with the voices of the
women coming out of it thin and high: "Glory! Glory!
Hallelujah!"

They were fighting now, the horses rearing and shoving against them, the troopers beating at them with
their scabbards, holding them clear of the bridge while
the last of the infantry began to cross; all of a sudden
there was an officer beside the wagon, holding his scab-
barded sword by the little end like a stick and hanging
onto the wagon and screaming at us. I don't know where
he came from, how he ever got to us, but there he was
with his little white face with a stubble of beard and a
long streak of blood on it, bareheaded and with his
mouth open. "Get back!" he shrieked. "Get back! We're
going to blow the bridge!" screaming right into Granny's
face while she shouted back at him with Mrs. Compson's hat knocked to one side of her head and hers and
the Yankee's faces not a yard apart:

"I want my silver! I'm John Sartoris' mother-in-law!

Send Colonel Dick to me!" Then the Yankee officer was gone, right in the middle of shouting and beating at the nigger heads with his sabre, with his little bloody shrieking face and all. I don't know where he went any more than I know where he came from; he just vanished still holding onto the wagon and flailing about him with the sabre, and then Cousin Drusilla was there on Bobolink; she had our nigh horse by the head-stall and was trying to turn the wagon sideways. I started to jump down to help. "Stay in the wagon," she said. She didn't shout; she just said it. "Take the lines and turn them." When we got the wagon turned sideways we stopped. And then for a minute I thought we were going backward, until I saw it was the niggers. Then I saw that the cavalry had broken; I saw the whole mob of it—horses and men and sabres and niggers—rolling on toward the end of the bridge like when a dam breaks, for about ten clear seconds behind the last of the infantry. And then the bridge vanished. I was looking right at it; I could see the clear gap between the infantry and the wave of niggers and cavalry, with a little empty thread of bridge joining them together in the air above the water, and then there was a bright glare and I felt my insides suck and a clap of wind hit me on the back of the head. I didn't hear anything at all. I just sat there in the wagon with a funny buzzing in my ears and a funny taste in my mouth, and watched little toy men and horses and pieces of plank floating along in the air above the water. But I didn't hear anything at all; I couldn't even hear Cousin Drusilla. She was right beside the wagon now, leaning toward us, her mouth urgent and wide and no sound coming out of it at all.

"What?" I said.

"Stay in the wagon!"

"I can't hear you!" I said. That's what I said, that's what I was thinking; I didn't realize even then that the wagon was moving again. But then I did; it was like the whole long bank of the river had turned and risen under us and was rushing us down toward the water, we sitting in the wagon and rushing down toward the water on another river of faces that couldn't see or hear either. Cousin Drusilla had the nigh horse by the bridle again, and I dragged at them, too, and Granny was standing up in the wagon and beating at the faces with Mrs. Compson's parasol, and then the whole rotten bridle came off in Cousin Drusilla's hand.

"Get away!" I said. "The wagon will float!"

"Yes," she said, "it will float. Just stay in it. Watch Aunt Rosa and Ringo."

"Yes," I said. Then she was gone. We passed her; turned, and holding Bobolink like a rock again and leaning down talking to him and patting his cheek, she was gone. Then maybe the bank did cave. I don't know. I didn't even know we were in the river. It was just like the earth had fallen out from under the wagon and the faces and all, and we all rushed down slow, with the faces looking up and their eyes blind and their mouths open and their arms held up. High up in the air across the river I saw a cliff and a big fire on it running fast sideways; and then all of a sudden the wagon was moving fast sideways, and then a dead horse came shining up from out of the yelling faces and went down slow again, exactly like a fish feeding, with, hanging over his rump by one stirrup, a man in a black uniform, and then I realized that the uniform was blue, only it was wet. They were screaming then, and now I could feel the wagon bed tilt and slide as they caught at it.

Granny was kneeling beside me now, hitting at the screaming faces with Mrs. Compson's parasol. Behind us they were still marching down the bank and into the river, singing.

III

A Yankee patrol helped Ringo and me cut the drowned horses out of the harness and drag the wagon ashore. We sprinkled water on Granny until she came to, and they rigged harness with ropes and hitched up two of their horses. There was a road on top of the bluff, and then we could see the fires along the bank. They were still singing on the other side of the river, but it was quieter now. But there were patrols still riding up and down the cliff on this side, and squads of infantry down at the water where the fires were. Then we began to pass between rows of tents, with Granny lying against me, and I could see her face then; it was white and still, and her eyes were shut. She looked old and tired; I hadn't realized how old and little she was. Then we began to pass big fires, with niggers in wet clothes crouching around them and soldiers going among them passing out food; then we came to a broad street, and stopped before a tent with a sentry at the door and a light inside. The soldiers looked at Granny.

"We better take her to the hospital," one of them said.

Granny opened her eyes; she tried to sit up. "No," she said. "Just take me to Colonel Dick. I will be all right then."

They carried her into the tent and put her in a chair. She hadn't moved; she was sitting there with her eyes closed and a strand of wet hair sticking to her face when Colonel Dick came in. I had never seen him before—only heard his voice while Ringo and I were

squatting under Granny's skirt and holding our breath
—but I knew him at once, with his bright beard and
his hard bright eyes, stooping over Granny and saying,
"Damn this war. Damn it. Damn it."

"They took the silver and the darkies and the mules,"
Granny said. "I have come to get them."

"Have them you shall," he said, "if they are anywhere in this corps. I'll see the general myself." He was
looking at Ringo and me now. "Ha!" he said. "I believe
we have met before also." Then he was gone again.

It was hot in the tent, and quiet, with three bugs
swirling around the lantern, and outside the sound of
the army like wind far away. Ringo was already asleep,
sitting on the ground with his head on his knees, and I
wasn't much better, because all of a sudden Colonel
Dick was back and there was an orderly writing at the
table, and Granny sitting again with her eyes closed in
her white face.

"Maybe you can describe them," Colonel Dick said
to me.

"I will do it," Granny said. She didn't open her eyes.
"The chest of silver tied with hemp rope. The rope was
new. Two darkies, Loosh and Philadelphy. The mules,
Old Hundred and Tinney."

Colonel Dick turned and watched the orderly writing.
"Have you got that?" he said.

The orderly looked at what he had written. "I guess
the general will be glad to give them twice the silver
and mules just for taking that many niggers," he said.

"Now I'll go see the general," Colonel Dick said.

Then we were moving again. I don't know how long
it had been, because they had to wake me and Ringo
both; we were in the wagon again, with two Army
horses pulling it on down the long broad street, and

there was another officer with us and Colonel Dick was gone. We came to a pile of chests and boxes that looked higher than a mountain. There was a rope pen behind it full of mules and then, standing to one side and waiting there, was what looked like a thousand niggers, men, women and children, with their wet clothes dried on them. And now it began to go fast again; there was Granny in the wagon with her eyes wide open now and the lieutenant reading from the paper and the soldiers jerking chests and trunks out of the pile. "Ten chests tied with hemp rope," the lieutenant read. "Got them? . . . A hundred and ten mules. It says from Philadelphia—that's in Mississippi. Get these Mississippi mules. They are to have rope and halters."

"We ain't got a hundred and ten Mississippi mules," the sergeant said.

"Get what we have got. Hurry." He turned to Granny. "And there are your niggers, madam."

Granny was looking at him with her eyes wide as Ringo's. She was drawn back a little, with her hand at her chest. "But they're not—they ain't——" she said.

"They ain't all yours?" the lieutenant said. "I know it. The general said to give you another hundred with his compliments."

"But that ain't—— We didn't——" Granny said.

"She wants the house back, too," the sergeant said. "We ain't got any houses, grandma," he said. "You'll just have to make out with trunks and niggers and mules. You wouldn't have room for it on the wagon, anyway."

We sat there while they loaded the ten trunks into the wagon. It just did hold them all. They got another set of trees and harness, and hitched four mules to it. "One of you darkies that can handle two span come here," the lieutenant said. One of the niggers came and got on the seat with Granny; none of us had ever seen him before. Behind us they were leading the mules out of the pen.

"You want to let some of the women ride?" the lieutenant said.

"Yes," Granny whispered.

"Come on," the lieutenant said. "Just one to a mule, now." Then he handed me the paper. "Here you are. There's a ford about twenty miles up the river; you can cross there. You better get on away from here before any more of these niggers decide to go with you."

We rode until daylight, with the ten chests in the wagon and the mules and our army of niggers behind. Granny had not moved, sitting there beside the strange nigger with Mrs. Compson's hat on and the parasol in her hand. But she was not asleep, because when it got light enough to see, she said, "Stop the wagon." The wagon stopped. She turned and looked at me. "Let me see that paper," she said.

We opened the paper and looked at it, at the neat writing:

> *Field Headquarters,*
> *———th Army Corps,*
> *Department of Tennessee,*
> *August 14, 1863.*

To all Brigade, Regimental and Other Commanders: You will see that bearer is repossessed in full of the following property, to wit: Ten (10) chests tied with hemp rope and containing silver. One hundred ten (110) mules captured loose near Philadelphia in Mississippi. One hundred ten (110) Negroes of both sexes belonging to and having strayed from the same locality.

You will further see that bearer is supplied with necessary food and forage to expedite his passage to his destination.

By order of the General Commanding.

We looked at one another in the gray light. "I reckon you gonter take um back now," Ringo said.

Granny looked at me. "We can get food and fodder too," I said.

"Yes," Granny said. "I tried to tell them better. You and Ringo heard me. It's the hand of God."

We stopped and slept until noon. That afternoon we came to the ford. We had already started down the bluff when we saw the troop of cavalry camped there. It was too late to stop.

"They done found hit out and headed us off," Ringo said. It was too late; already an officer and two men were riding toward us.

"I will tell them the truth," Granny said. "We have done nothing." She sat there, drawn back a little again, with her hand already raised and holding the paper out in the other when they rode up. The officer was a heavy-built man with a red face; he looked at us and took the paper and read it and began to swear. He sat there on his horse swearing while we watched him.

"How many do you lack?" he said.

"How many do I what?" Granny said.

"Mules!" the officer shouted. "Mules! Mules! Do I look like I had any chests of silver or niggers tied with hemp rope?"

"Do we——" Granny said, with her hand to her chest, looking at him; I reckon it was Ringo that knew first what he meant.

"We like fifty," Ringo said.

"Fifty, hey?" the officer said. He cursed again; he

turned to one of the men behind him and cursed him now. "Count 'em!" he said. "Do you think I'm going to take their word for it?"

The man counted the mules; we didn't move; I don't think we even breathed hardly. "Sixty-three," the man said.

The officer looked at us. "Sixty-three from a hundred and ten leaves forty-seven," he said. He cursed. "Get forty-seven mules! Hurry!" He looked at us again. "Think you can beat me out of three mules, hey?"

"Forty-seven will do," Ringo said. "Only I reckon maybe we better eat something, like the paper mention."

We crossed the ford. We didn't stop; we went on as soon as they brought up the other mules, and some more of the women got on them. We went on. It was after sundown then, but we didn't stop.

"Hah!" Ringo said. "Whose hand was that?"

We went on until midnight before we stopped. This time it was Ringo that Granny was looking at. "Ringo," she said.

"I never said nothing the paper never said," Ringo said. "Hit was the one that said it; hit wasn't me. All I done was to told him how much the hundred and ten liked; I never said we liked that many. 'Sides, hit ain't no use in praying about hit now; ain't no telling what we gonter run into 'fore we gits home. The main thing now is, whut we gonter do with all these niggers."

"Yes," Granny said. We cooked and ate the food the cavalry officer gave us; then Granny told all the niggers that lived in Alabama to come forward. It was about half of them. "I suppose you all want to cross some more rivers and run after the Yankee Army, don't you?" Granny said. They stood there, moving their feet in the dust. "What? Don't any of you want to?" They just stood there. "Then who are you going to mind from now on?"

After a while, one of them said, "You, missy."

"All right," Granny said. "Now listen to me. Go home. And if I ever hear of any of you straggling off like this again, I'll see to it. Now line up and come up here one at a time while we divide the food."

It took a long time until the last one was gone; when we started again, we had almost enough mules for everybody to ride, but not quite, and Ringo drove now. He didn't ask; he just got in and took the reins, with Granny on the seat by him; it was just once that she told him not to go so fast. So I rode in the back then, on one of the chests, and that afternoon I was asleep; it was the wagon stopping that woke me. We had just come down a hill onto a flat, and then I saw them beyond a field, about a dozen of them, cavalry in blue coats. They hadn't seen us yet, trotting along, while Granny and Ringo watched them.

"They ain't hardly worth fooling with," Ringo said. "Still, they's horses."

"We've already got a hundred and ten," Granny said. "That's all the paper calls for."

"All right," Ringo said. "You wanter go on?" Granny didn't answer, sitting there drawn back a little, with her hand at her breast again. "Well, what you wanter do?" Ringo said. "You got to 'cide quick, or they be gone." He looked at her; she didn't move. Ringo leaned out of the wagon. "Hey!" he hollered. They looked back quick and saw us and whirled about. "Granny say come here!" Ringo hollered.

"You, Ringo," Granny whispered.

"All right," Ringo said. "You want me to tell um to never mind?" She didn't answer; she was looking past Ringo at the two Yankees who were riding toward us across the field, with that kind of drawn-back look on her face and her hand holding the front of her dress. It was a lieutenant and a sergeant; the lieutenant didn't look much older than Ringo and me. He saw Granny and took off his hat. And then all of a sudden she took her hand away from her chest; it had the paper in it; she held it out to the lieutenant without saying a word. The lieutenant opened it, the sergeant looking over his shoulder. Then the sergeant looked at us.

"This says mules, not horses," he said.

"Just the first hundred was mules," Ringo said. "The extra twelve is horses."

"Damn it!" the lieutenant said. He sounded like a girl swearing. "I told Captain Bowen not to mount us with captured stock!"

"You mean you're going to give them the horses?" the sergeant said.

"What else can I do?" the lieutenant said. He looked like he was fixing to cry. "It's the general's signature!"

So then we had enough stock for all of them to ride except about fifteen or twenty. We went on. The soldiers stood under a tree by the road, with their saddles and bridles on the ground beside them—all but the lieutenant. When we started again, he ran along by the wagon; he looked like he was going to cry, trotting along by the wagon with his hat in his hand, looking at Granny.

"You'll meet some troops somewhere," he said. "I know you will. Will you tell them where we are and to send us something—mounts or wagons—anything we can ride in? You won't forget?"

"They's some of yawl about twenty or thirty miles back that claim to have three extry mules," Ringo said. "But when we sees any more of um, we'll tell um about yawl."

We went on. We came in sight of a town, but we went around it; Ringo didn't even want to stop and send the lieutenant's message in, but Granny made him stop and we sent the message in by one of the niggers.

"That's one more mouth to feed we got shed of," Ringo said.

We went on. We went fast now, changing the mules every few miles; a woman told us we were in Mississippi again, and then, in the afternoon, we came over the hill, and there our chimneys were, standing up into the sunlight, and the cabin behind them and Louvinia bending over a washtub and the clothes on the line, flapping bright and peaceful.

"Stop the wagon," Granny said.

We stopped—the wagon, the hundred and twenty-two mules and horses, and the niggers we never had had time to count.

Granny got out slow and turned to Ringo. "Get out," she said; then she looked at me. "You too," she said. "Because you said nothing at all." We got out of the wagon. She looked at us. "We have lied," she said.

"Hit was the paper that lied; hit wasn't us," Ringo said.

"The paper said a hundred and ten. We have a hundred and twenty-two," Granny said. "Kneel down."

"But they stole them 'fore we did," Ringo said.

"But we lied," Granny said. "Kneel down." She knelt first. Then we all three knelt by the road while she prayed. The washing blew soft and peaceful and bright on the clothesline. And then Louvinia saw us; she was already running across the pasture while Granny was praying.

SUTPEN stood above the pallet bed on which the mother and child lay. Between the shrunken planking of the wall the early sunlight fell in long pencil strokes, breaking upon his straddled legs and upon the riding whip in his hand, and lay across the still shape of the mother, who lay looking up at him from still, inscrutable, sullen eyes, the child at her side wrapped in a piece of dingy though clean cloth. Behind them an old Negro woman squatted beside the rough hearth where a meager fire smoldered.

"Well, Milly," Sutpen said, "too bad you're not a mare. Then I could give you a decent stall in the stable."

Still the girl on the pallet did not move. She merely continued to look up at him without expression, with a young, sullen, inscrutable face still pale from recent travail. Sutpen moved, bringing into the splintered pencils of sunlight the face of a man of sixty. He said quietly to the squatting Negress, "Griselda foaled this morning."

"Horse or mare?" the Negress said.

"A horse. A damned fine colt. . . . What's this?" He indicated the pallet with the hand which held the whip.

"That un's a mare, I reckon."

"Hah," Sutpen said. "A damned fine colt. Going to be the spit and image of old Rob Roy when I rode him North in '61. Do you remember?"

"Yes, Marster."

"Hah." He glanced back towards the pallet. None

could have said if the girl still watched him or not. Again his whip hand indicated the pallet. "Do whatever they need with whatever we've got to do it with." He went out, passing out the crazy doorway and stepping down into the rank weeds (there yet leaned rusting against the corner of the porch the scythe which Wash had borrowed from him three months ago to cut them with) where his horse waited, where Wash stood holding the reins.

When Colonel Sutpen rode away to fight the Yankees, Wash did not go. "I'm looking after the Kernel's place and niggers," he would tell all who asked him and some who had not asked—a gaunt, malaria-ridden man with pale, questioning eyes, who looked about thirty-five, though it was known that he had not only a daughter but an eight-year-old granddaughter as well. This was a lie, as most of them—the few remaining men between eighteen and fifty—to whom he told it, knew, though there were some who believed that he himself really believed it, though even these believed that he had better sense than to put it to the test with Mrs. Sutpen or the Sutpen slaves. Knew better or was just too lazy and shiftless to try it, they said, knowing that his sole connection with the Sutpen plantation lay in the fact that for years now Colonel Sutpen had allowed him to squat in a crazy shack on a slough in the river bottom on the Sutpen place, which Sutpen had built for a fishing lodge in his bachelor days and which had since fallen in dilapidation from disuse, so that now it looked like an aged or sick wild beast crawled terrifically there to drink in the act of dying.

The Sutpen slaves themselves heard of his statement. They laughed. It was not the first time they had laughed at him, calling him white trash behind his back. They began to ask him themselves, in groups, meeting him in the faint road which led up from the slough and the old fish camp, "Why ain't you at de war, white man?"

Pausing, he would look about the ring of black faces and white eyes and teeth behind which derision lurked. "Because I got a daughter and family to keep," he said. "Git out of my road, niggers."

"Niggers?" they repeated; "niggers?" laughing now. "Who him, calling us niggers?"

"Yes," he said. "I ain't got no niggers to look after my folks if I was gone."

"Nor nothing else but dat shack down yon dat Cunnel wouldn't *let* none of us live in."

Now he cursed them; sometimes he rushed at them, snatching up a stick from the ground while they scattered before him, yet seeming to surround him still with that black laughing, derisive, evasive, inescapable, leaving him panting and impotent and raging. Once it happened in the very back yard of the big house itself. This was after bitter news had come down from the Tennessee mountains and from Vicksburg, and Sherman had passed through the plantation, and most of the Negroes had followed him. Almost everything else had gone with the Federal troops, and Mrs. Sutpen had sent word to Wash that he could have the scuppernongs ripening in the arbor in the back yard. This time it was a house servant, one of the few Negroes who remained; this time the Negress had to retreat up the kitchen steps, where she turned. "Stop right dar, white man. Stop right whar you is. You ain't never crossed dese steps whilst Cunnel here, and you ain't ghy' do hit now."

This was true. But there was this of a kind of pride: he had never tried to enter the big house, even though he believed that if he had, Sutpen would have received

him, permitted him. "But I ain't going to give no black
nigger the chance to tell me I can't go nowhere," he
said to himself. "I ain't even going to give Kernel the
chance to have to cuss a nigger on my account." This,
though he and Sutpen had spent more than one afternoon together on those rare Sundays when there would
be no company in the house. Perhaps his mind knew
that it was because Sutpen had nothing else to do, being
a man who could not bear his own company. Yet the
fact remained that the two of them would spend whole
afternoons in the scuppernong arbor, Sutpen in the
hammock and Wash squatting against a post, a pail of
cistern water between them, taking drink for drink
from the same demijohn. Meanwhile on weekdays he
would see the fine figure of the man—they were the
same age almost to a day, though neither of them (perhaps because Wash had a grandchild while Sutpen's
son was a youth in school) ever thought of himself as
being so—on the fine figure of the black stallion, galloping about the plantation. For that moment his heart
would be quiet and proud. It would seem to him that
that world in which Negroes, whom the Bible told him
had been created and cursed by God to be brute and
vassal to all men of white skin, were better found and
housed and even clothed than he and his; that world in
which he sensed always about him mocking echoes of
black laughter was but a dream and an illusion, and
that the actual world was this one across which his own
lonely apotheosis seemed to gallop on the black
thoroughbred, thinking how the Book said also that all
men were created in the image of God and hence all
men made the same image in God's eyes at least; so
that he could say, as though speaking of himself, "A
fine proud man. If God Himself was to come down

and ride the natural earth, that's what He would aim to look like."

Sutpen returned in 1865, on the black stallion. He seemed to have aged ten years. His son had vanished the same winter in which his wife had died. He returned with his citation for gallantry from the hand of General Lee to a ruined plantation, where for a year now his daughter had subsisted partially on the meager bounty of the man to whom fifteen years ago he had granted permission to live in that tumbledown fishing camp whose very existence he had at the time forgotten. Wash was there to meet him, unchanged: still gaunt, still ageless, with his pale, questioning gaze, his air diffident, a little servile, a little familiar. "Well, Kernel," Wash said, "they kilt us but they ain't whupped us yit, air they?"

That was the tenor of their conversation for the next five years. It was inferior whiskey which they drank now together from a stoneware jug, and it was not in the scuppernong arbor. It was in the rear of the little store which Sutpen managed to set up on the highroad: a frame shelved room where, with Wash for clerk and porter, he dispensed kerosene and staple foodstuffs and stale gaudy candy and cheap beads and ribbons to Negroes or poor whites of Wash's own kind, who came afoot or on gaunt mules to haggle tediously for dimes and quarters with a man who at one time could gallop (the black stallion was still alive; the stable in which his jealous get lived was in better repair than the house where the master himself lived) for ten miles across his own fertile land and who had led troops gallantly in battle; until Sutpen in fury would empty the store, close and lock the doors from the inside. Then he and Wash would repair to the rear and the jug. But the talk would not be quiet now, as when Sutpen lay in the hammock, delivering an arrogant monologue while Wash squatted guffawing against his post. They both sat now, though Sutpen had the single chair while Wash used whatever box or keg was handy, and even this for just a little while, because soon Sutpen would reach that stage of impotent and furious undefeat in which he would rise, swaying and plunging, and declare again that he would take his pistol and the black stallion and ride single-handed into Washington and kill Lincoln, dead now, and Sherman, now a private citizen. "Kill them!" he would shout. "Shoot them down like the dogs they are—"

"Sho, Kernel; sho, Kernel," Wash would say, catching Sutpen as he fell. Then he would commandeer the first passing wagon or, lacking that, he would walk the mile to the nearest neighbor and borrow one and return and carry Sutpen home. He entered the house now. He had been doing so for a long time, taking Sutpen home in whatever borrowed wagon might be, talking him into locomotion with cajoling murmurs as though he were a horse, a stallion himself. The daughter would meet them and hold open the door without a word. He would carry his burden through the once white formal entrance, surmounted by a fanlight imported piece by piece from Europe and with a board now nailed over a missing pane, across a velvet carpet from which all nap was now gone, and up a formal stairs, now but a fading ghost of bare boards between two strips of fading paint, and into the bedroom. It would be dusk by now, and he would let his burden sprawl onto the bed and undress it and then he would sit quietly in a chair beside. After a time the daughter would come to the door. "We're all right now," he would tell her. "Don't you worry none, Miss Judith."

Then it would become dark, and after a while he would lie down on the floor beside the bed, though not to sleep, because after a time—sometimes before midnight—the man on the bed would stir and groan and then speak. "Wash?"

"Hyer I am, Kernel. You go back to sleep. We ain't whupped yit, air we? Me and you kin do hit."

Even then he had already seen the ribbon about his granddaughter's waist. She was now fifteen, already mature, after the early way of her kind. He knew where the ribbon came from; he had been seeing it and its kind daily for three years, even if she had lied about where she got it, which she did not, at once bold, sullen, and fearful.

"Sho now," he said. "Ef Kernel wants to give hit to you, I hope you minded to thank him."

His heart was quiet, even when he saw the dress, watching her secret, defiant, frightened face when she told him that Miss Judith, the daughter, had helped her to make it. But he was quite grave when he approached Sutpen after they closed the store that afternoon, following the other to the rear.

"Get the jug," Sutpen directed.

"Wait," Wash said. "Not yit for a minute."

Neither did Sutpen deny the dress. "What about it?" he said.

But Wash met his arrogant stare; he spoke quietly. "I've knowed you for going on twenty years. I ain't never yit denied to do what you told me to do. And I'm a man nigh sixty. And she ain't nothing but a fifteen-year-old gal."

"Meaning that I'd harm a girl? I, a man as old as you are?"

"If you was ara other man, I'd say you was as old as me. And old or no old, I wouldn't let her keep that dress nor nothing else that come from your hand. But you are different."

"How different?" But Wash merely looked at him with his pale, questioning, sober eyes. "So that's why you are afraid of me?"

Now Wash's gaze no longer questioned. It was tranquil, serene. "I ain't afraid. Because you air brave. It ain't that you were a brave man at one minute or day of your life and got a paper to show hit from General Lee. But you air brave, the same as you air alive and breathing. That's where hit's different. Hit don't need no ticket from nobody to tell me that. And I know that whatever you handle or tech, whether hit's a regiment of men or a ignorant gal or just a hound dog, that you will make hit right."

Now it was Sutpen who looked away, turning suddenly, brusquely. "Get the jug," he said sharply.

"Sho, Kernel," Wash said.

So on that Sunday dawn two years later, having watched the Negro midwife, whom he had walked three miles to fetch, enter the crazy door beyond which his granddaughter lay wailing, his heart was still quiet though concerned. He knew what they had been saying—the Negroes in cabins about the land, the white men who loafed all day long about the store, watching quietly the three of them: Sutpen, himself, his granddaughter with her air of brazen and shrinking defiance as her condition become daily more and more obvious, like three actors that came and went upon a stage. "I know what they say to one another," he thought. "I can almost hyear them: *Wash Jones has fixed old Sutpen at last. Hit taken him twenty years, but he has done hit at last.*"

It would be dawn after a while, though not yet.

From the house, where the lamp shone dim beyond the warped door frame, his granddaughter's voice came steadily as though run by a clock, while thinking went slowly and terrifically, fumbling, involved somehow with a sound of galloping hooves, until there broke suddenly free in mid-gallop the fine proud figure of the man on the fine proud stallion, galloping; and then that at which thinking fumbled, broke free too and quite clear, not in justification nor even explanation, but as the apotheosis, lonely, explicable, beyond all fouling by human touch: "He is bigger than all them Yankees that kilt his son and his wife and taken his niggers and ruined his land, bigger than this hyer durn country that he fit for and that has denied him into keeping a little country store; bigger than the denial which hit helt to his lips like the bitter cup in the Book. And how could I have lived this nigh to him for twenty years without being teched and changed by him? Maybe I ain't as big as him and maybe I ain't done none of the galloping. But at least I done been drug along. Me and him kin do hit, if so be he will show me what he aims for me to do."

Then it was dawn. Suddenly he could see the house, and the old Negress in the door looking at him. Then he realized that his granddaughter's voice had ceased. "It's a girl," the Negress said. "You can go tell him if you want to." She reëntered the house.

"A girl," he repeated; "a girl"; in astonishment, hearing the galloping hooves, seeing the proud galloping figure emerge again. He seemed to watch it pass, galloping through avatars which marked the accumulation of years, time, to the climax where it galloped beneath a brandished sabre and a shot-torn flag rushing down a sky in color like thunderous sulphur, thinking for the first time in his life that perhaps Sutpen was an old man like himself. "Gittin a gal," he thought in that astonishment; then he thought with the pleased surprise of a child: "Yes, sir. Be dawg if I ain't lived to be a great-grand-paw after all."

He entered the house. He moved clumsily, on tiptoe, as if he no longer lived there, as if the infant which had just drawn breath and cried in light had dispossessed him, be it of his own blood too though it might. But even above the pallet he could see little save the blur of his granddaughter's exhausted face. Then the Negress squatting at the hearth spoke, "You better gawn tell him if you going to. Hit's daylight now."

But this was not necessary. He had no more than turned the corner of the porch where the scythe leaned which he had borrowed three months ago to clear away the weeds through which he walked, when Sutpen himself rode up on the old stallion. He did not wonder how Sutpen had got the word. He took it for granted that this was what had brought the other out at this hour on Sunday morning, and he stood while the other dismounted, and he took the reins from Sutpen's hand, an expression on his gaunt face almost imbecile with a kind of weary triumph, saying, "Hit's a gal, Kernel. I be dawg if you ain't as old as I am—" until Sutpen passed him and entered the house. He stood there with the reins in his hand and heard Sutpen cross the floor to the pallet. He heard what Sutpen said, and something seemed to stop dead in him before going on.

The sun was now up, the swift sun of Mississippi latitudes, and it seemed to him that he stood beneath a strange sky, in a strange scene, familiar only as things are familiar in dream, like the dreams of falling to one who has never climbed. "I kain't have heard what I thought I heard," he thought quietly. "I know I kain't." Yet the voice, the familiar voice which had said the words was still speaking, talking now to the old Negress about a colt foaled that morning. "That's why he was up so early," he thought. "That was hit. Hit ain't me and mine. Hit ain't even hisn that got him outen bed."

Sutpen emerged. He descended into the weeds, moving with that heavy deliberation which would have been haste when he was younger. He had not yet looked full at Wash. He said, "Dicey will stay and tend to her. You better—" Then he seemed to see Wash facing him and paused. "What?" he said.

"You said—" To his own ears Wash's voice sounded flat and ducklike, like a deaf man's. "You said if she was a mare, you could give her a good stall in the stable."

"Well?" Sutpen said. His eyes widened and narrowed, almost like a man's fists flexing and shutting, as Wash began to advance towards him, stooping a little. Very astonishment kept Sutpen still for the moment, watching that man whom in twenty years he had no more known to make any motion save at command than he had the horse which he rode. Again his eyes narrowed and widened; without moving he seemed to rear suddenly upright. "Stand back," he said suddenly and sharply. "Don't you touch me."

"I'm going to tech you, Kernel," Wash said in that flat, quiet, almost soft voice, advancing.

Sutpen raised the hand which held the riding whip; the old Negress peered around the crazy door with her black gargoyle face of a worn gnome. "Stand back, Wash," Sutpen said. Then he struck. The old Negress leaped down into the weeds with the agility of a goat and fled. Sutpen slashed Wash again across the face with the whip, striking him to his knees. When Wash rose and advanced once more he held in his hands the scythe which he had borrowed from Sutpen three months ago and which Sutpen would never need again.

When he reëntered the house his granddaughter stirred on the pallet bed and called his name fretfully. "What was that?" she said.

"What was what, honey?"

"That ere racket out there."

"'Twarn't nothing," he said gently. He knelt and touched her hot forehead clumsily. "Do you want ara thing?"

"I want a sup of water," she said querulously. "I been laying here wanting a sup of water a long time, but don't nobody care enough to pay me no mind."

"Sho now," he said soothingly. He rose stiffly and fetched the dipper of water and raised her head to drink and laid her back and watched her turn to the child with an absolutely stonelike face. But a moment later he saw that she was crying quietly. "Now, now," he said, "I wouldn't do that. Old Dicey says hit's a right fine gal. Hit's all right now. Hit's all over now. Hit ain't no need to cry now."

But she continued to cry quietly, almost sullenly, and he rose again and stood uncomfortably above the pallet for a time, thinking as he had thought when his own wife lay so and then his daughter in turn: "Women. Hit's a mystry to me. They seem to want em, and yit when they git em they cry about hit. Hit's a mystry to me. To ara man." Then he moved away and drew a chair up to the window and sat down.

Through all that long, bright, sunny forenoon he sat at the window, waiting. Now and then he rose and tiptoed to the pallet. But his granddaughter slept now, her face sullen and calm and weary, the child in the crook of her arm. Then he returned to the chair and sat again, waiting, wondering why it took them so long, until he remembered that it was Sunday. He was sitting there at mid-afternoon when a half-grown white boy came around the corner of the house upon the body and gave a choked cry and looked up and glared for a mesmerized instant at Wash in the window before he turned and fled. Then Wash rose and tiptoed again to the pallet.

The granddaughter was awake now, wakened perhaps by the boy's cry without hearing it. "Milly," he said, "air you hungry?" She didn't answer, turning her face away. He built up the fire on the hearth and cooked the food which he had brought home the day before: fatback it was, and cold corn pone; he poured water into the stale coffee pot and heated it. But she would not eat when he carried the plate to her, so he ate himself, quietly, alone, and left the dishes as they were and returned to the window.

Now he seemed to sense, feel, the men who would be gathering with horses and guns and dogs—the curious, and the vengeful: men of Sutpen's own kind, who had made the company about Sutpen's table in the time when Wash himself had yet to approach nearer to the house than the scuppernong arbor—men who had also shown the lesser ones how to fight in battle, who maybe also had signed papers from the generals saying that they were among the first of the brave; who had also galloped in the old days arrogant and proud on the fine horses across the fine plantations—symbols also of admiration and hope; instruments too of despair and grief.

That was who they would expect him to run from. It seemed to him that he had no more to run from than he had to run to. If he ran, he would merely be fleeing one set of bragging and evil shadows for another just like them, since they were all of a kind throughout all the earth which he knew, and he was old, too old to flee far even if he were to flee. He could never escape them, no matter how much or how far he ran: a man going on sixty could not run that far. Not far enough to escape beyond the boundaries of earth where such men lived, set the order and the rule of living. It seemed to him that he now saw for the first time, after five years, how it was that Yankees or any other living armies had managed to whip them: the gallant, the proud, the brave; the acknowledged and chosen best among them all to carry courage and honor and pride. Maybe if he had gone to the war with them he would have discovered them sooner. But if he had discovered them sooner, what would he have done with his life since? How could he have borne to remember for five years what his life had been before?

Now it was getting toward sunset. The child had been crying; when he went to the pallet he saw his granddaughter nursing it, her face still bemused, sullen, inscrutable. "Air you hungry yit?" he said.

"I don't want nothing."

"You ought to eat."

This time she did not answer at all, looking down at the child. He returned to his chair and found that the sun had set. "Hit kain't be much longer," he thought. He could feel them quite near now, the curious and the vengeful. He could even seem to hear what they were saying about him, the undercurrent of believing beyond the immediate fury: *Old Wash Jones he come a tumble at last. He thought he had Sutpen, but Sutpen fooled him. He thought he had Kernel where he would have to marry the gal or pay up. And Kernel refused.* "But I never expected that, Kernel!" he cried aloud, catching himself at the sound of his own voice, glancing quickly back to find his granddaughter watching him.

"Who you talking to now?" she said.

"Hit ain't nothing. I was just thinking and talked out before I knowed hit."

Her face was becoming indistinct again, again a sullen blur in the twilight. "I reckon so. I reckon you'll have to holler louder than that before he'll hear you, up yonder at that house. And I reckon you'll need to do more than holler before you get him down here too."

"Sho now," he said. "Don't you worry none." But already thinking was going smoothly on: "You know I never. You know how I ain't never expected or asked nothing from ara living man but what I expected from you. And I never asked that. I didn't think hit would need. I said, *I don't need to. What need has a fellow like Wash Jones to question or doubt the man that General Lee himself says in a handwrote ticket that he was brave?* Brave," he thought. "Better if nara one of them had never rid back home in '65"; thinking *Better if his kind and mine too had never drawn the breath of life on this earth. Better that all who remain of us be blasted from the face of earth than that another Wash Jones should see his whole life shredded from him and shrivel away like a dried shuck thrown onto the fire.*

He ceased, became still. He heard the horses, suddenly and plainly; presently he saw the lantern and the movement of men, the glint of gun barrels, in its moving light. Yet he did not stir. It was quite dark now, and he listened to the voices and the sounds of underbrush as they surrounded the house. The lantern itself came on; its light fell upon the quiet body in the weeds and stopped, the horses tall and shadowy. A man descended and stooped in the lantern light, above the body. He held a pistol; he rose and faced the house. "Jones," he said.

"I'm here," Wash said quietly from the window. "That you, Major?"

"Come out."

"Sho," he said quietly. "I just want to see to my granddaughter."

"We'll see to her. Come on out."

"Sho, Major. Just a minute."

"Show a light. Light your lamp."

"Sho. In just a minute." They could hear his voice retreat into the house, though they could not see him as he went swiftly to the crack in the chimney where he kept the butcher knife: the one thing in his slovenly life and house in which he took pride, since it was razor sharp. He approached the pallet, his granddaughter's voice:

"Who is it? Light the lamp, grandpaw."

"Hit won't need no light, honey. Hit won't take but a minute," he said, kneeling, fumbling toward her voice, whispering now, "Where air you?"

"Right here," she said fretfully. "Where would I be? What is. . . ." His hand touched her face. "What is. . . . Grandpaw! Grand. . . ."

"Jones!" the sheriff said. "Come out of there!"

"In just a minute, Major," he said. Now he rose and moved swiftly. He knew where in the dark the can of kerosene was, just as he knew that it was full, since it was not two days ago that he had filled it at the store and held it there until he got a ride home with it, since the five gallons were heavy. There were still coals on the hearth; besides the crazy building itself was like tinder: the coals, the hearth, the walls exploding in a single blue glare. Against it the waiting men saw him in a wild instant springing toward them with the lifted scythe before the horses reared and whirled. They checked the horses and turned them back toward the glare, yet still in wild relief against it the gaunt figure ran toward them with the lifted scythe.

"Jones!" the sheriff shouted. "Stop! Stop, or I'll shoot. Jones! *Jones!*" Yet still the gaunt, furious figure came on against the glare and roar of the flames. With the scythe lifted, it bore down upon them, upon the wild glaring eyes of the horses and the swinging glints of gun barrels, without any cry, any sound.

1874.   AN ODOR OF
VERBENA

IT WAS just after supper. I had just opened my *Coke*
on the table beneath the lamp; I heard Professor
Wilkins' feet in the hall and then the instant of silence
as he put his hand to the doorknob, and I should have
known. People talk glibly of presentiment, but I had
none. I heard his feet on the stairs and then in the hall
approaching and there was nothing in the feet because
although I had lived in his house for three college
years now and although both he and Mrs. Wilkins
called me Bayard in the house, he would no more have
entered my room without knocking than I would have
entered his—or hers. Then he flung the door violently
inward against the doorstop with one of those gestures
with or by which an almost painfully unflagging pre-
ceptory of youth ultimately aberrates, and stood there
saying, "Bayard. Bayard, my son, my dear son."

I should have known; I should have been prepared.
Or maybe I was prepared because I remember how I
closed the book carefully, even marking the place,
before I rose. He (Professor Wilkins) was doing something, bustling at something; it was my hat and cloak
which he handed me and which I took although I would
not need the cloak, unless even then I was thinking
(although it was October, the equinox had not occurred) that the rains and the cool weather would
arrive before I should see this room again and so I

186

would need the cloak anyway to return to it if I returned, thinking "God, if he had only done this last
night, flung that door crashing and bouncing against
the stop last night without knocking so I could have
gotten there before it happened, been there when it
did, beside him on whatever spot, wherever it was that
he would have to fall and lie in the dust and dirt."

"Your boy is downstairs in the kitchen," he said. It
was not until years later that he told me (someone did;
it must have been Judge Wilkins) how Ringo had
apparently flung the cook aside and come on into the
house and into the library where he and Mrs. Wilkins
were sitting and said without preamble and already
turning to withdraw: "They shot Colonel Sartoris
this morning. Tell him I be waiting in the kitchen,"
and was gone before either of them could move. "He
has ridden forty miles yet he refuses to eat anything."
We were moving toward the door now—the door on
my side of which I had lived for three years now with
what I knew, what I knew now I must have believed
and expected, yet beyond which I had heard the approaching feet yet heard nothing in the feet. "If there
was just anything I could do."

"Yes, sir," I said. "A fresh horse for my boy. He will
want to go back with me."

"By all means take mine—Mrs. Wilkins'," he cried.
His tone was no different yet he did cry it and I suppose that at the same moment we both realized that was
funny—a short-legged, deep-barrelled mare who looked
exactly like a spinster music teacher, which Mrs.
Wilkins drove to a basket phaeton—which was good for
me, like being doused with a pail of cold water would
have been good for me.

"Thank you, sir," I said. "We won't need it. I will
get a fresh horse for him at the livery stable when I get

my mare." Good for me, because even before I finished
speaking I knew that would not be necessary either,
that Ringo would have stopped at the livery stable before he came out to the college and attended to that and
that the fresh horse for him and my mare both would
be saddled and waiting now at the side fence and we
would not have to go through Oxford at all. Loosh
would not have thought of that if he had come for me,
he would have come straight to the college, to Professor
Wilkins', and told his news and then sat down and let
me take charge from then on. But not Ringo.

He followed me from the room. From now until
Ringo and I rode away into the hot, thick, dusty darkness, quick and strained for the overdue equinox like a
laboring delayed woman, he would be somewhere
either just beside me or just behind me and I never to
know exactly nor care which. He was trying to find the
words with which to offer me his pistol too. I could
almost hear him: "Ah, this unhappy land, not ten
years recovered from the fever yet still men must kill
one another, still we must pay Cain's price in his own
coin." But he did not actually say it. He just followed
me, somewhere beside or behind me as we descended
the stairs toward where Mrs. Wilkins waited in the
hall beneath the chandelier—a thin gray woman who
reminded me of Granny, not that she looked like Granny
probably but because she had known Granny—a lifted,
anxious, still face which was thinking *Who lives by the
sword shall die by it* just as Granny would have thought,
toward which I walked, had to walk not because I was
Granny's grandson and had lived in her house for
three college years and was about the age of her son
when he was killed in almost the last battle nine years
ago, but because I was now The Sartoris. (The Sartoris:
that had been one of the concomitant flashes, along with

the *at last it has happened* when Professor Wilkins
opened my door.) She didn't offer me a horse and pistol,
not because she liked me any less than Professor Wilkins
but because she was a woman and so wiser than any
man, else the men would not have gone on with the
War for two years after they knew they were whipped.
She just put her hands (a small woman, no bigger than
Granny had been) on my shoulders and said, "Give my
love to Drusilla and your Aunt Jenny. And come back
when you can."

"Only I don't know when that will be," I said. "I
don't know how many things I will have to attend to."
Yes, I lied even to her; it had not been but a minute yet
since he had flung that door bouncing into the stop
yet already I was beginning to realize, to become aware
of that which I still had no yardstick to measure save
that one consisting of what, despite myself, despite my
raising and background (or maybe because of them)
I had for some time known I was becoming and had
feared the test of it; I remember how I thought while
her hands still rested on my shoulders: *At least this
will be my chance to find out if I am what I think I
am or if I just hope; if I am going to do what I have
taught myself is right or if I am just going to wish I
were.*

We went on to the kitchen, Professor Wilkins still
somewhere beside or behind me and still offering me
the pistol and horse in a dozen different ways. Ringo
was waiting; I remember how I thought then that no
matter what might happen to either of us, I would
never be The Sartoris to him. He was twenty-four too,
but in a way he had changed even less than I had since
that day when we had nailed Grumby's body to the
door of the old compress. Maybe it was because he had
outgrown me, had changed so much that summer while

he and Granny traded mules with the Yankees that since then I had had to do most of the changing just to catch up with him. He was sitting quietly in a chair beside the cold stove, spent-looking too who had ridden forty miles (at one time, either in Jefferson or when he was alone at last on the road somewhere, he had cried; dust was now caked and dried in the tear-channels on his face) and would ride forty more yet would not eat, looking up at me a little red-eyed with weariness (or maybe it was more than just weariness and so I would never catch up with him) then rising without a word and going on toward the door and I following and Professor Wilkins still offering the horse and the pistol without speaking the words and still thinking (I could feel that too) *Dies by the sword. Dies by the sword.*

Ringo had the two horses saddled at the side gate, as I had known he would—the fresh one for himself and my mare Father had given me three years ago, that could do a mile under two minutes any day and a mile every eight minutes all day long. He was already mounted when I realized that what Professor Wilkins wanted was to shake my hand. We shook hands; I knew he believed he was touching flesh which might not be alive tomorrow night, and I thought for a second how if I told him what I was going to do, since we had talked about it, about how if there was anything at all in the Book, anything of hope and peace for His blind and bewildered spawn which He had chosen above all others to offer immortality, *Thou shalt not kill* must be it, since maybe he even believed that he had taught it to me, except that he had not, nobody had, not even myself, since it went further than just having been learned. But I did not tell him. He was too old to be forced so, to condone even in principle such a decision; he was too old to have to stick to principle in the face of blood and raising and background, to be faced without warning and made to deliver like by a highwayman out of the dark: only the young could do that—one still young enough to have his youth supplied him gratis as a reason (not an excuse) for cowardice.

So I said nothing. I just shook his hand and mounted too, and Ringo and I rode on. We would not have to pass through Oxford now and so soon (there was a thin sickle of moon like the heel print of a boot in wet sand) the road to Jefferson lay before us, the road which I had travelled for the first time three years ago with Father and travelled twice at Christmas time and then in June and September and twice at Christmas time again and then June and September again each college term since alone on the mare, not even knowing that this was peace; and now this time and maybe last time who would not die (I knew that) but who maybe forever after could never again hold up his head. The horses took the gait which they would hold for forty miles. My mare knew the long road ahead and Ringo had a good beast too, had talked Hilliard at the livery stable out of a good horse too. Maybe it was the tears, the channels of dried mud across which his strain-reddened eyes had looked at me, but I rather think it was that same quality which used to enable him to replenish his and Granny's supply of United States Army letterheads during that time—some outrageous assurance gained from too long and too close association with white people: the one whom he called Granny, the other with whom he had slept from the time we were born until Father rebuilt the house. We spoke one time, then no more:

"We could bushwhack him," he said. "Like we done Grumby that day. But I reckon that wouldn't suit that white skin you walks around in."

"No," I said. We rode on; it was October; there was plenty of time still for verbena although I would have to reach home before I would realize there was a need for it; plenty of time for verbena yet from the garden where Aunt Jenny puttered beside old Joby, in a pair of Father's old cavalry gauntlets, among the coaxed and ordered beds, the quaint and odorous old names, for though it was October no rain had come yet and hence no frost to bring (or leave behind) the first half-warm half-chill nights of Indian Summer—the drowsing air cool and empty for geese yet languid still with the old hot dusty smell of fox grape and sassafras—the nights when before I became a man and went to college to learn law Ringo and I, with lantern and axe and croker-sack and six dogs (one to follow the trail and five more just for the tonguing, the music) would hunt possum in the pasture where, hidden, we had seen our first Yankee that afternoon on the bright horse, where for the last year now you could hear the whistling of the trains which had no longer belonged to Mr. Redmond for a long while now and which at some instant, some second during the morning Father too had relinquished along with the pipe which Ringo said he was smoking, which slipped from his hand as he fell. We rode on, toward the house where he would be lying in the parlor now, in his regimentals (sabre too) and where Drusilla would be waiting for me beneath all the festive glitter of the chandeliers, in the yellow ball gown and the sprig of verbena in her hair, holding the two loaded pistols (I could see that too, who had had no presentiment; I could see her, in the formal brilliant room arranged formally for obsequy, not tall, not slender as a woman is but as a youth, a boy, is, motion-less, in yellow, the face calm, almost bemused, the head simple and severe, the balancing sprig of verbena above each ear, the two arms bent at the elbows, the two hands shoulder high, the two identical duelling pistols lying upon, not clutched in, one to each: the Greek amphora priestess of a succinct and formal violence).

II

Drusilla said that he had a dream. I was twenty then and she and I would walk in the garden in the summer twilight while we waited for Father to ride in from the railroad. I was just twenty then: that summer before I entered the University to take the law degree which Father decided I should have and four years after the one, the day, the evening when Father and Drusilla had kept old Cash Benbow from becoming United States Marshal and returned home still unmarried and Mrs. Habersham herded them into her carriage and drove them back to town and dug her husband out of his little dim hole in the new bank and made him sign Father's peace bond for killing the two carpet baggers, and took Father and Drusilla to the minister herself and saw that they were married. And Father had rebuilt the house too, on the same blackened spot, over the same cellar, where the other had burned, only larger, much larger: Drusilla said that the house was the aura of Father's dream just as a bride's trousseau and veil is the aura of hers. And Aunt Jenny had come to live with us now so we had the garden (Drusilla would no more have bothered with flowers than Father himself would have, who even now, even four years after it was over, still seemed to exist, breathe, in that last year of it while she had ridden in man's clothes and with her hair cut short like any other member of Father's troop, across Georgia and both Carolinas in front of Sherman's army) for her to gather sprigs of

verbena from to wear in her hair because she said
verbena was the only scent you could smell above the
smell of horses and courage and so it was the only one
that was worth the wearing. The railroad was hardly
begun then and Father and Mr. Redmond were not
only still partners, they were still friends, which as
George Wyatt said was easily a record for Father, and
he would leave the house at daybreak on Jupiter, riding
up and down the unfinished line with two saddlebags of
gold coins borrowed on Friday to pay the men on Saturday, keeping just two cross-ties ahead of the sheriff as
Aunt Jenny said. So we walked in the dusk, slowly between Aunt Jenny's flower beds while Drusilla (in a
dress now, who still would have worn pants all the time
if Father had let her) leaned lightly on my arm and I
smelled the verbena in her hair as I had smelled the rain
in it and in Father's beard that night four years ago
when he and Drusilla and Uncle Buck McCaslin found
Grumby and then came home and found Ringo and
me more than just asleep: escaped into that oblivion
which God or Nature or whoever it was had supplied
us with for the time being, who had had to perform
more than should be required of children because
there should be some limit to the age, the youth at
least below which one should not have to kill. This
was just after the Saturday night when he returned and
I watched him clean the derringer and reload it and we
learned that the dead man was almost a neighbor, a
hill man who had been in the first infantry regiment
when it voted Father out of command: and we never to
know if the man actually intended to rob Father or not
because Father had shot too quick, but only that he
had a wife and several children in a dirt-floored cabin
in the hills, to whom Father the next day sent some
money and she (the wife) walked into the house two

days later while we were sitting at the dinner table and flung the money at Father's face.

"But nobody could have had more of a dream than Colonel Sutpen," I said. He had been Father's second-in-command in the first regiment and had been elected colonel when the regiment deposed Father after Second Manassas, and it was Sutpen and not the regiment whom father never forgave. He was underbred, a cold ruthless man who had come into the country about thirty years before the War, nobody knew from where except Father said you could look at him and know he would not dare to tell. He had got some land and nobody knew how he did that either, and he got money from somewhere—Father said they all believed he robbed steamboats, either as a card sharper or as an out-and-out highwayman—and built a big house and married and set up as a gentleman. Then he lost everything in the War like everybody else, all hope of descendants too (his son killed his daughter's fiancé on the eve of the wedding and vanished), yet he came back home and set out singlehanded to rebuild his plantation. He had no friends to borrow from and he had nobody to leave it to and he was past sixty years old, yet he set out to rebuild his place like it used to be; they told how he was too busy to bother with politics or anything; how when Father and the other men organized the night riders to keep the carpet baggers from organizing the Negroes into an insurrection, he refused to have anything to do with it. Father stopped hating him long enough to ride out to see Sutpen himself and he (Sutpen) came to the door with a lamp and did not even invite them to come in and discuss it; Father said, "Are you with us or against us?" and he said, "I'm for my land. If every man of you would rehabilitate his own land, the country will take care of itself" and Father challenged him to bring the lamp out and set it on a stump where they could both see to shoot and Sutpen would not. "Nobody could have more of a dream than that."

"Yes. But his dream was just Sutpen. John's is not. He is thinking of this whole country which he is trying to raise by its bootstraps, so that all the people in it, not just his kind nor his old regiment, but all the people, black and white, the women and children back in the hills who don't even own shoes— Don't you see?"

"But how can they get any good from what he wants to do for them if they are—after he has——"

"Killed some of them? I suppose you include those two carpet baggers he had to kill to hold that first election, don't you?"

"They were men. Human beings."

"They were Northerners, foreigners who had no business here. They were pirates." We walked on, her weight hardly discernible on my arm, her head just reaching my shoulder. I had always been a little taller than she, even on that night at Hawkhurst while we listened to the niggers passing in the road, and she had changed but little since—the same boy-hard body, the close implacable head with its savagely cropped hair which I had watched from the wagon above the tide of crazed singing niggers as we went down into the river—the body not slender as women are but as boys are slender. "A dream is not a very safe thing to be near, Bayard. I know; I had one once. It's like a loaded pistol with a hair trigger: if it stays alive long enough, somebody is going to be hurt. But if it's a good dream, it's worth it. There are not many dreams in the world, but there are a lot of human lives. And one human life or two dozen——"

"Are not worth anything?"

"No. Not anything.—Listen. I hear Jupiter. I'll beat you to the house." She was already running, the skirts she did not like to wear lifted almost to her knees, her legs beneath it running as boys run just as she rode like men ride.

I was twenty then. But the next time I was twenty-four; I had been three years at the University and in another two weeks I would ride back to Oxford for the final year and my degree. It was just last summer, last August, and Father had just beat Redmond for the State legislature. The railroad was finished now and the partnership between Father and Redmond had been dissolved so long ago that most people would have forgotten they were ever partners if it hadn't been for the enmity between them. There had been a third partner but nobody hardly remembered his name now; he and his name both had vanished in the fury of the conflict which set up between Father and Redmond almost before they began to lay the rails, between Father's violent and ruthless dictatorialness and will to dominate (the idea was his; he did think of the railroad first and then took Redmond in) and that quality in Redmond (as George Wyatt said, he was not a coward or Father would never have teamed with him) which permitted him to stand as much as he did from Father, to bear and bear and bear until something (not his will nor his courage) broke in him. During the War Redmond had not been a soldier, he had had something to do with cotton for the Government; he could have made money himself out of it but he had not and everybody knew he had not, Father knew it, yet Father would even taunt him with not having smelled powder. He was wrong; he knew he was when it was too late for him to stop just as a drunkard reaches a point where it is too late for him to stop, where he promises himself that he will and maybe believes he will or can but it is too late. Finally they reached the point (they had both put everything they could mortgage or borrow into it for Father to ride up and down the line, paying the work-men and the waybills on the rails at the last possible in-stant) where even Father realized that one of them would have to get out. So (they were not speaking then; it was arranged by Judge Benbow) they met and agreed to buy or sell, naming a price which, in reference to what they had put into it, was ridiculously low but which each believed the other could not raise—at least Father claimed that Redmond did not believe he could raise it. So Redmond accepted the price, and found out that Father had the money. And according to Father, that's what started it, although Uncle Buck McCaslin said Father could not have owned a half interest in even one hog, let alone a railroad, and not dissolve the business either sworn enemy or death-pledged friend to his recent partner. So they parted and Father finished the road. By that time, seeing that he was going to finish it, some Northern people sold him a locomotive on credit which he named for Aunt Jenny, with a silver oil can in the cab with her name engraved on it; and last summer the first train ran into Jefferson, the engine decorated with flowers and Father in the cab blowing blast after blast on the whistle when he passed Redmond's house; and there were speeches at the station, with more flowers and a Confederate flag and girls in white dresses and red sashes and a band, and Father stood on the pilot of the engine and made a direct and absolutely needless allu-sion to Mr. Redmond. That was it. He wouldn't let him alone. George Wyatt came to me right afterward and told me. "Right or wrong," he said, "us boys and most of the other folks in this county know John's right. But he ought to let Redmond alone. I know what's wrong: he's had to kill too many folks, and that's bad for a man. We all know Colonel's brave as a lion, but Redmond ain't no coward either and there ain't any use in making a brave man that made one mistake eat crow all the time. Can't you talk to him?"

"I don't know," I said. "I'll try." But I had no chance. That is, I could have talked to him and he would have listened, but he could not have heard me because he had stepped straight from the pilot of that engine into the race for the Legislature. Maybe he knew that Redmond would have to oppose him to save his face even though he (Redmond) must have known that, after that train ran into Jefferson, he had no chance against Father, or maybe Redmond had already announced his candidacy and Father entered the race just because of that, I don't remember. Anyway they ran, a bitter contest in which Father continued to badger Redmond without reason or need, since they both knew it would be a landslide for Father. And it was, and we thought he was satisfied. Maybe he thought so himself, as the drunkard believes that he is done with drink; and it was that afternoon and Drusilla and I walked in the garden in the twilight and I said something about what George Wyatt had told me and she released my arm and turned me to face her and said, "This from you? You? Have you forgotten Grumby?"

"No," I said. "I never will forget him."

"You never will. I wouldn't let you. There are worse things than killing men, Bayard. There are worse things than being killed. Sometimes I think the finest thing that can happen to a man is to love something, a woman preferably, well, hard hard hard, then to die young because he believed what he could not help but believe and was what he could not (could not? would not)

help but be." Now she was looking at me in a way she
never had before. I did not know what it meant then
and was not to know until tonight since neither of us
knew then that two months later Father would be dead.
I just knew that she was looking at me as she never had
before and that the scent of the verbena in her hair
seemed to have increased a hundred times, to have got
a hundred times stronger, to be everywhere in the dusk
in which something was about to happen which I had
never dreamed of. Then she spoke. "Kiss me, Bayard."

"No. You are Father's wife."

"And eight years older than you are. And your fourth
cousin, too. And I have black hair. Kiss me, Bayard."

"No."

"Kiss me, Bayard." So I leaned my face down to her.
But she didn't move, standing so, bent lightly back
from me from the waist, looking at me; now it was she
who said, "No." So I put my arms around her. Then
she came to me, melted as women will and can, the
arms with the wrist- and elbow-power to control horses
about my shoulders, using the wrists to hold my face to
hers until there was no longer need for the wrists; I
thought then of the woman of thirty, the symbol of the
ancient and eternal Snake and of the men who have
written of her, and I realized then the immitigable
chasm between all life and all print—that those who
can, do, those who cannot and suffer enough because
they can't, write about it. Then I was free, I could see
her again, I saw her still watching me with that dark
inscrutable look, looking up at me now across her down-
slanted face; I watched her arms rise with almost the
exact gesture with which she had put them around me
as if she were repeating the empty and formal gesture
of all promise so that I should never forget it, the elbows
angling outward as she put her hands to the sprig of

verbena in her hair, I standing straight and rigid facing
the slightly bent head, the short jagged hair, the rigid
curiously formal angle of the bare arms gleaming
faintly in the last of light as she removed the verbena
sprig and put it into my lapel, and I thought how the
War had tried to stamp all the women of her generation and class in the South into a type and how it had
failed—the suffering, the identical experience (hers and
Aunt Jenny's had been almost the same except that
Aunt Jenny had spent a few nights with her husband
before they brought him back home in an ammunition
wagon while Gavin Breckbridge was just Drusilla's
fiancé) was there in the eyes, yet beyond that was the
incorrigibly individual woman: not like so many men
who return from wars to live on Government reserva-
tions like so many steers, emasculate and empty of all
save an identical experience which they cannot forget
and dare not, else they would cease to live at that
moment, almost interchangeable save for the old habit
of answering to a given name.

"Now I must tell Father," I said.

"Yes," she said. "You must tell him. Kiss me." So
again it was like it had been before. No. Twice, a
thousand times and never like—the eternal and symbolical thirty to a young man, a youth, each time both
cumulative and retroactive, immitigably unrepetitive,
each wherein remembering excludes experience, each
wherein experience antedates remembering; the skill
without weariness, the knowledge virginal to surfeit,
the cunning secret muscles to guide and control just
as within the wrists and elbows lay slumbering the
mastery of horses: she stood back, already turning, not
looking at me when she spoke, never having looked at
me, already moving swiftly on in the dusk: "Tell John.
Tell him tonight."

I intended to. I went to the house and into the office at once; I went to the center of the rug before the cold hearth, I don't know why, and stood there rigid like soldiers stand, looking at eye level straight across the room and above his head and said "Father" and then stopped. Because he did not even hear me. He said, "Yes, Bayard?" but he did not hear me although he was sitting behind the desk doing nothing, immobile, as still as I was rigid, one hand on the desk with a dead cigar in it, a bottle of brandy and a filled and untasted glass beside his hand, clothed quiet and bemused in whatever triumph it was he felt since the last overwhelming return of votes had come in late in the afternoon. So I waited until after supper. We went to the dining-room and stood side by side until Aunt Jenny entered and then Drusilla, in the yellow ball gown, who walked straight to me and gave me one fierce inscrutable look then went to her place and waited for me to draw her chair while Father drew Aunt Jenny's. He had roused by then, not to talk himself but rather to sit at the head of the table and reply to Drusilla as she talked with a sort of feverish and glittering volubility—to reply now and then to her with that courteous intolerant pride which had lately become a little forensic, as if merely being in a political contest filled with fierce and empty oratory had retroactively made a lawyer of him who was anything and everything except a lawyer. Then Drusilla and Aunt Jenny rose and left us and he said, "Wait" to me who had made no move to follow and directed Joby to bring one of the bottles of wine which he had fetched back from New Orleans when he went there last to borrow money to liquidate his first private railroad bonds. Then I stood again like soldiers stand, gazing at eye level above his head while he sat half-turned from the table, a little paunchy now though not much, a little grizzled too in the hair though his beard was as strong as ever, with that spurious forensic air of lawyers and the intolerant eyes which in the last two years had acquired that transparent film which the eyes of carnivorous animals have and from behind which they look at a world which no ruminant ever sees, perhaps dares to see, which I have seen before on the eyes of men who have killed too much, who have killed so much that never again as long as they live will they ever be alone. I said again, "Father," then I told him.

"Hah?" he said. "Sit down." I sat down, I looked at him, watched him fill both glasses and this time I knew it was worse with him than not hearing: it didn't even matter. "You are doing well in the law, Judge Wilkins tells me. I am pleased to hear that. I have not needed you in my affairs so far, but from now on I shall. I have now accomplished the active portion of my aims in which you could not have helped me; I acted as the land and the time demanded and you were too young for that, I wished to shield you. But now the land and the time too are changing; what will follow will be a matter of consolidation, of pettifogging and doubtless chicanery in which I would be a babe in arms but in which you, trained in the law, can hold your own—our own. Yes. I have accomplished my aim, and now I shall do a little moral housecleaning. I am tired of killing men, no matter what the necessity or the end. Tomorrow, when I go to town and meet Ben Redmond, I shall be unarmed."

III

We reached home just before midnight; we didn't have to pass through Jefferson either. Before we turned in the gates I could see the lights, the chandeliers—

hall, parlor, and what Aunt Jenny (without any effort or perhaps even design on her part) had taught even Ringo to call the drawing room, the light falling outward across the portico, past the columns. Then I saw the horses, the faint shine of leather and buckle-glints on the black silhouettes and then the men too—Wyatt and others of Father's old troop—and I had forgot that they would be there. I had forgot that they would be there; I remember how I thought, since I was tired and spent with strain, *Now it will have to begin tonight. I won't even have until tomorrow in which to begin to resist.* They had a watchman, a picquet out, I suppose, because they seemed to know at once that we were in the drive. Wyatt met me, I halted the mare, I could look down at him and at the others gathered a few yards behind him with that curious vulture-like formality which Southern men assume in such situations.

"Well, boy," George said.

"Was it—" I said. "Was he——"

"It was all right. It was in front. Redmond ain't no coward. John had the derringer inside his cuff like always, but he never touched it, never made a move toward it." I have seen him do it, he showed me once: the pistol (it was not four inches long) held flat inside his left wrist by a clip he made himself of wire and an old clock spring; he would raise both hands at the same time, cross them, fire the pistol from beneath his left hand almost as if he were hiding from his own vision what he was doing; when he killed one of the men he shot a hole through his own coat sleeve. "But you want to get on to the house," Wyatt said. He began to stand aside, then he spoke again: "We'll take this off your hands, any of us. Me." I hadn't moved the mare yet and I had made no move to speak, yet he continued quickly, as if he had already rehearsed all this, his speech and mine, and knew what I would say and only spoke himself as he would have removed his hat on entering a house or used "sir" in conversing with a stranger: "You're young, just a boy, you ain't had any experience in this kind of thing. Besides, you got them two ladies in the house to think about. He would understand, all right."

"I reckon I can attend to it," I said.

"Sure," he said; there was no surprise, nothing at all, in his voice because he had already rehearsed this: "I reckon we all knew that's what you would say." He stepped back then; almost it was as though he and not I bade the mare to move on. But they all followed, still with that unctuous and voracious formality. Then I saw Drusilla standing at the top of the front steps, in the light from the open door and the windows like a theatre scene, in the yellow ball gown and even from here I believed that I could smell the verbena in her hair, standing there motionless yet emanating something louder than the two shots must have been—something voracious too and passionate. Then, although I had dismounted and someone had taken the mare, I seemed to be still in the saddle and to watch myself enter that scene which she had postulated like another actor while in the background for chorus Wyatt and the others stood with the unctuous formality which the Southern man shows in the presence of death—that Roman holiday engendered by mist-born Protestantism grafted onto this land of violent sun, of violent alteration from snow to heat-stroke which has produced a race impervious to both. I mounted the steps toward the figure straight and yellow and immobile as a candle which moved only to extend one hand; we stood together and looked down at them where they stood clumped, the horses too gathered in a tight group be-

yond them at the rim of light from the brilliant door
and windows. One of them stamped and blew his breath
and jangled his gear.

"Thank you, gentlemen," I said. "My aunt and my—
Drusilla thank you. There's no need for you to stay.
Good night." They murmured, turning. George Wyatt
paused, looking back at me.

"Tomorrow?" he said.

"Tomorrow." Then they went on, carrying their hats
and tiptoeing, even on the ground, the quiet and resili-
ent earth, as though anyone in that house awake would
try to sleep, anyone already asleep in it whom they
could have wakened. Then they were gone and Drusilla
and I turned and crossed the portico, her hand lying
light on my wrist yet discharging into me with a shock
like electricity that dark and passionate voracity, the
face at my shoulder—the jagged hair with a verbena
sprig above each ear, the eyes staring at me with that
fierce exaltation. We entered the hall and crossed it,
her hand guiding me without pressure, and entered the
parlor. Then for the first time I realized it—the alteration which is death—not that he was now just clay
but that he was lying down. But I didn't look at him
yet because I knew that when I did I would begin to
pant; I went to Aunt Jenny who had just risen from a
chair behind which Louvinia stood. She was Father's
sister, taller than Drusilla but no older, whose husband
had been killed at the very beginning of the War, by a
shell from a Federal frigate at Fort Moultrie, come to us
from Carolina six years ago. Ringo and I went to Tennessee Junction in the wagon to meet her. It was January, cold and clear and with ice in the ruts; we
returned just before dark with Aunt Jenny on the seat
beside me holding a lace parasol and Ringo in the wagon
bed nursing a hamper basket containing two bottles

of old sherry and the two jasmine cuttings which were bushes in the garden now, and the panes of colored glass which she had salvaged from the Carolina house where she and Father and Uncle Bayard were born and which Father had set in a fanlight about one of the drawing room windows for her—who came up the drive and Father (home now from the railroad) went down the steps and lifted her from the wagon and said, "Well, Jenny," and she said, "Well, Johnny," and began to cry. She stood too, looking at me as I approached— the same hair, the same high nose, the same eyes as Father's except that they were intent and very wise instead of intolerant. She said nothing at all, she just kissed me, her hands light on my shoulders. Then Drusilla spoke, as if she had been waiting with a sort of dreadful patience for the empty ceremony to be done, in a voice like a bell: clear, unsentient, on a single pitch, silvery and triumphant: "Come, Bayard."

"Hadn't you better go to bed now?" Aunt Jenny said.

"Yes," Drusilla said in that silvery ecstatic voice, "Oh yes. There will be plenty of time for sleep." I followed her, her hand again guiding me without pressure; now I looked at him. It was just as I had imagined it—sabre, plumes, and all—but with that alteration, that irrevocable difference which I had known to expect yet had not realized, as you can put food into your stomach which for a while the stomach declines to assimilate—the illimitable grief and regret as I looked down at the face which I knew—the nose, the hair, the eyelids closed over the intolerance—the face which I realized I now saw in repose for the first time in my life; the empty hands still now beneath the invisible stain of what had been (once, surely) needless blood, the hands now appearing clumsy in their very inertness, too clumsy to have performed the fatal actions which for-

ever afterward he must have waked and slept with and
maybe was glad to lay down at last—those curious
appendages clumsily conceived to begin with yet with
which man has taught himself to do so much, so much
more than they were intended to do or could be forgiven for doing, which had now surrendered that life
to which his intolerant heart had fiercely held; and then
I knew that in a minute I would begin to pant. So
Drusilla must have spoken twice before I heard her
and turned and saw in the instant Aunt Jenny and
Louvinia watching us, hearing Drusilla now, the unsentient bell quality gone now, her voice whispering into
that quiet death-filled room with a passionate and dying
fall: "Bayard." She faced me, she was quite near;
again the scent of the verbena in her hair seemed to
have increased a hundred times as she stood holding out
to me, one in either hand, the two duelling pistols. "Take
them, Bayard," she said, in the same tone in which she
had said "Kiss me" last summer, already pressing them
into my hands, watching me with that passionate and
voracious exaltation, speaking in a voice fainting and
passionate with promise: "Take them. I have kept them
for you. I give them to you. Oh you will thank me,
you will remember me who put into your hands what
they say is an attribute only of God's, who took what
belongs to heaven and gave it to you. Do you feel them?
the long true barrels true as justice, the triggers (you
have fired them) quick as retribution, the two of them
slender and invincible and fatal as the physical shape of
love?" Again I watched her arms angle out and upward
as she removed the two verbena sprigs from her hair
in two motions faster than the eye could follow, already
putting one of them into my lapel and crushing the
other in her other hand while she still spoke in that
rapid passionate voice not much louder than a whisper:

"There. One I give to you to wear tomorrow (it will not fade), the other I cast away, like this—" dropping the crushed bloom at her feet. "I abjure it. I abjure verbena forever more; I have smelled it above the odor of courage; that was all I wanted. Now let me look at you." She stood back, staring at me—the face tearless and exalted, the feverish eyes brilliant and voracious. "How beautiful you are: do you know it? How beautiful: young, to be permitted to kill, to be permitted vengeance, to take into your bare hands the fire of heaven that cast down Lucifer. No; I. I gave it to you; I put it into your hands; Oh you will thank me, you will remember me when I am dead and you are an old man saying to himself, 'I have tasted all things.'—It will be the right hand, won't it?" She moved; she had taken my right hand which still held one of the pistols before I knew what she was about to do; she had bent and kissed it before I comprehended why she took it. Then she stopped dead still, still stooping in that attitude of fierce exultant humility, her hot lips and her hot hands still touching my flesh, light on my flesh as dead leaves yet communicating to it that battery charge, dark, passionate, and damned forever of all peace. Because they are wise, women are—a touch, lips or fingers, and the knowledge, even clairvoyance, goes straight to the heart without bothering the laggard brain at all. She stood erect now, staring at me with intolerable and amazed incredulity which occupied her face alone for a whole minute while her eyes were completely empty; it seemed to me that I stood there for a full minute while Aunt Jenny and Louvinia watched us, waiting for her eyes to fill. There was no blood in her face at all, her mouth open a little and pale as one of those rubber rings women seal fruit jars with. Then her eyes filled with an expression of bitter and passionate betrayal.

"Why, he's not—" she said. "He's not— And I kissed his hand," she said in an aghast whisper; "*I kissed his hand!*" beginning to laugh, the laughter rising, becoming a scream yet still remaining laughter, screaming with laughter, trying herself to deaden the sound by putting her hand over her mouth, the laughter spilling between her fingers like vomit, the incredulous betrayed eyes still watching me across the hand.

"Louvinia!" Aunt Jenny said. They both came to her. Louvinia touched and held her and Drusilla turned her face to Louvinia.

"I kissed his hand, Louvinia!" she cried. "Did you see it? *I kissed his hand!*" the laughter rising again, becoming the scream again yet still remaining laughter, she still trying to hold it back with her hand like a small child who has filled its mouth too full.

"Take her upstairs," Aunt Jenny said. But they were already moving toward the door, Louvinia half-carrying Drusilla, the laughter diminishing as they neared the door as though it waited for the larger space of the empty and brilliant hall to rise again. Then it was gone; Aunt Jenny and I stood there and I knew soon that I would begin to pant. I could feel it beginning like you feel regurgitation beginning, as though there were not enough air in the room, the house, not enough air anywhere under the heavy hot low sky where the equinox couldn't seem to accomplish, nothing in the air for breathing, for the lungs. Now it was Aunt Jenny who said, "Bayard," twice before I heard her. "You are not going to try to kill him. All right."

"All right?" I said.

"Yes. All right. Don't let it be Drusilla, a poor hysterical young woman. And don't let it be him, Bayard, because he's dead now. And don't let it be George

Wyatt and those others who will be waiting for you tomorrow morning. I know you are not afraid."

"But what good will that do?" I said. "What good will that do?" It almost began then; I stopped it just in time. "I must live with myself, you see."

"Then it's not just Drusilla? Not just him? Not just George Wyatt and Jefferson?"

"No," I said.

"Will you promise to let me see you before you go to town tomorrow?" I looked at her; we looked at one another for a moment. Then she put her hands on my shoulders and kissed me and released me, all in one motion. "Good night, son," she said. Then she was gone too and now it could begin. I knew that in a minute I would look at him and it would begin and I did look at him, feeling the long-held breath, the hiatus before it started, thinking how maybe I should have said, "Good-bye, Father," but did not. Instead I crossed to the piano and laid the pistols carefully on it, still keeping the panting from getting too loud too soon. Then I was outside on the porch and (I don't know how long it had been) I looked in the window and saw Simon squatting on a stool beside him. Simon had been his body servant during the War and when they came home Simon had a uniform too—a Confederate private's coat with a Yankee brigadier's star on it and he had put it on now, too, like they had dressed Father, squatting on the stool beside him, not crying, not weeping the facile tears which are the white man's futile trait and which Negroes know nothing about but just sitting there, motionless, his lower lip slacked down a little; he raised his hand and touched the coffin, the black hand rigid and fragile-looking as a clutch of dead twigs, then dropped the hand; once he turned his head and I saw his eyes roll red and unwinking in his skull like those of a cornered fox. It had begun by that time; I panted, standing there, and this was it—the regret and grief, the despair out of which the tragic mute insensitive bones stand up that can bear anything, anything.

IV

After a while the whippoorwills stopped and I heard the first day bird, a mockingbird. It had sung all night too but now it was the day song, no longer the drowsy moony fluting. Then they all began—the sparrows from the stable, the thrush that lived in Aunt Jenny's garden, and I heard a quail too from the pasture and now there was light in the room. But I didn't move at once. I still lay on the bed (I hadn't undressed) with my hands under my head and the scent of Drusilla's verbena faint from where my coat lay on a chair, watching the light grow, watching it turn rosy with the sun. After a while I heard Louvinia come up across the back yard and go into the kitchen; I heard the door and then the long crash of her armful of stovewood into the box. Soon they would begin to arrive—the carriages and buggies in the drive—but not for a while yet because they too would wait first to see what I was going to do. So the house was quiet when I went down to the dining-room, no sound in it except Simon snoring in the parlor, probably still sitting on the stool though I didn't look in to see. Instead I stood at the dining-room window and drank the coffee which Louvinia brought me, then I went to the stable; I saw Joby watching me from the kitchen door as I crossed the yard and in the stable Loosh looked up at me across Betsy's head, a curry comb in his hand, though Ringo didn't look at me at all. We curried Jupiter then. I didn't know if we would be able to without trouble or not, since always Father

would come in first and touch him and tell him to stand
and he would stand like a marble horse (or pale
bronze rather) while Loosh curried him. But he stood
for me too, a little restive but he stood, then that was
done and now it was almost nine o'clock and soon they
would begin to arrive and I told Ringo to bring Betsy on
to the house.

I went on to the house and into the hall. I had not
had to pant in some time now but it was there, waiting,
a part of the alteration, as though by being dead and
no longer needing air he had taken all of it, all that he
had compassed and claimed and postulated between
the walls which he had built, along with him. Aunt
Jenny must have been waiting; she came out of the
dining-room at once, without a sound, dressed, the hair
that was like Father's combed and smooth above the
eyes that were different from Father's eyes because
they were not intolerant but just intent and grave and
(she was wise too) without pity. "Are you going now?"
she said.

"Yes." I looked at her. Yes, thank God, without pity.
"You see, I want to be thought well of."

"I do," she said. "Even if you spend the day hidden
in the stable loft, I still do."

"Maybe if she knew that I was going. Was going to
town anyway."

"No," she said. "No, Bayard." We looked at one
another. Then she said quietly, "All right. She's awake."
So I mounted the stairs. I mounted steadily, not fast
because if I had gone fast the panting would have
started again or I might have had to slow for a second
at the turn or at the top and I would not have gone on.
So I went slowly and steadily, across the hall to her
door and knocked and opened it. She was sitting at the
window, in something soft and loose for morning in her

bedroom, only she never did look like morning in a bedroom because here was no hair to fall about her shoulders. She looked up, she sat there looking at me with her feverish brilliant eyes and I remembered I still had the verbena sprig in my lapel and suddenly she began to laugh again. It seemed to come not from her mouth but to burst out all over her face like sweat does and with a dreadful and painful convulsion as when you have vomited until it hurts you yet still you must vomit again—burst out all over her face except her eyes, the brilliant, incredulous eyes looking at me out of the laughter as if they belonged to somebody else, as if they were two inert fragments of tar or coal lying on the bottom of a receptacle filled with turmoil: "I kissed his hand! *I kissed his hand!*" Louvinia entered, Aunt Jenny must have sent her directly after me; again I walked slowly and steadily so it would not start yet, down the stairs where Aunt Jenny stood beneath the chandelier in the hall as Mrs. Wilkins had stood yesterday at the University. She had my hat in her hand. "Even if you hid all day in the stable, Bayard," she said. I took the hat; she said quietly, pleasantly, as if she were talking to a stranger, a guest: "I used to see a lot of blockade runners in Charleston. They were heroes in a way, you see—not heroes because they were helping to prolong the Confederacy but heroes in the sense that David Crockett or John Sevier would have been to small boys or fool young women. There was one of them, an Englishman. He had no business there; it was the money of course, as with all of them. But he was the Davy Crockett to us because by that time we had all forgot what money was, what you could do with it. He must have been a gentleman once or associated with gentlemen before he changed his name, and he had a vocabulary of seven words, though I must admit he got along quite well with them. The first four were, 'I'll have rum, thanks,' and then, when he had the rum, he would use the other three—across the champagne, to whatever ruffled bosom or low gown: 'No bloody moon.' No bloody moon, Bayard."

Ringo was waiting with Betsy at the front steps. Again he did not look at me, his face sullen, downcast even while he handed me the reins. But he said nothing, nor did I look back. And sure enough I was just in time; I passed the Compson carriage at the gates, General Compson lifted his hat as I did mine as we passed. It was four miles to town but I had not gone two of them when I heard the horse coming up behind me and I did not look back because I knew it was Ringo. I did not look back; he came up on one of the carriage horses, he rode up beside me and looked me full in the face for one moment, the sullen determined face, the eyes rolling at me defiant and momentary and red; we rode on. Now we were in town—the long shady street leading to the square, the new courthouse at the end of it; it was eleven o'clock now: long past breakfast and not yet noon so there were only women on the street, not to recognize me perhaps, or at least not the walking stopped sudden and dead in midwalking as if the legs contained the sudden eyes, the caught breath, that not to begin until we reached the square, and I thinking *If I could only be invisible until I reach the stairs to his office and begin to mount.* But I could not, I was not; we rode up to the Holston House and I saw the row of feet along the gallery rail come suddenly and quietly down and I did not look at them; I stopped Betsy and waited until Ringo was down; then I dismounted and gave him the reins. "Wait for me here," I said.

"I'm going with you," he said, not loud; we stood there under the still circumspect eyes and spoke quietly to one another like two conspirators. Then I saw the pistol, the outline of it inside his shirt, probably the one we had taken from Grumby that day we killed him.

"No you ain't," I said.

"Yes I am."

"No you ain't." So I walked on, along the street in the hot sun. It was almost noon now and I could smell nothing except the verbena in my coat, as if it had gathered all the sun, all the suspended fierce heat in which the equinox could not seem to occur and were distilling it, so that I moved in a cloud of verbena as I might have moved in a cloud of smoke from a cigar. Then George Wyatt was beside me (I don't know where he came from) and five or six others of Father's old troop a few yards behind, George's hand on my arm, drawing me into a doorway out of the avid eyes like caught breaths.

"Have you got that derringer?" George said.

"No," I said.

"Good," George said. "They are tricky things to fool with. Couldn't nobody but Colonel ever handle one right; I never could. So you take this. I tried it this morning and I know it's right. Here." He was already fumbling the pistol into my pocket, then the same thing seemed to happen to him that happened to Drusilla last night when she kissed my hand—something communicated by touch straight to the simple code by which he lived, without going through the brain at all: so that he too stood suddenly back, the pistol in his hand, staring at me with his pale outraged eyes and speaking in a whisper thin with fury: "Who are you? Is your name Sartoris? By God, if you don't kill him, I'm going to." Now it was not panting, it was a terrible desire to laugh, to laugh as Drusilla had, and say, "That's what Drusilla said." But I didn't. I said,

"I'm tending to this. You stay out of it. I don't need any help." Then his fierce eyes faded gradually, exactly as you turn a lamp down.

"Well," he said, putting the pistol back into his pocket. "You'll have to excuse me, son. I should have knowed you wouldn't do anything that would keep John from laying quiet. We'll follow you and wait at the foot of the steps. And remember: he's a brave man, but he's been sitting in that office by himself since yesterday morning waiting for you and his nerves are on edge."

"I'll remember," I said. "I don't need any help." I had started on when suddenly I said it without having any warning that I was going to: "No bloody moon."

"What?" he said. I didn't answer. I went on across the square itself now, in the hot sun, they following though not close so that I never saw them again until afterward, surrounded by the remote still eyes not following me yet either, just stopped where they were before the stores and about the door to the courthouse, waiting. I walked steadily on enclosed in the now fierce odor of the verbena sprig. Then shadow fell upon me; I did not pause, I looked once at the small faded sign nailed to the brick *B. J. Redmond. Atty at Law* and began to mount the stairs, the wooden steps scuffed by the heavy bewildered boots of countrymen approaching litigation and stained by tobacco spit, on down the dim corridor to the door which bore the name again, *B. J. Redmond* and knocked once and opened it. He sat behind the desk, not much taller than Father but thicker as a man gets who spends most of his time sitting and listening to people, freshly shaven and with fresh linen; a lawyer yet it was not a lawyer's face— a face much thinner than the body would indicate, strained (and yes, tragic; I know that now) and ex-

hausted beneath the neat recent steady strokes of the
razor, holding a pistol flat on the desk before him,
loose beneath his hand and aimed at nothing. There
was no smell of drink, not even of tobacco in the neat
clean dingy room although I knew he smoked. I didn't
pause. I walked steadily toward him. It was not twenty
feet from door to desk yet I seemed to walk in a dreamlike state in which there was neither time nor distance,
as though the mere act of walking was no more intended to encompass space than was his sitting. We
didn't speak. It was as if we both knew what the passage of words would be and the futility of it; how he
might have said, "Go out, Bayard. Go away, boy" and
then, "Draw then. I will allow you to draw" and it
would have been the same as if he had never said it. So
we did not speak; I just walked steadily toward him as
the pistol rose from the desk. I watched it, I could see
the foreshortened slant of the barrel and I knew it
would miss me though his hand did not tremble. I
walked toward him, toward the pistol in the rocklike
hand, I heard no bullet. Maybe I didn't even hear the
explosion though I remember the sudden orange bloom
and smoke as they appeared against his white shirt as
they had appeared against Grumby's greasy Confederate coat; I still watched that foreshortened slant of
barrel which I knew was not aimed at me and saw the
second orange flash and smoke and heard no bullet that
time either. Then I stopped; it was done then. I
watched the pistol descend to the desk in short jerks;
I saw him release it and sit back, both hands on the
desk, I looked at his face and I knew too what it was
to want air when there was nothing in the circumambience for the lungs. He rose, shoved the chair back
with a convulsive motion and rose, with a queer ducking

motion of his head; with his head still ducked aside and one arm extended as though he couldn't see and the other hand resting on the desk as if he couldn't stand alone, he turned and crossed to the wall and took his hat from the rack and with his head still ducked aside and one hand extended he blundered along the wall and passed me and reached the door and went through it. He was brave; no one denied that. He walked down those stairs and out onto the street where George Wyatt and the other six of Father's old troop waited and where the other men had begun to run now; he walked through the middle of them with his hat on and his head up (they told me how someone shouted at him: "Have you killed that boy too?"), saying no word, staring straight ahead and with his back to them, on to the station where the south-bound train was just in and got on it with no baggage, nothing, and went away from Jefferson and from Mississippi and never came back.

I heard their feet on the stairs then in the corridor then in the room, but for a while yet (it wasn't that long, of course) I still sat behind the desk as he had sat, the flat of the pistol still warm under my hand, my hand growing slowly numb between the pistol and my forehead. Then I raised my head; the little room was full of men. "My God!" George Wyatt cried. "You took the pistol away from him and then missed him, missed him *twice*?" Then he answered himself—that same rapport for violence which Drusilla had and which in George's case was actual character judgment: "No; wait. You walked in here without even a pocket knife and let him miss you twice. My God in heaven." He turned, shouting: "Get to hell out of here! You, White, ride out to Sartoris and tell his folks it's all over and he's all right. Ride!" So they departed, went away; presently only George was left, watching me with that pale bleak stare which was speculative yet not at all ratiocinative. "Well by God," he said. "—Do you want a drink?"

"No," I said. "I'm hungry. I didn't eat any breakfast."

"I reckon not, if you got up this morning aiming to do what you did. Come on. We'll go to the Holston House."

"No," I said. "No. Not there."

"Why not? You ain't done anything to be ashamed of. I wouldn't have done it that way, myself. I'd a shot at him once, anyway. But that's your way or you wouldn't have done it."

"Yes," I said. "I would do it again."

"Be damned if I would.—You want to come home with me? We'll have time to eat and then ride out there in time for the——" But I couldn't do that either.

"No," I said. "I'm not hungry after all. I think I'll go home."

"Don't you want to wait and ride out with me?"

"No. I'll go on."

"You don't want to stay here, anyway." He looked around the room again, where the smell of powder smoke still lingered a little, still lay somewhere on the hot dead air though invisible now, blinking a little with his fierce pale unintroverted eyes. "Well by God," he said again. "Maybe you're right, maybe there has been enough killing in your family without— Come on." We left the office. I waited at the foot of the stairs and soon Ringo came up with the horses. We crossed the square again. There were no feet on the Holston House railing now (it was twelve o'clock) but a group of men stood before the door who raised their hats and I raised mine and Ringo and I rode on.

We did not go fast. Soon it was one, maybe after; the carriages and buggies would begin to leave the

square soon, so I turned from the road at the end of the
pasture and I sat the mare, trying to open the gate without dismounting, until Ringo dismounted and opened
it. We crossed the pasture in the hard fierce sun; I
could have seen the house now but I didn't look. Then
we were in the shade, the close thick airless shade of
the creek bottom; the old rails still lay in the undergrowth where we had built the pen to hide the Yankee
mules. Presently I heard the water, then I could see the
sunny glints. We dismounted. I lay on my back, I
thought *Now it can begin again if it wants to*. But it did
not. I went to sleep. I went to sleep almost before I had
stopped thinking. I slept for almost five hours and I
didn't dream anything at all yet I waked myself up crying, crying too hard to stop it. Ringo was squatting beside me and the sun was gone though there was a bird
of some sort still singing somewhere and the whistle of
the north-bound evening train sounded and the short
broken puffs of starting where it had evidently stopped
at our flag station. After a while I began to stop and
Ringo brought his hat full of water from the creek but
instead I went down to the water myself and bathed
my face.

There was still a good deal of light in the pasture,
though the whippoorwills had begun, and when we
reached the house there was a mockingbird singing in
the magnolia, the night song now, the drowsy moony
one, and again the moon like the rim print of a heel in
wet sand. There was just one light in the hall now and
so it was all over though I could still smell the flowers
even above the verbena in my coat. I had not looked
at him again. I had started to before I left the house but
I did not, I did not see him again and all the pictures
we had of him were bad ones because a picture could
no more have held him dead than the house could have

kept his body. But I didn't need to see him again because he was there, he would always be there; maybe what Drusilla meant by his dream was not something which he possessed but something which he had bequeathed us which we could never forget, which would even assume the corporeal shape of him whenever any of us, black or white, closed our eyes. I went into the house. There was no light in the drawing room except the last of the afterglow which came through the western window where Aunt Jenny's colored glass was; I was about to go on upstairs when I saw her sitting there beside the window. She didn't call me and I didn't speak Drusilla's name, I just went to the door and stood there. "She's gone," Aunt Jenny said. "She took the evening train. She has gone to Montgomery, to Dennison." Denny had been married about a year now; he was living in Montgomery, reading law.

"I see," I said. "Then she didn't——" But there wasn't any use in that either; Jed White must have got there before one o'clock and told them. And besides, Aunt Jenny didn't answer. She could have lied to me but she didn't, she said,

"Come here." I went to her chair. "Kneel down. I can't see you."

"Don't you want the lamp?"

"No. Kneel down." So I knelt beside the chair. "So you had a perfectly splendid Saturday afternoon, didn't you? Tell me about it." Then she put her hands on my shoulders. I watched them come up as though she were trying to stop them; I felt them on my shoulders as if they had a separate life of their own and were trying to do something which for my sake she was trying to restrain, prevent. Then she gave up or she was not strong enough because they came up and took my face between them, hard, and suddenly the tears sprang and

streamed down her face like Drusilla's laughing had.
"Oh, damn you Sartorises!" she said. "Damn you!
Damn you!"

As I passed down the hall the light came up in the
dining-room and I could hear Louvinia laying the table
for supper. So the stairs were lighted quite well. But
the upper hall was dark. I saw her open door (that
unmistakable way in which an open door stands open
when nobody lives in the room any more) and I
realized I had not believed that she was really gone. So
I didn't look into the room. I went on to mine and
entered. And then for a long moment I thought it was
the verbena in my lapel which I still smelled. I thought
that until I had crossed the room and looked down at
the pillow on which it lay—the single sprig of it (without looking she would pinch off a half dozen of them
and they would be all of a size, almost all of a shape,
as if a machine had stamped them out) filling the room,
the dusk, the evening with that odor which she said
you could smell alone above the smell of horses.

3. The Last Wilderness

EDITOR'S NOTE

THE county built a marble monument to Colonel Sartoris; it stands on the highest site in the Jefferson cemetery, overlooking the railroad he built. Drusilla disappeared from the family records. Young Bayard Sartoris lost control of his father's railroad, but he founded a bank in Jefferson and was its president during the rest of his long life. Years afterward, with the death of Major Cassius de Spain, he became the county's leading citizen.

Major de Spain, as a result of tax sales and mortgage foreclosures, had acquired most of the hundred square miles that Colonel Sutpen once owned. He remodeled the shack where Wash Jones had died into a hunting lodge; and there, late every fall, he used to entertain a group of his friends, including General Compson and McCaslin Edmonds and young Isaac McCaslin, the son of Uncle Buck and Miss Sophonsiba. Sam Fathers

was their guide through the wild lands in the Tallahatchie River bottom. It was on the north bank of the
river that Boon Hogganbeck, who also had Chickasaw
ancestors, finally killed Old Ben, the black bear.

"The Bear," which was included in *Go Down, Moses*,
is the longest of Faulkner's stories and in many ways
the best. It is divided into five parts. If you want to
read simply a hunting story, and one of the greatest in
the language, you should confine yourself to the first
three parts and the last, which are written in Faulkner's
simplest style. The long fourth part is harder to read
and deals with more complicated matters. In it Faulkner carries to an extreme his effort toward putting the
whole world into one sentence, between one capital
letter and one period. There is a sentence in the fourth
part of "The Bear" that occupies six pages of the present volume (295-301), with a two-page parenthesis in
the middle. Containing several paragraphs, each of
which begins with a small letter, and a quantity of
quoted matter, it runs to more than sixteen hundred
words; it is probably the longest sentence in American
fiction, and longer than any in English or Irish fiction,
except for Molly Bloom's soliloquy. In all this section of
"The Bear," the reader may have difficulty in fitting the
subjects to the predicates and in disentangling the sub-
ordinate clauses; and yet, if he perseveres, he will discover one of Faulkner's most impressive themes: the
belief in Isaac McCaslin's heart that the land itself had
been cursed by slavery, and that the only way for him to
escape the curse was to relinquish the land.

1883.   *THE BEAR*

I

THERE was a man and a dog too this time. Two beasts, counting Old Ben, the bear, and two men, counting Boon Hogganbeck, in whom some of the same blood ran which ran in Sam Fathers, even though Boon's was a plebeian strain of it and only Sam and Old Ben and the mongrel Lion were taintless and incorruptible.

Isaac McCaslin was sixteen. For six years now he had been a man's hunter. For six years now he had heard the best of all talking. It was of the wilderness, the big woods, bigger and older than any recorded document— of white man fatuous enough to believe he had bought any fragment of it, of Indian ruthless enough to pretend that any fragment of it had been his to convey; bigger than Major de Spain and the scrap he pretended to, knowing better; older than old Thomas Sutpen of whom Major de Spain had had it and who knew better; older even than old Ikkemotubbe, the Chickasaw chief, of whom old Sutpen had had it and who knew better in his turn. It was of the men, not white nor black nor red, but men, hunters, with the will and hardihood to endure and the humility and skill to survive, and the dogs and the bear and deer juxtaposed and reliefed against it, ordered and compelled by and within the wilderness in the ancient and unremitting contest according to the ancient and immitigable rules which voided all regrets and brooked no quarter;—the best game of all, the best

of all breathing and forever the best of all listening, the
voices quiet and weighty and deliberate for retrospec-
tion and recollection and exactitude among the concrete
trophies—the racked guns and the heads and skins—in
the libraries of town houses or the offices of plantation
houses or (and best of all) in the camps themselves
where the intact and still-warm meat yet hung, the men
who had slain it sitting before the burning logs on
hearths, when there were houses and hearths, or about
the smoky blazing of piled wood in front of stretched
tarpaulins when there were not. There was always a
bottle present, so that it would seem to him that those
fine fierce instants of heart and brain and courage and
wiliness and speed were concentrated and distilled into
that brown liquor which not women, not boys and children, but only hunters drank, drinking not of the blood
they spilled but some condensation of the wild immortal spirit, drinking it moderately, humbly even, not
with the pagan's base and baseless hope of acquiring
thereby the virtues of cunning and strength and speed
but in salute to them. Thus it seemed to him on this
December morning not only natural but actually fitting
that this should have begun with whiskey.

He realized later that it had begun long before that.
It had already begun on that day when he first wrote his
age in two ciphers and his cousin McCaslin brought
him for the first time to the camp, the big woods, to
earn for himself from the wilderness the name and state
of hunter provided he in his turn were humble and enduring enough. He had already inherited then, without
ever having seen it, the big old bear with one trap-
ruined foot that in an area almost a hundred miles
square had earned for himself a name, a definite designation like a living man:—the long legend of corn-
cribs broken down and rifled, of shoats and grown pigs

and even calves carried bodily into the woods and devoured, and traps and deadfalls overthrown and dogs
mangled and slain, and shotgun and even rifle shots
delivered at point-blank range yet with no more effect
than so many peas blown through a tube by a child—a
corridor of wreckage and destruction beginning back
before the boy was born, through which sped, not fast
but rather with the ruthless and irresistible deliberation
of a locomotive, the shaggy tremendous shape. It ran in
his knowledge before he ever saw it. It loomed and
towered in his dreams before he even saw the unaxed
woods where it left its crooked print, shaggy, tremendous, red-eyed, not malevolent but just big, too big for
the dogs which tried to bay it, for the horses which
tried to ride it down, for the men and the bullets they
fired into it; too big for the very country which was its
constricting scope. It was as if the boy had already
divined what his senses and intellect had not encom-
passed yet: that doomed wilderness whose edges were
being constantly and punily gnawed at by men with
plows and axes who feared it because it was wilderness,
men myriad and nameless even to one another in the
land where the old bear had earned a name, and
through which ran not even a mortal beast but an ana-
chronism indomitable and invincible out of an old,
dead time, a phantom, epitome and apotheosis of the
old, wild life which the little puny humans swarmed
and hacked at in a fury of abhorrence and fear, like
pygmies about the ankles of a drowsing elephant;—the
old bear, solitary, indomitable, and alone; widowered,
childless, and absolved of mortality—old Priam reft of
his old wife and outlived all his sons.

Still a child, with three years, then two years, then
one year yet before he too could make one of them, each
November he would watch the wagon containing the

dogs and the bedding and food and guns and his cousin McCaslin and Tennie's Jim and Sam Fathers too, until Sam moved to the camp to live, depart for the Big Bottom, the big woods. To him, they were going not to hunt bear and deer but to keep yearly rendezvous with the bear which they did not even intend to kill. Two weeks later they would return, with no trophy, no skin. He had not expected it. He had not even feared that it might be in the wagon this time with the other skins and heads. He did not even tell himself that in three years or two years or one year more he would be present and that it might even be his gun. He believed that only after he had served his apprenticeship in the woods which would prove him worthy to be a hunter, would he even be permitted to distinguish the crooked print, and that even then for two November weeks he would merely make another minor one, along with his cousin and Major de Spain and General Compson and Walter Ewell and Boon and the dogs which feared to bay it, and the shotguns and rifles which failed even to bleed it, in the yearly pageant-rite of the old bear's furious immortality.

His day came at last. In the surrey with his cousin and Major de Spain and General Compson he saw the wilderness through a slow drizzle of November rain just above the ice point, as it seemed to him later he always saw it or at least always remembered it—the tall and endless wall of dense November woods under the dissolving afternoon and the year's death, sombre, impenetrable (he could not even discern yet how, at what point they could possibly hope to enter it even though he knew that Sam Fathers was waiting there with the wagon), the surrey moving through the skeleton stalks of cotton and corn in the last of open country, the last trace of man's puny gnawing at the immemorial flank, until, dwarfed by that perspective into an almost ridiculous diminishment, the surrey itself seemed to have ceased to move (this too to be completed later, years later, after he had grown to a man and had seen the sea) as a solitary small boat hangs in lonely immobility, merely tossing up and down, in the infinite waste of the ocean, while the water and then the apparently impenetrable land which it nears without appreciable progress, swings slowly and opens the widening inlet which is the anchorage. He entered it. Sam was waiting, wrapped in a quilt on the wagon seat behind the patient and steaming mules. He entered his novitiate to the true wilderness with Sam beside him as he had begun his apprenticeship in miniature to manhood after the rabbits and such with Sam beside him, the two of them wrapped in the damp, warm, Negro-rank quilt, while the wilderness closed behind his entrance as it had opened momentarily to accept him, opening before his advancement as it closed behind his progress, no fixed path the wagon followed but a channel nonexistent ten yards ahead of it and ceasing to exist ten yards after it had passed, the wagon progressing not by its own volition but by attrition of their intact yet fluid circumambience, drowsing, earless, almost lightless.

It seemed to him that at the age of ten he was witnessing his own birth. It was not even strange to him. He had experienced it all before, and not merely in dreams. He saw the camp—a paintless six-room bungalow set on piles above the spring high-water—and he knew already how it was going to look. He helped in the rapid orderly disorder of their establishment in it, and even his motions were familiar to him, foreknown. Then for two weeks he ate the coarse, rapid food—the shapeless sour bread, the wild strange meat, venison and bear and turkey and coon which he had never tasted before—which men ate, cooked by men who were hunters first and cooks afterward; he slept in harsh sheetless blankets as hunters slept. Each morning the gray of dawn found him and Sam Fathers on the stand, the crossing, which had been allotted him. It was the poorest one, the most barren. He had expected that; he had not dared yet to hope even to himself that he would even hear the running dogs this first time. But he did hear them. It was on the third morning—a murmur, sourceless, almost indistinguishable, yet he knew what it was although he had never before heard that many dogs running at once, the murmur swelling into separate and distinct voices until he could call the five dogs which his cousin owned from among the others. "Now," Sam said, "slant your gun up a little and draw back the hammers and then stand still."

But it was not for him, not yet. The humility was there; he had learned that. And he could learn the patience. He was only ten, only one week. The instant had passed. It seemed to him that he could actually see the deer, the buck, smoke-colored, elongated with speed, vanished, the woods, the gray solitude still ringing even when the voices of the dogs had died away; from far away across the sombre woods and the gray half-liquid morning there came two shots. "Now let your hammers down," Sam said.

He did so. "You knew it too," he said.

"Yes," Sam said. "I want you to learn how to do when you didn't shoot. It's after the chance for the bear or the deer has done already come and gone that men and dogs get killed."

"Anyway, it wasn't him," the boy said. "It wasn't even a bear. It was just a deer."

"Yes," Sam said, "it was just a deer."

Then one morning, it was in the second week, he

heard the dogs again. This time before Sam even spoke he readied the too-long, too-heavy, man-size gun as Sam had taught him, even though this time he knew the dogs and the deer were coming less close than ever, hardly within hearing even. They didn't sound like any running dogs he had ever heard before even. Then he found that Sam, who had taught him first of all to cock the gun and take position where he could see best in all directions and then never to move again, had himself moved up beside him. "There," he said. "Listen." The boy listened, to no ringing chorus strong and fast on a free scent but, a moiling yapping an octave too high and with something more than indecision and even abjectness in it which he could not yet recognize, reluctant, not even moving very fast, taking a long time to pass out of hearing, leaving even then in the air that echo of thin and almost human hysteria, abject, almost humanly grieving, with this time nothing ahead of it, no sense of a fleeing unseen smoke-colored shape. He could hear Sam breathing at his shoulder. He saw the arched curve of the old man's inhaling nostrils.

"It's Old Ben!" he cried, whispering.

Sam didn't move save for the slow gradual turning of his head as the voices faded on and the faint steady rapid arch and collapse of his nostrils. "Hah," he said. "Not even running. Walking."

"But up here!" the boy cried. "Way up here!"

"He do it every year," Sam said. "Once. Ash and Boon say he comes up here to run the other little bears away. Tell them to get to hell out of here and stay out until the hunters are gone. Maybe." The boy no longer heard anything at all, yet still Sam's head continued to turn gradually and steadily until the back of it was toward him. Then it turned back and looked down at him—the same face, grave, familiar, expressionless until it smiled, the same old man's eyes from which as he watched there faded slowly a quality darkly and fiercely lambent, passionate and proud. "He don't care no more for bears than he does for dogs or men neither. He come to see who's here, who's new in camp this year, whether he can shoot or not, can stay or not. Whether we got the dog yet that can bay and hold him until a man gets there with a gun. Because he's the head bear. He's the man." It faded, was gone; again they were the eyes as he had known them all his life. "He'll let them follow him to the river. Then he'll send them home. We might as well go too; see how they look when they get back to camp."

The dogs were there first, ten of them huddled back under the kitchen, himself and Sam squatting to peer back into the obscurity where they crouched, quiet, the eyes rolling and luminous, vanishing, and no sound, only that effluvium which the boy could not quite place yet, of something more than dog, stronger than dog and not just animal, just beast even. Because there had been nothing in front of the abject and painful yapping except the solitude, the wilderness, so that when the eleventh hound got back about mid-afternoon and he and Tennie's Jim held the passive and still trembling bitch while Sam daubed her tattered ear and raked shoulder with turpentine and axle-grease, it was still no living creature but only the wilderness which, leaning for a moment, had patted lightly once her temerity. "Just like a man," Sam said. "Just like folks. Put off as long as she could having to be brave, knowing all the time that sooner or later she would have to be brave once so she could keep on calling herself a dog, and knowing beforehand what was going to happen when she done it."

He did not know just when Sam left. He only knew

that he was gone. For the next three mornings he rose and ate breakfast and Sam was not waiting for him. He went to his stand alone; he found it without help now and stood on it as Sam had taught him. On the third morning he heard the dogs again, running strong and free on a true scent again, and he readied the gun as he had learned to do and heard the hunt sweep past on since he was not ready yet, had not deserved other yet in just one short period of two weeks as compared to all the long life which he had already dedicated to the wilderness with patience and humility; he heard the shot again, one shot, the single clapping report of Walter Ewell's rifle. By now he could not only find his stand and then return to camp without guidance, by using the compass his cousin had given him he reached Walter, waiting beside the buck and the moiling of dogs over the cast entrails, before any of the others except Major de Spain and Tennie's Jim on the horses, even before Uncle Ash arrived with the one-eyed wagon-mule which did not mind the smell of blood or even, so they said, of bear.

It was not Uncle Ash on the mule. It was Sam, returned. And Sam was waiting when he finished his dinner and, himself on the one-eyed mule and Sam on the other one of the wagon team, they rode for more than three hours through the rapid shortening sunless afternoon, following no path, no trail even that he could discern, into a section of country he had never seen before. Then he understood why Sam had made him ride the one-eyed mule which would not spook at the smell of blood, of wild animals. The other one, the sound one, stopped short and tried to whirl and bolt even as Sam got down, jerking and wrenching at the rein while Sam held it, coaxing it forward with his voice since he did not dare risk hitching it, drawing it forward while the boy dismounted from the marred one which would stand. Then, standing beside Sam in the thick great gloom of ancient woods and the winter's dying afternoon, he looked quietly down at the rotted log scored and gutted with claw-marks and, in the wet earth beside it, the print of the enormous warped two-toed foot. Now he knew what he had heard in the hounds' voices in the woods that morning and what he had smelled when he peered under the kitchen where they huddled. It was in him too, a little different because they were brute beasts and he was not, but only a little different—an eagerness, passive; an abjectness, a sense of his own fragility and impotence against the timeless woods, yet without doubt or dread; a flavor like brass in the sudden run of saliva in his mouth, a hard sharp constriction either in his brain or his stomach, he could not tell which and it did not matter; he knew only that for the first time he realized that the bear which had run in his listening and loomed in his dreams since before he could remember and which therefore must have existed in the listening and the dreams of his cousin and Major de Spain and even old General Compson before they began to remember in their turn, was a mortal animal and that they had departed for the camp each November with no actual intention of slaying it, not because it could not be slain but because so far they had no actual hope of being able to. "It will be tomorrow," he said.

"You mean we will try tomorrow," Sam said. "We ain't got the dog yet."

"We've got eleven," he said. "They ran him Monday."

"And you heard them," Sam said. "Saw them too. We ain't got the dog yet. It won't take but one. But he ain't there. Maybe he ain't nowhere. The only other

way will be for him to run by accident over somebody
that had a gun and knowed how to shoot it."

"That wouldn't be me," the boy said. "It would be
Walter or Major or——"

"It might," Sam said. "You watch close tomorrow. Because he's smart. That's how come he has lived this
long. If he gets hemmed up and has got to pick out
somebody to run over, he will pick out you."

"How?" he said. "How will he know. . . ." He
ceased. "You mean he already knows me, that I ain't
never been to the big bottom before, ain't had time to
find out yet whether I . . ." He ceased again, staring
at Sam; he said humbly, not even amazed: "It was me
he was watching. I don't reckon he did need to come
but once."

"You watch tomorrow," Sam said. "I reckon we better start back. It'll be long after dark now before we
get to camp."

The next morning they started three hours earlier
than they had ever done. Even Uncle Ash went, the
cook, who called himself by profession a camp cook
and who did little else save cook for Major de Spain's
hunting and camping parties, yet who had been marked
by the wilderness from simple juxtaposition to it until
he responded as they all did, even the boy who until
two weeks ago had never even seen the wilderness, to a
hound's ripped ear and shoulder and the print of a
crooked foot in a patch of wet earth. They rode. It was
too far to walk: the boy and Sam and Uncle Ash in the
wagon with the dogs, his cousin and Major de Spain
and General Compson and Boon and Walter and Tennie's Jim riding double on the horses; again the first
gray light found him, as on that first morning two
weeks ago, on the stand where Sam had placed and left

him. With the gun which was too big for him, the breech-loader which did not even belong to him but to Major de Spain and which he had fired only once, at a stump on the first day to learn the recoil and how to reload it with the paper shells, he stood against a big gum tree beside a little bayou whose black still water crept without motion out of a cane-brake, across a small clearing and into the cane again, where, invisible, a bird, the big woodpecker called Lord-to-God by Negroes, clattered at a dead trunk. It was a stand like any other stand, dissimilar only in incidentals to the one where he had stood each morning for two weeks; a territory new to him yet no less familiar than that other one which after two weeks he had come to believe he knew a little—the same solitude, the same loneliness through which frail and timorous man had merely passed without altering it, leaving no mark nor scar, which looked exactly as it must have looked when the first ancestor of Sam Fathers' Chickasaw predecessors crept into it and looked about him, club or stone axe or bone arrow drawn and ready, different only because, squatting at the edge of the kitchen, he had smelled the dogs huddled and cringing beneath it and saw the raked ear and side of the bitch that, as Sam had said, had to be brave once in order to keep on calling herself a dog, and saw yesterday in the earth beside the gutted log, the print of the living foot. He heard no dogs at all. He never did certainly hear them. He only heard the drumming of the woodpecker stop short off, and knew that the bear was looking at him. He never saw it. He did not know whether it was facing him from the cane or behind him. He did not move, holding the useless gun which he knew now he would never fire at it, now or ever, tasting in his saliva that taint of brass which he had smelled in the huddled dogs when he peered under the kitchen.

Then it was gone. As abruptly as it had stopped, the woodpecker's dry hammering set up again, and after a while he believed he even heard the dogs—a murmur, scarce a sound even, which he had probably been hearing for a time, perhaps a minute or two, before he remarked it, drifting into hearing and then out again, dying away. They came nowhere near him. If it was dogs he heard, he could not have sworn to it; if it was a bear they ran, it was another bear. It was Sam himself who emerged from the cane and crossed the bayou, the injured bitch following at heel as a bird dog is taught to walk. She came and crouched against his leg, trembling. "I didn't see him," he said. "I didn't, Sam."

"I know it," Sam said. "He done the looking. You didn't hear him neither, did you?"

"No," the boy said. "I——"

"He's smart," Sam said. "Too smart." Again the boy saw in his eyes that quality of dark and brooding lambence as Sam looked down at the bitch trembling faintly and steadily against the boy's leg. From her raked shoulder a few drops of fresh blood clung like bright berries. "Too big. We ain't got the dog yet. But maybe some day."

Because there would be a next time, after and after. He was only ten. It seemed to him that he could see them, the two of them, shadowy in the limbo from which time emerged and became time: the old bear absolved of mortality and himself who shared a little of it. Because he recognized now what he had smelled in the huddled dogs and tasted in his own saliva, recognized fear as a boy, a youth, recognizes the existence of love and passion and experience which is his heritage but not yet his patrimony, from entering by chance the presence or perhaps even merely the bedroom of a woman who has loved and been loved by many men. *So I will have to see him,* he thought, without dread or even hope. *I will have to look at him.* So it was in June of the next summer. They were at the camp again, celebrating Major de Spain's and General Compson's birthdays. Although the one had been born in September and the other in the depth of winter and almost thirty years earlier, each June the two of them and McCaslin and Boon and Walter Ewell (and the boy too from now on) spent two weeks at the camp, fishing and shooting squirrels and turkey and running coons and wildcats with the dogs at night. That is, Boon and the Negroes (and the boy too now) fished and shot squirrels and ran the coons and cats, because the proven hunters, not only Major de Spain and old General Compson (who spent those two weeks sitting in a rocking chair before a tremendous iron pot of Brunswick stew, stirring and tasting, with Uncle Ash to quarrel with about how he was making it and Tennie's Jim to pour whiskey into the tin dipper from which he drank it), but even McCaslin and Walter Ewell who were still young enough, scorned such, other than shooting the wild gobblers with pistols for wagers or to test their marksmanship.

That is, his cousin McCaslin and the others thought he was hunting squirrels. Until the third evening he believed that Sam Fathers thought so too. Each morning he would leave the camp right after breakfast. He had his own gun now, a new breech-loader, a Christmas gift; he would own and shoot it for almost seventy years, through two new pairs of barrels and locks and one new stock, until all that remained of the original gun was the silver-inlaid trigger-guard with his and McCaslin's engraved names and the date in 1878. He found the tree beside the little bayou where he had stood that morning. Using the compass he ranged from that point; he was teaching himself to be better than a fair woodsman without even knowing he was doing it. On the third day he even found the gutted log where he had first seen the print. It was almost completely crumbled now, healing with unbelievable speed, a passionate and almost visible relinquishment, back into the earth from which the tree had grown. He ranged the summer woods now, green with gloom, if anything actually dimmer than they had been in November's gray dissolution, where even at noon the sun fell only in windless dappling upon the earth which never completely dried and which crawled with snakes—moccasins and watersnakes and rattlers, themselves the color of the dappled gloom so that he would not always see them until they moved; returning to camp later and later and later, first day, second day, passing in the twilight of the third evening the little log pen enclosing the log barn where Sam was putting up the stock for the night.

"You ain't looked right yet," Sam said.

He stopped. For a moment he didn't answer. Then he said peacefully, in a peaceful rushing burst, as when a boy's miniature dam in a little brook gives way: "All right. Yes. But how? I went to the bayou. I even found that log again. I——"

"I reckon that was all right. Likely he's been watching you. You never saw his foot?"

"I . . ." the boy said. "I didn't . . . I never thought . . ."

"It's the gun," Sam said. He stood beside the fence, motionless, the old man, son of a Negro slave and a Chickasaw chief, in the battered and faded overalls and the frayed five-cent straw hat which had been the badge of the Negro's slavery and was now the regalia of his freedom. The camp—the clearing, the house, the barn and its tiny lot with which Major de Spain in his turn had scratched punily and evanescently at the wilderness—faded in the dusk, back into the immemorial darkness of the woods. *The gun,* the boy thought. *The gun.* "You will have to choose," Sam said.

He left the next morning before light, without breakfast, long before Uncle Ash would wake in his quilts on the kitchen floor and start the fire. He had only the compass and a stick for the snakes. He could go almost a mile before he would need to see the compass. He sat on a log, the invisible compass in his hand, while the secret night-sounds which had ceased at his movements, scurried again and then fell still for good and the owls ceased and gave over to the waking day birds and there was light in the gray wet woods and he could see the compass. He went fast yet still quietly, becoming steadily better and better as a woodsman without yet having time to realize it; he jumped a doe and a fawn, walked them out of the bed, close enough to see them—the crash of undergrowth, the white scut, the fawn scudding along behind her, faster than he had known it could have run. He was hunting right, upwind, as Sam had taught him, but that didn't matter now. He had left the gun; by his own will and relinquishment he had accepted not a gambit, not a choice, but a condition in which not only the bear's heretofore inviolable anonymity but all the ancient rules and balances of hunter and hunted had been abrogated. He would not even be afraid, not even in the moment when the fear would take him completely: blood, skin, bowels, bones, memory from the long time before it even became his memory—all save that thin clear quenchless lucidity which alone differed him from this bear and from all

the other bears and bucks he would follow during
almost seventy years, to which Sam had said: "Be
scared. You can't help that. But don't be afraid. Ain't
nothing in the woods going to hurt you if you don't
corner it or it don't smell that you are afraid. A bear or
a deer has got to be scared of a coward the same as a
brave man has got to be."

By noon he was far beyond the crossing on the little
bayou, farther into the new and alien country than he
had ever been, travelling now not only by the compass
but by the old, heavy, biscuit-thick silver watch which
had been his father's. He had left the camp nine hours
ago; nine hours from now, dark would already have
been an hour old. He stopped, for the first time since he
had risen from the log when he could see the compass
face at last, and looked about, mopping his sweating
face on his sleeve. He had already relinquished, of his
will, because of his need, in humility and peace and
without regret, yet apparently that had not been
enough, the leaving of the gun was not enough. He
stood for a moment—a child, alien and lost in the green
and soaring gloom of the markless wilderness. Then he
relinquished completely to it. It was the watch and the
compass. He was still tainted. He removed the linked
chain of the one and the looped thong of the other from
his overalls and hung them on a bush and leaned the
stick beside them and entered it.

When he realized he was lost, he did as Sam had
coached and drilled him: made a cast to cross his back-
track. He had not been going very fast for the last two
or three hours, and he had gone even less fast since he
left the compass and watch on the bush. So he went
slower still now, since the tree could not be very far;
in fact, he found it before he really expected to and
turned and went to it. But there was no bush beneath

it, no compass nor watch, so he did next as Sam had
coached and drilled him: made this next circle in the
opposite direction and much larger, so that the pattern
of the two of them would bisect his track somewhere,
but crossing no trace nor mark anywhere of his feet or
any feet, and now he was going faster though still not
panicked, his heart beating a little more rapidly but
strong and steady enough, and this time it was not even
the tree because there was a down log beside it which
he had never seen before and beyond the log a little
swamp, a seepage of moisture somewhere between
earth and water, and he did what Sam had coached
and drilled him as the next and the last, seeing as he
sat down on the log the crooked print, the warped indentation in the wet ground which while he looked at
it continued to fill with water until it was level full and
the water began to overflow and the sides of the print
began to dissolve away. Even as he looked up he saw
the next one, and, moving, the one beyond it; moving,
not hurrying, running, but merely keeping pace with
them as they appeared before him as though they were
being shaped out of thin air just one constant pace
short of where he would lose them forever and be lost
forever himself, tireless, eager, without doubt or dread,
panting a little above the strong rapid little hammer of
his heart, emerging suddenly into a little glade, and the
wilderness coalesced. It rushed, soundless, and solidi-
fied—the tree, the bush, the compass and the watch
glinting where a ray of sunlight touched them. Then he
saw the bear. It did not emerge, appear: it was just
there, immobile, fixed in the green and windless noon's
hot dappling, not as big as he had dreamed it but as
big as he had expected, bigger, dimensionless against
the dappled obscurity, looking at him. Then it moved.
It crossed the glade without haste, walking for an in-

stant into the sun's full glare and out of it, and stopped
again and looked back at him across one shoulder. Then
it was gone. It didn't walk into the woods. It faded,
sank back into the wilderness without motion as he had
watched a fish, a huge old bass, sink back into the dark
depths of its pool and vanish without even any movement of its fins.

II

So he should have hated and feared Lion. He was
thirteen then. He had killed his buck and Sam Fathers
had marked his face with the hot blood, and in the
next November he killed a bear. But before that acco-
lade he had become as competent in the woods as
many grown men with the same experience. By now he
was a better woodsman than most grown men with
more. There was no territory within twenty-five miles
of the camp that he did not know—bayou, ridge, landmark trees and path; he could have led anyone direct to
any spot in it and brought him back. He knew game
trails that even Sam Fathers had never seen; in the third
fall he found a buck's bedding-place by himself and
unbeknown to his cousin he borrowed Walter Ewell's
rifle and lay in wait for the buck at dawn and killed it
when it walked back to the bed as Sam had told him
how the old Chickasaw fathers did.

By now he knew the old bear's footprint better than
he did his own, and not only the crooked one. He could
see any one of the three sound prints and distinguish it
at once from any other, and not only because of its size.
There were other bears within that fifty miles which
left tracks almost as large, or at least so near that the
one would have appeared larger only by juxtaposition.
It was more than that. If Sam Fathers had been his
mentor and the backyard rabbits and squirrels his kin-

dergarten, then the wilderness the old bear ran was his college and the old male bear itself, so long unwifed and childless as to have become its own ungendered progenitor, was his alma mater.

He could find the crooked print now whenever he wished, ten miles or five miles or sometimes closer than that, to the camp. Twice while on stand during the next three years he heard the dogs strike its trail and once even jump it by chance, the voices high, abject, almost human in their hysteria. Once, still-hunting with Walter Ewell's rifle, he saw it cross a long corridor of down timber where a tornado had passed. It rushed through rather than across the tangle of trunks and branches as a locomotive would, faster than he had ever believed it could have moved, almost as fast as a deer even because the deer would have spent most of that distance in the air; he realized then why it would take a dog not only of abnormal courage but size and speed too ever to bring it to bay. He had a little dog at home, a mongrel, of the sort called fyce by Negroes, a ratter, itself not much bigger than a rat and possessing that sort of courage which had long since stopped being bravery and had become foolhardiness. He brought it with him one June and, timing them as if they were meeting an appointment with another human being, himself carrying the fyce with a sack over its head and Sam Fathers with a brace of the hounds on a rope leash, they lay downwind of the trail and actually ambushed the bear. They were so close that it turned at bay although he realized later this might have been from surprise and amazement at the shrill and frantic uproar of the fyce. It turned at bay against the trunk of a big cypress, on its hind feet; it seemed to the boy that it would never stop rising, taller and taller, and even the two hounds

seemed to have taken a kind of desperate and despairing courage from the fyce. Then he realized that the
fyce was actually not going to stop. He flung the gun
down and ran. When he overtook and grasped the shrill,
frantically pinwheeling little dog, it seemed to him that
he was directly under the bear. He could smell it, strong
and hot and rank. Sprawling, he looked up where it
loomed and towered over him like a thunderclap. It was
quite familiar, until he remembered: this was the way
he had used to dream about it.

Then it was gone. He didn't see it go. He knelt, holding the frantic fyce with both hands, hearing the abased
wailing of the two hounds drawing further and further
away, until Sam came up, carrying the gun. He laid it
quietly down beside the boy and stood looking down at
him. "You've done seed him twice now, with a gun in
your hands," he said. "This time you couldn't have
missed him."

The boy rose. He still held the fyce. Even in his arms
it continued to yap frantically, surging and straining toward the fading sound of the hounds like a collection of
live-wire springs. The boy was panting a little. "Neither
could you," he said. "You had the gun. Why didn't you
shoot him?"

Sam didn't seem to have heard. He put out his hand
and touched the little dog in the boy's arms which still
yapped and strained even though the two hounds were
out of hearing now. "He's done gone," Sam said. "You
can slack off and rest now, until next time." He stroked
the little dog until it began to grow quiet under his
hand. "You's almost the one we wants," he said. "You
just ain't big enough. We ain't got that one yet. He will
need to be just a little bigger than smart, and a little
braver than either." He withdrew his hand from the

fyce's head and stood looking into the woods where the bear and the hounds had vanished. "Somebody is going to, some day."

"I know it," the boy said. "That's why it must be one of us. So it won't be until the last day. When even he don't want it to last any longer."

So he should have hated and feared Lion. It was in the fourth summer, the fourth time he had made one in the celebration of Major de Spain's and General Compson's birthday. In the early spring Major de Spain's mare had foaled a horse colt. One evening when Sam brought the horses and mules up to stable them for the night, the colt was missing and it was all he could do to get the frantic mare into the lot. He had thought at first to let the mare lead him back to where she had become separated from the foal. But she would not do it. She would not even feint toward any particular part of the woods or even in any particular direction. She merely ran, as if she couldn't see, still frantic with terror. She whirled and ran at Sam once, as if to attack him in some ultimate desperation, as if she could not for the moment realize that he was a man and a long-familiar one. He got her into the lot at last. It was too dark by that time to back-track her, to unravel the erratic course she had doubtless pursued.

He came to the house and told Major de Spain. It was an animal, of course, a big one, and the colt was dead now, wherever it was. They all knew that. "It's a panther," General Compson said at once. "The same one. That doe and fawn last March." Sam had sent Major de Spain word of it when Boon Hogganbeck came to the camp on a routine visit to see how the stock had wintered—the doe's throat torn out, and the beast had run down the helpless fawn and killed it too.

"Sam never did say that was a panther," Major de

Spain said. Sam said nothing now, standing behind Major de Spain where they sat at supper, inscrutable, as if he were just waiting for them to stop talking so he could go home. He didn't even seem to be looking at anything. "A panther might jump a doe, and he wouldn't have much trouble catching the fawn afterward. But no panther would have jumped that colt with the dam right there with it. It was Old Ben," Major de Spain said. "I'm disappointed in him. He has broken the rules. I didn't think he would have done that. He has killed mine and McCaslin's dogs, but that was all right. We gambled the dogs against him; we gave each other warning. But now he has come into my house and destroyed my property, out of season too. He broke the rules. It was Old Ben, Sam." Still Sam said nothing, standing there until Major de Spain should stop talking. "We'll back-track her tomorrow and see," Major de Spain said.

Sam departed. He would not live in the camp; he had built himself a little hut something like Joe Baker's, only stouter, tighter, on the bayou a quarter-mile away, and a stout log crib where he stored a little corn for the shoat he raised each year. The next morning he was waiting when they waked. He had already found the colt. They did not even wait for breakfast. It was not far, not five hundred yards from the stable—the three-months' colt lying on its side, its throat torn out and the entrails and one ham partly eaten. It lay not as if it had been dropped but as if it had been struck and hurled, and no cat-mark, no claw-mark where a panther would have gripped it while finding its throat. They read the tracks where the frantic mare had circled and at last rushed in with that same ultimate desperation with which she had whirled on Sam Fathers yesterday evening, and the long tracks of dead and terrified running and those of the beast which had not even rushed at her when she advanced but had merely walked three or four paces toward her until she broke, and General Compson said, "Good God, what a wolf!"

Still Sam said nothing. The boy watched him while the men knelt, measuring the tracks. There was something in Sam's face now. It was neither exultation nor joy nor hope. Later, a man, the boy realized what it had been, and that Sam had known all the time what had made the tracks and what had torn the throat out of the doe in the spring and killed the fawn. It had been foreknowledge in Sam's face that morning. *And he was glad,* he told himself. *He was old. He had no children, no people, none of his blood anywhere above earth that he would ever meet again. And even if he were to, he could not have touched it, spoken to it, because for seventy years now he had had to be a Negro. It was almost over now and he was glad.*

They returned to camp and had breakfast and came back with guns and the hounds. Afterward the boy realized that they also should have known then what killed the colt as well as Sam Fathers did. But that was neither the first nor the last time he had seen men rationalize from and even act upon their misconceptions. After Boon, standing astride the colt, had whipped the dogs away from it with his belt, they snuffed at the tracks. One of them, a young dog hound without judgment yet, bayed once, and they ran for a few feet on what seemed to be a trail. Then they stopped, looking back at the men, eager enough, not baffled, merely questioning, as if they were asking "Now what?" Then they rushed back to the colt, where Boon, still astride it, slashed at them with the belt.

"I never knew a trail to get cold that quick," General Compson said.

"Maybe a single wolf big enough to kill a colt with the dam right there beside it don't leave scent," Major de Spain said.

"Maybe it was a hant," Walter Ewell said. He looked at Tennie's Jim. "Hah, Jim?"

Because the hounds would not run it, Major de Spain had Sam hunt out and find the tracks a hundred yards farther on and they put the dogs on it again and again the young one bayed and not one of them realized then that the hound was not baying like a dog striking game but was merely bellowing like a country dog whose yard has been invaded. General Compson spoke to the boy and Boon and Tennie's Jim: to the squirrel hunters. "You boys keep the dogs with you this morning. He's probably hanging around somewhere, waiting to get his breakfast off the colt. You might strike him."

But they did not. The boy remembered how Sam stood watching them as they went into the woods with the leashed hounds—the Indian face in which he had never seen anything until it smiled, except that faint arching of the nostrils on that first morning when the hounds had found Old Ben. They took the hounds with them on the next day, though when they reached the place where they hoped to strike a fresh trail, the carcass of the colt was gone. Then on the third morning Sam was waiting again, this time until they had finished breakfast. He said, "Come." He led them to his house, his little hut, to the corn-crib beyond it. He had removed the corn and had made a deadfall of the door, baiting it with the colt's carcass; peering between the logs, they saw an animal almost the color of a gun or pistol barrel, what little time they had to examine its color or shape. It was not crouched nor even standing. It was in motion, in the air, coming toward them—a heavy body crashing with tremendous force against

the door so that the thick door jumped and clattered in
its frame, the animal, whatever it was, hurling itself
against the door again seemingly before it could have
touched the floor and got a new purchase to spring
from. "Come away," Sam said, "fore he break his neck."
Even when they retreated the heavy and measured
crashes continued, the stout door jumping and clattering
each time, and still no sound from the beast itself—no
snarl, no cry.

"What in hell's name is it?" Major de Spain said.

"It's a dog," Sam said, his nostrils arching and collapsing faintly and steadily and that faint, fierce milki-
ness in his eyes again as on that first morning when
the hounds had struck the old bear. "It's the dog."

"*The* dog?" Major de Spain said.

"That's gonter hold Old Ben."

"Dog the devil," Major de Spain said. "I'd rather
have Old Ben himself in my pack than that brute. Shoot
him."

"No," Sam said.

"You'll never tame him. How do you ever expect to
make an animal like that afraid of you?"

"I don't want him tame," Sam said; again the boy
watched his nostrils and the fierce milky light in his
eyes. "But I almost rather he be tame than scared, of
me or any man or any thing. But he won't be neither,
of nothing."

"Then what are you going to do with it?"

"You can watch," Sam said.

Each morning through the second week they would
go to Sam's crib. He had removed a few shingles from
the roof and had put a rope on the colt's carcass and
had drawn it out when the trap fell. Each morning
they would watch him lower a pail of water into the
crib while the dog hurled itself tirelessly against the

door and dropped back and leaped again. It never made any sound and there was nothing frenzied in the act but only a cold and grim indomitable determination. Toward the end of the week it stopped jumping at the door. Yet it had not weakened appreciably and it was not as if it had rationalized the fact that the door was not going to give. It was as if for that time it simply disdained to jump any longer. It was not down. None of them had ever seen it down. It stood, and they could see it now—part mastiff, something of Airedale and something of a dozen other strains probably, better than thirty inches at the shoulders and weighing as they guessed almost ninety pounds, with cold yellow eyes and a tremendous chest and over all that strange color like a blued gun-barrel.

Then the two weeks were up. They prepared to break camp. The boy begged to remain and his cousin let him. He moved into the little hut with Sam Fathers. Each morning he watched Sam lower the pail of water into the crib. By the end of that week the dog was down. It would rise and half stagger, half crawl to the water and drink and collapse again. One morning it could not even reach the water, could not raise its forequarters even from the floor. Sam took a short stick and prepared to enter the crib. "Wait," the boy said. "Let me get the gun——"

"No," Sam said. "He can't move now." Nor could it. It lay on its side while Sam touched it, its head and the gaunted body, the dog lying motionless, the yellow eyes open. They were not fierce and there was nothing of petty malevolence in them, but a cold and almost impersonal malignance like some natural force. It was not even looking at Sam nor at the boy peering at it between the logs.

Sam began to feed it again. The first time he had to

raise its head so it could lap the broth. That night he left a bowl of broth containing lumps of meat where the dog could reach it. The next morning the bowl was empty and the dog was lying on its belly, its head up, the cold yellow eyes watching the door as Sam entered, no change whatever in the cold yellow eyes and still no sound from it even when it sprang, its aim and coordination still bad from weakness so that Sam had time to strike it down with the stick and leap from the crib and slam the door as the dog, still without having had time to get its feet under it to jump again seemingly, hurled itself against the door as if the two weeks of starving had never been.

At noon that day someone came whooping through the woods from the direction of the camp. It was Boon. He came and looked for a while between the logs, at the tremendous dog lying again on its belly, its head up, the yellow eyes blinking sleepily at nothing: the indomitable and unbroken spirit. "What we better do," Boon said, "is to let that sonofabitch go and catch Old Ben and run him on the dog." He turned to the boy his weather-reddened and beetling face. "Get your traps together. Cass says for you to come on home. You been in here fooling with that horse-eating varmint long enough."

Boon had a borrowed mule at the camp; the buggy was waiting at the edge of the bottom. He was at home that night. He told McCaslin about it. "Sam's going to starve him again until he can go in and touch him. Then he will feed him again. Then he will starve him again, if he has to."

"But why?" McCaslin said. "What for? Even Sam will never tame that brute."

"We don't want him tame. We want him like he is. We just want him to find out at last that the only way

he can get out of that crib and stay out of it is to do
what Sam or somebody tells him to do. He's the dog
that's going to stop Old Ben and hold him. We've already named him. His name is Lion."

Then November came at last. They returned to the
camp. With General Compson and Major de Spain and
his cousin and Walter and Boon he stood in the yard
among the guns and bedding and boxes of food and
watched Sam Fathers and Lion come up the lane from
the lot—the Indian, the old man in battered overalls
and rubber boots and a worn sheepskin coat and a hat
which had belonged to the boy's father; the tremendous
dog pacing gravely beside him. The hounds rushed out
to meet them and stopped, except the young one which
still had but little of judgment. It ran up to Lion, fawn-
ing. Lion didn't snap at it. He didn't even pause. He
struck it rolling and yelping for five or six feet with a
blow of one paw as a bear would have done and came
on into the yard and stood, blinking sleepily at nothing,
looking at no one, while Boon said, "Jesus. Jesus.—
Will he let me touch him?"

"You can touch him," Sam said. "He don't care. He
don't care about nothing or nobody."

The boy watched that too. He watched it for the
next two years from that moment when Boon touched
Lion's head and then knelt beside him, feeling the
bones and muscles, the power. It was as if Lion were a
woman—or perhaps Boon was the woman. That was
more like it—the big, grave, sleepy-seeming dog which,
as Sam Fathers said, cared about no man and no thing;
and the violent, insensitive, hard-faced man with his
touch of remote Indian blood and the mind almost of a
child. He watched Boon take over Lion's feeding from
Sam and Uncle Ash both. He would see Boon squatting
in the cold rain beside the kitchen while Lion ate.

Because Lion neither slept nor ate with the other dogs though none of them knew where he did sleep until in the second November, thinking until then that Lion slept in his kennel beside Sam Fathers' hut, when the boy's cousin McCaslin said something about it to Sam by sheer chance and Sam told him. And that night the boy and Major de Spain and McCaslin with a lamp entered the back room where Boon slept—the little, tight, airless room rank with the smell of Boon's unwashed body and his wet hunting-clothes—where Boon, snoring on his back, choked and waked and Lion raised his head beside him and looked back at them from his cold, slumbrous yellow eyes.

"Damn it, Boon," McCaslin said. "Get that dog out of here. He's got to run Old Ben tomorrow morning. How in hell do you expect him to smell anything fainter than a skunk after breathing you all night?"

"The way I smell ain't hurt my nose none that I ever noticed," Boon said.

"It wouldn't matter if it had," Major de Spain said. "We're not depending on you to trail a bear. Put him outside. Put him under the house with the other dogs."

Boon began to get up. "He'll kill the first one that happens to yawn or sneeze in his face or touches him."

"I reckon not," Major de Spain said. "None of them are going to risk yawning in his face or touching him either, even asleep. Put him outside. I want his nose right tomorrow. Old Ben fooled him last year. I don't think he will do it again."

Boon put on his shoes without lacing them; in his long soiled underwear, his hair still tousled from sleep, he and Lion went out. The others returned to the front room and the poker game where McCaslin's and Major de Spain's hands waited for them on the table. After a while McCaslin said, "Do you want me to go back and look again?"

"No," Major de Spain said. "I call," he said to Walter Ewell. He spoke to McCaslin again. "If you do, don't tell me. I am beginning to see the first sign of my increasing age: I don't like to know that my orders have been disobeyed, even when I knew when I gave them that they would be.—A small pair," he said to Walter Ewell.

"How small?" Walter said.

"Very small," Major de Spain said.

And the boy, lying beneath his piled quilts and blankets waiting for sleep, knew likewise that Lion was already back in Boon's bed, for the rest of that night and the next one and during all the nights of the next November and the next one. He thought then: *I wonder what Sam thinks. He could have Lion with him, even if Boon is a white man. He could ask Major or McCaslin either. And more than that. It was Sam's hand that touched Lion first and Lion knows it.* Then he became a man and he knew that too. It had been all right. That was the way it should have been. Sam was the chief, the prince; Boon, the plebeian, was his huntsman. Boon should have nursed the dogs.

On the first morning that Lion led the pack after Old Ben, seven strangers appeared in the camp. They were swampers: gaunt, malaria-ridden men appearing from nowhere, who ran trap-lines for coons or perhaps farmed little patches of cotton and corn along the edge of the bottom, in clothes but little better than Sam Fathers' and nowhere near as good as Tennie's Jim's, with worn shotguns and rifles, already squatting patiently in the cold drizzle in the side yard when day broke. They had a spokesman; afterward Sam Fathers told Major de

Spain how all during the past summer and fall they had drifted into the camp singly or in pairs and threes, to look quietly at Lion for a while and then go away: "Mawnin, Major. We heerd you was aimin to put that ere blue dawg on that old two-toed bear this mawnin. We figgered we'd come up and watch, if you don't mind. We won't do no shooting, lessen he runs over us."

"You are welcome," Major de Spain said. "You are welcome to shoot. He's more your bear than ours."

"I reckon that ain't no lie. I done fed him enough cawn to have a sheer in him. Not to mention a shoat three years ago."

"I reckon I got a sheer too," another said. "Only it ain't in the bear." Major de Spain looked at him. He was chewing tobacco. He spat. "Hit was a heifer calf. Nice un too. Last year. When I finally found her, I reckon she looked about like that colt of yourn looked last June."

"Oh," Major de Spain said. "Be welcome. If you see game in front of my dogs, shoot it."

Nobody shot Old Ben that day. No man saw him. The dogs jumped him within a hundred yards of the glade where the boy had seen him that day in the summer of his eleventh year. The boy was less than a quarter-mile away. He heard the jump but he could distinguish no voice among the dogs that he did not know and therefore would be Lion's, and he thought, believed, that Lion was not among them. Even the fact that they were going much faster than he had ever heard them run behind Old Ben before and that the high thin note of hysteria was missing now from their voices was not enough to disabuse him. He didn't comprehend until that night, when Sam told him that Lion would never cry on a trail. "He gonter growl when he catches Old Ben's throat," Sam said. "But he ain't gonter never holler, no more than he ever done when he was jumping at that two-inch door. It's that blue dog in him. What you call it?"

"Airedale," the boy said.

Lion was there; the jump was just too close to the river. When Boon returned with Lion about eleven that night, he swore that Lion had stopped Old Ben once but that the hounds would not go in and Old Ben broke away and took to the river and swam for miles down it and he and Lion went down one bank for about ten miles and crossed and came up the other but it had begun to get dark before they struck any trail where Old Ben had come up out of the water, unless he was still in the water when he passed the ford where they crossed. Then he fell to cursing the hounds and ate the supper Uncle Ash had saved for him and went off to bed and after a while the boy opened the door of the little stale room thunderous with snoring and the great grave dog raised its head from Boon's pillow and blinked at him for a moment and lowered its head again.

When the next November came and the last day, the day which it was now becoming traditional to save for Old Ben, there were more than a dozen strangers waiting. They were not all swampers this time. Some of them were townsmen, from other county seats like Jefferson, who had heard about Lion and Old Ben and had come to watch the great blue dog keep his yearly rendezvous with the old two-toed bear. Some of them didn't even have guns and the hunting-clothes and boots they wore had been on a store shelf yesterday.

This time Lion jumped Old Ben more than five miles from the river and bayed and held him and this time the hounds went in, in a sort of desperate emulation. The boy heard them; he was that near. He heard Boon whooping; he heard the two shots when General Compson delivered both barrels, one containing five buckshot, the other a single ball, into the bear from as close as he could force his almost unmanageable horse. He heard the dogs when the bear broke free again. He was running now; panting, stumbling, his lungs bursting, he reached the place where General Compson had fired and where Old Ben had killed two of the hounds. He saw the blood from General Compson's shots, but he could go no further. He stopped, leaning against a tree for his breathing to ease and his heart to slow, hearing the sound of the dogs as it faded on and died away.

In camp that night—they had as guests five of the still terrified strangers in new hunting coats and boots who had been lost all day until Sam Fathers went out and got them—he heard the rest of it: how Lion had stopped and held the bear again but only the one-eyed mule which did not mind the smell of wild blood would approach and Boon was riding the mule and Boon had never been known to hit anything. He shot at the bear five times with his pump gun, touching nothing, and Old Ben killed another hound and broke free once more and reached the river and was gone. Again Boon and Lion hunted as far down one bank as they dared. Too far; they crossed in the first of dusk and dark overtook them within a mile. And this time Lion found the broken trail, the blood perhaps, in the darkness where Old Ben had come up out of the water, but Boon had him on a rope, luckily, and he got down from the mule and fought Lion hand-to-hand until he got him back to camp. This time Boon didn't even curse. He stood in the door, muddy, spent, his huge gargoyle's face tragic and still amazed. "I missed him," he said. "I was in twenty-five feet of him and I missed him five times."

"But we have drawn blood," Major de Spain said.

"General Compson drew blood. We have never done that before."

"But I missed him," Boon said. "I missed him five times. With Lion looking right at me."

"Never mind," Major de Spain said. "It was a damned fine race. And we drew blood. Next year we'll let General Compson or Walter ride Katie, and we'll get him."

Then McCaslin said, "Where is Lion, Boon?"

"I left him at Sam's," Boon said. He was already turning away. "I ain't fit to sleep with him."

So he should have hated and feared Lion. Yet he did not. It seemed to him that there was a fatality in it. It seemed to him that something, he didn't know what, was beginning; had already begun. It was like the last act on a set stage. It was the beginning of the end of something, he didn't know what except that he would not grieve. He would be humble and proud that he had been found worthy to be a part of it too or even just to see it too.

III

It was December. It was the coldest December he had ever remembered. They had been in camp four days over two weeks, waiting for the weather to soften so that Lion and Old Ben could run their yearly race. Then they would break camp and go home. Because of these unforeseen additional days which they had had to pass waiting on the weather, with nothing to do but play poker, the whiskey had given out and he and Boon were being sent to Memphis with a suitcase and a note from Major de Spain to Mr. Semmes, the distiller, to get more. That is, Major de Spain and McCaslin were sending Boon to get the whiskey and sending him to see that Boon got back with it or most of it or at least some of it.

Tennie's Jim waked him at three. He dressed rapidly, shivering, not so much from the cold because a fresh fire already boomed and roared on the hearth, but in that dead winter hour when the blood and the heart are slow and sleep is incomplete. He crossed the gap between house and kitchen, the gap of iron earth beneath the brilliant and rigid night where dawn would not begin for three hours yet, tasting, tongue, palate, and to the very bottom of his lungs, the searing dark, and entered the kitchen, the lamp-lit warmth where the stove glowed, fogging the windows, and where Boon already sat at the table at breakfast, hunched over his plate, almost in his plate, his working jaws blue with stubble and his face innocent of water and his coarse, horse-mane hair innocent of comb—the quarter Indian, grandson of a Chickasaw squaw, who on occasion resented with his hard and furious fists the intimation of one single drop of alien blood and on others, usually after whiskey, affirmed with the same fists and the same fury that his father had been the full-blood Chickasaw and even a chief and that even his mother had been only half white. He was four inches over six feet; he had the mind of a child, the heart of a horse, and little hard shoe-button eyes without depth or meanness or generosity or viciousness or gentleness or anything else, in the ugliest face the boy had ever seen. It looked like somebody had found a walnut a little larger than a football and with a machinist's hammer had shaped features into it and then painted it, mostly red; not Indian red but a fine bright ruddy color which whiskey might have had something to do with but which was mostly just happy and violent out-of-doors, the wrinkles

in it not the residue of the forty years it had survived
but from squinting into the sun or into the gloom of
cane-brakes where game had run, baked into it by the
camp fires before which he had lain trying to sleep on
the cold November or December ground while waiting
for daylight so he could rise and hunt again, as though
time were merely something he walked through as he
did through air, aging him no more than air did. He
was brave, faithful, improvident and unreliable; he had
neither profession job nor trade and owned one vice
and one virtue: whiskey, and that absolute and unquestioning fidelity to Major de Spain and the boy's cousin
McCaslin. "Sometimes I'd call them both virtues," Major
de Spain said once. "Or both vices," McCaslin said.

He ate his breakfast, hearing the dogs under the
kitchen, wakened by the smell of frying meat or perhaps by the feet overhead. He heard Lion once, short
and peremptory, as the best hunter in any camp has
only to speak once to all save the fools, and none other
of Major de Spain's and McCaslin's dogs were Lion's
equal in size and strength and perhaps even in courage,
but they were not fools; Old Ben had killed the last
fool among them last year.

Tennie's Jim came in as they finished. The wagon
was outside. Ash decided he would drive them over to
the log-line where they would flag the outbound log-
train and let Tennie's Jim wash the dishes. The boy
knew why. It would not be the first time he had listened
to old Ash badgering Boon.

It was cold. The wagon wheels banged and clattered
on the frozen ground; the sky was fixed and brilliant.
He was not shivering, he was shaking, slow and steady
and hard, the food he had just eaten still warm and
solid inside him while his outside shook slow and steady

around it as though his stomach floated loose. "They won't run this morning," he said. "No dog will have any nose today."

"Cep Lion," Ash said. "Lion don't need no nose. All he need is a bear." He had wrapped his feet in towsacks and he had a quilt from his pallet bed on the kitchen floor drawn over his head and wrapped around him until in the thin brilliant starlight he looked like nothing at all that the boy had ever seen before. "He run a bear through a thousand-acre ice-house. Catch him too. Them other dogs don't matter because they ain't going to keep up with Lion nohow, long as he got a bear in front of him."

"What's wrong with the other dogs?" Boon said. "What the hell do you know about it anyway? This is the first time you've had your tail out of that kitchen since we got here except to chop a little wood."

"Ain't nothing wrong with them," Ash said. "And long as it's left up to them, ain't nothing going to be. I just wish I had knowed all my life how to take care of my health good as them hounds knows."

"Well, they ain't going to run this morning," Boon said. His voice was harsh and positive. "Major promised they wouldn't until me and Ike get back."

"Weather gonter break today. Gonter soft up. Rain by night." Then Ash laughed, chuckled, somewhere inside the quilt which concealed even his face. "Hum up here, mules!" he said, jerking the reins so that the mules leaped forward and snatched the lurching and banging wagon for several feet before they slowed again into their quick, short-paced, rapid plodding. "Sides, I like to know why Major need to wait on you. It's Lion he aiming to use. I ain't never heard tell of you bringing no bear nor no other kind of meat into this camp."

Now Boon's going to curse Ash or maybe even hit

him, the boy thought. But Boon never did, never had; the boy knew he never would even though four years ago Boon had shot five times with a borrowed pistol at a Negro on the street in Jefferson, with the same result as when he had shot five times at Old Ben last fall. "By God," Boon said, "he ain't going to put Lion or no other dog on nothing until I get back tonight. Because he promised me. Whip up them mules and keep them whipped up. Do you want me to freeze to death?"

They reached the log-line and built a fire. After a while the log-train came up out of the woods under the paling east and Boon flagged it. Then in the warm caboose the boy slept again while Boon and the conductor and brakeman talked about Lion and Old Ben as people later would talk about Sullivan and Kilrain and, later still, about Dempsey and Tunney. Dozing, swaying as the springless caboose lurched and clattered, he would hear them still talking, about the shoats and calves Old Ben had killed and the cribs he had rifled and the traps and deadfalls he had wrecked and the lead he probably carried under his hide—Old Ben, the two-toed bear in a land where bears with trap-ruined feet had been called Two-Toe or Three-Toe or Cripple-Foot for fifty years, only Old Ben was an extra bear (the head bear, General Compson called him) and so had earned a name such as a human man could have worn and not been sorry.

They reached Hoke's at sunup. They emerged from the warm caboose in their hunting clothes, the muddy boots and stained khaki and Boon's blue unshaven jowls. But that was all right. Hoke's was a sawmill and commissary and two stores and a loading-chute on a sidetrack from the main line, and all the men in it wore boots and khaki too. Presently the Memphis train came. Boon bought three packages of popcorn-and-molasses and a bottle of beer from the news butch and the boy went to sleep again to the sound of his chewing.

But in Memphis it was not all right. It was as if the high buildings and the hard pavements, the fine carriages and the horse cars and the men in starched collars and neckties made their boots and khaki look a little rougher and a little muddier and made Boon's beard look worse and more unshaven and his face look more and more like he should never have brought it out of the woods at all or at least out of reach of Major de Spain or McCaslin or someone who knew it and could have said, "Don't be afraid. He won't hurt you." He walked through the station, on the slick floor, his face moving as he worked the popcorn out of his teeth with his tongue, his legs spraddled and stiff in the hips as if he were walking on buttered glass, and that blue stubble on his face like the filings from a new gun-barrel. They passed the first saloon. Even through the closed doors the boy could seem to smell the sawdust and the reek of old drink. Boon began to cough. He coughed for something less than a minute. "Damn this cold," he said. "I'd sure like to know where I got it."

"Back there in the station," the boy said.

Boon had started to cough again. He stopped. He looked at the boy. "What?" he said.

"You never had it when we left camp nor on the train either." Boon looked at him, blinking. Then he stopped blinking. He didn't cough again. He said quietly:

"Lend me a dollar. Come on. You've got it. If you ever had one, you've still got it. I don't mean you are tight with your money because you ain't. You just don't never seem to ever think of nothing you want. When I was sixteen a dollar bill melted off of me before I even

had time to read the name of the bank that issued it."
He said quietly: "Let me have a dollar, Ike."

"You promised Major. You promised McCaslin. Not
till we get back to camp."

"All right," Boon said in that quiet and patient voice.
"What can I do on just one dollar? You ain't going to
lend me another."

"You're damn right I ain't," the boy said, his voice
quiet too, cold with rage which was not at Boon, remembering: Boon snoring in a hard chair in the kitchen
so he could watch the clock and wake him and McCaslin and drive them the seventeen miles in to Jefferson to
catch the train to Memphis; the wild, never-bridled
Texas paint pony which he had persuaded McCaslin to
let him buy and which he and Boon had bought at auction for four dollars and seventy-five cents and fetched
home wired between two gentle old mares with pieces
of barbed wire and which had never even seen shelled
corn before and didn't even know what it was unless the
grains were bugs maybe, and at last (he was ten and
Boon had been ten all his life) Boon said the pony was
gentled and with a towsack over its head and four
Negroes to hold it they backed it into an old two-
wheeled cart and hooked up the gear and he and Boon
got up and Boon said, "All right, boys. Let him go" and
one of the Negroes—it was Tennie's Jim—snatched the
towsack off and leaped for his life and they lost the first
wheel against a post of the open gate only at that moment Boon caught him by the scruff of the neck and
flung him into the roadside ditch so he only saw the
rest of it in fragments: the other wheel as it slammed
through the side gate and crossed the back yard and
leaped up onto the gallery and scraps of the cart here
and there along the road and Boon vanishing rapidly on

his stomach in the leaping and spurting dust and still
holding the reins until they broke too and two days
later they finally caught the pony seven miles away still
wearing the hames and the headstall of the bridle
around its neck like a duchess with two necklaces at
one time. He gave Boon the dollar.

"All right," Boon said. "Come on in out of the cold."

"I ain't cold," he said.

"You can have some lemonade."

"I don't want any lemonade."

The door closed behind him. The sun was well up
now. It was a brilliant day, though Ash had said it
would rain before night. Already it was warmer; they
could run tomorrow. He felt the old lift of the heart, as
pristine as ever, as on the first day; he would never lose
it, no matter how old in hunting and pursuit: the best,
the best of all breathing, the humility and the pride. He
must stop thinking about it. Already it seemed to him
that he was running, back to the station, to the tracks
themselves: the first train going south; he must stop
thinking about it. The street was busy. He watched the
big Norman draft horses, the Percherons; the trim carriages from which the men in the fine overcoats and the
ladies rosy in furs descended and entered the station.
(They were still next door to it but one.) Twenty years
ago his father had ridden into Memphis as a member of
Colonel Sartoris' horse in Forrest's command, up Main
street and (the tale told) into the lobby of the Gayoso
Hotel where the Yankee officers sat in the leather chairs
spitting into the tall bright cuspidors and then out again,
scot-free——

The door opened behind him. Boon was wiping his
mouth on the back of his hand. "All right," he said.
"Let's go tend to it and get the hell out of here."

They went and had the suitcase packed. He never

knew where or when Boon got the other bottle. Doubtless Mr. Semmes gave it to him. When they reached Hoke's again at sundown, it was empty. They could get a return train to Hoke's in two hours; they went straight back to the station as Major de Spain and then McCaslin had told Boon to do and then ordered him to do and had sent the boy along to see that he did. Boon took the first drink from his bottle in the washroom. A man in a uniform cap came to tell him he couldn't drink there and looked at Boon's face once and said nothing. The next time he was pouring into his water glass beneath the edge of a table in the restaurant when the manager (she was a woman) did tell him he couldn't drink there and he went back to the washroom. He had been telling the Negro waiter and all the other people in the restaurant who couldn't help but hear him and who had never heard of Lion and didn't want to, about Lion and Old Ben. Then he happened to think of the zoo. He had found out that there was another train to Hoke's at three o'clock and so they would spend the time at the zoo and take the three o'clock train until he came back from the washroom for the third time. Then they would take the first train back to camp, get Lion and come back to the zoo where, he said, the bears were fed on ice cream and lady fingers and he would match Lion against them all.

So they missed the first train, the one they were supposed to take, but he got Boon onto the three o'clock train and they were all right again, with Boon not even going to the washroom now but drinking in the aisle and talking about Lion and the men he buttonholed no more daring to tell Boon he couldn't drink there than the man in the station had dared.

When they reached Hoke's at sundown, Boon was asleep. The boy waked him at last and got him and the suitcase off the train and he even persuaded him to eat some supper at the sawmill commissary. So he was all right when they got in the caboose of the log-train to go back into the woods, with the sun going down red and the sky already overcast and the ground would not freeze tonight. It was the boy who slept now, sitting behind the ruby stove while the springless caboose jumped and clattered and Boon and the brakeman and the conductor talked about Lion and Old Ben because they knew what Boon was talking about because this was home. "Overcast and already thawing," Boon said. "Lion will get him tomorrow."

It would have to be Lion, or somebody. It would not be Boon. He had never hit anything bigger than a squirrel that anybody ever knew, except the Negro woman that day when he was shooting at the Negro man. He was a big Negro and not ten feet away but Boon shot five times with the pistol he had borrowed from Major de Spain's Negro coachman and the Negro he was shooting at outed with a dollar-and-a-half mail-order pistol and would have burned Boon down with it only it never went off, it just went snicksnicksnicksnicksnick five times and Boon still blasting away and he broke a plate-glass window that cost McCaslin forty-five dollars and hit a Negro woman who happened to be passing in the leg only Major de Spain paid for that; he and McCaslin cut cards, the plate-glass window against the Negro woman's leg. And the first day on stand this year, the first morning in camp, the buck ran right over Boon; he heard Boon's old pump gun go whow. whow. whow. whow. whow. and then his voice: "God damn, here he comes! Head him! Head him!" and when he got there the buck's tracks and the five exploded shells were not twenty paces apart.

There were five guests in camp that night from Jefferson: Mr. Bayard Sartoris and his son and General Compson's son and two others. And the next morning he looked out the window, into the gray thin drizzle of daybreak which Ash had predicted, and there they were, standing and squatting beneath the thin rain, almost two dozen of them who had fed Old Ben corn and shoats and even calves for ten years, in their worn hats and hunting coats and overalls which any town Negro would have thrown away or burned and only the rubber boots strong and sound, and the worn and blueless guns, and some even without guns. While they ate breakfast a dozen more arrived, mounted and on foot: loggers from the camp thirteen miles below and sawmill men from Hoke's and the only gun among them that one which the log-train conductor carried: so that when they went into the woods this morning Major de Spain led a party almost as strong, excepting that some of them were not armed, as some he had led in the last darkening days of '64 and '65. The little yard would not hold them. They overflowed it, into the lane where Major de Spain sat his mare while Ash in his dirty apron thrust the greasy cartridges into his carbine and passed it up to him and the great grave blue dog stood at his stirrup not as a dog stands but as a horse stands, blinking his sleepy topaz eyes at nothing, deaf even to the yelling of the hounds which Boon and Tennie's Jim held on leash.

"We'll put General Compson on Katie this morning," Major de Spain said. "He drew blood last year; if he'd had a mule then that would have stood, he would have——"

"No," General Compson said. "I'm too old to go helling through the woods on a mule or a horse or any-

thing else any more. Besides, I had my chance last year
and missed it. I'm going on a stand this morning. I'm
going to let that boy ride Katie."

"No, wait," McCaslin said. "Ike's got the rest of his
life to hunt bears in. Let somebody else——"

"No," General Compson said. "I want Ike to ride
Katie. He's already a better woodsman than you or me
either and in another ten years he'll be as good as
Walter."

At first he couldn't believe it, not until Major de
Spain spoke to him. Then he was up, on the one-eyed
mule which would not spook at wild blood, looking
down at the dog motionless at Major de Spain's stirrup,
looking in the gray streaming light bigger than a calf,
bigger than he knew it actually was—the big head, the
chest almost as big as his own, the blue hide beneath
which the muscles flinched or quivered to no touch
since the heart which drove blood to them loved no man
and no thing, standing as a horse stands yet different
from a horse which infers only weight and speed while
Lion inferred not only courage and all else that went
to make up the will and desire to pursue and kill, but
endurance, the will and desire to endure beyond all
imaginable limits of flesh in order to overtake and slay.
Then the dog looked at him. It moved its head and
looked at him across the trivial uproar of the hounds,
out of the yellow eyes as depthless as Boon's, as free as
Boon's of meanness or generosity or gentleness or
viciousness. They were just cold and sleepy. Then it
blinked, and he knew it was not looking at him and
never had been, without even bothering to turn its
head away.

That morning he heard the first cry. Lion had already vanished while Sam and Tennie's Jim were putting saddles on the mule and horse which had drawn

the wagon and he watched the hounds as they crossed and cast, snuffing and whimpering, until they too disappeared. Then he and Major de Spain and Sam and Tennie's Jim rode after them and heard the first cry out of the wet and thawing woods not two hundred yards ahead, high, with that abject, almost human quality he had come to know, and the other hounds joining in until the gloomed woods rang and clamored. They rode then. It seemed to him that he could actually see the big blue dog boring on, silent, and the bear too: the thick, locomotive-like shape which he had seen that day four years ago crossing the blow-down, crashing on ahead of the dogs faster than he had believed it could have moved, drawing away even from the running mules. He heard a shotgun, once. The woods had opened, they were going fast, the clamor faint and fading on ahead; they passed the man who had fired— a swamper, a pointing arm, a gaunt face, the small black orifice of his yelling studded with rotten teeth.

He heard the changed note in the hounds' uproar and two hundred yards ahead he saw them. The bear had turned. He saw Lion drive in without pausing and saw the bear strike him aside and lunge into the yelling hounds and kill one of them almost in its tracks and whirl and run again. Then they were in a streaming tide of dogs. He heard Major de Spain and Tennie's Jim shouting and the pistol sound of Tennie's Jim's leather thong as he tried to turn them. Then he and Sam Fathers were riding alone. One of the hounds had kept on with Lion though. He recognized its voice. It was the young hound which even a year ago had had no judgment and which, by the lights of the other hounds anyway, still had none. *Maybe that's what courage is,* he thought. "Right," Sam said behind him. "Right. We got to turn him from the river if we can."

Now they were in cane: a brake. He knew the path through it as well as Sam did. They came out of the undergrowth and struck the entrance almost exactly. It would traverse the brake and come out onto a high open ridge above the river. He heard the flat clap of Walter Ewell's rifle, then two more. "No," Sam said. "I can hear the hound. Go on."

They emerged from the narrow roofless tunnel of snapping and hissing cane, still galloping, onto the open ridge below which the thick yellow river, reflectionless in the gray and streaming light, seemed not to move. Now he could hear the hound too. It was not running. The cry was a high frantic yapping and Boon was running along the edge of the bluff, his old gun leaping and jouncing against his back on its sling made of a piece of cotton plowline. He whirled and ran up to them, wild-faced, and flung himself onto the mule behind the boy. "That damn boat!" he cried. "It's on the other side! He went straight across! Lion was too close to him! That little hound too! Lion was so close I couldn't shoot! Go on!" he cried, beating his heels into the mule's flanks. "Go on!"

They plunged down the bank, slipping and sliding in the thawed earth, crashing through the willows and into the water. He felt no shock, no cold, he on one side of the swimming mule, grasping the pommel with one hand and holding his gun above the water with the other, Boon opposite him. Sam was behind them somewhere, and then the river, the water about them, was full of dogs. They swam faster than the mules; they were scrabbling up the bank before the mules touched bottom. Major de Spain was whooping from the bank they had just left and, looking back, he saw Tennie's Jim and the horse as they went into the water.

Now the woods ahead of them and the rain-heavy air

were one uproar. It rang and clamored; it echoed and broke against the bank behind them and reformed and clamored and rang until it seemed to the boy that all the hounds which had ever bayed game in this land were yelling down at him. He got his leg over the mule as it came up out of the water. Boon didn't try to mount again. He grasped one stirrup as they went up the bank and crashed through the undergrowth which fringed the bluff and saw the bear, on its hind feet, its back against a tree while the bellowing hounds swirled around it and once more Lion drove in, leaping clear of the ground.

This time the bear didn't strike him down. It caught the dog in both arms, almost loverlike, and they both went down. He was off the mule now. He drew back both hammers of the gun but he could see nothing but moiling spotted houndbodies until the bear surged up again. Boon was yelling something, he could not tell what; he could see Lion still clinging to the bear's throat and he saw the bear, half erect, strike one of the hounds with one paw and hurl it five or six feet and then, rising and rising as though it would never stop, stand erect again and begin to rake at Lion's belly with its forepaws. Then Boon was running. The boy saw the gleam of the blade in his hand and watched him leap among the hounds, hurdling them, kicking them aside as he ran, and fling himself astride the bear as he had hurled himself onto the mule, his legs locked around the bear's belly, his left arm under the bear's throat where Lion clung, and the glint of the knife as it rose and fell.

It fell just once. For an instant they almost resembled a piece of statuary: the clinging dog, the bear, the man astride its back, working and probing the buried blade. Then they went down, pulled over backward by Boon's weight, Boon underneath. It was the bear's back which reappeared first but at once Boon was astride it again. He had never released the knife and again the boy saw the almost infinitesimal movement of his arm and shoulder as he probed and sought; then the bear surged erect, raising with it the man and the dog too, and turned and still carrying the man and the dog it took two or three steps toward the woods on its hind feet as a man would have walked and crashed down. It didn't collapse, crumple. It fell all of a piece, as a tree falls, so that all three of them, man dog and bear, seemed to bounce once.

He and Tennie's Jim ran forward. Boon was kneeling at the bear's head. His left ear was shredded, his left coat sleeve was completely gone, his right boot had been ripped from knee to instep; the bright blood thinned in the thin rain down his leg and hand and arm and down the side of his face which was no longer wild but was quite calm. Together they prized Lion's jaws from the bear's throat. "Easy, goddamn it," Boon said. "Can't you see his guts are all out of him?" He began to remove his coat. He spoke to Tennie's Jim in that calm voice: "Bring the boat up. It's about a hundred yards down the bank there. I saw it." Tennie's Jim rose and went away. Then, and he could not remember if it had been a call or an exclamation from Tennie's Jim or if he had glanced up by chance, he saw Tennie's Jim stooping and saw Sam Fathers lying motionless on his face in the trampled mud.

The mule had not thrown him. He remembered that Sam was down too even before Boon began to run. There was no mark on him whatever and when he and Boon turned him over, his eyes were open and he said something in that tongue which he and Joe Baker had

used to speak together. But he couldn't move. Tennie's
Jim brought the skiff up; they could hear him shouting
to Major de Spain across the river. Boon wrapped Lion
in his hunting coat and carried him down to the skiff
and they carried Sam down and returned and hitched
the bear to the one-eyed mule's saddle-bow with Tennie's Jim's leash-thong and dragged him down to the
skiff and got him into it and left Tennie's Jim to swim
the horse and the two mules back across. Major de
Spain caught the bow of the skiff as Boon jumped out
and past him before it touched the bank. He looked at
Old Ben and said quietly: "Well." Then he walked into
the water and leaned down and touched Sam and Sam
looked up at him and said something in that old tongue
he and Joe Baker spoke. "You don't know what happened?" Major de Spain said.

"No, sir," the boy said. "It wasn't the mule. It wasn't
anything. He was off the mule when Boon ran in on the
bear. Then we looked up and he was lying on the
ground." Boon was shouting at Tennie's Jim, still in the
middle of the river.

"Come on, goddamn it!" he said. "Bring me that
mule!"

"What do you want with a mule?" Major de Spain
said.

Boon didn't even look at him. "I'm going to Hoke's to
get the doctor," he said in that calm voice, his face quite
calm beneath the steady thinning of the bright blood.

"You need a doctor yourself," Major de Spain said.
"Tennie's Jim——"

"Damn that," Boon said. He turned on Major de
Spain. His face was still calm, only his voice was a pitch
higher. "Can't you see his goddamn guts are all out of
him?"

"Boon!" Major de Spain said. They looked at one another. Boon was a good head taller than Major de Spain; even the boy was taller now than Major de Spain.

"I've got to get the doctor," Boon said. "His goddamn guts——"

"All right," Major de Spain said. Tennie's Jim came up out of the water. The horse and the sound mule had already scented Old Ben; they surged and plunged all the way up to the top of the bluff, dragging Tennie's Jim with them, before he could stop them and tie them and come back. Major de Spain unlooped the leather thong of his compass from his buttonhole and gave it to Tennie's Jim. "Go straight to Hoke's," he said. "Bring Doctor Crawford back with you. Tell him there are two men to be looked at. Take my mare. Can you find the road from here?"

"Yes, sir," Tennie's Jim said.

"All right," Major de Spain said. "Go on." He turned to the boy. "Take the mules and the horse and go back and get the wagon. We'll go on down the river in the boat to Coon bridge. Meet us there. Can you find it again?"

"Yes, sir," the boy said.

"All right. Get started."

He went back to the wagon. He realized then how far they had run. It was already afternoon when he put the mules into the traces and tied the horse's lead-rope to the tail-gate. He reached Coon bridge at dusk. The skiff was already there. Before he could see it and almost before he could see the water he had to leap from the tilting wagon, still holding the reins, and work around to where he could grasp the bit and then the ear of the plunging sound mule and dig his heels and hold it until Boon came up the bank. The rope of the led horse had already snapped and it had already disappeared up the road toward camp. They turned the wagon around and took the mules out and he led the sound mule a hundred yards up the road and tied it. Boon had already brought Lion up to the wagon and Sam was sitting up in the skiff now and when they raised him he tried to walk, up the bank and to the wagon and he tried to climb into the wagon but Boon did not wait; he picked Sam up bodily and set him on the seat. Then they hitched Old Ben to the one-eyed mule's saddle again and dragged him up the bank and set two skid-poles into the open tail-gate and got him into the wagon and he went and got the sound mule and Boon fought it into the traces, striking it across its hard hollow-sounding face until it came into position and stood trembling. Then the rain came down, as though it had held off all day waiting on them.

They returned to camp through it, through the streaming and sightless dark, hearing long before they saw any light the horn and the spaced shots to guide them. When they came to Sam's dark little hut he tried to stand up. He spoke again in the tongue of the old fathers; then he said clearly: "Let me out. Let me out."

"He hasn't got any fire," Major said. "Go on!" he said sharply.

But Sam was struggling now, trying to stand up. "Let me out, master," he said. "Let me go home."

So he stopped the wagon and Boon got down and lifted Sam out. He did not wait to let Sam try to walk this time. He carried him into the hut and Major de Spain got light on a paper spill from the buried embers on the hearth and lit the lamp and Boon put Sam on his bunk and drew off his boots and Major de Spain covered him and the boy was not there, he was holding the mules, the sound one which was trying again to bolt since when the wagon stopped Old Ben's scent drifted forward again along the streaming blackness of air, but Sam's eyes were probably open again on that profound look which saw further than them or the hut, further than the death of a bear and the dying of a dog. Then they went on, toward the long wailing of the horn and the shots which seemed each to linger intact somewhere in the thick streaming air until the next spaced report joined and blended with it, to the lighted house, the bright streaming windows, the quiet faces as Boon entered, bloody and quite calm, carrying the bundled coat. He laid Lion, blood coat and all, on his stale sheetless pallet bed which not even Ash, as deft in the house as a woman, could ever make smooth.

The sawmill doctor from Hoke's was already there. Boon would not let the doctor touch him until he had seen to Lion. He wouldn't risk giving Lion chloroform. He put the entrails back and sewed him up without it while Major de Spain held his head and Boon his feet. But he never tried to move. He lay there, the yellow eyes open upon nothing while the quiet men in the new hunting clothes and in the old ones crowded into the little airless room rank with the smell of Boon's body and garments, and watched. Then the doctor cleaned and disinfected Boon's face and arm and leg and bandaged them and, the boy in front with a lantern and the doctor and McCaslin and Major de Spain and General Compson following, they went to Sam Fathers' hut. Tennie's Jim had built up the fire; he squatted before it, dozing. Sam had not moved since Boon had put him in the bunk and Major de Spain had covered him with the blankets, yet he opened his eyes and looked from one to another of the faces and when McCaslin touched his shoulder and said, "Sam. The doctor wants to look at you," he even drew his hands out of the blanket and began to fumble at his shirt buttons until

McCaslin said, "Wait. We'll do it." They undressed him. He lay there—the copper-brown, almost hairless body, the old man's body, the old man, the wild man not even one generation from the woods, childless, kinless, peopleless—motionless, his eyes open but no longer looking at any of them, while the doctor examined him and drew the blankets up and put the stethoscope back into his bag and snapped the bag and only the boy knew that Sam too was going to die.

"Exhaustion," the doctor said. "Shock maybe. A man his age swimming rivers in December. He'll be all right. Just make him stay in bed for a day or two. Will there be somebody here with him?"

"There will be somebody here," Major de Spain said.

They went back to the house, to the rank little room where Boon still sat on the pallet bed with Lion's head under his hand while the men, the ones who had hunted behind Lion and the ones who had never seen him before today, came quietly in to look at him and went away. Then it was dawn and they all went out into the yard to look at Old Ben, with his eyes open too and his lips snarled back from his worn teeth and his mutilated foot and the little hard lumps under his skin which were the old bullets (there were fifty-two of them, buckshot rifle and ball) and the single almost invisible slit under his left shoulder where Boon's blade had finally found his life. Then Ash began to beat on the bottom of the dishpan with a heavy spoon to call them to breakfast and it was the first time he could remember hearing no sound from the dogs under the kitchen while they were eating. It was as if the old bear, even dead there in the yard, was a more potent terror still than they could face without Lion between them.

The rain had stopped during the night. By midmorn-

ing the thin sun appeared, rapidly burning away mist and cloud, warming the air and the earth; it would be one of those windless Mississippi December days which are a sort of Indian summer's Indian summer. They moved Lion out to the front gallery, into the sun. It was Boon's idea. "Goddamn it," he said, "he never did want to stay in the house until I made him. You know that." He took a crowbar and loosened the floor boards under his pallet bed so it could be raised, mattress and all, without disturbing Lion's position, and they carried him out to the gallery and put him down facing the woods.

Then he and the doctor and McCaslin and Major de Spain went to Sam's hut. This time Sam didn't open his eyes and his breathing was so quiet, so peaceful that they could hardly see that he breathed. The doctor didn't even take out his stethoscope nor even touch him. "He's all right," the doctor said. "He didn't even catch cold. He just quit."

"Quit?" McCaslin said.

"Yes. Old people do that sometimes. Then they get a good night's sleep or maybe it's just a drink of whiskey, and they change their minds."

They returned to the house. And then they began to arrive—the swamp-dwellers, the gaunt men who ran trap-lines and lived on quinine and coons and river water, the farmers of little corn- and cotton-patches along the bottom's edge whose fields and cribs and pig-pens the old bear had rifled, the loggers from the camp, and the sawmill men from Hoke's, and the town men from further away than that, whose hounds the old bear had slain and whose traps and deadfalls he had wrecked and whose lead he carried. They came up mounted and on foot and in wagons, to enter the yard

and look at him and then go on to the front where
Lion lay, filling the little yard and overflowing it until
there were almost a hundred of them squatting and
standing in the warm and drowsing sunlight, talking
quietly of hunting, of the game and the dogs which ran
it, of hounds and bear and deer and men of yesterday
vanished from the earth, while from time to time the
great blue dog would open his eyes, not as if he were
listening to them but as though to look at the woods
for a moment before closing his eyes again, to remember
the woods or to see that they were still there. He died
at sundown.

Major de Spain broke camp that night. They carried
Lion into the woods, or Boon carried him that is,
wrapped in a quilt from his bed, just as he had refused
to let anyone else touch Lion yesterday until the doctor
got there; Boon carrying Lion, and the boy and General
Compson and Walter and still almost fifty of them following with lanterns and lighted pine-knots—men from
Hoke's and even further, who would have to ride out of
the bottom in the dark, and swampers and trappers
who would have to walk even, scattering toward the
little hidden huts where they lived. And Boon would let
nobody else dig the grave either and lay Lion in it and
cover him, and then General Compson stood at the head
of it while the blaze and smoke of the pine-knots
streamed away among the winter branches and spoke as
he would have spoken over a man. Then they returned
to camp. Major de Spain and McCaslin and Ash had
rolled and tied all the bedding. The mules were hitched
to the wagon and pointed out of the bottom and the
wagon was already loaded and the stove in the kitchen
was cold and the table was set with scraps of cold food
and bread and only the coffee was hot when the boy ran

into the kitchen where Major de Spain and McCaslin had already eaten. "What?" he cried. "What? I'm not going."

"Yes," McCaslin said, "we're going out tonight. Major wants to get on back home."

"No!" he said. "I'm going to stay."

"You've got to be back in school Monday. You've already missed a week more than I intended. It will take you from now until Monday to catch up. Sam's all right. You heard Doctor Crawford. I'm going to leave Boon and Tennie's Jim both to stay with him until he feels like getting up."

He was panting. The others had come in. He looked rapidly and almost frantically around at the other faces. Boon had a fresh bottle. He upended it and started the cork by striking the bottom of the bottle with the heel of his hand and drew the cork with his teeth and spat it out and drank. "You're damn right you're going back to school," Boon said. "Or I'll burn the tail off of you myself if Cass don't, whether you are sixteen or sixty. Where in hell do you expect to get without education? Where would Cass be? Where in hell would I be if I hadn't never went to school?"

He looked at McCaslin again. He could feel his breath coming shorter and shorter and shallower and shallower, as if there were not enough air in the kitchen for that many to breathe. "This is just Thursday. I'll come home Sunday night on one of the horses. I'll come home Sunday, then. I'll make up the time I lost studying Sunday night, McCaslin," he said, without even despair.

"No, I tell you," McCaslin said. "Sit down here and eat your supper. We're going out to——"

"Hold up, Cass," General Compson said. The boy did not know General Compson had moved until he put his hand on his shoulder. "What is it, bud?" he said.

"I've got to stay," he said. "I've got to."

"All right," General Compson said. "You can stay. If missing an extra week of school is going to throw you so far behind you'll have to sweat to find out what some hired pedagogue put between the covers of a book, you better quit altogether.—And you shut up, Cass," he said, though McCaslin had not spoken. "You've got one foot straddled into a farm and the other foot straddled into a bank; you ain't even got a good hand-hold where this boy was already an old man long before you damned Sartorises and Edmondses invented farms and banks to keep yourselves from having to find out what this boy was born knowing, and fearing too maybe, but without being afraid, that could go ten miles on a compass because he wanted to look at a bear none of us had ever got near enough to put a bullet in and looked at the bear and came the ten miles back on the compass in the dark; maybe by God that's the why and the wherefore of farms and banks.—I reckon you still ain't going to tell what it is?"

But still he could not. "I've got to stay," he said.

"All right," General Compson said. "There's plenty of grub left. And you'll come home Sunday, like you promised McCaslin? Not Sunday night: Sunday."

"Yes, sir," he said.

"All right," General Compson said. "Sit down and eat, boys," he said. "Let's get started. It's going to be cold before we get home."

They ate. The wagon was already loaded and ready to depart; all they had to do was to get into it. Boon would drive them out to the road, to the farmer's stable where the surrey had been left. He stood beside the wagon, in silhouette on the sky, turbaned like a Paythan and taller than any there, the bottle tilted. Then he flung the bottle from his lips without even lowering it, spinning and glinting in the faint starlight, empty. "Them that's going," he said, "get in the goddamn wagon. Them that ain't, get out of the goddamn way." The others got in. Boon mounted to the seat beside General Compson and the wagon moved, on into the obscurity until the boy could no longer see it, even the moving density of it amid the greater night. But he could still hear it, for a long while: the slow, deliberate banging of the wooden frame as it lurched from rut to rut. And he could hear Boon even when he could no longer hear the wagon. He was singing, harsh, tuneless, loud.

That was Thursday. On Saturday morning Tennie's Jim left on McCaslin's woods-horse which had not been out of the bottom one time now in six years, and late that afternoon rode through the gate on the spent horse and on to the commissary where McCaslin was rationing the tenants and the wage-hands for the coming week, and this time McCaslin forestalled any necessity or risk of having to wait while Major de Spain's surrey was being horsed and harnessed. He took their own, and with Tennie's Jim already asleep in the back seat he drove in to Jefferson and waited while Major de Spain changed to boots and put on his overcoat, and they drove the thirty miles in the dark of that night and at daybreak on Sunday morning they swapped to the waiting mare and mule and as the sun rose they rode out of the jungle and onto the low ridge where they had buried Lion: the low mound of unannealed earth where Boon's spade-marks still showed, and beyond the grave the platform of freshly cut saplings bound between four posts and the blanket-wrapped bundle upon the platform and Boon and the boy squatting between the platform and the grave until Boon, the bandage removed, ripped from his head so that the long scoriations of Old Ben's claws resembled crusted tar in the sunlight, sprang up and threw down upon them with the old gun with which he had never been known to hit anything although McCaslin was already off the mule, kicked both feet free of the irons and vaulted down before the mule had stopped, walking toward Boon.

"Stand back," Boon said. "By God, you won't touch him. Stand back, McCaslin." Still McCaslin came on, fast yet without haste.

"Cass!" Major de Spain said. Then he said, "Boon! You, Boon!" and he was down too and the boy rose too, quickly, and still McCaslin came on not fast but steady and walked up to the grave and reached his hand steadily out, quickly yet still not fast, and took hold the gun by the middle so that he and Boon faced one another across Lion's grave, both holding the gun, Boon's spent indomitable amazed and frantic face almost a head higher than McCaslin's beneath the black scoriations of beast's claws and then Boon's chest began to heave as though there were not enough air in all the woods, in all the wilderness, for all of them, for him and anyone else, even for him alone.

"Turn it loose, Boon," McCaslin said.

"You damn little spindling—" Boon said. "Don't you know I can take it away from you? Don't you know I can tie it around your neck like a damn cravat?"

"Yes," McCaslin said. "Turn it loose, Boon."

"This is the way he wanted it. He told us. He told us exactly how to do it. And by God you ain't going to move him. So we did it like he said, and I been sitting here ever since to keep the damn wildcats and varmints away from him and by God—" Then McCaslin had the gun, downslanted while he pumped the slide, the five shells snicking out of it so fast that the last one was

almost out before the first one touched the ground and
McCaslin dropped the gun behind him without once
having taken his eyes from Boon's.

"Did you kill him, Boon?" he said. Then Boon moved.
He turned, he moved like he was still drunk and then
for a moment blind too, one hand out as he blundered
toward the big tree and seemed to stop walking before
he reached the tree so that he plunged, fell toward it,
flinging up both hands and catching himself against the
tree and turning until his back was against it, backing
with the tree's trunk his wild spent scoriated face and
the tremendous heave and collapse of his chest, Mc-
Caslin following, facing him again, never once having
moved his eyes from Boon's eyes. "Did you kill him,
Boon?"

"No!" Boon said. "No!"

"Tell the truth," McCaslin said. "I would have done it
if he had asked me to." Then the boy moved. He was
between them, facing McCaslin; the water felt as if it
had burst and sprung not from his eyes alone but from
his whole face, like sweat.

"Leave him alone!" he cried. "Goddamn it! Leave him
alone!"

IV

then he was twenty-one. He could say it, himself and
his cousin juxtaposed not against the wilderness but
against the tamed land which was to have been his
heritage, the land which old Carothers McCaslin, his
grandfather, had bought with white man's money from
the wild men whose grandfathers without guns hunted
it, and tamed and ordered, or believed he had tamed
and ordered it, for the reason that the human beings
he held in bondage and in the power of life and death
had removed the forest from it and in their sweat

scratched the surface of it to a depth of perhaps fourteen
inches in order to grow something out of it which had
not been there before, and which could be translated
back into the money he who believed he had bought it
had had to pay to get it and hold it, and a reasonable
profit too: and for which reason old Carothers McCaslin,
knowing better, could raise his children, his descendants
and heirs, to believe the land was his to hold and bequeath, since the strong and ruthless man has a cynical
foreknowledge of his own vanity and pride and strength
and a contempt for all his get: just as, knowing better,
Major de Spain had his fragment of that wilderness
which was bigger and older than any recorded deed:
just as, knowing better, old Thomas Sutpen, from whom
Major de Spain had had his fragment for money: just
as Ikkemotubbe, the Chickasaw chief, from whom
Thomas Sutpen had had the fragment for money or
rum or whatever it was, knew in his turn that not even
a fragment of it had been his to relinquish or sell

not against the wilderness but against the land, not
in pursuit and lust but in relinquishment; and in the
commissary as it should have been, not the heart perhaps but certainly the solar-plexus of the repudiated and
relinquished: the square, galleried, wooden building
squatting like a portent above the fields whose laborers
it still held in thrall, '65 or no, and placarded over with
advertisements for snuff and cures for chills and salves
and potions manufactured and sold by white men to
bleach the pigment and straighten the hair of Negroes
that they might resemble the very race which for two
hundred years had held them in bondage and from
which for another hundred years not even a bloody
civil war would have set them completely free

himself and his cousin amid the old smells of cheese
and salt meat and kerosene and harness, the ranked

shelves of tobacco and overalls and bottled medicine and thread and plow-bolts, the barrels and kegs of flour and meal and molasses and nails, the wall pegs dependant with plowlines and plow-collars and hames and trace-chains, and the desk and the shelf above it on which rested the ledgers in which McCaslin recorded the slow outward trickle of food and supplies and equipment which returned each fall as cotton made and ginned and sold (two threads frail as truth and impalpable as equators yet cable-strong to bind for life them who made the cotton to the land their sweat fell on), and the older ledgers, clumsy and archaic in size and shape, on the yellowed pages of which were recorded in the faded hand of his father Theophilus and his uncle Amodeus during the two decades before the Civil War the manumission, in title at least, of Carothers McCaslin's slaves:

'Relinquish,' McCaslin said. 'Relinquish. You, the direct male descendant of him who saw the opportunity and took it, bought the land, took the land, got the land no matter how, held it to bequeath, no matter how, out of the old grant, the first patent, when it was a wilderness of wild beasts and wilder men, and cleared it, translated it into something to bequeath to his children, worthy of bequeathment for his descendants' ease and security and pride, and to perpetuate his name and accomplishments. Not only the male descendant but the only and last descendant in the male line and in the third generation, while I am not only four generations from old Carothers, I derived through a woman and the very McCaslin in my name is mine only by sufferance and courtesy and my grandmother's pride in what that man accomplished, whose legacy and monument you think you can repudiate.' and he

'I can't repudiate it. It was never mine to repudiate.

It was never Father's and Uncle Buddy's to bequeath me to repudiate, because it was never Grandfather's to bequeath them to bequeath me to repudiate, because it was never old Ikkemotubbe's to sell to Grandfather for bequeathment and repudiation. Because it was never Ikkemotubbe's fathers' fathers' to bequeath Ikkemotubbe to sell to Grandfather or any man because on the instant when Ikkemotubbe discovered, realized, that he could sell it for money, on that instant it ceased ever to have been his forever, father to father to father, and the man who bought it bought nothing.'

'Bought nothing?' and he

'Bought nothing. Because He told in the Book how He created the earth, made it and looked at it and said it was all right, and then He made man. He made the earth first and peopled it with dumb creatures, and then He created man to be His overseer on the earth and to hold suzerainty over the earth and the animals on it in His name, not to hold for himself and his descendants inviolable title forever, generation after generation, to the oblongs and squares of the earth, but to hold the earth mutual and intact in the communal anonymity of brotherhood, and all the fee He asked was pity and humility and sufferance and endurance and the sweat of his face for bread. And I know what you are going to say,' he said: 'That nevertheless Grandfather—' and McCaslin

'—did own it. And not the first. Not alone and not the first since, as your Authority states, man was dispossessed of Eden. Nor yet the second and still not alone, on down through the tedious and shabby chronicle of His chosen sprung from Abraham; and of the sons of them who dispossessed Abraham, and of the five hundred years during which half the known world and all it contained was chattel to one city, as this plantation and all the life it contained was chattel and revokeless thrall to this commissary store and those ledgers yonder during your grandfather's life; and the next thousand years while men fought over the fragments of that collapse until at last even the fragments were exhausted and men snarled over the gnawed bones of the old world's worthless evening until an accidental egg discovered to them a new hemisphere. So let me say it: That nevertheless and notwithstanding old Carothers did own it. Bought it, got it, no matter; kept it, held it, no matter; bequeathed it: else why do you stand here relinquishing and repudiating? Held it, kept it for fifty years until you could repudiate it, while He—this Arbiter, this Architect, this Umpire—condoned—or did He? looked down and saw—or did He? Or at least did nothing: saw, and could not, or did not see; saw, and would not, or perhaps He would not see—perverse, impotent, or blind: which?' and he

'Dispossessed.' and McCaslin

'What?' and he

'Dispossessed. Not impotent: He didn't condone; not blind, because He watched it. And let me say it. Dispossessed of Eden. Dispossessed of Canaan, and those who dispossessed him dispossessed him dispossessed, and the five hundred years of absentee landlords in the Roman bagnios, and the thousand years of wild men from the northern woods who dispossessed them and devoured their ravished substance ravished in turn again and then snarled in what you call the old world's worthless twilight over the old world's gnawed bones, blasphemous in His name until He used a simple egg to discover to them a new world where a nation of people could be founded in humility and pity and sufferance and pride of one to another. And Grandfather did own the land nevertheless and notwithstanding because He permitted it, not impotent and not condoning and not blind, because He ordered and watched it. He saw the land already accursed even as Ikkemotubbe and Ikkemotubbe's father old Issetibbeha and old Issetibbeha's fathers too held it, already tainted even before any white man owned it by what Grandfather and his kind, his fathers, had brought into the new land which He had vouchsafed them out of pity and sufferance, on condition of pity and humility and sufferance and endurance, from that old world's corrupt and worthless twilight as though in the sailfuls of the old world's tainted wind which drove the ships—' and McCaslin

'Ah.'

'—and no hope for the land anywhere so long as Ikkemotubbe and Ikkemotubbe's descendants held it in unbroken succession. Maybe He saw that only by voiding the land for a time of Ikkemotubbe's blood and substituting for it another blood, could He accomplish His purpose. Maybe He knew already what that other blood would be, maybe it was more than justice that only the white man's blood was available and capable to raise the white man's curse, more than vengeance when—' and McCaslin

'Ah.'

'—when He used the blood which had brought in the evil to destroy the evil as doctors use fever to burn up fever, poison to slay poison. Maybe He chose Grandfather out of all of them He might have picked. Maybe He knew that Grandfather himself would not serve His purpose because Grandfather was born too soon too, but that Grandfather would have descendants, the right descendants; maybe He had foreseen already the descendants Grandfather would have, maybe He saw already in Grandfather the seed progenitive of the three generations He saw it would take to set at least some of His lowly people free—' and McCaslin

'The sons of Ham. You who quote the Book: the sons of Ham.' and he

'There are some things He said in the Book, and some things reported of Him that He did not say. And I know what you will say now: That if truth is one thing to me and another thing to you, how will we choose which is truth? You don't need to choose. The heart already knows. He didn't have His Book written to be read by what must elect and choose, but by the heart, not by the wise of the earth because maybe they don't need it or maybe the wise no longer have any heart, but by the doomed and lowly of the earth who have nothing else to read with but the heart. Because the men who wrote His Book for Him were writing about truth and there is only one truth and it covers all things that touch the heart.' and McCaslin

'So these men who transcribed His Book for Him were sometime liars.' and he

'Yes. Because they were human men. They were trying to write down the heart's truth out of the heart's driving complexity, for all the complex and troubled hearts which would beat after them. What they were trying to tell, what He wanted said, was too simple. Those for whom they transcribed His words could not have believed them. It had to be expounded in the everyday terms which they were familiar with and could comprehend, not only those who listened but those who told it too, because if they who were that near to Him as to have been elected from among all who breathed and spoke language to transcribe and relay His words, could comprehend truth only through

the complexity of passion and lust and hate and fear
which drives the heart, what distance back to truth must
they traverse whom truth could only reach by word-of-
mouth?' and McCaslin

'I might answer that, since you have taken to proving
your points and disproving mine by the same text, I
don't know. But I don't say that, because you have answered yourself: No time at all if, as you say, the heart
knows truth, the infallible and unerring heart. And perhaps you are right, since although you admitted three
generations from old Carothers to you, there were not
three. There were not even completely two. Uncle Buck
and Uncle Buddy. And they not the first and not alone.
A thousand other Bucks and Buddies in less than two
generations and sometimes less than one in this land
which so you claim God created and man himself cursed
and tainted. Not to mention 1865.' and he

'Yes. More men than Father and Uncle Buddy,' not
even glancing toward the shelf above the desk, nor did
McCaslin. They did not need to. To him it was as
though the ledgers in their scarred cracked leather
bindings were being lifted down one by one in their
fading sequence and spread open on the desk or perhaps upon some apocryphal Bench, or even Altar, or
perhaps before the Throne Itself for a last perusal and
contemplation and refreshment of the Allknowledge-
able, before the yellowed pages and the brown thin
ink in which was recorded the injustice and a little at
least of its amelioration and restitution faded back
forever into the anonymous communal original dust

the yellowed pages scrawled in fading ink by the
hand first of his grandfather and then of his father and
uncle, bachelors up to and past fifty and then sixty, the
one who ran the plantation and the farming of it, and

the other who did the housework and the cooking and continued to do it even after his twin married and the boy himself was born

the two brothers who as soon as their father was buried moved out of the tremendously-conceived, the almost barnlike edifice which he had not even completed, into a one-room log cabin which the two of them built themselves and added other rooms to while they lived in it, refusing to allow any slave to touch any timber of it other than the actual raising into place the logs which two men alone could not handle, and domiciled all the slaves in the big house some of the windows of which were still merely boarded up with odds and ends of plank or with the skins of bear and deer nailed over the empty frames: each sundown the brother who superintended the farming would parade the Negroes as a first sergeant dismisses a company, and herd them willynilly, man woman and child, without question protest or recourse, into the tremendous abortive edifice scarcely yet out of embryo, as if even old Carothers McCaslin had paused aghast at the concrete indication of his own vanity's boundless conceiving: he would call his mental roll and herd them in and with a hand-wrought nail as long as a flenching-knife and suspended from a short deer-hide thong attached to the door-jamb for that purpose, he would nail to the door of that house which lacked half its windows and had no hinged back door at all, so that presently, and for fifty years afterward, when the boy himself was big to hear and remember it, there was in the land a sort of folk-tale: of the countryside all night long full of skulking McCaslin slaves dodging the moonlit roads and the Patrol-riders to visit other plantations, and of the unspoken gentlemen's agreement between the two white men and the

two dozen black ones that, after the white man had
counted them and driven the home-made nail into the
front door at sundown, neither of the white men would
go around behind the house and look at the back door,
provided that all the Negroes were behind the front
one when the brother who drove it drew out the nail
again at daybreak

the twins who were identical even in their hand-
writing, unless you had specimens side by side to
compare, and even when both hands appeared on the
same page (as often happened, as if, long since past
any oral intercourse, they had used the diurnally advancing pages to conduct the unavoidable business of
the compulsion which had traversed all the waste wilderness of North Mississippi in 1830 and '40 and singled
them out to drive) they both looked as though they had
been written by the same perfectly normal ten-year-old
boy, even to the spelling, except that the spelling did
not improve as one by one the slaves which Carothers
McCaslin had inherited and purchased— Roscius and
Phoebe and Thucydides and Eunice and their descendants, and Sam Fathers and his mother for both of whom
he had swapped an underbred trotting gelding to old
Ikkemotubbe, the Chickasaw chief, from whom he had
likewise bought the land, and Tennie Beauchamp whom
the twin Amodeus had won from a neighbor in a poker-
game, and the anomaly calling itself Percival Brownlee
which the twin Theophilus had purchased, neither he
nor his brother ever knew why apparently, from Bedford
Forrest while he was still only a slave-dealer and not
yet a general (It was a single page, not long and covering less than a year, not seven months in fact, begun in
the hand which the boy had learned to distinguish as
that of his father:

> *Percavil Brownly 26yr Old. cleark @ Bookepper.*
> *bought from N.B.Forest at Cold Water 3 Mar*
> *1856 $265. dolars*

and beneath that, in the same hand:

> *5 mar 1856 No bookepper any way Cant read.*
> *Can write his Name but I already put that down*
> *My self Says he can Plough but dont look like it*
> *to Me. sent to Feild to day Mar 5 1856*

and the same hand:

> *6 Mar 1856 Cant plough either Says he aims to be*
> *a Precher so may be he can lead live stock to Crick*
> *to Drink*

and this time it was the other, the hand which he now
recognized as his uncle's when he could see them both
on the same page:

> *Mar 23th 1856 Cant do that either Except one at*
> *a Time Get shut of him*

then the first again:

> *24 Mar 1856 Who in hell would buy him*

then the second:

> *19th of Apr 1856 Nobody You put yourself out of*
> *Market at Cold Water two months ago I never*
> *said sell him Free him*

the first:

> *22 Apr 1856 Ill get it out of him*

the second:

> *Jun 13th 1856 How $1 per yr 265$ 265 yrs Whol*
> *sign his Free paper*

then the first again:

> *1 Oct 1856 Mule josephine Broke Leg @ shot Wrong stall wrong niger wrong everything $100. dolars*

and the same:

> *2 Oct 1856 Freed Debit McCaslin @ McCaslin $265. dolars*

then the second again:

> *Oct 3th Debit Theophilus McCaslin Niger 265$ Mule 100$ 365$ He hasnt gone yet Father should be here*

then the first:

> *3 Oct 1856 Son of a bitch wont leave What would father done*

the second:

> *29th of Oct 1856 Renamed him*

the first:

> *31 Oct 1856 Renamed him what*

the second:

> *Chrstms 1856 Spintrius*

) took substance and even a sort of shadowy life with their passions and complexities too, as page followed page and year year; all there, not only the general and condoned injustice and its slow amortization but the specific tragedy which had not been condoned and could never be amortized; the new page and the new ledger, the hand which he could now recognize at first glance as his father's:

> *Father dide Lucius Quintus Carothers McCaslin,*
> *Callina 1772 Missippy 1837. Dide and burid 27*
> *June 1837*
> *Roskus. rased by Granfather in Callina Dont know*
> *how old. Freed 27 June 1837 Dont want to leave.*
> *Dide and Burid 12 Jan 1841*
> *Fibby Roskus Wife. bought by granfather in Cal-*
> *lina says Fifty Freed 27 June 1837 Dont want to*
> *leave. Dide and burd 1 Aug 1849*
> *Thucydus Roskus @ Fibby Son born in Callina*
> *1779. Refused 10acre peace fathers Will 28 Jun*
> *1837 Refused Cash offer $200. dolars from A.*
> *@ T. McCaslin 28 Jun 1837 Wants to stay and*
> *work it out*

and beneath this and covering the next five pages and
almost that many years, the slow, day-by-day accru-
ment of the wages allowed him and the food and
clothing—the molasses and meat and meal, the cheap
durable shirts and jeans and shoes, and now and then a
coat against rain and cold—charged against the slowly
yet steadily mounting sum of balance (and it would
seem to the boy that he could actually see the black
man, the slave whom his white owner had forever manu-
mitted by the very act from which the black man could
never be free so long as memory lasted, entering the
commissary, asking permission perhaps of the white
man's son to see the ledger-page which he could not
even read, not even asking for the white man's word,
which he would have had to accept for the reason that
there was absolutely no way under the sun for him to
test it, as to how the account stood, how much longer
before he could go and never return, even if only as far
as Jefferson seventeen miles away), on to the double
pen-stroke closing the final entry:

3 Nov 1841 By Cash to Thucydus McCaslin $200. dolars Set Up blaksmith in J. Dec 1841 Dide and burid in J. 17 feb 1854

Eunice Bought by Father in New Orleans 1807 $650. dolars. Marrid to Thucydus 1809 Drownd in Crick Cristmas Day 1832

and then the other hand appeared, the first time he had seen it in the ledger to distinguish it as his uncle's, the cook and housekeeper whom even McCaslin, who had known him and the boy's father for sixteen years before the boy was born, remembered as sitting all day long in the rocking chair from which he cooked the food, before the kitchen fire on which he cooked it:

June 21th 1833 Drownd herself

and the first:

23 Jun 1833 Who in hell ever heard of a niger drownding him self

and the second, unhurried, with a complete finality; the two identical entries might have been made with a rubber stamp save for the date:

Aug 13th 1833 Drownd herself

and he thought *But why? But why?* He was sixteen then. It was neither the first time he had been alone in the commissary nor the first time he had taken down the old ledgers familiar on their shelf above the desk ever since he could remember. As a child and even after nine and ten and eleven, when he had learned to read, he would look up at the scarred and cracked backs and ends but with no particular desire to open them, and though he intended to examine them someday because he realized that they probably contained a chronological and much more comprehensive though doubtless tedious record than he would ever get from any other source, not alone of his own flesh and blood but of all his people, not only the whites but the black ones too, who were as much a part of his ancestry as his white progenitors, and of the land which they had all held and used in common and fed from and on and would continue to use in common without regard to color or titular ownership, it would only be on some idle day when he was old and perhaps even bored a little, since what the old books contained would be after all these years fixed immutably, finished, unalterable, harmless. Then he was sixteen. He knew what he was going to find before he found it. He got the commissary key from McCaslin's room after midnight while McCaslin was asleep and with the commissary door shut and locked behind him and the forgotten lantern stinking anew the rank dead icy air, he leaned above the yellowed page and thought not *Why drowned herself*, but thinking what he believed his father had thought when he found his brother's first comment: *Why did Uncle Buddy think she had drowned herself?* finding, beginning to find on the next succeeding page what he knew he would find, only this was still not it because he already knew this:

> *Tomasina called Tomy Daughter of Thucydus @*
> *Eunice Born 1810 dide in Child bed June 1833*
> *and Burd. Yr stars fell*

nor the next:

> *Turl Son of Thucydus @ Eunice Tomy born Jun*
> *1833 yr stars fell Fathers will*

and nothing more, no tedious recording filling this page of wages, day by day, and food and clothing charged against them, no entry of his death and burial because he had outlived his white half-brothers and the books which McCaslin kept did not include obituaries: just *Fathers will* and he had seen that too: old Carothers' bold cramped hand far less legible than his sons' even and not much better in spelling, who while capitalizing almost every noun and verb, made no effort to punctuate or construct whatever, just as he made no effort either to explain or obfuscate the thousand-dollar legacy to the son of an unmarried slave-girl, to be paid only at the child's coming-of-age, bearing the consequence of the act of which there was still no definite incontrovertible proof that he acknowledged, not out of his own substance, but penalizing his sons with it, charging them a cash forfeit on the accident of their own paternity; not even a bribe for silence toward his own fame since his fame would suffer only after he was no longer present to defend it, flinging almost contemptuously, as he might a cast-off hat or pair of shoes, the thousand dollars which could have had no more reality to him under those conditions than it would have to the Negro, the slave who would not even see it until he came of age, twenty-one years too late to begin to learn what money was. *So I reckon that was cheaper than saying My son to a nigger,* he thought. *Even if My son wasn't but just two words. But there must have been love,* he thought. *Some sort of love. Even what he would have called love: not just an afternoon's or a night's spittoon.* There was the old man, old, within five years of his life's end, long a widower and, since his sons were not only bachelors but were approaching middleage, lonely in the house and doubtless even bored, since his plantation was established now and functioning and there was enough money now, too much of it probably for a man whose vices even apparently remained below his means;

there was the girl, husbandless and young, only twenty-three when the child was born: perhaps he had sent for her at first out of loneliness, to have a young voice and movement in the house, summoned her, bade her mother send her each morning to sweep the floors and make the beds and the mother acquiescing since that was probably already understood, already planned: the only child of a couple who were not field hands and who held themselves something above the other slaves, not alone for that reason but because the husband and his father and mother too had been inherited by the white man from his father, and the white man himself had travelled three hundred miles and better to New Orleans in a day when men travelled by horseback or steamboat, and bought the girl's mother as a wife for him

and that was all. The old frail pages seemed to turn of their own accord even while he thought, *His own daughter His own daughter. No. No Not even him,* back to that one where the white man (not even a widower then) who never went anywhere, any more than his sons in their time ever did, and who did not need another slave, had gone all the way to New Orleans and bought one. And Tomey's Terrel was still alive when the boy was ten years old and he knew from his own observation and memory that there had already been some white in Tomey's Terrel's blood before his father gave him the rest of it; and looking down at the yellowed page spread beneath the yellow glow of the lantern smoking and stinking in that rank chill midnight room fifty years later, he seemed to see her actually walking into the icy creek on that Christmas day six months before her daughter's and her lover's (*Her first lover's,* he thought. *Her first*) child was born, solitary, inflexible, griefless, ceremonial, in formal and succinct repudiation of grief and despair, who had already had to repudiate belief and hope

that was all. He would never need look at the ledgers again nor did he; the yellowed pages in their fading and implacable succession were as much a part of his consciousness and would remain so forever, as the fact of his own nativity:

Tennie Beauchamp 21yrs Won by Amodeus McCaslin from Hubert Beauchamp Esqre Possible Strait against three Treys in sigt Not called 1859 Marrid to Tomys Turl 1859

and no date of freedom because her freedom, as well as that of her first surviving child, derived not from Buck and Buddy McCaslin in the commissary but from a stranger in Washington, and no date of death and burial, not only because McCaslin kept no obituaries in his books, but because in this year 1883 she was still alive and would remain so to see a grandson by her last surviving child:

Amodeus McCaslin Beauchamp Son of tomys Turl @ Tennie Beauchamp 1859 dide 1859

then his uncle's hand entire, because his father was now a member of the cavalry command of that man whose name as a slave-dealer he could not even spell: and not even a page and not even a full line:

Dauter Tomes Turl and tenny 1862

and not even a line and not even a sex and no cause given though the boy could guess it because McCaslin was thirteen then and he remembered how there was not always enough to eat in more places than Vicksburg:

Child of tomes Turl and Tenny 1863

and the same hand again and this one lived, as though
Tennie's perseverance and the fading and diluted ghost
of old Carothers' ruthlessness had at last conquered even
starvation: and clearer, fuller, more carefully written
and spelled than the boy had yet seen it, as if the old
man, who should have been a woman to begin with,
trying to run what was left of the plantation in his
brother's absence in the intervals of cooking and caring
for himself and the fourteen-year-old orphan, had taken
as an omen for renewed hope the fact that this nameless inheritor of slaves was at least remaining alive long
enough to receive a name:

> *James Thucydus Beauchamp Son of Tomes Turl
> and Tenny Beauchamp Born 29th december 1864
> and both Well Wanted to call him Theophilus but
> Tride Amodeus McCaslin and Callina McCaslin
> and both dide so Disswaded Them Born at Two
> clock A,m, both Well*

but no more, nothing; it would be another two years
yet before the boy, almost a man now, would return
from the abortive trip into Tennessee with the still-
intact third of old Carothers' legacy to his Negro son
and his descendants, which as the three surviving children established at last one by one their apparent
intention of surviving, their white half-uncles had increased to a thousand dollars each, conditions permit-
ting, as they came of age, and completed the page
himself as far as it would even be completed when
that day was long passed beyond which a man born in
1864 (or 1867 either, when he himself saw light) could
have expected or himself hoped or even wanted to be
still alive; his own hand now, queerly enough resembling neither his father's nor his uncle's nor even

McCaslin's, but like that of his grandfather's save for the spelling:

> *Vanished sometime on night of his twenty-first birthday Dec 29 1885. Traced by Isaac McCaslin to Jackson Tenn. and there lost. His third of legacy $1000.00 returned to McCaslin Edmonds Trustee this day Jan 12 1886*

but not yet: that would be two years yet, and now his father's again, whose old commander was now quit of soldiering and slave-trading both; once more in the ledger and then not again, and more illegible than ever, almost indecipherable at all from the rheumatism which now crippled him, and almost completely innocent now even of any sort of spelling as well as punctuation, as if the four years during which he had followed the sword of the only man ever breathing who ever sold him a Negro, let alone beat him in a trade, had convinced him not only of the vanity of faith and hope, but of orthography too:

> *Miss sophonsiba b dtr t t @ t 1869*

but not of belief and will because it was there, written, as McCaslin had told him, with the left hand, but there in the ledger one time more and then not again, for the boy himself was a year old, and when Lucas was born six years later, his father and uncle had been dead inside the same twelve-months almost five years; his own hand again, who was there and saw it, 1886, she was just seventeen, two years younger than himself, and he was in the commissary when McCaslin entered out of the first of dusk and said, 'He wants to marry Fonsiba,' like that: and he looked past McCaslin and saw the man, the stranger, taller than McCaslin and wearing better clothes than McCaslin and most of the other white men the boy knew habitually wore, who entered the room like a white man and stood in it like a white man, as though he had let McCaslin precede him into it not because McCaslin's skin was white but simply because McCaslin lived there and knew the way, and who talked like a white man too, looking at him past McCaslin's shoulder rapidly and keenly once and then no more, without further interest, as a mature and contained white man not impatient but just pressed for time might have looked. 'Marry Fonsiba?' he cried. 'Marry Fonsiba?' and then no more either, just watching and listening while McCaslin and the Negro talked:

'To live in Arkansas, I believe you said.'

'Yes. I have property there. A farm.'

'Property? A farm? You own it?'

'Yes.'

'You don't say Sir, do you?'

'To my elders, yes.'

'I see. You are from the North.'

'Yes. Since a child.'

'Then your father was a slave.'

'Yes. Once.'

'Then how do you own a farm in Arkansas?'

'I have a grant. It was my father's. From the United States. For military service.'

'I see,' McCaslin said. 'The Yankee army.'

'The United States army,' the stranger said; and then himself again, crying it at McCaslin's back:

'Call aunt Tennie! I'll go get her! I'll—' But McCaslin was not even including him; the stranger did not even glance back toward his voice, the two of them speaking to one another again as if he were not even there:

'Since you seem to have it all settled,' McCaslin said,

'why have you bothered to consult my authority at all?'

'I don't,' the stranger said. 'I acknowledge your authority only so far as you admit your responsibilty toward her as a female member of the family of which you are the head. I don't ask your permission. I——'

'That will do!' McCaslin said. But the stranger did not falter. It was neither as if he were ignoring McCaslin nor as if he had failed to hear him. It was as though he were making, not at all an excuse and not exactly a justification, but simply a statement which the situation absolutely required and demanded should be made in McCaslin's hearing whether McCaslin listened to it or not. It was as if he were talking to himself, for himself to hear the words spoken aloud. They faced one another, not close yet at slightly less than foils' distance, erect, their voices not raised, not impactive, just succinct:

'—I inform you, notify you in advance as chief of her family. No man of honor could do less. Besides, you have, in your way, according to your lights and upbringing——'

'That's enough, I said,' McCaslin said. 'Be off this place by full dark. Go.' But for another moment the other did not move, contemplating McCaslin with that detached and heatless look, as if he were watching reflected in McCaslin's pupils the tiny image of the figure he was sustaining.

'Yes,' he said. 'After all, this is your house. And in your fashion you have. . . . But no matter. You are right. This is enough.' He turned back toward the door; he paused again but only for a second, already moving while he spoke: 'Be easy. I will be good to her.' Then he was gone.

'But how did she ever know him?' the boy cried. 'I

never even heard of him before! And Fonsiba, that's never been off this place except to go to church since she was born——'

'Ha,' McCaslin said. 'Even their parents don't know until too late how seventeen-year-old girls ever met the men who marry them too, if they are lucky.' And the next morning they were both gone, Fonsiba too. McCaslin never saw her again, nor did he, because the woman he found at last, five months later, was no one he had ever known. He carried a third of the three-thousand-dollar fund in gold in a money-belt, as when he had vainly traced Tennie's Jim into Tennessee a year ago. They—the man—had left an address of some sort with Tennie, and three months later a letter came, written by the man although McCaslin's wife, Alice, had taught Fonsiba to read and write too a little. But it bore a different postmark from the address the man had left with Tennie, and he travelled by rail as far as he could and then by contracted stage and then by a hired livery rig and then by rail again for a distance: an experienced traveller by now and an experienced blood-hound too, and a successful one this time because he would have to be; as the slow interminable empty muddy December miles crawled and crawled and night followed night in hotels, in roadside taverns of rough logs and containing little else but a bar, and in the cabins of strangers, and the hay of lonely barns, in none of which he dared undress because of his secret golden girdle like that of a disguised one of the Magi travelling incognito and not even hope to draw him, but only determination and desperation, he would tell himself: *I will have to find her. I will have to. We have already lost one of them. I will have to find her this time.* He did. Hunched in the slow and icy rain, on a spent hired horse splashed to the chest and higher, he saw it—a single log edifice with a clay chimney, which seemed in process of being flattened by the rain to a nameless and valueless rubble of dissolution in that roadless and even pathless waste of unfenced fallow and wilderness jungle—no barn, no stable, not so much as a hen-coop: just a log cabin built by hand and no clever hand either, a meagre pile of clumsily-cut firewood sufficient for about one day and not even a gaunt hound to come bellowing out from under the house when he rode up—a farm only in embryo, perhaps a good farm, maybe even a plantation someday, but not now, not for years yet and only then with labor, hard and enduring and unflagging work and sacrifice; he shoved open the crazy kitchen door in its awry frame and entered an icy gloom where not even a fire for cooking burned, and after another moment saw, crouched into the wall's angle behind a crude table, the coffee-colored face which he had known all his life but knew no more, the body which had been born within a hundred yards of the room that he was born in and in which some of his own blood ran, but which was now completely inheritor of generation after generation to whom an unannounced white man on a horse was a white man's hired Patroller wearing a pistol sometimes and a blacksnake whip always; he entered the next room, the only other room the cabin owned, and found, sitting in a rocking chair before the hearth, the man himself, reading—sitting there in the only chair in the house, before that miserable fire for which there was not wood sufficient to last twenty-four hours, in the same ministerial clothing in which he had entered the commissary five months ago and a pair of gold-framed spectacles which, when he looked up and then rose to his feet, the boy saw did not even contain lenses, reading a book in the midst of that desolation, that muddy waste, fenceless and even pathless and without even a walled shed for stock to stand beneath: and over all, permeant, clinging to the man's very clothing and exuding from his skin itself, that rank stink of baseless and imbecile delusion, that boundless rapacity and folly, of the carpet-bagger followers of victorious armies.

'Don't you see?' he cried. 'Don't you see? This whole land, the whole South, is cursed, and all of us who derive from it, whom it ever suckled, white and black both, lie under the curse? Granted that my people brought the curse onto the land: maybe for that reason their descendants alone can—not resist it, not combat it—maybe just endure and outlast it until the curse is lifted. Then your peoples' turn will come because we have forfeited ours. But not now. Not yet. Don't you see?'

The other stood now, the unfrayed garments still ministerial even if not quite so fine, the book closed upon one finger to keep the place, the lenseless spectacles held like a music master's wand in the other workless hand while the owner of it spoke his measured and sonorous imbecility of the boundless folly and the baseless hope: 'You're wrong. The curse you whites brought into this land has been lifted. It has been voided and discharged. We are seeing a new era, an era dedicated, as our founders intended it, to freedom, liberty and equality for all, to which this country will be the new Canaan——'

'Freedom from what? From work? Canaan?' He jerked his arm, comprehensive, almost violent: whereupon it all seemed to stand there about them, intact and complete and visible in the drafty, damp, heatless, Negro-stale Negro-rank sorry room—the empty fields without plow or seed to work them, fenceless against the stock which did not exist within or without the

walled stable which likewise was not there. 'What corner
of Canaan is this?'

'You are seeing it at a bad time. This is winter. No
man farms this time of year.'

'I see. And of course her need for food and clothing
will stand still while the land lies fallow.'

'I have a pension,' the other said. He said it as a man
might say *I have grace* or *I own a gold mine.* 'I have my
father's pension too. It will arrive on the first of the
month. What day is this?'

'The eleventh,' he said. 'Twenty days more. And until
then?'

'I have a few groceries in the house from my credit
account with the merchant in Midnight who banks my
pension check for me. I have executed to him a power
of attorney to handle it for me as a matter of mutual—'

'I see. And if the groceries don't last the twenty
days?'

'I still have one more hog.'

'Where?'

'Outside,' the other said. 'It is customary in this country to allow stock to range free during the winter for
food. It comes up from time to time. But no matter if it
doesn't; I can probably trace its footprints when the
need——'

'Yes!' he cried. 'Because no matter: you still have the
pension check. And the man in Midnight will cash it
and pay himself out of it for what you have already
eaten and if there is any left over, it is yours. And the
hog will be eaten by then or you still can't catch it, and
then what will you do?'

'It will be almost spring then,' the other said. 'I am
planning in the spring——'

'It will be January,' he said. 'And then February. And
then more than half of March—' and when he stopped

again in the kitchen she had not moved, she did not even seem to breathe or to be alive except her eyes watching him; when he took a step toward her it was still not movement because she could have retreated no further: only the tremendous, fathomless, ink-colored eyes in the narrow, thin, too thin, coffee-colored face watching him without alarm, without recognition, without hope. 'Fonsiba,' he said. 'Fonsiba. Are you all right?'

'I'm free,' she said. Midnight was a tavern, a livery stable, a big store (that would be where the pension check banked itself as a matter of mutual elimination of bother and fret, he thought) and a little one, a saloon and a blacksmith shop. But there was a bank there too. The president (the owner, for all practical purposes) of it was a translated Mississippian who had been one of Forrest's men too: and his body lightened of the golden belt for the first time since he left home eight days ago, with pencil and paper he multiplied three dollars by twelve months and divided it into one thousand dollars; it would stretch that way over almost twenty-eight years and for twenty-eight years at least she would not starve, the banker promising to send the three dollars himself by a trusty messenger on the fifteenth of each month and put it into her actual hand, and he returned home and that was all because in 1874 his father and his uncle were both dead and the old ledgers never again came down from the shelf above the desk to which his father had returned them for the last time that day in 1869. But he could have completed it:

Lucas Quintus Carothers McCaslin Beauchamp.
Last surviving son and child of Tomey's Terrel
and Tennie Beauchamp. March 17, 1874

except that there was no need: not *Lucius Quintus* @c @c @c, but *Lucas Quintus,* not refusing to be called

Lucius, because he simply eliminated that word from the name; not denying, declining the name itself, because he used three quarters of it; but simply taking the name and changing, altering it, making it no longer the white man's but his own, by himself composed, himself selfprogenitive and nominate, by himself ancestored, as, for all the old ledgers recorded to the contrary, old Carothers himself was

and that was all: 1874 the boy; 1888 the man, repudiated denied and free; 1895 and husband but no father, unwidowered but without a wife, and found long since that no man is ever free and probably could not bear it if he were; married then and living in Jefferson in the little new jerrybuilt bungalow which his wife's father had given them: and one morning Lucas stood suddenly in the doorway of the room where he was reading the Memphis paper and he looked at the paper's dateline and thought *It's his birthday. He's twenty-one today* and Lucas said: 'Whar's the rest of that money old Carothers left? I wants it. All of it.'

that was all: and McCaslin

'More men than that one Buck and Buddy to fumbleheed that truth so mazed for them that spoke it and so confused for them that heard yet still there was 1865:' and he

'But not enough. Not enough of even Father and Uncle Buddy to fumble-heed in even three generations not even three generations fathered by Grandfather not even if there had been nowhere beneath His sight any but Grandfather and so He would not even have needed to elect and choose. But He tried and I know what you will say. That having Himself created them He could have known no more of hope than He could have pride and grief, but He didn't hope He just waited because He had made them: not just because He had set them alive and in motion but because He had already worried with them so long: worried with them so long because He had seen how in individual cases they were capable of anything, any height or depth remembered in mazed incomprehension out of heaven where hell was created too, and so He must admit them or else admit his equal somewhere and so be no longer God and therefore must accept responsibility for what He Himself had done in order to live with Himself in His lonely and paramount heaven. And He probably knew it was vain but He had created them and knew them capable of all things because He had shaped them out of the primal Absolute which contained all and had watched them since in their individual exaltation and baseness, and they themselves not knowing why nor how nor even when: until at last He saw that they were all Grandfather all of them and that even from them the elected and chosen the best the very best He could expect (not hope mind: not hope) would be Bucks and Buddies and not even enough of them and in the third generation not even Bucks and Buddies but—' and McCaslin

'Ah:' and he

'Yes. If He could see Father and Uncle Buddy in Grandfather He must have seen me too. —an Isaac born into a later life than Abraham's and repudiating immolation: fatherless and therefore safe declining the altar because maybe this time the exasperated Hand might not supply the kid—' and McCaslin

'Escape:' and he

'All right. Escape.—Until one day He said what you told Fonsiba's husband that afternoon here in this room: *This will do. This is enough:* not in exasperation or rage or even just sick to death as you were sick that day: just *This is enough* and looked about for one last time, for one time more since He had created them, upon this land this South for which He had done so much with woods for game and streams for fish and deep rich soil for seed and lush springs to sprout it and long summers to mature it and serene falls to harvest it and short mild winters for men and animals, and saw no hope anywhere and looked beyond it where hope should have been, where to East North and West lay illimitable that whole hopeful continent dedicated as a refuge and sanctuary of liberty and freedom from what you called the old world's worthless evening, and saw the rich descendants of slavers, females of both sexes, to whom the black they shrieked of was another specimen another example like the Brazilian macaw brought home in a cage by a traveller, passing resolutions about horror and outrage in warm and air-proof halls: and the thundering cannonade of politicians earning votes and the medicine-shows of pulpiteers earning Chatauqua fees, to whom the outrage and the injustice were as much abstractions as Tariff or Silver or Immortality and who employed the very shackles of its servitude and the sorry rags of its regalia as they did the other beer and banners and mottoes, redfire and brimstone and sleight-of-hand and musical handsaws: and the whirling wheels which manufactured for a profit the pristine replacements of the shackles and shoddy garments as they wore out, and spun the cotton and made the gins which ginned it and the cars and ships which hauled it, and the men who ran the wheels for that profit and established and collected the taxes it was taxed with and the rates for hauling it and the commissions for selling it: and He could have repudiated them since they were his creation now and forever more throughout all their generations, until not only that old world from which He had rescued them but this new one too which He had revealed and led them to as a sanctuary and refuge were become the same worthless tideless rock cooling in the last crimson evening, except that out of all that empty sound and bootless fury one silence, among that loud and moiling all of them just one simple enough to believe that horror and outrage were first and last simply horror and outrage and crude enough to act upon that, illiterate and had no words for talking or perhaps was just busy and had no time to, one out of them all who did not bother Him with cajolery and adjuration then pleading then threat, and had not even bothered to inform Him in advance what he was about so that a lesser than He might have even missed the simple act of lifting the long ancestral musket down from the deerhorns above the door, whereupon He said *My name is Brown too* and the other *So is mine* and He *Then mine or yours can't be because I am against it* and the other *So am I* and He triumphantly *Then where are you going with that gun?* and the other told him in one sentence one word and He: amazed: Who knew neither hope nor pride nor grief *But your Association, your Committee, your Officers. Where are your Minutes, your Motions, your Parliamentary Procedures?* and the other *I ain't against them. They are all right I reckon for them that have the time. I am just against the weak because they are niggers being held in bondage by the strong just because they are white.* So He turned once more to this land which He still intended to save because He had done so much for it—' and McCaslin

'What?' and he

'—to these people He was still committed to because they were his creations—' and McCaslin

'Turned back to us? His face to us?' and he

'—whose wives and daughters at least made soups

and jellies for them when they were sick, and carried
the trays through the mud and the winter too into the
stinking cabins, and sat in the stinking cabins and kept
fires going until crises came and passed, but that was
not enough: and when they were very sick had them
carried into the big house itself into the company room
itself maybe and nursed them there, which the white
man would have done too for any other of his cattle
that was sick but at least the man who hired one from a
livery wouldn't have, and still that was not enough: so
that He said and not in grief either, Who had made
them and so could know no more of grief than He could
of pride or hope: *Apparently they can learn nothing
save through suffering, remember nothing save when
underlined in blood—*' and McCaslin

'Ashby on an afternoon's ride, to call on some remote
maiden cousins of his mother or maybe just acquaint-
ances of hers, comes by chance upon a minor engage-
ment of outposts and dismounts and with his crimson-
lined cloak for target leads a handful of troops he never
saw before against an entrenched position of back-
woods-trained riflemen. Lee's battle-order, wrapped
maybe about a handful of cigars and doubtless thrown
away when the last cigar was smoked, found by a Yankee Intelligence officer on the floor of a saloon behind
the Yankee lines after Lee had already divided his forces
before Sharpsburg. Jackson on the Plank Road, already
rolled up the flank which Hooker believed could not be
turned and, waiting only for night to pass to continue
the brutal and incessant slogging which would fling
that whole wing back into Hooker's lap where he sat
on a front gallery in Chancellorsville drinking rum
toddies and telegraphing Lincoln that he had defeated
Lee, is shot from among a whole covey of minor officers
and in the blind night by one of his own patrols, leaving

as next by seniority Stuart, that gallant man born apparently already horsed and sabred and already knowing all there was to know about war except the slogging and brutal stupidity of it: and that same Stuart off raiding Pennsylvania hen-roosts when Lee should have known of all of Meade just where Hancock was on Cemetery Ridge: and Longstreet too at Gettysburg and that same Longstreet shot out of saddle by his own men in the dark by mistake just as Jackson was. His face to us? His face to us?' and he

'How else have made them fight? Who else but Jacksons and Stuarts and Ashbys and Morgans and Forrests?—the farmers of the central and middle-west, holding land by the acre instead of the tens or maybe even the hundreds, farming it themselves and to no single crop of cotton or tobacco or cane, owning no slaves and needing and wanting none, and already looking toward the Pacific coast, not always as long as two generations there and having stopped where they did stop only through the fortuitous mischance that an ox died or a wagon-axle broke. And the New England mechanics who didn't even own land and measured all things by the weight of water and the cost of turning wheels, and the narrow fringe of traders and shipowners still looking backward across the Atlantic and attached to the continent only by their counting-houses. And those who should have had the alertness to see: the wildcat manipulators of mythical wilderness townsites; and the astuteness to rationalize: the bankers who held the mortgages on the land which the first were only waiting to abandon, and on the railroads and steamboats to carry them still further west, and on the factories and the wheels and the rented tenements those who ran them lived in; and the leisure and scope to comprehend and fear in time and even anticipate: the Boston-bred

(even when not born in Boston) spinster, descendants
of long lines of similarly-bred and likewise spinster
aunts and uncles whose hands knew no callus except
that of the indicting pen, to whom the wilderness itself
began at the top of tide and who looked, if at anything
other than Beacon Hill, only toward heaven—not to
mention all the loud rabble of the camp-followers of
pioneers: the bellowing of politicians, the mellifluous
choiring of self-styled men of God, the—' and McCaslin

'Here, here. Wait a minute:' And he

'Let me talk now. I'm trying to explain to the head
of my family something which I have got to do which
I don't quite understand myself, not in justification of
it but to explain it if I can. I could say I don't know
why I must do it but that I do know I have got to because I have got myself to have to live with for the rest
of my life and all I want is peace to do it in. But you
are the head of my family. More. I knew a long time
ago that I would never have to miss my father, even if
you are just finding out that you have missed your son
—the drawers of bills and the shavers of notes and the
schoolmasters and the self-ordained to teach and lead
and all that horde of the semi-literate with a white shirt
but no change for it, with one eye on themselves and
watching each other with the other one. Who else could
have made them fight: could have struck them so aghast
with fear and dread as to turn shoulder to shoulder and
face one way and even stop talking for a while and even
after two years of it keep them still so wrung with
terror that some among them would seriously propose
moving their very capital into a foreign country lest it
be ravaged and pillaged by a people whose entire white
male population would have little more than filled any
one of their larger cities: except Jackson in the Valley
and three separate armies trying to catch him and none

of them ever knowing whether they were just retreating from a battle or just running into one, and Stuart riding his whole command entirely around the biggest single armed force this continent ever saw in order to see what it looked like from behind, and Morgan leading a cavalry charge against a stranded man-of-war. Who else could have declared a war against a power with ten times the area and a hundred times the men and a thousand times the resources, except men who could believe that all necessary to conduct a successful war was not acumen nor shrewdness nor politics nor diplomacy nor money nor even integrity and simple arithmetic, but just love of land and courage——'

'And an unblemished and gallant ancestry and the ability to ride a horse,' McCaslin said. 'Don't leave that out.' It was evening now, the tranquil sunset of October mazy with windless woodsmoke. The cotton was long since picked and ginned, and all day now the wagons loaded with gathered corn moved between field and crib, processional across the enduring land. 'Well, maybe that's what He wanted. At least, that's what He got.' This time there was no yellowed procession of fading and harmless ledger-pages. This was chronicled in a harsher book, and McCaslin, fourteen and fifteen and sixteen, had seen it and the boy himself had inherited it as Noah's grandchildren had inherited the Flood although they had not been there to see the deluge: that dark corrupt and bloody time while three separate peoples had tried to adjust not only to one another but to the new land which they had created and inherited too and must live in for the reason that those who had lost it were no less free to quit it than those who had gained it were:—those upon whom freedom and equality had been dumped overnight and without warning or preparation or any training in how to employ it or even

just endure it and who misused it, not as children would
nor yet because they had been so long in bondage and
then so suddenly freed, but misused it as human beings
always misuse freedom, so that he thought *Apparently
there is a wisdom beyond even that learned through
suffering necessary for a man to distinguish between
liberty and license;* those who had fought for four years
and lost to preserve a condition under which that
franchisement was anomaly and paradox, not because
they were opposed to freedom as freedom but for the
old reasons for which man (not the generals and politicians but man) has always fought and died in wars: to
preserve a status quo or to establish a better future one
to endure for his children; and lastly, as if that were
not enough for bitterness and hatred and fear, that third
race even more alien to the people whom they resembled
in pigment and in whom even the same blood ran, than
to the people whom they did not,—that race threefold
in one and alien even among themselves save for a
single fierce will for rapine and pillage, composed of
the sons of middleaged Quartermaster lieutenants and
Army sutlers and contractors in military blankets and
shoes and transport mules, who followed the battles
they themselves had not fought and inherited the con-
quest they themselves had not helped to gain, sanc-
tioned and protected even if not blessed, and left their
bones and in another generation would be engaged in a
fierce economic competition of small sloven farms with
the black men they were supposed to have freed and
the white descendants of fathers who had owned no
slaves anyway whom they were supposed to have dis-
inherited, and in the third generation would be back
once more in the little lost county seats as barbers and
garage mechanics and deputy sheriffs and mill- and gin-
hands and power-plant firemen, leading, first in mufti

then later in an actual formalized regalia of hooded sheets and passwords and fiery Christian symbols, lynching mobs against the race their ancestors had come to save: and of all that other nameless horde of speculators in human misery, manipulators of money and politics and land, who follow catastrophe and are their own protection as grasshoppers are and need no blessing and sweat no plow or axe-helve and batten and vanish and leave no bones, just as they derived apparently from no ancestry, no mortal flesh, no act even of passion or even of lust: and the Jew who came without protection too, since after two thousand years he had got out of the habit of being or needing it, and solitary, without even the solidarity of the locusts, and in this a sort of courage since he had come thinking not in terms of simple pillage but in terms of his great-grandchildren, seeking yet some place to establish them to endure even though forever alien: and unblessed: a pariah about the face of the Western earth which twenty centuries later was still taking revenge on him for the fairy tale with which he had conquered it. McCaslin had actually seen it, and the boy even at almost eighty would never be able to distinguish certainly between what he had seen and what had been told him: a lightless and gutted and empty land where women crouched with the huddled children behind locked doors and men armed in sheets and masks rode the silent roads and the bodies of white and black both, victims not so much of hate as of desperation and despair, swung from lonely limbs: and men shot dead in polling-booths with the still wet pen in one hand and the unblotted ballot in the other: and a United States marshal in Jefferson who signed his official papers with a crude cross, an ex-slave called Sickymo, not at all because his ex-owner was a doctor and apothecary but because, still a slave, he would steal his mas-

ter's grain alcohol and dilute it with water and peddle
it in pint bottles from a cache beneath the roots of a
big sycamore tree behind the drug store, who had attained his high office because his half-white sister was
the concubine of the Federal A.P.M.: and this time Mc-
Caslin did not even say Look but merely lifted one hand,
not even pointing, not even specifically toward the shelf
of ledgers but toward the desk, toward the corner where
it sat beside the scuffed patch on the floor where two
decades of heavy shoes had stood while the white man
at the desk added and multiplied and subtracted. And
again he did not need to look because he had seen this
himself and, twenty-three years after the Surrender and
twenty-four after the Proclamation, was still watching
it: the ledgers, new ones now and filled rapidly, succeeding one another rapidly and containing more names
than old Carothers or even his father and Uncle Buddy
had ever dreamed of; new names and new faces to go
with them, among which the old names and faces that
even his father and uncle would have recognized, were
lost, vanished—Tomey's Terrel dead, and even the
tragic and miscast Percival Brownlee, who couldn't
keep books and couldn't farm either, found his true
niche at last, reappeared in 1862 during the boy's
father's absence and had apparently been living on the
plantation for at least a month before his uncle found
out about it, conducting impromptu revival meetings
among Negroes, preaching and leading the singing also
in his high sweet true soprano voice and disappeared
again on foot and at top speed, not behind but ahead of
a body of raiding Federal horse and reappeared for the
third and last time in the entourage of a travelling Army
paymaster, the two of them passing through Jefferson
in a surrey at the exact moment when the boy's father
(it was 1866) also happened to be crossing the Square,

the surrey and its occupants traversing rapidly that quiet and bucolic scene and even in that fleeting moment, and to others beside the boy's father, giving an illusion of flight and illicit holiday like a man on an excursion during his wife's absence with his wife's personal maid, until Brownlee glanced up and saw his late co-master and gave him one defiant female glance and then broke again, leaped from the surrey and disappeared this time for good, and it was only by chance that McCaslin, twenty years later, heard of him again, an old man now and quite fat, as the well-to-do proprietor of a select New Orleans brothel; and Tennie's Jim gone, nobody knew where, and Fonsiba in Arkansas with her three dollars each month and the scholar-husband with his lenseless spectacles and frock coat and his plans for the spring; and only Lucas was left, the baby, the last save himself of old Carothers' doomed and fatal blood which in the male derivation seemed to destroy all it touched, and even he was repudiating and at least hoping to escape it;—Lucas, the boy of fourteen whose name would not even appear for six years yet among those rapid pages in the bindings new and dustless too since McCaslin lifted them down daily now to write into them the continuation of that record which two hundred years had not been enough to complete, and another hundred would not be enough to discharge; that chronicle which was a whole land in miniature, which multiplied and compounded was the entire South, twenty-three years after surrender and twenty-four from emancipation—that slow trickle of molasses and meal and meat, of shoes and straw hats and overalls, of plowlines and collars and heel-bolts and buckheads and clevises, which returned each fall as cotton—the two threads frail as truth and impalpable as equators yet cable-strong to bind for life them who made the cotton to the land their sweat fell on: and he

'Yes. Binding them for a while yet, a little while yet. Through and beyond that life and maybe through and beyond the life of that life's sons and maybe even through and beyond that of the sons of those sons. But not always, because they will endure. They will outlast us because they are—' it was not a pause, barely a falter even, possibly appreciable only to himself, as if he couldn't speak even to McCaslin, even to explain his repudiation, that which to him too, even in the act of escaping (and maybe this was the reality and the truth of his need to escape), was heresy: so that even in escaping he was taking with him more of that evil and unregenerate old man who could summon, because she was his property, a human being because she was old enough and female, to his widower's house and get a child on her and then dismiss her because she was of an inferior race, and then bequeath a thousand dollars to the infant because he would be dead then and wouldn't have to pay it, than even he had feared. 'Yes. He didn't want to. He had to. Because they will endure. They are better than we are. Stronger than we are. Their vices are vices aped from white men or that white men and bondage have taught them: improvidence and intemperance and evasion—not laziness: evasion: of what white men had set them to, not for their aggrandizement or even comfort but his own—' and McCaslin

'All right. Go on: Promiscuity. Violence. Instability and lack of control. Inability to distinguish between mine and thine—' and he

'How distinguish, when for two hundred years mine did not even exist for them?' and McCaslin

'All right. Go on. And their virtues—' and he

'Yes. Their own. Endurance—' and McCaslin

'So have mules:' and he

'—and pity and tolerance and forbearance and fidelity
and love of children—' and McCaslin

'So have dogs:' and he

'—whether their own or not or black or not. And
more: what they got not only not from white people but
not even despite white people because they had it already from the old free fathers a longer time free than
us because we have never been free—' and it was in
McCaslin's eyes too, he had only to look at McCaslin's
eyes and it was there, that summer twilight seven years
ago, almost a week after they had returned from the
camp before he discovered that Sam Fathers had told
McCaslin: an old bear, fierce and ruthless not just to
stay alive but ruthless with the fierce pride of liberty
and freedom, jealous and proud enough of liberty and
freedom to see it threatened not with fear nor even
alarm but almost with joy, seeming deliberately to put
it into jeopardy in order to savor it and keep his old
strong bones and flesh supple and quick to defend and
preserve it; an old man, son of a Negro slave and an
Indian king, inheritor on the one hand of the long
chronicle of a people who had learned humility through
suffering and learned pride through the endurance
which survived the suffering, and on the other side the
chronicle of a people even longer in the land than the
first, yet who now existed there only in the solitary
brotherhood of an old and childless Negro's alien blood
and the wild and invincible spirit of an old bear; a boy
who wished to learn humility and pride in order to become skillful and worthy in the woods but found himself becoming so skillful so fast that he feared he would
never become worthy, because he had not learned humility and pride though he had tried, until one day an
old man, who could not have defined either, led him as
though by the hand to where an old bear and a little

mongrel dog showed him that, by possessing one thing other, he would possess them both; and a little dog, nameless and mongrel and many-fathered, grown yet weighing less than six pounds, who couldn't be dangerous because there was nothing anywhere much smaller, not fierce because that would have been called just noise, not humble because it was already too near the ground to genuflect, and not proud because it would not have been close enough for anyone to discern what was casting that shadow, and which didn't even know it was not going to heaven since they had already decided it had no immortal soul, so that all it could be was brave, even though they would probably call that too just noise. 'And you didn't shoot,' McCaslin said. 'How close were you?'

'I don't know,' he said. 'There was a big wood tick just inside his off hind leg. I saw that. But I didn't have the gun then.'

'But you didn't shoot when you had the gun,' McCaslin said. 'Why?' But McCaslin didn't wait, rising and crossing the room, across the pelt of the bear he had killed two years ago and the bigger one McCaslin had killed before he was born, to the bookcase beneath the mounted head of his first buck, and returned with the book and sat down again and opened it. 'Listen,' he said. He read the five stanzas aloud and closed the book on his finger and looked up. 'All right,' he said. 'Listen,' and read again, but only one stanza this time and closed the book and laid it on the table. 'She cannot fade, though thou hast not thy bliss,' McCaslin said: 'Forever wilt thou love, and she be fair.'

'He's talking about a girl,' he said.

'He had to talk about something,' McCaslin said. Then he said, 'He was talking about truth. Truth is one. It doesn't change. It covers all things which touch the

*heart—honor and pride and pity and justice and cour-
age and love. Do you see now?' He didn't know. Somehow it had seemed simpler than that, simpler than somebody talking in a book about a young man and a girl he
would never need to grieve over because he could never
approach any nearer and would never have to get any
further away. He had heard about an old bear and
finally got big enough to hunt it and he hunted it four
years and at last met it with a gun in his hands and he
didn't shoot. Because a little dog—But he could have
shot long before the fyce covered the twenty yards to
where the bear waited, and Sam Fathers could have
shot at any time during the interminable minute while
Old Ben stood on his hind legs over them. . . . He
ceased. McCaslin watched him, still speaking, the voice,
the words as quiet as the twilight itself was: 'Courage
and honor and pride, and pity and love of justice and
of liberty. They all touch the heart, and what the heart
holds to becomes truth, as far as we know truth. Do you
see now?'*

and he could still hear them, intact in this twilight as
in that one seven years ago, no louder still because they
did not need to be because they would endure: and he
had only to look at McCaslin's eyes beyond the thin
and bitter smiling, the faint lip-lift which would have
had to be called smiling;—his kinsman, his father almost, who had been born too late into the old time and
too soon for the new, the two of them juxtaposed and
alien now to each other against their ravaged patrimony, the dark and ravaged fatherland still prone and
panting from its etherless operation:

'Habet then.—So this land is, indubitably, of and by
itself cursed:' and he

'Cursed:' and again McCaslin merely lifted one hand,
not even speaking and not even toward the ledgers: so

that, as the stereopticon condenses into one instantaneous field the myriad minutiae of its scope, so did that slight and rapid gesture establish in the small cramped and cluttered twilit room not only the ledgers but the whole plantation in its mazed and intricate entirety—the land, the fields and what they represented in terms of cotton ginned and sold, the men and women whom they fed and clothed and even paid a little cash money at Christmas-time in return for the labor which planted and raised and picked and ginned the cotton, the machinery and mules and gear with which they raised it and their cost and upkeep and replacement—that whole edifice intricate and complex and founded upon injustice and erected by ruthless rapacity and carried on even yet with at times downright savagery not only to the human beings but the valuable animals too, yet solvent and efficient and, more than that: not only still intact but enlarged, increased; brought still intact by McCaslin, himself little more than a child then, through and out of the debacle and chaos of twenty years ago where hardly one in ten survived, and enlarged and increased and would continue so, solvent and efficient and intact and still increasing so long as McCaslin and his McCaslin successors lasted, even though their surnames might not even be Edmonds then: and he

'Habet too. Because that's it: not the land, but us. Not only the blood, but the name too; not only its color but its designation: Edmonds, white, but, a female line, could have no other but the name his father bore; Beauchamp, the elder line and the male one, but, black, could have had any name he liked and no man would have cared, except the name his father bore who had no name—' and McCaslin

'And since I know too what you know I will say now, once more let me say it: And one other, and in the third generation too, and the male, the eldest, the direct and sole and white and still McCaslin even, father to son to son—' and he

'I am free:' and this time McCaslin did not even gesture, no inference of fading pages, no postulation of the stereoptic whole, but the frail and iron thread strong as truth and impervious as evil and longer than life itself and reaching beyond record and patrimony both to join him with the lusts and passions, the hopes and dreams and griefs, of bones whose names while still fleshed and capable even old Carothers' grandfather had never heard: and he:

'And of that too:' and McCaslin

'Chosen, I suppose (I will concede it) out of all your time by Him, as you say Buck and Buddy were from theirs. And it took Him a bear and an old man and four years just for you. And it took you fourteen years to reach that point and about that many, maybe more, for Old Ben, and more than seventy for Sam Fathers. And you are just one. How long then? How long?' and he

'It will be long. I have never said otherwise. But it will be all right because they will endure—' and McCaslin

'And anyway, you will be free.—No, not now nor ever, we from them nor they from us. So I repudiate too. I would deny even if I knew it were true. I would have to. Even you can see that I could do no else. I am what I am; I will be always what I was born and have always been. And more than me. More than me, just as there were more than Buck and Buddy in what you called His first plan which failed:' and he

'And more than me:' and McCaslin

'No. Not even you. Because mark. You said how on that instant when Ikkemotubbe realized that he could sell the land to Grandfather, it ceased forever to have been his. All right; go on: Then it belonged to Sam Fathers, old Ikkemotubbe's son. And who inherited from Sam Fathers, if not you? co-heir perhaps with Boon, if not of his life maybe, at least of his quitting it?' and he

'Yes. Sam Fathers set me free.'

and Isaac McCaslin, not yet Uncle Ike, a long time yet before he would be uncle to half a county and still father to none, living in one small cramped fireless rented room in a Jefferson boardinghouse where petit juries were domiciled during court terms and itinerant horse- and mule-traders stayed, with his kit of brand-new carpenter's tools and the shotgun McCaslin had given him with his name engraved in silver and old General Compson's compass (and, when the General died, his silver-mounted horn too) and the iron cot and mattress and the blankets which he would take each fall into the woods for more than sixty years and the bright tin coffee-pot

there had been a legacy, from his Uncle Hubert Beauchamp, his godfather, that bluff burly roaring childlike man from whom Uncle Buddy had won Tomey's Terrel's wife Tennie in the poker-game in 1859—'possible strait against three Treys in sigt Not called'—; no pale sentence or paragraph scrawled in cringing fear of death by a weak and trembling hand as a last desperate sop flung backward at retribution, but a Legacy, a Thing, possessing weight to the hand and bulk to the eye and even audible: a silver cup filled with gold pieces and wrapped in burlap and sealed with his godfather's ring in the hot wax, which (intact still) even before his Uncle Hubert's death and long before his own majority, when it would be his, had become not only a legend but one of the family lares. After his father's and his

Uncle Hubert's sister's marriage they moved back into the big house, the tremendous cavern which old Carothers had started and never finished, cleared the remaining Negroes out of it and with his mother's dowry completed it, at least the rest of the windows and doors and moved into it, all of them save Uncle Buddy who declined to leave the cabin he and his twin had built, the move being the bride's notion and more than just a notion, and none ever to know if she really wanted to live in the big house or if she knew beforehand that Uncle Buddy would refuse to move: and two weeks after his birth in 1867, the first time he and his mother came down stairs one night, and the silver cup sitting on the cleared dining-room table beneath the bright lamp, and while his mother and his father and McCaslin and Tennie (his nurse: carrying him)—all of them again but Uncle Buddy—watched, his Uncle Hubert rang one by one into the cup the bright and glinting mintage and wrapped it into the burlap envelope and heated the wax and sealed it and carried it back home with him where he lived alone now without even his sister either to hold him down as McCaslin said or to try to raise him up as Uncle Buddy said, and (dark times then in Mississippi) Uncle Buddy said most of the niggers gone and the ones that didn't go even Hub Beauchamp could not have wanted: but the dogs remained and Uncle Buddy said Beauchamp fiddled while Nero fox-hunted

they would go and see it there; at last his mother would prevail and they would depart in the surrey, once more all save Uncle Buddy and McCaslin to keep Uncle Buddy company, until one winter Uncle Buddy began to fail and from then on it was himself, beginning to remember now, and his mother and Tennie and Tomey's Terrel to drive: the twenty-two miles into the

next county, the twin gateposts on one of which Mc-
Caslin could remember the half-grown boy blowing a
fox-horn at breakfast, dinner, and supper-time and
jumping down to open to any passer who happened to
hear it, but where there were no gates at all now, the
shabby and overgrown entrance to what his mother
still insisted that people call Warwick because her
brother was, if truth but triumphed and justice but prevailed, the rightful earl of it, the paintless house which
outwardly did not change but which on the inside
seemed each time larger because he was too little to
realize then that there was less and less in it of the fine
furnishings, the rosewood and mahogany and walnut,
which for him had never existed anywhere anyway save
in his mother's tearful lamentations, and the occasional
piece small enough to be roped somehow onto the rear
or the top of the carriage on their return (And he remembered this, he had seen it: an instant, a flash, his
mother's soprano 'Even my dress! Even my dress!' loud
and outraged in the barren unswept hall; a face young
and female and even lighter in color than Tomey's Terrel's for an instant in a closing door; a swirl, a glimpse
of the silk gown and the flick and glint of an ear-ring:
an apparition rapid and tawdry and illicit, yet somehow
even to the child, the infant still almost, breathless and
exciting and evocative: as though, like two limpid and
pellucid streams meeting, the child which he still was
had made serene and absolute and perfect rapport and
contact through that glimpsed nameless illicit hybrid
female flesh with the boy which had existed at that
stage of inviolable and immortal adolescence in his
uncle for almost sixty years; the dress, the face, the ear-
rings gone in that same aghast flash and his uncle's
voice: 'She's my cook! She's my new cook! I had to
have a cook, didn't I?' then the uncle himself, the face

alarmed and aghast too yet still innocently and somehow even indomitably of a boy, they retreating in their
turn now, back to the front gallery, and his uncle again,
pained and still amazed, in a sort of desperate re-
surgence if not of courage at least of self-assertion:
'They're free now; They're folks too just like we are!'
and his mother: 'That's why! That's why! My mother's
house! Defiled! Defiled!' and his uncle: 'Damn it, Sibbey, at least give her time to pack her grip:' then over,
finished, the loud uproar and all, himself and Tennie
and he remembered Tennie's inscrutable face at the
broken shutterless window of the bare room which had
once been the parlor while they watched, hurrying
down the lane at a stumbling trot, the routed com-
pounder of his uncle's uxory: the back, the nameless
face which he had seen only for a moment, the once-
hooped dress ballooning and flapping below a man's
overcoat, the worn heavy carpet-bag jouncing and banging against her knee, routed and in retreat true enough
and in the empty lane, solitary, young-looking, and forlorn, yet withal still exciting and evocative and wearing still the silken banner captured inside the very citadel of respectability, and unforgettable.)

the cup, the sealed inscrutable burlap, sitting on the
shelf in the locked closet, Uncle Hubert unlocking the
door and lifting it down and passing it from hand to
hand: his mother, his father, McCaslin and even Tennie, insisting that each take it in turn and heft it for
weight and shake it again to prove the sound, Uncle
Hubert himself standing spraddled before the cold unswept hearth in which the very bricks themselves were
crumbling into a litter of soot and dust and mortar and
the droppings of chimney-sweeps, still roaring and still
innocent and still indomitable: and for a long time he
believed nobody but himself had noticed that his uncle

now put the cup only into his hands, unlocked the door
and lifted it down and put it into his hands and stood
over him until he had shaken it obediently until it
sounded then took it from him and locked it back into
the closet before anyone else could have offered to
touch it, and even later, when competent not only to
remember but to rationalize, he could not say what it
was or even if it had been anything because the parcel
was still heavy and still rattled, not even when, Uncle
Buddy dead and his father, at last and after almost
seventy-five years in bed after the sun rose, said: 'Go
get that damn cup. Bring that damn Hub Beauchamp
too if you have to:' because it still rattled though his
uncle no longer put it even into his hands now but
carried it himself from one to the other, his mother,
McCaslin, Tennie, shaking it before each in turn, saying: 'Hear it? Hear it?' his face still innocent, not quite
baffled but only amazed and not very amazed and still
indomitable:

and, his father and Uncle Buddy both gone now, one
day without reason or any warning the almost completely empty house in which his uncle and Tennie's
ancient and quarrelsome great-grandfather (who
claimed to have seen Lafayette and McCaslin said in
another ten years would be remembering God) lived,
cooked and slept in one single room, burst into peaceful
conflagration, a tranquil instantaneous sourceless una-
nimity of combustion, walls floors and roof: at sunup
it stood where his uncle's father had built it sixty years
ago, at sundown the four blackened and smokeless
chimneys rose from a light white powder of ashes and
a few charred ends of planks which did not even appear
to have been very hot: and out of the last of evening,
the last one of the twenty-two miles, on the old white
mare which was the last of that stable which McCaslin

remembered, the two old men riding double up to the sister's door, the one wearing his fox-horn on its braided deerhide thong and the other carrying the burlap parcel wrapped in a shirt, the tawny wax-daubed shapeless lump sitting again and on an almost identical shelf and his uncle holding the half-opened door now, his hand not only on the knob but one foot against it and the key waiting in the other hand, the face urgent and still not baffled but still and even indomitably not very amazed and himself standing in the half-opened door looking quietly up at the burlap shape, become almost three times its original height and a good half less than its original thickness, and turning away, and he would remember not his mother's look this time nor yet Tennie's inscrutable expression but McCaslin's dark and aquiline face grave insufferable and bemused:

then one night they waked him and fetched him still half-asleep into the lamp light, the smell of medicine which was familiar by now in that room and the smell of something else which he had not smelled before and knew at once and would never forget, the pillow, the worn and ravaged face from which looked out still the boy innocent and immortal and amazed and urgent, looking at him and trying to tell him until McCaslin moved and leaned over the bed and drew from the top of the night shirt the big iron key on the greasy cord which suspended it, the eyes saying Yes Yes Yes now, and cut the cord and unlocked the closet and brought the parcel to the bed, the eyes still trying to tell him even when he took the parcel so that was still not it, the hands still clinging to the parcel even while relinquishing it, the eyes more urgent than ever trying to tell him but they never did; and he was ten and his mother was dead too and McCaslin said, 'You are almost half-way now. You might as well open it:' and he: 'No. He said twenty-one:' and he was twenty-one and McCaslin shifted the bright lamp to the center of the cleared dining-room table and set the parcel beside it and laid his open knife beside the parcel and stood back with that expression of old grave intolerant and repudiating and he lifted it, the burlap lump which fifteen years ago had changed its shape completely overnight, which shaken gave forth a thin weightless not-quite-musical curiously muffled clatter, the bright knife-blade hunting amid the mazed intricacy of string, the knobby gouts of wax bearing his uncle's Beauchamp seal rattling onto the table's polished top and, standing amid the collapse of burlap folds, the unstained tin coffee-pot still brand new, the handful of copper coins and now he knew what had given them the muffled sound: a collection of minutely folded scraps of paper sufficient almost for a rat's nest, of good linen bond, of the crude ruled paper such as Negroes use, of raggedly-torn ledger-pages and the margins of newspapers and once the paper label from a new pair of overalls, all dated and all signed, beginning with the first one not six months after they had watched him seal the silver cup into the burlap on this same table in this same room by the light even of this same lamp almost twenty-one years ago:

I owe my Nephew Isaac Beauchamp McCaslin five (5) pieces Gold which I,O.U constitues My note of hand with Interest at 5 percent.

  Hubert Fitz-Hubert Beauchamp
at Warwick 27 Nov 1867

and he: 'Anyway he called it Warwick:' once at least, even if no more. But there was more:

Isaac 24 Dec 1867 I.O.U. 2 pieces Gold H.Fh.B. I.O.U. Isaac 1 piece Gold 1 Jan 1868 H.Fh.B.

then five again then three then one then one then a
long time and what dream, what dreamed splendid re-
coup, not of any injury or betrayal of trust because it
had been merely a loan: nay, a partnership:

> I.O.U. Beauchamp McCaslin or his heirs twenty-
> five (25) pieces Gold This & All preceeding con-
> stituting My notes of hand at twenty (20) per-
> centum compounded annually. This date of 19th
> January 1873
>
> Beauchamp

no location save that in time and signed by the single
not name but word as the old proud earl himself might
have scrawled Nevile: and that made forty-three and
he could not remember himself of course but the legend
had it at fifty, which balanced: one: then one: then
one: then one and then the last three and then the last
chit, dated after he came to live in the house with them
and written in the shaky hand not of a beaten old man
because he had never been beaten to know it but of a
tired old man maybe and even at that tired only on the
outside and still indomitable, the simplicity of the last
one the simplicity not of resignation but merely of
amazement, like a simple comment or remark, and not
very much of that:

> One silver cup. Hubert Beauchamp

and McCaslin: 'So you have plenty of coppers anyway.
But they are still not old enough yet to be either rarities
or heirlooms. So you will have to take the money:' except that he didn't hear McCaslin, standing quietly beside the table and looking peacefully at the coffee-pot
and the pot sitting one night later on the mantel above
what was not even a fireplace in the little cramped ice-
like room in Jefferson as McCaslin tossed the folded

banknotes onto the bed and, still standing (there was nowhere to sit save on the bed) did not even remove his hat and overcoat: and he

'As a loan. From you. This one:' and McCaslin

'You can't. I have no money that I can lend to you. And you will have to go to the bank and get it next month because I won't bring it to you:' and he could not hear McCaslin now either, looking peacefully at McCaslin, his kinsman, his father almost yet no kin now as, at the last, even fathers and sons are no kin: and he

'It's seventeen miles, horseback and in the cold. We could both sleep here:' and McCaslin

'Why should I sleep here in my house when you won't sleep yonder in yours?' and gone, and he looking at the bright rustless unstained tin and thinking, and not for the first time, how much it takes to compound a man (Isaac McCaslin for instance) and of the devious intricate choosing yet unerring path that man's (Isaac McCaslin's for instance) spirit takes among all that mass to make him at last what he is to be, not only to the astonishment of them (the ones who sired the McCaslin who sired his father and Uncle Buddy and their sister, and the ones who sired the Beauchamp who sired his Uncle Hubert and his Uncle Hubert's sister) who believed they had shaped him, but to Isaac McCaslin too

as a loan and used it though he would not have had to: Major de Spain offered him a room in his house as long as he wanted it and asked nor would ever ask any question, and old General Compson more than that, to take him into his own room, to sleep in half of his own bed and more than Major de Spain because he told him baldly why: 'You sleep with me and before this winter is out, I'll know the reason. You'll tell me. Because I don't believe you just quit. It looks like you just quit but I have watched you in the woods too much and I don't believe you just quit even if it does look damn like it:' using it as a loan, paid his board and rent for a month and bought the tools, not simply because he was good with his hands because he had intended to use his hands and it could have been with horses, and not in mere static and hopeful emulation of the Nazarene, as the young gambler buys a spotted shirt because the old gambler won in one yesterday, but (without the arrogance of false humility and without the false humbleness of pride, who intended to earn his bread, didn't especially want to earn it but had to earn it and for more than just bread) because if the Nazarene had found carpentering good for the life and ends He had assumed and elected to serve, it would be all right too for Isaac McCaslin even though Isaac McCaslin's ends, although simple enough in their apparent motivation, were and would be always incomprehensible to him, and his life, invincible enough in its needs, if he could have helped himself, not being the Nazarene, he would not have chosen it: and paid it back. He had forgotten the thirty dollars which McCaslin put into the bank in his name each month, fetched it in to him and flung it onto the bed that first one time but no more; he had a partner now or rather he was the partner: a blasphemous profane clever old dipsomaniac who had built blockade-runners in Charleston in '62 and '63 and had been a ship's carpenter since and appeared in Jefferson two years ago, nobody knew from where nor why, and spent a good part of his time since recovering from delirium tremens in the jail; they had put a new roof on the stable of the bank's president and (the old man in jail again still celebrating that job) he went to the bank to collect for it and the president said, 'I should borrow from you instead of paying you:' and it had been seven months now and he remembered for the first time, two-hundred-and-ten dollars, and this was the first job of any size and when he left the bank the account stood at two-twenty, two-forty to balance, only twenty dollars more to go, then it did balance though by then the total had increased to three hundred and thirty and he said, 'I will transfer it now:' and the president said, 'I can't do that. McCaslin told me not to. Haven't you got another initial you could use and open another account?' but that was all right, the coins the silver and the bills as they accumulated knotted into a handkerchief and the coffee-pot wrapped in an old shirt as when Tennie's great-grandfather had fetched it from Warwick eighteen years ago, in the bottom of the iron-bound trunk which old Carothers had brought from Carolina and his landlady said, 'Not even a lock! And you don't even lock your door, not even when you leave!' and himself looking at her as peacefully as he had looked at McCaslin that first night in this same room, no kin to him at all yet more than kin as those who serve you even for pay are your kin and those who injure you are more than brother or wife

and he had the wife now; got the old man out of jail and fetched him to the rented room and sobered him by superior strength, did not even remove his own shoes for twenty-four hours, got him up and got food into him and they built the barn this time from the ground up and he married her: an only child, a small girl yet curiously bigger than she seemed at first, solider perhaps, with dark eyes and a passionate heart-shaped face, who had time even on that farm to watch most of the day while he sawed timbers to the old man's measurements: and she: 'Papa told me about you. That farm is really yours, isn't it?' and he

'And McCaslin's:' and she

'Was there a will leaving half of it to him?' and he

'There didn't need to be a will. His grandmother was my father's sister. We were the same as brothers:' and she

'You are the same as second cousins and that's all you ever will be. But I don't suppose it matters:' and they were married, they were married and it was the new country, his heritage too as it was the heritage of all, out of the earth, beyond the earth yet of the earth because his too was of the earth's long chronicle, his too because each must share with another in order to come into it, and in the sharing they become one: for that while, one: for that little while at least, one: indivisible, that while at least irrevocable and unrecoverable, living in a rented room still but for just a little while and that room wall-less and topless and floorless in glory for him to leave each morning and return to at night; her father already owned the lot in town and furnished the material and he and his partner would build it, her dowry from one: her wedding-present from three, she not to know it until the bungalow was finished and ready to be moved into and he never know who told her, not her father and not his partner and not even in drink though for a while he believed that, himself coming home from work and just time to wash and rest a moment before going down to supper, entering no rented cubicle since it would still partake of glory even after they would have grown old and lost it: and he saw her face then, just before she spoke: 'Sit down:' the two of them sitting on the bed's edge, not even touching yet, her face strained and terrible, her voice a passionate and expiring whisper of immeasurable promise: 'I love you. You know I love you. When are we going to move?' and he

'I didn't—I didn't know—Who told you—' the hot

fierce palm clapped over his mouth, crushing his lips
into his teeth, the fierce curve of fingers digging into his
cheek and only the palm slacked off enough for him to
answer:

'The farm. Our farm. Your farm:' and he

'I——' then the hand again, finger and palm, the
whole enveloping weight of her although she still was
not touching him save the hand, the voice: 'No! No!'
and the fingers themselves seeming to follow through
the cheek the impulse to speech as it died in his mouth,
then the whisper, the breath again, of love and of incredible promise, the palm slackening again to let him
answer:

'When?' and he

'I——' then she was gone, the hand too, standing,
her back to him and her head bent, the voice so calm
now that for an instant it seemed no voice of hers that
he ever remembered: 'Stand up and turn your back and
shut your eyes:' and repeated before he understood and
stood himself with his eyes shut and heard the bell ring
for supper below stairs, and the calm voice again: 'Lock
the door:' and he did so and leaned his forehead against
the cold wood, his eyes closed, hearing his heart and
the sound he had begun to hear before he moved until
it ceased and the bell rang again below stairs and he
knew it was for them this time, and he heard the bed
and turned and he had never seen her naked before, he
had asked her to once, and why: that he wanted to see
her naked because he loved her and he wanted to see
her looking at him naked because he loved her, but
after that he never mentioned it again, even turning his
face when she put the nightgown on over her dress to
undress at night and putting the dress on over the gown
to remove it in the morning, and she would not let him
get into bed beside her until the lamp was out and even

in the heat of summer she would draw the sheet up
over them both before she would let him turn to her:
and the landlady came up the stairs up the hall and
rapped on the door and then called their names but she
didn't move, lying still on the bed outside the covers,
her face turned away on the pillow, listening to nothing, thinking of nothing, not of him anyway he thought:
then the landlady went away and she said, 'Take off
your clothes:' her head still turned away, looking at
nothing, thinking of nothing, waiting for nothing, not
even him, her hand moving as though with volition and
vision of its own, catching his wrist at the exact moment
when he paused beside the bed so that he never paused
but merely changed the direction of moving, downward now, the hand drawing him and she moved at
last, shifted, a movement one single complete inherent
not practiced and one time older than man, looking at
him now, drawing him still downward with the one
hand down and down and he neither saw nor felt it
shift, palm flat against his chest now and holding him
away with the same apparent lack of any effort or any
need for strength, and not looking at him now, she
didn't need to, the chaste woman, the wife, already
looked upon all the men who ever rutted and now her
whole body had changed, altered, he had never seen it
but once and now it was not even the one he had seen
but composite of all woman-flesh since man that ever
of its own will reclined on its back and opened, and
out of it somewhere, without any movement of lips
even, the dying and invincible whisper: 'Promise:' and
he

    'Promise?'

'The farm.' He moved. He had moved, the hand shifting from his chest once more to his wrist, grasping it,
the arm still lax and only the light increasing pressure

of the fingers as though arm and hand were a piece of wire cable with one looped end, only the hand tightening as he pulled against it. 'No,' he said. 'No:' and she was not looking at him still but not like the other, but still the hand: 'No, I tell you. I won't. I can't. Never:' and still the hand and he said, for the last time, he tried to speak clearly and he knew it was still gently and he thought, *She already knows more than I with all the man-listening in camps where there was nothing to read ever even heard of. They are born already bored with what a boy approaches only at fourteen and fifteen with blundering and aghast trembling:* 'I can't. Not ever. Remember:' and still the steady and invincible hand and he said 'Yes' and he thought, *She is lost. She was born lost. We were all born lost* then he stopped thinking and even saying Yes, it was like nothing he had ever dreamed, let alone heard in mere man-talking until after a no-time he returned and lay spent on the insatiate immemorial beach and again with a movement one time more older than man she turned and freed herself and on their wedding night she had cried and he thought she was crying now at first, into the tossed and wadded pillow, the voice coming from somewhere between the pillow and the cachinnation: 'And that's all. That's all from me. If this don't get you that son you talk about, it won't be mine:' lying on her side, her back to the empty rented room, laughing and laughing

v

He went back to the camp one more time before the lumber company moved in and began to cut the timber. Major de Spain himself never saw it again. But he made them welcome to use the house and hunt the land whenever they liked, and in the winter following the last hunt when Sam Fathers and Lion died, General Compson and Walter Ewell invented a plan to corporate themselves, the old group, into a club and lease the camp and the hunting privileges of the woods—an invention doubtless of the somewhat childish old General but actually worthy of Boon Hogganbeck himself. Even the boy, listening, recognized it for the subterfuge it was: to change the leopard's spots when they could not alter the leopard, a baseless and illusory hope to which even McCaslin seemed to subscribe for a while, that once they had persuaded Major de Spain to return to the camp he might revoke himself, which even the boy knew he would not do. And he did not. The boy never knew what occurred when Major de Spain declined. He was not present when the subject was broached and McCaslin never told him. But when June came and the time for the double birthday celebration there was no mention of it and when November came no one spoke of using Major de Spain's house and he never knew whether or not Major de Spain knew they were going on the hunt though without doubt old Ash probably told him: he and McCaslin and General Compson (and that one was the General's last hunt too) and Walter and Boon and Tennie's Jim and old Ash loaded two wagons and drove two days and almost forty miles beyond any country the boy had ever seen before and lived in tents for the two weeks. And the next spring they heard (not from Major de Spain) that he had sold the timber-rights to a Memphis lumber company and in June the boy came to town with McCaslin one Saturday and went to Major de Spain's office—the big, airy, book-lined, second-storey room with windows at one end opening upon the shabby hinder purlieus of stores and at the other a door giving onto the railed balcony above

the Square, with its curtained alcove where sat a cedar
water-bucket and a sugar-bowl and spoon and tumbler
and a wicker-covered demijohn of whiskey, and the
bamboo-and-paper punkah swinging back and forth
above the desk while old Ash in a tilted chair beside the
entrance pulled the cord.

"Of course," Major de Spain said. "Ash will probably
like to get off in the woods himself for a while, where
he won't have to eat Daisy's cooking. Complain about
it, anyway. Are you going to take anybody with you?"

"No sir," he said. "I thought that maybe Boon—"
For six months now Boon had been town-marshal at
Hoke's; Major de Spain had compounded with the
lumber company—or perhaps compromised was closer,
since it was the lumber company who had decided that
Boon might be better as a town-marshal than head of
a logging gang.

"Yes," Major de Spain said. "I'll wire him today. He
can meet you at Hoke's. I'll send Ash on by the train
and they can take some food in and all you will have to
do will be to mount your horse and ride over."

"Yes sir," he said. "Thank you." And he heard his
voice again. He didn't know he was going to say it yet
he did know, he had known it all the time: "Maybe if
you . . ." His voice died. It was stopped, he never
knew how because Major de Spain did not speak and
it was not until his voice ceased that Major de Spain
moved, turned back to the desk and the papers spread
on it and even that without moving because he was
sitting at the desk with a paper in his hand when the
boy entered, the boy standing there looking down at
the short plumpish gray-haired man in sober fine broadcloth and an immaculate glazed shirt whom he was
used to seeing in boots and muddy corduroy, unshaven,
sitting the shaggy powerful long-hocked mare with the

worn Winchester carbine across the saddlebow and the great blue dog standing motionless as bronze at the stirrup, the two of them in that last year and to the boy anyway coming to resemble one another somehow as two people competent for love or for business who have been in love or in business together for a long time sometimes do. Major de Spain did not look up again.

"No. I will be too busy. But good luck to you. If you have it, you might bring me a young squirrel."

"Yes sir," he said. "I will."

He rode his mare, the three-year-old filly he had bred and raised and broken himself. He left home a little after midnight and six hours later, without even having sweated her, he rode into Hoke's, the tiny log-line junction which he had always thought of as Major de Spain's property too although Major de Spain had merely sold the company (and that many years ago) the land on which the sidetracks and loading-platforms and the commissary store stood, and looked about in shocked and grieved amazement even though he had had forewarning and had believed himself prepared: a new planing-mill already half completed which would cover two or three acres and what looked like miles and miles of stacked steel rails red with the light bright rust of newness and of piled crossties sharp with creosote, and wire corrals and feeding-troughs for two hundred mules at least and the tents for the men who drove them; so that he arranged for the care and stabling of his mare as rapidly as he could and did not look any more, mounted into the log-train caboose with his gun and climbed into the cupola and looked no more save toward the wall of wilderness ahead within which he would be able to hide himself from it once more anyway.

Then the little locomotive shrieked and began to

move: a rapid churning of exhaust, a lethargic deliberate clashing of slack couplings travelling backward along the train, the exhaust changing to the deep slow clapping bites of power as the caboose too began to move and from the cupola he watched the train's head complete the first and only curve in the entire line's length and vanish into the wilderness, dragging its length of train behind it so that it resembled a small dingy harmless snake vanishing into weeds, drawing him with it too until soon it ran once more at its maximum clattering speed between the twin walls of unaxed wilderness as of old. It had been harmless once. Not five years ago Walter Ewell had shot a six-point buck from this same moving caboose, and there was the story of the half-grown bear: the train's first trip in to the cutting thirty miles away, the bear between the rails, its rear end elevated like that of a playing puppy while it dug to see what sort of ants or bugs they might contain or perhaps just to examine the curious symmetrical squared barkless logs which had appeared apparently from nowhere in one endless mathematical line overnight, still digging until the driver on the braked engine not fifty feet away blew the whistle at it, whereupon it broke frantically and took the first tree it came to: an ash sapling not much bigger than a man's thigh and climbed as high as it could and clung there, its head ducked between its arms as a man (a woman perhaps) might have done while the brakeman threw chunks of ballast at it, and when the engine returned three hours later with the first load of outbound logs the bear was halfway down the tree and once more scrambled back up as high as it could and clung again while the train passed and was still there when the engine went in again in the afternoon and still there when it came back out at dusk; and Boon had been in Hoke's with the

wagon after a barrel of flour that noon when the train-
crew told about it and Boon and Ash, both twenty
years younger then, sat under the tree all that night to
keep anybody from shooting it and the next morning
Major de Spain had the log-train held at Hoke's and
just before sundown on the second day, with not only
Boon and Ash but Major de Spain and General Compson and Walter and McCaslin, twelve then, watching,
it came down the tree after almost thirty-six hours without even water and McCaslin told him how for a minute
they thought it was going to stop right there at the
barrow-pit where they were standing and drink, how it
looked at the water and paused and looked at them and
at the water again, but did not, gone, running, as bears
run, the two sets of feet, front and back, tracking two
separate though parallel courses.

It had been harmless then. They would hear the passing log-train sometimes from the camp; sometimes,
because nobody bothered to listen for it or not. They
would hear it going in, running light and fast, the light
clatter of the trucks, the exhaust of the diminutive
locomotive and its shrill peanut-parcher whistle flung
for one petty moment and absorbed by the brooding and
inattentive wilderness without even an echo. They
would hear it going out, loaded, not quite so fast now
yet giving its frantic and toylike illusion of crawling
speed, not whistling now to conserve steam, flinging its
bitten laboring miniature puffing into the immemorial
woodsface with frantic and bootless vainglory, empty
and noisy and puerile, carrying to no destination or
purpose sticks which left nowhere any scar or stump,
as the child's toy loads and transports and unloads its
dead sand and rushes back for more, tireless and unceasing and rapid yet never quite so fast as the Hand which
plays with it moves the toy burden back to load the

toy again. But it was different now. It was the same
train, engine cars and caboose, even the same engine-
men brakeman and conductor to whom Boon, drunk
then sober then drunk again then fairly sober once
more all in the space of fourteen hours, had bragged
that day two years ago about what they were going to
do to Old Ben tomorrow, running with its same illusion
of frantic rapidity between the same twin walls of impenetrable and impervious woods, passing the old
landmarks, the old game crossings over which he had
trailed bucks wounded and not wounded and more
than once seen them, anything but wounded, bot out
of the woods and up and across the embankment which
bore the rails and ties then down and into the woods
again as the earth-bound supposedly move but crossing
as arrows travel, groundless, elongated, three times its
actual length and even paler, different in color, as if
there were a point between immobility and absolute
motion where even mass chemically altered, changing
without pain or agony not only in bulk and shape but in
color too, approaching the color of wind, yet this time
it was as though the train (and not only the train but
himself, not only his vision which had seen it and his
memory which remembered it but his clothes too, as
garments carry back into the clean edgeless blowing of
air the lingering effluvium of a sick-room or of death)
had brought with it into the doomed wilderness, even
before the actual axe, the shadow and portent of the
new mill not even finished yet and the rails and ties
which were not even laid; and he knew now what he
had known as soon as he saw Hoke's this morning but
had not yet thought into words: why Major de Spain
had not come back, and that after this time he himself,
who had had to see it one time other, would return no
more.

Now they were near. He knew it before the engine-driver whistled to warn him. Then he saw Ash and the wagon, the reins without doubt wrapped once more about the brake-lever as within the boy's own memory Major de Spain had been forbidding him for eight years to do, the train slowing, the slackened couplings jolting and clashing again from car to car, the caboose slowing past the wagon as he swung down with his gun, the conductor leaning out above him to signal the engine, the caboose still slowing, creeping, although the engine's exhaust was already slatting in mounting tempo against the unechoing wilderness, the crashing of draw-bars once more travelling backward along the train, the caboose picking up speed at last. Then it was gone. It had not been. He could no longer hear it. The wilderness soared, musing, inattentive, myriad, eternal, green; older than any mill-shed, longer than any spur-line. "Mr. Boon here yet?" he said.

"He beat me in," Ash said. "Had the wagon loaded and ready for me at Hoke's yistiddy when I got there and setting on the front steps at camp last night when I got in. He already been in the woods since fo daylight this morning. Said he gwine up to the Gum Tree and for you to hunt up that way and meet him." He knew where that was: a single big sweet-gum just outside the woods, in an old clearing; if you crept up to it very quietly this time of year and then ran suddenly into the clearing, sometimes you caught as many as a dozen squirrels in it, trapped, since there was no other tree near they could jump to. So he didn't get into the wagon at all.

"I will," he said.

"I figured you would," Ash said, "I fotch you a box of shells." He passed the shells down and began to unwrap the lines from the brake-pole.

"How many times up to now do you reckon Major has told you not to do that?" the boy said.

"Do which?" Ash said. Then he said: "And tell Boon Hogganbeck dinner gonter be on the table in a hour and if yawl want any to come on and eat it."

"In an hour?" he said. "It ain't nine o'clock yet." He drew out his watch and extended it face-toward Ash. "Look." Ash didn't even look at the watch.

"That's town time. You ain't in town now. You in the woods."

"Look at the sun then."

"Nemmine the sun too," Ash said. "If you and Boon Hogganbeck want any dinner, you better come on in and get it when I tole you. I aim to get done in that kitchen because I got my wood to chop. And watch your feet. They're crawling."

"I will," he said.

Then he was in the woods, not alone but solitary; the solitude closed about him, green with summer. They did not change, and, timeless, would not, any more than would the green of summer and the fire and rain of fall and the iron cold and sometimes even snow

the day, the morning when he killed the buck and Sam marked his face with its hot blood, they returned to camp and he remembered old Ash's blinking and disgruntled and even outraged disbelief until at last McCaslin had had to affirm the fact that he had really killed it: and that night Ash sat snarling and unapproachable behind the stove so that Tennie's Jim had to serve the supper and waked them with breakfast already on the table the next morning and it was only half-past one o'clock and at last out of Major de Spain's angry cursing and Ash's snarling and sullen rejoinders the fact emerged that Ash not only wanted to go into the woods and shoot a deer also but he intended to and Major de Spain said, 'By God, if we don't let him we will probably have to do the cooking from now on:' and Walter Ewell said, 'Or get up at midnight to eat what Ash cooks:' and since he had already killed his buck for this hunt and was not to shoot again unless they needed meat, he offered his gun to Ash until Major de Spain took command and allotted that gun to Boon for the day and gave Boon's unpredictable pump gun to Ash, with two buckshot shells but Ash said, 'I got shells:' and showed them, four: one buck, one of number three shot for rabbits, two of bird-shot and told one by one their history and their origin and he remembered not Ash's face alone but Major de Spain's and Walter's and General Compson's too, and Ash's voice: 'Shoot? In course they'll shoot! Genl Cawmpson guv me this un'—the buckshot—'right outen the same gun he kilt that big buck with eight years ago. And this un'— it was the rabbit shell: triumphantly—'is oldern thisyer boy!' And that morning he loaded the gun himself, re- versing the order: the bird-shot, the rabbit, then the buck so that the buckshot would feed first into the chamber, and himself without a gun, he and Ash walked beside Major de Spain's and Tennie's Jim's horses and the dogs (that was the snow) until they cast and struck, the sweet strong cries ringing away into the muffled falling air and gone almost immediately, as if the constant and unmurmuring flakes had already buried even the unformed echoes beneath their myriad

*and weightless falling, Major de Spain and Tennie's
Jim gone too, whooping on into the woods; and then
it was all right, he knew as plainly as if Ash had told
him that Ash had now hunted his deer and that even
his tender years had been forgiven for having killed
one, and they turned back toward home through the
falling snow—that is, Ash said, 'Now whut?' and he
said. 'This way'—himself in front because, although
they were less than a mile from camp, he knew that
Ash, who had spent two weeks of his life in the camp
each year for the last twenty, had no idea whatever
where they were, until quite soon the manner in which
Ash carried Boon's gun was making him a good deal
more than just nervous and he made Ash walk in front,
striding on, talking now, an old man's garrulous monologue beginning with where he was at the moment
then of the woods and of camping in the woods and of
eating in camps then of eating then of cooking it and of
his wife's cooking then briefly of his old wife and almost
at once and at length of a new light-colored woman who
nursed next door to Major de Spain's and if she didn't
watch out who she was switching her tail at he would
show her how old was an old man or not if his wife
just didn't watch him all the time, the two of them in
a game trail through a dense brake of cane and brier
which would bring them out within a quarter-mile of
camp, approaching a big fallen tree-trunk lying athwart
the path and just as Ash, still talking, was about to step
over it the bear, the yearling, rose suddenly beyond the
log, sitting up, its forearms against its chest and its*

wrists limply arrested as if it had been surprised in the act of covering its face to pray: and after a certain time Ash's gun yawed jerkily up and he said, 'You haven't got a shell in the barrel yet. Pump it:' but the gun already snicked and he said, 'Pump it. You haven't got a shell in the barrel yet:' and Ash pumped the action and in a certain time the gun steadied again and snicked and he said, 'Pump it:' and watched the buckshot shell jerk, spinning heavily, into the cane. This is the rabbit shot: he thought and the gun snicked and he thought: The next is bird-shot: and he didn't have to say Pump it; he cried, 'Don't shoot! Don't shoot!' but that was already too late too, the light dry vicious snick! before he could speak and the bear turned and dropped to allfours and then was gone and there was only the log, the cane, the velvet and constant snow and Ash said, 'Now whut?' and he said, 'This way. Come on:' and began to back away down the path and Ash said, 'I got to find my shells:' and he said, 'Goddamn it, goddamn it, come on:' but Ash leaned the gun against the log and returned and stooped and fumbled among the cane roots until he came back and stooped and found the shells and they rose and at that moment the gun, untouched, leaning against the log six feet away and for that while even forgotten by both of them, roared, bellowed and flamed, and ceased: and he carried it now, pumped out the last mummified shell and gave that one also to Ash and, the action still open, himself carried the gun until he stood it in the corner behind Boon's bed at the camp

—; summer, and fall, and snow, and wet and sap-rife spring in their ordered immortal sequence, the deathless and immemorial phases of the mother who had shaped him if any had toward the man he almost was, mother and father both to the old man born of a Negro slave and a Chickasaw chief who had been his spirit's father if any had, whom he had revered and harkened to and loved and lost and grieved: and he would marry some-day and they too would own for their brief while that brief unsubstanced glory which inherently of itself cannot last and hence why glory: and they would, might, carry even the remembrance of it into the time when flesh no longer talks to flesh because memory at least does last: but still the woods would be his mis-tress and his wife.

He was not going toward the Gum Tree. Actually he was getting farther from it. Time was and not so long ago either when he would not have been allowed here without someone with him, and a little later, when he had begun to learn how much he did not know, he would not have dared be here without someone with him, and later still, beginning to ascertain, even if only dimly, the limits of what he did not know, he could have attempted and carried it through with a compass, not because of any increased belief in himself but be-cause McCaslin and Major de Spain and Walter and General Compson too had taught him at last to believe the compass regardless of what it seemed to state. Now he did not even use the compass but merely the sun and that only subconsciously, yet he could have taken a scaled map and plotted at any time to within a hundred feet of where he actually was; and sure enough, at almost the exact moment when he expected it, the earth began to rise faintly, he passed one of the four concrete markers set down by the lumber company's surveyor

to establish the four corners of the plot which Major de
Spain had reserved out of the sale, then he stood on the
crest of the knoll itself, the four corner-markers all
visible now, blanched still even beneath the winter's
weathering, lifeless and shockingly alien in that place
where dissolution itself was a seething turmoil of
ejaculation tumescence conception and birth, and death
did not even exist. After two winters' blanketings of
leaves and the flood-waters of two springs, there was
no trace of the two graves any more at all. But those
who would have come this far to find them would not
need headstones but would have found them as Sam
Fathers himself had taught him to find such: by bear-
ings on trees: and did, almost the first thrust of the
hunting knife finding (but only to see if it was still
there) the round tin box manufactured for axle-grease
and containing now Old Ben's dried mutilated paw,
resting above Lion's bones.

He didn't disturb it. He didn't even look for the other
grave where he and McCaslin and Major de Spain and
Boon had laid Sam's body, along with his hunting horn
and his knife and his tobacco-pipe, that Sunday morning two years ago; he didn't have to. He had stepped
over it, perhaps on it. But that was all right. *He probably knew I was in the woods this morning long before I
got here,* he thought, going on to the tree which had
supported one end of the platform where Sam lay when
McCaslin and Major de Spain found them—the tree,
the other axle-grease tin nailed to the trunk, but
weathered, rusted, alien too yet healed already into the
wilderness' concordant generality, raising no tuneless
note, and empty, long since empty of the food and tobacco he had put into it that day, as empty of that as it
would presently be of this which he drew from his
pocket—the twist of tobacco, the new bandanna hand-

kerchief, the small paper sack of the peppermint candy
which Sam had used to love; that gone too, almost before he had turned his back, not vanished but merely
translated into the myriad life which printed the dark
mold of these secret and sunless places with delicate
fairy tracks, which, breathing and biding and immobile,
watched him from beyond every twig and leaf until he
moved, moving again, walking on; he had not stopped,
he had only paused, quitting the knoll which was no
abode of the dead because there was no death, not
Lion and not Sam: not held fast in earth but free in
earth and not in earth but of earth, myriad yet undif-
fused of every myriad part, leaf and twig and particle,
air and sun and rain and dew and night, acorn oak and
leaf and acorn again, dark and dawn and dark and
dawn again in their immutable progression, and, being
myriad, one: and Old Ben too. Old Ben too; they would
give him his paw back even, certainly they would give
him his paw back: then the long challenge and the
long chase, no heart to be driven and outraged, no flesh
to be mauled and bled— Even as he froze himself, he
seemed to hear Ash's parting admonition. He could even
hear the voice as he froze, immobile, one foot just taking
his weight, the toe of the other just lifted behind him,
not breathing, feeling again and as always the sharp
shocking inrush from when Isaac McCaslin long yet
was not, and so it was fear all right but not fright as he
looked down at it. It had not coiled yet and the buzzer
had not sounded either, only one thick rapid contraction,
one loop cast sideways as though merely for purchase
from which the raised head might start slightly backward, not in fright either, not in threat quite yet, more
than six feet of it, the head raised higher than his
knee and less than his knee's length away, and old, the
once-bright markings of its youth dulled now to a mono-

tone concordant too with the wilderness it crawled and lurked: the old one, the ancient and accursed about the earth, fatal and solitary and he could smell it now: the thin sick smell of rotting cucumbers and something else which had no name, evocative of all knowledge and an old weariness and of pariah-hood and of death. At last it moved. Not the head. The elevation of the head did not change as it began to glide away from him, moving erect yet off the perpendicular as if the head and that elevated third were complete and all: an entity walking on two feet and free of all laws of mass and balance, and should have been because even now he could not quite believe that all that shift and flow of shadow behind that walking head could have been one snake: going and then gone; he put the other foot down at last and didn't know it, standing with one hand raised as Sam had stood that afternoon six years ago when Sam led him into the wilderness and showed him and he ceased to be a child, speaking the old tongue which Sam had spoken that day without premeditation either: "Chief," he said: "Grandfather."

He couldn't tell when he first began to hear the sound, because when he became aware of it, it seemed to him that he had been already hearing it for several seconds —a sound as though someone were hammering a gun-barrel against a piece of railroad iron, a sound loud and heavy and not rapid yet with something frenzied about it, as the hammerer were not only a strong man and an earnest one but a little hysterical too. Yet it couldn't be on the logline because, although the track lay in that direction, it was at least two miles from him and this sound was not three hundred yards away. But even as he thought that, he realized where the sound must be coming from: whoever the man was and whatever he was doing, he was somewhere near the edge of the clearing where the Gum Tree was and where he was to meet Boon. So far, he had been hunting as he advanced, moving slowly and quietly and watching the ground and the trees both. Now he went on, his gun unloaded and the barrel slanted up and back to facilitate its passage through brier and undergrowth, approaching as it grew louder and louder that steady savage somehow queerly hysterical beating of metal on metal, emerging from the woods, into the old clearing, with the solitary gum tree directly before him. At first glance the tree seemed to be alive with frantic squirrels. There appeared to be forty or fifty of them leaping and darting from branch to branch until the whole tree had become one green maelstrom of mad leaves, while from time to time, singly or in twos and threes, squirrels would dart down the trunk then whirl without stopping and rush back up again as though sucked violently back by the vacuum of their fellows' frenzied vortex. Then he saw Boon, sitting, his back against the trunk, his head bent, hammering furiously at something on his lap. What he hammered with was the barrel of his dismembered gun, what he hammered at was the breech of it. The rest of the gun lay scattered about him in a half-dozen pieces while he bent over the piece on his lap his scarlet and streaming walnut face, hammering the disjointed barrel against the gun-breech with the frantic abandon of a madman. He didn't even look up to see who it was. Still hammering, he merely shouted back at the boy in a hoarse strangled voice:

"Get out of here! Don't touch them! Don't touch a one of them! They're mine!"

4. The Peasants

ABOUT thirty years after the Civil War, Flem Snopes appeared in the little community of Frenchman's Bend, in the southeastern corner of Faulkner's county. Flem was the son of a Civil War bushwhacker and horse thief. A lumpish and silent young man, with eyes the color of stagnant water, he never drank or smoked, but sometimes he chewed a nickel's worth of tobacco until the suption was out of it. "Flem Snopes don't even tell himself what he is up to," said one of his neighbors. "Not if he was laying in bed with himself in the dark of the moon."

In his own surreptitious fashion, Flem managed to get control of the general store, the cotton gin, and the blacksmith shop, the only three money-making enterprises in Frenchman's Bend; and one by one he introduced a horde of his relatives to take charge of them. Lump Snopes, the storekeeper; I.O. Snopes, the schoolmaster; Mink Snopes, the killer; Ike Snopes, the idiot boy who fell in love with a cow; Eck Snopes, the stupid and good-natured blacksmith: all together they descended on the community like field mice, devouring everything, cheating everybody, cheating one another; and when Flem had cheated even Ratliff, the sewing-machine agent, known as the shrewdest man in the county, they all moved on to Jefferson, like mice into an untouched field of grain.

Faulkner once planned to devote two or three volumes to the rise and proliferation of the Snopes tribe; but so far he has published only *The Hamlet* (1940), which is halfway between a novel and a cycle of stories. It was a book that took him a dozen years to write. When he first began working on the idea, it produced one story, "Spotted Horses," but went no further. About two years later, he wrote two other stories with the same background, "The Hound" and "Lizards in Jamshyd's Courtyard." "I wrote them mainly," he said in a letter, "because 'Spotted Horses' had created a character I fell in love with: the itinerant sewing-machine agent named Suratt. Later a man of that name turned up at home, so I changed my man to Ratliff. . . . Meanwhile my book had created Snopes and his clan, who produced stories in their saga which are to fall in later volumes: 'Mule in the Yard,' 'Brass,' etc. This over about ten years, until one day I decided I had better start on the first volume or I'd never get any of it down."

The version of "Spotted Horses" used in *The Hamlet,* and reprinted here, is nearly three times as long as the magazine version printed ten years earlier in *Scribner's,* as well as being nearly three times as good. I don't think it would be too much to call it the funniest American story since Mark Twain.

1900. SPOTTED HORSES

I

A LITTLE while before sundown the men loung-
ing about the gallery of the store saw, coming up
the road from the south, a covered wagon drawn by
mules and followed by a considerable string of obviously alive objects which in the levelling sun resembled
vari-sized and -colored tatters torn at random from
large billboards—circus posters, say—attached to the
rear of the wagon and inherent with its own separate
and collective motion, like the tail of a kite.

"What in the hell is that?" one said.

"It's a circus," Quick said. They began to rise, watching the wagon. Now they could see that the animals
behind the wagon were horses. Two men rode in the
wagon.

"Hell fire," the first man—his name was Freeman—
said. "It's Flem Snopes." They were all standing when
the wagon came up and stopped and Snopes got down
and approached the steps. He might have departed only
this morning. He wore the same cloth cap, the minute
bow tie against the white shirt, the same gray trousers.
He mounted the steps.

"Howdy, Flem," Quick said. The other looked briefly
at all of them and none of them, mounting the steps.
"Starting you a circus?"

"Gentlemen," he said. He crossed the gallery; they
made way for him. Then they descended the steps
and approached the wagon, at the tail of which the

horses stood in a restive clump, larger than rabbits and gaudy as parrots and shackled to one another and to the wagon itself with sections of barbed wire. Calico-coated, small-bodied, with delicate legs and pink faces in which their mismatched eyes rolled wild and sub-dued, they huddled, gaudy, motionless, and alert, wild as deer, deadly as rattlesnakes, quiet as doves. The men stood at a respectful distance, looking at them. At that moment Jody Varner came through the group, shoul-dering himself to the front of it.

"Watch yourself, doc," a voice said from the rear. But it was already too late. The nearest animal rose on its hind legs with lightning rapidity and struck twice with its forefeet at Varner's face, faster than a boxer, the movement of its surge against the wire which held it travelling backward among the rest of the band in a wave of thuds and lunges. "Hup, you broom-tailed, hay-burning sidewinders," the same voice said. This was the second man who had arrived in the wagon. He was a stranger. He wore a heavy, densely black moustache, a wide pale hat. When he thrust himself through and turned to herd them back from the horses they saw, thrust into the hip pockets of his tight jeans pants, the butt of a heavy pearl-handled pistol and a florid carton such as small cakes come in. "Keep away from them, boys," he said. "They've got kind of skittish, they ain't been rode in so long."

"Since when have they been rode?" Quick said. The stranger looked at Quick. He had a broad, quite cold, wind-gnawed face and bleak, cold eyes. His belly fitted neat and smooth as a peg into the tight trousers.

"I reckon that was when they were rode on the ferry to get across the Mississippi River," Varner said. The stranger looked at him. "My name's Varner," Jody said.

"Hipps," the other said. "Call me Buck." Across the

left side of his head, obliterating the tip of that ear, was a savage and recent gash gummed over with a blackish substance like axle-grease. They looked at the scar. Then they watched him remove the carton from his pocket and tilt a gingersnap into his hand and put the gingersnap into his mouth, beneath the moustache.

"You and Flem have some trouble back yonder?" Quick said. The stranger ceased chewing. When he looked directly at anyone, his eyes became like two pieces of flint turned suddenly up in dug earth.

"Back where?" he said.

"Your nigh ear," Quick said.

"Oh," the other said. "That." He touched his ear. "That was my mistake. I was absent-minded one night when I was staking them out. Studying about something else and forgot how long the wire was." He chewed. They looked at his ear. "Happen to any man careless around a horse. Put a little axle-dope on it and you won't notice it tomorrow though. They're pretty lively now, lazing along all day doing nothing. It'll work out of them in a couple of days." He put another gingersnap into his mouth, chewing, "Don't you believe they'll gentle?" No one answered. They looked at the ponies, grave and noncommittal. Jody turned and went back into the store. "Them's good, gentle ponies," the stranger said. "Watch now." He put the carton back into his pocket and approached the horses, his hand extended. The nearest one was standing on three legs now. It appeared to be asleep. Its eyelid drooped over the cerulean eye; its head was shaped like an ironing-board. Without even raising the eyelid it flicked its head, the yellow teeth cropped. For an instant it and the man appeared to be inextricable in one violence. Then they became motionless, the stranger's high heels dug into the earth, one hand gripping the animal's nostrils, holding the horse's head wrenched half around while it breathed in hoarse, smothered groans. "See?" the stranger said in a panting voice, the veins standing white and rigid in his neck and along his jaw. "See? All you got to do is handle them a little and work hell out of them for a couple of days. Now look out. Give me room back there." They gave back a little. The stranger gathered himself then sprang away. As he did so, a second horse slashed at his back, severing his vest from collar to hem down the back exactly as the trick swordsman severs a floating veil with one stroke.

"Sho now," Quick said. "But suppose a man don't happen to own a vest."

At that moment Jody Varner, followed by the blacksmith, thrust through them again. "All right, Buck," he said. "Better get them on into the lot. Eck here will help you." The stranger, the severed halves of the vest swinging from either shoulder, mounted to the wagon seat, the blacksmith following.

"Get up, you transmogrified hallucinations of Job and Jezebel," the stranger said. The wagon moved on, the tethered ponies coming gaudily into motion behind it, behind which in turn the men followed at a respectful distance, on up the road and into the lane and so to the lot gate behind Mrs. Littlejohn's. Eck got down and opened the gate. The wagon passed through but when the ponies saw the fence the herd surged backward against the wire which attached it to the wagon, standing on its collective hind legs and then trying to turn within itself, so that the wagon moved backward for a few feet until the Texan, cursing, managed to saw the mules about and so lock the wheels. The men following had already fallen rapidly back. "Here, Eck," the Texan said. "Get up here and take the reins." The blacksmith got back in the wagon and took the reins. Then they watched the Texan descend, carrying a looped-up blacksnake whip, and go around to the rear of the herd and drive it through the gate, the whip snaking about the harlequin rumps in methodical and pistol-like reports. Then the watchers hurried across Mrs. Littlejohn's yard and mounted to the veranda, one end of which overlooked the lot.

"How you reckon he ever got them tied together?" Freeman said.

"I'd a heap rather watch how he aims to turn them loose," Quick said. The Texan had climbed back into the halted wagon. Presently he and Eck both appeared at the rear end of the open hood. The Texan grasped the wire and began to draw the first horse up to the wagon, the animal plunging and surging back against the wire as though trying to hang itself, the contagion passing back through the herd from animal to animal until they were rearing and plunging again against the wire.

"Come on, grab a holt," the Texan said. Eck grasped the wire also. The horses laid back against it, the pink faces tossing above the back-surging mass. "Pull him up, pull him up," the Texan said sharply. "They couldn't get up here in the wagon even if they wanted to." The wagon moved gradually backward until the head of the first horse was snubbed up to the tail-gate. The Texan took a turn of the wire quickly about one of the wagon stakes. "Keep the slack out of it," he said. He vanished and reappeared, almost in the same second, with a pair of heavy wire-cutters. "Hold them like that," he said, and leaped. He vanished, broad hat, flapping vest, wire-cutters and all, into a kaleidoscopic maelstrom of long teeth and wild eyes and slashing feet, from which presently the horses began to burst one by one like partridges flushing, each wearing a necklace of barbed wire. The first one crossed the lot at top speed, on a straight line. It galloped into the fence without any diminution whatever. The wire gave, recovered, and slammed the horse to earth where it lay for a moment, glaring, its legs still galloping in air. It scrambled up without having ceased to gallop and crossed the lot and galloped into the opposite fence and was slammed again to earth. The others were now freed. They whipped and whirled about the lot like dizzy fish in a bowl. It had seemed like a big lot until now, but now the very idea that all that fury and motion should be transpiring inside any one fence was something to be repudiated with contempt, like a mirror trick. From the ultimate dust the stranger, carrying the wire-cutters and his vest completely gone now, emerged. He was not running, he merely moved with a light-poised and watchful celerity, weaving among the calico rushes of the animals, feinting and dodging like a boxer until he reached the gate and crossed the yard and mounted to the veranda. One sleeve of his shirt hung only at one point from his shoulder. He ripped it off and wiped his face with it and threw it away and took out the paper carton and shook a gingersnap into his hand. He was breathing only a little heavily. "Pretty lively now," he said. "But it'll work out of them in a couple of days." The ponies still streaked back and forth through the growing dusk like hysterical fish, but not so violently now.

"What'll you give a man to reduce them odds a little for you?" Quick said. The Texan looked at him, the eyes bleak, pleasant and hard above the chewing jaw, the heavy moustache. "To take one of them off your hands?" Quick said.

At that moment the little periwinkle-eyed boy came

along the veranda, saying, "Papa, papa; where's papa?"

"Who you looking for, sonny?" one said.

"It's Eck's boy," Quick said. "He's still out yonder in the wagon. Helping Mr. Buck here." The boy went on to the end of the veranda, in diminutive overalls—a miniature replica of the men themselves.

"Papa," he said. "Papa." The blacksmith was still leaning from the rear of the wagon, still holding the end of the severed wire. The ponies, bunched for the moment, now slid past the wagon, flowing, stringing out again so that they appeared to have doubled in number, rushing on; the hard, rapid, light patter of unshod hooves came out of the dust. "Mamma says to come on to supper," the boy said.

The moon was almost full then. When supper was over and they had gathered again along the veranda, the alteration was hardly one of visibility even. It was merely a translation from the lapidary-dimensional of day to the treacherous and silver receptivity in which the horses huddled in mazy camouflage, or singly or in pairs rushed, fluid, phantom, and unceasing, to huddle again in mirage-like clumps from which came high, abrupt squeals and the vicious thudding of hooves.

Ratliff was among them now. He had returned just before supper. He had not dared to take his team into the lot at all. They were now in Bookwright's stable a half mile from the store. "So Flem has come home again," he said. "Well, well, well. Will Varner paid to get him to Texas, so I reckon it ain't no more than fair for you fellows to pay the freight on him back." From the lot there came a high, thin squeal. One of the animals emerged. It seemed not to gallop but to flow, bodiless, without dimension. Yet there was the rapid light beat of hard hooves on the packed earth.

"He ain't said they was his yet," Quick said.

"He ain't said they ain't neither," Freeman said.

"I see," Ratliff said. "That's what you are holding back on. Until he tells you whether they are his or not. Or maybe you can wait until the auction's over and split up and some can follow Flem and some can follow that Texas fellow and watch to see which one spends the money. But then, when a man's done got trimmed, I don't reckon he cares who's got the money."

"Maybe if Ratliff would leave here tonight, they wouldn't make him buy one of them ponies tomorrow," a third said.

"That's fact," Ratliff said. "A fellow can dodge a Snopes if he just starts lively enough. In fact, I don't believe he would have to pass more than two folks before he would have another victim intervened betwixt them. You folks ain't going to buy them things sho enough, are you?" Nobody answered. They sat on the steps, their backs against the veranda posts, or on the railing itself. Only Ratliff and Quick sat in chairs, so that to them the others were black silhouettes against the dreaming lambence of the moonlight beyond the veranda. The pear tree across the road opposite was now in full and frosty bloom, the twigs and branches springing not outward from the limbs but standing motionless and perpendicular above the horizontal boughs like the separate and upstreaming hair of a drowned woman sleeping upon the uttermost floor of the windless and tideless sea.

"Anse McCallum brought two of them horses back from Texas once," one of the men on the steps said. He did not move to speak. He was not speaking to anyone. "It was a good team. A little light. He worked it for ten years. Light work, it was."

"I mind it," another said. "Anse claimed he traded fourteen rifle cartridges for both of them, didn't he?"

"It was the rifle too, I heard," a third said.

"No, it was just the shells," the first said. "The fellow wanted to swap him four more for the rifle too, but Anse said he never needed them. Cost too much to get six of them back to Mississippi."

"Sho," the second said. "When a man don't have to invest so much into a horse or a team, he don't need to expect so much from it." The three of them were not talking any louder, they were merely talking among themselves, to one another, as if they sat there alone. Ratliff, invisible in the shadow against the wall, made a sound, harsh, sardonic, not loud.

"Ratliff's laughing," a fourth said.

"Don't mind me," Ratliff said. The three speakers had not moved. They did not move now, yet there seemed to gather about the three silhouettes something stubborn, convinced, and passive, like children who have been chidden. A bird, a shadow, fleet and dark and swift, curved across the moonlight, upward into the pear tree and began to sing; a mockingbird.

"First one I've noticed this year," Freeman said.

"You can hear them along Whiteleaf every night," the first man said. "I heard one in February. In that snow. Singing in a gum."

"Gum is the first tree to put out," the third said. "That was why. It made it feel like singing, fixing to put out that way. That was why it taken a gum."

"Gum first to put out?" Quick said. "What about willow?"

"Willow ain't a tree," Freeman said. "It's a weed."

"Well, I don't know what it is," the fourth said. "But it ain't no weed. Because you can grub up a weed and you are done with it. I been grubbing up a clump of willows outen my spring pasture for fifteen years. They are the same size every year. Only difference is, it's just two or three more trees every time."

"And if I was you," Ratliff said, "that's just exactly where I would be come sunup tomorrow. Which of course you ain't going to do. I reckon there ain't nothing under the sun or in Frenchman's Bend neither that can keep you folks from giving Flem Snopes and that Texas man your money. But I'd sholy like to know just exactly who I was giving my money to. Seems like Eck here would tell you. Seems like he'd do that for his neighbors, don't it? Besides being Flem's cousin, him and that boy of his, Wallstreet, helped that Texas man tote water for them tonight and Eck's going to help him feed them in the morning too. Why, maybe Eck will be the one that will catch them and lead them up one at a time for you folks to bid on them. Ain't that right, Eck?"

The other man sitting on the steps with his back against the post was the blacksmith. "I don't know," he said.

"Boys," Ratliff said, "Eck knows all about them horses. Flem's told him, how much they cost and how much him and that Texas man aim to get for them, make off of them. Come on, Eck. Tell us." The other did not move, sitting on the top step, not quite facing them, sitting there beneath the successive layers of their quiet and intent concentrated listening and waiting.

"I don't know," he said. Ratliff began to laugh. He sat in the chair, laughing while the others sat or lounged upon the steps and the railing, sitting beneath his laughing as Eck had sat beneath their listening and waiting. Ratliff ceased laughing. He rose. He yawned, quite loud.

"All right. You folks can buy them critters if you want to. But me, I'd just as soon buy a tiger or a rattle-snake. And if Flem Snopes offered me either one of them, I would be afraid to touch it for fear it would turn out to be a painted dog or a piece of garden hose when I went up to take possession of it. I bid you one and all goodnight." He entered the house. They did not look after him, though after a while they all shifted a little and looked down into the lot, upon the splotchy, sporadic surge and flow of the horses, from among which from time to time came an abrupt squeal, a thudding blow. In the pear tree the mockingbird's idiot reiteration pulsed and purled.

"Anse McCallum made a good team outen them two of hisn," the first man said. "They was a little light. That was all."

When the sun rose the next morning a wagon and three saddled mules stood in Mrs. Littlejohn's lane and six men and Eck Snopes' son were already leaning on the fence, looking at the horses which huddled in a quiet clump before the barn door, watching the men in their turn. A second wagon came up the road and into the lane and stopped, and then there were eight men beside the boy standing at the fence, beyond which the horses stood, their blue-and-brown eyeballs rolling alertly in their gaudy faces. "So this here is the Snopes circus, is it?" one of the newcomers said. He glanced at the faces, then he went to the end of the row and stood beside the blacksmith and the little boy. "Are them Flem's horses?" he said to the blacksmith.

"Eck don't know who them horses belong to any more than we do," one of the others said. "He knows that Flem come here on the same wagon with them, be-cause he saw him. But that's all."

"And all he will know," a second said. "His own kin will be the last man in the world to find out anything about Flem Snopes' business."

"No," the first said. "He wouldn't even be that. The first man Flem would tell his business to would be the man that was left after the last man died. Flem Snopes don't even tell himself what he is up to. Not if he was laying in bed with himself in a empty house in the dark of the moon."

"That's a fact," a third said. "Flem would trim Eck or any other of his kin quick as he would us. Ain't that right, Eck?"

"I don't know," Eck said. They were watching the horses, which at that moment broke into a high-eared, stiff-kneed swirl and flowed in a patchwork wave across the lot and brought up again, facing the men along the fence, so they did not hear the Texan until he was among them. He wore a new shirt and another vest a little too small for him and he was just putting the paper carton back into his hip pocket.

"Morning, morning," he said. "Come to get an early pick, have you? Want to make me an offer for one or two before the bidding starts and runs the prices up?" They had not looked at the stranger long. They were not looking at him now, but at the horses in the lot, which had lowered their heads, snuffing into the dust.

"I reckon we'll look a while first," one said.

"You are in time to look at them eating breakfast, anyhow," the Texan said. "Which is more than they done without they staid up all night." He opened the gate and entered it. At once the horses jerked their heads up, watching him. "Here, Eck," the Texan said over his shoulder, "two or three of you boys help me drive them into the barn." After a moment Eck and two others approached the gate, the little boy at his father's heels, though the other did not see him until he turned to shut the gate.

"You stay out of here," Eck said. "One of them things will snap your head off same as a acorn before you even know it." He shut the gate and went on after the others, whom the Texan had now waved fanwise outward as he approached the horses which now drew into a restive huddle, beginning to mill slightly, watching the men. Mrs. Littlejohn came out of the kitchen and crossed the yard to the woodpile, watching the lot. She picked up two or three sticks of wood and paused, watching the lot again. Now there were two more men standing at the fence.

"Come on, come on," the Texan said. "They won't hurt you. They just ain't never been in under a roof before."

"I just as lief let them stay out here, if that's what they want to do," Eck said.

"Get yourself a stick—there's a bunch of wagon stakes against the fence yonder—and when one of them tries to rush you, bust him over the head so he will understand what you mean." One of the men went to the fence and got three of the stakes and returned and distributed them. Mrs. Littlejohn, her armful of wood complete now, paused again halfway back to the house, looking into the lot. The little boy was directly behind his father again, though this time the father had not discovered him yet. The men advanced toward the horses, the huddle of which began to break into gaudy units turning inward upon themselves. The Texan was cursing them in a loud steady cheerful voice. "Get in there, you banjo-faced jack rabbits. Don't hurry them, now. Let them take their time. Hi! Get in there. What do you think that barn is—a law court maybe? Or maybe a church and somebody is going to take up a collection on you?" The animals fell slowly back. Now and then one feinted to break from the huddle, the Texan driving it back each time with skillfully thrown bits of dirt. Then one at the rear saw the barn door just behind it but before the herd could break the Texan snatched the wagon stake from Eck and, followed by one of the other men, rushed at the horses and began to lay about the heads and shoulders, choosing by unerring instinct the point animal and striking it first square in the face then on the withers as it turned and then on the rump as it turned further, so that when the break came it was reversed and the entire herd rushed into the long open hallway and brought up against the further wall with a hollow, thunderous sound like that of a collapsing mine-shaft. "Seems to have held all right," the Texan said. He and the other man slammed the half-length doors and looked over them into the tunnel of the barn, at the far end of which the ponies were now a splotchy, phantom moiling punctuated by crackings of wooden partitions and the dry reports of hooves which gradually died away. "Yep, it held all right," the Texan said. The other two came to the doors and looked over them. The little boy came up beside his father now, trying to see through a crack, and Eck saw him.

"Didn't I tell you to stay out of here?" Eck said. "Don't you know them things will kill you quicker than you can say scat? You go and get outside of that fence and stay there."

"Why don't you get your paw to buy you one of them, Wall?" one of the men said.

"Me buy one of them things?" Eck said. "When I can go to the river anytime and catch me a snapping turtle or a moccasin for nothing? You go on, now. Get out of here and say out." The Texan had entered the barn.

One of the men closed the doors after him and put the bar up again and over the top of the doors they watched the Texan go on down the hallway, toward the ponies which now huddled like gaudy phantoms in the gloom, quiet now and already beginning to snuff experimentally into the long lipworn trough fastened against the rear wall. The little boy had merely gone around behind his father, to the other side, where he stood peering now through a knot-hole in a plank. The Texan opened a smaller door in the wall and entered it, though almost immediately he reappeared.

"I don't see nothing but shelled corn in here," he said. "Snopes said he would send some hay up here last night."

"Won't they eat corn either?" one of the men said.

"I don't know," the Texan said. "They ain't never seen any that I know of. We'll find out in a minute though." He disappeared, though they could still hear him in the crib. Then he emerged once more, carrying a big double-ended feed-basket, and retreated into the gloom where the parti-colored rumps of the horses were now ranged quietly along the feeding-trough. Mrs. Littlejohn appeared once more, on the veranda this time, carrying a big brass dinner bell. She raised it to make the first stroke. A small commotion set up among the ponies as the Texan approached but he began to speak to them at once, in a brisk loud unemphatic mixture of cursing and cajolery, disappearing among them. The men at the door heard the dry rattling of the corn-pellets into the trough, a sound broken by a single snort of amazed horror. A plank cracked with a loud report; before their eyes the depths of the hallway dissolved in loud fury, and while they stared over the doors, unable yet to begin to move, the entire interior exploded into mad tossing shapes like a downrush of flames.

"Hell fire," one of them said. "Jump!" he shouted. The three turned and ran frantically for the wagon, Eck last. Several voices from the fence were now shouting something but Eck did not even hear them until, in the act of scrambling madly at the tail-gate, he looked behind him and saw the little boy still leaning to the knot-hole in the door which in the next instant vanished into matchwood, the knot-hole itself exploding from his eye and leaving him, motionless in the diminutive overalls and still leaning forward a little until he vanished utterly beneath the towering parti-colored wave full of feet and glaring eyes and wild teeth which, overtopping, burst into scattering units, revealing at last the gaping orifice and the little boy still standing in it, unscratched, his eye still leaned to the vanished knot-hole.

"Wall!" Eck roared. The little boy turned and ran for the wagon. The horses were whipping back and forth across the lot, as if while in the barn they had once more doubled their number; two of them rushed up quattering and galloped all over the boy again without touching him as he ran, earnest and diminutive and seemingly without progress, though he reached the wagon at last, from which Eck, his sunburned skin now a sickly white, reached down and snatched the boy into the wagon by the straps of his overalls and slammed him face down across his knees and caught up a coiled hitching-rope from the bed of the wagon.

"Didn't I tell you to get out of here?" Eck said in a shaking voice. "Didn't I tell you?"

"If you're going to whip him, you better whip the rest of us too and then one of us can frail hell out of you," one of the others said.

"Or better still, take the rope and hang that durn fellow yonder," the second said. The Texan was now standing in the wrecked door of the barn, taking the gingersnap carton from his hip pocket. "Before he kills the rest of Frenchman's Bend too."

"You mean Flem Snopes," the first said. The Texan tilted the carton above his other open palm. The horses still rushed and swirled back and forth but they were beginning to slow now, trotting on high, stiff legs, although their eyes were still rolling whitely and various.

"I misdoubted that damn shell corn all along," the Texan said. "But at least they have seen what it looks like. They can't claim they ain't got nothing out of this trip." He shook the carton over his open hand. Nothing came out of it. Mrs. Littlejohn on the veranda made the first stroke with the dinner bell; at the sound the horses rushed again, the earth of the lot becoming vibrant with the light dry clatter of hooves. The Texan crumpled the carton and threw it aside. "Chuck wagon," he said. There were three more wagons in the lane now and there were twenty or more men at the fence when the Texan, followed by his three assistants and the little boy, passed through the gate. The bright cloudless early sun gleamed upon the pearl butt of the pistol in his hip pocket and upon the bell which Mrs. Littlejohn still rang, peremptory, strong, and loud.

When the Texan, picking his teeth with a splintered kitchen match, emerged from the house twenty minutes later, the tethered wagons and riding horses and mules extended from the lot gate to Varner's store, and there were more than fifty men now standing along the fence beside the gate, watching him quietly, a little covertly, as he approached, rolling a little, slightly bowlegged, the high heels of his carved boots printing neatly into the dust. "Morning, gents," he said. "Here, Bud," he said to the little boy, who stood slightly behind him, looking at the protruding butt of the pistol. He took a coin from his pocket and gave it to the boy. "Run to the store and get me a box of gingersnaps." He looked about at the quiet faces, protuberant, sucking his teeth. He rolled the match from one side of his mouth to the other without touching it. "You boys done made your picks, have you? Ready to start her off, hah?" They did not answer. They were not looking at him now. That is, he began to have the feeling that each face had stopped looking at him the second before his gaze reached it. After a moment Freeman said:

"Ain't you going to wait for Flem?"

"Why?" the Texan said. Then Freeman stopped looking at him too. There was nothing in Freeman's face either. There was nothing, no alteration, in the Texan's voice. "Eck, you done already picked out yours. So we can start her off when you are ready."

"I reckon not," Eck said. "I wouldn't buy nothing I was afraid to walk up and touch."

"Them little ponies?" the Texan said. "You helped water and feed them. I bet that boy of yours could walk up to any one of them."

"He better not let me catch him," Eck said. The Texan looked about at the quiet faces, his gaze at once abstract and alert, with an impenetrable surface quality like flint, as though the surface were impervious or perhaps there was nothing behind it.

"Them ponies is gentle as a dove, boys. The man that buys them will get the best piece of horseflesh he ever forked or druv for the money. Naturally they got spirit; I ain't selling crowbait. Besides, who'd want Texas crowbait anyway, with Mississippi full of it?" His stare was still absent and unwinking; there was no mirth or humor in his voice and there was neither mirth nor humor in the single guffaw which came from the rear of the group. Two wagons were now drawing out of the road at the same time, up to the fence. The men got down from them and tied them to the fence and approached. "Come up, boys," the Texan said. "You're just in time to buy a good gentle horse cheap."

"How about that one that cut your vest off last night?" a voice said. This time three or four guffawed. The Texan looked toward the sound, bleak and unwinking.

"What about it?" he said. The laughter, if it had been laughter, ceased. The Texan turned to the nearest gatepost and climbed to the top of it, his alternate thighs deliberate and bulging in the tight trousers, the butt of the pistol catching and losing the sun in pearly gleams. Sitting on the post, he looked down at the faces along the fence which were attentive, grave, reserved and not looking at him. "All right," he said. "Who's going to start her off with a bid? Step right up; take your pick and make your bid, and when the last one is sold, walk in that lot and put your rope on the best piece of horse-flesh you ever forked or druv for the money. There ain't a pony there that ain't worth fifteen dollars. Young, sound, good for saddle or work stock, guaranteed to outlast four ordinary horses; you couldn't kill one of them with a axle-tree—" There was a small violent commotion at the rear of the group. The little boy appeared, burrowing among the motionless overalls. He approached the post, the new and unbroken paper carton lifted. The Texan leaned down and took it and tore the end from it and shook three or four of the cakes into the boy's hand, a hand as small and almost as black as that of a coon. He held the carton in his hand while he talked, pointing out the horses with it as he indicated them. "Look at that one with the three stocking-feet and the frost-bit ear; watch him now when they pass again. Look at that shoulder-action; that horse is worth twenty dollars of any man's money. Who'll make me a bid on him to start her off?" His voice was harsh, ready, forensic. Along the fence below him the men stood with, buttoned close in their overalls, the tobacco-sacks and worn purses the sparse silver and frayed bills hoarded a coin at a time in the cracks of chimneys or chinked into the logs of walls. From time to time the horses broke and rushed with purposeless violence and huddled again, watching the faces along the fence with wild mismatched eyes. The lane was full of wagons now. As the others arrived they would have to stop in the road beyond it and the occupants came up the lane on foot. Mrs. Littlejohn came out of her kitchen. She crossed the yard, looking toward the lot gate. There was a blackened wash pot set on four bricks in the corner of the yard. She built a fire beneath the pot and came to the fence and stood there for a time, her hands on her hips and the smoke from the fire drifting blue and slow behind her. Then she turned and went back into the house. "Come on, boys," the Texan said. "Who'll make me a bid?"

"Four bits," a voice said. The Texan did not even glance toward it.

"Or, if he don't suit you, how about that fiddle-head horse without no mane to speak of? For a saddle pony, I'd rather have him than that stocking-foot. I heard somebody say fifty cents just now. I reckon he meant five dollars, didn't he? Do I hear five dollars?"

"Four bits for the lot," the same voice said. This time there were no guffaws. It was the Texan who laughed, harshly, with only his lower face, as if he were reciting a multiplication table.

"Fifty cents for the dried mud offen them, he means," he said. "Who'll give a dollar more for the genuine Texas cockle-burrs?" Mrs. Littlejohn came out of the kitchen, carrying the sawn half of a wooden hogshead which she set on a stump beside the smoking pot, and

stood with her hands on her hips, looking into the lot
for a while without coming to the fence this time. Then
she went back into the house. "What's the matter with
you boys?" the Texan said. "Here, Eck, you been helping me and you know them horses. How about making
me a bid on that wall-eyed one you picked out last
night? Here. Wait a minute." He thrust the paper carton
into his other hip pocket and swung his feet inward and
dropped, cat-light, into the lot. The ponies, huddled,
watched him. Then they broke before him and slid stiffly
along the fence. He turned them and they whirled and
rushed back across the lot; whereupon, as though he
had been waiting his chance when they should have
turned their backs on him, the Texan began to run too,
so that when they reached the opposite side of the lot
and turned, slowing to huddle again, he was almost
upon them. The earth became thunderous; dust arose,
out of which the animals began to burst like flushed
quail and into which, with that apparently unflagging
faith in his own invulnerability, the Texan rushed. For
an instant the watchers could see them in the dust—
the pony backed into the angle of the fence and the
stable, the man facing it, reaching toward his hip. Then
the beast rushed at him in a sort of fatal and hopeless
desperation and he struck it between the eyes with the
pistol-butt and felled it and leaped onto its prone head.
The pony recovered almost at once and pawed itself to
its knees and heaved at its prisoned head and fought
itself up, dragging the man with it; for an instant in the
dust the watchers saw the man free of the earth and in
violent lateral motion like a rag attached to the horse's
head. Then the Texan's feet came back to earth and the
dust blew aside and revealed them, motionless, the
Texan's sharp heels braced into the ground, one hand
gripping the pony's forelock and the other its nostrils,

the long evil muzzle wrung backward over its scarred shoulder while it breathed in labored and hollow groans. Mrs. Littlejohn was in the yard again. No one had seen her emerge this time. She carried an armful of clothing and a metal-ridged washboard and she was standing motionless at the kitchen steps, looking into the lot. Then she moved across the yard, still looking into the lot, and dumped the garments into the tub, still looking into the lot. "Look him over, boys," the Texan panted, turning his own suffused face and the protuberant glare of his eyes toward the fence. "Look him over quick. Them shoulders and—" He had relaxed for an instant apparently. The animal exploded again; again for an instant the Texan was free of the earth, though he was still talking: "—and legs you whoa I'll tear your face right look him over quick boys worth fifteen dollars of let me get a holt of who'll make me a bid whoa you blare-eyed jack rabbit, whoa!" They were moving now—a kaleidoscope of inextricable and incredible violence on the periphery of which the metal clasps of the Texan's suspenders sun-glinted in ceaseless orbit, with terrific slowness across the lot. Then the broad clay-colored hat soared deliberately outward; an instant later the Texan followed it, though still on his feet, and the pony shot free in mad, staglike bounds. The Texan picked up the hat and struck the dust from it against his leg, and returned to the fence and mounted the post again. He was breathing heavily. Still the faces did not look at him as he took the carton from his hip and shook a cake from it and put the cake into his mouth, chewing, breathing harshly. Mrs. Littlejohn turned away and began to bail water from the pot into the tub, though after each bucketful she turned her head and looked into the lot again. "Now, boys," the Texan said. "Who says that pony ain't worth fifteen dollars? You couldn't buy that much dynamite for just fifteen dollars. There ain't one of them can't do a mile in three minutes; turn them into pasture and they will board themselves; work them like hell all day and every time you think about it, lay them over the head with a single-tree and after a couple of days every jack rabbit one of them will be so tame you will have to put them out of the house at night like a cat." He shook another cake from the carton and ate it. "Come on, Eck," he said. "Start her off. How about ten dollars for that horse, Eck?"

"What need I got for a horse I would need a bear-trap to catch?" Eck said.

"Didn't you just see me catch him?"

"I seen you," Eck said. "And I don't want nothing as big as a horse if I got to wrastle with it every time it finds me on the same side of a fence it's on."

"All right," the Texan said. He was still breathing harshly, but now there was nothing of fatigue or breathlessness in it. He shook another cake into his palm and inserted it beneath his moustache. "All right. I want to get this auction started. I ain't come here to live, no matter how good a country you folks claim you got. I'm going to give you that horse." For a moment there was no sound, not even that of breathing except the Texan's.

"You going to give it to me?" Eck said.

"Yes. Provided you will start the bidding on the next one." Again there was no sound save the Texan's breathing, and then the clash of Mrs. Littlejohn's pail against the rim of the pot.

"I just start the bidding," Eck said. "I don't have to buy it lessen I ain't over-topped." Another wagon had come up the lane. It was battered and paintless. One wheel had been repaired by crossed planks bound to the spokes with baling wire and the two underfed mules wore a battered harness patched with bits of cotton rope; the reins were ordinary cotton plowlines, not new. It contained a woman in a shapeless gray garment and a faded sunbonnet, and a man in faded and patched though clean overalls. There was not room for the wagon to draw out of the lane so the man left it standing where it was and got down and came forward—a thin man, not large, with something about his eyes, something strained and washed-out, at once vague and intense, who shoved into the crowd at the rear, saying,

"What? What's that? Did he give him that horse?"

"All right," the Texan said. "That wall-eyed horse with the scarred neck belongs to you. Now. That one that looks like he's had his head in a flour barrel. What do you say? Ten dollars?"

"Did he give him that horse?" the newcomer said.

"A dollar," Eck said. The Texan's mouth was still open for speech; for an instant his face died so behind the hard eyes.

"A dollar?" he said. "One dollar? Did I actually hear that?"

"Durn it," Eck said. "Two dollars then. But I ain't ____"

"Wait," the newcomer said. "You, up there on the post." The Texan looked at him. When the others turned, they saw that the woman had left the wagon too, though they had not known she was there since they had not seen the wagon drive up. She came among them behind the man, gaunt in the gray shapeless garment and the sunbonnet, wearing stained canvas gymnasium shoes. She overtook the man but she did not touch him, standing just behind him, her hands rolled before her into the gray dress.

"Henry," she said in a flat voice. The man looked over his shoulder.

"Get back to that wagon," he said.

"Here, missus," the Texan said. "Henry's going to get the bargain of his life in about a minute. Here, boys, let the missus come up close where she can see. Henry's going to pick out that saddle-horse the missus has been wanting. Who says ten——"

"Henry," the woman said. She did not raise her voice. She had not once looked at the Texan. She touched the man's arm. He turned and struck her hand down.

"Get back to that wagon like I told you." The woman stood behind him, her hands rolled again into her dress. She was not looking at anything, speaking to anyone.

"He ain't no more despair than to buy one of them things," she said. "And us not but five dollars away from the poorhouse, he ain't no more despair." The man turned upon her with that curious air of leashed, of dreamlike fury. The others lounged along the fence in attitudes gravely inattentive, almost oblivious. Mrs. Littlejohn had been washing for some time now, pumping rhythmically up and down above the washboard in the sud-foamed tub. She now stood erect again, her soap-raw hands on her hips, looking into the lot.

"Shut your mouth and get back in that wagon," the man said. "Do you want me to take a wagon stake to you?" He turned and looked up at the Texan. "Did you give him that horse?" he said. The Texan was looking at the woman. Then he looked at the man; still watching him, he tilted the paper carton over his open palm. A single cake came out of it.

"Yes," he said.

"Is the fellow that bids in this next horse going to get that first one too?"

"No," the Texan said.

"All right," the other said. "Are you going to give a horse to the man that makes the first bid on the next one?"

"No," the Texan said.

"Then if you were just starting the auction off by giving away a horse, why didn't you wait till we were all here?" The Texan stopped looking at the other. He raised the empty carton and squinted carefully into it, as if it might contain a precious jewel or perhaps a deadly insect. Then he crumpled it and dropped it carefully beside the post on which he sat.

"Eck bids two dollars," he said. "I believe he still thinks he's bidding on them scraps of bob-wire they come here in instead of on one of the horses. But I got to accept it. But are you boys——"

"So Eck's going to get two horses at a dollar a head," the newcomer said. "Three dollars." The woman touched him again. He flung her hand off without turning and she stood again, her hands rolled into her dress across her flat stomach, not looking at anything.

"Misters," she said, "we got chaps in the house that never had shoes last winter. We ain't got corn to feed the stock. We got five dollars I earned weaving by fire-light after dark. And he ain't no more despair."

"Henry bids three dollars," the Texan said. "Raise him a dollar, Eck, and the horse is yours." Beyond the fence the horses rushed suddenly and for no reason and as suddenly stopped, staring at the faces along the fence.

"Henry," the woman said. The man was watching Eck. His stained and broken teeth showed a little beneath his lip. His wrists dangled into fists below the faded sleeves of his shirt too short from many washings.

"Four dollars," Eck said.

"Five dollars!" the husband said, raising one clenched

hand. He shouldered himself forward toward the gate-post. The woman did not follow him. She now looked at the Texan for the first time. Her eyes were a washed gray also, as though they had faded too like the dress and the sunbonnet.

"Mister," she said, "if you take that five dollars I earned my chaps a-weaving for one of them things, it'll be a curse on you and yours during all the time of man."

"Five dollars!" the husband shouted. He thrust himself up to the post, his clenched hand on a level with the Texan's knees. He opened it upon a wad of frayed banknotes and silver. "Five dollars! And the man that raises it will have to beat my head off or I'll beat hisn."

"All right," the Texan said. "Five dollars is bid. But don't you shake your hand at me."

At five o'clock that afternoon the Texan crumpled the third paper carton and dropped it to the earth beneath him. In the copper slant of the levelling sun which fell also upon the line of limp garments in Mrs. Littlejohn's backyard and which cast his shadow and that of the post on which he sat long across the lot where now and then the ponies still rushed in purposeless and tireless surges, the Texan straightened his leg and thrust his hand into his pocket and took out a coin and leaned down to the little boy. His voice was now hoarse, spent. "Here, bud," he said. "Run to the store and get me a box of ginger-snaps." The men still stood along the fence, tireless, in their overalls and faded shirts. Flem Snopes was there now, appeared suddenly from nowhere, standing beside the fence with a space the width of three or four men on either side of him, standing there in his small yet definite isolation, chewing tobacco, in the same gray trousers and minute bow tie in which he had departed last summer but in a new cap, gray too like the other, but new, and overlaid with a bright golfer's plaid, looking also at the horses in the lot. All of them save two had been sold for sums ranging from three dollars and a half to eleven and twelve dollars. The purchasers, as they had bid them in, had gathered as though by instinct into a separate group on the other side of the gate, where they stood with their hands lying upon the top strand of the fence, watching with a still more sober intensity the animals which some of them had owned for seven and eight hours now but had not yet laid hands upon. The husband, Henry, stood beside the post on which the Texan sat. The wife had gone back to the wagon, where she sat gray in the gray garment, motionless, looking at nothing, still, she might have been something inanimate which he had loaded into the wagon to move it somewhere, waiting now in the wagon until he should be ready to go on again, patient, insensate, timeless.

"I bought a horse and I paid cash for it," he said. His voice was harsh and spent too, the mad look in his eyes had a quality glazed now and even sightless. "And yet you expect me to stand around here till they are all sold before I can get my horse. Well, you can do all the expecting you want. I'm going to take my horse out of there and go home." The Texan looked down at him. The Texan's shirt was blotched with sweat. His big face was cold and still, his voice level.

"Take your horse then." After a moment Henry looked away. He stood with his head bent a little, swallowing from time to time.

"Ain't you going to catch him for me?"

"It ain't my horse," the Texan said in that flat still voice. After a while Henry raised his head. He did not look at the Texan.

"Who'll help me catch my horse?" he said. Nobody answered. They stood along the fence, looking quietly into the lot where the ponies huddled, already beginning to fade a little where the long shadow of the house lay upon them, deepening. From Mrs. Littlejohn's kitchen the smell of frying ham came. A noisy cloud of sparrows swept across the lot and into a chinaberry tree beside the house, and in the high soft vague blue swallows stooped and whirled in erratic indecision, their cries like strings plucked at random. Without looking back, Henry raised his voice: "Bring that ere plowline." After a time the wife moved. She got down from the wagon and took a coil of new cotton rope from it and approached. The husband took the rope from her and moved toward the gate. The Texan began to descend from the post, stiffly, as Henry put his hand on the latch. "Come on here," he said. The wife had stopped when he took the rope from her. She moved again, obediently, her hands rolled into the dress across her stomach, passing the Texan without looking at him.

"Don't go in there, missus," he said. She stopped, not looking at him, not looking at anything. The husband opened the gate and entered the lot and turned, holding the gate open but without raising his eyes.

"Come on here," he said.

"Don't you go in there, missus," the Texan said. The wife stood motionless between them, her face almost concealed by the sunbonnet, her hands folded across her stomach.

"I reckon I better," she said. The other men did not look at her at all, at her or Henry either. They stood along the fence, grave and quiet and inattentive, almost bemused. Then the wife passed through the gate; the husband shut it behind them and turned and began to move toward the huddled ponies, the wife following in the gray and shapeless garment within which she moved without inference of locomotion, like something on a moving platform, a float. The horses were watching them. They clotted and blended and shifted among themselves, on the point of breaking though not breaking yet. The husband shouted at them. He began to curse them, advancing, the wife following. Then the huddle broke, the animals moving with high, stiff knees, circling the two people who turned and followed again as the herd flowed and huddled again at the opposite side of the lot.

"There he is," the husband said. "Get him into that corner." The herd divided; the horse which the husband had bought jolted on stiff legs. The wife shouted at it; it spun and poised, plunging, then the husband struck it across the face with the coiled rope and it whirled and slammed into the corner of the fence. "Keep him there now," the husband said. He shook out the rope, advancing. The horse watched him with wild, glaring eyes; it rushed again, straight toward the wife. She shouted at it and waved her arms but it soared past her in a long bound and rushed again into the huddle of its fellows. They followed and hemmed it again into another corner; again the wife failed to stop its rush for freedom and the husband turned and struck her with the coiled rope. "Why didn't you head him?" he said. "Why didn't you?" He struck her again; she did not move, not even to fend the rope with a raised arm. The men along the fence stood quietly, their faces lowered as though brooding upon the earth at their feet. Only Flem Snopes was still watching—if he ever had been looking into the lot at all, standing in his little island of isolation, chewing with his characteristic faint sidewise thrust beneath the new plaid cap.

The Texan said something, not loud, harsh and short. He entered the lot and went to the husband and jerked the uplifted rope from his hand. The husband whirled as though he were about to spring at the Texan.

crouched slightly, his knees bent and his arms held slightly away from his sides, though his gaze never mounted higher than the Texan's carved and dusty boots. Then the Texan took the husband by the arm and led him back toward the gate, the wife following, and through the gate which he held open for the woman and then closed. He took a wad of banknotes from his trousers and removed a bill from it and put it into the woman's hand. "Get him into the wagon and get him on home," he said.

"What's that for?" Flem Snopes said. He had approached. He now stood beside the post on which the Texan had been sitting. The Texan did not look at him.

"Thinks he bought one of them ponies," the Texan said. He spoke in a flat still voice, like that of a man after a sharp run. "Get him on away, missus."

"Give him back that money," the husband said, in his lifeless, spent tone. "I bought that horse and I aim to have him if I got to shoot him before I can put a rope on him." The Texan did not even look at him.

"Get him on away from here, missus," he said.

"You take your money and I take my horse," the husband said. He was shaking slowly and steadily now, as though he were cold. His hands open and shut below the frayed cuffs of his shirt. "Give it back to him," he said.

"You don't own no horse of mine," the Texan said. "Get him on home, missus." The husband raised his spent face, his mad glazed eyes. He reached out his hand. The woman held the banknote in her folded hands across her stomach. For a while the husband's shaking hand merely fumbled at it. Then he drew the banknote free.

"It's my horse," he said. "I bought it. These fellows saw me. I paid for it. It's my horse. Here." He turned and extended the banknote toward Snopes. "You got something to do with these horses. I bought one. Here's the money for it. I bought one. Ask him." Snopes took the banknote. The others stood, gravely inattentive, in relaxed attitudes along the fence. The sun had gone now; there was nothing save violet shadow upon them and upon the lot where once more and for no reason the ponies rushed and flowed. At that moment the little boy came up, tireless and indefatigable still, with the new paper carton. The Texan took it, though he did not open it at once. He had dropped the rope and now the husband stooped for it, fumbling at it for some time before he lifted it from the ground. Then he stood with his head bent, his knuckles whitening on the rope. The woman had not moved. Twilight was coming fast now; there was a last mazy swirl of swallows against the high and changing azure. Then the Texan tore the end from the carton and tilted one of the cakes into his hand; he seemed to be watching the hand as it shut slowly upon the cake until a fine powder of snuff-colored dust began to rain from his fingers. He rubbed the hand carefully on his thigh and raised his head and glanced about until he saw the little boy and handed the carton back to him.

"Here, Bud," he said. Then he looked at the woman, his voice flat, quiet again. "Mr. Snopes will have your money for you tomorrow. Better get him in the wagon and get him on home. He don't own no horse. You can get your money tomorrow from Mr. Snopes." The wife turned and went back to the wagon and got into it. No one watched her, nor the husband who still stood, his head bent, passing the rope from one hand to the other. They leaned along the fence, grave and quiet, as though the fence were in another land, another time.

"How many you got left?" Snopes said. The Texan roused; they all seemed to rouse then, returning, listening again.

"Got three now," the Texan said. "Swap all three of them for a buggy or a——"

"It's out in the road," Snopes said, a little shortly, a little quickly, turning away. "Get your mules." He went on up the lane. They watched the Texan enter the lot and cross it, the horses flowing before him but without the old irrational violence, as if they too were spent, vitiated with the long day, and enter the barn and then emerge, leading the two harnessed mules. The wagon had been backed under the shed beside the barn. The Texan entered this and came out a moment later, carrying a bedding-roll and his coat, and led the mules back toward the gate, the ponies huddled again and watching him with their various unmatching eyes, quietly now, as if they too realized there was not only an armistice between them at last but that they would never look upon each other again in both their lives. Someone opened the gate. The Texan led the mules through it and they followed in a body, leaving the husband standing beside the closed gate, his head still bent and the coiled rope in his hand. They passed the wagon in which the wife sat, her gray garment fading into the dusk, almost the same color and as still, looking at nothing; they passed the clothesline with its limp and unwinded drying garments, walking through the hot vivid smell of ham from Mrs. Littlejohn's kitchen. When they reached the end of the lane they could see the moon, almost full, tremendous and pale and still lightless in the sky from which day had not quite gone. Snopes was standing at the end of the lane beside an empty buggy. It was the one with the glittering wheels

and the fringed parasol top in which he and Will Varner
had used to drive. The Texan was motionless too, looking at it.

"Well well well," he said. "So this is it."

"If it don't suit you, you can ride one of the mules
back to Texas," Snopes said.

"You bet," the Texan said. "Only I ought to have a
powder puff or at least a mandolin to ride it with." He
backed the mules onto the tongue and lifted the breast-
yoke. Two of them came forward and fastened the
traces for him. Then they watched him get into the
buggy and raise the reins.

"Where you heading for?" one said. "Back to Texas?"

"In this?" the Texan said. "I wouldn't get past the
first Texas saloon without starting the vigilance committee. Besides, I ain't going to waste all this here lace-
trimmed top and these spindle wheels just on Texas.
Long as I am this far, I reckon I'll go on a day or two
and look-see them Northern towns. Washington and
New York and Baltimore. What's the short way to New
York from here?" They didn't know. But they told him
how to reach Jefferson.

"You're already headed right," Freeman said. "Just
keep right on up the road past the schoolhouse."

"All right," the Texan said. "Well, remember about
busting them ponies over the head now and then until
they get used to you. You won't have any trouble with
them then." He lifted the reins again. As he did so
Snopes stepped forward and got into the buggy.

"I'll ride as far as Varner's with you," he said.

"I didn't know I was going past Varner's," the Texan
said.

"You can go to town that way," Snopes said. "Drive
on." The Texan shook the reins. Then he said,

"Whoa." He straightened his leg and put his hand

into his pocket. "Here, Bud," he said to the little boy, "run to the store and— Never mind. I'll stop and get it myself, long as I am going back that way. Well, boys," he said. "Take care of yourselves." He swung the team around. The buggy went on. They looked after it.

"I reckon he aims to kind of come up on Jefferson from behind," Quick said.

"He'll be lighter when he gets there," Freeman said. "He can come up to it easy from any side he wants."

"Yes," Bookwright said. "His pockets won't rattle." They went back to the lot; they passed on through the narrow way between the two lines of patient and motionless wagons, which at the end was completely closed by the one in which the woman sat. The husband was still standing beside the gate with his coiled rope, and now night had completely come. The light itself had not changed so much; if anything, it was brighter but with that other-worldly quality of moonlight, so that when they stood once more looking into the lot, the splotchy bodies of the ponies had a distinctness, almost a brilliance, but without individual shape and without depth—no longer horses, no longer flesh and bone directed by a principle capable of calculated violence, no longer inherent with the capacity to hurt and harm.

"Well, what are we waiting for?" Freeman said. "For them to go to roost?"

"We better all get our ropes first," Quick said. "Get your ropes everybody." Some of them did not have ropes. When they left home that morning, they had not heard about the horses, the auction. They had merely happened through the village by chance and learned of it and stopped.

"Go to the store and get some then," Freeman said.

"The store will be closed now," Quick said.

"No it won't," Freeman said. "If it was closed, Lump Snopes would a been up here." So while the ones who had come prepared got their ropes from the wagons, the others went down to the store. The clerk was just closing it.

"You all ain't started catching them yet, have you?" he said. "Good; I was afraid I wouldn't get there in time." He opened the door again and amid the old strong sunless smells of cheese and leather and molasses he measured and cut off sections of plow-line for them and in a body and the clerk in the center and still talking, voluble and unlistened to, they returned up the road. The pear tree before Mrs. Littlejohn's was like drowned silver now in the moon. The mockingbird of last night, or another one, was already singing in it, and they now saw, tied to the fence, Ratliff's buckboard and team.

"I thought something was wrong all day," one said. "Ratliff wasn't there to give nobody advice." When they passed down the lane, Mrs. Littlejohn was in her backyard, gathering the garments from the clothesline; they could still smell the ham. The others were waiting at the gate, beyond which the ponies, huddled again, were like phantom fish, suspended apparently without legs now in the brilliant treachery of the moon.

"I reckon the best way will be for us all to take and catch them one at a time," Freeman said.

"One at a time," the husband, Henry, said. Apparently he had not moved since the Texan had led his mules through the gate, save to lift his hands to the top of the gate, one of them still clutching the coiled rope. "One at a time," he said. He began to curse in a harsh, spent monotone. "After I've stood around here all day, waiting for that—" He cursed. He began to jerk at the gate, shaking it with spent violence until one of the others slid the latch back and it swung open and Henry entered it, the others following, the little boy pressing close behind his father until Eck became aware of him and turned.

"Here," he said. "Give me that rope. You stay out of here."

"Aw, paw," the boy said.

"No sir. Them things will kill you. They almost done it this morning. You stay out of here."

"But we got two to catch." For a moment Eck stood looking down at the boy.

"That's right," he said. "We got two. But you stay close to me now. And when I holler run, you run. You hear me?"

"Spread out, boys," Freeman said. "Keep them in front of us." They began to advance across the lot in a ragged crescent-shaped line, each one with his rope. The ponies were now at the far side of the lot. One of them snorted; the mass shifted within itself but without breaking. Freeman, glancing back, saw the little boy. "Get that boy out of here," he said.

"I reckon you better," Eck said to the boy. "You go and get in the wagon yonder. You can see us catch them from there." The little boy turned and trotted toward the shed beneath which the wagon stood. The line of men advanced, Henry a little in front.

"Watch them close now," Freeman said. "Maybe we better try to get them into the barn first—" At that moment the huddle broke. It parted and flowed in both directions along the fence. The men at the ends of the line began to run, waving their arms and shouting. "Head them," Freeman said tensely. "Turn them back." They turned them, driving them back upon themselves again; the animals merged and spun in short, huddling rushes, phantom and inextricable. "Hold them now,"

Freeman said. "Don't let them get by us." The line advanced again. Eck turned; he did not know why— whether a sound, what. The little boy was just behind him again.

"Didn't I tell you to get in that wagon and stay there?" Eck said.

"Watch out, paw!" the boy said. "There he is! There's ourn!" It was the one the Texan had given Eck. "Catch him, paw!"

"Get out of my way," Eck said. "Get back to that wagon." The line was still advancing. The ponies milled, clotting, forced gradually backward toward the open door of the barn. Henry was still slightly in front, crouched slightly, his thin figure, even in the mazy moonlight, emanating something of that spent fury. The splotchy huddle of animals seemed to be moving before the advancing line of men like a snowball which they might have been pushing before them by some invisible means, gradually nearer and nearer to the black yawn of the barn door. Later it was obvious that the ponies were so intent upon the men that they did not realize the barn was even behind them until they backed into the shadow of it. Then an indescribable sound, a movement desperate and despairing, arose among them; for an instant of static horror men and animals faced one another, then the men whirled and ran before a gaudy vomit of long wild faces and splotched chests which overtook and scattered them and flung them sprawling aside and completely obliterated from sight Henry and the little boy, neither of whom had moved though Henry had flung up both arms, still holding his coiled rope, the herd sweeping on across the lot, to crash through the gate which the last man through it had neglected to close, leaving it slightly ajar, carrying all of the gate save the upright to which the hinges were nailed with

them, and so among the teams and wagons which
choked the lane, the teams springing and lunging too,
snapping hitch-reins and tongues. Then the whole inextricable mass crashed among the wagons and eddied
and divided about the one in which the woman sat,
and rushed on down the lane and into the road, dividing, one half going one way and one half the other.

The men in the lot, except Henry, got to their feet
and ran toward the gate. The little boy once more had
not been touched, not even thrown off his feet; for a
while his father held him clear of the ground in one
hand, shaking him like a rag doll. "Didn't I tell you to
stay in that wagon?" Eck cried. "Didn't I tell you?"

"Look out, paw!" the boy chattered out of the violent
shaking, "there's ourn! There he goes!" It was the horse
the Texan had given them again. It was as if they owned
no other, the other one did not exist; as if by some absolute and instantaneous rapport of blood they had rele-
gated to oblivion the one for which they had paid
money. They ran to the gate and down the lane where
the other men had disappeared. They saw the horse the
Texan had given them whirl and dash back and rush
through the gate into Mrs. Littlejohn's yard and run up
the front steps and crash once on the wooden veranda
and vanish through the front door. Eck and the boy ran
up onto the veranda. A lamp sat on a table just inside
the door. In its mellow light they saw the horse fill the
long hallway like a pinwheel, gaudy, furious and thunderous. A little further down the hall there was a
varnished yellow melodeon. The horse crashed into it;
it produced a single note, almost a chord, in bass,
resonant and grave, of deep and sober astonishment;
the horse with its monstrous and antic shadow whirled
again and vanished through another door. It was a bedroom; Ratliff, in his underclothes and one sock and with

the other sock in his hand and his back to the door, was leaning out the open window facing the lane, the lot. He looked back over his shoulder. For an instant he and the horse glared at one another. Then he sprang through the window as the horse backed out of the room and into the hall again and whirled and saw Eck and the little boy just entering the front door, Eck still carrying his rope. It whirled again and rushed on down the hall and onto the back porch just as Mrs. Littlejohn, carrying an armful of clothes from the line and the washboard, mounted the steps.

"Get out of here, you son of a bitch," she said. She struck with the washboard; it divided neatly on the long mad face and the horse whirled and rushed back up the hall, where Eck and the boy now stood.

"Get to hell out of here, Wall!" Eck roared. He dropped to the floor, covering his head with his arms. The boy did not move, and for the third time the horse soared above the unwinking eyes and the unbowed and untouched head and onto the front veranda again just as Ratliff, still carrying the sock, ran around the corner of the house and up the steps. The horse whirled without breaking or pausing. It galloped to the end of the veranda and took the railing and soared outward, hob-goblin and floating, in the moon. It landed in the lot still running and crossed the lot and galloped through the wrecked gate and among the overturned wagons and the still intact one in which Henry's wife still sat, and on down the lane and into the road.

A quarter of a mile further on, the road gashed pallid and moony between the moony shadows of the bordering trees, the horse still galloping, galloping its shadow into the dust, the road descending now toward the creek and the bridge. It was of wood, just wide enough for a single vehicle. When the horse reached it, it was occupied by a wagon coming from the opposite direction and drawn by two mules already asleep in the harness and the soporific motion. On the seat was Tull and his wife, in splint chairs in the wagon behind them sat their four daughters, all returning belated from an all-day visit with some of Mrs. Tull's kin. The horse neither checked nor swerved. It crashed once on the wooden bridge and rushed between the two mules which waked lunging in opposite directions in the traces, the horse now apparently scrambling along the wagon-tongue itself like a mad squirrel and scrabbling at the end-gate of the wagon with its forefeet as if it intended to climb into the wagon while Tull shouted at it and struck at its face with his whip. The mules were now trying to turn the wagon around in the middle of the bridge. It slewed and tilted, the bridge-rail cracked with a sharp report above the shrieks of the women; the horse scrambled at last across the back of one of the mules and Tull stood up in the wagon and kicked at its face. Then the front end of the wagon rose, flinging Tull, the reins now wrapped several times about his wrist, backward into the wagon bed among the overturned chairs and the exposed stockings and undergarments of his women. The pony scrambled free and crashed again on the wooden planking, galloping again. The wagon lurched again; the mules had finally turned it on the bridge where there was not room for it to turn and were now kicking themselves free of the traces. When they came free, they snatched Tull bodily out of the wagon. He struck the bridge on his face and was dragged for several feet before the wrist-wrapped reins broke. Far up the road now, distancing the frantic mules, the pony faded on. While the five women still shrieked above Tull's unconscious body, Eck and the little boy came up, trotting, Eck still carrying his rope. He was panting. "Which way'd he go?" he said.

In the now empty and moon-drenched lot, his wife and Mrs. Littlejohn and Ratliff and Lump Snopes, the clerk, and three other men raised Henry out of the trampled dust and carried him into Mrs. Littlejohn's back yard. His face was blanched and stony, his eyes were closed, the weight of his head tautened his throat across the protruding larynx; his teeth glinted dully beneath his lifted lip. They carried him on toward the house, through the dappled shade of the chinaberry trees. Across the dreaming and silver night a faint sound like remote thunder came and ceased. "There's one of them on the creek bridge," one of the men said.

"It's that one of Eck Snopes'," another said. "The one that was in the house." Mrs. Littlejohn had preceded them into the hall. When they entered with Henry, she had already taken the lamp from the table and she stood beside an open door, holding the lamp high.

"Bring him in here," she said. She entered the room first and set the lamp on the dresser. They followed with clumsy scufflings and pantings and laid Henry on the bed and Mrs. Littlejohn came to the bed and stood looking down at Henry's peaceful and bloodless face. "I'll declare," she said. "You men." They had drawn back a little, clumped, shifting from one foot to another, not looking at her nor at his wife either, who stood at the foot of the bed, motionless, her hands folded into her dress. "You all get out of here, V. K.," she said to Ratliff. "Go outside. See if you can't find something else to play with that will kill some more of you."

"All right," Ratliff said. "Come on, boys. Ain't no more horses to catch in here." They followed him toward the door, on tiptoe, their shoes scuffling, their shadows monstrous on the wall.

"Go get Will Varner," Mrs. Littlejohn said. "I reckon you can tell him it's still a mule." They went out; they didn't look back. They tiptoed up the hall and crossed the veranda and descended into the moonlight. Now that they could pay attention to it, the silver air seemed to be filled with faint and sourceless sounds—shouts, thin and distant, again a brief thunder of hooves on a wooden bridge, more shouts faint and thin and earnest and clear as bells; once they even distinguished the words: "Whooey. Head him."

"He went through that house quick," Ratliff said. "He must have found another woman at home." Then Henry screamed in the house behind them. They looked back into the dark hall where a square of light fell through the bedroom door, listening while the scream sank into a harsh respiration: "Ah. Ah. Ah" on a rising note about to become screaming again. "Come on," Ratliff said. "We better get Varner." They went up the road in a body, treading the moon-blanched dust in the tremulous April night murmurous with the moving of sap and the wet bursting of burgeoning leaf and bud and constant with the thin and urgent cries and the brief and fading bursts of galloping hooves. Varner's house was dark, blank and without depth in the moonlight. They stood, clumped darkly in the silver yard and called up at the blank windows until suddenly someone was standing in one of them. It was Flem Snopes' wife. She was in a white garment; the heavy braided club of her hair looked almost black against it. She did not lean out, she merely stood there, full in the moon, apparently blank-eyed or certainly not looking downward at them—the heavy gold hair, the mask not tragic and perhaps not even doomed: just damned, the strong faint lift of breasts beneath marblelike fall of the garment; to those below what Brunhilde, what Rhinemaiden on what spurious river-rock of papier-mache, what Helen returned to what topless and shoddy Argos, waiting for no one. "Evening, Mrs. Snopes," Ratliff said. "We want Uncle Will. Henry Armstid is hurt at Mrs. Littlejohn's." She vanished from the window. They waited in the moonlight, listening to the faint remote shouts and cries, until Varner emerged, sooner than they had actually expected, hunching into his coat and buttoning his trousers over the tail of his nightshirt, his suspenders still dangling in twin loops below the coat. He was carrying the battered bag which contained the plumber-like tools with which he drenched and wormed and blistered and floated or drew the teeth of horses and mules; he came down the steps, lean and loosejointed, his shrewd ruthless head cocked a little as he listened also to the faint bell-like cries and shouts with which the silver air was full.

"Are they still trying to catch them rabbits?" he said.

"All of them except Henry Armstid," Ratliff said. "He caught his."

"Hah," Varner said. "That you, V. K.? How many did you buy?"

"I was too late," Ratliff said. "I never got back in time."

"Hah," Varner said. They moved on to the gate and into the road again. "Well, it's a good bright cool night for running them." The moon was now high overhead, a pearled and mazy yawn in the soft sky, the ultimate ends of which rolled onward, whorl on whorl, beyond the pale stars and by pale stars surrounded. They walked in a close clump, tramping their shadows into the road's mild dust, blotting the shadows of the burgeoning trees which soared, trunk branch and twig against the pale sky, delicate and finely thinned. They passed the dark store. Then the pear tree came in sight. It rose in mazed and silver immobility like exploding snow; the mockingbird still sang in it. "Look at that tree," Varner said. "It ought to make this year, sho."

"Corn'll make this year too," one said.

"A moon like this is good for every growing thing outen earth," Varner said. "I mind when me and Mrs. Varner was expecting Eula. Already had a mess of children and maybe we ought to quit then. But I wanted some more gals. Others had done married and moved away, and a passel of boys, soon as they get big enough to be worth anything, they ain't got time to work. Got to set around the store and talk. But a gal will stay home and work until she does get married. So there was a old woman told my mammy once that if a woman showed her belly to the full moon after she had done caught, it would be a gal. So Mrs. Varner taken and laid every night with the moon on her nekid belly, until it fulled and after. I could lay my ear to her belly and hear Eula kicking and scrouging like all get-out, feeling the moon."

"You mean it actually worked sho enough, Uncle Will?" the other said.

"Hah," Varner said. "You might try it. You get enough women showing their nekid bellies to the moon or the sun either or even just to your hand fumbling around often enough and more than likely after a while there will be something in it you can lay your ear and listen to, provided something come up and you ain't got away by that time. Hah, V. K.?" Someone guffawed.

"Don't ask me," Ratliff said. "I can't even get nowhere in time to buy a cheap horse." Two or three guf-

fawed this time. Then they began to hear Henry's res-
pirations from the house: "Ah. Ah. Ah." and they ceased
abruptly, as if they had not been aware of their close-
ness to it. Varner walked on in front, lean, shambling,
yet moving quite rapidly, though his head was still
slanted with listening as the faint, urgent, indomitable
cries murmured in the silver lambence, sourceless, at
times almost musical, like fading bell-notes; again there
was a brief rapid thunder of hooves on wooden planking.

"There's another one on the creek bridge," one said.

"They are going to come out even on them things,
after all," Varner said. "They'll get the money back in
exercise and relaxation. You take a man that ain't got
no other relaxation all year long except dodging mule-
dung up and down a field furrow. And a night like this
one, when a man ain't old enough yet to lay still and
sleep, and yet he ain't young enough anymore to be
tomcatting in and out of other folks' back windows,
something like this is good for him. It'll make him sleep
tomorrow night anyhow, provided he gets back home
by then. If we had just knowed about this in time, we
could have trained up a pack of horse-dogs. Then we
could have held one of these field trials."

"That's one way to look at it, I reckon," Ratliff said.
"In fact, it might be a considerable comfort to Bookwright and Quick and Freeman and Eck Snopes and
them other new horse-owners if that side of it could be
brought to their attention, because the chances are
ain't none of them thought to look at it in that light yet.
Probably there ain't a one of them that believes now
there's any cure a tall for that Texas disease Flem
Snopes and that Dead-eye Dick brought here."

"Hah," Varner said. He opened Mrs. Littlejohn's gate.

The dim light still fell outward across the hall from the
bedroom door; beyond it, Armstid was saying "Ah. Ah.
Ah" steadily. "There's a pill for every ill but the last
one."

"Even if there was always time to take it," Ratliff said.

"Hah," Varner said again. He glanced back at Ratliff
for an instant, pausing. But the little hard bright eyes
were invisible now; it was only the bushy overhang of
the brows which seemed to concentrate downward
toward him in writhen immobility, not frowning but
with a sort of fierce risibility. "Even if there was time to
take it. Breathing is a sight-draft dated yesterday."

11

At nine o'clock on the second morning after that, five
men were sitting or squatting along the gallery of the
store. The sixth was Ratliff. He was standing up, and
talking: "Maybe there wasn't but one of them things in
Mrs. Littlejohn's house that night, like Eck says. But it
was the biggest drove of just one horse I ever seen. It
was in my rooms and it was on the front porch and I
could hear Mrs. Littlejohn hitting it over the head with
that washboard in the back yard all at the same time.
And still it was missing everybody everytime. I reckon
that's what that Texas man meant by calling them bar-
gains: that a man would need to be powerful unlucky
to ever get close enough to one of them to get hurt."
They laughed, all except Eck himself. He and the little
boy were eating. When they mounted the steps, Eck
had gone on into the store and emerged with a paper
sack, from which he took a segment of cheese and with
his pocket knife divided it carefully into two exact
halves and gave one to the boy and took a handful of

crackers from the sack and gave them to the boy, and now they squatted against the wall, side by side and, save for the difference in size, identical, eating.

"I wonder what that horse thought Ratliff was," one said. He held a spray of peach bloom between his teeth. It bore four blossoms like miniature ballet skirts of pink tulle. "Jumping out windows and running indoors in his shirt-tail? I wonder how many Ratliffs that horse thought he saw."

"I don't know," Ratliff said. "But if he saw just half as many of me as I saw of him, he was sholy surrounded. Everytime I turned my head, that thing was just running over me or just swirling to run back over that boy again. And that boy there, he stayed right under it one time to my certain knowledge for a full one-and-one-half minutes without ducking his head or even batting his eyes. Yes sir, when I looked around and seen that varmint in the door behind me blaring its eyes at me, I'd a made sho Flem Snopes had brought a tiger back from Texas except I knowed that couldn't no just one tiger completely fill a entire room." They laughed again, quietly. Lump Snopes, the clerk, sitting in the only chair tilted back against the door-facing and partly blocking the entrance, cackled suddenly.

"If Flem had knowed how quick you fellows was going to snap them horses up, he'd a probably brought some tigers," he said. "Monkeys too."

"So they was Flem's horses," Ratliff said. The laughter stopped. The other three had open knives in their hands, with which they had been trimming idly at chips and slivers of wood. Now they sat apparently absorbed in the delicate and almost tedious movements of the knife-blades. The clerk had looked quickly up and found Ratliff watching him. His constant expression of incorrigible and mirthful disbelief had left him now;

only the empty wrinkles of it remained about his mouth and eyes.

"Has Flem ever said they was?" he said. "But you town fellows are smarter than us country folks. Likely you done already read Flem's mind." But Ratliff was not looking at him now.

"And I reckon we'd a bought them," he said. He stood above them again, easy, intelligent, perhaps a little sombre but still perfectly impenetrable. "Eck here, for instance. With a wife and family to support. He owns two of them, though to be sho he never had to pay money for but one. I heard folks chasing them things up until midnight last night, but Eck and that boy ain't been home at all in two days." They laughed again, except Eck. He pared off a bit of cheese and speared it on the knife-point and put it into his mouth.

"Eck caught one of hisn," the second man said.

"That so?" Ratliff said. "Which one was it, Eck? The one he give you or the one you bought?"

"The one he give me," Eck said, chewing.

"Well, well," Ratliff said. "I hadn't heard about that. But Eck's still one horse short. And the one he had to pay money for. Which is pure proof enough that them horses wasn't Flem's because wouldn't no man even give his own blood kin something he couldn't even catch." They laughed again, but they stopped when the clerk spoke. There was no mirth in his voice at all.

"Listen," he said. "All right. We done all admitted you are too smart for anybody to get ahead of. You never bought no horse from Flem or nobody else, so maybe it ain't none of your business and maybe you better just leave it at that."

"Sholy," Ratliff said. "It's done already been left at that two nights ago. The fellow that forgot to shut that lot gate done that. With the exception of Eck's horse.

And we know that wasn't Flem's, because that horse was give to Eck for nothing."

"There's others besides Eck that ain't got back home yet," the man with the peach spray said. "Bookwright and Quick are still chasing theirs. They was reported three miles west of Burtsboro Old Town at eight o'clock last night. They ain't got close enough to it yet to tell which one it belongs to."

"Sholy," Ratliff said. "The only new horse-owner in this country that could a been found without blood-hounds since whoever it was left that gate open two nights ago, is Henry Armstid. He's laying right there in Mrs. Littlejohn's bedroom where he can watch the lot so that any time the one he bought happens to run back into it, all he's got to do is to holler at his wife to run out with the rope and catch it—" He ceased, though he said, "Morning, Flem," so immediately afterward and with no change whatever in tone, that the pause was not even discernible. With the exception of the clerk, who sprang up, vacated the chair with a sort of servile alacrity, and Eck and the little boy who continued to eat, they watched above their stilled hands as Snopes in the gray trousers and the minute tie and the new cap with its bright overplaid mounted the steps. He was chewing; he already carried a piece of white pine board; he jerked his head at them, looking at nobody, and took the vacated chair and opened his knife and began to whittle. The clerk now leaned in the opposite side of the door, rubbing his back against the facing. The expression of merry and invincible disbelief had returned to his face, with a quality watchful and secret.

"You're just in time," he said. "Ratliff here seems to be in a considerable sweat about who actually owned them horses." Snopes drew his knife-blade neatly along the board, the neat, surgeon-like sliver curling before it.

The others were whittling again, looking carefully at nothing, except Eck and the boy, who were still eating, and the clerk rubbing his back against the door-facing and watching Snopes with that secret and alert intensity. "Maybe you could put his mind at rest." Snopes turned his head slightly and spat, across the gallery and the steps and into the dust beyond them. He drew the knife back and began another curling sliver.

"He was there too," Snopes said. "He knows as much as anybody else." This time the clerk guffawed, chortling, his features gathering toward the center of his face as though plucked there by a hand. He slapped his leg, cackling.

"You might as well to quit," he said. "You can't beat him."

"I reckon not," Ratliff said. He stood above them, not looking at any of them, his gaze fixed apparently on the empty road beyond Mrs. Littlejohn's house, impenetrable, brooding even. A hulking, half-grown boy in overalls too small for him, appeared suddenly from nowhere in particular. He stood for a while in the road, just beyond spitting-range of the gallery, with the air of having come from nowhere in particular and of not knowing where he would go next when he should move again and of not being troubled by that fact. He was looking at nothing, certainly not toward the gallery, and no one on the gallery so much as looked at him except the little boy, who now watched the boy in the road, his periwinkle eyes grave and steady above the bitten cracker in his halted hand. The boy in the road moved on, thickly undulant in the tight overalls, and vanished beyond the corner of the store, the round head and the unwinking eyes of the little boy on the gallery turning steadily to watch him out of sight. Then the little boy bit the cracker again, chewing. "Of course there's Mrs.

Tull," Ratliff said. "But that's Eck she's going to sue for damaging Tull against that bridge. And as for Henry Armstid——"

"If a man ain't got gumption enough to protect himself, it's his own look-out," the clerk said.

"Sholy," Ratliff said, still in that dreamy, abstracted tone, actually speaking over his shoulder even. "And Henry Armstid, that's all right because from what I hear of the conversation that taken place, Henry had already stopped owning that horse he thought was his before that Texas man left. And as for that broke leg, that won't put him out none because his wife can make his crop." The clerk had ceased to rub his back against the door. He watched the back of Ratliff's head, unwinking too, sober and intent; he glanced at Snopes who, chewing, was watching another sliver curl away from the advancing knife-blade, then he watched the back of Ratliff's head again.

"It won't be the first time she has made their crop," the man with the peach spray said. Ratliff glanced at him.

"You ought to know. This won't be the first time I ever saw you in their field, doing plowing Henry never got around to. How many days have you already given them this year?" The man with the peach spray removed it and spat carefully and put the spray back between his teeth.

"She can run a furrow straight as I can," the second said.

"They're unlucky," the third said. "When you are unlucky, it don't matter much what you do."

"Sholy," Ratliff said. "I've heard laziness called bad luck so much that maybe it is."

"He ain't lazy," the third said. "When their mule died three or four years ago, him and her broke their land working time about in the traces with the other mule. They ain't lazy."

"So that's all right," Ratliff said, gazing up the empty road again. "Likely she will begin right away to finish the plowing; that oldest gal is pretty near big enough to work with a mule, ain't she? or at least to hold the plow steady while Mrs. Armstid helps the mule?" He glanced again toward the man with the peach spray as though for an answer, but he was not looking at the other and he went on talking without any pause. The clerk stood with his rump and back pressed against the door-facing as if he had paused in the act of scratching, watching Ratliff quite hard now, unwinking. If Ratliff had looked at Flem Snopes, he would have seen nothing below the down-slanted peak of the cap save the steady motion of his jaws. Another sliver was curling with neat deliberation before the moving knife. "Plenty of time now because all she's got to do after she finishes washing Mrs. Littlejohn's dishes and sweeping out the house to pay hers and Henry's board, is to go out home and milk and cook up enough vittles to last the children until tomorrow and feed them and get the littlest ones to sleep and wait outside the door until that biggest gal gets the bar up and gets into bed herself with the axe——"

"The axe?" the man with the peach spray said.

"She takes it to bed with her. She's just twelve, and what with this country still more or less full of them uncaught horses that never belonged to Flem Snopes, likely she feels maybe she can't swing a mere washboard like Mrs. Littlejohn can—and then come back and wash up the supper dishes. And after that, not nothing to do until morning except to stay close enough where Henry can call her until it's light enough to chop the wood to cook breakfast and then help Mrs. Littlejohn wash the dishes and make the beds and sweep while watching the road. Because likely any time now Flem Snopes will get back from wherever he has been since the auction, which of course is to town naturally to see about his cousin that's got into a little legal trouble, and so get that five dollars. 'Only maybe he won't give it back to me,' she says, and maybe that's what Mrs. Littlejohn thought too, because she never said nothing. I could hear her——"

"And where did you happen to be during all this?" the clerk said.

"Listening," Ratliff said. He glanced back at the clerk, then he was looking away again, almost standing with his back to them. "——could hear her dumping the dishes into the pan like she was throwing them at it. 'Do you reckon he will give it back to me?' Mrs. Armstid says. 'That Texas man give it to him and said he would. All the folks there saw him give Mr. Snopes the money and heard him say I could get it from Mr. Snopes tomorrow.' Mrs. Littlejohn was washing the dishes now, washing them like a man would, like they was made out of iron. 'No,' she says. 'But asking him won't do no hurt.'—'If he wouldn't give it back, it ain't no use to ask,' Mrs. Armstid says.—'Suit yourself,' Mrs. Littlejohn says. 'It's your money.' Then I couldn't hear nothing but the dishes for a while. 'Do you reckon he might give it back to me?' Mrs. Armstid says. 'That Texas man said he would. They all heard him say it.'—'Then go and ask him for it,' Mrs. Littlejohn says. Then I couldn't hear nothing but the dishes again. 'He won't give it back to me,' Mrs. Armstid says.—'All right,' Mrs. Littlejohn says. 'Don't ask him, then.' Then I just heard the dishes. They would have two pans, both washing. 'You don't reckon he would, do you?' Mrs. Armstid says. Mrs. Littlejohn never said nothing. It sounded like she was throwing the dishes at one another. 'Maybe I better go and talk to Henry,' Mrs. Armstid says.—'I would,' Mrs. Littlejohn says. And I be dog if it didn't sound exactly like she had two plates in her hands, beating them together like these here brass bucket-lids in a band. 'Then Henry can buy another five-dollar horse with it. Maybe he'll buy one next time that will out and out kill him. If I just thought he would, I'd give him back that money, myself.'—'I reckon I better talk to him first,' Mrs. Armstid says. And then it sounded just like Mrs. Littlejohn taken up the dishes and pans and all and throwed the whole business at the cookstove—" Ratliff ceased. Behind him the clerk was hissing "Psst! Psst! Flem. Flem!" Then he stopped, and all of them watched Mrs. Armstid approach and mount the steps, gaunt in the shapeless gray garment, the stained tennis shoes hissing faintly on the boards. She came among them and stood, facing Snopes but not looking at anyone, her hands rolled into her apron.

"He said that day he wouldn't sell Henry that horse," she said in a flat toneless voice. "He said you had the money and I could get it from you." Snopes raised his head and turned it slightly again and spat neatly past the woman, across the gallery and into the road.

"He took all the money with him when he left," he said. Motionless, the gray garment hanging in rigid, almost formal folds like drapery in bronze, Mrs. Armstid appeared to be watching something near Snopes' feet, as though she had not heard him, or as if she had quitted her body as soon as she finished speaking and although her body, hearing, had received the words, they would have no life nor meaning until she returned. The clerk was rubbing his back steadily against the door-facing again, watching her. The little boy was watching her too with his unwinking ineffable gaze, but nobody else was. The man with the peach spray removed it and spat and put the twig back into his mouth.

"He said Henry hadn't bought no horse," she said. "He said I could get the money from you."

"I reckon he forgot it," Snopes said. "He took all the money away with him when he left." He watched her a moment longer, then he trimmed again at the stick. The clerk rubbed his back gently against the door, watching her. After a time Mrs. Armstid raised her head and looked up the road where it went on, mild with spring dust, past Mrs. Littlejohn's, beginning to rise, on past the not-yet-bloomed (that would be in June) locust grove across the way, on past the schoolhouse, the weathered roof of which, rising beyond an orchard of peach and pear trees, resembled a hive swarmed about by a cloud of pink-and-white bees, ascending, mounting toward the crest of the hill where the church stood among its sparse gleam of marble headstones in the sombre cedar grove where during the long afternoons of summer the constant mourning doves called back and forth. She moved; once more the rubber soles hissed on the gnawed boards.

"I reckon it's about time to get dinner started," she said.

"How's Henry this morning, Mrs. Armstid?" Ratliff said. She looked at him, pausing, the blank eyes waking for an instant.

"He's resting, I thank you kindly," she said. Then the eyes died again and she moved again. Snopes rose from the chair, closing his knife with his thumb and brushing a litter of minute shavings from his lap.

"Wait a minute," he said. Mrs. Armstid paused again, half-turning, though still not looking at Snopes nor at any of them. Because she can't possibly actually believe it, Ratliff told himself, any more than I do. Snopes entered the store, the clerk, motionless again, his back and rump pressed against the door-facing as though waiting to start rubbing again, watched him enter, his head turning as the other passed him like the head of an owl, the little eyes blinking rapidly now. Jody Varner came up the road on his horse. He did not pass but instead turned in beside the store, toward the mulberry tree behind it where he was in the habit of hitching his horse. A wagon came up the road, creaking past. The man driving it lifted his hand; one or two of the men on the gallery lifted theirs in response. The wagon went on. Mrs. Armstid looked after it. Snopes came out of the door, carrying a small striped paper bag and approached Mrs. Armstid. "Here," he said. Her hand turned just enough to receive it. "A little sweetening for the chaps," he said. His other hand was already in his pocket, and as he turned back to the chair, he drew something from his pocket and handed it to the clerk, who took it. It was a five-cent piece. He sat down in the chair and tilted it back against the door again. He now had the knife in his hand again, already open. He turned his head slightly and spat again, neatly past the gray garment, into the road. The little boy was watching the sack in Mrs. Armstid's hand. Then she seemed to discover it also, rousing.

"You're right kind," she said. She rolled the sack into the apron, the little boy's unwinking gaze fixed upon the lump her hands made beneath the cloth. She moved again. "I reckon I better get on and help with dinner," she said. She descended the steps, though as soon as she reached the level earth and began to retreat, the gray folds of the garment once more lost all inference and intimation of locomotion, so that she seemed to progress without motion like a figure on a retreating and diminishing float; a gray and blasted tree-trunk moving, somehow intact and upright, upon an unhurried flood. The clerk in the doorway cackled suddenly, explosively, chortling. He slapped his thigh.

"By God," he said, "You can't beat him."

Jody Varner, entering the store from the rear, paused in midstride like a pointing bird-dog. Then, on tiptoe, in complete silence and with astonishing speed, he darted behind the counter and sped up the gloomy tunnel, at the end of which a hulking, bear-shaped figure stooped, its entire head and shoulders wedged into the glass case which contained the needles and thread and snuff and tobacco and the stale gaudy candy. He snatched the boy savagely and viciously out; the boy gave a choked cry and struggled flabbily, cramming a final handful of something into his mouth, chewing. But he ceased to struggle almost at once and became slack and inert save for his jaws. Varner dragged him around the counter as the clerk entered, seemed to bounce suddenly into the store with a sort of alert concern. "You, Saint Elmo!" he said.

"Ain't I told you and told you to keep him out of here?" Varner demanded, shaking the boy. "He's damn near eaten that candy-case clean. Stand up!" The boy hung like a half-filled sack from Varner's hand, chewing with a kind of fatalistic desperation, the eyes shut tight in the vast flaccid colorless face, the ears moving steadily and faintly to the chewing. Save for the jaw and the ears, he appeared to have gone to sleep chewing.

"You, Saint Elmo!" the clerk said. "Stand up!" The boy assumed his own weight, though he did not open his eyes yet nor cease to chew. Varner released him. "Git on home," the clerk said. The boy turned obediently to re-enter the store. Varner jerked him about again.

"Not that way," he said. The boy crossed the gallery

and descended the steps, the tight overalls undulant and reluctant across his flabby thighs. Before he reached the ground, his hand rose from his pocket to his mouth; again his ears moved faintly to the motion of chewing.

"He's worse than a rat, ain't he?" the clerk said.

"Rat, hell," Varner said, breathing harshly. "He's worse than a goat. First thing I know, he'll graze on back and work through that lace leather and them hame-strings and lap-links and ring-bolts and eat me and you and him all three clean out the back door. And then be damned if I wouldn't be afraid to turn my back for fear he would cross the road and start in on the gin and the blacksmith shop. Now you mind what I say. If I catch him hanging around here one more time, I'm going to set a bear-trap for him."

He went out onto the gallery, the clerk following. "Well, Eck," he said, "I hear you caught one of your horses."

"That's right," Eck said. He and the little boy had finished the crackers and cheese and he had sat for some time now, holding the empty bag.

"It was the one he give you, wasn't it?" Varner said.

"That's right," Eck said.

"Give the other one to me, paw," the little boy said.

"What happened?" Varner said.

"He broke his neck," Eck said.

"I know," Varner said. "But how?" Eck did not move. Watching him, they could almost see him visibly gathering and arranging words, speech. Varner, looking down at him, began to laugh steadily and harshly, sucking his teeth. "I'll tell you what happened. Eck and that boy finally run it into that blind lane of Freeman's, after a chase of about twenty-four hours. They figured it couldn't possibly climb them eight-foot fences of Freeman's so him and the boy tied their rope across the end

of the lane, about three feet off the ground. And sho
enough, soon as the horse come to the end of the lane
and seen Freeman's barn, it whirled just like Eck figured
it would and come helling back up that lane like a
scared hen-hawk. It probably never even seen the rope
at all. Mrs. Freeman was watching from where she had
run up onto the porch. She said that when it hit that
rope, it looked just like one of these here great big
Christmas pinwheels. But the one you bought got clean
away, didn't it?"

"That's right," Eck said. "I never had time to see
which way the other one went."

"Give him to me, paw," the little boy said.

"You wait till we catch him," Eck said. "We'll see
about it then."

III

The two actions of Armstid pl. vs. Snopes, and Tull
pl. vs. Eckrum Snopes (and anyone else named Snopes
or Varner either which Tull's irate wife could contrive
to involve, as the village well knew) were accorded a
change of venue by mutual agreement and arrangement
among the litigants. Three of the parties did, that is,
because Flem Snopes flatly refused to recognise the
existence of the suit against himself, stating once and
without heat and first turning his head slightly aside to
spit, "They wasn't none of my horses," then fell to
whittling again while the baffled and helpless bailiff
stood before the tilted chair with the papers he was trying to serve.

So the Varner surrey was not among the wagons,
the buggies, and the saddled horses and mules which
moved out of the village on that May Saturday morning, to converge upon Whiteleaf store eight miles away.

coming not only from Frenchman's Bend but from other directions too, since by that time what Ratliff had called 'that Texas sickness,' that spotted corruption of frantic and uncatchable horses, had spread as far as twenty and thirty miles. By the time the Frenchman's Bend people began to arrive, there were two dozen wagons, the teams reversed and eased of harness and tied to the rear wheels in order to pass the day, and twice that many saddled animals already standing about the locust grove beside the store and the site of the hearing had already been transferred from the store to an adjacent shed where in the fall cotton would be stored. But by nine o'clock it was seen that even the shed would not hold them all, so the palladium was moved again, from the shed to the grove itself. The horses and mules and wagons were cleared from it; the single chair, the gnawed table bearing a thick Bible which had the appearance of loving and constant use of a piece of old and perfectly-kept machinery and an almanac and a copy of Mississippi Reports dated 1881 and bearing along its opening edge a single thread-thin line of soilure, as if during all the time of his possession its owner (or user) had opened it at only one page though that quite often, were fetched from the shed to the grove; a wagon and four men were dispatched and returned presently from the church a mile away with four wooden pews for the litigants and their clansmen and witnesses; behind these in turn the spectators stood— the men, the women, the children, sober, attentive, and neat, not in their Sunday clothes to be sure, but in the clean working garments donned that morning for the Saturday's diversion of sitting about the country stores or trips into the county seat, and in which they would return to the field on Monday morning and would wear all that week until Friday night came round again.

The Justice of the Peace was a neat, small, plump old man resembling a tender caricature of all grandfathers who ever breathed, in a beautifully laundered though collarless white shirt with immaculate starch-gleaming cuffs and bosom, and steel-framed spectacles and neat, faintly curling white hair. He sat behind the table and looked at them—at the gray woman in the gray sunbonnet and dress, her clasped and motionless hands on her lap resembling a gnarl of pallid and drowned roots from a drained swamp; at Tull in his faded but absolutely clean shirt and the overalls which his womenfolks not only kept immaculately washed but starched and ironed also, and not creased through the legs but flat across them from seam to seam, so that on each Saturday morning they resembled the short pants of a small boy, and the sedate and innocent blue of his eyes above the month-old corn-silk beard which concealed most of his abraded face and which gave him an air of incredible and paradoxical dissoluteness, not as though at last and without warning he had appeared in the sight of his fellowmen in his true character, but as if an old Italian portrait of a child saint had been defaced by a vicious and idle boy; at Mrs. Tull, a strong, full-bosomed though slightly dumpy woman with an expression of grim and seething outrage which the elapsed four weeks had apparently neither increased nor diminished but had merely set, an outrage which curiously and almost at once began to give the impression of being directed not at any Snopes or at any other man in particular but at all men, all males, and of which Tull himself was not at all the victim but the subject, who sat on one side of her husband while the biggest of the four daughters sat on the other as if they (or Mrs. Tull at least) were not so much convinced that Tull might leap up and flee, as determined that he would not; and at Eck and the little boy, identical save for size, and Lump, the clerk, in a gray cap which someone actually recognized as being the one which Flem Snopes had worn when he went to Texas last year, who between spells of rapid blinking would sit staring at the Justice with the lidless intensity of a rat—and into the lens-distorted and irisless old-man's eyes of the Justice there grew an expression not only of amazement and bewilderment but, as in Ratliff's eyes while he stood on the store gallery four weeks ago, something very like terror.

"This—" he said. "I didn't expect—I didn't look to see—. I'm going to pray," he said. "I ain't going to pray aloud. But I hope—" He looked at them. "I wish. . . . Maybe some of you all anyway had better do the same." He bowed his head. They watched him, quiet and grave, while he sat motionless behind the table, the light morning wind moving faintly in his thin hair and the shadow-stipple of windy leaves gliding and flowing across the starched bulge of bosom and the gleaming bone-buttoned cuffs, as rigid and almost as large as sections of six-inch stovepipe, at his joined hands. He raised his head. "Armstid against Snopes," he said. Mrs. Armstid spoke. She did not move, she looked at nothing, her hands clasped in her lap, speaking in that flat, toneless and hopeless voice:

"That Texan man said——"

"Wait," the Justice said. He looked about at the faces, the blurred eyes fleeing behind the thick lenses. "Where is the defendant? I don't see him."

"He wouldn't come," the bailiff said.

"Wouldn't come?" the Justice said. "Didn't you serve the papers on him?"

"He wouldn't take them," the bailiff said. "He said ——"

"Then he is in contempt!" the Justice cried.

"What for?" Lump Snopes said. "Ain't nobody proved yet they was his horses." The Justice looked at him.

"Are you representing the defendant?" he said. Snopes blinked at him for a moment.

"What's that mean?" he said. "That you aim for me to pay whatever fine you think you can clap onto him?"

"So he refuses to defend himself," the Justice said. "Don't he know that I can find against him for that reason, even if pure justice and decency ain't enough?"

"It'll be pure something," Snopes said. "It don't take no mind-reader to see how your mind is——"

"Shut up, Snopes," the bailiff said. "If you ain't in this case, you keep out of it." He turned back to the Justice. "What you want me to do: go over to the Bend and fetch Snopes here anyway? I reckon I can do it."

"No," the Justice said. "Wait." He looked about at the sober faces again with that bafflement, that dread. "Does anybody here know for sho who them horses belonged to? Anybody?" They looked back at him, sober, attentive—at the neat immaculate old man sitting with his hands locked together on the table before him to still the trembling. "All right, Mrs. Armstid," he said. "Tell the court what happened." She told it, unmoving, in the flat, inflectionless voice, looking at nothing, while they listened quietly, coming to the end and ceasing without even any fall of voice, as though the tale mattered nothing and came to nothing. The Justice was looking down at his hands. When she ceased, he looked up at her. "But you haven't showed yet that Snopes owned the horses. The one you want to sue is that Texas man. And he's gone. If you got a judgment against him, you couldn't collect the money. Don't you see?"

"Mr. Snopes brought him here," Mrs. Armstid said. "Likely that Texas man wouldn't have knowed where

Frenchman's Bend was if Mr. Snopes hadn't showed him."

"But it was the Texas man that sold the horses and collected the money for them." The Justice looked about again at the faces. "Is that right? You, Bookwright, is that what happened?"

"Yes," Bookwright said. The Justice looked at Mrs. Armstid again, with that pity and grief. As the morning increased the wind had risen, so that from time to time gusts of it ran through the branches overhead, bringing a faint snow of petals, prematurely bloomed as the spring itself had condensed with spendthrift speed after the hard winter, and the heavy and drowsing scent of them, about the motionless heads.

"He give Mr. Snopes Henry's money. He said Henry hadn't bought no horse. He said I could get the money from Mr. Snopes tomorrow."

"And you have witnesses that saw and heard him?"

"Yes, sir. The other men that was there saw him give Mr. Snopes the money and say that I could get it——"

"And you asked Snopes for the money?"

"Yes, sir. He said that Texas man taken it away with him when he left. But I would. . . ." She ceased again, perhaps looking down at her hands also. Certainly she was not looking at anyone.

"Yes?" the Justice said. "You would what?"

"I would know them five dollars. I earned them myself, weaving at night after Henry and the chaps was asleep. Some of the ladies in Jefferson would save up string and such and give it to me and I would weave things and sell them. I earned that money a little at a time and I would know it when I saw it because I would take the can outen the chimney and count it now and then while it was making up to enough to buy my chaps some shoes for next winter. I would know it if I was to see it again. If Mr. Snopes would just let——"

"Suppose there was somebody seen Flem give that money back to that Texas fellow," Lump Snopes said suddenly.

"Did anybody here see that?" the Justice said.

"Yes," Snopes said, harshly and violently. "Eck here did." He looked at Eck. "Go on. Tell him." The Justice looked at Eck; the four Tull girls turned their heads as one head and looked at him, and Mrs. Tull leaned forward to look past her husband, her face cold, furious, and contemptuous, and those standing shifted to look past one another's heads at Eck sitting motionless on the bench.

"Did you see Snopes give Armstid's money back to the Texas man, Eck?" the Justice said. Still Eck did not answer nor move, Lump Snopes made a gross violent sound through the side of his mouth.

"By God, I ain't afraid to say it if Eck is. I seen him do it."

"Will you swear that as testimony?" Snopes looked at the Justice. He did not blink now.

"So you won't take my word," he said.

"I want the truth," the Justice said. "If I can't find that, I got to have sworn evidence of what I will have to accept as truth." He lifted the Bible from the two other books.

"All right," the bailiff said. "Step up here." Snopes rose from the bench and approached. They watched him, though now there was no shifting nor craning, no movement at all among the faces, the still eyes. Snopes at the table looked back at them once, his gaze traversing swiftly the crescent-shaped rank; he looked at the Justice again. The bailiff grasped the Bible; though the Justice did not release it yet.

"You are ready to swear you saw Snopes give that Texas man back the money he took from Henry Armstid for that horse?" he said.

"I said I was, didn't I?" Snopes said. The Justice released the Bible.

"Swear him," he said.

"Put your left hand on the Book raise your right hand you solemnly swear and affirm—" the bailiff said rapidly. But Snopes had already done so, his left hand clapped onto the extended Bible and the other hand raised and his head turned away as once more his gaze went rapidly along the circle of expressionless and intent faces, saying in that harsh and snarling voice:

"Yes. I saw Flem Snopes give back to that Texas man whatever money Henry Armstid or anybody else thinks Henry Armstid or anybody else paid Flem for any of them horses. Does that suit you?"

"Yes," the Justice said. Then there was no movement, no sound anywhere among them. The bailiff placed the Bible quietly on the table beside the Justice's locked hands, and there was no movement save the flow and recover of the windy shadows and the drift of the locust petals. Then Mrs. Armstid rose; she stood once more (or still) looking at nothing, her hands clasped across her middle.

"I reckon I can go now, can't I?" she said.

"Yes," the Justice said, rousing. "Unless you would like——"

"I better get started," she said. "It's a right far piece." She had not come in the wagon, but on one of the gaunt and underfed mules. One of the men followed her across the grove and untied the mule for her and led it up to a wagon, from one hub of which she mounted. Then they looked at the Justice again. He sat behind the table, his hands still joined before him, though his head was not bowed now. Yet he did not move until the bailiff leaned and spoke to him, when he roused, came suddenly awake without starting, as an old man wakes from an old man's light sleep. He removed his hands from the table and, looking down, he spoke exactly as if he were reading from a paper:

"Tull against Snopes. Assault and——"

"Yes!" Mrs. Tull said. "I'm going to say a word before you start." She leaned, looking past Tull at Lump Snopes again. "If you think you are going to lie and perjure Flem and Eck Snopes out of——"

"Now, mamma," Tull said. Now she spoke to Tull, without changing her position or her tone or even any break or pause in her speech:

"Don't you say hush to me! You'll let Eck Snopes or Flem Snopes or that whole Varner tribe snatch you out of the wagon and beat you half to death against a wooden bridge. But when it comes to suing them for your just rights and a punishment, oh no. Because that wouldn't be neighborly. What's neighborly got to do with you lying flat on your back in the middle of planting time while we pick splinters out of your face?" By this time the bailiff was shouting,

"Order! Order! This here's a law court!" Mrs. Tull ceased. She sat back, breathing hard, staring at the Justice, who sat and spoke again as if he were reading aloud:

"——assault and battery on the person of Vernon Tull, through the agency and instrument of one horse, unnamed, belonging to Eckrum Snopes. Evidence of physical detriment and suffering, defendant himself. Witnesses, Mrs. Tull and daughters——"

"Eck Snopes saw it too," Mrs. Tull said, though with less violence now. "He was there. He got there in plenty of time to see it. Let him deny it. Let him look me in the face and deny it if he——"

"If you please, ma'am," the Justice said. He said it so quietly that Mrs. Tull hushed and became quite calm, almost a rational and composed being. "The injury to your husband ain't disputed. And the agency of the horse ain't disputed. The law says that when a man owns a creature which he knows to be dangerous and if that creature is restrained and restricted from the public commons by a pen or enclosure capable of restraining and restricting it, if a man enter that pen or enclosure, whether he knows the creature in it is dangerous or not dangerous, then that man has committed trespass and the owner of that creature is not liable. But if that creature known to him to be dangerous ceases to be restrained by that suitable pen or enclosure, either by accident or design and either with or without the owner's knowledge, then that owner is liable. That's the law. All necessary now is to establish first, the ownership of the horse, and second, that the horse was a dangerous creature within the definition of the law as provided."

"Hah," Mrs. Tull said. She said it exactly as Bookwright would have. "Dangerous. Ask Vernon Tull. Ask Henry Armstid if them things was pets."

"If you please, ma'am," the Justice said. He was looking at Eck. "What is the defendant's position? Denial of ownership?"

"What?" Eck said.

"Was that your horse that ran over Mr. Tull?"

"Yes," Eck said. "It was mine. How much do I have to p——"

"Hah," Mrs. Tull said again. "Denial of ownership. When there were at least forty men—fools too, or they wouldn't have been there. But even a fool's word is good about what he saw and heard—at least forty men heard that Texas murderer give that horse to Eck Snopes. Not sell it to him, mind; give it to him."

"What?" the Justice said. "Gave it to him?"

"Yes," Eck said. "He give it to me. I'm sorry Tull happened to be using that bridge too at the same time. How much do I——"

"Wait," the Justice said. "What did you give him? a note? a swap of some kind?"

"No," Eck said. "He just pointed to it in the lot and told me it belonged to me."

"And he didn't give you a bill of sale or a deed or anything in writing?"

"I reckon he never had time," Eck said. "And after Lon Quick forgot and left that gate open, never nobody had time to do no writing even if we had a thought of it."

"What's all this?" Mrs. Tull said. "Eck Snopes has just told you he owned that horse. And if you won't take his word, there were forty men standing at that gate all day long doing nothing, that heard that murdering card-playing whiskey-drinking anti-christ—" This time the Justice raised one hand, in its enormous pristine cuff, toward her. He did not look at her.

"Wait," he said. "Then what did he do?" he said to Eck. "Just lead the horse up and put the rope in your hand?"

"No," Eck said. "Him nor nobody else never got no ropes on none of them. He just pointed to the horse in the lot and said it was mine and auctioned off the rest of them and got into the buggy and said good-bye and druv off. And we got our ropes and went into the lot, only Lon Quick forgot to shut the gate. I'm sorry it made Tull's mules snatch him outen the wagon. How

much do I owe him?" Then he stopped, because the
Justice was no longer looking at him and, as he realized
a moment later, no longer listening either. Instead, he
was sitting back in the chair, actually leaning back in
it for the first time, his head bent slightly and his hands
resting on the table before him, the fingers lightly over-
lapped. They watched him quietly for almost a halfminute before anyone realized that he was looking
quietly and steadily at Mrs. Tull.

"Well, Mrs. Tull," he said, "by your own testimony,
Eck never owned that horse."

"What?" Mrs. Tull said. It was not loud at all. "What
did you say?"

"In the law, ownership can't be conferred or invested
by word-of-mouth. It must be established either by
recorded or authentic document, or by possession or
occupation. By your testimony and his both, he never
gave that Texan anything in exchange for that horse,
and by his testimony the Texas man never gave him
any paper to prove he owned it, and by his testimony
and by what I know myself from these last four weeks,
nobody yet has ever laid hand or rope either on any one
of them. So that horse never came into Eck's possession
at all. That Texas man could have given that same horse
to a dozen other men standing around that gate that
day, without even needing to tell Eck he had done it;
and Eck himself could have transferred all his title and
equity in it to Mr. Tull right there while Mr. Tull was
lying unconscious on that bridge just by thinking it to
himself, and Mr. Tull's title would be just as legal as
Eck's."

"So I get nothing," Mrs. Tull said. Her voice was still
calm, quiet, though probably no one but Tull realized
that it was too calm and quiet. "My team is made to
run away by a wild spotted mad dog, my wagon is

wrecked; by husband is jerked out of it and knocked
unconscious and unable to work for a whole week with
less than half of our seed in the ground, and I get
nothing."

"Wait," the Justice said. "The law——"

"The law," Mrs. Tull said. She stood suddenly up—
a short, broad, strong woman, balanced on the balls of
her planted feet.

"Now, mamma," Tull said.

"Yes, ma'am," the Justice said. "Your damages are
fixed by statute. The law says that when a suit for
damages is brought against the owner of an animal
which has committed damage or injury, if the owner
of the animal either can't or won't assume liability, the
injured or damaged party shall find recompense in the
body of the animal. And since Eck Snopes never owned
that horse at all, and since you just heard a case here
this morning that failed to prove that Flem Snopes had
any equity in any of them, that horse still belongs to
that Texas man. Or did belong. Because now that horse
that made your team run away and snatch your husband out of the wagon, belongs to you and Mr. Tull."

"Now, mamma!" Tull said. He rose quickly. But
Mrs. Tull was still quiet, only quite rigid and breathing
hard, until Tull spoke. Then she turned on him, not
screaming: shouting; presently the bailiff was banging
the table-top with his hand-polished hickory cane and
roaring "Order! Order!" while the neat old man, thrust
backward in his chair as though about to dodge and
trembling with an old man's palsy, looked on with
amazed unbelief.

"The horse!" Mrs. Tull shouted. "We see it for five
seconds, while it is climbing into the wagon with us
and then out again. Then it's gone, God don't know
where and thank the Lord He don't! And the mules

gone with it and the wagon wrecked and you laying there on the bridge with your face full of kindling-wood and bleeding like a hog and dead for all we knew. And he gives us the horse! Don't hush me! Get on to that wagon, fool that would sit there behind a pair of young mules with the reins tied around his wrist! Get on to that wagon, all of you!"

"I can't stand no more!" the old Justice cried. "I won't! This court's adjourned! Adjourned!"

5. The End of an Order

EDITOR'S NOTE

IT IS the burden of Faulkner's novels that the old South was defeated from within. After four years of fighting against hopeless odds, the landowners of Yoknapatawpha County had remained "the unvanquished"; and all of them had tried, like Colonel Sutpen, to restore their houses, their plantations, and their whole society to the image of what they had been before the war. Moreover, they achieved a partial success. There were years in Jefferson when the prewar standards prevailed; when a Sartoris was mayor, a Benbow was county judge, and Major de Spain was the local magnate. But the heirs of the men who had withstood the Northern armies and defeated the carpetbaggers were driven from their posts of influence by Southern renegades, or rather by a coalition between Northern business and a new class of Southerners descended in part from the bushwhackers of Civil War days. Jefferson itself was overrun, infested by the tribe of Snopes: there were Snopeses in the bank, in the power company, in politics, Snopeses everywhere gnawing like rats at the standards by which the South had lived.

The Snopeses are the destructive element in Faulkner's novels. The Negroes are an element of stability: they endured. Faulkner's favorite characters are the Negro cooks and matriarchs who hold a white family together: Elnora and Clytie and Dilsey and Aunt Mollie Beauchamp. After the Compson family has gone to pieces, in *The Sound and the Fury*, it is Dilsey the cook who is left behind to mourn. Looking up at the square, unpainted house with its rotting portico, she thinks, "Ise seed de first en de last"; and later in the kitchen she says, looking at the cold stove, "I seed de first en de last."

Of the four stories in this section, "That Evening Sun" belongs to the cycle dealing with the Compson children. "Ad Astra" is part of another cycle describing the adventures of Bayard Sartoris' twin grandsons in the Royal Air Force: John was killed at the front, and Bayard, named for his grandfather, came home feeling that he too had died on the night of the Armistice; that he was now wandering like a disembodied spirit in a dead land. In "A Rose for Emily," often anthologized, Faulkner has found one of his most effective symbols for the decay of the old order. These three stories were all included in *These Thirteen* (1931). "Dilsey" comes from the fourth and last part of *The Sound and the Fury* (1929), which describes the going to pieces of the Compson family and which is still Faulkner's favorite among his novels. For the earlier history of the Compsons and the fate of the survivors, see the Compson genealogy printed as an appendix to this volume.

1902. THAT EVENING SUN

I

MONDAY is no different from any other week-day in Jefferson now. The streets are paved now, and the telephone and electric companies are cutting down more and more of the shade trees—the water oaks, the maples and locusts and elms—to make room for iron poles bearing clusters of bloated and ghostly and bloodless grapes, and we have a city laundry which makes the rounds on Monday morning, gathering the bundles of clothes into bright-colored, specially made motorcars: the soiled wearing of a whole week now flees apparitionlike behind alert and irritable electric horns, with a long diminishing noise of rubber and asphalt like tearing silk, and even the Negro women who still take in white people's washing after the old custom, fetch and deliver it in automobiles.

But fifteen years ago, on Monday morning the quiet, dusty, shady streets would be full of Negro women with, balanced on their steady, turbaned heads, bundles of clothes tied up in sheets, almost as large as cotton bales, carried so without touch of hand between the kitchen door of the white house and the blackened washpot beside a cabin door in Negro Hollow.

Nancy would set her bundle on the top of her head, then upon the bundle in turn she would set the black straw sailor hat which she wore winter and summer. She was tall, with a high, sad face sunken a little where her teeth were missing. Sometimes we would go a part of the way down the lane and across the pasture with her, to watch the balanced bundle and the hat that never bobbed nor wavered, even when she walked down into the ditch and up the other side and stooped through the fence. She would go down on her hands and knees and crawl through the gap, her head rigid, uptilted, the bundle steady as a rock or a balloon, and rise to her feet again and go on.

Sometimes the husbands of the washing women would fetch and deliver the clothes, but Jesus never did that for Nancy, even before Father told him to stay away from our house, even when Dilsey was sick and Nancy would come to cook for us.

And then about half the time we'd have to go down the lane to Nancy's cabin and tell her to come on and cook breakfast. We would stop at the ditch, because Father told us to not have anything to do with Jesus— he was a short black man, with a razor scar down his face—and we would throw rocks at Nancy's house until she came to the door, leaning her head around it without any clothes on.

"What yawl mean, chunking my house?" Nancy said. "What you little devils mean?"

"Father says for you to come on and get breakfast," Caddy said. "Father says it's over a half an hour now, and you've got to come this minute."

"I ain't studying no breakfast," Nancy said. "I going to get my sleep out."

"I bet you're drunk," Jason said. "Father says you're drunk. Are you drunk, Nancy?"

"Who says I is?" Nancy said. "I got to get my sleep out. I ain't studying no breakfast."

So after a while we quit chunking the cabin and went back home. When she finally came, it was too late for me to go to school. So we thought it was

whiskey until that day they arrested her again and they
were taking her to jail and they passed Mr. Stovall. He
was the cashier in the bank and a deacon in the Baptist
church, and Nancy began to say:

"When you going to pay me, white man? When you
going to pay me, white man? It's been three times now
since you paid me a cent—" Mr. Stovall knocked her
down, but she kept on saying, "When you going to pay
me, white man? It's been three times now since—"
until Mr. Stovall kicked her in the mouth with his heel
and the marshal caught Mr. Stovall back, and Nancy
lying in the street, laughing. She turned her head and
spat out some blood and teeth and said, "It's been three
times now since he paid me a cent."

That was how she lost her teeth, and all that day
they told about Nancy and Mr. Stovall, and all that
night the ones that passed the jail could hear Nancy
singing and yelling. They could see her hands holding
to the window bars, and a lot of them stopped along
the fence, listening to her and to the jailer trying to
make her stop. She didn't shut up until almost daylight, when the jailer began to hear a bumping and
scraping upstairs and he went up there and found
Nancy hanging from the window bar. He said that it
was cocaine and not whiskey, because no nigger would
try to commit suicide unless he was full of cocaine,
because a nigger full of cocaine wasn't a nigger any
longer.

The jailer cut her down and revived her; then he
beat her, whipped her. She had hung herself with her
dress. She had fixed it all right, but when they arrested
her she didn't have on anything except a dress and so
she didn't have anything to tie her hands with and she
couldn't make her hands let go of the window ledge.
So the jailer heard the noise and ran up there and

found Nancy hanging from the window, stark naked, her belly already swelling out a little, like a little balloon.

When Dilsey was sick in her cabin and Nancy was cooking for us, we could see her apron swelling out; that was before father told Jesus to stay away from the house. Jesus was in the kitchen, sitting behind the stove, with his razor scar on his black face like a piece of dirty string. He said it was a watermelon that Nancy had under her dress.

"It never come off of your vine, though," Nancy said.

"Off of what vine?" Caddy said.

"I can cut down the vine it did come off of," Jesus said.

"What makes you want to talk like that before these chillen?" Nancy said. "Whyn't you go on to work? You done et. You want Mr. Jason to catch you hanging around his kitchen, talking that way before these chillen?"

"Talking what way?" Caddy said. "What vine?"

"I can't hang around white man's kitchen," Jesus said. "But white man can hang around mine. White man can come in my house, but I can't stop him. When white man want to come in my house, I ain't got no house. I can't stop him, but he can't kick me outen it. He can't do that."

Dilsey was still sick in her cabin. Father told Jesus to stay off our place. Dilsey was still sick. It was a long time. We were in the library after supper.

"Isn't Nancy through in the kitchen yet?" Mother said. "It seems to me that she has had plenty of time to have finished the dishes."

"Let Quentin go and see," Father said. "Go and see if Nancy is through, Quentin. Tell her she can go on home."

I went to the kitchen. Nancy was through. The dishes were put away and the fire was out. Nancy was sitting in a chair, close to the cold stove. She looked at me.

"Mother wants to know if you are through," I said.

"Yes," Nancy said. She looked at me. "I done finished." She looked at me.

"What is it?" I said. "What is it?"

"I ain't nothing but a nigger," Nancy said. "It ain't none of my fault."

She looked at me, sitting in the chair before the cold stove, the sailor hat on her head. I went back to the library. It was the cold stove and all, when you think of a kitchen being warm and busy and cheerful. And with a cold stove and the dishes all put away, and nobody wanting to eat at that hour.

"Is she through?" Mother said.

"Yessum," I said.

"What is she doing?" Mother said.

"She's not doing anything. She's through."

"I'll go and see," Father said.

"Maybe she's waiting for Jesus to come and take her home," Caddy said.

"Jesus is gone," I said. Nancy told us how one morning she woke up and Jesus was gone.

"He quit me," Nancy said. "Done gone to Memphis, I reckon. Dodging them city po-lice for a while, I reckon."

"And a good riddance," Father said. "I hope he stays there."

"Nancy's scaired of the dark," Jason said.

"So are you," Caddy said.

"I'm not," Jason said.

"Scairy cat," Caddy said.

"I'm not," Jason said.

"You, Candace!" Mother said. Father came back.

"I am going to walk down the lane with Nancy," he said. "She says that Jesus is back."

"Has she seen him?" Mother said.

"No. Some Negro sent her word that he was back in town. I won't be long."

"You'll leave me alone, to take Nancy home?" Mother said. "Is her safety more precious to you than mine?"

"I won't be long," Father said.

"You'll leave these children unprotected, with that Negro about?"

"I'm going too," Caddy said. "Let me go, Father."

"What would he do with them, if he were unfortunate enough to have them?" Father said.

"I want to go, too," Jason said.

"Jason!" Mother said. She was speaking to Father. You could tell that by the way she said the name. Like she believed that all day Father had been trying to think of doing the thing she wouldn't like the most, and that she knew all the time that after a while he would think of it. I stayed quiet, because Father and I both knew that Mother would want him to make me stay with her if she just thought of it in time. So Father didn't look at me. I was the oldest. I was nine and Caddy was seven and Jason was five.

"Nonsense," Father said. "We won't be long."

Nancy had her hat on. We came to the lane. "Jesus always been good to me," Nancy said. "Whenever he had two dollars, one of them was mine." We walked in the lane. "If I can just get through the lane," Nancy said, "I be all right then."

The lane was always dark. "This is where Jason got scaired on Hallowe'en," Caddy said.

"I didn't," Jason said.

"Can't Aunt Rachel do anything with him?" Father

said. Aunt Rachel was old. She lived in a cabin beyond Nancy's, by herself. She had white hair and she smoked a pipe in the door, all day long; she didn't work any more. They said she was Jesus' mother. Sometimes she said she was and sometimes she said she wasn't any kin to Jesus.

"Yes you did," Caddy said. "You were scairder than Frony. You were scairder than T.P. even. Scairder than niggers."

"Can't nobody do nothing with him," Nancy said. "He say I done woke up the devil in him and ain't but one thing going to lay it down again."

"Well, he's gone now," Father said. "There's nothing for you to be afraid of now. And if you'd just let white men alone."

"Let what white men alone?" Caddy said. "How let them alone?"

"He ain't gone nowhere," Nancy said. "I can feel him. I can feel him now, in this lane. He hearing us talk, every word, hid somewhere, waiting. I ain't seen him, and I ain't going to see him again but once more, with that razor in his mouth. That razor on that string down his back, inside his shirt. And then I ain't going to be even surprised."

"I wasn't scaired," Jason said.

"If you'd behave yourself, you'd have kept out of this," Father said. "But it's all right now. He's probably in Saint Louis now. Probably got another wife by now and forgot all about you."

"If he has, I better not find out about it," Nancy said. "I'd stand there right over them, and every time he wropped her, I'd cut that arm off. I'd cut his head off and I'd slit her belly and I'd shove—"

"Hush," Father said.

"Slit whose belly, Nancy?" Caddy said.

"I wasn't scaired," Jason said. "I'd walk right down this lane by myself."

"Yah," Caddy said. "You wouldn't dare to put your foot down in it if we were not here too."

II

Dilsey was still sick, so we took Nancy home every night until Mother said, "How much longer is this going on? I to be left alone in this big house while you take home a frightened Negro?"

We fixed a pallet in the kitchen for Nancy. One night we waked up, hearing the sound. It was not singing and it was not crying, coming up the dark stairs. There was a light in Mother's room and we heard Father going down the hall, down the back stairs, and Caddy and I went into the hall. The floor was cold. Our toes curled away from it while we listened to the sound. It was like singing and it wasn't like singing, like the sounds that Negroes make.

Then it stopped and we heard Father going down the back stairs, and we went to the head of the stairs. Then the sound began again, in the stairway, not loud, and we could see Nancy's eyes halfway up the stairs, against the wall. They looked like cat's eyes do, like a big cat against the wall, watching us. When we came down the steps to where she was, she quit making the sound again, and we stood there until Father came back up from the kitchen, with his pistol in his hand. He went back down with Nancy and they came back with Nancy's pallet.

We spread the pallet in our room. After the light in Mother's room went off, we could see Nancy's eyes again. "Nancy," Caddy whispered, "are you asleep, Nancy?"

Nancy whispered something. It was oh or no, I don't know which. Like nobody had made it, like it came from nowhere and went nowhere, until it was like Nancy was not there at all; that I had looked so hard at her eyes on the stairs that they had got printed on my eyeballs, like the sun does when you have closed your eyes and there is no sun. "Jesus," Nancy whispered. "Jesus."

"Was it Jesus?" Caddy said. "Did he try to come into the kitchen?"

"Jesus," Nancy said. Like this: Jeeeeeeeeeeeeeeeesus, until the sound went out, like a match or a candle does.

"It's the other Jesus she means," I said.

"Can you see us, Nancy?" Caddy whispered. "Can you see our eyes too?"

"I ain't nothing but a nigger," Nancy said. "God knows. God knows."

"What did you see down there in the kitchen?" Caddy whispered. "What tried to get in?"

"God knows," Nancy said. We could see her eyes. "God knows."

Dilsey got well. She cooked dinner. "You'd better stay in bed a day or two longer," Father said.

"What for?" Dilsey said. "If I had been a day later, this place would be to rack and ruin. Get on out of here now, and let me get my kitchen straight again."

Dilsey cooked supper too. And that night, just before dark, Nancy came into the kitchen.

"How do you know he's back?" Dilsey said. "You ain't seen him."

"Jesus is a nigger," Jason said.

"I can feel him," Nancy said. "I can feel him laying yonder in the ditch."

"Tonight?" Dilsey said. "Is he there tonight?"

"Dilsey's a nigger too," Jason said.

"You try to eat something," Dilsey said.

"I don't want nothing," Nancy said.

"I ain't a nigger," Jason said.

"Drink some coffee," Dilsey said. She poured a cup of coffee for Nancy. "Do you know he's out there tonight? How come you know it's tonight?"

"I know," Nancy said. "He's there, waiting. I know. I done lived with him too long. I know what he is fixing to do fore he know it himself."

"Drink some coffee," Dilsey said. Nancy held the cup to her mouth and blew into the cup. Her mouth pursed out like a spreading adder's, like a rubber mouth, like she had blown all the color out of her lips with blowing the coffee.

"I ain't a nigger," Jason said. "Are you a nigger, Nancy?"

"I hellborn, child," Nancy said. "I won't be nothing soon. I going back where I come from soon."

III

She began to drink the coffee. While she was drinking, holding the cup in both hands, she began to make the sound again. She made the sound into the cup and the coffee sploshed out onto her hands and her dress. Her eyes looked at us and she sat there, her elbows on her knees, holding the cup in both hands, looking at us across the wet cup, making the sound.

"Look at Nancy," Jason said. "Nancy can't cook for us now. Dilsey's got well now."

"You hush up," Dilsey said. Nancy held the cup in both hands, looking at us, making the sound, like there were two of them: one looking at us and the other making the sound. "Whyn't you let Mr. Jason telefoam the marshal?" Dilsey said. Nancy stopped then, holding the cup in her long brown hands. She tried to drink some coffee again, but it sploshed out of the cup, onto her hands and her dress, and she put the cup down. Jason watched her.

"I can't swallow it," Nancy said. "I swallows but it won't go down me."

"You go down to the cabin," Dilsey said. "Frony will fix you a pallet and I'll be there soon."

"Won't no nigger stop him," Nancy said.

"I ain't a nigger," Jason said. "Am I, Dilsey?"

"I reckon not," Dilsey said. She looked at Nancy. "I don't reckon so. What you going to do, then?"

Nancy looked at us. Her eyes went fast, like she was afraid there wasn't time to look, without hardly moving at all. She looked at us, at all three of us at one time. "You member that night I stayed in yawls' room?" she said. She told about how we waked up early the next morning, and played. We had to play quiet, on her pallet, until Father woke up and it was time to get breakfast. "Go and ask your maw to let me stay here tonight," Nancy said. "I won't need no pallet. We can play some more."

Caddy asked Mother. Jason went too. "I can't have Negroes sleeping in the bedrooms," Mother said. Jason cried. He cried until Mother said he couldn't have any dessert for three days if he didn't stop. Then Jason said he would stop if Dilsey would make a chocolate cake. Father was there.

"Why don't you do something about it?" Mother said. "What do we have officers for?"

"Why is Nancy afraid of Jesus?" Caddy said. "Are you afraid of Father, Mother?"

"What could the officers do?" Father said. "If Nancy hasn't seen him, how could the officers find him?"

"Then why is she afraid?" Mother said.

"She says he is there. She says she knows he is there tonight."

"Yet we pay taxes," Mother said. "I must wait here alone in this big house while you take a Negro woman home."

"You know that I am not lying outside with a razor," Father said.

"I'll stop if Dilsey will make a chocolate cake," Jason said. Mother told us to go out and Father said he didn't know if Jason would get a chocolate cake or not, but he knew what Jason was going to get in about a minute. We went back to the kitchen and told Nancy.

"Father said for you to go home and lock the door, and you'll be all right," Caddy said. "All right from what, Nancy? Is Jesus mad at you?" Nancy was holding the coffee cup in her hands again, her elbows on her knees and her hands holding the cup between her knees. She was looking into the cup. "What have you done that made Jesus mad?" Caddy said. Nancy let the cup go. It didn't break on the floor, but the coffee spilled out, and Nancy sat there with her hands still making the shape of the cup. She began to make the sound again, not loud. Not singing and not unsinging. We watched her.

"Here," Dilsey said. "You quit that, now. You get aholt of yourself. You wait here. I going to get Versh to walk home with you." Dilsey went out.

We looked at Nancy. Her shoulders kept shaking, but she quit making the sound. We stood and watched her.

"What's Jesus going to do to you?" Caddy said. "He went away."

Nancy looked at us. "We had fun that night I stayed in yawls' room, didn't we?"

"I didn't," Jason said. "I didn't have any fun."

"You were asleep in Mother's room," Caddy said. "You were not there."

"Let's go down to my house and have some more fun," Nancy said.

"Mother won't let us," I said. "It's too late now."

"Don't bother her," Nancy said. "We can tell her in the morning. She won't mind."

"She wouldn't let us," I said.

"Don't ask her now," Nancy said. "Don't bother her now."

"She didn't say we couldn't go," Caddy said.

"We didn't ask," I said.

"If you go, I'll tell," Jason said.

"We'll have fun," Nancy said. "They won't mind, just to my house. I been working for yawl a long time. They won't mind."

"I'm not afraid to go," Caddy said. "Jason is the one that's afraid. He'll tell."

"I'm not," Jason said.

"Yes, you are," Caddy said. "You'll tell."

"I won't tell," Jason said. "I'm not afraid."

"Jason ain't afraid to go with me," Nancy said. "Is you, Jason?"

"Jason is going to tell," Caddy said. The lane was dark. We passed the pasture gate. "I bet if something was to jump out from behind that gate, Jason would holler."

"I wouldn't," Jason said. We walked down the lane. Nancy was talking loud.

"What are you talking so loud for, Nancy?" Caddy said.

"Who; me?" Nancy said. "Listen at Quentin and Caddy and Jason saying I'm talking loud."

"You talk like there was five of us here," Caddy said. "You talk like Father was here too."

"Who; me talking loud, Mr. Jason?" Nancy said.

"Nancy called Jason 'Mister,'" Caddy said.

"Listen how Caddy and Quentin and Jason talk," Nancy said.

"We're not talking loud," Caddy said. "You're the one that's talking like Father—"

"Hush," Nancy said; "hush, Mr. Jason."

"Nancy called Jason 'Mister' aguh—"

"Hush," Nancy said. She was talking loud when we crossed the ditch and stooped through the fence where she used to stoop through with the clothes on her head. Then we came to her house. We were going fast then. She opened the door. The smell of the house was like the lamp and the smell of Nancy was like the wick, like they were waiting for one another to begin to smell. She lit the lamp and closed the door and put the bar up. Then she quit talking loud, looking at us.

"What're we going to do?" Caddy said.

"What do yawl want to do?" Nancy said.

"You said we would have some fun," Caddy said.

There was something about Nancy's house; something you could smell besides Nancy and the house. Jason smelled it, even. "I don't want to stay here," he said. "I want to go home."

"Go home, then," Caddy said.

"I don't want to go by myself," Jason said.

"We're going to have some fun," Nancy said.

"How?" Caddy said.

Nancy stood by the door. She was looking at us, only it was like she had emptied her eyes, like she had quit using them. "What do you want to do?" she said.

"Tell us a story," Caddy said. "Can you tell a story?"

"Yes," Nancy said.

"Tell it," Caddy said. We looked at Nancy. "You don't know any stories."

"Yes," Nancy said. "Yes I do."

She came and sat in a chair before the hearth. There was a little fire there. Nancy built it up, when it was already hot inside. She built a good blaze. She told a story. She talked like her eyes looked, like her eyes watching us and her voice talking to us did not belong to her. Like she was living somewhere else, waiting somewhere else. She was outside the cabin. Her voice was inside and the shape of her, the Nancy that could stoop under a barbed wire fence with a bundle of clothes balanced on her head as though without weight, like a balloon, was there. But that was all. "And so this here queen come walking up to the ditch, where that bad man was hiding. She was walking up to the ditch, and she say, 'If I can just get past this here ditch,' was what she say . . ."

"What ditch?" Caddy said. "A ditch like that one out there? Why did a queen want to go into a ditch?"

"To get to her house," Nancy said. She looked at us. "She had to cross the ditch to get into her house quick and bar the door."

"Why did she want to go home and bar the door?" Caddy said.

IV

Nancy looked at us. She quit talking. She looked at us. Jason's legs stuck straight out of his pants where he sat on Nancy's lap. "I don't think that's a good story," he said. "I want to go home."

"Maybe we had better," Caddy said. She got up from the floor. "I bet they are looking for us right now." She went toward the door.

"No," Nancy said. "Don't open it." She got up quick and passed Caddy. She didn't touch the door, the wooden bar.

"Why not?" Caddy said.

"Come back to the lamp," Nancy said. "We'll have fun. You don't have to go."

"We ought to go," Caddy said. "Unless we have a lot of fun." She and Nancy came back to the fire, the lamp.

"I want to go home," Jason said. "I'm going to tell."

"I know another story," Nancy said. She stood close to the lamp. She looked at Caddy, like when your eyes look up at a stick balanced on your nose. She had to look down to see Caddy, but her eyes looked like that, like when you are balancing a stick.

"I won't listen to it," Jason said. "I'll bang on the floor."

"It's a good one," Nancy said. "It's better than the other one."

"What's it about?" Caddy said. Nancy was standing by the lamp. Her hand was on the lamp, against the light, long and brown.

"Your hand is on that hot globe," Caddy said. "Don't it feel hot to your hand?"

Nancy looked at her hand on the lamp chimney. She took her hand away, slow. She stood there, looking at Caddy, wringing her long hand as though it were tied to her wrist with a string.

"Let's do something else," Caddy said.

"I want to go home," Jason said.

"I got some popcorn," Nancy said. She looked at Caddy and then at Jason and then at me and then at Caddy again. "I got some popcorn."

"I don't like popcorn," Jason said. "I'd rather have candy."

Nancy looked at Jason. "You can hold the popper." She was still wringing her hand; it was long and limp and brown.

"All right," Jason said. "I'll stay a while if I can do

that. Caddy can't hold it. I'll want to go home again if Caddy holds the popper."

Nancy built up the fire. "Look at Nancy putting her hands in the fire," Caddy said. "What's the matter with you, Nancy?"

"I got popcorn," Nancy said. "I got some." She took the popper from under the bed. It was broken. Jason began to cry.

"Now we can't have any popcorn," he said.

"We ought to go home, anyway," Caddy said. "Come on, Quentin."

"Wait," Nancy said; "wait. I can fix it. Don't you want to help me fix it?"

"I don't think I want any," Caddy said. "It's too late now."

"You help me, Jason," Nancy said. "Don't you want to help me?"

"No," Jason said. "I want to go home."

"Hush," Nancy said; "hush. Watch. Watch me. I can fix it so Jason can hold it and pop the corn." She got a piece of wire and fixed the popper.

"It won't hold good," Caddy said.

"Yes it will," Nancy said. "Yawl watch. Yawl help me shell some corn."

The popcorn was under the bed too. We shelled it into the popper and Nancy helped Jason hold the popper over the fire.

"It's not popping," Jason said. "I want to go home."

"You wait," Nancy said. "It'll begin to pop. We'll have fun then."

She was sitting close to the fire. The lamp was turned up so high it was beginning to smoke. "Why don't you turn it down some?" I said.

"It's all right," Nancy said. "I'll clean it. Yawl wait. The popcorn will start in a minute."

"I don't believe it's going to start," Caddy said. "We ought to start home, anyway. They'll be worried."

"No," Nancy said. "It's going to pop. Dilsey will tell um yawl with me. I been working for yawl long time. They won't mind if yawl at my house. You wait, now. It'll start popping any minute now."

Then Jason got some smoke in his eyes and he began to cry. He dropped the popper into the fire. Nancy got a wet rag and wiped Jason's face, but he didn't stop crying.

"Hush," she said. "Hush." But he didn't hush. Caddy took the popper out of the fire.

"It's burned up," she said. "You'll have to get some more popcorn, Nancy."

"Did you put all of it in?" Nancy said.

"Yes," Caddy said. Nancy looked at Caddy. Then she took the popper and opened it and poured the cinders into her apron and began to sort the grains, her hands long and brown, and we watching her.

"Haven't you got any more?" Caddy said.

"Yes," Nancy said; "yes. Look. This here ain't burnt. All we need to do is—"

"I want to go home," Jason said. "I'm going to tell."

"Hush," Caddy said. We all listened. Nancy's head was already turned toward the barred door, her eyes filled with red lamplight. "Somebody is coming," Caddy said.

Then Nancy began to make that sound again, not loud, sitting there above the fire, her long hands dangling between her knees; all of a sudden water began to come out on her face in big drops, running down her face, carrying in each one a little turning ball of fire-light like a spark until it dropped off her chin. "She's not crying," I said.

"I ain't crying," Nancy said. Her eyes were closed. "I ain't crying. Who is it?"

"I don't know," Caddy said. She went to the door and looked out. "We've got to go now," she said. "Here comes Father."

"I'm going to tell," Jason said. "Yawl made me come."

The water still ran down Nancy's face. She turned in her chair. "Listen. Tell him. Tell him we going to have fun. Tell him I take good care of yawl until in the morning. Tell him to let me come home with yawl and sleep on the floor. Tell him I won't need no pallet. We'll have fun. You member last time how we had so much fun?"

"I didn't have fun," Jason said. "You hurt me. You put smoke in my eyes. I'm going to tell."

v

Father came in. He looked at us. Nancy did not get up.

"Tell him," she said.

"Caddy made us come down here," Jason said. "I didn't want to."

Father came to the fire. Nancy looked up at him. "Can't you go to Aunt Rachel's and stay?" he said. Nancy looked up at Father, her hands between her knees. "He's not here," Father said. "I would have seen him. There's not a soul in sight."

"He in the ditch," Nancy said. "He waiting in the ditch yonder."

"Nonsense," Father said. He looked at Nancy. "Do you know he's there?"

"I got the sign," Nancy said.

"What sign?"

"I got it. It was on the table when I come in. It was a hogbone, with blood meat still on it, laying by the lamp. He's out there. When yawl walk out that door, I gone."

"Gone where, Nancy?" Caddy said.

"I'm not a tattletale," Jason said.

"Nonsense," Father said.

"He out there," Nancy said. "He looking through that window this minute, waiting for yawl to go. Then I gone."

"Nonsense," Father said. "Lock up your house and we'll take you on to Aunt Rachel's."

" 'Twon't do no good," Nancy said. She didn't look at Father now, but he looked down at her, at her long, limp, moving hands. "Putting it off won't do no good."

"Then what do you want to do?" Father said.

"I don't know," Nancy said. "I can't do nothing. Just put it off. And that don't do no good. I reckon it belong to me. I reckon what I going to get ain't no more than mine."

"Get what?" Caddy said. "What's yours?"

"Nothing," Father said. "You all must get to bed."

"Caddy made me come," Jason said.

"Go on to Aunt Rachel's," Father said.

"It won't do no good," Nancy said. She sat before the fire, her elbows on her knees, her long hands between her knees. "When even your own kitchen wouldn't do no good. When even if I was sleeping on the floor in the room with your chillen, and the next morning there I am, and blood—"

"Hush," Father said. "Lock the door and put out the lamp and go to bed."

"I scaired of the dark," Nancy said. "I scaired for it to happen in the dark."

"You mean you're going to sit right here with the

lamp lighted?" Father said. Then Nancy began to make the sound again, sitting before the fire, her long hands between her knees. "Ah, damnation," Father said. "Come along, chillen. It's past bedtime."

"When yawl go home, I gone," Nancy said. She talked quieter now, and her face looked quiet, like her hands. "Anyway, I got my coffin money saved up with Mr. Lovelady." Mr. Lovelady was a short, dirty man who collected the Negro insurance, coming around to the cabins or the kitchens every Saturday morning, to collect fifteen cents. He and his wife lived at the hotel. One morning his wife committed suicide. They had a child, a little girl. He and the child went away. After a week or two he came back alone. We would see him going along the lanes and the back streets on Saturday mornings.

"Nonsense," Father said. "You'll be the first thing I'll see in the kitchen tomorrow morning."

"You'll see what you'll see, I reckon," Nancy said. "But it will take the Lord to say what that will be."

VI

We left her sitting before the fire.

"Come and put the bar up," Father said. But she didn't move. She didn't look at us again, sitting quietly there between the lamp and the fire. From some distance down the lane we could look back and see her through the open door.

"What, Father?" Caddy said. "What's going to happen?"

"Nothing," Father said. Jason was on Father's back, so Jason was the tallest of all of us. We went down into the ditch. I looked at it, quiet. I couldn't see much where the moonlight and the shadows tangled.

"If Jesus *is* hid here, he can see us, can't he?" Caddy said.

"He's not there," Father said. "He went away a long time ago."

"You made me come," Jason said, high; against the sky it looked like Father had two heads, a little one and a big one. "I didn't want to."

We went up out of the ditch. We could still see Nancy's house and the open door, but we couldn't see Nancy now, sitting before the fire with the door open, because she was tired. "I just done got tired," she said. "I just a nigger. It ain't no fault of mine."

But we could hear her, because she began just after we came up out of the ditch, the sound that was not singing and not unsinging. "Who will do our washing now, Father?" I said.

"I'm not a nigger," Jason said, high and close above Father's head.

"You're worse," Caddy said, "you are a tattletale. If something was to jump out, you'd be scairder than a nigger."

"I wouldn't," Jason said.

"You'd cry," Caddy said.

"Caddy," Father said.

"I wouldn't!" Jason said.

"Scairy cat," Caddy said.

"Candace!" Father said.

1918.   AD ASTRA

I DON'T know what we were. With the exception
of Comyn, we had started out Americans, but after
three years, in our British tunics and British wings and
here and there a ribbon, I don't suppose we had even
bothered in three years to wonder what we were, to
think or to remember.

And on that day, that evening, we were even less
than that, or more than that: either beneath or beyond
the knowledge that we had not even wondered in three
years. The subadar—after a while he was there, in his
turban and his trick major's pips—said that we were
like men trying to move in water. "But soon it will clear
away," he said. "The effluvium of hatred and of words.
We are like men trying to move in water, with held
breath watching our terrific and infinitesimal limbs,
watching one another's terrific stasis without touch,
without contact, robbed of all save the impotence and
the need."

We were in the car then, going to Amiens, Sartoris
driving and Comyn sitting half a head above him in
the front seat like a tackling dummy, the subadar,
Bland and I in back, each with a bottle or two in his
pockets. Except the subadar, that is. He was squat,
small and thick, yet his sobriety was colossal. In that
maelstrom of alcohol where the rest of us had fled our
inescapable selves he was like a rock, talking quietly
in a grave bass four sizes too big for him: "In my country I was prince. But all men are brothers."

465

But after twelve years I think of us as bugs in the surface of the water, isolant and aimless and unflagging. Not on the surface; in it, within that line of demarcation not air and not water, sometimes submerged, sometimes not. You have watched an unbreaking groundswell in a cove, the water shallow, the cove quiet, a little sinister with satiate familiarity, while beyond the darkling horizon the dying storm has raged on. That was the water, we the flotsam. Even after twelve years it is no clearer than that. It had no beginning and no ending. Out of nothing we howled, unwitting the storm which we had escaped and the foreign strand which we could not escape; that in the interval between two surges of the swell we died who had been too young to have ever lived.

We stopped in the middle of the road to drink again. The land was dark and empty. And quiet: that was what you noticed, remarked. You could hear the earth breathe, like coming out of ether, like it did not yet know, believe, that it was awake. "But now it is peace," the subadar said. "All men are brothers."

"You spoke before the Union once," Bland said. He was blond and tall. When he passed through a room where women were he left a sighing wake like a ferry boat entering the slip. He was a Southerner, too, like Sartoris; but unlike Sartoris, in the five months he had been out, no one had ever found a bullet hole in his machine. But he had transferred out of an Oxford battalion—he was a Rhodes scholar—with a barnacle and a wound-stripe. When he was tight he would talk about his wife, though we all knew that he was not married.

He took the bottle from Sartoris and drank. "I've got the sweetest little wife," he said. "Let me tell you about her."

"Don't tell us," Sartoris said. "Give her to Comyn. He wants a girl."

"All right," Bland said. "You can have her, Comyn."

"Is she blonde?" Comyn said.

"I don't know," Bland said. He turned back to the subadar. "You spoke before the Union once. I remember you."

"Ah," the subadar said. "Oxford. Yes."

"He can attend their schools among the gentleborn, the bleach-skinned," Bland said. "But he cannot hold their commission, because gentility is a matter of color and not lineage or behavior."

"Fighting is more important than truth," the subadar said. "So we must restrict the prestige and privileges of it to the few so that it will not lose popularity with the many who have to die."

"Why more important?" I said. "I thought this one was being fought to end war forevermore."

The subadar made a brief gesture, dark, deprecatory, tranquil. "I was a white man also for that moment. It is more important for the Caucasian because he is only what he can do; it is the sum of him."

"So you see further than we see?"

"A man sees further looking out of the dark upon the light than a man does in the light and looking out upon the light. That is the principle of the spyglass. The lens is only to tease him with that which the sense that suffers and desires can never affirm."

"What do you see, then?" Bland said.

"I see girls," Comyn said. "I see acres and acres of the yellow hair of them like wheat and me among the wheat. Have ye ever watched a hidden dog quartering a wheat field, any of yez?"

"Not hunting bitches," Bland said.

Comyn turned in the seat, thick and huge. He was big as all outdoors. To watch two mechanics shoe-horning him into the cockpit of a Dolphin like two chambermaids putting an emergency bolster into a case too small for it, was a sight to see. "I will beat the head off ye for a shilling," he said.

"So you believe in the rightness of man?" I said.

"I will beat the heads off yez all for a shilling," Comyn said.

"I believe in the pitiableness of man," the subadar said. "That is better."

"I will give yez the shilling, then," Comyn said.

"All right," Sartoris said. "Did you ever try a little whiskey for the night air, any of you all?"

Comyn took the bottle and drank. "Acres and acres of them," he said, "with their little round white woman parts gleaming among the moiling wheat."

So we drank again, on the lonely road between two beet fields, in the dark quiet, and the turn of the inebriation began to make. It came back from wherever it had gone, rolling down upon us and upon the grave sober rock of the subadar until his voice sounded remote and tranquil and dreamlike, saying that we were brothers. Monaghan was there then, standing beside our car in the full glare of the headlights of his car, in a R.F.C. cap and an American tunic with both shoulder straps flapping loose, drinking from Comyn's bottle. Beside him stood a second man, also in a tunic shorter and trimmer than ours, with a bandage about his head.

"I'll fight you," Comyn told Monaghan. "I'll give you the shilling."

"All right," Monaghan said. He drank again.

"We are all brothers," the subadar said. "Sometimes we pause at the wrong inn. We think it is night and we stop, when it is not night. That is all."

"I'll give you a sovereign," Comyn told Monaghan.

"All right," Monaghan said. He extended the bottle to the other man, the one with the bandaged head.

"I thangk you," the man said. "I haf plenty yet."

"I'll fight him," Comyn said.

"It is because we can do only within the heart," the subadar said. "While we see beyond the heart."

"I'll be damned if you will," Monaghan said. "He's mine." He turned to the man with the bandaged head. "Aren't you mine? Here; drink."

"I haf plenty, I thangk you, gentlemen," the other said. But I don't think any of us paid much attention to him until we were inside the Cloche-Clos. It was crowded, full of noise and smoke. When we entered all the noise ceased, like a string cut in two, the end raveling back into a sort of shocked consternation of pivoting faces, and the waiter—an old man in a dirty apron—falling back before us, slack-jawed, with an expression of outraged unbelief, like an atheist confronted with either Christ or the devil. We crossed the room, the waiter retreating before us, paced by the turning outraged faces, to a table adjacent to one where three French officers sat watching us with that same expression of astonishment and then outrage and then anger. As one they rose; the whole room, the silence, became staccato with voices, like machine guns. That was when I turned and looked at Monaghan's companion for the first time, in his green tunic and his black snug breeks and his black boots and his bandage. He had cut himself recently shaving, and with his bandaged head and his face polite and dazed and bloodless and sick, he looked like Monaghan had been using him pretty hard. Roundfaced, not old, with his immaculately turned bandage which served only to emphasize the generations of difference between him and the turbaned subadar, flanked by Monaghan with his wild face and wild tunic and surrounded by the French people's shocked and outraged faces, he appeared to contemplate with a polite and alert concern his own struggle against the inebriation which Monaghan was forcing upon him. There was something Anthony-like about him: rigid, soldierly, with every button in place, with his unblemished bandage and his fresh razor cuts, he appeared to muse furiously upon a clear flame of a certain conviction of individual behavior above a violent and inexplicable chaos. Then I remarked Monaghan's second companion: an American military policeman. He was not drinking. He sat beside the German, rolling cigarettes from a cloth sack.

On the German's other side Monaghan was filling his glass. "I brought him down this morning," he said. "I'm going to take him home with me."

"Why?" Bland said. "What do you want with him?"

"Because he belongs to me," Monaghan said. He set the full glass before the German. "Here; drink."

"I once thought about taking one home to my wife," Bland said. "So I could prove to her that I have only been to a war. But I never could find a good one. A whole one, I mean."

"Come on," Monaghan said. "Drink."

"I haf plenty," the German said. "All day I haf plenty."

"Do you want to go to America with him?" Bland said.

"Yes. I would ligk it. Thanks."

"Sure you'll like it," Monaghan said. "I'll make a man of you. Drink."

The German raised the glass, but he merely held it in his hand. His face was strained, deprecatory, yet with a kind of sereneness, like that of a man who has conquered himself. I imagine some of the old martyrs must have looked at the lions with that expression. He was sick, too. Not from the liquor: from his head. "I haf in Bayreuth a wife and a little wohn. Mine son. I haf not him yet seen."

"Ah," the subadar said. "Bayreuth. I was there one spring."

"Ah," the German said. He looked quickly at the subadar. "So? The music?"

"Yes," the subadar said. "In your music a few of you have felt, tasted, lived, the true brotherhood. The rest of us can only look beyond the heart. But we can follow them for a little while in the music."

"And then we must return," the German said. "That iss not good. Why must we yet return always?"

"It is not the time for that yet," the subadar said. "But soon . . . It is not as far as it once was. Not now."

"Yes," the German said. "Defeat will be good for us. Defeat iss good for art; victory, it iss not good."

"So you admit you were whipped," Comyn said. He was sweating again, and Sartoris' nostrils were quite white. I thought of what the subadar had said about men in water. Only our water was drunkenness: that isolation of alcoholism which drives men to shout and laugh and fight, not with one another but with their unbearable selves which, drunk, they are even more fain and still less fell to escape. Loud and overloud, unwitting the black thunderhead of outraged France (steadily the other tables were being emptied; the other customers were now clotted about the high desk where the *patronne,* an old woman in steel spectacles, sat, a wad of knitting on the ledge before her), we shouted at one another, speaking in foreign tongues out of our inescapable isolations, reiterant, unlistened to by one another; while submerged by us and more foreign still, the German and the subadar talked quietly of music, art, the victory born of defeat. And outside in the chill November darkness was the suspension, the not-quite-believing, not-quite-awakened nightmare, the breathing spell of the old verbiaged lusts and the buntinged and panoplied greeds.

"By God, I'm shanty Irish," Monaghan said. "That's what I am."

"What about it?" Sartoris said, his nostrils like chalk against his high-colored face. His twin brother had been killed in July. He was in a Camel squadron below us, and Sartoris was down there when it happened. For a week after that, as soon as he came in from patrol he would fill his tanks and drums and go out again, alone. One day somebody saw him, roosting about five thousand feet above an old Ak.W. I suppose the other guy who was with his brother that morning had seen the markings on the Hun patrol leader's crate; anyway, that's what Sartoris was doing, using the Ak.W. for bait. Where he got it and who he got to fly it, we didn't know. But he got three Huns that week, catching them dead when they dived on the Ak.W., and on the eighth day he didn't go out again. "He must have got him," Hume said. But we didn't know. He never told us. But after that, he was all right again. He never did talk much; just did his patrols and maybe once a week he'd sit and drink his nostrils white in a quiet sort of way.

Bland was filling his glass, a drop at a time almost, with a catlike indolence. I could see why men didn't like him and why women did. Comyn, his arms crossed on the table, his cuff in a pool of spilt liquor, was staring at the German. His eyes were bloodshot, a little protuberant. Beneath his downcrushed monkey cap the American M.P. smoked his meager cigarettes, his face quite blank. The steel chain of his whistle looped into his breast pocket, his pistol was hunched forward onto his lap. Beyond, the French people, the soldiers, the waiter, the *patronne,* clotted at the desk. I could hear their voices like from a distance, like crickets in September grass, the shadows of their hands jerking up the wall and flicking away.

"I'm not a soldier," Monaghan said. "I'm not a gentleman. I'm not anything." At the base of each flapping shoulder strap there was a small rip; there were two longer ones parallel above his left pocket where his wings and ribbon had been. "I don't know what I am. I have been in this damn war for three years and all I know is, I'm not dead. I—"

"How do you know you're not dead?" Bland said.

Monaghan looked at Bland, his mouth open upon his uncompleted word.

"I'll kill you for a shilling," Comyn said. "I don't like your bloody face, Lootenant. Bloody lootenant."

"I'm shanty Irish," Monaghan said. "That's what I am. My father was shanty Irish, by God. And I don't know what my grandfather was. I don't know if I had one. My father don't remember one. Likely it could have been one of several. So he didn't even have to be a gentleman. He never had to be. That's why he could make a million dollars digging sewers in the ground. So he could look up at the tall glittering windows and say—I've heard him, and him smoking the pipe would gas the puking guts out of you damn, niggling, puny—"

"Are you bragging about your father's money or about his sewers?" Bland said.

"—would look up at them and he'd say to me, he'd say, 'When you're with your fine friends, the fathers and mothers and sisters of them you met at Yale, ye might just remind them that every man is the slave of his own refuse and so your old dad they would be sending around to the forty-storey back doors of their kitchens is the king of them all—' What did you say?" He looked at Bland.

"Look here, buddy," the M.P. said. "This is about enough of this. I've got to report this prisoner."

"Wait," Monaghan said. He did not cease to look at Bland. "What did you say?"

"Are you bragging about your father's money or about his sewers?" Bland said.

"No," Monaghan said. "Why should I? Any more than I would brag about the thirteen Huns I got, or the two ribbons, one of which his damned king—" he jerked his head at Comyn—"gave me."

"Don't call him my damned king," Comyn said, his cuff soaking slowly in the spilt liquor.

"Look," Monaghan said. He jerked his hand at the rips on his flapping shoulder straps, at the two parallel rips on his breast. "That's what I think of it. Of all your goddamn twaddle about glory and gentlemen. I was young; I thought you had to be. Then I was in it and there wasn't time to stop even when I found it didn't count. But now it's over; finished now. Now I can be what I am. Shanty Irish; son of an immigrant that knew naught but shovel and pick until youth and the time for pleasuring was wore out of him before his time. Out of a peat bog he came, and his son went to their gentlemen's school and returned across the water to swank it with any of them that owned the peat bogs and the bitter sweat of them that mired it, and the king said him well."

"I will give yez the shilling and I will beat the head off yez," Comyn said.

"But why do you want to take him back with you?" Bland said. Monaghan just looked at Bland. There was something of the crucified about Monaghan, too: furi-

ous, inarticulate not with stupidity but at it, like into
him more than any of us had distilled the ceased drums
of the old lust and greed waking at last aghast at its
own impotence and accrued despair. Bland sat on his
spine, legs extended, his hands in his slacks, his handsome face calmly insufferable. "What stringed pick
would he bow? maybe a shovel strung with the gut of
an alley-cat? he will create perhaps in music the flushed
toilets of Manhattan to play for your father after supper
of an evening?" Monaghan just looked at Bland with
that wild, rapt expression. Bland turned his lazy face a
little to the German.

"Look here," the M.P. said.

"You have a wife, Herr Leutnant?" Bland said.

The German looked up. He glanced swiftly from face
to face. "Yes, thank you," he said. He still had not
touched his full glass save to hold it in his hand. But he
was no nearer sober than before, the liquor become the
hurting of his head, his head the pulse and beat of
alcohol in him. "My people are of Prussia little barons.
There are four brothers: the second for the Army, the
third who did nothing in Berlin, the little one a cadet of
dragoons; I, the eldest, in the University. There I
learned. There wass a time then. It wass as though we,
young from the quiet land, were brought together,
chosen and worthy to witness a period quick like a
woman with a high destiny of the earth and of man. It
iss as though the old trash, the old litter of man's blundering iss to be swept away for a new race that will in
the heroic simplicity of olden time to walk the new
earth. You knew that time, not? when the eye sparkled,
the blut ran quick?" He looked about at our faces. "No?
Well, in America perhaps not. America iss new; in a
new house it iss not the litter so much as in old." He
looked at his glass for a moment, his face tranquil. "I

return home; I say to my father, in the University I haf learned it iss not good; baron I will not be. He cannot believe. He talks of Germany, the fatherland; I say to him, It iss there; so. You say fatherland; I, brotherland. I say, the word *father* iss that barbarism which will be first swept away; it iss the symbol of that hierarchy which hass stained the history of man with injustice of arbitrary instead of moral; force instead of love.

"From Berlin they send for that one; from the Army that one comes. I still say baron I will not be, for it iss not good. We are in the little hall where my ancestors on the walls hang; I stand before them like court-martial; I say that Franz must be baron, for I will not be. My father says you can; you will; it iss for Germany. Then I say, For Germany then will my wife be baroness? And like a court-martial I tell them I haf married the daughter of a musician who wass peasant.

"So it iss that. That one of Berlin iss to be baron. He and Franz are twin, but Franz iss captain already, and the most humble of the Army may eat meat with our kaiser; he does not need to be baron. So I am in Bayreuth with my wife and my music. It iss as though I am dead. I do not get letter until to say my father iss dead and I haf killed him, and that one iss now home from Berlin to be baron. But he does not stay at home. In 1912 he iss in Berlin newspaper dead of a lady's husband and so Franz iss baron after all.

"Then it iss war. But I am in Bayreuth with my wife and my music, because we think that it will not be long, since it was not long before. The fatherland in its pride needed us of the schools, but when it needed us it did not know it. And when it did realize that it needed us it wass too late and any peasant who would be hard to die would do. And so—"

"Why did you go, then?" Bland said. "Did the women make you? throw eggs at you, maybe?"

The German looked at Bland. "I am German; that iss beyond the I, the I am. Not for baron and kaiser." Then he quit looking at Bland without moving his eyes. "There wass a Germany before there wass barons," he said. "And after, there will be."

"Even after this?"

"More so. Then it was pride, a word in the mouth. Now it is a—how you call it? . . ."

"A nation vanquishes its banners," the subadar said. "A man conquers himself."

"Or a woman a child bears," the German said.

"Out of the lust, the travail," the subadar said; "out of the travail, the affirmation, the godhead; truth."

The M.P. was rolling another cigarette. He watched the subadar, upon his face an expression savage, restrained, and cold. He licked the cigarette and looked at me.

"When I came to this goddamn country," he said, "I thought niggers were niggers. But now I'll be damned if I know what they are. What's he? snake-charmer?"

"Yes," I said. "Snake-charmer."

"Then he better get his snake out and beat it. I've got to report this prisoner. Look at those frogs yonder." As I turned and looked three of the Frenchmen were leaving the room, insult and outrage in the shapes of their backs. The German was talking again.

"I hear by the newspapers how Franz is colonel and then general, and how the cadet, who wass still the round-headed boy part of a gun always when I last saw him, iss now ace with iron cross by the Kaiser's own hand. Then it iss 1916. I see by the paper how the cadet iss killed by your Bishop—" he bowed slightly to Comyn—"that good man. So now I am cadet myself. It iss as though I know. It iss as though I see what iss to be. So I transfer to be aviator, and yet though I know now that Franz iss general of staff and though to myself each night I say, 'You have again returned,' I know that it iss no good.

"That, until our Kaiser fled. Then I learn that Franz iss now in Berlin; I believe that there iss a truth, that we haf not forfeited all in pride, because we know it will not be much longer now, and Franz in Berlin safe, the fighting away from.

"Then it iss this morning. Then comes the letter in my mother's hand that I haf not seen in seven years, addressed to me as baron. Franz iss shot from his horse by German soldier in Berlin street. It iss as though all had been forgotten, because women can forget all that quick, since to them nothing iss real—truth, justice, all —nothing that cannot be held in the hands or cannot die. So I burn all my papers, the picture of my wife and my son that I haf not yet seen, destroy my identity disk and remove all insignia from my tunic—" he gestured toward his collar.

"You mean," Bland said, "that you had no intention of coming back? Why didn't you take a pistol to yourself and save your government an aeroplane?"

"Suicide iss just for the body," the German said. "The body settles nothing. It iss of no importance. It iss just to be kept clean when possible."

"It is merely a room in the inn," the subadar said. "It is just where we hide for a little while."

"The lavatory," Bland said; "the toilet."

The M.P. rose. He tapped the German on the shoulder. Comyn was staring at the German.

"So you admit you were whipped," he said.

"Yes," the German said. "It wass our time first, because we were the sickest. It will be your England's next. Then she too will be well."

"Don't say my England," Comyn said. "I am of the Irish nation." He turned to Monaghan. "You said, my damned king. Don't say my damned king. Ireland has had no king since the Ur Neill, God bless the redhaired stern of him."

Rigid, controlled, the German made a faint gesture. "You see?" he said to no one at all.

"The victorious lose that which the vanquished gain," the subadar said.

"And what will you do now?" Bland said.

The German did not answer. He sat bolt upright with his sick face and his immaculate bandage.

"What will you do?" the subadar said to Bland. "What will any of us do? All this generation which fought in the war are dead tonight. But we do not yet know it."

We looked at the subadar: Comyn with his bloodshot pig's eyes, Sartoris with his white nostrils, Bland slumped in his chair, indolent, insufferable, with his air of a spoiled woman. Above the German the M.P. stood.

"It seems to worry you a hell of a lot," Bland said.

"You do not believe?" the subadar said. "Wait. You will see."

"Wait?" Bland said. "I don't think I've done anything in the last three years to have acquired that habit. In the last twenty-six years. Before that I don't remember. I may have."

"Then you will see sooner than waiting," the subadar said. "You will see." He looked about at us, gravely serene. "Those who have been four years rotting out yonder—" he waved his short thick arm—"are not more dead than we."

Again the M.P. touched the German's shoulder. "Hell," he said. "Come along, buddy." Then he turned his head and we all looked up at the two Frenchmen, an officer and a sergeant, standing beside the table. For a while we just remained so. It was like all the little bugs had suddenly found that their orbits had coincided and they wouldn't even have to be aimless any more or even to keep on moving. Beneath the alcohol I could feel that hard, hot ball beginning in my stomach, like in combat, like when you know something is about to happen; that instant when you think Now. Now I can dump everything overboard and just be. Now. Now. It is quite pleasant.

"Why is that here, monsieur?" the officer said. Monaghan looked up at him, thrust backward and sideways in his chair, poised on the balls of his thighs as though they were feet, his arm lying upon the table. "Why do you make desagreable for France, monsieur, eh?" the officer said.

Someone grasped Monaghan as he rose; it was the M.P. behind him, holding him half risen. "Wa-a-a-i-daminute," the M.P. said; "wa-a-a-i-daminute." The cigarette bobbed on his lower lip as he talked, his hands on Monaghan's shoulders, the brassard on his arm lifted into bold relief. "What's it to you, Frog?" he said. Behind the officer and the sergeant the other French people stood, and the old woman. She was trying to push through the circle. "This is my prisoner," the M.P. said. "I'll take him anywhere I please and keep him there as long as I like. What do you think about that?"

"By which authority, monsieur?" the officer said. He was tall, with a gaunt tragic face. I saw then that one of his eyes was glass. It was motionless, rigid in a face that looked even deader than the spurious eye.

The M.P. glanced toward his brassard, then instead he looked at the officer again and tapped the pistol swinging low now against his flank. "I'll take him all over your goddamn lousy country. I'll take him into your goddamn senate and kick your president up for a chair for him and you can suck your chin until I come back to wipe the latrine off your feet again."

"Ah," the officer said, "a devil-dog, I see." He said "dehvil-dahg" between his teeth, with no motion of his dead face, in itself insult. Behind him the *patronne* began to shriek in French:

"Boche! Boche! Broken! Broken! Every cup, every saucer, glass, plate—all, all! I will show you! I have kept them for this day. Eight months since the shelling I have kept them in a box against this day: plates, cups, saucers, glasses, all that I have had since thirty years, all gone, broken at one time! And it costing me fifty centimes the glass for such that I shame myself to have my patrons—"

There is an unbearable point, a climax, in weariness. Even alcohol cannot approach it. Mobs are motivated by it, by a sheer attenuation of sameness become unbearable. As Monaghan rose, the M.P. flung him back. Then it was as though we all flung everything overboard at once, facing unabashed and without shame the specter which for four years we had been decking out in high words, leaping forward with concerted and orderly promptitude each time the bunting slipped. I saw the M.P. spring at the officer, then Comyn rose and met him. I saw the M.P. hit Comyn three times on the point of the jaw with his fist before Comyn picked him up bodily and threw him clean over the crowd, where he vanished, horizontal in mid-air, tugging at his pistol. I saw three poilus on Monaghan's back and the officer trying to hit him with a bottle, and Sartoris leaping upon the officer from behind. Comyn was gone; through the gap which he had made the *patronne* emerged, shrieking. Two men caught at her and she strove forward, trying to spit on the German. "Boche! Boche!" she shrieked, spitting and slobbering, her gray hair broken loose about her face; she turned and spat full at me. "Thou, too!" she shrieked, "it was not England that was devastated! Thou, too, come to pick the bones of France. Jackal! Vulture! Animal! Broken, broken! All! All! All!" And beneath it all, unmoved, unmoving, alert, watchful and contained, the German and the subadar sat, the German with his high sick face, the subadar tranquil as a squat idol, the both of them turbaned like prophets in the Old Testament.

It didn't take long. There was no time in it. Or rather, we were outside of time; within, not on, that surface, that demarcation between the old where we knew we had not died and the new where the subadar said that we were dead. Beyond the brandished bottles, the blue sleeves and the grimed hands, the faces like masks grimaced into rigid and soundless shouts to frighten children, I saw Comyn again. He came plowing up like a laden ship in a chop sea; beneath his arm was the ancient waiter, to his lips he held the M.P.'s whistle. Then Sartoris swung a chair at the single light.

It was cold in the street, a cold that penetrated the clothing, the alcohol-distended pores, and murmured to the skeleton itself. The plaza was empty, the lights infrequent and remote. So quiet it was that I could hear the faint water in the fountain. From some distance away came sound, remote too under the thick low sky—shouting, far-heard, on a thin female note like all shouting, even a mob of men, broken now and then by the sound of a band. In the shadow of the wall

Monaghan and Comyn held the German on his feet. He
was unconscious; the three of them invisible save for
the faint blur of the bandage, inaudible save for the
steady monotone of Monaghan's cursing.

"There should never have been an alliance between
Frenchmen and Englishmen," the subadar said. He
spoke without effort; invisible, his effortless voice had
an organ quality, out of all proportion to his size. "Different nations should never join forces to fight for the
same object. Let each fight for something different;
ends that do not conflict, each in his own way." Sartoris
passed us, returning from the fountain, carrying his
bulging cap carefully before him, bottom-up. We could
hear the water dripping from it between his footsteps.
He became one of the blob of thicker shadow where
the bandage gleamed and where Monaghan cursed
steadily and quietly. "And each after his own tradition,"
the subadar said. "My people. The English gave them
rifles. They looked at them and came to me: 'This spear
is too short and too heavy: how can a man slay a swift
enemy with a spear of this size and weight?' They gave
them tunics with buttons to be kept buttoned; I have
passed a whole trench of them squatting, motionless,
buried to the ears in blankets, straw, empty sand bags,
their faces gray with cold; I have lifted the blankets
away from patient torsos clad only in a shirt.

"The English officers would say to them, 'Go there
and do thus'; they would not stir. Then one day at fall
noon the whole battalion, catching movement beyond a
crater, sprang from the trench, carrying me and an officer with it. We carried the trench without firing a
shot; what was left of us—the officer, I, and seventeen
others—lived three days in a traverse of the enemy's
front line; it required a whole brigade to extricate us.
'Why didn't you shoot?' the officer said. 'You let them

pick you off like driven pheasant.' They did not look at him. Like children they stood, murmurous, alert, without shame. I said to the headman, 'Were the rifles loaded, O Das?' Like children they stood, diffident, without shame. 'O Son of many kings,' Das said. 'Speak the truth of thy knowing to the sahib,' I said. 'They were not loaded, sahib,' Das said."

Again the band came, remote, thudding in the thick air. They were giving the German drink from a bottle. Monaghan said: "Now. Feel better now?"

"It iss mine head," the German said. They spoke quietly, like they were discussing wallpaper.

Monaghan cursed again. "I'm going back. By God, I—"

"No, no," the German said. "I will not permit. You haf already obligated—"

We stood in the shadow beneath the wall and drank. We had one bottle left. Comyn crashed it, empty, against the wall.

"Now what?" Bland said.

"Girls," Comyn said. "Would ye watch Comyn of the Irish nation among the yellow hair of them like a dog among the wheat?"

We stood there, hearing the far band, the far shouting. "You sure you feel all right?" Monaghan said.

"Thanks," the German said. "I feel goot."

"Come on, then," Comyn said.

"You going to take him with you?" Bland said.

"Yes," Monaghan said. "What of it?"

"Why not take him on to the A.P.M.? He's sick."

"Do you want me to bash your bloody face in?" Monaghan said.

"All right," Bland said.

"Come on," Comyn said. "What fool would rather

fight than fush? All men are brothers, and all their wives are sisters. So come along, yez midnight fusileers."

"Look here," Bland said to the German, "do you want to go with them?" With his bandaged head, he and the subadar alone were visible, like two injured men among five spirits.

"Hold him up a minute," Monaghan told Comyn. Monaghan approached Bland. He cursed Bland. "I like fighting," he said, in that same monotone. "I even like being whipped."

"Wait," the German said. "Again I will not permit." Monaghan halted, he and Bland not a foot apart. "I haf wife and son in Bayreuth," the German said. He was speaking to me. He gave me the address, twice, carefully.

"I'll write to her," I said. "What shall I tell her?"

"Tell her it iss nothing. You will know."

"Yes. I'll tell her you are all right."

"Tell her this life iss nothing."

Comyn and Monaghan took his arms again, one on either side. They turned and went on, almost carrying him. Comyn looked back once. "Peace be with you," he said.

"And with you, peace," the subadar said. They went on. We watched them come into silhouette in the mouth of an alley where a light was. There was an arch there, and the faint cold pale light on the arch and on the walls so that it was like a gate and they entering the gate, holding the German up between them.

"What will they do with him?" Bland said. "Prop him in the corner and turn the light off? Or do French brothels have he-beds too?"

"Who the hell's business is that?" I said.

The sound of the band came, thudding; it was cold.

Each time my flesh jerked with alcohol and cold I believed that I could hear it rasp on the bones.

"Since seven years now I have been in this climate," the subadar said. "But still I do not like the cold." His voice was deep, quiet, like he might be six feet tall. It was like when they made him they said among themselves, "We'll give him something to carry his message around with." "Why? Who'll listen to his message?" "He will. So we'll give him something to hear it with."

"Why don't you go back to India, then?" Bland said.

"Ah," the subadar said. "I am like him; I too will not be baron."

"So you clear out and let foreigners who will treat the people like oxen or rabbits come in and take it."

"By removing myself I undid in one day what it took two thousand years to do. Is not that something?"

We shook with the cold. Now the cold was the band, the shouting, murmuring with cold hands to the skeleton, not the ears.

"Well," Bland said, "I suppose the English government is doing more to free your people than you could."

The subadar touched Bland on the chest, lightly. "You are wise, my friend. Let England be glad that all Englishmen are not so wise."

"So you will be an exile for the rest of your days, eh?"

The subadar jerked his short, thick arm toward the empty arch where Comyn and the German and Monaghan had disappeared. "Did you not hear what he said? This life is nothing."

"You can think so," Bland said. "But, by God, I'd hate to think that what I saved out of the last three years is nothing."

"You saved a dead man," the subadar said serenely. "You will see."

"I saved my destiny," Bland said. "You nor nobody else knows what that will be."

"What is your destiny except to be dead? It is unfortunate that your generation had to be the one. It is unfortunate that for the better part of your days you will walk the earth a spirit. But that was your destiny." From far away came the shouting, on that sustained note, feminine and childlike all at once, and then the band again, brassy, thudding, like the voices, forlornly gay, hysteric, but most of all forlorn. The arch in the cold glow of the light yawned empty, profound, silent, like the gate to another city, another world. Suddenly Sartoris left us. He walked steadily to the wall and leaned against it on his propped arms, vomiting.

"Hell," Bland said. "I want a drink." He turned to me. "Where's your bottle?"

"It's gone."

"Gone where? You had two."

"I haven't got one now, though. Drink water."

"Water?" he said. "Who the hell drinks water?"

Then the hot hard ball came into my stomach again, pleasant, unbearable, real; again that instant when you say Now. Now I can dump everything. "You will, you goddamn son," I said.

Bland was not looking at me. "Twice," he said in a quiet, detached tone. "Twice in an hour. How's that for high?" He turned and went toward the fountain. Sartoris came back, walking steadily erect. The band blent with the cold along the bones.

"What time is it?" I said.

Sartoris peered at his wrist. "Twelfth."

"It's later than midnight," I said. "It must be."

"I said it was the twelfth," Sartoris said.

Bland was stooping at the fountain. There was a

little light there. As we reached him he stood up, mopping at his face. The light was on his face and I thought for some time that he must have had his whole head under to be mopping that high up his face before I saw that he was crying. He stood there, mopping at his face, crying hard but quiet.

"My poor little wife," he said. "My poor little wife."

1924. A ROSE FOR EMILY

I

WHEN Miss Emily Grierson died, our whole
town went to her funeral: the men through a
sort of respectful affection for a fallen monument, the
women mostly out of curiosity to see the inside of her
house, which no one save an old manservant—a com-
bined gardener and cook—had seen in at least ten years.

It was a big, squarish frame house that had once
been white, decorated with cupolas and spires and
scrolled balconies in the heavily lightsome style of the
seventies, set on what had once been our most select
street. But garages and cotton gins had encroached and
obliterated even the august names of that neighborhood; only Miss Emily's house was left, lifting its stubborn and coquettish decay above the cotton wagons and
the gasoline pumps—an eyesore among eyesores. And
now Miss Emily had gone to join the representatives of
those august names where they lay in the cedar-
bemused cemetery among the ranked and anonymous
graves of Union and Conferedate soldiers who fell at
the battle of Jefferson.

Alive, Miss Emily had been a tradition, a duty, and
a care; a sort of hereditary obligation upon the town,
dating from that day in 1894 when Colonel Sartoris, the
mayor—he who fathered the edict that no Negro
woman should appear on the streets without an apron
—remitted her taxes, the dispensation dating from the
death of her father on into perpetuity. Not that Miss

Emily would have accepted charity. Colonel Sartoris invented an involved tale to the effect that Miss Emily's father had loaned money to the town, which the town, as a matter of business, preferred this way of repaying. Only a man of Colonel Sartoris' generation and thought could have invented it, and only a woman could have believed it.

When the next generation, with its more modern ideas, became mayors and aldermen, this arrangement created some little dissatisfaction. On the first of the year they mailed her a tax notice. February came, and there was no reply. They wrote her a formal letter, asking her to call at the sheriff's office at her convenience. A week later the mayor wrote her himself, offering to call or to send his car for her, and received in reply a note on paper of an archaic shape, in a thin, flowing calligraphy in faded ink, to the effect that she no longer went out at all. The tax notice was also enclosed, without comment.

They called a special meeting of the Board of Aldermen. A deputation waited upon her, knocked at the door through which no visitor had passed since she ceased giving china-painting lessons eight or ten years earlier. They were admitted by the old Negro into a dim hall from which a stairway mounted into still more shadow. It smelled of dust and disuse—a close, dank smell. The Negro led them into the parlor. It was furnished in heavy, leather-covered furniture. When the Negro opened the blinds of one window, they could see that the leather was cracked; and when they sat down, a faint dust rose sluggishly about their thighs, spinning with slow motes in the single sun-ray. On a tarnished gilt easel before the fireplace stood a crayon portrait of Miss Emily's father.

They rose when she entered—a small, fat woman in

black, with a thin gold chain descending to her waist and vanishing into her belt, leaning on an ebony cane with a tarnished gold head. Her skeleton was small and spare; perhaps that was why what would have been merely plumpness in another was obesity in her. She looked bloated, like a body long submerged in motionless water, and of that pallid hue. Her eyes, lost in the fatty ridges of her face, looked like two small pieces of coal pressed into a lump of dough as they moved from one face to another while the visitors stated their errand.

She did not ask them to sit. She just stood in the door and listened quietly until the spokesman came to a stumbling halt. Then they could hear the invisible watch ticking at the end of the gold chain.

Her voice was dry and cold. "I have no taxes in Jefferson. Colonel Sartoris explained it to me. Perhaps one of you can gain access to the city records and satisfy yourselves."

"But we have. We are the city authorities, Miss Emily. Didn't you get a notice from the sheriff, signed by him?"

"I received a paper, yes," Miss Emily said. "Perhaps he considers himself the sheriff . . . I have no taxes in Jefferson."

"But there is nothing on the books to show that, you see. We must go by the—"

"See Colonel Sartoris. I have no taxes in Jefferson."

"But, Miss Emily—"

"See Colonel Sartoris." (Colonel Sartoris had been dead almost ten years.) "I have no taxes in Jefferson. Tobe!" The Negro appeared. "Show these gentlemen out."

II

So she vanquished them, horse and foot, just as she had vanquished their fathers thirty years before about the smell. That was two years after her father's death and a short time after her sweetheart—the one we believed would marry her—had deserted her. After her father's death she went out very little; after her sweetheart went away, people hardly saw her at all. A few of the ladies had the temerity to call, but were not received, and the only sign of life about the place was the Negro man—a young man then—going in and out with a market basket.

"Just as if a man—any man—could keep a kitchen properly," the ladies said; so they were not surprised when the smell developed. It was another link between the gross, teeming world and the high and mighty Griersons.

A neighbor, a woman, complained to the mayor, Judge Stevens, eighty years old.

"But what will you have me do about it, madam?" he said.

"Why, send her word to stop it," the woman said. "Isn't there a law?"

"I'm sure that won't be necessary," Judge Stevens said. "It's probably just a snake or a rat that nigger of hers killed in the yard. I'll speak to him about it."

The next day he received two more complaints, one from a man who came in diffident deprecation. "We really must do something about it, Judge. I'd be the last one in the world to bother Miss Emily, but we've got to do something." That night the Board of Aldermen met—three graybeards and one younger man, a member of the rising generation.

"It's simple enough," he said. "Send her word to have

her place cleaned up. Give her a certain time to do it in, and if she don't . . ."

"Dammit, sir," Judge Stevens said, "will you accuse a lady to her face of smelling bad?"

So the next night, after midnight, four men crossed Miss Emily's lawn and slunk about the house like burglars, sniffing along the base of the brickwork and at the cellar openings while one of them performed a regular sowing motion with his hand out of a sack slung from his shoulder. They broke open the cellar door and sprinkled lime there, and in all the outbuildings. As they recrossed the lawn, a window that had been dark was lighted and Miss Emily sat in it, the light behind her, and her upright torso motionless as that of an idol. They crept quietly across the lawn and into the shadow of the locusts that lined the street. After a week or two the smell went away.

That was when people had begun to feel really sorry for her. People in our town, remembering how old lady Wyatt, her great-aunt, had gone completely crazy at last, believed that the Griersons held themselves a little too high for what they really were. None of the young men were quite good enough to Miss Emily and such. We had long thought of them as a tableau; Miss Emily a slender figure in white in the background, her father a spraddled silhouette in the foreground, his back to her and clutching a horsewhip, the two of them framed by the back-flung front door. So when she got to be thirty and was still single, we were not pleased exactly, but vindicated; even with insanity in the family she wouldn't have turned down all of her chances if they had really materialized.

When her father died, it got about that the house was all that was left to her; and in a way, people were glad. At last they could pity Miss Emily. Being left alone, and a pauper, she had become humanized. Now she too would know the old thrill and the old despair of a penny more or less.

The day after his death all the ladies prepared to call at the house and offer condolence and aid, as is our custom. Miss Emily met them at the door, dressed as usual and with no trace of grief on her face. She told them that her father was not dead. She did that for three days, with the ministers calling on her, and the doctors, trying to persuade her to let them dispose of the body. Just as they were about to resort to law and force, she broke down, and they buried her father quickly.

We did not say she was crazy then. We believed she had to do that. We remembered all the young men her father had driven away, and we knew that with nothing left, she would have to cling to that which had robbed her, as people will.

III

She was sick for a long time. When we saw her again, her hair was cut short, making her look like a girl, with a vague resemblance to those angels in colored church windows—sort of tragic and serene.

The town had just let the contracts for paving the sidewalks, and in the summer after her father's death they began the work. The construction company came with niggers and mules and machinery, and a foreman named Homer Barron, a Yankee—a big, dark, ready man, with a big voice and eyes lighter than his face. The little boys would follow in groups to hear him cuss the niggers, and the niggers singing in time to the rise and fall of picks. Pretty soon he knew everybody in town. Whenever you heard a lot of laughing anywhere about the square, Homer Barron would be in the center of the group. Presently we began to see him and Miss Emily on Sunday afternoons driving in the yellow-wheeled buggy and the matched team of bays from the livery stable.

At first we were glad that Miss Emily would have an interest, because the ladies all said, "Of course a Grierson would not think seriously of a Northerner, a day laborer." But there were still others, older people, who said that even grief could not cause a real lady to forget *noblesse oblige*—without calling it *noblesse oblige*. They just said, "Poor Emily. Her kinsfolk should come to her." She had some kin in Alabama; but years ago her father had fallen out with them over the estate of old lady Wyatt, the crazy woman, and there was no communication between the two families. They had not even been represented at the funeral.

And as soon as the old people said, "Poor Emily," the whispering began. "Do you suppose it's really so?" they said to one another. "Of course it is. What else could . . ." This behind their hands; rustling of craned silk and satin behind jalousies closed upon the sun of Sunday afternoon as the thin, swift clop-clop-clop of the matched team passed: "Poor Emily."

She carried her head high enough—even when we believed that she was fallen. It was as if she demanded more than ever the recognition of her dignity as the last Grierson; as if it had wanted that touch of earthiness to reaffirm her imperviousness. Like when she bought the rat poison, the arsenic. That was over a year after they had begun to say "Poor Emily," and while the two female cousins were visiting her.

"I want some poison," she said to the druggist. She was over thirty then, still a slight woman, though thinner than usual, with cold, haughty black eyes in a face the flesh of which was strained across the temples and about the eye-sockets as you imagine a lighthouse-keeper's face ought to look. "I want some poison," she said.

"Yes, Miss Emily. What kind? For rats and such? I'd recom—"

"I want the best you have. I don't care what kind."

The druggist named several. "They'll kill anything up to an elephant. But what you want is—"

"Arsenic," Miss Emily said. "Is that a good one?"

"Is . . . arsenic? Yes, ma'am. But what you want—"

"I want arsenic."

The druggist looked down at her. She looked back at him, erect, her face like a strained flag. "Why, of course," the druggist said. "If that's what you want. But the law requires you to tell what you are going to use it for."

Miss Emily just stared at him, her head tilted back in order to look him eye for eye, until he looked away and went and got the arsenic and wrapped it up. The Negro delivery boy brought her the package; the druggist didn't come back. When she opened the package at home there was written on the box, under the skull and bones: "For rats."

IV

So the next day we all said, "She will kill herself"; and we said it would be the best thing. When she had first begun to be seen with Homer Barron, we had said, "She will marry him." Then we said, "She will persuade him yet," because Homer himself had remarked—he liked men, and it was known that he drank with the younger men in the Elks' Club—that he was not a marrying man. Later we said, "Poor Emily" behind the jalousies as they passed on Sunday afternoon in the glittering buggy, Miss Emily with her head high and Homer Barron with his hat cocked and a cigar in his teeth, reins and whip in a yellow glove.

Then some of the ladies began to say that it was a disgrace to the town and a bad example to the young people. The men did not want to interfere, but at last the ladies forced the Baptist minister—Miss Emily's people were Episcopal—to call upon her. He would never divulge what happened during that interview, but he refused to go back again. The next Sunday they again drove about the streets, and the following day the minister's wife wrote to Miss Emily's relations in Alabama.

So she had blood-kin under her roof again and we sat back to watch developments. At first nothing happened. Then we were sure that they were to be married. We learned that Miss Emily had been to the jeweler's and ordered a man's toilet set in silver, with the letters H. B. on each piece. Two days later we learned that she had bought a complete outfit of men's clothing, including a nightshirt, and we said, "They are married." We were really glad. We were glad because the two female cousins were even more Grierson than Miss Emily had ever been.

So we were not surprised when Homer Barron— the streets had been finished some time since—was gone. We were a little disappointed that there was not a public blowing-off, but we believed that he had gone on to prepare for Miss Emily's coming, or to give her a chance to get rid of the cousins. (By that time it was a cabal, and we were all Miss Emily's allies to help circumvent the cousins.) Sure enough, after another week they departed. And, as we had expected all along, within three days Homer Barron was back in town. A neighbor saw the Negro man admit him at the kitchen door at dusk one evening.

And that was the last we saw of Homer Barron. And of Miss Emily for some time. The Negro man went in and out with the market basket, but the front door remained closed. Now and then we would see her at a window for a moment, as the men did that night when they sprinkled the lime, but for almost six months she did not appear on the streets. Then we knew that this was to be expected too; as if that quality of her father which had thwarted her woman's life so many times had been too virulent and too furious to die.

When we next saw Miss Emily, she had grown fat and her hair was turning gray. During the next few years it grew grayer and grayer until it attained an even pepper-and-salt iron-gray, when it ceased turning. Up to the day of her death at seventy-four it was still that vigorous iron-gray, like the hair of an active man.

From that time on her front door remained closed, save for a period of six or seven years, when she was about forty, during which she gave lessons in china-painting. She fitted up a studio in one of the downstairs rooms, where the daughters and granddaughters of Colonel Sartoris' contemporaries were sent to her with the same regularity and in the same spirit that they were sent to church on Sundays with a twenty-five cent piece for the collection plate. Meanwhile her taxes had been remitted.

Then the newer generation became the backbone and the spirit of the town, and the painting pupils grew up and fell away and did not send their children to her with boxes of color and tedious brushes and pictures cut from the ladies' magazines. The front door closed upon the last one and remained closed for good. When the town got free postal delivery,

Miss Emily alone refused to let them fasten the metal numbers above her door and attach a mailbox to it. She would not listen to them.

Daily, monthly, yearly we watched the Negro grow grayer and more stooped, going in and out with the market basket. Each December we sent her a tax notice, which would be returned by the post office a week later, unclaimed. Now and then we would see her in one of the downstairs windows—she had evidently shut up the top floor of the house—like the carven torso of an idol in a niche, looking or not looking at us, we could never tell which. Thus she passed from generation to generation—dear, inescapable, impervious, tranquil, and perverse.

And so she died. Fell ill in the house filled with dust and shadows, with only a doddering Negro man to wait on her. We did not even know she was sick; we had long since given up trying to get any information from the Negro. He talked to no one, probably not even to her, for his voice had grown harsh and rusty, as if from disuse.

She died in one of the downstairs rooms, in a heavy walnut bed with a curtain, her gray head propped on a pillow yellow and moldy with age and lack of sunlight.

v

The Negro met the first of the ladies at the front door and let them in, with their hushed, sibilant voices and their quick, curious glances, and then he disappeared. He walked right through the house and out the back and was not seen again.

The two female cousins came at once. They held the funeral on the second day, with the town coming to look at Miss Emily beneath a mass of bought flowers, with the crayon face of her father musing profoundly above the bier and the ladies sibilant and macabre; and the very old men—some in their brushed Confederate uniforms—on the porch and the lawn, talking of Miss Emily as if she had been a contemporary of theirs, believing that they had danced with her and courted her perhaps, confusing time with its mathematical progression, as the old do, to whom all the past is not a diminishing road but, instead, a huge meadow which no winter ever quite touches, divided from them now by the narrow bottle-neck of the most recent decade of years.

Already we knew that there was one room in that region above stairs which no one had seen in forty years, and which would have to be forced. They waited until Miss Emily was decently in the ground before they opened it.

The violence of breaking down the door seemed to fill this room with pervading dust. A thin, acrid pall as of the tomb seemed to lie everywhere upon this room decked and furnished as for a bridal: upon the valence curtains of faded rose color, upon the rose-shaded lights, upon the dressing table, upon the delicate array of crystal and the man's toilet things backed with tarnished silver, silver so tarnished that the monogram was obscured. Among them lay a collar and tie, as if they had just been removed, which, lifted, left upon the surface a pale crescent in the dust. Upon a chair hung the suit, carefully folded; beneath it the two mute shoes and the discarded socks.

The man himself lay in the bed.

For a long while we just stood there, looking down at the profound and fleshless grin. The body had apparently once lain in the attitude of an embrace, but now the long sleep that outlasts love, that conquers even the grimace of love, had cuckolded him. What was left of him, rotted beneath what was left of the nightshirt, had become inextricable from the bed in which he lay; and upon him and upon the pillow beside him lay that even coating of the patient and biding dust.

Then we noticed that in the second pillow was the indentation of a head. One of us lifted something from it, and leaning forward, that faint and invisible dust dry and acrid in the nostrils, we saw a long strand of iron-gray hair.

THE day dawned bleak and chill, a moving wall of gray light out of the northeast which, instead of dissolving into moisture, seemed to disintegrate into minute and venomous particles like dust that, when Dilsey opened the door of the cabin and emerged, needled laterally into her flesh, precipitating not so much a moisture as a substance partaking of the quality of thin, not quite congealed oil. She wore a stiff black straw hat perched upon her turban, and a maroon velvet cape with a border of mangy and anonymous fur above a dress of purple silk, and she stood in the door for a while with her myriad and sunken face lifted to the weather, and one gaunt hand flac-soled as the belly of a fish, then she moved the cape aside and examined the bosom of her gown.

The gown fell gauntly from her shoulders, across her fallen breasts, then tightened upon her paunch and fell again, ballooning a little above the nether garments which she would remove layer by layer as the spring accomplished and the warm days, in color regal and moribund. She had been a big woman once but now her skeleton rose, draped loosely in unpadded skin that tightened again upon a paunch almost dropsical, as though muscle and tissue had been courage or fortitude which the days or the years had consumed until only the indomitable skeleton was left rising like a ruin or a landmark above the somnolent and impervious guts, and above that the collapsed face that gave the impression of the bones themselves being outside the flesh, lifted into the driving day with an expression at once fatalistic and of a child's astonished disappointment, until she turned and entered the house again and closed the door.

The earth immediately about the door was bare. It had a patina, as though from the soles of bare feet in generations, like old silver or the walls of Mexican houses which have been plastered by hand. Beside the house, shading it in summer, stood three mulberry trees, the fledged leaves that would later be broad and placid as the palms of hands steaming flatly undulant upon the driving air. A pair of jaybirds came up from nowhere, whirled up on the blast like gaudy scraps of cloth or paper and lodged in the mulberries, where they swung in raucous tilt and recover, screaming into the wind that ripped their harsh cries onward and away like scraps of paper or of cloth in turn. Then three more joined them and they swung and tilted in the wrung branches for a time, screaming. The door of the cabin opened and Dilsey emerged once more, this time in a man's felt hat and an army overcoat, beneath the frayed skirts of which her blue gingham dress fell in uneven balloonings, streaming too about her as she crossed the yard and mounted the steps to the kitchen door.

A moment later she emerged, carrying an open umbrella now, which she slanted ahead into the wind, and crossed to the woodpile and laid the umbrella down, still open. Immediately she caught at it and arrested it and held to it for a while, looking about her. Then she closed it and laid it down and stacked stovewood into her crooked arm, against her breast, and picked up the umbrella and got it open at last and returned to the steps and held the wood precariously balanced while she contrived to close the umbrella, which she propped in the corner just within the door. She dumped the wood into the box behind the stove. Then she removed the overcoat and hat and took a soiled apron down from the wall and put it on and built a fire in the stove. While she was doing so, rattling the grate bars and clattering the lids, Mrs. Compson began to call her from the head of the stairs.

She wore a dressing gown of quilted black satin, holding it close under her chin. In the other hand she held a red rubber hot water bottle and she stood at the head of the back stairway, calling, "Dilsey," at steady and inflectionless intervals into the quiet stairwell that descended into complete darkness, then opened again where a gray window fell across it. "Dilsey," she called, without inflection or emphasis or haste, as though she were not listening for a reply at all. "Dilsey."

Dilsey answered and ceased clattering the stove, but before she could cross the kitchen Mrs. Compson called her again, and before she crossed the dining room and brought her head into relief against the gray splash of the window, still again.

"All right," Dilsey said, "all right, here I is. I'll fill hit soon ez I git some hot water." She gathered up her skirts and mounted the stairs, wholly blotting the gray light. "Put hit down dar en g'awn back to bed."

"I couldn't understand what was the matter," Mrs. Compson said. "I've been lying awake for an hour at least, without hearing a sound from the kitchen."

"You put hit down and g'awn back to bed," Dilsey said. She toiled painfully up the steps, shapeless, breathing heavily. "I'll have de fire gwine in a minute, en de water hot in two mo'."

"I've been lying there for an hour, at least," Mrs.

Compson said. "I thought maybe you were waiting for me to come down and start the fire."

Dilsey reached the top of the stairs and took the water bottle. "I'll fix hit in a minute," she said. "Luster overslep' dis mawnin, up half de night at dat show. I gwine build de fire myself. Go on now, so you won't wake de others twell I ready."

"If you permit Luster to do things that interfere with his work, you'll have to suffer for it yourself," Mrs. Compson said. "Jason won't like this if he hears about it. You know he won't."

"Twusn't none of Jason's money he went on," Dilsey said. "Dat's one thing sho." She went on down the stairs. Mrs. Compson returned to her room. As she got into bed again she could hear Dilsey yet descending the stairs with a sort of painful and terrific slowness that would have become maddening had it not presently ceased beyond the flapping diminishment of the pantry door.

She entered the kitchen and built up the fire and began to prepare breakfast. In the midst of this she ceased and went to the window and looked out toward her cabin, then she went to the door and opened it and shouted into the driving weather.

"Luster!" she shouted, standing to listen, tilting her face from the wind. "You, Luster?" She listened, then as she prepared to shout again Luster appeared around the corner of the kitchen.

"Ma'am?" he said innocently, so innocently that Dilsey looked down at him, for a moment motionless, with something more than mere surprise.

"Whar you at?" she said.

"Nowhere," he said. "Jes in de cellar."

"Whut you doin' in de cellar?" she said. "Don't stand dar in de rain, fool," she said.

"Ain't doin' nothing'," he said. He came up the steps.

"Don't you dare come in dis do' widout a armful of wood," she said. "Here I done had to tote yo wood en build yo fire bofe. Didn't I tole you not to leave dis place last night befo' dat woodbox was full to de top?"

"I did," Luster said. "I filled hit."

"Whar hit gone to, den?"

"I don't know'm. I ain't teched hit."

"Well, you git hit full up now," she said. "And git on up den en see 'bout Benjy."

She shut the door. Luster went to the woodpile. The five jaybirds whirled over the house, screaming, and into the mulberries again. He watched them. He picked up a rock and threw it. "Whoo," he said, "git on back to hell, whar you belong at. 'Tain't Monday yit."

He loaded himself mountainously with stove wood. He could not see over it, and he staggered to the steps and up them and blundered crashing against the door, shedding billets. Then Dilsey came and opened the door for him and he blundered across the kitchen. "You, Luster!" she shouted, but he had already hurled the wood into the box with a thunderous crash. "Hah!" he said.

"Is you tryin' to wake up de whole house?" Dilsey said. She hit him on the back of his head with the flat of her hand. "Go on up dar and git Benjy dressed, now."

"Yessum," he said. He went toward the outer door.

"Whar you gwine?" Dilsey said.

"I thought I better go round de house en in by de front, so I won't wake up Miss Cahline en dem."

"You go on up dem back stairs like I tole you en git Benjy's clothes on him," Dilsey said. "Go on, now."

"Yessum," Luster said. He returned and left by the

dining-room door. After a while it ceased to flap. Dilsey prepared to make biscuit. As she ground the sifter steadily above the breadboard, she sang, to herself at first, something without particular tune or words, repetitive, mournful and plaintive, austere, as she ground a faint, steady snowing of flour onto the breadboard. The stove had begun to heat the room and to fill it with murmurous minors of the fire, and presently she was singing louder, as if her voice too had been thawed out by the growing warmth, and then Mrs. Compson called her name again from within the house. Dilsey raised her face as if her eyes could and did penetrate the walls and ceiling and saw the old woman in her quilted dressing gown at the head of the stairs, calling her name with machine-like regularity.

"Oh, Lawd," Dilsey said. She set the sifter down and swept up the hem of her apron and wiped her hands and caught up the bottle from the chair on which she had laid it and gathered her apron about the handle of the kettle which was now jetting faintly. "Jes a minute," she called. "De water jes dis minute got hot."

It was not the bottle which Mrs. Compson wanted, however, and clutching it by the neck like a dead hen Dilsey went to the foot of the stairs and looked upward.

"Ain't Luster up dar wid him?" she said.

"Luster hasn't been in the house. I've been lying here listening for him. I knew he would be late, but I did hope he'd come in time to keep Benjamin from disturbing Jason on Jason's one day in the week to sleep in the morning."

"I don't see how you expect anybody to sleep, wid you standin' in de hall, holl'in at folks fum de crack of dawn," Dilsey said. She began to mount the stairs, toiling heavily. "I sont dat boy up dar half hour ago."

Mrs. Compson watched her, holding the dressing gown under her chin. "What are you going to do?" she said.

"Gwine git Benjy dressed en bring him down to de kitchen, whar he won't wake Jason en Quentin," Dilsey said.

"Haven't you started breakfast yet?"

"I'll tend to dat too," Dilsey said. "You better git back in bed twell Luster make yo fire. Hit cold dis mawnin."

"I know it," Mrs. Compson said. "My feet are like ice. They were so cold they waked me up." She watched Dilsey mount the stairs. It took her a long while. "You know how it frets Jason when breakfast is late," Mrs. Compson said.

"I can't do but one thing at a time," Dilsey said. "You git on back to bed, fo I has you on my hands dis mawnin too."

"If you're going to drop everything to dress Benjamin, I'd better come down and get breakfast. You know as well as I do how Jason acts when it's late."

"En who gwine eat yo messin'?" Dilsey said. "Tell me dat. Go on now," she said, toiling upward. Mrs. Compson stood watching her as she mounted, steadying herself against the wall with one hand, holding her skirts up with the other.

"Are you going to wake him up just to dress him?" she said.

Dilsey stopped. With her foot lifted to the next step she stood there, her hand against the wall and the gray splash of the window behind her, motionless and shapeless she looked.

"He ain't awake den?" she said.

"He wasn't when I looked in," Mrs. Compson said.

"But it's past his time. He never does sleep after half past seven. You know he doesn't."

Dilsey said nothing. She made no further move, but though she could not see her save as a blobby shape without depth, Mrs. Compson knew that she had lowered her face a little and that she stood now like a cow in the rain, as she held the empty water bottle by its neck.

"You're not the one who has to bear it," Mrs. Compson said. "It's not your responsibility. You can go away. You don't have to bear the brunt of it day in and day out. You owe nothing to them, to Mr. Compson's memory. I know you have never had any tenderness for Jason. You've never tried to conceal it."

Dilsey said nothing. She turned slowly and descended, lowering her body from step to step, as a small child does, her hand against the wall. "You go on and let him alone," she said. "Don't go in dar no mo', now. I'll send Luster up soon as I find him. Let him alone, now."

She returned to the kitchen. She looked into the stove, then she drew her apron over her head and donned the overcoat and opened the outer door and looked up and down the yard. The weather drove upon her flesh, harsh and minute, but the scene was empty of all else that moved. She descended the steps, gingerly, as if for silence, and went around the corner of the kitchen. As she did so Luster emerged quickly and innocently from the cellar door.

Dilsey stopped. "What you up to?" she said.

"Nothin'," Luster said. "Mr. Jason say fer me to find out whar dat water leak in de cellar fum."

"En when wus hit he say fer you to do dat?" Dilsey said. "Last New Year's day, wasn't hit?"

"I thought I jes be lookin whiles dey sleep," Luster said. Dilsey went to the cellar door. He stood aside and she peered down into the obscurity odorous of dank earth and mold and rubber.

"Huh," Dilsey said. She looked at Luster again. He met her gaze blandly, innocent and open. "I don't know what you up to, but you ain't got no business doin' hit. You jes trying me too dis mawnin cause de others is, ain't you? You git on up dar en see to Benjy, you hear?"

"Yessum," Luster said. He went on toward the kitchen steps, swiftly.

"Here," Dilsey said, "you git me another armful of wood while I got you."

"Yessum," he said. He passed her on the steps and went to the woodpile. When he blundered again at the door a moment later, again invisible and blind within and beyond his wooden avatar, Dilsey opened the door and guided him across the kitchen with a firm hand.

"Jes thow hit at dat box again," she said, "Jes thow hit."

"I got to," Luster said, panting, "I can't put hit down no other way."

"Den you stand dar en hold hit a while," Dilsey said. She unloaded him a stick at a time. "Whut got into you dis mawnin? Here I sont you fer wood en you ain't never brought mo'n six sticks at a time to save yo life twell today. Whut you fixin to ax me kin you do now? Ain't dat show left town yit?"

"Yessum. Hit done gone."

She put the last stick into the box. "Now you go on up dar wid Benjy, like I tole you befo," she said. "And I don't want nobody else yellin' down dem stairs at me twell I rings de bell. You hear me."

"Yessum," Luster said. He vanished through the

swing door. Dilsey put some more wood in the stove and returned to the breadboard. Presently she began to sing again.

The room grew warmer. Soon Dilsey's skin had taken on a rich, lustrous quality as compared with that as of a faint dusting of wood ashes which both it and Luster's had worn, as she moved about the kitchen, gathering about her the raw materials of food, coördinating the meal. On the wall above a cupboard, invisible save at night, by lamplight and even then evincing an enigmatic profundity because it had but one hand, a cabinet clock ticked, then with a preliminary sound as if it had cleared its throat, struck five times.

"Eight o'clock," Dilsey said. She ceased and tilted her head upward, listening. But there was no sound save the clock and the fire. She opened the oven and looked at the pan of bread, then stooping she paused while someone descended the stairs. She heard the feet cross the dining-room, then the swing door opened and Luster entered, followed by a big man who appeared to have been shaped of some substance whose particles would not or did not cohere to one another or to the frame which supported it. His skin was dead looking and hairless; dropsical too, he moved with a shambling gait like a trained bear. His hair was pale and fine. It had been brushed smoothly down upon his brow like that of children in daguerreotypes. His eyes were clear, of the pale sweet blue of cornflowers, his thick mouth hung open, drooling a little.

"Is he cold?" Dilsey said. She wiped her hands on her apron and touched his hand.

"Ef he ain't, I is," Luster said. "Always cold Easter. Ain't never seen hit fail. Miss Cahline say ef you ain't got time to fix her hot water bottle to never mind about hit."

"Oh, Lawd," Dilsey said. She drew a chair into the corner between the woodbox and the stove. The man went obediently and sat in it. "Look in de dinin' room and see whar I laid dat bottle down," Dilsey said. Luster fetched the bottle from the dining-room and Dilsey filled it and gave it to him. "Hurry up, now," she said. "See ef Jason 'wake now. Tell em hit's all ready."

Luster went out. Ben sat beside the stove. He sat loosely, utterly motionless save for his head, which made a continual bobbing sort of movement as he watched Dilsey with his sweet vague gaze as she moved about. Luster returned.

"He up," he said, "Miss Cahline say put hit on de table." He came to the stove and spread his hands palm down above the firebox. "He up, too," he said. "Gwine hit wid bofe feet dis mawnin."

"Whut's de matter now?" Dilsey said. "Git away fum dar. How kin I do anything wid you standing over de stove?"

"I cold," Luster said.

"You ought to thought about dat whiles you wus down dar in dat cellar," Dilsey said. "Whut de matter wid Jason?"

"Sayin' me en Benjy broke dat winder in his room."

"Is dey one broke?" Dilsey said.

"Dat's whut he sayin'," Luster said. "Say I broke hit."

"How could you, when he keep hit locked all day en night?"

"Say I broke hit chunkin' rocks at hit," Luster said.

"En did you?"

"Nome," Luster said.

"Don't lie to me, boy," Dilsey said.

"I never done hit," Luster said. "Ask Benjy ef I did. I ain't stud'in' dat winder."

"Who could a broke hit, den?" Dilsey said. "He jes tryin hisself, to wake Quentin up," she said, taking the pan of biscuits out of the stove.

"Reckin so," Luster said. "Dese is funny folks. Glad I ain't none of em."

"Ain't none of who?" Dilsey said. "Lemme tell you somethin', nigger boy, you got jes es much Compson devilment in you es any of em. Is you right sho you never broke dat window?"

"Whut I want to break hit fur?"

"Whut you do any of yo devilment fur?" Dilsey said. "Watch him now, so he can't burn his hand again twell I git de table set."

She went to the dining-room, where they heard her moving about, then she returned and set a plate at the kitchen table and set food there. Ben watched her, slobbering, making a faint, eager sound.

"All right, honey," she said. "Here yo breakfast. Bring his chair, Luster." Luster moved the chair up and Ben sat down, whimpering and slobbering. Dilsey tied a cloth about his neck and wiped his mouth with the end of it. "And see kin you kep fum messin' up his clothes one time," she said, handing Luster a spoon.

Ben ceased whimpering. He watched the spoon as it rose to his mouth. It was as if even eagerness were muscle-bound in him too, and hunger itself inarticulate, not knowing it is hunger. Luster fed him with skill and detachment. Now and then his attention would return long enough to enable him to feint the spoon and cause Ben to close his mouth upon the empty air, but it was apparent that Luster's mind was elsewhere. His other hand lay on the back of the chair and upon that dead surface it moved tentatively, delicately, as if he were picking an inaudible tune out of the dead void, and once he even forgot to tease Ben with the spoon while his fingers teased out of the slain wood a soundless and involved arpeggio until Ben recalled him by whimpering again.

In the dining-room Dilsey moved back and forth. Presently she rang a small clear bell, then in the kitchen Luster heard Mrs. Compson and Jason descending, and Jason's voice, and he rolled his eyes whitely with listening.

"Sure, I know they didn't break it," Jason said. "Sure, I know that. Maybe the change of weather broke it."

"I don't see how it could have," Mrs. Compson said. "Your room stays locked all day long, just as you leave it when you go to town. None of us ever go in there except Sunday, to clean it. I don't want you to think that I would go where I'm not wanted, or that I would permit anyone else to."

"I never said you broke it, did I?" Jason said.

"I don't want to go in your room," Mrs. Compson said. "I respect anybody's private affairs. I wouldn't put my foot over the threshold, even if I had a key."

"Yes," Jason said, "I know your keys won't fit. That's why I had the lock changed. What I want to know is, how that window got broken."

"Luster say he didn't do hit," Dilsey said.

"I knew that without asking him," Jason said. "Where's Quentin?" he said.

"Where she is ev'y Sunday mawnin," Dilsey said. "Whut got into you de last few days, anyhow?"

"Well, we're going to change all that," Jason said. "Go up and tell her breakfast is ready."

"You leave her alone now, Jason," Dilsey said. "She gits up fer breakfast ev'y week mawnin, en Cahline lets her stay in bed ev'y Sunday. You knows dat."

"I can't keep a kitchen full of niggers to wait on

her pleasure, much as I'd like to," Jason said. "Go and tell her to come down to breakfast."

"Ain't nobody have to wait on her," Dilsey said. "I puts her breakfast in de warmer en she—"

"Did you hear me?" Jason said.

"I hears you," Dilsey said. "All I been hearin', when you in de house. Ef hit ain't Quentin er yo maw, hit's Luster en Benjy. Whut you let him go on dat way fer, Miss Cahline?"

"You'd better do as he says," Mrs. Compson said. "He's head of the house now. It's his right to require us to respect his wishes. I try to do it, and if I can, you can too."

" 'Tain't no sense in him bein' so bad tempered he got to make Quentin git up jes to suit him," Dilsey said. "Maybe you think she broke dat window."

"She would, if she happened to think of it," Jason said. "You go and do what I told you."

"En I wouldn't blame her none ef she did," Dilsey said, going toward the stairs. "Wid you naggin' at her all de blessed time you in de house."

"Hush, Dilsey," Mrs. Compson said. "It's neither your place nor mine to tell Jason what to do. Sometimes I think he is wrong, but I try to obey his wishes for you all's sakes. If I'm strong enough to come to the table, Quentin can too."

Dilsey went out. They heard her mounting the stairs. They heard her a long while on the stairs.

"You've got a prize set of servants," Jason said. He helped his mother and himself to food. "Did you ever have one that was worth killing? You must have had some before I was big enough to remember."

"I have to humor them," Mrs. Compson said. "I have to depend on them so completely. It's not as if I were strong. I wish I were. I wish I could do all the house-work myself. I could at least take that much off your shoulders."

"And a fine pigsty we'd live in, too," Jason said. "Hurry up, Dilsey," he shouted.

"I know you blame me," Mrs. Compson said, "for letting them off to go to church today."

"Go where?" Jason said. "Hasn't that damn show left yet?"

"To church," Mrs. Compson said. "The darkies are having a special Easter service. I promised Dilsey two weeks ago that they could get off."

"Which means we'll eat cold dinner," Jason said, "or none at all."

"I know it's my fault," Mrs. Compson said. "I know you blame me."

"For what?" Jason said. "You never resurrected Christ, did you?"

They heard Dilsey mount the final stair, then her slow feet overhead.

"Quentin," she said. When she called the first time Jason laid his knife and fork down and he and his mother appeared to wait across the table from one another, in identical attitudes; the one cold and shrewd, with close-thatched brown hair curled into two stub-born hooks, one on either side of his forehead like a bartender in caricature, and hazel eyes with black-ringed irises like marbles, the other cold and querulous, with perfectly white hair and eyes pouched and baffled and so dark as to appear to be all pupil or all iris.

"Quentin," Dilsey said, "get up, honey. Dey waitin' breakfast on you."

"I can't understand how that window got broken," Mrs. Compson said. "Are you sure it was done yester-day? It could have been like that a long time, with the warm weather. The upper sash, behind the shade like that."

"I've told you for the last time that it happened yesterday," Jason said. "Don't you reckon I know the room I live in? Do you reckon I could have lived in it a week with a hole in the window you could stick your hand—" his voice ceased, ebbed, left him staring at his mother with eyes that for an instant were quite empty of anything. It was as though his eyes were holding their breath, while his mother looked at him, her face flaccid and querulous, interminable, clairvoyant yet obtuse. As they sat so Dilsey said,

"Quentin. Don't play wid me, honey. Come on to breakfast, honey. Dey waitin' fer you."

"I can't understand it," Mrs. Compson said. "It's just as if somebody had tried to break into the house —" Jason sprang up. His chair crashed over backward. "What—" Mrs. Compson said, staring at him as he ran past her and went jumping up the stairs, where he met Dilsey. His face was now in shadow, and Dilsey said,

"She sullin. Yo ma ain't unlocked—" But Jason ran on past her and along the corridor to a door. He didn't call. He grasped the knob and tried it, then he stood with the knob in his hand and his head bent a little, as if he were listening to something much further away than the dimensioned room beyond the door, and which he already heard. His attitude was that of one who goes through the motions of listening in order to deceive himself as to what he already hears. Behind him Mrs. Compson mounted the stairs, calling his name. Then she saw Dilsey and she quit calling him and began to call Dilsey instead.

"I told you she ain't unlocked dat do' yit," Dilsey said. When she spoke he turned and ran toward her, but his voice was quiet, matter of fact. "She carry the key with her?" he said. "Has she got it now, I mean, or will she have—"

"Dilsey," Mrs. Compson said on the stairs.

"Is which?" Dilsey said. "Whyn't you let—"

"The key," Jason said, "to that room. Does she carry it with her all the time. Mother." Then he saw Mrs. Compson and he went down the stairs and met her. "Give me the key," he said. He fell to pawing at the pockets of the rusty black dressing sacque she wore. She resisted.

"Jason," she said, "Jason! Are you and Dilsey trying to put me to bed again?" she said, trying to fend him off. "Can't you even let me have Sunday in peace?"

"The key," Jason said, pawing at her. "Give it here." He looked back at the door, as if he expected it to fly open before he could get back to it with the key he did not yet have.

"You, Dilsey!" Mrs. Compson said, clutching her sacque about her.

"Give me the key, you old fool!" Jason cried suddenly. From her pocket he tugged a huge bunch of rusted keys on an iron ring like a medieval jailer's and ran back up the hall with the two women behind him.

"You, Jason!" Mrs. Compson said. "He will never find the right one," she said. "You know I never let anyone take my keys, Dilsey," she said. She began to wail.

"Hush," Dilsey said. "He ain't gwine do nothin' to her. I ain't gwine let him."

"But on Sunday morning, in my own house," Mrs. Compson said. "When I've tried so hard to raise them Christians. Let me find the right key, Jason," she said. She put her hand on his arm. Then she began to struggle with him, but he flung her aside with a motion of his elbow and looked around at her for a moment, his eyes cold and harried, then he turned to the door again and the unwieldy keys.

"Hush," Dilsey said. "You, Jason!"

"Something terrible has happened," Mrs. Compson said, wailing again. "I know it has. You, Jason," she said, grasping at him again. "He won't even let me find the key to a room in my own house!"

"Now, now," Dilsey said, "whut kin happen? I right here. I ain't gwine let him hurt her. Quentin," she said, raising her voice, "don't you be skeered, honey, I'se right here."

The door opened, swung inward. He stood in it for a moment, hiding the room, then he stepped aside. "Go in," he said in a thick, light voice. They went in. It was not a girl's room. It was not anybody's room, and the faint scent of cheap cosmetics and the few feminine objects and the other evidences of crude and hopeless efforts to feminize it but added to its anonymity, giving it that dead and stereotyped transience of rooms in assignation houses. The bed had not been disturbed. On the floor lay a soiled undergarment of cheap silk a little too pink; from a half-open bureau drawer dangled a single stocking.

The window was open. A pear tree grew there, close against the house. It was in bloom and the branches scraped and rasped against the house and the myriad air, driving in the window, brought into the room the forlorn scent of the blossoms.

"Dar now," Dilsey said, "didn't I told you she all right?"

"All right?" Mrs. Compson said. Dilsey followed her into the room and touched her.

"You come on and lay down, now," she said. "I find her in ten minutes."

Mrs. Compson shook her off. "Find the note," she said. "Quentin left a note when he did it."

"All right," Dilsey said, "I'll find hit. You come on to yo room, now."

"I knew the minute they named her Quentin this would happen," Mrs. Compson said. She went to the bureau and began to turn over the scattered objects there—scent bottles, a box of powder, a chewed pencil, a pair of scissors with one broken blade lying upon a darned scarf dusted with powder and stained with rouge. "Find the note," she said.

"I is," Dilsey said. "You come on, now. Me and Jason'll find hit. You come on to yo' room."

"Jason," Mrs. Compson said, "where is he?" She went to the door. Dilsey followed her on down the hall, to another door. It was closed. "Jason," she called through the door. There was no answer. She tried the knob, then she called him again. But there was still no answer, for he was hurling things backward out of the closet: garments, shoes, a suitcase. Then he emerged carrying a sawn section of tongue-and-groove planking and laid it down and entered the closet again and emerged with a metal box. He set it on the bed and stood looking at the broken lock while he dug a key ring from his pocket and selected a key, and for a time longer he stood with the selected key, in his hand, looking at the broken lock, then he put the keys back in his pocket and carefully tilted the contents of the box out upon the bed. Still carefully he sorted the papers, taking them up one at a time and shaking them. Then he upended the box and shook it too and slowly replaced the papers and stood again, looking at the broken lock, with the box in his hands and his head bent. Outside the window he heard some jaybirds swirl shrieking past, and away, their cries whipping away along the wind, and an automobile passed somewhere and died away also. His mother spoke his name again beyond the door, but he didn't move. He heard Dilsey lead her away up the hall, and then a door closed. Then he replaced the box in the closet and flung the garments back into it and went downstairs to the telephone. While he stood there with the receiver to his ear, waiting, Dilsey came down the stairs. She looked at him, without stopping, and went on.

The wire opened. "This is Jason Compson," he said, his voice so harsh and thick that he had to repeat himself. "Jason Compson," he said, controlling his voice. "Have a car ready, with a deputy, if you can't go, in ten minutes. I'll be there— What?—Robbery. My house. I know who it— Robbery, I say. Have a car read— What? Aren't you a paid law enforcement— Yes, I'll be there in five minutes. Have that car ready to leave at once. If you don't, I'll report it to the governor."

He clapped the receiver back and crossed the dining-room, where the scarce-broken meal now lay cold on the table, and entered the kitchen. Dilsey was filling the hot water bottle. Ben sat, tranquil and empty. Beside him Luster looked like a fyce dog, brightly watchful. He was eating something. Jason went on across the kitchen.

"Ain't you going to eat no breakfast?" Dilsey said. He paid her no attention. "Go on and eat yo breakfast, Jason." He went on. The outer door banged behind him. Luster rose and went to the window and looked out.

"Whoo," he said, "whut happenin' up dar? He been beatin' Miss Quentin?"

"You hush yo mouf," Dilsey said. "You git Benjy started now en I beat yo head off. You keep him quiet es you kin twell I get back, now." She screwed the cap on the bottle and went out. They heard her go up the stairs, then they heard Jason pass the house in his car. Then there was no sound in the kitchen save the simmering murmur of the kettle and the clock.

"You know whut I bet?" Luster said. "I bet he beat her. I bet he knock her in de head en now he gone fer de doctor. Dat's whut I bet." The clock ticktocked, solemn and profound. It might have been the dry pulse of the decaying house itself; after a while it whirred and cleared its throat and struck six times. Ben looked up at it, then he looked at the bullet-like silhouette of Luster's head in the window and he began to bob his head again, drooling. He whimpered.

"Hush up, loony," Luster said without turning. "Look like we ain't gwine git to go to no church today." But Ben sat in the chair, his big soft hands dangling between his knees, moaning faintly. Suddenly he wept, a slow bellowing sound, meaningless and sustained. "Hush," Luster said. He turned and lifted his hand. "You want me to whup you?" But Ben looked at him, bellowing slowly with each expiration. Luster came and shook him. "You hush dis minute!" he shouted. "Here," he said. He hauled Ben out of the chair and dragged the chair around facing the stove and opened the door to the firebox and shoved Ben into the chair. They looked like a tug nudging at a clumsy tanker in a narrow dock. Ben sat down again facing the rosy door. He hushed. Then they heard the clock again, and Dilsey slow on the stairs. When she entered he began to whimper again. Then he lifted his voice.

"Whut you done to him?" Dilsey said. "Why can't you let him 'lone dis mawnin, of all times?"

"I ain't doin' nothin' to him," Luster said. "Mr. Jason skeered him, dat's whut hit is. He ain't kilt Miss Quentin, is he?"

"Hush, Benjy," Dilsey said. He hushed. She went to

the window and looked out. "Is it quit rainin'?" she said.

"Yessum," Luster said. "Quit long time ago."

"Den y'all go out do's awhile," she said. "I jes got Miss Cahline quiet now."

"Is we gwine to church?" Luster said.

"I let you know bout dat when de time come. You keep him away fum de house twell I calls you."

"Kin we go to de pastuh?" Luster said.

"All right. Only you keep him away fum de house. I done stood all I kin."

"Yessum," Luster said. "Whar Mr. Jason gone, mammy?"

"Dat's some mo' of yo' business, ain't it?" Dilsey said. She began to clear the table. "Hush, Benjy. Luster gwine take you out to play."

"Whut he done to Miss Quentin, mammy?" Luster said.

"Ain't done nothin' to her. You all git on outen here?"

"I bet she ain't here," Luster said.

Dilsey looked at him. "How you know she ain't here?"

"Me and Benjy seed her clamb out de window last night. Didn't us, Benjy?"

"You did?" Dilsey said, looking at him.

"We sees her doin' hit ev'y night," Luster said. "Clamb right down dat pear tree."

"Don't you lie to me, nigger boy," Dilsey said.

"I ain't lyin'. Ask Benjy ef I is."

"Whyn't you say somethin' about it, den?"

"'Twarn't none o' my business," Luster said. "I ain't gwine git mixed up in white folks' business. Come on here, Benjy, les go out do's."

They went out. Dilsey stood for a while at the table, then she went and cleared the breakfast things from the dining-room and ate her breakfast and cleaned up the kitchen. Then she removed her apron and hung it up and went to the foot of the stairs and listened for a moment. There was no sound. She donned the overcoat and the hat and went across to her cabin.

The rain had stopped. The air now drove out of the southeast, broken overhead into blue patches. Upon the crest of a hill beyond the trees and roofs and spires of town sunlight lay like a pale scrap of cloth, was blotted away. Upon the air a bell came, then as if at a signal, other bells took up the sound and repeated it.

The cabin door opened and Dilsey emerged, again in the maroon cape and the purple gown, and wearing soiled white elbow-length gloves and minus her headcloth now. She came into the yard and called Luster. She waited a while, then she went to the house and around it to the cellar door, moving close to the wall, and looked into the door. Ben sat on the steps. Before him Luster squatted on the damp floor. He held a saw in his left hand, the blade sprung a little by pressure of his hand, and he was in the act of striking the blade with the worn wooden mallet with which she had been making beaten biscuit for more than thirty years. The saw gave forth a single sluggish twang that ceased with lifeless alacrity, leaving the blade in a thin clean curve between Luster's hand and the floor. Still, inscrutable, it bellied.

"Dat's de way he done hit," Luster said. "I jes ain't foun' de right thing to hit it wid."

"Dat's whut you doin', is it?" Dilsey said. "Bring me dat mallet," she said.

"I ain't hurt hit," Luster said.

"Bring hit here," Dilsey said. "Put dat saw whar you got hit first."

He put the saw away and brought the mallet to her. Then Ben wailed again, hopeless and prolonged. It was nothing. Just sound. It might have been all time and injustice and sorrow become vocal for an instant by a conjunction of planets.

"Listen at him," Luster said. "He been gwine on dat way ev'y since you sont us outen de house. I don't know whut got into him dis mawnin."

"Bring him here," Dilsey said.

"Come on, Benjy," Luster said. He went back down the steps and took Ben's arm. He came obediently, wailing, that slow hoarse sound that ships make, that seems to begin before the sound itself has started, seems to cease before the sound itself has stopped.

"Run and git his cap," Dilsey said. "Don't make no noise Miss Cahline kin hear. Hurry, now. We already late."

"She gwine hear him anyhow, ef you don't stop him," Luster said.

"He stop when we git off de place," Dilsey said. "He smellin' hit. Dat's whut hit is."

"Smell whut, mammy?" Luster said.

"You go git dat cap," Dilsey said. Luster went on. They stood in the cellar door, Ben one step below her. The sky was broken now into scudding patches that dragged their swift shadows up out of the shabby garden, over the broken fence and across the yard. Dilsey stroked Ben's head, slowly and steadily, smoothing the bang upon his brow. He wailed quietly, unhurriedly. "Hush," Dilsey said. "Hush, now. We be gone in a minute. Hush, now." He wailed quietly and steadily.

Luster returned, wearing a stiff new straw hat with a colored band and carrying a cloth cap. The hat seemed to isolate Luster's skull, in the beholder's eye as a spotlight would, in all its individual planes and angles. So peculiarly individual was its shape that at first glance the hat appeared to be on the head of someone standing immediately behind Luster. Dilsey looked at the hat.

"Whyn't you wear yo' old hat?" she said.

"Couldn't find hit," Luster said.

"I bet you couldn't. I bet you fixed hit last night so you couldn't find hit. You fixin' to ruin dat un."

"Aw, mammy," Luster said, "hit ain't gwine rain."

"How you know? You go git dat old hat en put dat new un away."

"Aw, mammy."

"Den you go git de umbreller."

"Aw, mammy."

"Take yo choice," Dilsey said. "Git yo old hat, er de umbreller. I don't keer which."

Luster went to the cabin. Ben wailed quietly.

"Come on," Dilsey said, "dey kin ketch up wid us. We gwine to hear de singin'." They went around the house, toward the gate. "Hush," Dilsey said from time to time as they went down the drive. They reached the gate. Dilsey opened it. Luster was coming down the drive behind them, carrying the umbrella. A woman was with him. "Here dey come," Dilsey said. They passed out the gate. "Now, den," she said. Ben ceased. Luster and his mother overtook them. Frony wore a dress of bright blue silk and a flowered hat. She was a thin woman, with a flat, pleasant face.

"You got six weeks' work right dar on yo back," Dilsey said. "Whut you gwine do ef hit rain?"

"Git wet, I reckon," Frony said. "I ain't never stopped no rain yit."

"Mammy always talkin' bout hit gwine rain," Luster said.

"Ef I don't worry bout y'all, I don't know who is," Dilsey said. "Come on, we already late."

"Rev'un Shegog gwine preach today," Frony said.

"Is?" Dilsey said. "Who him?"

"He fum Saint Looey," Frony said. "Dat big preacher."

"Huh," Dilsey said. "Whut dey needs is a man kin put de fear of God into dese here triflin' young niggers."

"Rev'un Shegog gwine preach today," Frony said. "So dey tells."

They went on along the street. Along its quiet length white people in bright clumps moved churchward, under the windy bells, walking now and then in the random and tentative sun. The wind was gusty, out of the southeast, chill and raw after the warm days.

"I wish you wouldn't keep on bringin' him to church, mammy," Frony said. "Folks talkin."

"Whut folks?" Dilsey said.

"I hears em," Frony said.

"And I knows whut kind of folks," Dilsey said. "Trash white folks. Dat's who it is. Thinks he ain't good enough fer white church, but nigger church ain't good enough fer him."

"Dey talks, jes de same," Frony said.

"Den you send um to me," Dilsey said. "Tell um de good Lawd don't keer whether he smart er not. Don't nobody but white trash keer dat."

A street turned off at right angles, descending, and became a dirt road. On either hand the land dropped more sharply; a broad flat dotted with small cabins whose weathered roofs were on a level with the crown of the road. They were set in small grassless plots littered with broken things, bricks, planks, crockery, things of a once utilitarian value. What growth there was consisted of rank weeds and the trees were mulberries and locusts and sycamores—trees that partook also of the foul desiccation which surrounded the houses; trees whose very burgeoning seemed to be the sad and stubborn remnant of September, as if even spring had passed them by, leaving them to feed upon the rich and unmistakable smell of Negroes in which they grew.

From the doors Negroes spoke to them as they passed, to Dilsey usually:

"Sis' Gibson! How you dis mawnin?"

"I'm well. Is you well?"

"I'm right well, I thank you."

They emerged from the cabins and struggled up the shading levee to the road—men in staid, hard brown or black, with gold watch chains and now and then a stick; young men in cheap, violent blues or stripes and swaggering hats; women a little stiffly sibilant, and children in garments bought second hand of white people, who looked at Ben with the covertness of nocturnal animals:

"I bet you won't go up en tech him."

"How come I won't?"

"I bet you won't. I bet you skeered to."

"He won't hurt folks. He des a loony."

"How come a loony won't hurt folks?"

"Dat un won't. I teched him."

"I bet you won't now."

"Case Miss Dilsey lookin'."

"You won't no ways."

"He don't hurt folks. He des a loony."

And steadily the older people speaking to Dilsey, though, unless they were quite old, Dilsey permitted Frony to respond.

"Mammy ain't feelin' well dis mawnin."

"Dat's too bad. But Rev'un Shegog'll cure dat. He'll give her de comfort en de unburdenin'."

The road rose again, to a scene like a painted backdrop. Notched into a cut of red clay crowned with oaks the road appeared to stop short off, like a cut ribbon. Beside it a weathered church lifted its crazy steeple like a painted church, and the whole scene was as flat and without perspective as a painted cardboard set upon the ultimate edge of the flat earth, against the windy sunlight of space and April and a midmorning filled with bells. Toward the church they thronged with slow sabbath deliberation. The women and children went on in, the men stopped outside and talked in quiet groups until the bell ceased ringing. Then they too entered.

The church had been decorated, with sparse flowers from kitchen gardens and hedgerows, and with streamers of colored crepe paper. Above the pulpit hung a battered Christmas bell, the accordion sort that collapses. The pulpit was empty, though the choir was already in place, fanning themselves although it was not warm.

Most of the women were gathered on one side of the room. They were talking. Then the bell struck one time and they dispersed to their seats and the congregation sat for an instant, expectant. The bell struck again one time. The choir rose and began to sing and the congregation turned its head as one, as six small children—four girls with tight pigtails bound with small scraps of cloth like butterflies, and two boys with close-napped heads—entered and marched up the aisle, strung together in a harness of white ribbons and flowers, and followed by two men in single file. The second man was huge, of a light coffee color, imposing in a frock coat and white tie. His head was magisterial and profound, his neck rolled above his collar in rich folds. But he was familiar to them, and so the heads were still reverted when he had passed, and it was not until the choir ceased singing that they realized that the visiting clergy-man had already entered, and when they saw the man who had preceded their minister enter the pulpit still ahead of him an indescribable sound went up, a sigh, a sound of astonishment and disappointment.

The visitor was undersized, in a shabby alpaca coat. He had a wizened, black face like a small, aged monkey. And all the while that the choir sang again and while the six children rose and sang in thin, frightened, tune-less whispers, they watched the insignificant-looking man sitting dwarfed and countrified by the minister's imposing bulk, with something like consternation. They were still looking at him with consternation and unbe-lief when the minister rose and introduced him in rich, rolling tones whose very unction served to increase the visitor's insignificance.

"En dey brung dat all de way fum Saint Looey," Frony whispered.

"I've knowed de Lawd to use cuiser tools dan dat," Dilsey said. "Hush, now," she said to Ben. "Dey fixin' to sing again in a minute."

When the visitor rose to speak he sounded like a white man. His voice was level and cold. It sounded too big to have come from him and they listened at first through curiosity, as they would have to a monkey talking. They began to watch him as they would a man on a tightrope. They even forgot his insignificant ap-pearance in the virtuosity with which he ran and poised and swooped upon the cold inflectionless wire of his voice, so that at last, when with a sort of swooping glide he came to rest again beside the reading desk with one arm resting upon it at shoulder height and his monkey body as reft of all motion as a mummy or an emptied vessel, the congregation sighed as if it waked from a collective dream and moved a little in its seats.

Behind the pulpit the choir fanned steadily. Dilsey whispered, "Hush, now. Dey fixin' to sing in a minute."

Then a voice said, "Brethren."

The preacher had not moved. His arm lay yet across the desk, and he still held that pose while the voice died in sonorous echoes between the walls. It was as different as day and dark from his former tone, with a sad, timbrous quality like an alto horn, sinking into their hearts and speaking there again when it had ceased in fading and cumulate echoes.

"Brethren and sisteren," it said again. The preacher removed his arm and he began to walk back and forth before the desk, his hands clasped behind him, a meagre figure, hunched over upon itself like that of one long immured in striving with the implacable earth, "I got the recollection and the blood of the Lamb!" He tramped steadily back and forth beneath the twisted paper and the Christmas bell, hunched, his hands clasped behind him. He was like a worn, small rock whelmed by the successive waves of his voice. With his body he seemed to feed the voice that, succubus like, had fleshed its teeth in him. And the congregation seemed to watch with its own eyes while the voice consumed him, until he was nothing and they were nothing and there was not even a voice, but instead their hearts were speaking to one another in chanting measures beyond the need for words, so that when he came to rest against the reading desk, his monkey face lifted and his whole attitude that of a serene, tortured crucifix that transcended its shabbiness and insignificance and made it of no moment, a long, moaning expulsion of breath rose from them, and a woman's single soprano: "Yes, Jesus!"

As the scudding day passed overhead the dingy windows glowed and faded in ghostly retrograde. A car passed along the road outside, laboring in the sand, died away. Dilsey sat bolt upright, her hand on Ben's knee. Two tears slid down her fallen cheeks, in and out of the myriad coruscations of immolation and abnegation and time.

"Brethren," the minister said in a harsh whisper, without moving.

"Yes, Jesus!" the woman's voice said, hushed yet.

"Breddren en sistuhn!" His voice rang again, with the horns. He removed his arm and stood erect and raised his hands. "I got de ricklickshun en de blood of de Lamb!" They did not mark just when his intonation, his pronunciation, became Negroid, they just sat swaying a little in their seats as the voice took them into itself.

"When de long, cold— Oh, I tells you, breddren, when de long, cold—I sees de light en I sees de word, po' sinner! Dey passed away in Egypt, de swingin' chariots; de generations passed away. Wus a rich man: whar he now, O breddren? Wus a po' man: whar he now, O sistuhn? Oh I tells you, ef you ain't got de milk en de dew of de old salvation when de long, cold years rolls away!"

"Yes, Jesus!"

"I tells you, breddren, en I tells you, sistuhn, dey'll come a time. Po' sinner saying Let me lay down wid de Lawd, lemme lay down my load. Den whut Jesus gwine say, O breddren? O sistuhn? Is you got de ricklickshun en de blood of de Lamb? Case I ain't gwine load down heaven!"

He fumbled in his coat and took out a handkerchief and mopped his face. A low, concerted sound rose from the congregation: Mmmmmmmmmmmmmm! The woman's voice said, "Yes, Jesus! Jesus!"

"Breddren! Look at dem little chillen settin dar.

Jesus wus like dat once. He mammy suffered de glory en de pangs. Sometime maybe she helt him at de night-fall, whilst de angels singin' him to sleep; maybe she look out de do' en see de Roman po-lice passin'." He tramped back and forth, mopping his face. "Listen breddren! I sees de day. Ma'y settin in de do' wid Jesus on her lap, de little Jesus. Like dem chillen dar, de little Jesus. I hears de angels singin' de peaceful songs en de glory; I sees de closin' eyes; sees Mary jump up, sees de sojer face: We gwine to kill! We gwine to kill! We gwine to kill yo little Jesus! I hears de weepin' en de lamentation of de po' mammy widout de salvation en de word of God!"

"Mmmmmmmmmmmmmmmmm! Jesus! Little Jesus!" and another voice, rising:

"I sees, O Jesus! Oh I sees!" and still another, without words, like bubbles rising in water.

"I sees hit, breddren! I sees hit! Sees de blastin', blindin' sight! I sees Calvary, wid de sacred trees, sees de thief en de murderer en de least of dese; I hears de boastin' en de braggin': Ef you be Jesus, lif up yo' tree en walk! I hears de wailin' of women en de evenin' lamentations; I hears de weepin' en de cryin' en de turnt-away face of God: dey done kilt Jesus; dey done kilt my Son!"

"Mmmmmmmmmmmmmmm. Jesus! I sees, O Jesus!"

"O blind sinner! Breddren, I tells you; sistuhn, I says to you, when de Lawd did turn His mighty face, say, Ain't gwine overload heaven! I can see de widowed God shet His do'; I sees de whelmin' flood roll between; I sees de darkness en de death everlastin' upon de generations. Den, lo! Breddren! Yes, breddren! Whut I see? Whut I see, O sinner? I sees de resurrection en de light; sees de meek Jesus sayin' Dey kilt Me dat ye shall live again; I died dat dem whut sees en believes shall never die. Breddren, O breddren! I sees de doom crack en hears de golden horns shoutin' down de glory, en de arisen dead whut got de blood en de ricklickshun of de Lamb!"

In the midst of the voices and the hands Ben sat, rapt in his sweet blue gaze. Dilsey sat bolt upright beside, crying rigidly and quietly in the annealment and the blood of the remembered Lamb.

As they walked through the bright noon, up the sandy road with the dispersing congregation talking, easily again, group to group, she continued to weep, unmindful of the talk.

"He sho a preacher, mon! He didn't look like much at first, but hush!"

"He seed de power en de glory."

"Yes, suh. He seed hit. Face to face he seed hit."

Dilsey made no sound, her face did not quiver as the tears took their sunken and devious courses, walking with her head up, making no effort to dry them away even.

"Whyn't you quit dat, mammy?" Frony said. "Wid all dese people lookin'. We be passin' white folks soon."

"I've seed de first en de last," Dilsey said. "Never you mind me."

"First en last whut?" Frony said.

"Never you mind," Dilsey said. "I seed de beginnin', en now I sees de endin'."

Before they reached the street, though, she stopped and lifted her skirt and dried her eyes on the hem of her topmost underskirt. Then they went on. Ben shambled along beside Dilsey, watching Luster who anticked along ahead, the umbrella in his hand and his new straw hat slanted viciously in the sunlight, like a big foolish dog watching a small clever one. They reached the gate and entered. Immediately Ben began to whimper again, and for a while all of them looked up the drive at the square, paintless house with its rotting portico.

"Whut's gwine on up dar today?" Frony said. "Somethin' is."

"Nothin'," Dilsey said. "You tend to yo business en let de white folks tend to deir'n."

"Somethin' is," Frony said. "I heard him first thing dis mawnin. 'Taint none of my business, dough."

"En I knows whut, too," Luster said.

"You knows mo dan you got any use fer," Dilsey said. "Ain't you jes heard Frony say hit ain't none of yo business? You take Benjy on to de back and keep him quiet twell I put dinner on."

"I knows whar Miss Quentin is," Luster said.

"Den jes keep hit," Dilsey said. "Soon es Quentin need any of yo' egvice, I'll let you know. Y'all g'awn en play in de back, now."

"You know whut gwine happen soon es dey start playin' dat ball over yonder," Luster said.

"Dey won't start fer a while yit. By dat time T.P. be here to take him ridin'. Here, you gimme dat new hat."

Luster gave her the hat and he and Ben went on across the back yard. Ben was still whimpering, though not loud. Dilsey and Frony went to the cabin. After a while Dilsey emerged, again in the faded calico dress, and went to the kitchen. The fire had died down. There was no sound in the house. She put on the apron and went upstairs. There was no sound anywhere. Quentin's room was as they had left it. She entered and picked up the undergarment and put the stocking back in the drawer and closed it. Mrs. Compson's door was closed. Dilsey stood beside it for a moment, listening. Then she opened it and entered, entered a pervading reek of camphor. The shades were drawn, the room in half-light, and the bed, so that at first she thought Mrs. Compson was asleep and was about to close the door when the other spoke.

"Well?" she said. "What is it?"

"Hit's me," Dilsey said. "You want anything?"

Mrs. Compson didn't answer. After a while, without moving her head at all, she said: "Where's Jason?"

"He ain't come back yit," Dilsey said. "Whut you want?"

Mrs. Compson said nothing. Like so many cold, weak people, when faced at last by the incontrovertible disaster she exhumed from somewhere a sort of fortitude, strength. In her case it was an unshakable conviction regarding the yet unplumbed event. "Well," she said presently, "did you find it?"

"Find whut? Whut you talkin' about?"

"The note. At least she would have enough consideration to leave a note. Even Quentin did that."

"Whut you talkin' about?" Dilsey said. "Don't you know she all right? I bet she be walkin' right in dis do' befo' dark."

"Fiddlesticks," Mrs. Compson said. "It's in the blood. Like uncle, like niece. Or mother. I don't know which would be worse. I don't seem to care."

"Whut you keep on talkin' that way fur?" Dilsey said. "Whut she want to do anything like that fur?"

"I don't know. What reason did Quentin have? Under God's heaven what reason did he have? It can't be simply to flout and hurt me. Whoever God is, He would not permit that. I'm a lady. You might not believe that from my offspring, but I am."

"You des wait en see," Dilsey said. "She be here by night, right dar in her bed." Mrs. Compson said nothing. The camphor-soaked cloth lay upon her brow. The black robe lay across the foot of the bed. Dilsey stood with her hand on the doorknob.

"Well," Mrs. Compson said. "What do you want? Are you going to fix some dinner for Jason and Benjamin, or not?"

"Jason ain't come yit," Dilsey said. "I gwine fix somethin'. You sho you don't want nothin? Yo' bottle still hot enough?"

"You might hand me my Bible."

"I give hit to you dis mawnin, befo' I left."

"You laid it on the edge of the bed. How long did you expect it to stay there?"

Dilsey crossed to the bed and groped among the shadows beneath the edge of it and found the Bible, face down. She smoothed the bent pages and laid the book on the bed again. Mrs. Compson didn't open her eyes. Her hair and the pillow were the same color, beneath the wimple of the medicated cloth she looked like an old nun praying. "Don't put it there again," she said, without opening her eyes. "That's where you put it before. Do you want me to have to get out of bed to pick it up?"

Dilsey reached the book across her and laid it on the broad side of the bed. "You can't see to read, noways," she said. "You want me to raise de shade a little?"

"No. Let them alone. Go on and fix Jason something to eat."

Dilsey went out. She closed the door and returned to the kitchen. The stove was almost cold. While she stood there the clock above the cupboard struck ten times. "One o'clock," she said aloud. "Jason ain't comin' home. Ise seed de first en de last," she said, looking at the cold stove. "I seed de first en de last."

FROM

Sea of Cortez

Written in Collaboration with Edward F. Ricketts

OLD MAN OF THE SEA

HOMING

Episodes from the scientific travelogue of an expedition in the Gulf of California, published in 1941.

6. Mississippi Flood

EDITOR'S NOTE

EARLY in April 1927, the big river overflowed its banks, and the entire population of the state prison farm at Parchman, Mississippi, was set to work on a threatened levee. One tall convict was ordered out in a rowboat to look for a woman in a cypress snag and a man on the ridgepole of a cottonhouse. The water continued to rise. It was the worst flood in the history of the river: for six weeks more than 20,000 square miles were under water, including the whole of the rich Delta, and 600,000 persons were driven from their homes. Several hundreds were drowned, in addition to 25,000 horses, 50,000 cattle, 148,000 hogs, 1300 sheep, and 1,300,000 chickens; 400,000 acres of crops were destroyed and hundreds of miles of levees. A few weeks after the river had returned to its bed, the tall convict rowed back to the state prison farm. "Yonder's your boat," he said, "and here's the woman. But I never did find that bastard on the cottonhouse."

The tall convict was born in the pine hills southeast of Frenchman's Bend, but otherwise "Old Man," the story that follows, stands apart from the Yoknapatawpha County saga. It is, as it were, the connection between Yoknapatawpha County and the rest of the South: our horizons widen as the convict floats down the river. Originally the story formed half of a novel published in 1939. The other half was a completely separate story called "The Wild Palms," which was also the title of the novel as a whole. Faulkner had tried the experiment of writing two unrelated stories of about the same length, cutting each of them into five parts, and printing the parts alternately: one chapter of "The Wild Palms," then a chapter of "Old Man," then another chapter of "The Wild Palms." What he gained was an effect of contrast or counterpoint: in "The Wild Palms," a man sacrificed everything for freedom and love, and lost them both; in "Old Man," the convict sacrificed everything to escape from freedom and love and return to the womanless security of the state prison farm. This second story, however, is much more effective than the first and gains by standing alone, as in the present volume. It isn't as good as *Huckleberry Finn*, by a long distance; but it is the only other story of the Mississippi that can be set beside *Huckleberry Finn* without shriveling under the comparison; it is the only other story in American literature that gives the same impression of the power and legendary sweep of the River.

1927. OLD MAN

I

ONCE (it was in Mississippi, in May, in the flood year 1927) there were two convicts. One of them was about twenty-five, tall, lean, flat-stomached, with a sunburned face and Indian-black hair and pale, china-colored, outraged eyes—an outrage directed not at the men who had foiled his crime, not even at the lawyers and judges who had sent him here, but at the writers, the uncorporeal names attached to the stories, the paper novels—the Diamond Dicks and Jesse Jameses and such—whom he believed had led him into his present predicament through their own ignorance and gullibility regarding the medium in which they dealt and took money for, in accepting information on which they placed the stamp of verisimilitude and authenticity (this so much the more criminal since there was no sworn notarized statement attached and hence so much the quicker would the information be accepted by one who expected the same unspoken good faith, demanding, asking, expecting no certification, which he extended along with the dime or fifteen cents to pay for it) and retailed for money and which, on actual application, proved to be impractical and (to the convict) criminally false; there would be times when he would halt his mule and plow in midfurrow (there is no walled penitentiary in Mississippi; it is a cotton plantation which the convicts work under the rifles and shotguns of guards and trusties) and muse with a kind

541

of enraged impotence, fumbling among the rubbish
left him by his one and only experience with courts and
law, fumbling until the meaningless and verbose shib-
boleth took form at last (himself seeking justice at the
same blind font where he had met justice and been
hurled back and down): Using the mails to defraud:
who felt that he had been defrauded by the third-class
mail system not of crass and stupid money which he did
not particularly want anyway, but of liberty and honor
and pride.

He was in for fifteen years (he had arrived shortly
after his nineteenth birthday) for attempted train robbery. He had laid his plans in advance, he had followed
his printed (and false) authority to the letter; he had
saved the paper-backs for two years, reading and re-
reading them, memorizing them, comparing and weighing story and method against story and method, taking
the good from each and discarding the dross as his work-
able plan emerged, keeping his mind open to make the
subtle last-minute changes, without haste and without
impatience, as the newer pamphlets appeared on their
appointed days, as a conscientious dressmaker makes
the subtle alterations in a court presentation costume as
the newer bulletins appear. And then when the day
came, he did not even have a chance to go through the
coaches and collect the watches and the rings, the
brooches and the hidden money-belts, because he had
been captured as soon as he entered the express car
where the safe and the gold would be. He had shot no
one because the pistol which they took away from him
was not that kind of a pistol although it was loaded;
later he admitted to the District Attorney that he had
got it, as well as the dark lantern in which a candle
burned and the black handkerchief to wear over the
face, by peddling among his pinehill neighbors sub-

scriptions to the *Detectives' Gazette.* So now from time to time (he had ample leisure for it) he mused with that raging impotence, because there was something else he could not tell them at the trial, did not know how to tell them. It was not the money he had wanted. It was not riches, not the crass loot; that would have been merely a bangle to wear upon the breast of his pride like the Olympic runner's amateur medal—a symbol, a badge to show that he too was the best at his chosen gambit in the living and fluid world of his time. So that at times as he trod the richly shearing black earth behind his plow or with a hoe thinned the sprouting cotton and corn or lay on his sullen back in his bunk after supper, he cursed in a harsh steady unrepetitive stream, not at the living men who had put him where he was but at what he did not even know were pen-names, did not even know were not actual men but merely the designations of shades who had written about shades.

The second convict was short and plump. Almost hairless, he was quite white. He looked like something exposed to light by turning over rotting logs or planks and he too carried (though not in his eyes like the first convict) a sense of burning and impotent outrage. So it did not show on him and hence none knew it was there. But then nobody knew very much about him, including the people who had sent him here. His outrage was directed at no printed word but at the paradoxical fact that he had been forced to come here of his own free choice and will. He had been forced to choose between the Mississippi State penal farm and the Federal Penitentiary at Atlanta, and the fact that he, who resembled a hairless and pallid slug, had chosen the out-of-doors and the sunlight was merely another manifestation of the close-guarded and solitary enigma of his character, as something recognizable roils momentarily into view from beneath stagnant and opaque water, then sinks again. None of his fellow prisoners knew what his crime had been, save that he was in for a hundred and ninety-nine years—this incredible and impossible period of punishment or restraint itself carrying a vicious and fabulous quality which indicated that his reason for being here was such that the very men, the paladins and pillars of justice and equity who had sent him here had during that moment become blind apostles not of mere justice but of all human decency, blind instruments not of equity but of all human outrage and vengeance, acting in a savage personal concert, judge, lawyer and jury, which certainly abrogated justice and possibly even law.

Possibly only the Federal and State's Attorneys knew what the crime actually was. There had been a woman in it, and a stolen automobile transported across a State line, a filling station robbed and the attendant shot to death. There had been a second man in the car at the time and anyone could have looked once at the convict (as the two attorneys did) and known he would not even have had the synthetic courage of alcohol to pull trigger on anyone. But he and the woman and the stolen car had been captured while the second man, doubtless the actual murderer, had escaped, so that, brought to bay at last in the State's Attorney's office, harried, dishevelled, and snarling, the two grimly implacable and viciously gleeful attorneys in his front and the now raging woman held by two policemen in the anteroom in his rear, he was given his choice. He could be tried in Federal Court under the Mann Act and for the automobile, that is, by electing to pass through the anteroom where the woman raged he could take his chances on the lesser crime in Federal Court, or by ac-

cepting a sentence for manslaughter in the State Court
he would be permitted to quit the room by a back entrance, without having to pass the woman. He had
chosen; he stood at the bar and heard a judge (who
looked down at him as if the District Attorney actually
had turned over a rotten plank with his toe and exposed
him) sentence him to a hundred and ninety-nine years
at the State Farm. Thus (he had ample leisure too; they
had tried to teach him to plow and had failed, they had
put him in the blacksmith shop and the foreman trusty
himself had asked to have him removed: so that now, in
a long apron like a woman, he cooked and swept and
dusted in the deputy wardens' barracks) he too mused
at times with that sense of impotence and outrage
though it did not show on him as on the first convict
since he leaned on no halted broom to do it and so
none knew it was there.

It was this second convict who, toward the end of
April, began to read aloud to the others from the daily
newspapers when, chained ankle to ankle and herded
by armed guards, they had come up from the fields and
had eaten supper and were gathered in the bunkhouse.
It was the Memphis newspaper which the deputy wardens had read at breakfast; the convict read aloud
from it to his companions who could have had but little
active interest in the outside world, some of whom could
not have read it for themselves at all and did not even
know where the Ohio and Missouri river basins were,
some of whom had never even seen the Mississippi
River, although for past periods ranging from a few
days to ten and twenty and thirty years (and for future
periods ranging from a few months to life) they had
plowed and planted and eaten and slept beneath the
shadow of the levee itself, knowing only that there was
water beyond it from hearsay and because now and

then they heard the whistles of steamboats from beyond it and, during the last week or so had seen the stacks and pilot houses moving along the sky sixty feet above their heads.

But they listened, and soon even those who, like the taller convict, had probably never before seen more water than a horse pond would hold, knew what thirty feet on a river gauge at Cairo or Memphis meant and could (and did) talk glibly of sandboils. Perhaps what actually moved them were the accounts of the conscripted levee gangs, mixed blacks and whites working in double shifts against the steadily rising water; stories of men, even though they were Negroes, being forced like themselves to do work for which they received no other pay than coarse food and a place in a mudfloored tent to sleep on—stories, pictures, which emerged from the shorter convict's reading voice: the mudsplashed white men with the inevitable shot-guns, the antlike lines of Negroes carrying sandbags, slipping and crawling up the steep face of the revetment to hurl their futile ammunition into the face of a flood and return for more. Or perhaps it was more than this. Perhaps they watched the approach of the disaster with that same amazed and incredulous hope of the slaves—the lions and bears and elephants, the grooms and bathmen and pastrycooks—who watched the mounting flames of Rome from Ahenobarbus' gardens. But listen they did and presently it was May and the wardens' newspaper began to talk in headlines two inches tall—those black staccato slashes of ink which, it would almost seem, even the illiterate should be able to read: *Crest Passes Memphis at Midnight 4000 Homeless in White River Basin Governor Calls out National Guard Martial Law Declared in Following Counties Red Cross Train with*

President Hoover Leaves Washington Tonight; then, three evenings later (It had been raining all day—not the vivid brief thunderous downpours of April and May, but the slow steady gray rain of November and December before a cold north wind. The men had not gone to the fields at all during the day, and the very second-hand optimism of the almost twenty-four-hour-old news seemed to contain its own refutation.): *Crest Now Below Memphis 22,000 Refugees Safe at Vicksburg Army Engineers Say Levees Will Hold.*

"I reckon that means it will bust tonight," one convict said.

"Well, maybe this rain will hold on until the water gets here," a second said. They all agreed to this because what they meant, the living unspoken thought among them, was that if the weather cleared, even though the levees broke and the flood moved in upon the Farm itself, they would have to return to the fields and work, which they would have had to do. There was nothing paradoxical in this, although they could not have expressed the reason for it which they instinctively perceived: that the land they farmed and the substance they produced from it belonged neither to them who worked it nor to those who forced them at guns' point to do so, that as far as either—convicts or guards—were concerned, it could have been pebbles they put into the ground and papier-mâché cotton- and corn-sprouts which they thinned. So it was that, what between the sudden wild hoping and the idle day and the evening's headlines, they were sleeping restlessly beneath the sound of the rain on the tin roof when at midnight the sudden glare of the electric bulbs and the guards' voices waked them and they heard the throbbing of the waiting trucks.

"Turn out of there!" the deputy shouted. He was fully dressed—rubber boots, slicker and shotgun. "The levee went out at Mound's Landing an hour ago. Get up out of it!"

II

When the belated and streaming dawn broke the two convicts, along with twenty others, were in a truck. A trusty drove, two armed guards sat in the cab with him. Inside the high, stall-like, topless body the convicts stood, packed like matches in an upright box or like the pencil-shaped ranks of cordite in a shell, shackled by the ankles to a single chain which wove among the motionless feet and swaying legs and a clutter of picks and shovels among which they stood, and was riveted by both ends to the steel body of the truck.

Then, and without warning, they saw the flood about which the plump convict had been reading and they listening for two weeks or more. The road ran south. It was built on a raised levee, known locally as a dump, about eight feet above the flat surrounding land, bordered on both sides by the barrow pits from which the earth of the levee had been excavated. These barrow pits had held water all winter from the fall rains, not to speak of the rain of yesterday, but now they saw that the pit on either side of the road had vanished and instead there lay a flat still sheet of brown water which extended into the fields beyond the pits, ravelled out into long motionless shreds in the bottom of the plow furrows and gleamed faintly in the gray light like the bars of a prone and enormous grating. And then (the truck was moving at good speed) as they watched quietly (they had not been talking much anyway but now they were all silent and quite grave, shifting and craning as one to look soberly off to the west side of the road) the crests of the furrows vanished too, and they now looked at a single perfectly flat and motionless steel-colored sheet in which the telephone poles and the straight hedgerows which marked section lines seemed to be fixed and rigid as though set in concrete.

It was perfectly motionless, perfectly flat. It looked, not innocent, but bland. It looked almost demure. It looked as if you could walk on it. It looked so still that they did not realize it possessed motion until they came to the first bridge. There was a ditch under the bridge, a small stream, but ditch and stream were both invisible now, indicated only by the rows of cypress and bramble which marked its course. Here they both saw and heard movement—the slow profound eastward and upstream ("It's running backward," one convict said quietly) set of the still rigid surface, from beneath which came a deep faint subaquean rumble which (though none in the truck could have made the comparison) sounded like a subway train passing far beneath the street, and which suggested a terrific and secret speed. It was as if the water itself were in three strata, separate and distinct, the bland and unhurried surface bearing a frothy scum and a miniature flotsam of twigs and screening, as though by vicious calculation, the rush and fury of the flood itself, and beneath this in turn the original stream trickle, murmuring along in the opposite direction, following undisturbed and unaware of its appointed course and serving its Lilliputian end, like a thread of ants between the rails on which an express train passes, they (the ants) as unaware of the power and fury as if it were a cyclone crossing Saturn.

Now there was water on both sides of the road and now, as if once they had become aware of movement in the water it had given over deception and concealment, they seemed to be able to watch it rising up the flanks of the dump; trees which a few miles back had stood on tall trunks above the water now seemed to burst from the surface at the level of the lower branches like decorative shrubs on barbered lawns. The truck passed a Negro cabin. The water was up to the window ledges. A woman clutching two children squatted on the ridgepole, a man and a halfgrown youth, standing waistdeep, were hoisting a squealing pig onto the slanting roof of a barn, on the ridgepole of which sat a row of chickens and a turkey. Near the barn was a haystack on which a cow stood tied by a rope to the center pole and bawling steadily; a yelling Negro boy on a saddleless mule which he flogged steadily, his legs clutching the mule's barrel and his body leaned to the drag of a rope attached to a second mule, approached the haystack, splashing and floundering. The woman on the housetop began to shriek at the passing truck, her voice carrying faint and melodious across the brown water, becoming fainter and fainter as the truck passed and went on, ceasing at last, whether because of distance or because she had stopped screaming those in the truck did not know.

Then the road vanished. There was no perceptible slant to it yet it had slipped abruptly beneath the brown surface with no ripple, no ridgy demarcation, like a flat thin blade slipped obliquely into flesh by a delicate hand, annealed into the water without disturbance, as if it had existed so for years, had been built that way. The truck stopped. The trusty descended from the cab and came back and dragged two shovels from among their feet, the blades clashing against the serpentining of the chain about their ankles. "What is it?" one said. "What are you fixing to do?" The trusty didn't answer. He returned to the cab, from which one of the guards had descended, without his shotgun. He and the trusty, both

in hip boots and each carrying a shovel, advanced into
the water, gingerly, probing and feeling ahead with the
shovel handles. The same convict spoke again. He was a
middle-aged man with a wild thatch of iron-gray hair
and a slightly mad face. "What the hell are they doing?"
he said. Again nobody answered him. The truck moved,
on into the water, behind the guard and the trusty, beginning to push ahead of itself a thick slow viscid ridge
of chocolate water. Then the gray-haired convict began
to scream. "God damn it, unlock the chain!" He began
to struggle, thrashing violently about him, striking at
the men nearest him until he reached the cab, the roof
of which he now hammered on with his fists, screaming.
"God damn it, unlock us! Unlock us! Son of a bitch!"
he screamed, addressing no one. "They're going to
drown us! Unlock the chain!" But for all the answer he
got the men within radius of his voice might have been
dead. The truck crawled on, the guard and the trusty
feeling out the road ahead with the reversed shovels,
the second guard at the wheel, the twenty-two convicts
packed like sardines into the truck bed and padlocked
by the ankles to the body of the truck itself. They
crossed another bridge—two delicate and paradoxical
iron railings slanting out of the water, travelling parallel
to it for a distance, then slanting down into it again
with an outrageous quality almost significant yet apparently meaningless like something in a dream not quite
nightmare. The truck crawled on.

Along toward noon they came to a town, their destination. The streets were paved; now the wheels of the
truck made a sound like tearing silk. Moving faster
now, the guard and the trusty in the cab again, the
truck even had a slight bone in its teeth, its bow-wave
spreading beyond the submerged sidewalks and across
the adjacent lawns, lapping against the stoops and

porches of houses where people stood among piles of furniture. They passed through the business district; a man in hip boots emerged knee-deep in water from a store, dragging a flat-bottomed skiff containing a steel safe.

At last they reached the railroad. It crossed the street at right angles, cutting the town in two. It was on a dump, a levee, also, eight or ten feet above the town itself; the street ran blankly into it and turned at right angles beside a cotton compress and a loading platform on stilts at the level of a freight-car door. On this platform was a khaki army tent and a uniformed National Guard sentry with a rifle and bandolier.

The truck turned and crawled out of the water and up the ramp which cotton wagons used and where trucks and private cars filled with household goods came and unloaded onto the platform. They were unlocked from the chain in the truck and, shackled ankle to ankle in pairs, they mounted the platform and into an apparently inextricable jumble of beds and trunks, gas and electric stoves, radios and tables and chairs and framed pictures, which a chain of Negroes under the eye of an unshaven white man in muddy corduroy and hip boots carried piece by piece into the compress, at the door of which another guardsman stood with his rifle, they (the convicts) not stopping here but herded on by the two guards with their shotguns into the dim and cavernous building where, among the piled heterogeneous furniture, the ends of cotton bales and the mirrors on dressers and sideboards gleamed with an identical mute and unreflecting concentration of pallid light.

They passed on through, onto the loading platform where the army tent and the first sentry were. They waited here. Nobody told them for what nor why.

While the two guards talked with the sentry before the tent, the convicts sat in a line along the edge of the platform like buzzards on a fence, their shackled feet dangling above the brown motionless flood out of which the railroad embankment rose, pristine and intact, in a kind of paradoxical denial and repudiation of change and portent; not talking, just looking quietly across the track to where the other half of the amputated town seemed to float, house, shrub, and tree, ordered and pageant-like and without motion, upon the limitless liquid plain beneath the thick gray sky.

After a while the other four trucks from the Farm arrived. They came up, bunched closely, radiator to tail light, with their four separate sounds of tearing silk and vanished beyond the compress. Presently the ones on the platform heard the feet, the mute clashing of the shackles. The first truckload emerged from the compress, the second, the third; there were more than a hundred of them now in their bed-ticking overalls and jumpers and fifteen or twenty guards with rifles and shotguns. The first lot rose and they mingled, paired, twinned by their clanking and clashing umbilicals; then it began to rain, a slow steady gray drizzle like November instead of May. Yet not one of them made any move toward the open door of the compress. They did not even look toward it, with longing or hope or without it. If they thought at all, they doubtless knew that the available space in it would be needed for furniture, even if it were not already filled. Or perhaps they knew that, even if there were room in it, it would not be for them, not that the guards would wish them to get wet but that the guards would not think about getting them out of the rain. So they just stopped talking and, with their jumper collars turned up and shackled in braces like dogs at a field trial, they stood, immobile, patient, almost ruminant, their backs turned to the rain as sheep and cattle do.

After another while they became aware that the number of soldiers had increased to a dozen or more, warm and dry beneath rubberized ponchos, there was an officer with a pistol at his belt, then and without making any more toward it, they began to smell food and, turning to look, saw an army field kitchen set up just inside the compress door. But they made no move, they waited until they were herded into line, they inched forward, their heads lowered and patient in the rain, and received each a bowl of stew, a mug of coffee, two slices of bread. They ate this in the rain. They did not sit down because the platform was wet, they squatted on their heels as country men do, hunching forward, trying to shield the bowls and mugs into which nevertheless the rain splashed steadily as into miniature ponds and soaked, invisible and soundless, into the bread.

After they had stood on the platform for three hours, a train came for them. Those nearest the edge saw it, watched it—a passenger coach apparently running under its own power and trailing a cloud of smoke from no visible stack, a cloud which did not rise but instead shifted slowly and heavily aside and lay upon the surface of the aqueous earth with a quality at once weightless and completely spent. It came up and stopped, a single old-fashioned open-ended wooden car coupled to the nose of a pushing switch engine considerably smaller. They were herded into it, crowding forward to the other end where there was a small cast-iron stove. There was no fire in it, nevertheless they crowded about it—the cold and voiceless lump of iron stained with fading tobacco and hovered about by the ghosts of a thousand Sunday excursions to Memphis or Moor-head and return—the peanuts, the bananas, the soiled garments of infants—huddling, shoving for places near it. "Come on, come on," one of the guards shouted. "Sit down, now." At last three of the guards, laying aside their guns, came among them and broke up the huddle, driving them back and into seats.

There were not enough seats for all. The others stood in the aisle, they stood braced, they heard the air hiss out of the released brakes, the engine whistled four blasts, the car came into motion with a snapping jerk; the platform, the compress fled violently as the train seemed to transpose from immobility to full speed with that same quality of unreality with which it had appeared, running backward now though with the engine in front where before it had moved forward but with the engine behind.

When the railroad in its turn ran beneath the surface of the water, the convicts did not even know it. They felt the train stop, they heard the engine blow a long blast which wailed away unechoed across the waste, wild and forlorn, and they were not even curious; they sat or stood behind the rain-streaming windows as the train crawled on again, feeling its way as the truck had while the brown water swirled between the trucks and among the spokes of the driving wheels and lapped in cloudy steam against the dragging fire-filled belly of the engine; again it blew four short harsh blasts filled with the wild triumph and defiance yet also with repudiation and even farewell, as if the articulated steel itself knew it did not dare stop and would not be able to return. Two hours later in the twilight they saw through the streaming windows a burning plantation house. Juxtaposed to nowhere and neighbored by nothing it stood, a clear steady pyre-like flame rigidly fleeing its own reflection, burning in the dusk above the watery desolation with a quality paradoxical, outrageous and bizarre.

Sometime after dark the train stopped. The convicts did not know where they were. They did not ask. They would no more have thought of asking where they were than they would have asked why and what for. They couldn't even see, since the car was unlighted and the windows fogged on the outside by rain and on the inside by the engendered heat of the packed bodies. All they could see was a milky and sourceless flick and glare of flashlights. They could hear shouts and commands, then the guards inside the car began to shout; they were herded to their feet and toward the exit, the ankle chains clashing and clanking. They descended into a fierce hissing of steam, through ragged whisps of it blowing past the car. Laid-to alongside the train and resembling a train itself was a thick blunt motor launch to which was attached a string of skiffs and flat boats. There were more soldiers; the flashlights played on the rifle barrels and bandolier buckles and flicked and glinted on the ankle chains of the convicts as they stepped gingerly down into knee-deep water and entered the boats; now car and engine both vanished completely in steam as the crew began dumping the fire from the firebox.

After another hour they began to see lights ahead—a faint wavering row of red pin-pricks extending along the horizon and apparently hanging low in the sky. But it took almost another hour to reach them while the convicts squatted in the skiffs, huddled into the soaked garments (they no longer felt the rain any more at all as separate drops) and watched the lights draw nearer and nearer until at last the crest of the levee defined itself; now they could discern a row of army tents stretching along it and people squatting about the fires, the wavering reflections from which, stretching across the water, revealed an involved mass of other skiffs tied against the flank of the levee which now stood high and dark overhead. Flashlights glared and winked along the base, among the tethered skiffs; the launch, silent now, drifted in.

When they reached the top of the levee they could see the long line of khaki tents, interspersed with fires about which people—men, women and children, Negro and white—crouched or stood among shapeless bales of clothing, their heads turning, their eyeballs glinting in the firelight as they looked quietly at the striped garments and the chains; further down the levee, huddled together too though untethered, was a drove of mules and two or three cows. Then the taller convict became conscious of another sound. He did not begin to hear it all at once, he suddenly became aware that he had been hearing it all the time, a sound so much beyond all his experience and his powers of assimilation that up to this point he had been as oblivious of it as an ant or a flea might be of the sound of the avalanche on which it rides; he had been travelling upon water since early afternoon and for seven years now he had run his plow and harrow and planter within the very shadow of the levee on which he now stood, but this profound deep whisper which came from the further side of it he did not at once recognize. He stopped. The line of convicts behind jolted into him like a line of freight cars stopping, with an iron clashing like cars. "Get on!" a guard shouted.

"What's that?" the convict said. A Negro man squatting before the nearest fire answered him:

"Dat's him. Dat's de Ole Man."

"The old man?" the convict said.

"Get on! Get on up there!" the guard shouted. They

went on; they passed another huddle of mules, the eyeballs rolling too, the long morose faces turning into and out of the firelight; they passed them and reached a section of empty tents, the light pup tents of a military campaign, made to hold two men. The guards herded the convicts into them, three brace of shackled men to each tent.

They crawled in on all fours, like dogs into cramped kennels, and settled down. Presently the tent became warm from their bodies. Then they became quiet and then all of them could hear it, they lay listening to the bass whisper deep, strong, and powerful. "The old man?" the train-robber convict said.

"Yah," another said. "He don't have to brag."

At dawn the guards waked them by kicking the soles of the projecting feet. Opposite the muddy landing and the huddle of skiffs an army field kitchen was set up, already they could smell the coffee. But the taller convict at least, even though he had had but one meal yesterday and that at noon in the rain, did not move at once toward the food. Instead and for the first time he looked at the River within whose shadow he had spent the last seven years of his life but had never seen before; he stood in quiet and amazed surmise and looked at the rigid steel-colored surface not broken into waves but merely slightly undulant. It stretched from the levee on which he stood, further than he could see—a slowly and heavily roiling chocolate-frothy expanse broken only by a thin line a mile away as fragile in appearance as a single hair, which after a moment he recognized. *It's another levee,* he thought quietly. *That's what we look like from there. That's what I am standing on looks like from there.* He was prodded from the rear; a guard's voice carried forward: "Go on! Go on! You'll have plenty of time to look at that!"

They received the same stew and coffee and bread as the day before; they squatted again with their bowls and mugs as yesterday, though it was not raining yet. During the night an intact wooden barn had floated up. It now lay jammed by the current against the levee while a crowd of Negroes swarmed over it, ripping off the shingles and planks and carrying them up the bank; eating steadily and without haste, the taller convict watched the barn dissolve rapidly down to the very water-line exactly as a dead fly vanished beneath the moiling industry of a swarm of ants.

They finished eating. Then it began to rain again, as upon a signal, while they stood or squatted in their harsh garments which had not dried out during the night but had merely become slightly warmer than the air. Presently they were haled to their feet and told off into two groups, one of which was armed from a stack of mud-clogged picks and shovels nearby, and marched away up the levee. A little later the motor launch with its train of skiffs came up across what was, fifteen feet beneath its keel, probably a cotton field, the skiffs loaded to the gunwales with Negroes and a scattering of white people nursing bundles on their laps. When the engine shut off the faint plinking of a guitar came across the water. The skiffs warped in and unloaded; the convicts watched the men and women and children struggle up the muddy slope, carrying heavy towsacks and bundles wrapped in quilts. The sound of the guitar had not ceased and now the convicts saw him—a young, black, lean-hipped man, the guitar slung by a piece of cotton plow line about his neck. He mounted the levee, still picking it. He carried nothing else, no food, no change of clothes, not even a coat.

The taller convict was so busy watching this that he did not hear the guard until the guard stood directly beside him shouting his name. "Wake up!" the guard shouted. "Can you fellows paddle a boat?"

"Paddle a boat where?" the taller convict said.

"In the water," the guard said. "Where in hell do you think?"

"I ain't going to paddle no boat nowhere out yonder," the tall convict said, jerking his head toward the invisible river beyond the levee behind him.

"No, it's on this side," the guard said. He stooped swiftly and unlocked the chain which joined the tall convict and the plump hairless one. "It's just down the road a piece." He rose. The two convicts followed him down to the boats. "Follow them telephone poles until you come to a filling station. You can tell it, the roof is still above water. It's on a bayou and you can tell the bayou because the tops of the trees are sticking up. Follow the bayou until you come to a cypress snag with a woman in it. Pick her up and then cut straight back west until you come to a cottonhouse with a fellow sitting on the ridgepole—" He turned, looking at the two convicts, who stood perfectly still, looking first at the skiff and then at the water with intense sobriety. "Well? What are you waiting for?"

"I can't row a boat," the plump convict said.

"Then it's high time you learned," the guard said. "Get in."

The tall convict shoved the other forward. "Get in," he said. "That water ain't going to hurt you. Ain't nobody going to make you take a bath."

As, the plump one in the bow and the other in the stern, they shoved away from the levee, they saw other pairs being unshackled and manning the other skiffs. "I wonder how many more of them fellows are seeing this much water for the first time in their lives too," the tall convict said. The other did not answer. He knelt in the bottom of the skiff, pecking gingerly at the water now and then with his paddle. The very shape of his thick soft back seemed to wear that expression of wary and tense concern.

Some time after midnight a rescue boat filled to the guard rail with homeless men and women and children docked at Vicksburg. It was a steamer, shallow of draft; all day long it had poked up and down cypress- and gum-choked bayous and across cotton fields (where at times instead of swimming it waded) gathering its sorry cargo from the tops of houses and barns and even out of trees, and now it warped into that mushroom city of the forlorn and despairing, where kerosene flares smoked in the drizzle and hurriedly strung electrics glared upon the bayonets of martial policemen and the Red-Cross brassards of doctors and nurses and canteen-workers. The bluff overhead was almost solid with tents, yet still there were more people than shelter for them; they sat or lay, single and by whole families, under what shelter they could find, or sometimes under the rain itself, in the little death of profound exhaustion while the doctors and the nurses and the soldiers stepped over and around and among them.

Among the first to disembark was one of the penitentiary deputy wardens, followed closely by the plump convict and another white man—a small man with a gaunt unshaven wan face still wearing an expression of incredulous outrage. The deputy warden seemed to know exactly where he wished to go. Followed closely by his two companions he threaded his way swiftly among the piled furniture and the sleeping bodies and stood presently in a fiercely lighted and hastily established temporary office, almost a military post of command in fact, where the Warden of the Penitentiary sat with two army officers wearing majors' leaves. The deputy warden spoke without preamble. "We lost a man," he said. He called the tall convict's name.

"Lost him?" the Warden said.

"Yah. Drowned." Without turning his head he spoke to the plump convict. "Tell him," he said.

"He was the one that said he could row a boat," the plump convict said. "I never. I told him myself—" he indicated the deputy warden with a jerk of his head "—I couldn't. So when we got to the bayou—"

"What's this?" the Warden said.

"The launch brought word in," the deputy warden said. "Woman in a cypress snag on the bayou, then this fellow—" he indicated the third man; the Warden and the two officers looked at the third man "—on a cotton-house. Never had room in the launch to pick them up. Go on."

"So we come to where the bayou was," the plump convict continued in a voice perfectly flat, without any inflection whatever. "Then the boat got away from him. I don't know what happened. I was just sitting there because he was so positive he could row a boat. I never saw any current. Just all of a sudden the boat whirled clean around and begun to run fast backward like it was hitched to a train and it whirled around again and I happened to look up and there was a limb right over my head and I grabbed it just in time and that boat was snatched out from under me like you'd snatch off a sock and I saw it one time more upside down and that fellow that said he knew all about rowing holding to it with one hand and still holding the paddle in the other—" He ceased. There was no dying fall to his voice, it just ceased and the convict stood looking quietly at a half-full quart of whiskey sitting on the table.

"How do you know he's drowned?" the Warden said

to the deputy. "How do you know he didn't just see his chance to escape, and took it?"

"Escape where?" the other said. "The whole Delta's flooded. There's fifteen foot of water for fifty miles, clean back to the hills. And that boat was upside down."

"That fellow's drowned," the plump convict said. "You don't need to worry about him. He's got his pardon; it won't cramp nobody's hand signing it, neither."

"And nobody else saw him?" the Warden said. "What about the woman in the tree?"

"I don't know," the deputy said. "I ain't found her yet. I reckon some other boat picked her up. But this is the fellow on the cotton house."

Again the Warden and the two officers looked at the third man, at the gaunt, unshaven wild face in which an old terror, an old blending of fear and impotence and rage still lingered. "He never came for you?" the Warden said. "You never saw him?"

"Never nobody came for me," the refugee said. He began to tremble though at first he spoke quietly enough. "I set there on that sonabitching cotton house, expecting hit to go any minute. I saw that launch and them boats come up and they never had no room for me. Full of bastard niggers and one of them setting there playing a guitar but there wasn't no room for me. A guitar!" he cried; now he began to scream, trembling, slavering, his face twitching and jerking. "Room for a bastard nigger guitar but not for me—"

"Steady now," the Warden said. "Steady now."

"Give him a drink," one of the officers said. The Warden poured the drink. The deputy handed it to the refugee, who took the glass in both jerking hands and tried to raise it to his mouth. They watched him for perhaps twenty seconds, then the deputy took the glass from him and held it to his lips while he gulped, though even then a thin trickle ran from each corner of his mouth, into the stubble on his chin.

"So we picked him and—" the deputy called the plump convict's name now "—both up just before dark and come on in. But that other fellow is gone."

"Yes," the Warden said. "Well. Here I haven't lost a prisoner in ten years, and now, like this—I'm sending you back to the Farm tomorrow. Have his family notified, and his discharge papers filled out at once."

"All right," the deputy said. "And listen, chief. He wasn't a bad fellow and maybe he never had no business in that boat. Only he did say he could paddle one. Listen. Suppose I write on his discharge, Drowned while trying to save lives in the great flood of nineteen twenty-seven, and send it down for the Governor to sign it. It will be something nice for his folks to have, to hang on the wall when neighbors come in or something. Maybe they will even give his folks a cash bonus because after all they sent him to the Farm to raise cotton, not to fool around in a boat in a flood."

"All right," the Warden said. "I'll see about it. The main thing is to get his name off the books as dead before some politician tries to collect his food allowance."

"All right," the deputy said. He turned and herded his companions out. In the drizzling darkness again he said to the plump convict: "Well, your partner beat you. He's free. He's done served his time out but you've got a right far piece to go yet."

"Yah," the plump convict said. "Free. He can have it."

III

As the short convict had testified, the tall one, when he returned to the surface, still retained what the short one called the paddle. He clung to it, not instinctively against the time when he would be back inside the boat and would need it, because for a time he did not believe he would ever regain the skiff or anything else that would support him, but because he did not have time to think about turning it loose. Things had moved too fast for him. He had not been warned, he had felt the first snatching tug of the current, he had seen the skiff begin to spin and his companion vanish violently upward like in a translation out of Isaiah, then he himself was in the water, struggling against the drag of the paddle which he did not know he still held each time he fought back to the surface and grasped at the spinning skiff which at one instant was ten feet away and the next poised above his head as though about to brain him, until at last he grasped the stern, the drag of his body becoming a rudder to the skiff, the two of them, man and boat and with the paddle perpendicular above them like a jackstaff, vanishing from the view of the short convict (who had vanished from that of the tall one with the same celerity though in a vertical direction) like a tableau snatched offstage intact with violent and incredible speed.

He was now in the channel of a slough, a bayou, in which until today no current had run probably since the old subterranean outrage which had created the country. There was plenty of current in it now though; from his trough behind the stern he seemed to see the trees and sky rushing past with vertiginous speed, looking down at him between the gouts of cold yellow in lugubrious and mournful amazement. But they were fixed and secure in something; he thought of that, he remembered in an instant of despairing rage the firm earth fixed and founded strong and cemented fast and stable forever by the generations of laborious sweat, somewhere beneath him, beyond the reach of his feet, when, and again without warning, the stern of the skiff struck him a stunning blow across the bridge of his nose. The instinct which had caused him to cling to it now caused him to fling the paddle into the boat in order to grasp the gunwale with both hands just as the skiff pivoted and spun away again. With both hands free he now dragged himself over the stern and lay prone on his face, streaming with blood and water and panting, not with exhaustion but with that furious rage which is terror's aftermath.

But he had to get up at once because he believed he had come much faster (and so further) than he had. So he rose, out of the watery scarlet puddle in which he had lain, streaming, the soaked denim heavy as iron on his limbs, the black hair plastered to his skull, the blood-infused water streaking his jumper, and dragged his forearm gingerly and hurriedly across his lower face and glanced at it then grasped the paddle and began to try to swing the skiff back upstream. It did not even occur to him that he did not know where his companion was, in which tree among all which he had passed or might pass. He did not even speculate on that for the reason that he knew so incontestably that the other was upstream from him, and after his recent experience the mere connotation of the term upstream carried a sense of such violence and force and speed that the conception of it as other than a straight line was something which the intelligence, reason, simply refused to harbor, like the notion of a rifle bullet the width of a cotton field.

The bow began to swing back upstream. It turned readily, it outpaced the aghast and outraged instant in which he realized it was swinging far too easily, it had swung on over the arc and lay broadside to the current and began again that vicious spinning while he sat, his teeth bared in his bloody streaming face while his spent arms flailed the impotent paddle at the water, that innocent-appearing medium which at one time had held him in ironlike and shifting convolutions like an anaconda yet which now seemed to offer no more resistance to the thrust of his urge and need than so much air, like air; the boat which had threatened him and at last actually struck him in the face with the shocking violence of a mule's hoof now seemed to poise weightless upon it like a thistle bloom, spinning like a wind vane while he flailed at the water and thought of, envisioned, his companion safe, inactive, and at ease in the tree with nothing to do but wait, musing with impotent and terrified fury upon that arbitrariness of human affairs which had abrogated to the one the secure tree and to the other the hysterical and unmanageable boat for the very reason that it knew that he alone of the two of them would make any attempt to return and rescue his companion.

The skiff had paid off and now ran with the current again. It seemed again to spring from immobility into incredible speed, and he thought he must already be miles away from where his companion had quitted him, though actually he had merely described a big circle since getting back into the skiff, and the object (a clump of cypress trees choked by floating logs and debris) which the skiff was now about to strike was the same one it had careened into before when the stern had struck him. He didn't know this because he had not yet ever looked higher than the bow of the boat. He didn't look higher now, he just saw that he was going to strike; he seemed to feel run through the very insentient fabric of the skiff a current of eager gleeful vicious incorrigible wilfulness; and he who had never ceased to flail at the bland treacherous water with what he had be-

lieved to be the limit of his strength now from somewhere, some ultimate absolute reserve, produced a final
measure of endurance, will to endure, which adum-
brated mere muscle and nerves, continuing to flail the
paddle right up to the instant of striking, completing
one last reach, thrust and recover out of pure desperate
reflex, as a man slipping on ice reaches for his hat and
money-pocket, as the skiff struck and hurled him once
more flat on his face in the bottom of it.

This time he did not get up at once. He lay flat on his
face, slightly spread-eagled and in an attitude almost
peaceful, a kind of abject meditation. He would have
to get up sometime, he knew that, just as all life consists
of having to get up sooner or later and then having to
lie down again sooner or later after a while. And he
was not exactly exhausted and he was not particularly
without hope and he did not especially dread getting
up. It merely seemed to him that he had accidentally
been caught in a situation in which time and environment, not himself, were mesmerized; he was being toyed
with by a current of water going nowhere, beneath a
day which would wane toward no evening; when it was
done with him it would spew him back into the comparatively safe world he had been snatched violently
out of, and in the meantime it did not much matter just
what he did or did not do. So he lay on his face, now not
only feeling but hearing the strong quiet rustling of the
current on the underside of the planks, for a while
longer. Then he raised his head and this time touched
his palm gingerly to his face and looked at the blood
again, then he sat up onto his heels and leaning over
the gunwale he pinched his nostrils between thumb and
finger and expelled a gout of blood and was in the act
of wiping his fingers on his thigh when a voice slightly
above his line of sight said quietly, "It's taken you a

while," and he who up to this moment had had neither reason nor time to raise his eyes higher than the bows looked up and saw, sitting in a tree and looking at him, a woman. She was not ten feet away. She sat on the lowest limb of one of the trees holding the jam he had grounded on, in a calico wrapper and an army private's tunic and a sunbonnet, a woman whom he did not even bother to examine since that first startled glance had been ample to reveal to him all the generations of her life and background, who could have been his sister if he had a sister, his wife if he had not entered the penitentiary at an age scarcely out of adolescence and some years younger than that at which even his prolific and monogamous kind married—a woman who sat clutching the trunk of the tree, her stockingless feet in a pair of man's unlaced brogans less than a yard from the water, who was very probably somebody's sister and quite certainly (or certainly should have been) somebody's wife, though this too he had entered the penitentiary too young to have had more than mere theoretical female experience to discover yet. "I thought for a minute you wasn't aiming to come back."

"Come back?"

"After the first time. After you run into this brush pile the first time and got into the boat and went on." He looked about, touching his face tenderly again; it could very well be the same place where the boat had hit him in the face.

"Yah," he said. "I'm here now though."

"Could you maybe get the boat a little closer? I taken a right sharp strain getting up here; maybe I better . . ." He was not listening; he had just discovered that the paddle was gone; this time when the skiff hurled him forward he had flung the paddle not into it but beyond it. "It's right there in them brush tops," the

woman said. "You can get it. Here. Catch a holt of
this." It was a grapevine. It had grown up into the tree
and the flood had torn the roots loose. She had taken a
turn with it about her upper body; she now loosed it
and swung it out until he could grasp it. Holding to the
end of the vine he warped the skiff around the end of
the jam, picking up the paddle, and warped the skiff on
beneath the limb and held it and now he watched her
move, gather herself heavily and carefully to descend—
that heaviness which was not painful but just excru-
ciatingly careful, that profound and almost lethargic
awkwardness which added nothing to the sum of that
first aghast amazement which had served already for
the catafalque of invincible dream since even in durance
he had continued (and even with the old avidity, even
though they had caused his downfall) to consume the
impossible pulp-printed fables carefully censored and
as carefully smuggled into the penitentiary; and who to
say what Helen, what living Garbo, he had not dreamed
of rescuing from what craggy pinnacle or dragoned
keep when he and his companion embarked in the skiff.
He watched her, he made no further effort to help her
beyond holding the skiff savagely steady while she lowered herself from the limb—the entire body, the de-
formed swell of belly bulging the calico, suspended by
its arms, thinking, *And this is what I get. This, out of
all the female meat that walks, is what I have to be
caught in a runaway boat with.*

"Where's that cottonhouse?" he said.

"Cottonhouse?"

"With that fellow on it. The other one."

"I don't know. It's a right smart of cottonhouses
around here. With folks on them too, I reckon." She
was examining him. "You're bloody as a hog," she said.
"You look like a convict."

"Yah," he said, snarled. "I feel like I done already been hung. Well, I got to pick up my pardner and then find that cottonhouse." He cast off. That is, he released his hold on the vine. That was all he had to do, for even while the bow of the skiff hung high on the log jam and even while he held it by the vine in the comparatively dead water behind the jam, he felt steadily and constantly the whisper, the strong purring power of the water just one inch beyond the frail planks on which he squatted and which, as soon as he released the vine, took charge of the skiff not with one powerful clutch but in a series of touches light, tentative, and catlike; he realized now that he had entertained a sort of foundationless hope that the added weight might make the skiff more controllable. During the first moment or two he had a wild (and still foundationless) belief that it had; he had got the head upstream and managed to hold it so by terrific exertion continued even after he discovered that they were travelling straight enough but stern-first and continued somehow even after the bow began to wear away and swing: the old irresistible movement which he knew well by now, too well to fight against it, so that he let the bow swing on downstream with the hope of utilizing the skiff's own momentum to bring it through the full circle and so upstream again, the skiff travelling broadside then bow-first then broadside again, diagonally across the channel, toward the other wall of submerged trees; it began to flee beneath him with terrific speed, they were in an eddy but did not know it; he had no time to draw conclusions or even wonder; he crouched, his teeth bared in his blood-caked and swollen face, his lungs bursting, flailing at the water while the trees stooped hugely down at him. The skiff struck, spun, struck again; the woman half lay in the bow, clutching the gunwales, as if she were trying to crouch behind her own pregnancy; he banged now not at the water but at the living sapblooded wood with the paddle, his desire now not to go anywhere, reach any destination, but just to keep the skiff from beating itself to fragments against the tree trunks. Then something exploded, this time against the back of his head, and stooping trees and dizzy water, the woman's face and all, fled together and vanished in bright soundless flash and glare.

An hour later the skiff came slowly up an old logging road and so out of the bottom, the forest, and into (or onto) a cottonfield—a gray and limitless desolation now free of turmoil, broken only by a thin line of telephone poles like a wading millipede. The woman was now paddling, steadily and deliberately, with that curious lethargic care, while the convict squatted, his head between his knees, trying to stanch the fresh and apparently inexhaustible flow of blood from his nose with handfuls of water. The woman ceased paddling, the skiff drifted on, slowing, while she looked about. "We're done out," she said.

The convict raised his head and also looked about. "Out where?"

"I thought maybe you might know."

"I don't even know where I used to be. Even if I knowed which way was north, I wouldn't know if that was where I wanted to go." He cupped another handful of water to his face and lowered his hand and regarded the resulting crimson marbling on his palm, not with dejection, not with concern, but with a kind of sardonic and vicious bemusement. The woman watched the back of his head.

"We got to get somewhere."

"Don't I know it? A fellow on a cottonhouse. Another in a tree. And now that thing in your lap."

"It wasn't due yet. Maybe it was having to climb that tree quick yesterday, and having to set in it all night. I'm doing the best I can. But we better get somewhere soon."

"Yah," the convict said. "I thought I wanted to get somewhere too and I ain't had no luck at it. You pick out a place to get to now and we'll try yours. Gimme that oar." The woman passed him the paddle. The boat was a double-ender; he had only to turn around.

"Which way you fixing to go?" the woman said.

"Never you mind that. You just keep on holding on." He began to paddle, on across the cottonfield. It began to rain again, though not hard at first. "Yah," he said. "Ask the boat. I been in it since breakfast and I ain't never knowed, where I aimed to go or where I was going either."

That was about one o'clock. Toward the end of the afternoon the skiff (they were in a channel of some sort again, they had been in it for some time; they had got into it before they knew it and too late to get out again, granted there had been any reason to get out, as, to the convict anyway, there was certainly none and the fact that their speed had increased again was reason enough to stay in it) shot out upon a broad expanse of debris-filled water which the convict recognized as a river and, from its size, the Yazoo River, though it was little enough he had seen of this country which he had not quitted for so much as one single day in the last seven years of his life. What he did not know was that it was now running backward. So as soon as the drift of the skiff indicated the set of the current, he began to paddle in that direction which he believed to be downstream, where he knew there were towns—Yazoo City, and as a last resort, Vicksburg, if his luck was that bad, if not, smaller towns whose names he did not know but where there would be people, houses, something, anything he might reach and surrender his charge to and turn his back on her forever, on all pregnant and female life forever and return to that monastic existence of shotguns and shackles where he would be secure from it. Now, with the imminence of habitations, release from her, he did not even hate her. When he looked upon the swelling and unmanageable body before him it seemed to him that it was not the woman at all but rather a separate demanding threatening inert yet living mass of which both he and she were equally victims; thinking, as he had been for the last three or four hours, of that minute's—nay, second's—aberration of eye or hand which would suffice to precipitate her into the water to be dragged down to death by that senseless millstone which, in its turn, would not even have to feel agony, he no longer felt any glow of revenge toward her as its custodian, he felt sorry for her as he would for the living timber in a barn which had to be burned to rid itself of vermin.

He paddled on, helping the current, steadily and strongly, with a calculated husbandry of effort, toward what he believed was downstream, towns, people, something to stand upon, while from time to time the woman raised herself to bail the accumulated rain from the skiff. It was raining steadily now though still not hard, still without passion, the sky, the day itself dissolving without grief; the skiff moved in a nimbus, an aura of gray gauze which merged almost without demarcation with the roiling spittle-frothed debris-choked water. Now the day, the light, definitely began to end and the convict permitted himself an extra notch or two of effort because it suddenly seemed to him that the speed of the skiff had lessened. This was actually the case though the convict did not know it. He merely took it as a phe-

nomenon of the increasing obfuscation, or at most as a
result of the long day's continuous effort with no food,
complicated by the ebbing and fluxing phases of anxiety
and impotent rage at his absolutely gratuitous predicament. So he stepped up his stroke a beat or so, not from
alarm but on the contrary, since he too had received
that lift from the mere presence of a known stream, a
river known by its ineradicable name to generations of
men who had been drawn to live beside it as man
always has been drawn to dwell beside water, even
before he had a name for water and fire, drawn to the
living water, the course of his destiny and his actual
physical appearance rigidly coerced and postulated by
it. So he was not alarmed. He paddled on, upstream
without knowing it, unaware that all the water which
for forty hours now had been pouring through the levee
break to the north was somewhere ahead of him, on its
way back to the River.

It was full dark now. That is, night had completely
come, the gray dissolving sky had vanished, yet as
though in perverse ratio surface visibility had sharp-
ened, as though the light which the rain of the afternoon
had washed out of the air had gathered upon the water
as the rain itself had done, so that the yellow flood
spread on before him now with a quality almost phosphorescent, right up to the instant where vision ceased.
The darkness in fact had its advantages; he could now
stop seeing the rain. He and his garments had been wet
for more than twenty-four hours now so he had long
since stopped feeling it, and now that he could no longer
see it either it had in a certain sense ceased for him.
Also, he now had to make no effort even not to see the
swell of his passenger's belly. So he was paddling on,
strongly and steadily, not alarmed and not concerned
but just exasperated because he had not yet begun to

see any reflection on the clouds which would indicate the city or cities which he believed he was approaching but which were actually now miles behind him, when he heard a sound. He did not know what it was because he had never heard it before and he would never be expected to hear such again, since it is not given to every man to hear such at all and to none to hear it more than once in his life. And he was not alarmed now either because there was not time, for although the visibility ahead, for all its clarity, did not extend very far, yet in the next instant to the hearing he was also seeing something such as he had never seen before. This was that the sharp line where the phosphorescent water met the darkness was now about ten feet higher than it had been an instant before and that it was curled forward upon itself like a sheet of dough being rolled out for a pudding. It reared, stooping; the crest of it swirled like the mane of a galloping horse and, phosphorescent too, fretted and flickered like fire. And while the woman huddled in the bows, aware or not aware the convict did not know which, he (the convict), his swollen and blood-streaked face gaped in an expression of aghast and incredulous amazement, continued to paddle directly into it. Again he simply had not had time to order his rhythm-hypnotized muscles to cease. He continued to paddle though the skiff had ceased to move forward at all but seemed to be hanging in space, while the paddle still reached, thrust, recovered and reached again; now instead of space the skiff became abruptly surrounded by a welter of fleeing debris—planks, small buildings, the bodies of drowned yet antic animals, entire trees leaping and diving like porpoises, above which the skiff seemed to hover in weightless and airy indecision like a bird above a fleeing countryside, undecided where to light or whether to light at all, while the convict squatted in it still going through the motions of paddling, waiting for an opportunity to scream. He never found it. For an instant the skiff seemed to stand erect on its stern and then shoot scrabbling and scrambling up the curling wall of water like a cat, and soared on above the licking crest itself and hung cradled into the high actual air in the limbs of a tree, from which bower of new-leafed boughs and branches the convict, like a bird in its nest and still waiting his chance to scream and still going through the motions of paddling though he no longer even had the paddle now, looked down upon a world turned to furious motion and in incredible retrograde.

Some time about midnight, accompanied by a rolling cannonade of thunder and lightning like a battery going into action, as though some forty hours' constipation of the elements, the firmament itself, were discharging in clapping and glaring salute to the ultimate acquiescence to desperate and furious motion, and still leading its charging welter of dead cows and mules and outhouses and cabins and hencoops, the skiff passed Vicksburg. The convict didn't know it. He wasn't looking high enough above the water; he still squatted, clutching the gunwales and glaring at the yellow turmoil about him, out of which entire trees, the sharp gables of houses, the long mournful heads of mules which he fended off with a splintered length of plank snatched from he knew not where in passing (and which seemed to glare reproachfully back at him with sightless eyes, in limber-lipped and incredulous amazement) rolled up and then down again, the skiff now travelling forward, now sideways, now sternward, sometimes in the water, sometimes riding for yards upon the roofs of houses and trees and even upon the backs of the mules as though even in death they were not to escape that burden-bearing doom with which their eunuch race was cursed. But he didn't see Vicksburg; the skiff, travelling at express speed, was in a seething gut between soaring and dizzy banks with a glare of light above them but he did not see it; he saw the flotsam ahead of him divide violently and begin to climb upon itself, mounting, and he was sucked through the resulting gap too fast to recognize it as the trestling of a railroad bridge; for a horrible moment the skiff seemed to hang in static indecision before the looming flank of a steamboat as though undecided whether to climb over it or dive under it, then a hard icy wind filled with the smell and taste and sense of wet and boundless desolation blew upon him; the skiff made one long bounding lunge as the convict's native state, in a final paroxysm, regurgitated him onto the wild bosom of the Father of Waters.

This is how he told about it seven weeks later, sitting in new bedticking garments, shaved and with his hair cut again, on his bunk in the barracks:

During the next three or four hours after the thunder and lightning had spent itself, the skiff ran in pitch streaming darkness upon a roiling expanse which, even if he could have seen, apparently had no boundaries. Wild and invisible, it tossed and heaved about and beneath the boat, ridged with dirty phosphorescent foam and filled with a debris of destruction—objects nameless and enormous and invisible, which struck and slashed at the skiff and whirled on. He did not know he was now upon the River. At that time he would have refused to believe it, even if he had known. Yesterday he had known he was in a channel by the regularity of the spacing between the bordering trees. Now, since even by daylight he could have seen no boundaries, the last place under the sun (or the streaming sky rather) he would have suspected himself to be would have been a river; if he had pondered at all about his present whereabouts, about the geography beneath him, he would merely have taken himself to be travelling at dizzy and inexplicable speed above the largest cotton-field in the world; if he who yesterday had known he was in a river, had accepted that fact in good faith and earnest, then had seen that river turn without warning and rush back upon him with furious and deadly intent like a frenzied stallion in a lane—if he had suspected for one second that the wild and limitless expanse on which he now found himself was a river, consciousness would simply have refused; he would have fainted.

When daylight—a gray and ragged dawn filled with driving scud between icy rain-squalls—came and he could see again, he knew he was in no cottonfield. He knew that the wild water on which the skiff tossed and fled flowed above no soil tamely trod by man, behind the straining and surging buttocks of a mule. That was when it occurred to him that its present condition was no phenomenon of a decade, but that the intervening years during which it consented to bear upon its placid and sleepy bosom the frail mechanicals of man's clumsy contriving was the phenomenon and this the norm and the River was now doing what it liked to do, had waited patiently the ten years in order to do, as a mule will work for you ten years for the privilege of kicking you once. And he also learned something else about fear too, something he had even failed to discover on that other occasion when he was really afraid—that three or four seconds of that night in his youth while he looked down the twice-flashing pistol barrel of the terrified mail clerk before the clerk could be persuaded that his (the con-vict's) pistol would not shoot: that if you just held on long enough a time would come in fear after which it would no longer be agony at all but merely a kind of horrible outrageous itching, as after you have been burned bad.

He did not have to paddle now, he just steered (who had been without food for twenty-four hours now and without any sleep to speak of for fifty) while the skiff sped on across that boiling desolation where he had long since begun to not dare believe he could possibly be where he could not doubt he was, trying with his fragment of splintered plank merely to keep the skiff intact and afloat among the houses and trees and dead animals (the entire towns, stores, residences, parks and farmyards, which leaped and played about him like fish), not trying to reach any destination, just trying to keep the skiff afloat until he did. He wanted so little. He wanted nothing for himself. He just wanted to get rid of the woman, the belly, and he was trying to do that in the right way, not for himself, but for her. He could have put her back into another tree at any time—

"Or you could have jumped out of the boat and let her and it drown," the plump convict said. "Then they could have given you the ten years for escaping and then hung you for the murder and charged the boat to your folks."

"Yah," the tall convict said.—But he had not done that. He wanted to do it the right way, find somebody, anybody he could surrender her to, something solid he could set her down on and then jump back into the river, if that would please anyone. That was all he wanted—just to come to something, anything. That didn't seem like a great deal to ask. And he couldn't do it. He told how the skiff fled on—

"Didn't you pass nobody?" the plump convict said. "No steamboat, nothing?"

"I don't know," the tall one said.—while he tried

merely to keep it afloat, until the darkness thinned and lifted and revealed—

"Darkness?" the plump convict said. "I thought you said it was already daylight."

"Yah," the tall one said. He was rolling a cigarette, pouring the tobacco carefully from a new sack, into the creased paper. "This was another one. They had several while I was gone."—the skiff to be moving still rapidly up a winding corridor bordered by drowned trees which the convict recognized again to be a river running again in the direction that, until two days ago, had been upstream. He was not exactly warned through instinct that this one, like that of two days ago, was in reverse. He would not say that he now believed himself to be in the same river, though he would not have been surprised to find that he did believe this, existing now, as he did and had and apparently was to continue for an unnamed period, in a state in which he was toy and pawn on a vicious and inflammable geography. He merely realized that he was in a river again, with all the subsequent inferences of a comprehensible, even if not familiar, portion of the earth's surface. Now he believed that all he had to do would be to paddle far enough and he would come to something horizontal and above water even if not dry and perhaps even populated; and, if fast enough, in time, and that his only other crying urgency was to refrain from looking at the woman who, as vision, the incontrovertible and apparently inescapable presence of his passenger, returned with dawn, had ceased to be a human being and (you could add twenty-four more hours to the first twenty-four and the first fifty now, even counting the hen. It was dead, drowned, caught by one wing under a shingle on a roof which had rolled momentarily up beside the skiff yesterday and he had eaten some of it raw though the woman would not) had become instead one single inert monstrous sentient womb from which, he now believed, if he could only turn his gaze away and keep it away, would disappear, and if he could only keep his gaze from pausing again at the spot it had occupied, would not return. That's what he was doing this time when he discovered the wave was coming.

He didn't know how he discovered it was coming back. He heard no sound, it was nothing felt nor seen. He did not even believe that finding the skiff to be now in slack water—that is, that the motion of the current which, whether right or wrong, had at least been horizontal, had now stopped that and assumed a vertical direction—was sufficient to warn him. Perhaps it was just an invincible and almost fanatic faith in the inventiveness and innate viciousness of that medium on which his destiny was now cast, apparently forever; a sudden conviction far beyond either horror or surprise that now was none too soon for it to prepare to do whatever it was it intended doing. So he whirled the skiff, spun it on its heel like a running horse, whereupon, reversed, he could not even distinguish the very channel he had come up. He did not know whether he simply could not see it or if it had vanished some time ago and he not aware at the time; whether the river had become lost in a drowned world or if the world had become drowned in one limitless river. So now he could not tell if he were running directly before the wave or quartering across its line of charge; all he could do was keep that sense of swiftly accumulating ferocity behind him and paddle as fast as his spent and now numb muscles could be driven, and try not to look at the woman, to wrench his gaze from her and keep it away until he reached something flat and above water. So, gaunt, hollow-eyed, striving and wrenching almost physically at his eyes as if they were two of those suction-tipped rubber arrows shot from the toy gun of a child, his spent muscles obeying not will now, but that attenuation beyond mere exhaustion which, mesmeric, can continue easier than cease, he once more drove the skiff full tilt into something it could not pass and, once more hurled violently forward onto his hands and knees, crouching, he glared with his wild swollen face up at the man with the shotgun and said in a harsh, croaking voice: "Vicksburg? Where's Vicksburg?"

Even when he tried to tell it, even after the seven weeks and he safe, secure, riveted warranted and doubly guaranteed by the ten years they had added to his sentence for attempted escape, something of the old hysteric incredulous outrage came back into his face, his voice, his speech. He never did even get on the other boat. He told how he clung to a strake (it was a dirty unpainted shanty boat with a drunken rake of tin stove pipe, it had been moving when he struck it and apparently it had not even changed course even though the three people on it must have been watching him all the while—a second man, barefoot and with matted hair and beard also at the steering sweep, and then—he did not know how long—a woman leaning in the door, in a filthy assortment of men's garments, watching him too with the same cold speculation) being dragged violently along, trying to state and explain his simple (and to him at least) reasonable desire and need; telling it, trying to tell it, he could feel again the old unforgettable affronting like an ague fit as he watched the abortive tobacco rain steadily and faintly from between his shaking hands and then the paper itself part with a thin dry snapping report:

"Burn my clothes?" the convict cried. "Burn them?"

"How in hell do you expect to escape in them bill-boards?" the man with the shotgun said. He (the convict) tried to tell it, tried to explain as he had tried to explain not to the three people on the boat alone but to the entire circumambience—desolate water and forlorn trees and sky—not for justification because he needed none and knew that his hearers, the other convicts, required none from him, but rather as, on the point of exhaustion, he might have picked dreamily and incredulously at a suffocation. He told the man with the gun how he and his partner had been given the boat and told to pick up a man and a woman, how he had lost his partner and failed to find the man, and now all in the world he wanted was something flat to leave the woman on until he could find an officer, a sheriff. He thought of home, the place where he had lived almost since childhood, his friends of years whose ways he knew and who knew his ways, the familiar fields where he did work he had learned to do well and to like, the mules with characters he knew and respected as he knew and respected the characters of certain men; he thought of the barracks at night, with screens against the bugs in summer and good stoves in winter and someone to supply the fuel and the food too; the Sunday ball games and the picture shows—things which, with the exception of the ball games, he had never known before. But most of all, his own character (Two years ago they had offered to make a trusty of him. He would no longer need to plow or feed stock, he would only follow those who did with a loaded gun, but he declined. "I reckon I'll stick to plowing," he said, absolutely without humor. "I done already tried to use a gun one time too many.") his good name, his responsibility not only toward those who were responsible toward him but to himself, his own honor in the doing of what was asked of him, his pride in being able to do it, no matter what it was. He thought of this and listened to the man with the gun talking about escape and it seemed to him that, hanging there, being dragged violently along (It was here he said that he first noticed the goats' beards of moss in the trees, though it could have been there for several days so far as he knew. It just happened that he first noticed it here.) that he would simply burst.

"Can't you get it into your head that the last thing I want to do is run away?" he cried. "You can set there with that gun and watch me; I give you fair lief. All I want is to put this woman—"

"And I told you she could come aboard," the man with the gun said in his level voice. "But there ain't no room on no boat of mine for nobody hunting a sheriff in no kind of clothes, let alone a penitentiary suit."

"When he steps aboard, knock him in the head with the gun barrel," the man at the sweep said. "He's drunk."

"He ain't coming aboard," the man with the gun said. "He's crazy."

Then the woman spoke. She didn't move, leaning in the door, in a pair of faded and patched and filthy overalls like the two men: "Give them some grub and tell them to get out of here." She moved, she crossed the deck and looked down at the convict's companion with her cold sullen face. "How much more time have you got?"

"It wasn't due till next month," the woman in the boat said. "But I—" The woman in overalls turned to the man with the gun.

"Give them some grub," she said. But the man with the gun was still looking down at the woman in the boat.

"Come on," he said to the convict. "Put her aboard, and beat it."

"And what'll happen to you," the woman in overalls said, "when you try to turn her over to an officer. When you lay alongside a sheriff and the sheriff asks you who you are?" Still the man with the gun didn't even look at her. He hardly even shifted the gun across his arm as he struck the woman across the face with the back of his other hand, hard. "You son of a bitch," she said. Still the man with the gun did not even look at her.

"Well?" he said to the convict.

"Don't you see I can't?" the convict cried. "Can't you see that?"

Now, he said, he gave up. He was doomed. That is, he knew now that he had been doomed from the very start never to get rid of her, just as the ones who sent him out with the skiff knew that he never would actually give up; when he recognized one of the objects which the woman in overalls was hurling into the skiff to be a can of condensed milk, he believed it to be a presage, gratuitous and irrevocable as a death-notice over the telegraph, that he was not even to find a flat stationary surface in time for the child to be born on it. So he told how he held the skiff alongside the shanty-boat while the first tentative toying of the second wave made up beneath him, while the woman in overalls passed back and forth between house and rail, flinging the food— the hunk of salt meat, the ragged and filthy quilt, the scorched lumps of cold bread which she poured into the skiff from a heaped dishpan like so much garbage— while he clung to the strake against the mounting pull of the current, the new wave which for the moment he had forgotten because he was still trying to state the incredible simplicity of his desire and need until the man with the gun (the only one of the three who wore shoes) began to stamp at his hands, he snatching his hands away one at a time to avoid the heavy shoes, then grasping the rail again until the man with the gun kicked at his face, he flinging himself sideways to avoid the shoe and so breaking his hold on the rail, his weight canting the skiff off at a tangent on the increasing current so that it began to leave the shanty boat behind and he paddling again now, violently, as a man hurries toward the precipice for which he knows at last he is doomed, looking back at the other boat, the three faces sullen, derisive, and grim and rapidly diminishing across the widening water and at last, apoplectic, suffocating with the intolerable fact not that he had been refused but that he had been refused so little, had wanted so little, asked for so little, yet there had been demanded of him in return the one price out of all breath which (they must have known) if he could have paid it, he would not have been where he was, asking what he asked, raising the paddle and shaking it and screaming curses back at them even after the shotgun flashed and the charge went scuttering past along the water to one side.

So he hung there, he said, shaking the paddle and howling, when suddenly he remembered that other wave, the second wall of water full of houses and dead mules building up behind him back in the swamp. So he quit yelling then and went back to paddling. He was not trying to outrun it. He just knew from experience that when it overtook him, he would have to travel in the same direction it was moving in anyway, whether he wanted to or not, and when it did overtake him, he would begin to move too fast to stop, no matter what places he might come to where he could leave the woman, land her in time. Time: that was his itch now, so his only chance was to stay ahead of it as long as he could and hope to reach something before it struck. So he went on, driving the skiff with muscles which had been too tired so long they had quit feeling it, as when a man has had bad luck for so long that he ceases to believe it is even bad, let alone luck. Even when he ate —the scorched lumps the size of baseballs and the weight and durability of cannel coal even after having lain in the skiff's bilge where the shanty boat woman had thrown them—the iron-like lead-heavy objects which no man would have called bread outside of the crusted and scorched pan in which they had cooked—it was with one hand, begrudging even that from the paddle.

He tried to tell that too—that day while the skiff fled on among the bearded trees while every now and then small quiet tentative exploratory feelers would come up from the wave behind and toy for a moment at the skiff, light and curious, then go on with a faint hissing sighing, almost a chuckling, sound, the skiff going on, driving on with nothing to see but trees and water and solitude: until after a while it no longer seemed to him that he was trying to put space and distance behind him or shorten space and distance ahead but that both he and the wave were now hanging suspended simultaneous and unprogressing in pure time, upon a dreamy desolation in which he paddled on not from any hope even to reach anything at all but merely to keep intact what little of distance the length of the skiff provided between himself and the inert and inescapable mass of female meat before him; then night and the skiff rushing on, fast since any speed over anything unknown and invisible is too fast, with nothing before him, and behind him the outrageous idea of a volume of moving water toppling forward, its crest frothed and shredded like fangs, and then dawn again (another of those dreamlike alterations day to dark then back to day again with that quality truncated, anachronic, and unreal as the waxing

and waning of lights in a theatre scene) and the skiff
emerging now with the woman no longer supine beneath the shrunken soaked private's coat but sitting bolt
upright, gripping the gunwales with both hands, her
eyes closed and her lower lip caught between her teeth
and he driving the splintered board furiously now, glaring at her out of his wild swollen sleepless face and
crying, croaking, "Hold on! For God's sake hold on!"

"I'm trying to," she said. "But hurry! Hurry!" He
told it, the unbelievable: hurry, hasten: the man falling
from a cliff being told to catch onto something and save
himself; the very telling of it emerging shadowy and
burlesque, ludicrous, comic, and mad, from the ague of
unbearable forgetting with a quality more dreamily
furious than any fable behind proscenium lights:

He was in a basin now— "A basin?" the plump convict said. "That's what you wash in."

"All right," the tall one said, harshly, above his hands.
"I did." With a supreme effort he stilled them long
enough to release the two bits of cigarette paper and
watched them waft in light fluttering indecision to the
floor between his feet, holding his hands motionless
even for a moment longer—a basin, a broad peaceful
yellow sea which had an abruptly and curiously ordered
air, giving him, even at that moment, the impression
that it was accustomed to water even if not total sub-
mersion; he even remembered the name of it, told to
him two or three weeks later by someone: Atchafalaya—

"Louisiana?" the plump convict said. "You mean you
were clean out of Mississippi? Hell fire." He stared at
the tall one. "Shucks," he said. "That ain't but just
across from Vicksburg."

"They never named any Vicksburg across from where
I was," the tall one said. "It was Baton Rouge they

named." And now he began to talk about a town, a little neat white portrait town nestling among enormous very green trees, appearing suddenly in the telling as it probably appeared in actuality, abrupt and airy and mirage-like and incredibly serene before him, behind a scattering of boats moored to a line of freight cars standing flush to the doors in water. And now he tried to tell that too: how he stood waist-deep in water for a moment looking back and down at the skiff in which the woman half lay, her eyes still closed, her knuckles white on the gunwales and a tiny thread of blood creeping down her chin from her chewed lip, and he looking down at her in a kind of furious desperation.

"How far will I have to walk?" she said.

"I don't know, I tell you!" he cried. "But it's land somewhere yonder! It's land, houses."

"If I try to move, it won't even be born inside a boat," she said. "You'll have to get closer."

"Yes," he cried, wild, desperate, incredulous. "Wait. I'll go and surrender, then they will have—" He didn't finish, wait to finish; he told that too: himself splashing, stumbling, trying to run, sobbing and gasping; now he saw it—another loading platform standing above the yellow flood, the khaki figures on it as before, identical, the same; he said how the intervening days since that first innocent morning telescoped, vanished as if they had never been, the two contiguous succeeding instants (succeeding? simultaneous) and he transported across no intervening space but merely turned in his own footsteps, plunging, splashing, his arms raised, croaking harshly. He heard the startled shout, "There's one of them!", the command, the clash of equipment, the alarmed cry: "There he goes! There he goes!"

"Yes!" he cried, running, plunging, "here I am! Here! Here!" running on, into the first scattered volley, stop-

ping among the bullets, waving his arms, shrieking, "I
want to surrender! I want to surrender!" watching not
in terror but in amazed and absolutely unbearable outrage as a squatting clump of the khaki figures parted
and he saw the machine gun, the blunt thick muzzle
slant and drop and probe toward him and he still
screaming in his hoarse crow's voice, "I want to surrender! Can't you hear me?" continuing to scream even
as he whirled and plunged splashing, ducking, went
completely under and heard the bullets going thuck-
thuck-thuck on the water above him and he scrabbling
still on the bottom, still trying to scream even before he
regained his feet and still all submerged save his plunging unmistakable buttocks, the outraged screaming
bubbling from his mouth and about his face since he
merely wanted to surrender. Then he was comparatively
screened, out of range, though not for long. That is
(he didn't tell how nor where) there was a moment in
which he paused, breathed for a second before running
again, the course back to the skiff open for the time
being though he could still hear the shouts behind him
and now and then a shot, and he panting, sobbing, a
long savage tear in the flesh of one hand, got when and
how he did not know, and he wasting precious breath,
speaking to no one now any more than the scream of the
dying rabbit is addressed to any mortal ear but rather
an indictment of all breath and its folly and suffering,
its infinite capacity for folly and pain, which seems to
be its only immortality: "All in the world I want is just
to surrender."

He returned to the skiff and got in and took up his
splintered plank. And now when he told this, despite
the fury of element which climaxed it, it (the telling)
became quite simple; he now even creased another
cigarette paper between fingers which did not tremble

at all and filled the paper from the tobacco sack without spilling a flake, as though he had passed from the machine-gun's barrage into a bourne beyond any more amazement: so that the subsequent part of his narrative seemed to reach his listeners as though from beyond a sheet of slightly milky though still transparent glass, as something not heard but seen—a series of shadows, edgeless yet distinct, and smoothly flowing, logical and unfrantic and making no sound: They were in the skiff, in the center of the broad placid trough which had no boundaries and down which the tiny forlorn skiff flew to the irresistible coercion of a current going once more he knew not where, the neat small liveoak-bowered towns unattainable and miragelike and apparently attached to nothing upon the airy and unchanging horizon. He did not believe them, they did not matter, he was doomed; they were less than the figments of smoke or of delirium, and he driving his unceasing paddle without destination or even hope now, looking now and then at the woman sitting with her knees drawn up and locked and her entire body one terrific clench while the threads of bloody saliva crept from her teeth-clenched lower lip. He was going nowhere and fleeing from nothing, he merely continued to paddle because he had paddled so long now that he believed if he stopped his muscles would scream in agony. So when it happened he was not surprised. He heard the sound which he knew well (he had heard it but once before, true enough, but no man needed hear it but once) and he had been expecting it; he looked back, still driving the paddle, and saw it, curled, crested with its strawlike flotsam of trees and debris and dead beasts and he glared over his shoulder at it for a full minute out of that attenuation far beyond the point of outragement where even suffering, the capability of being further affronted, had ceased, from which he now contemplated with savage and invulnerable curiosity the further extent to which his now anesthetized nerves could bear, what next could be invented for them to bear, until the wave actually began to rear above his head into its thunderous climax. Then only did he turn his head. His stroke did not falter, it neither slowed nor increased; still paddling with that spent hypnotic steadiness, he saw the swimming deer. He did not know what it was nor that he had altered the skiff's course to follow it, he just watched the swimming head before him as the wave boiled down and the skiff rose bodily in the old familiar fashion on a welter of tossing trees and houses and bridges and fences, he still paddling even while the paddle found no purchase save air and still paddled even as he and the deer shot forward side by side at arm's length, he watching the deer now, watching the deer begin to rise out of the water bodily until it was actually running along upon the surface, rising still, soaring clear of the water altogether, vanishing upward in a dying crescendo of splashings and snapping branches, its damp scut flashing upward, the entire animal vanishing upward as smoke vanishes. And now the skiff struck and canted and he was out of it too, standing knee-deep, springing out and falling to his knees, scrambling up, glaring after the vanished deer. "Land!" he croaked. "Land! Hold on! Just hold on!" He caught the woman beneath the arms, dragging her out of the boat, plunging and panting after the vanished deer. Now earth actually appeared—an acclivity smooth and swift and steep, bizarre, solid, and unbelievable; an Indian mound, and he plunging at the muddy slope, slipping back, the woman struggling in his muddy hands.

"Let me down!" she cried. "Let me down!" But he

held her, panting, sobbing, and rushed again at the muddy slope; he had almost reached the flat crest with his now violently unmanageable burden when a stick under his foot gathered itself with thick convulsive speed. *It was a snake,* he thought as his feet fled beneath him and with the indubitable last of his strength he half pushed and half flung the woman up the bank as he shot feet first and face down back into that medium upon which he had lived for more days and nights than he could remember and from which he himself had never completely emerged, as if his own failed and spent flesh were attempting to carry out his furious unflagging will for severance at any price, even that of drowning, from the burden with which, unwitting and without choice, he had been doomed. Later it seemed to him that he had carried back beneath the surface with him the sound of the infant's first mewling cry.

I V

When the woman asked him if he had a knife, standing there in the streaming bedticking garments which had got him shot at, the second time by a machine gun, on the two occasions when he had seen any human life after leaving the levee four days ago, the convict felt exactly as he had in the fleeing skiff when the woman suggested that they had better hurry. He felt the same outrageous affronting of a condition purely moral, the same raging impotence to find any answer to it; so that, standing above her, spent suffocating and inarticulate, it was a full minute before he comprehended that she was now crying, "The can! The can in the boat!" He did not anticipate what she could want with it; he did not even wonder nor stop to ask. He turned running; this time he thought, *It's another moccasin* as the thick

body truncated in that awkward reflex which had nothing of alarm in it but only alertness, he not even shifting his stride though he knew his running foot would
fall within a yard of the flat head. The bow of the skiff
was well up the slope now where the wave had set it
and there was another snake just crawling over the
stern into it and as he stooped for the bailing can he
saw something else swimming toward the mound, he
didn't know what—a head, a face at the apex of a vee
of ripples. He snatched up the can; by pure juxtaposition of it and water he scooped it full, already turning.
He saw the deer again, or another one. That is, he saw
a deer—a side glance, the light smoke-colored phantom
in a cypress vista then gone, vanished, he not pausing to
look after it, galloping back to the woman and kneeling
with the can to her lips until she told him better.

It had contained a pint of beans or tomatoes, something, hermetically sealed and opened by four blows of
an axe heel, the metal flap turned back, the jagged
edges razor-sharp. She told him how, and he used this
in lieu of a knife, he removed one of his shoelaces and
cut it in two with the sharp tin. Then she wanted warm
water—"If I just had a little hot water," she said in a
weak serene voice without particular hope; only when
he thought of matches it was again a good deal like
when she had asked him if he had a knife, until she
fumbled in the pocket of the shrunken tunic (it had a
darker double vee on one cuff and a darker blotch on
the shoulder where service stripes and a divisional em-
blem had been ripped off but this meant nothing to
him) and produced a match-box contrived by telescop-
ing two shotgun shells. So he drew her back a little from
the water and went to hunt wood dry enough to burn,
thinking this time, *It's just another snake,* only, he said,
he should have thought *ten thousand other snakes:* and

now he knew it was not the same deer because he saw three at one time, does or bucks, he did not know which since they were all antlerless in May, and besides he had never seen one of any kind anywhere before except on a Christmas card; and then the rabbit, drowned, dead anyway, already torn open, the bird, the hawk, standing upon it—the erected crest, the hard vicious patrician nose, the intolerant omnivorous yellow eye— and he kicking at it, kicking it lurching and broadwinged into the actual air.

When he returned with the wood and the dead rabbit, the baby, wrapped in the tunic, lay wedged between two cypress-knees and the woman was not in sight, though while the convict knelt in the mud, blowing and nursing his meagre flame, she came slowly and weakly from the direction of the water. Then, the water heated at last and there, produced from somewhere he was never to know, she herself perhaps never to know until the need comes, no woman perhaps ever to know, only no woman will even wonder, that square of something somewhere between sackcloth and silk—squatting, his own wet garments steaming in the fire's heat, he watched her bathe the child with a savage curiosity and interest that became amazed unbelief, so that at last he stood above them both, looking down at the tiny terracotta colored creature resembling nothing, and thought, *And this is all. This is what severed me violently from all I ever knew and did not wish to leave and cast me upon a medium I was born to fear, to fetch up at last in a place I never saw before and where I do not even know where I am.*

Then he returned to the water and refilled the bailing can. It was drawing toward sunset now (or what would have been sunset save for the high prevailing overcast) of this day whose beginning he could not even remember. When he returned to where the fire burned in the interlaced gloom of the cypresses, even after this short absence, evening had definitely come, as though darkness too had taken refuge upon that quarter-acre mound, that earthen Ark out of Genesis, that dim wet cypress-choked life-teeming constricted desolation, in what direction and how far from what and where he had no more idea than of the day of the month, and had now with the setting of the sun crept forth again to spread upon the waters. He stewed the rabbit in sections while the fire burned redder and redder in the darkness where the shy wild eyes of small animals—once the tall mild almost plate-sized stare of one of the deer—glowed and vanished and glowed again, the broth hot and rank after the four days; he seemed to hear the roar of his own saliva as he watched the woman sip the first canful. Then he drank too; they ate the other fragments which had been charring and scorching on willow twigs; it was full night now. "You and him better sleep in the boat," the convict said. "We want to get an early start tomorrow." He shoved the bow of the skiff off the land so it would lie level, he lengthened the painter with a piece of grapevine and returned to the fire and tied the grapevine about his wrist and lay down. It was mud he lay upon, but it was solid underneath, it was earth, it did not move; if you fell upon it you broke your bones against its incontrovertible passivity sometimes, but it did not accept you substanceless and enveloping and suffocating, down and down and down; it was hard at times to drive a plow through, it sent you spent, weary, and cursing its light-long insatiable demands, back to your bunk at sunset at times, but it did not snatch you violently out of all familiar knowing and sweep you, thrall and impotent, for days against any returning. *I don't know where I am and I don't reckon I know the way back to where I want to go,* he thought. *But at least the boat has stopped long enough to give me a chance to turn it around.*

He waked at dawn, the light faint, the sky jonquil-colored; the day would be fine. The fire had burned out; on the opposite side of the cold ashes lay three snakes motionless and parallel as underscoring, and in the swiftly making light others seemed to materialize: earth which an instant before had been mere earth broke up into motionless coils and loops, branches which a moment before had been mere branches now become immobile ophidian festoons, even as the convict stood thinking about food, about something hot before they started. But he decided against this, against wasting this much time, since there still remained in the skiff quite a few of the rocklike objects which the shanty woman had flung into it, besides (thinking this) no matter how fast nor successfully he hunted, he would never be able to lay up enough food to get them back to where they wanted to go. So he returned to the skiff, paying himself back to it by his vine-spliced painter, back to the water on which a low mist, thick as cotton batting (though apparently not very tall, deep), lay, into which the stern of the skiff was already beginning to disappear, although it lay with its prow almost touching the mound. The woman waked, stirred. "We fixing to start now?" she said.

"Yah," the convict said. "You ain't aiming to have another one this morning, are you?" He got in and shoved the skiff clear of the land, which immediately began to dissolve into the mist. "Hand me the oar," he said over his shoulder, not turning yet.

"The oar?"

He turned his head. "The oar. You're laying on it."

But she was not, and for an instant during which the mound, the island continued to fade slowly into the mist which seemed to enclose the skiff in weightless and impalpable wool like a precious or fragile bauble or jewel, the convict squatted not in dismay but in that frantic and astonished outrage of a man who, having just escaped a falling safe, is struck by the following two-ounce paper weight which was sitting on it: this the more unbearable because he knew that never in his life had he less time to give way to it. He did not hesitate. Grasping the grapevine end he sprang into the water, vanishing in the violent action of climbing and reappeared still climbing and (who had never learned to swim) plunged and threshed on toward the almost-vanished mound, moving through the water then upon it as the deer had done yesterday and scrabbled up the muddy slope and lay gasping and panting, still clutching the grapevine end.

Now the first thing he did was to choose what he believed to be the most suitable tree (for an instant in which he knew he was insane he thought of trying to saw it down with the flange of the bailing can) and build a fire against the butt of it. Then he went to seek food. He spent the next six days seeking it while the tree burned through and fell and burned through again at the proper length and he nursing little constant cunning flames along the flanks of the log to make it paddle-shaped, nursing them at night too while the woman and baby (it was eating, nursing now, he turning his back or even returning into the woods each time she prepared to open the faded tunic) slept in the skiff. He learned to watch for stooping hawks and so found more rabbits, and twice possums; they ate some drowned fish which gave them both a rash and then a violent flux and one snake which the woman thought was turtle and which did them no harm, and one night it rained and he got up and dragged brush, shaking the snakes (he no longer thought, *It ain't nothing but another moccasin*, he just stepped aside for them as they, when there was time, telescoped sullenly aside for him) out of it with the old former feeling of personal invulnerability and built a shelter and the rain stopped at once and did not recommence and the woman went back to the skiff.

Then one night—the slow tedious charring log was almost a paddle now—one night and he was in bed, in his bed in the bunkhouse, and it was cold, he was trying to pull the covers up only his mule wouldn't let him, prodding and bumping heavily at him, trying to get into the narrow bed with him, and now the bed was cold too and wet and he was trying to get out of it only the mule would not let him, holding him by his belt in its teeth, jerking and bumping him back into the cold wet bed and, leaning, gave him a long swipe across the face with its cold limber musculated tongue, and he waked to no fire, no coal even beneath where the almost-finished paddle had been charring, and something else prolonged and coldly limber passed swiftly across his body where he lay in four inches of water while the nose of the skiff alternately tugged at the grapevine tied about his waist and bumped and shoved him back into the water again. Then something else came up and began to nudge at his ankle (the log, the oar, it was) even as he groped frantically for the skiff, hearing the swift rustling going to and fro inside the hull as the woman began to thrash about and scream. "Rats!" she cried. "It's full of rats!"

"Lay still!" he cried. "It's just snakes. Can't you hold still long enough for me to find the boat?" Then he found it, he got into it with the unfinished paddle; again the thick muscular body convulsed under his foot; it did not strike; he would not have cared, glaring astern where he could see a little—the faint outer luminosity of the open water. He poled toward it, thrusting aside the snake-looped branches, the bottom of the skiff resounding faintly to thick solid plops, the woman shrieking steadily. Then the skiff was clear of the trees, the mound, and now he could feel the bodies whipping about his ankles and hear the rasp of them as they went over the gunwale. He drew the log in and scooped it forward along the bottom of the boat and up and out; against the pallid water he could see three more of them in lashing convolutions before they vanished. "Shut up!" he cried. "Hush! I wish I was a snake so I could get out too!"

When once more the pale and heatless wafer disc of the early sun stared down at the skiff (whether they were moving or not the convict did not know) in its nimbus of fine cotton batting, the convict was hearing again that sound which he had heard twice before and would never forget—that sound of deliberate and irresistible and monstrously disturbed water. But this time he could not tell from what direction it came. It seemed to be everywhere, waxing and fading; it was like a phantom behind the mist, at one instant miles away, the next on the point of overwhelming the skiff within the next second; suddenly, in the instant he would believe (his whole weary body would spring and scream) that he was about to drive the skiff point-blank into it and with the unfinished paddle of the color and texture of sooty bricks, like something gnawed out of an old chimney by beavers and weighing twenty-five pounds, he would whirl the skiff frantically and find the sound dead ahead of him again. Then something bellowed tremendously above his head, he heard human voices, a bell jangled and the sound ceased and the mist vanished as when you draw your hand across a frosted pane, and the skiff now lay upon a sunny glitter of brown water flank to flank with, and about thirty yards away from, a steamboat. The decks were crowded and packed with men, women, and children sitting or standing beside and among a homely conglomeration of hurried furniture, who looked mournfully and silently down into the skiff while the convict and the man with a megaphone in the pilot house talked to each other in alternate puny shouts and roars above the chuffing of the reversed engines:

"What in hell are you trying to do? Commit suicide?"

"Which is the way to Vicksburg?"

"Vicksburg? Vicksburg? Lay alongside and come aboard."

"Will you take the boat too?"

"Boat? Boat?" Now the megaphone cursed, the roaring waves of blasphemy and biological supposition empty cavernous and bodiless in turn, as if the water, the air, the mist had spoken it, roaring the words then taking them back to itself and no harm done, no scar, no insult left anywhere. "If I took aboard every floating sardine can you sonabitchin mushrats want me to I wouldn't even have room forrard for a leadsman. Come aboard! Do you expect me to hang here on stern engines till hell freezes?"

"I ain't coming without the boat," the convict said. Now another voice spoke, so calm and mild and sensible that for a moment it sounded more foreign and out of place than even the megaphone's bellowing and bodiless profanity:

"Where is it you are trying to go?"

"I ain't trying," the convict said. "I'm going. Parchman." The man who had spoken last turned and appeared to converse with a third man in the pilot house. Then he looked down at the skiff again.

"Carnarvon?"

"What?" the convict said. "Parchman?"

"All right. We're going that way. We'll put you off where you can get home. Come aboard."

"The boat too?"

"Yes, yes. Come along. We're burning coal just to talk to you." So the convict came alongside then and watched them help the woman and baby over the rail and he came aboard himself, though he still held to the end of the vine-spliced painter until the skiff was hoisted onto the boiler deck. "My God," the man, the gentle one, said, "is that what you have been using for a paddle?"

"Yah," the convict said. "I lost the plank."

"The plank," the mild man (the convict told how he seemed to whisper it), "the plank. Well. Come along and get something to eat. Your boat is all right now."

"I reckon I'll wait here," the convict said. Because now, he told them, he began to notice for the first time that the other people, the other refugees who crowded the deck, who had gathered in a quiet circle about the upturned skiff on which he and the woman sat, the grapevine painter wrapped several times about his wrist and clutched in his hand, staring at him and the woman with queer hot mournful intensity, were not white people—

"You mean niggers?" the plump convict said.

"No. Not Americans."

"Not Americans? You was clean out of *America* even?"

"I don't know," the tall one said. "They called it Atchafalaya."—Because after a while he said, "What?" to the man and the man did it again, gobble-gobble—

"Gobble-gobble?" the plump convict said.

"That's the way they talked," the tall one said. "Gobble-gobble, whang, caw-caw-to-to."—And he sat there and watched them gobbling at one another and then looking at him again, then they fell back and the mild man (he wore a Red-Cross brassard) entered, followed by a waiter with a tray of food. The mild man carried two glasses of whiskey.

"Drink this," the mild man said. "This will warm you." The woman took hers and drank it but the convict told how he looked at his and thought, *I ain't tasted whiskey in seven years*. He had not tasted it but once before that; it was at the still itself back in a pine hollow; he was seventeen, he had gone there with four companions, two of whom were grown men, one of twenty-two or -three, the other about forty; he remembered it. That is, he remembered perhaps a third of that evening—a fierce turmoil in the hell-colored firelight, the shock and shock of blows about his head (and likewise of his own fists on other hard bone), then the waking to a splitting and blinding sun in a place, a cowshed, he had never seen before and which later turned out to be twenty miles from his home. He said he thought of this and he looked about at the faces watching him and he said,

"I reckon not."

"Come, come," the mild man said. "Drink it."

"I don't want it."

"Nonsense," the mild man said. "I'm a doctor. Here. Then you can eat." So he took the glass and even then he hesitated but again the mild man said, "Come along, down with it; you're still holding us up," in that voice still calm and sensible but a little sharp too—the voice of a man who could keep calm and affable because he wasn't used to being crossed—and he drank the whiskey and even in the second between the sweet full fire in his belly and when it began to happen he was trying to say, "I tried to tell you! I tried to!" But it was too late now in the pallid sun-glare of the tenth day of terror and hopelessness and despair and impotence and rage and outrage and it was himself and the mule, his mule (they had let him name it—John Henry) which no man save he had plowed for five years now and whose ways and habits he knew and respected and who knew his ways and habits so well that each of them could anticipate the other's very movements and intentions; it was himself and the mule, the little gobbling faces flying before them, the familiar hard skull-bones shocking against his fists, his voice shouting, "Come on, John Henry! Plow them down! Gobble them down, boy!" even as the bright hot red wave turned back, meeting it joyously, happily, lifted, poised, then hurling through space, triumphant and yelling, then again the old shocking blow at the back of his head: he lay on the deck, flat on his back and pinned arm and leg and cold sober again, his nostrils gushing again, the mild man stooping over him with behind the thin rimless glasses the coldest eyes the convict had ever seen—eyes which the convict said were not looking at him but at the gushing blood with nothing in the world in them but complete impersonal interest.

"Good man," the mild man said. "Plenty of life in the old carcass yet, eh? Plenty of good red blood too. Did anyone ever suggest to you that you were hemophilic?"

—"What?" the plump convict said. "Hemophilic? You know what that means?" The tall convict had his cigarette going now, his body jackknifed backward into the coffinlike space between the upper and lower bunks, lean, clean, motionless, the blue smoke wreathing across his lean dark aquiline shaven face. "That's a calf that's a bull and a cow at the same time."

"No, it ain't," a third convict said. "It's a calf or a colt that ain't neither one."

"Hell fire," the plump one said. "He's got to be one or the other to keep from drounding." He had never ceased to look at the tall one in the bunk; now he spoke to him again: "You let him call you that?"—The tall one had done so. He did not answer the doctor (this was where he stopped thinking of him as the mild man) at all. He could not move either, though he felt fine, he felt better than he had in ten days. So they helped him to his feet and steadied him over and lowered him onto the upturned skiff beside the woman, where he sat bent forward, elbows on knees in the immemorial attitude, watching his own bright crimson staining the mud-trodden deck, until the doctor's clean clipped hand appeared under his nose with a phial.

"Smell," the doctor said. "Deep." The convict inhaled, the sharp ammoniac sensation burned up his nostrils and into his throat. "Again," the doctor said. The convict inhaled obediently. This time he choked and spat a gout of blood, his nose now had no more feeling than a toenail, other than it felt about the size of a ten-inch shovel, and as cold.

"I ask you to excuse me," he said. "I never meant—"

"Why?" the doctor said. "You put up as pretty a scrap against forty or fifty men as I ever saw. You lasted a good two seconds. Now you can eat something. Or do you think that will send you haywire again?"

They both ate, sitting on the skiff, the gobbling faces no longer watching them now, the convict gnawing slowly and painfully at the thick sandwich, hunched, his face laid sideways to the food and parallel to the earth as a dog chews; the steamboat went on. At noon there were bowls of hot soup and bread and more coffee; they ate this too, sitting side by side on the skiff, the grape-

vine still wrapped about the convict's wrist. The baby
waked and nursed and slept again and they talked
quietly:

"Was it Parchman he said he was going to take us?"

"That's where I told him I wanted to go."

"It never sounded exactly like Parchman to me. It
sounded like he said something else." The convict had
thought that too. He had been thinking about that fairly
soberly ever since they boarded the steamboat and soberly indeed ever since he had remarked the nature of
the other passengers, those men and women definitely a
little shorter than he and with skin a little different in
pigmentation from any sunburn, even though the eyes
were sometimes blue or gray, who talked to one another in a tongue he had never heard before and who
apparently did not understand his own, people the like
of whom he had never seen about Parchman nor anywhere else and whom he did not believe were going
there or beyond there either. But after his hill-billy
country fashion and kind he would not ask, because, to
his raising, asking information was asking a favor and
you did not ask favors of strangers; if they offered them
perhaps you accepted and you expressed gratitude almost tediously recapitulant, but you did not ask. So he
would watch and wait, as he had done before, and do
or try to do to the best of his ability what the best of his
judgment dictated.

So he waited, and in midafternoon the steamboat
chuffed and thrust through a willow-choked gorge and
emerged from it, and now the convict knew it was the
River. He could believe it now—the tremendous reach,
yellow and sleepy in the afternoon—"Because it's too
big," he told them soberly. "Ain't no flood in the world
big enough to make it do more than stand a little higher
so it can look back and see just where the flea is, just

exactly where to scratch. It's the little ones, the little piddling creeks, that run backward one day and forward the next and come busting down on a man full of dead mules and hen houses."—and the steamboat moving up this now (*like a ant crossing a plate,* the convict thought, sitting beside the woman on the upturned skiff, the baby nursing again, apparently looking too out across the water where, a mile away on either hand, the twin lines of levee resembled parallel unbroken floating thread) and then it was nearing sunset and he began to hear, to notice, the voices of the doctor and of the man who had first bawled at him through the megaphone now bawling again from the pilot house overhead:

"Stop? Stop? Am I running a street car?"

"Stop for the novelty then," the doctor's pleasant voice said. "I don't know how many trips back and forth you have made in yonder nor how many of what you call mushrats you have fetched out. But this is the first time you ever had two people—no, three—who not only knew the name of some place they wished to go to but were actually trying to go there." So the convict waited while the sun slanted more and more and the steamboat-ant crawled steadily on across its vacant and gigantic plate turning more and more to copper. But he did not ask, he just waited. *Maybe it was Carrollton he said,* he thought. *It begun with a C.* But he did not believe that either. He did not know where he was, but he did know that this was not anywhere near the Carrollton he remembered from that day seven years ago when, shackled wrist to wrist with the deputy sheriff, he had passed through it on the train—the slow spaced repeated shattering banging of trucks where two railroads crossed, a random scattering of white houses tranquil among trees on green hills lush with summer, a pointing spire, the finger of the hand of God. But there was no river there. *And you ain't never close to this river without knowing it,* he thought. *I don't care who you are nor where you have been all your life.* Then the head of the steamboat began to swing across the stream, its shadow swinging too, travelling long before it across the water, toward the vacant ridge of willow-massed earth empty of all life. There was nothing there at all, the convict could not even see either earth or water beyond it; it was as though the steamboat were about to crash slowly through the thin low frail willow barrier and embark into space, or lacking this, slow and back and fill and disembark him into space, granted it was about to disembark him, granted this was that place which was not near Parchman and was not Carrollton either, even though it did begin with C. Then he turned his head and saw the doctor stooping over the woman, pushing the baby's eyelid up with his forefinger, peering at it.

"Who else was there when he came?" the doctor said.

"Nobody," the convict said.

"Did it all yourselves, eh?"

"Yes," the convict said. Now the doctor stood up and looked at the convict.

"This is Carnarvon," he said.

"Carnarvon?" the convict said. "That ain't—" Then he stopped, ceased. And now he told about that—the intent eyes as dispassionate as ice behind the rimless glasses, the clipped quick-tempered face that was not accustomed to being crossed or lied to either.—"Yes," the plump convict said. "That's what I was aiming to ask. Them clothes. Anybody would know them. How if this doctor was as smart as you claim he was—"

"I had slept in them for ten nights, mostly in the mud," the tall one said. "I had been rowing since midnight with that sapling oar I had tried to burn out that I never had time to scrape the soot off. But it's being scared and worried and then scared and then worried again in clothes for days and days and days that changes the way they look. I don't mean just your pants." He did not laugh. "Your face too. That doctor knowed."

"All right," the plump one said. "Go on."—

"I know it," the doctor said. "I discovered that while you were lying on the deck yonder sobering up again. Now don't lie to me. I don't like lying. This boat is going to New Orleans."

"No," the convict said immediately, quietly, with absolute finality. He could hear them again—the thuck-thuck-thuck on the water where an instant before he had been. But he was not thinking of the bullets. He had forgotten them, forgiven them. He was thinking of himself crouching, sobbing, panting before running again—the voice, the indictment, the cry of final and irrevocable repudiation of the old primal faithless Manipulator of all the lust and folly and injustice: *All in the world I wanted was just to surrender;* thinking of it, remembering it but without heat now, without passion now and briefer than an epitaph: *No. I tried that once. They shot at me.*

"So you don't want to go to New Orleans. And you didn't exactly plan to go to Carnarvon. But you will take Carnarvon in preference to New Orleans." The convict said nothing. The doctor looked at him, the magnified pupils like the heads of two bridge nails. "What were you in for? Hit him harder than you thought, eh?"

"No. I tried to rob a train."

"Say that again." The convict said it again. "Well? Go on. You don't say that in the year 1927 and just stop, man." So the convict told it, dispassionately too

—about the magazines, the pistol which would not shoot, the mask and the dark lantern in which no draft had been arranged to keep the candle burning so that it died almost with the match but even then left the metal too hot to carry, won with subscriptions. *Only it ain't my eyes or my mouth either he's watching,* he thought. *It's like he is watching the way my hair grows on my head.* "I see," the doctor said. "But something went wrong. But you've had plenty of time to think about it since. To decide what was wrong, what you failed to do."

"Yes," the convict said. "I've thought about it a right smart since."

"So next time you are not going to make that mistake."

"I don't know," the convict said. "There ain't going to be a next time."

"Why? If you know what you did wrong, they won't catch you next time."

The convict looked at the doctor steadily. They looked at each other steadily; the two sets of eyes were not so different after all. "I reckon I see what you mean," the convict said presently. "I was eighteen then. I'm twenty-five now."

"Oh," the doctor said. Now (the convict tried to tell it) the doctor did not move, he just simply quit looking at the convict. He produced a pack of cheap cigarettes from his coat. "Smoke?" he said.

"I wouldn't care for none," the convict said.

"Quite," the doctor said in that affable clipped voice. He put the cigarettes away. "There has been conferred upon my race (the Medical race) also the power to bind and to loose, if not by Jehovah perhaps, certainly by the American Medical Association—on which incidentally, in this day of Our Lord, I would put my

money, at any odds, at any amount, at any time. I don't
know just how far out of bounds I am on this specific
occasion but I think we'll put it to the touch." He
cupped his hands to his mouth, toward the pilot house
overhead. "Captain!" he shouted. "We'll put these three
passengers ashore here." He turned to the convict again.
"Yes," he said, "I think I shall let your native State
lick its own vomit. Here." Again his hand emerged from
his pocket, this time with a bill in it.

"No," the convict said.

"Come, come; I don't like to be disputed either."

"No," the convict said. "I ain't got any way to pay it
back."

"Did I ask you to pay it back?"

"No," the convict said. "I never asked to borrow it
either."

So once more he stood on dry land, who had already
been toyed with twice by that risible and concentrated
power of water, once more than should have fallen to
the lot of any one man, any one lifetime, yet for whom
there was reserved still another unbelievable recapitu-
lation, he and the woman standing on the empty levee,
the sleeping child wrapped in the faded tunic and the
grapevine painter still wrapped about the convict's
wrist, watching the steamboat back away and turn and
once more crawl onward up the platter-like reach of
vacant water burnished more and more to copper, its
trailing smoke roiling in slow copper-edged gouts, thinning out along the water, fading, stinking, away across
the vast serene desolation, the boat growing smaller and
smaller until it did not seem to crawl at all but to hang
stationary in the airy substanceless sunset, dissolving
into nothing like a pellet of floating mud.

Then he turned and for the first time looked about
him, behind him, recoiling, not through fear but through

pure reflex and not physically but the soul, the spirit,
that profound sober alert attentiveness of the hillman
who will not ask anything of strangers, not even information, thinking quietly, *No. This ain't Carrollton
neither.* Because he now looked down the almost perpendicular landward slope of the levee through sixty
feet of absolute space, upon a surface, a terrain flat as
a waffle and of the color of a waffle, or perhaps of the
summer coat of a claybank horse, and possessing that
same piled density of a rug or peltry, spreading away
without undulation yet with that curious appearance of
imponderable solidity like fluid, broken here and there
by thick humps of arsenical green which nevertheless
still seemed to possess no height and by writhen veins
of the color of ink which he began to suspect to be actual
water but with judgment reserved, with judgment still
reserved even when presently he was walking in it.
That's what he said, told: So they went on. He didn't
tell how he got the skiff singlehanded up the revetment
and across the crown and down the opposite sixty foot
drop, he just said he went on, in a swirling cloud of
mosquitoes like hot cinders, thrusting and plunging
through the saw-edged grass which grew taller than his
head and which whipped back at his arms and face like
limber knives, dragging by the vine-spliced painter the
skiff in which the woman sat, slogging and stumbling
knee-deep in something less of earth than water, along
one of those black winding channels less of water than
earth: and then (he was in the skiff too now, paddling
with the charred log, what footing there had been having given away beneath him without warning thirty
minutes ago, leaving only the air-filled bubble of his
jumperback ballooning lightly on the twilit water until
he rose to the surface and scrambled into the skiff)
the house, the cabin a little larger than a horse-box, of

cypress boards and an iron roof, rising on ten-foot stilts slender as spiders' legs, like a shabby and death-stricken (and probably poisonous) wading creature which had got that far into that flat waste and died with nothing nowhere in reach or sight to lie down upon, a pirogue tied to the foot of a crude ladder, a man standing in the open door holding a lantern (it was that dark now) above his head, gobbling down at them.

He told it—of the next eight or nine or ten days, he did not remember which, while the four of them —himself and the woman and baby and the little wiry man with rotting teeth and soft wild bright eyes like a rat or a chipmunk, whose language neither of them could understand—lived in the room and a half. He did not tell it that way, just as he apparently did not consider it worth the breath to tell how he had got the hundred-and-sixty-pound skiff singlehanded up and across and down the sixty-foot levee. He just said, "After a while we come to a house and we stayed there eight or nine days then they blew up the levee with dynamite so we had to leave." That was all. But he remembered it, but quietly now, with the cigar now, the good one the Warden had given him (though not lighted yet) in his peaceful and steadfast hand, remembering that first morning when he waked on the thin pallet beside his host (the woman and baby had the one bed) with the fierce sun already latticed through the warped rough planking of the wall, and stood on the rickety porch looking out upon that flat fecund waste, neither earth nor water, where even the senses doubted which was which, which rich and massy air and which mazy and impalpable vegetation, and thought quietly, *He must do something here to eat and live. But I don't know what. And until I can go on again, until I can find where I am and how to pass that town without them see-*

*ing me I will have to help him do it so we can eat and
live too, and I don't know what.* And he had a change
of clothing too, almost at once on that first morning,
not telling any more than he had about the skiff and
the levee how he had begged borrowed or bought from
the man whom he had not laid eyes on twelve hours
ago and with whom on the day he saw him for the last
time he still could exchange no word, the pair of dungaree pants which even the Cajun had discarded as no
longer wearable, filthy, buttonless, the legs slashed and
frayed into fringe like that on an 1890 hammock, in
which he stood naked from the waist up and holding out
to her the mud-caked and soot-stained jumper and over-
all when the woman waked on that first morning in the
crude bunk nailed into one corner and filled with dried
grass, saying, "Wash them. Good. I want all them stains
out. All of them."

"But the jumper," she said. "Ain't he got ere old
shirt too? That sun and them mosquitoes—" But he did
not even answer, and she said no more either, though
when he and the Cajun returned at dark the garments
were clean, stained a little still with the old mud and
soot, but clean, resembling again what they were supposed to resemble as (his arms and back already a
fiery red which would be blisters by tomorrow) he
spread the garments out and examined them and then
rolled them up carefully in a six-months-old New Orleans paper and thrust the bundle behind a rafter, where
it remained while day followed day and the blisters on
his back broke and suppurated and he would sit with
his face expressionless as a wooden mask beneath the
sweat while the Cajun doped his back with something
on a filthy rag from a filthy saucer, she still saying nothing since she too doubtless knew what his reason was,
not from that rapport of the wedded conferred upon her

by the two weeks during which they had jointly suffered all the crises, emotional social economic and even moral, which do not always occur even in the ordinary fifty married years (the old married: you have seen them, the electroplate reproductions, the thousand identical coupled faces with only a collarless stud or a fichu out of Louisa Alcott to denote the sex, looking in pairs like the winning braces of dogs after a field trial, out from among the packed columns of disaster and alarm and baseless assurance and hope and incredible insensitivity and insulation from tomorrow, propped by a thousand morning sugar bowls or coffee urns; or singly, rocking on porches or sitting in the sun beneath the tobacco-stained porticoes of a thousand county courthouses, as though with the death of the other having inherited a sort of rejuvenescence, immortality; relict, they take a new lease on breath and seem to live forever, as though that flesh which the old ceremony or ritual had morally purified and made legally one had actually become so with long tedious habit and he or she who entered the ground first took all of it with him or her, leaving only the old permanent enduring bone, free and tramelless)—not because of this but because she too had stemmed at some point from the same dim hill-bred Abraham.

So the bundle remained behind the rafter and day followed day while he and his partner (he was in partnership now with his host, hunting alligators on shares, on the halvers he called it—"Halvers?" the plump convict said. "How could you make a business agreement with a man you claim you couldn't even talk to?"

"I never had to talk to him," the tall one said. "Money ain't got but one language."—departed at dawn each day, at first together in the pirogue but later singly, the one in the pirogue and the other in the skiff, the one

with the battered and pitted rifle, the other with the
knife and a piece of knotted rope and a lightwood club
the size and weight and shape of a Thuringian mace,
stalking their pleistocene nightmares up and down
the secret inky channels which writhed the flat brass-
colored land. He remembered that too: that first morning when turning in the sunrise from the rickety platform he saw the hide nailed drying to the wall and
stopped dead, looking at it quietly, thinking quietly
and soberly, *So that's it. That's what he does in order to
eat and live,* knowing it was a hide, a skin, but from
what animal, by association, ratiocination, or even memory of any picture out of his dead youth, he did not
know, but knowing that it was the reason, the explanation, for the little lost spider-legged house (which had
already begun to die, to rot from the legs upward almost
before the roof was nailed on) set in that teeming and
myriad desolation, enclosed and lost within the furious
embrace of flowing mare earth and stallion sun, divining through pure rapport of kind for kind, hill-billy and
bayou-rat, the two one and identical because of the same
grudged dispensation and niggard fate of hard and unceasing travail not to gain future security, a balance in
the bank or even in a buried soda can for slothful and
easy old age, but just permission to endure and endure
to buy air to feel and sun to drink for each's little while,
thinking (the convict), *Well, anyway I am going to find
out what it is sooner than I expected to,* and did so,
re-entered the house where the woman was just waking
in the one sorry built-in straw-filled bunk which the
Cajun had surrendered to her, and ate the breakfast
(the rice, a semi-liquid mess violent with pepper and
mostly fish considerably high, the chicory-thickened
coffee) and, shirtless, followed the little scuttling bobbing bright-eyed rotten-toothed man down the crude

ladder and into the pirogue. He had never seen a
pirogue either and he believed that it would not remain
upright—not that it was light and precariously balanced
with its open side upward but that there was inherent in
the wood, the very log, some dynamic and unsleeping
natural law, almost will, which its present position outraged and violated—yet accepting this too as he had
the fact that that hide had belonged to something larger
than any calf or hog, and that anything which looked
like that on the outside would be more than likely to
have teeth and claws too, accepting this, squatting in
the pirogue, clutching both gunwales, rigidly immobile
as though he had an egg filled with nitroglycerin in his
mouth and scarcely breathing, thinking, *If that's it, then
I can do it too and even if he can't tell me how I reckon
I can watch him and find out.* And he did this too, he
remembered it, quietly even yet, thinking, *I thought
that was how to do it and I reckon I would still think
that even if I had it to do again now for the first time*—
the brazen day already fierce upon his naked back, the
crooked channel like a voluted thread of ink, the pirogue
moving steadily to the paddle which both entered and
left the water without a sound; then the sudden cessation of the paddle behind him and the fierce hissing
gobble of the Cajun at his back, and he squatting bate-
breathed and with that intense immobility of complete
sobriety of a blind man listening, while the frail wooden
shell stole on at the dying apex of its own parted water.
Afterward he remembered the rifle too—the rust-pitted
single-shot weapon with a clumsily wired stock and a
muzzle you could have driven a whiskey cork into,
which the Cajun had brought into the boat—but not
now; now he just squatted, crouched, immobile, breathing with infinitesimal care, his sober unceasing gaze
going here and there constantly as he thought, *What?*

What? I not only don't know what I am looking for, I don't even know where to look for it. Then he felt the motion of the pirogue as the Cajun moved and then the tense gobbling hissing actually, hot rapid and repressed, against his neck and ear, and glancing downward saw projecting between his own arm and body from behind the Cajun's hand holding the knife, and glaring up again saw the flat thick spit of mud, which as he looked at it divided and became a thick mud-colored log which in turn seemed, still immobile, to leap suddenly against his retinae in three—no, four—dimensions: volume, solidity, shape, and another: not fear but pure and intense speculation and he looking at the scaled motionless shape, thinking not, *It looks dangerous* but *It looks big,* thinking, *Well, maybe a mule standing in a lot looks big to a man that never walked up to one with a halter before,* thinking, *Only if he could just tell me what to do it would save time,* the pirogue drawing nearer now, creeping now, with no ripple now even, and it seemed to him that he could even hear his companion's held breath, and he taking the knife from the other's hand now and not even thinking this since it was too fast, a flash; it was not a surrender, not a resignation, it was too calm, it was a part of him, he had drunk it with his mother's milk and lived with it all his life: *After all a man can't only do what he has to do, with what he has to do with, with what he has learned, to the best of his judgment. And I reckon a hog is still a hog, no matter what it looks like. So here goes,* sitting still for an instant longer until the bow of the pirogue grounded lighter than the falling of a leaf and stepped out of it and paused just for one instant while the words *It does look big* stood for just a second, unemphatic and trivial, somewhere where some fragment of his attention could see them and vanished, and stooped straddling, the knife driving even as he grasped the near foreleg, this all in the same instant when the lashing tail struck him a terrific blow upon the back. But the knife was home, he knew that even on his back in the mud, the weight of the thrashing beast longwise upon him, its ridged back clutched to his stomach, his arm about its throat, the hissing head clamped against his jaw, the furious tail lashing and flailing, the knife in his other hand probing for the life and finding it, the hot fierce gush: and now sitting beside the profound up-bellied carcass, his head again between his knees in the old attitude while his own blood freshened the other which drenched him, thinking, *It's my durn nose again.*

So he sat there, his head, his streaming face, bowed between his knees in an attitude not of dejection but profoundly bemused, contemplative, while the shrill voice of the Cajun seemed to buzz at him from an enormous distance; after a time he even looked up at the antic wiry figure bouncing hysterically about him, the face wild and grimacing, the voice gobbling and high; while the convict, holding his face carefully slanted so the blood would run free, looked at him with the cold intentness of a curator or custodian paused before one of his own glass cases, the Cajun threw up the rifle, cried "Boom-boom-boom!" flung it down and in pantomime re-enacted the recent scene then whirled his hands again, crying "Magnifique! Magnifique! Cent d'argent! mille d'argent! Tout l'argent sous le ciel de Dieu!" But the convict was already looking down again, cupping the coffee-colored water to his face, watching the constant bright carmine marble it, thinking, *It's a little late to be telling me that now,* and not even thinking this long because presently they were in the pirogue again, the convict squatting again with that unbreathing rigidity as though he were trying by holding his breath to decrease his very weight, the bloody skin in the bows before him and he looking at it, thinking, *And I can't even ask him how much my half will be.*

But this not for long either, because as he was to tell the plump convict later, money has but one language. He remembered that too (they were at home now, the skin spread on the platform, where for the woman's benefit now the Cajun once more went through the pantomime—the gun which was not used, the hand-to-hand battle; for the second time the invisible alligator was slain amid cries, the victor rose and found this time that not even the woman was watching him. She was looking at the once more swollen and inflamed face of the convict. "You mean it kicked you right in the face?" she said.

"Nah," the convict said harshly, savagely. "It never had to. I done seem to got to where if that boy was to shoot me in the tail with a bean blower my nose would bleed.")—remembered that too but he did not try to tell it. Perhaps he could not have—how two people who could not even talk to one another made an agreement which both not only understood but which each knew the other would hold true and protect (perhaps for this reason) better than any written and witnessed contract. They even discussed and agreed somehow that they should hunt separately, each in his own vessel, to double the chances of finding prey. But this was easy: the convict could almost understand the words in which the Cajun said, "You do not need me and the rifle; we will only hinder you, be in your way." And more than this, they even agreed about the second rifle: that there was someone, it did not matter who—friend, neighbor, perhaps one in business in that line—from whom they could rent a second rifle; in their two patois, the one bastard English, the other bastard French—the one volatile, with his wild bright eyes and his voluble mouth full of stumps of teeth, the other sober, almost grim, swollen-faced and with his naked back blistered and scoriated like so much beef—they discussed this, squatting on either side of the pegged-out hide like two members of a corporation facing each other across a mahogany board table, and decided against it, the convict deciding: "I reckon not," he said. "I reckon if I had knowed enough to wait to start out with a gun, I still would. But since I done already started out without one, I don't reckon I'll change." Because it was a question of the money in terms of time, days. (Strange to say, that was the one thing which the Cajun could not tell him: how much the half would be. But the convict knew it was half.) He had so little of them. He would have to move on soon, thinking (the convict), *All this durn foolishness will stop soon and I can get on back*, and then suddenly he found that he was thinking, *Will have to get on back*, and he became quite still and looked about at the rich strange desert which surrounded him, in which he was temporarily lost in peace and hope and into which the last seven years had sunk like so many trivial pebbles into a pool, leaving no ripple, and he thought quietly, with a kind of bemused amazement, *Yes. I reckon I had done forgot how good making money was. Being let to make it.*

So he used no gun, his the knotted rope and the Thuringian mace, and each morning he and the Cajun took their separate ways in the two boats to comb and creep the secret channels about the lost land from (or out of) which now and then still other pint-sized dark men appeared gobbling, abruptly and as though by magic from nowhere, in other hollowed logs, to follow quietly and watch him at his single combats—men named Tine and Toto and Theule, who were not much

larger than and looked a good deal like the muskrats
which the Cajun (the host did this too, supplied the
kitchen too; he expressed this too like the rifle business, in his own tongue, the convict comprehending this
too as though it had been English: "Do not concern
yourself about food, O Hercules. Catch alligators; I
will supply the pot.") took now and then from traps as
you take a shoat pig at need from a pen, and varied the
eternal rice and fish (the convict did tell this: how at
night, in the cabin, the door and one sashless window
battened against mosquitoes—a form, a ritual, as empty
as crossing the fingers or knocking on wood—sitting
beside the bug-swirled lantern on the plank table in a
temperature close to blood heat he would look down at
the swimming segment of meat on his sweating plate
and think, *It must be Theule. He was the fat one.*)—
day following day, unemphatic and identical, each like
the one before and the one which would follow while his
theoretical half of a sum to be reckoned in pennies,
dollars, or tens of dollars he did not know, mounted—
the mornings when he set forth to find waiting for him
like the *matador* his *aficionados* the small clump of
constant and deferential pirogues, the hard noons when
ringed half about by little motionless shells he fought
his solitary combats, the evenings, the return, the pirogues departing one by one into inlets and passages
which during the first few days he could not even distinguish, then the platform in the twilight where before
the static woman and the usually nursing infant and
the one or two bloody hides of the day's take the Cajun
would perform his ritualistic victorious pantomime before the two growing rows of knifemarks in one of the
boards of the wall; then the nights when, the woman
and child in the single bunk and the Cajun already
snoring on the pallet and the reeking lantern set close,

he (the convict) would sit on his naked heels, sweating
steadily, his face worn and calm, immersed and indomitable, his bowed back raw and savage as beef
beneath the suppurant old blisters and the fierce welts
of tails, and scrape and chip at the charred sapling
which was almost a paddle now, pausing now and then
to raise his head while the cloud of mosquitoes about it
whined and whirled, to stare at the wall before him
until after a while the crude boards themselves must
have dissolved away and let his blank unseeing gaze go
on and on unhampered, through the rich oblivious darkness, beyond it even perhaps, even perhaps beyond the
seven wasted years during which, so he had just realized, he had been permitted to toil but not to work.
Then he would retire himself, he would take a last look
at the rolled bundle behind the rafter and blow out the
lantern and lie down as he was beside his snoring partner, to lie sweating (on his stomach, he could not bear
the touch of anything to his back) in the whining oven-
like darkness filled with the forlorn bellowing of alligators, thinking not, *They never gave me time to learn*
but *I had forgot how good it is to work.*

Then on the tenth day it happened. It happened for
the third time. At first he refused to believe it, not that
he felt that now he had served out and discharged his
apprenticeship to mischance, had with the birth of the
child reached and crossed the crest of his Golgotha and
would now be, possibly not permitted so much as ig-
nored, to descend the opposite slope free-wheeling. That
was not his feeling at all. What he declined to accept
was the fact that a power, a force such as that which had
been consistent enough to concentrate upon him with
deadly undeviation for weeks, should with all the wealth
of cosmic violence and disaster to draw from, have been
so barren of invention and imagination, so lacking in

pride of artistry and craftmanship, as to repeat itself
twice. Once he had accepted, twice he even forgave, but
three times he simply declined to believe, particularly
when he was at last persuaded to realize that this third
time was to be instigated not by the blind potency of
volume and motion but by human direction and hands:
that now the cosmic joker, foiled twice, had stooped in
its vindictive concentration to the employing of dynamite.

He did not tell that. Doubtless he did not know himself how it happened, what was happening. But he
doubtless remembered it (but quietly above the thick,
rich-colored, pristine cigar in his clean, steady hand),
what he knew, divined of it. It would be evening, the
ninth evening, he and the woman on either side of their
host's empty place at the evening meal, he hearing the
voices from without but not ceasing to eat, still chewing
steadily, because it would be the same as though he
were seeing them anyway—the two or three or four
pirogues floating on the dark water beneath the platform
on which the host stood, the voices gobbling and jabber-
ing, incomprehensible and filled not with alarm and not
exactly with rage or ever perhaps absolute surprise but
rather just cacophony like those of disturbed marsh
fowl, he (the convict) not ceasing to chew but just
looking up quietly and maybe without a great deal of
interrogation or surprise too as the Cajun burst in and
stood before them, wild-faced, glaring, his blackened
teeth gaped against the inky orifice of his distended
mouth, watching (the convict) while the Cajun went
through his violent pantomime of violent evacuation,
ejection, scooping something invisible into his arms
and hurling it out and downward, and in the instant of
completing the gesture changing from instigator to
victim of that which he had set into pantomimic motion.

clasping his head and, bowed over and not otherwise moving, seeming to be swept on and away before it, crying "Boom! Boom! Boom!", the convict watching him, his jaw not chewing now, though for just that moment, thinking, *What? What is it he is trying to tell me?* thinking (this a flash too, since he could not have expressed this, and hence did not even know that he had ever thought it) that though his life had been cast here, circumscribed by this environment, accepted by this environment and accepting it in turn (and he had done well here—this quietly, soberly indeed, if he had been able to phrase it, think it instead of merely knowing it—better than he had ever done, who had not even known until now how good work, making money, could be), yet it was not his life, he still and would ever be no more than the water bug upon the surface of the pond, the plumbless and lurking depths of which he would never know, his only actual contact with it being the instants when on lonely and glaring mudspits under the pitiless sun and amphitheatred by his motionless and riveted semicircle of watching pirogues, he accepted the gambit which he had not elected, entered the lashing radius of the armed tail and beat at the thrashing and hissing head with his lightwood club, or this failing, embraced without hesitation the armored body itself with the frail web of flesh and bone in which he walked and lived, and sought the raging life with an eight-inch knife-blade.

So he and the woman merely watched the Cajun as he acted out the whole charade of eviction—the little wiry man, gesticulant and wild, his hysterical shadow leaping and falling upon the rough wall as he went through the pantomime of abandoning the cabin, gathering in pantomime his meagre belongings from the

walls and corners—objects which no other man would
want and only some power or force like blind water or
earthquake or fire would ever dispossess him of, the
woman watching too, her mouth slightly open upon a
mass of chewed food, on her face an expression of placid
astonishment, saying, "What? What's he saying?"

"I don't know," the convict said. "But I reckon if it's
something we ought to know we will find it out when it's
ready for us to." Because he was not alarmed, though
by now he had read the other's meaning plainly enough.
He's fixing to leave, he thought. *He's telling me to leave
too*—this later, after they had quitted the table and the
Cajun and the woman had gone to bed and the Cajun
had risen from the pallet and approached the convict
and once more went through the pantomime of abandoning the cabin, this time as one repeats a speech
which may have been misunderstood, tediously, carefully repetitional as to a child, seeming to hold the convict with one hand while he gestured, talked, with
the other, gesturing as though in single syllables, the
convict (squatting, the knife open and the almost-
finished paddle across his lap) watching, nodding his
head, even speaking in English: "Yah; sure. You bet.
I got you,"—trimming again at the paddle but no
faster, with no more haste than on any other night,
serene in his belief that when the time came for him to
know whatever it was, that would take care of itself,
having already and without even knowing it, even before the possibility, the question, ever arose, declined,
refused to accept even the thought of moving also,
thinking about the hides, thinking, *If there was just
some way he could tell me where to carry my share to
get the money,* but thinking this only for an instant
between two delicate strokes of the blade because al-

most at once he thought, *I reckon as long as I can catch them I won't have no big trouble finding whoever it is that will buy them.*

So the next morning he helped the Cajun load his few belongings—the pitted rifle, a small bundle of clothing (again they traded, who could not even converse with one another, this time the few cooking vessels, a few rusty traps by definite allocation, and something embracing and abstractional which included the stove, the crude bunk, the house or its occupancy—something— in exchange for one alligator hide)—into the pirogue, then, squatting and as two children divide sticks they divided the hides, separating them into two piles, one-for-me-and-one-for-you, two-for-me-and-two-for-you, and the Cajun loaded his share and shoved away from the platform and paused again, though this time he only put the paddle down, gathered something invisibly into his two hands and flung it violently upward, crying "Boom? Boom?" on a rising inflection, nodding violently to the half-naked and savagely scoriated man on the platform who stared with a sort of grim equability back at him and said, "Sure. Boom. Boom." Then the Cajun went on. He did not look back. They watched him, already paddling rapidly, or the woman did; the convict had already turned.

"Maybe he was trying to tell us to leave too," she said.

"Yah," the convict said. "I thought of that last night. Hand me the paddle." She fetched it to him—the sapling, the one he had been trimming at nightly, not quite finished yet though one more evening would do it (he had been using a spare one of the Cajun's. The other had offered to let him keep it, to include it perhaps with the stove and the bunk and the cabin's freehold, but the convict had declined. Perhaps he had computed it by volume against so much alligator hide, this weighed against one more evening with the tedious and careful blade) and he departed too with his knotted rope and mace, in the opposite direction, as though not only not content with refusing to quit the place he had been warned against, he must establish and affirm the irrevocable finality of his refusal by penetrating even further and deeper into it. And then, and without warning, the high fierce drowsing of his solitude gathered itself and struck at him.

He could not have told this if he had tried—this not yet midmorning and he going on, alone for the first time, no pirogue emerging anywhere to fall in behind him, but he had not expected this anyway, he knew that the others would have departed too; it was not this, it was his very solitude, his desolation which was now his alone and in full, since he had elected to remain; the sudden cessation of the paddle, the skiff shooting on for a moment yet while he thought, *What? What?* Then, *No. No. No,* as the silence and solitude and emptiness roared down upon him in a jeering bellow: and now reversed, the skiff spun violently on its heel, he the betrayed driving furiously back toward the platform where he knew it was already too late, that citadel where the very crux and dear breath of his life—the being allowed to work and earn money, that right and privilege which he believed he had earned to himself unaided, asking no favor of anyone or anything save the right to be let alone to pit his will and strength against the sauric protagonist of a land, a region, which he had not asked to be projected into—was being threatened, driving the home-made paddle in grim fury, coming in sight of the platform at last and seeing the motor launch lying alongside it with no surprise at all but actually with a kind of pleasure as though at a visible justification of his outrage and fear, the privilege of saying *I told you so*

to his own affronting, driving on toward it in a dreamlike state in which there seemed to be no progress at all,
in which, unimpeded and suffocating, he strove dreamily
with a weightless oar, with muscles without strength or
resiliency, at a medium without resistance, seeming to
watch the skiff creep infinitesimally across the sunny
water and up to the platform while a man in the launch
(there were five of them in all) gobbled at him in that
same tongue he had been hearing constantly now for
ten days and still knew no word of, just as a second man,
followed by the woman carrying the baby and dressed
again for departure in the faded tunic and the sunbonnet, emerged from the house, carrying (the man carried
several other things but the convict saw nothing else)
the paper-wrapped bundle which the convict had put
behind the rafter ten days ago and no other hand had
touched since, he (the convict) on the platform too
now, holding the skiff's painter in one hand and the
bludgeon-like paddle in the other, contriving to speak
to the woman at last in a voice dreamy and suffocating
and incredibly calm: "Take it away from him and carry
it back into the house."

"So you can talk English, can you?" the man in the
launch said. "Why didn't you come out like they told
you to last night?"

"Out?" the convict said. Again he even looked, glared,
at the man in the launch, contriving even again to control his voice: "I ain't got time to take trips. I'm busy,"
already turning to the woman again, his mouth already
open to repeat, as the dreamy buzzing voice of the man
came to him and he turning once more, in a terrific
and absolutely unbearable exasperation, crying, "Flood?
What flood? Hell a mile, it's done passed me twice
months ago! It's gone! What flood?" and then (he did
not think this in actual words either but he knew it,

suffered that flashing insight into his own character or destiny: how there was a peculiar quality of repetitiveness about his present fate, how not only the almost seminal crises recurred with a certain monotony, but the very physical circumstances followed a stupidly unimaginative pattern) the man in the launch said, "Take him," and he was on his feet for a few minutes yet, lashing and striking in panting fury, then once more on his back on hard unyielding planks while the four men swarmed over him in a fierce wave of hard bones and panting curses and at last the thin dry vicious snapping of handcuffs.

"Damn it, are you mad?" the man in the launch said. "Can't you understand they are going to dynamite that levee at noon today?—Come on," he said to the others. "Get him aboard. Let's get out of here."

"I want my hides and boat," the convict said.

"Damn your hides," the man in the launch said. "If they don't get that levee blowed pretty soon you can hunt plenty more of them on the capitol steps at Baton Rouge. And this is all the boat you will need and you can say your prayers about it."

"I ain't going without my boat," the convict said. He said it calmly and with complete finality, so calm, so final that for almost a minute nobody answered him, they just stood looking quietly down at him as he lay, half-naked, blistered and scarred, helpless and manacled hand and foot, on his back, delivering his ultimatum in a voice peaceful and quiet as that in which you talk to your bedfellow before going to sleep. Then the man in the launch moved; he spat quietly over the side and said in a voice as calm and quiet as the convict's:

"All right. Bring his boat." They helped the woman, carrying the baby and the paper-wrapped parcel, into the launch. Then they helped the convict to his feet and into the launch too, the shackles on his wrists and ankles clashing. "I'd unlock you if you'd promise to behave yourself," the man said. The convict did not answer this at all.

"I want to hold the rope," he said.

"The rope?"

"Yes," the convict said. "The rope." So they lowered him into the stern and gave him the end of the painter after it had passed the towing cleat, and they went on. The convict did not look back. But then, he did not look forward either, he lay half sprawled, his shackled legs before him, the end of the skiff's painter in one shackled hand. The launch made two other stops; when the hazy wafer of the intolerable sun began to stand once more directly overhead there were fifteen people in the launch; and then the convict, sprawled and motionless, saw the flat brazen land begin to rise and become a greenish-black mass of swamp, bearded and convoluted, this in turn stopping short off and there spread before him an expanse of water embraced by a blue dissolution of shore line and glittering thinly under the noon, larger than he had ever seen before, the sound of the launch's engine ceasing, the hull sliding on behind its fading bow-wave. "What are you doing?" the leader said.

"It's noon," the helmsman said. "I thought we might hear the dynamite." So they all listened, the launch lost of all forward motion, rocking slightly, the glitter-broken small waves slapping and whispering at the hull, but no sound, no tremble even, came anywhere under the fierce hazy sky; the long moment gathered itself and turned on and noon was past. "All right," the leader said. "Let's go." The engine started again, the hull began to gather speed. The leader came aft and stooped over the convict, key in hand. "I guess you'll have to behave now, whether you want to or not," he said, unlocking the manacles. "Won't you?"

"Yes," the convict said. They went on; after a time the shore vanished completely and a little sea got up. The convict was free now but he lay as before, the end of the skiff's painter in his hand, bent now with three or four turns about his wrist; he turned his head now and then to look back at the towing skiff as it slewed and bounced in the launch's wake; now and then he even looked out over the lake, the eyes alone moving, the face grave and expressionless, thinking, *This is a greater immensity of water, of waste and desolation, than I have ever seen before;* perhaps not; thinking three or four hours later, the shoreline raised again and broken into a clutter of sailing sloops and power cruisers, *These are more boats than I believed existed, a maritime race of which I also had no cognizance* or perhaps not thinking it but just watching as the launch opened the shored gut of the ship canal, the low smoke of the city beyond it, then a wharf, the launch slowing in; a quiet crowd of people watching with that same forlorn passivity he had seen before, and whose race he did recognize even though he had not seen Vicksburg when he passed it—the brand, the unmistakable hallmark of the violently homeless, he more so than any, who would have permitted no man to call him one of them.

"All right," the leader said to him. "Here you are."

"The boat," the convict said.

"You've got it. What do you want me to do—give you a receipt for it?"

"No," the convict said. "I just want the boat."

"Take it. Only you ought to have a bookstrap or something to carry it in."—"Carry it in?" the plump convict said. "Carry it where? Where would you have to carry it?"—

He (the tall one) told that: how he and the woman disembarked and how one of the men helped him haul the skiff up out of the water and how he stood there with the end of the painter wrapped around his wrist and the man bustled up, saying, "All right. Next load! Next load!" and how he told this man too about the boat and the man cried, "Boat? Boat?" and how he (the convict) went with them when they carried the skiff over and racked, berthed, it with the others and how he lined himself up by a coca-cola sign and the arch of a drawbridge so he could find the skiff again quick when he returned, and how he and the woman (he carrying the paper-wrapped parcel) were herded into a truck and after a while the truck began to run in traffic, between close houses, then there was a big building, an armory—

"Armory?" the plump one said. "You mean a jail."

"No. It was a kind of warehouse, with people with bundles laying on the floor."—And how he thought maybe his partner might be there and how he even looked about for the Cajun while waiting for a chance to get back to the door again, where the soldier was and how he got back to the door at last, the woman behind him and his chest actually against the dropped rifle.

"Gwan, gwan," the soldier said. "Get back. They'll give you some clothes in a minute. You can't walk around the streets that way. And something to eat too. Maybe your kinfolks will come for you by that time." And he told that too: how the woman said,

"Maybe if you told him you had some kinfolks here he would let us out." And how he did not; he could not have expressed this either, it too deep, too ingrained; he had never yet had to think it into words through all the long generations of himself—his hill-man's sober and jealous respect not for truth but for the power, the strength, of lying—not to be niggard with lying but rather to use it with respect and even care, delicate quick and strong, like a fine and fatal blade. And how they fetched him clothes—a blue jumper and overalls, and then food too (a brisk starched young woman saying, "But the baby must be bathed, cleaned. It will die if you don't" and the woman saying, "Yessum. He might holler some, he ain't never been bathed before. But he's a good baby.") and now it was night, the unshaded bulbs harsh and savage and forlorn above the snorers and he rising, gripping the woman awake, and then the window. He told that: how there were doors in plenty, leading he did not know where, but he had a hard time finding a window they could use but he found one at last, he carrying the parcel and the baby too while he climbed through first—"You ought to tore up a sheet and slid down it," the plump convict said.—But he needed no sheet, there were cobbles under his feet now, in the rich darkness. The city was there too but he had not seen it yet and would not—the low constant glare; Bienville had stood there too, it had been the figment of an emasculate also calling himself Napoleon but no more, Andrew Jackson had found it one step from Pennsylvania Avenue. But the convict found it considerably further than one step back to the ship canal and the skiff, the coca-cola sign dim now, the drawbridge arching spidery against the jonquil sky at dawn: nor did he tell, any more than about the sixty-foot levee, how he got the skiff back into the water.

The lake was behind him now; there was but one direction he could go. When he saw the River again he knew it at once. He should have; it was now ineradicably a part of his past, his life; it would be a part of what he would bequeath, if that were in store for him. But four weeks later it would look different from what it did now, and did: he (the Old Man) had recovered from his debauch, back in banks again, the Old Man, rippling placidly toward the sea, brown and rich as chocolate between levees whose inner faces were wrinkled as though in a frozen and aghast amazement, crowned with the rich green of summer in the willows; beyond them, sixty feet below, slick mules squatted against the broad pull of middle-busters in the richened soil which would not need to be planted, which would need only to be shown a cotton seed to sprout and make; there would be the symmetric miles of strong stalks by July, purple bloom in August, in September the black fields snowed over, spilled, the middles dragged smooth by the long sacks, the long black limber hands plucking, the hot air filled with the whine of gins, the September air then, but now June air heavy with locust and (the towns) the smell of new paint and the sour smell of the paste which holds wall paper—the towns, the villages, the little lost wood landings on stilts on the inner face of the levee, the lower storeys bright and rank under the new paint and paper and even the marks on spile and post and tree of May's raging water-height fading beneath each bright silver gust of summer's loud and inconstant rain; there was a store at the levee's lip, a few saddled and rope-bridled mules in the sleepy dust, a few dogs, a handful of Negroes sitting on the steps beneath the chewing tobacco and malaria medicine signs, and three white men, one of them a deputy sheriff canvassing for votes to beat his superior (who had given him his job) in the August primary, all pausing to watch the skiff emerge from the glitter-glare of the afternoon water and approach and land, a woman carrying a child stepping out, then a man, a tall

man who, approaching, proved to be dressed in a faded
but recently washed and quite clean suit of penitentiary
clothing, stopping in the dust where the mules dozed
and watching with pale cold humorless eyes while the
deputy sheriff was still making toward his armpit that
gesture which everyone present realized was to have
produced a pistol in one flashing motion for a considerable time while still nothing came of it. It was apparently enough for the newcomer, however.

"You a officer?" he said:

"You damn right I am," the deputy said. "Just let me
get this damn gun—"

"All right," the other said. "Yonder's your boat, and
here's the woman. But I never did find that bastard on
the cottonhouse."

v

One of the Governor's young men arrived at the
Penitentiary the next morning. That is, he was fairly
young (he would not see thirty again, though without
doubt he did not want to, there being that about him
which indicated a character which never had and never
would want anything it did not, or was not about to,
possess), a Phi Beta Kappa out of an Eastern university,
a colonel on the Governor's staff who did not buy it with
a campaign contribution, who had stood in his negligent
Eastern-cut clothes and his arched nose and lazy contemptuous eyes on the galleries of any number of little
lost backwoods stores and told his stories and received
the guffaws of his overalled and spitting hearers, and
with the same look in his eyes fondled infants named
in memory of the last administration and in honor (or
hope) of the next, and (it was said of him and doubtless not true) by lazy accident the behinds of some who

were not infants any longer though still not old enough
to vote. He was in the Warden's office with a briefcase,
and presently the deputy warden of the levee was there
too. He would have been sent for presently though not
yet, but he came anyhow, without knocking, with his
hat on, calling the Governor's young man loudly by a
nickname and striking him with a flat hand on the back,
and lifted one thigh to the Warden's desk, almost between the Warden and the caller, the emissary. Or the
vizier with the command, the knotted cord, as began to
appear immediately.

"Well," the Governor's young man said, "you've
played the devil, haven't you?" The Warden had a
cigar. He had offered the caller one. It had been refused,
though presently, while the Warden looked at the back
of his neck with hard immobility even a little grim, the
deputy leaned and reached back and opened the desk
drawer and took one.

"Seems straight enough to me," the Warden said. "He
got swept away against his will. He came back as soon
as he could and surrendered."

"He even brought that damn boat back," the deputy
said. "If he'd a throwed the boat away he could a
walked back in three days. But no sir. He's got to bring
the boat back. 'Here's your boat and here's the woman
but I never found no bastard on no cottonhouse.'" He
slapped his knee, guffawing. "Them convicts. A mule's
got twice as much sense."

"A mule's got twice as much sense as anything except
a rat," the emissary said in his pleasant voice. "But that's
not the trouble."

"What is the trouble?" the Warden said.

"This man is dead."

"Hell fire, he ain't dead," the deputy said. "He's up

yonder in that bunkhouse right now, lying his head off probly. I'll take you up there and you can see him." The Warden was looking at the deputy.

"Look," he said. "Bledsoe was trying to tell me something about that Kate mule's leg. You better go up to the stable and—"

"I done tended to it," the deputy said. He didn't even look at the Warden. He was watching, talking to, the emissary. "No sir. He ain't—"

"But he has received an official discharge as being dead. Not a pardon nor a parole either: a discharge. He's either dead, or free. In either case he doesn't belong here." Now both the Warden and the deputy looked at the emissary, the deputy's mouth open a little, the cigar poised in his hand to have its tip bitten off. The emissary spoke pleasantly, extremely distinctly: "On a report of death forwarded to the Governor by the Warden of the Penitentiary." The deputy closed his mouth, though otherwise he didn't move. "On the official evidence of the officer delegated at the time to the charge and returning of the body of the prisoner to the Penitentiary." Now the deputy put the cigar into his mouth and got slowly off the desk, the cigar rolling across his lip as he spoke:

"So that's it. I'm to be it, am I?" He laughed shortly, a stage laugh, two notes. "When I done been right three times running through three separate administrations? That's on a book somewhere too. Somebody in Jackson can find that too. And if they can't, I can show—"

"Three administrations?" the emissary said. "Well, well. That's pretty good."

"You damn right it's good," the deputy said. "The woods are full of folks that didn't." The Warden was again watching the back of the deputy's neck.

"Look," he said. "Why don't you step up to my house and get that bottle of whiskey out of the sideboard and bring it down here?"

"All right," the deputy said. "But I think we better settle this first. I'll tell you what we'll do—"

"We can settle it quicker with a drink or two," the Warden said. "You better step on up to your place and get a coat so the bottle—"

"That'll take too long," the deputy said. "I won't need no coat." He moved to the door, where he stopped and turned. "I'll tell you what to do. Just call twelve men in here and tell him it's a jury—he never seen but one before and he won't know no better—and try him over for robbing that train. Hamp can be the judge."

"You can't try a man twice for the same crime," the emissary said. "He might know that even if he doesn't know a jury when he sees one."

"Look," the Warden said.

"All right. Just call it a new train robbery. Tell him it happened yesterday, tell him he robbed another train while he was gone and just forgot it. He couldn't help himself. Besides, he won't care. He'd just as lief be here as out. He wouldn't have nowhere to go if he was out. None of them do. Turn one loose and be damned if he ain't right back here by Christmas like it was a reunion or something, for doing the very same thing they caught him at before." He guffawed again. "Them convicts."

"Look," the Warden said. "While you're there, why don't you open the bottle and see if the liquor's any good. Take a drink or two. Give yourself time to feel it. If it's not good, no use in bringing it."

"O. K.," the deputy said. He went out this time.

"Couldn't you lock the door?" the emissary said. The Warden squirmed faintly. That is, he shifted his position in his chair.

"After all, he's right," he said. "He's guessed right three times now. And he's kin to all the folks in Pittman County except the niggers."

"Maybe we can work fast then." The emissary opened the briefcase and took out a sheaf of papers. "So there you are," he said.

"There what are?"

"He escaped."

"But he came back voluntarily and surrendered."

"But he escaped."

"All right," the Warden said. "He escaped. Then what?" Now the emissary said look. That is, he said,

"Listen. I'm on per diem. That's tax-payers, votes. And if there's any possible chance for it to occur to anyone to hold an investigation about this, there'll be ten senators and twenty-five representatives here on a special train maybe. On per diem. And it will be mighty hard to keep some of them from going back to Jackson by way of Memphis or New Orleans—on per diem."

"All right," the Warden said. "What does he say to do?"

"This. The man left here in charge of one specific officer. But he was delivered back here by a different one."

"But he surren—" This time the Warden stopped of his own accord. He looked, stared almost, at the emissary. "All right. Go on."

"In specific charge of an appointed and delegated officer, who returned here and reported that the body of the prisoner was no longer in his possession; that, in fact, he did not know where the prisoner was. That's correct, isn't it?" The Warden said nothing. "Isn't that correct?" the emissary said, pleasantly, insistently.

"But you can't do that to him. I tell you he's kin to half the—"

"That's taken care of. The Chief has made a place for him on the highway patrol."

"Hell," the Warden said. "He can't ride a motorcycle. I don't even let him try to drive a truck."

"He won't have to. Surely an amazed and grateful State can supply the man who guessed right three times in succession in Mississippi general elections with a car to ride in and somebody to run it if necessary. He won't even have to stay in it all the time. Just so he's near enough so when an inspector sees the car and stops and blows the horn of it he can hear it and come out."

"I still don't like it," the Warden said.

"Neither do I. Your man could have saved all of this if he had just gone on and drowned himself, as he seems to have led everybody to believe he had. But he didn't. And the Chief says do. Can you think of anything better?" The Warden sighed.

"No," he said.

"All right." The emissary opened the papers and uncapped a pen and began to write. "Attempted escape from the Penitentiary, ten years' additional sentence," he said. "Deputy Warden Buckworth transferred to Highway Patrol. Call it for meritorious service even if you want to. It won't matter now. Done?"

"Done," the Warden said.

"Then suppose you send for him. Get it over with." So the Warden sent for the tall convict and he arrived presently, saturnine and grave, in his new bed-ticking, his jowls blue and close under the sunburn, his hair recently cut and neatly parted and smelling faintly of the prison barber's (the barber was in for life, for murdering his wife, still a barber) pomade. The Warden called him by name.

"You had bad luck, didn't you?" The convict said

nothing. "They are going to have to add ten years to your time."

"All right," the convict said.

"It's hard luck. I'm sorry."

"All right," the convict said. "If that's the rule." So they gave him the ten years more and the Warden gave him the cigar and now he sat, jackknifed backward into the space between the upper and lower bunks, the unlighted cigar in his hand while the plump convict and four others listened to him. Or questioned him, that is, since it was all done, finished, now and he was safe again, so maybe it wasn't even worth talking about any more.

"All right," the plump one said. "So you come back into the River. Then what?"

"Nothing. I rowed."

"Wasn't it pretty hard rowing coming back?"

"The water was still high. It was running pretty hard still. I never made much speed for the first week or two. After that it got better." Then, suddenly and quietly, something—the inarticulateness, the innate and inherited reluctance for speech, dissolved and he found himself, listened to himself, telling it quietly, the words coming not fast but easily to the tongue as he required them: How he paddled on (he found out by trying it that he could make better speed, if you could call it speed, next the bank—this after he had been carried suddenly and violently out to midstream before he could prevent it and found himself, the skiff, travelling back toward the region from which he had just escaped, and he spent the better part of the morning getting back inshore and up to the canal again from which he had emerged at dawn) until night came and they tied up to the bank and ate some of the food he had secreted in his jumper before leaving the armory in New Orleans, and the woman and the infant slept in the boat as usual and when daylight came they went on and tied up again that night too, and the next day the food gave out and he came to a landing, a town, he didn't notice the name of it, and he got a job. It was a cane farm—

"Cane?" one of the other convicts said. "What does anybody want to raise cane for? You cut cane. You have to fight it where I come from. You burn it just to get shut of it."

"It was sorghum," the tall convict said.

"Sorghum?" another said. "A whole farm just raising sorghum? *Sorghum?* What did they do with it?" The tall one didn't know. He didn't ask, he just came up the levee and there was a truck waiting full of niggers and a white man said, "You there. Can you run a shovel plow?" and the convict said, "Yes," and the man said, "Jump in then," and the convict said, "Only I've got a—"

"Yes," the plump one said. "That's what I been aiming to ask. What did—" The tall convict's face was grave, his voice was calm, just a little short:

"They had tents for the folks to live in. They were behind." The plump one blinked at him.

"Did they think she was your wife?"

"I don't know. I reckon so." The plump one blinked at him.

"Wasn't she your wife? Just from time to time kind of, you might say?" The tall one didn't answer this at all. After a moment he raised the cigar and appeared to examine a loosening of the wrapper because after another moment he licked the cigar carefully near the end. "All right," the plump one said. "Then what?" So he worked there four days. He didn't like it. Maybe that was why: that he too could not quite put credence in that much of what he believed to be sorghum. So when they told him it was Saturday and paid him and the white man told him about somebody who was going to Baton Rouge the next day in a motor boat, he went to see the man and took the six dollars he had earned and bought food with it and tied the skiff behind the motor boat and went to Baton Rouge. It didn't take long and even after they left the motor boat at Baton Rouge and he was paddling again it seemed to the convict that the River was lower and the current not so fast, so hard, so they made fair speed, tying up to the bank at night among the willows, the woman and baby sleeping in the skiff as of old. Then the food gave out again. This time it was a wood landing, the wood stacked and waiting, a wagon and team being unladen of another load. The men with the wagon told him about the sawmill and helped him drag the skiff up the levee; they wanted to leave it there but he would not so they loaded it onto the wagon too and he and the woman got on the wagon too and they went to the sawmill. They gave them one room in a house to live in here. They paid two dollars a day and furnish. The work was hard. He liked it. He stayed there eight days.

"If you liked it so well, why did you quit?" the plump one said. The tall convict examined the cigar again, holding it up where the light fell upon the rich chocolate-colored flank.

"I got in trouble," he said.

"What trouble?"

"Woman. It was a fellow's wife."

"You mean you had been toting one piece up and down the country day and night for over a month, and now the first time you have a chance to stop and catch your breath almost you got to get in trouble over another one?" The tall convict had thought of that. He remembered it: how there were times, seconds, at first when if it had not been for the baby he might have, might have tried. But they were just seconds because in the next instant his whole being would seem to flee the very idea in a kind of savage and horrified revulsion; he would find himself looking from a distance at this millstone which the force and power of blind and risible Motion had fastened upon him, thinking, saying aloud actually, with harsh and savage outrage even though it had been two years since he had had a woman and that a nameless and not young Negress, a casual, a straggler whom he had caught more or less by chance on one of the fifth-Sunday visiting days, the man—husband or sweetheart—whom she had come to see having been shot by a trusty a week or so previous and she had not heard about it: "She ain't even no good to me for that."

"But you got this one, didn't you?" the plump convict said.

"Yah," the tall one said. The plump one blinked at him.

"Was it good?"

"It's all good," one of the others said. "Well? Go on. How many more did you have on the way back? Sometimes when a fellow starts getting it it looks like he just can't miss even if—" That was all, the convict told them. They left the sawmill fast, he had no time to buy food until they reached the next landing. There he spent the whole sixteen dollars he had earned and they went on. The River was lower now, there was no doubt of it, and sixteen dollars' worth looked like a lot of food and he thought maybe it would do, would be enough. But maybe there was more current in the River still than it looked like. But this time it was Mississippi, it was cotton; the plow handles felt right to his palms again, the strain and squat of the slick buttocks against the middle-buster's blade was what he knew, even though they paid but a dollar a day here. But that did it. He told it: they told him it was Saturday again and paid him and he told about it—night, a smoked lantern in a disc of worn and barren earth as smooth as silver, a circle of crouching figures, the importunate murmurs and ejaculations, the meagre piles of worn bills beneath the crouching knees, the dotted cubes clicking and scuttering in the dust; that did it. "How much did you win?" the second convict said.

"Enough," the tall one said.

"But how much?"

"Enough," the tall one said. It was enough exactly; he gave it all to the man who owned the second motor boat (he would not need food now), he and the woman in the launch now and the skiff towing behind, the woman with the baby, and the paper-wrapped parcel beneath his peaceful hand, on his lap; almost at once he recognized, not Vicksburg because he had never seen Vicksburg, but the trestle beneath which on his roaring wave of trees and houses and dead animals he had shot, accompanied by thunder and lightning, a month and three weeks ago; he looked at it once without heat, even without interest as the launch went on. But now he began to watch the bank, the levee. He didn't know how he would know but he knew he would, and then it was early afternoon and sure enough the moment came and he said to the launch owner: "I reckon this will do."

"Here?" the launch owner said. "This don't look like anywhere to me."

"I reckon this is it," the convict said. So the launch put inshore, the engine ceased, it drifted up and lay against the levee and the owner cast the skiff loose.

"You better let me take you on until we come to something," he said. "That was what I promised."

"I reckon this will do," the convict said. So they got

out and he stood with the grapevine painter in his hand while the launch purred again and drew away, already curving; he did not watch it. He laid the bundle down and made the painter fast to a willow root and picked up the bundle and turned. He said no word, he mounted the levee, passing the mark, the tide-line of the old raging, dry now and lined, traversed by shallow and empty cracks like foolish and deprecatory senile grins, and entered a willow clump and removed the overalls and shirt they had given him in New Orleans and dropped them without even looking to see where they fell and opened the parcel and took out the other, the known, the desired, faded a little, stained and worn, but clean, recognizable, and put them on and returned to the skiff and took up the paddle. The woman was already in it.

The plump convict stood blinking at him. "So you come back," he said. "Well well." Now they all watched the tall convict as he bit the end from the cigar neatly and with complete deliberation and spat it out and licked the bite smooth and damp and took a match from his pocket and examined the match for a moment as though to be sure it was a good one, worthy of the cigar perhaps, and raked it up his thigh with the same deliberation—a motion almost too slow to set fire to it, it would seem—and held it until the flame burned clear and free of sulphur, then put it to the cigar. The plump one watched him, blinking rapidly and steadily. "And they give you ten years more for running. That's bad. A fellow can get used to what they give him at first, to start off with, I don't care how much it is, even a hundred and ninety-nine years. But ten more years. Ten years more, on top of that. When you never expected it. Ten more years to have to do without no society, no

female companionship—" He blinked steadily at the
tall convict. But he (the tall convict) had thought of
that too. He had had a sweetheart. That is, he had gone
to church singings and picnics with her—a girl a year
or so younger than he, short-legged, with ripe breasts
and a heavy mouth and dull eyes like ripe muscadines,
who owned a baking-powder can almost full of ear-rings
and brooches and rings bought (or presented at suggestion) from ten-cent stores. Presently he had divulged
his plan to her, and there were times later when, musing,
the thought occurred to him that possibly if it had not
been for her he would not actually have attempted it—
this a mere feeling, unworded, since he could not have
phrased this either: that who to know what Capone's
uncandled bridehood she might not have dreamed to be
her destiny and fate, what fast car filled with authentic
colored glass and machine guns, running traffic lights.
But that was all past and done when the notion first
occurred to him, and in the third month of his incarcera-
tion she came to see him. She wore ear-rings and a
bracelet or so which he had never seen before and it
never became quite clear how she had got that far from
home, and she cried violently for the first three minutes,
though presently (and without his ever knowing either
exactly how they had got separated or how she had
made the acquaintance) he saw her in animated conversation with one of the guards. But she kissed him
before she left that evening and said she would return
the first chance she got, clinging to him, sweating a
little, smelling of scent and soft young female flesh,
slightly pneumatic. But she didn't come back though he
continued to write to her, and seven months later he
got an answer. It was a postcard, a colored lithograph of
a Birmingham hotel, a childish X inked heavily across

one window, the heavy writing on the reverse slanted and primer-like too: *This is where were honnymonning at. Your friend (Mrs) Vernon Waldrip*

The plump convict stood blinking at the tall one, rapidly and steadily. "Yes, sir," he said. "It's them ten more years that hurt. Ten more years to do without a woman, no woman a tall a fellow wants—" He blinked steadily and rapidly, watching the tall one. The other did not move, jackknifed backward between the two bunks, grave and clean, the cigar burning smoothly and richly in his clean steady hand, the smoke wreathing upward across his face, saturnine, humorless, and calm. "Ten more years—"

"Women——!" the tall convict said.

7. Modern Times

EDITOR'S NOTE

BY THE END of the 1920's, the old slaveholding families had almost disappeared from Yoknapatawpha County. The name of Sartoris was borne only by a middle-aged woman and her half-grown son; the name of Compson only by an irascible bachelor; the name of McCaslin only by a childless hunter now in his seventies; while other names like Sutpen, Coldfield, and Beauchamp had survived, some of them in the Negro quarters, but most of them only in the courthouse records. With the old families had vanished the code they tried to observe in their human relations; almost the only code followed by their successors was that of grab-and-git. This was the age of machines, and of persons who reacted like machines, in spastic patterns of stimulus and response. Popeye, the impotent killer with his tight black clothes and his eyes like rubber pushbuttons, was the symbol of the time.

Of the four stories in this section, "Death Drag" first appeared in *Doctor Martino and Other Stories* (1934). It grew out of the same interest in the mechanized lives of barnstorming aviators that produced Faulkner's novel, *Pylon*. "Uncle Bud and the Three Madams" is Chapter XXV of *Sanctuary* (1931). "Percy Grimm" is taken from Chapter XIX of *Light in August* (1932); it is not the best passage in that fine novel, but it is the only one that tells a complete story in itself. Said Faulkner in a letter, "I invented Grimm in 1931. I didn't realize until after Hitler got into the newspapers that I had created a Nazi before he did." Incidentally the title of the novel has nothing to do with August sunlight; it refers to Lena Grove and her baby. In the Mississippi backwoods, it is sometimes said of a pregnant woman, but more often of a mare or a cow, that she will be *light* in August or September.

"Delta Autumn" comes from *Go Down, Moses* (1942). Old Ike McCaslin, the hero of that book, is the most admirable of Faulkner's characters in his life as a whole and in his relation to the Negroes. Through Sam Fathers, his master in woodlore, he had also become the spiritual heir of the Chickasaws; and therefore it is right that he should give the final judgment on the Yoknapatawpha story from the beginning. "No wonder," he thinks on his last trip into the wilderness, "the ruined woods I used to know don't cry for retribution! The people who have destroyed it will accomplish its revenge."

1928.   DEATH DRAG

THE airplane appeared over town with almost the abruptness of an apparition. It was travelling fast; almost before we knew it there it was already at the top of a loop; still over the square, in violation of both city and government ordinance. It was not a good loop either, performed viciously and slovenly and at top speed, as though the pilot were either a very nervous man or in a hurry, or (and this queerly: there is in our town an ex-army aviator. He was coming out of the post office when the airplane appeared going south; he watched the hurried and ungraceful loop and he made the comment) as though the pilot were trying to make the minimum of some specified maneuver in order to save gasoline. The airplane came over the loop with one wing down, as though about to make an Immelmann turn. Then it did a half roll, the loop three-quarters complete, and without any break in the whine of the full-throttled engine and still at top speed and with that apparition-like suddenness, it disappeared eastward toward our airport. When the first small boys reached the field, the airplane was on the ground, drawn up into a fence corner at the end of the field. It was motionless and empty. There was no one in sight at all. Resting there, empty and dead, patched and shabby and painted awkwardly with a single thin coat of dead black, it gave again that illusion of ghostliness, as though

653

it might have flown there and made that loop and landed by itself.

Our field is still in an embryonic state. Our town is built upon hills, and the field, once a cotton field, is composed of forty acres of ridge and gully, upon which, by means of grading and filling, we managed to build an X-shaped runway into the prevailing winds. The runways are long enough in themselves, but the field, like our town, is controlled by men who were of middle age when younger men first began to fly, and so the clearance is not always good. On one side is a grove of trees which the owner will not permit to be felled; on another is the barnyard of a farm: sheds and houses, a long barn with a roof of rotting shingles, a big haycock. The airplane had come to rest in the fence corner near the barn. The small boys and a Negro or two and a white man, descended from a halted wagon in the road, were standing quietly about it when two men in helmets and lifted goggles emerged suddenly around the corner of the barn. One was tall, in a dirty coverall. The other was quite short, in breeches and puttees and a soiled, brightly patterned overcoat which looked as if he had got wet in it and it had shrunk on him. He walked with a decided limp.

They had stopped at the corner of the barn. Without appearing to actually turn their heads, they seemed to take in at one glance the entire scene, quickly. The tall man spoke. "What town is this?"

One of the small boys told him the name of the town.

"Who lives here?" the tall man said.

"Who lives here?" the boy repeated.

"Who runs this field? Is it a private field?"

"Oh. It belongs to the town. They run it."

"Do they all live here? The ones that run it?"

The white man, the Negroes, the small boys, all watched the tall man.

"What I mean, is there anybody in this town that flies, that owns a ship? Any strangers here that fly?"

"Yes," the boy said. "There's a man lives here that flew in the war, the English army."

"Captain Warren was in the Royal Flying Corps," a second boy said.

"That's what I said," the first boy said.

"You said the English army," the second boy said.

The second man, the short one with the limp, spoke. He spoke to the tall man, quietly, in a dead voice, in the diction of Weber and Fields in vaudeville, making his *wh*'s into *v*'s and his *th*'s into *d*'s. "What does that mean?" he said.

"It's all right," the tall man said. He moved forward. "I think I know him." The short man followed, limping, terrific, crablike. The tall man had a gaunt face beneath a two days' stubble. His eyeballs looked dirty, too, with a strained, glaring expression. He wore a dirty helmet of cheap, thin cloth, though it was January. His goggles were worn, but even we could tell that they were good ones. But then everybody quit looking at him to look at the short man; later, when we older people saw him, we said among ourselves that he had the most tragic face we had ever seen; an expression of outraged and convinced and indomitable despair, like that of a man carrying through choice a bomb which, at a certain hour each day, may or may not explode. He had a nose which would have been out of proportion to a man six feet tall. As shaped by his close helmet, the entire upper half of his head down to the end of his nose would have fitted a six-foot body. But below that, below a lateral line bisecting his head from the end of his nose to the back of his skull, his jaw, the rest of his face, was not two inches deep. His jaw was a long, flat line clapping-to beneath his nose like the jaw of a shark, so that the tip of his nose and the tip of his jaw almost touched. His goggles were merely flat pieces of window-glass held in felt frames. His helmet was leather. Down the back of it, from the top to the hem, was a long savage tear, held together top and bottom by strips of adhesive tape almost black with dirt and grease.

From around the corner of the barn there now appeared a third man, again with that abrupt immobility, as though he had materialized there out of thin air; though when they saw him he was already moving toward the group. He wore an overcoat above a neat civilian suit; he wore a cap. He was a little taller than the limping man, and broad, heavily built. He was handsome in a dull, quiet way; from his face, a man of infrequent speech. When he came up the spectators saw that he, like the limping man, was also a Jew. That is, they knew at once that two of the strangers were of a different race from themselves, without being able to say what the difference was. The boy who had first spoken probably revealed by his next speech what they thought the difference was. He, as well as the other boys, was watching the man who limped.

"Were you in the war?" the boy said. "In the air war?"

The limping man did not answer. Both he and the tall man were watching the gate. The spectators looked also and saw a car enter the gate and come down the edge of the field toward them. Three men got out of the car and approached. Again the limping man spoke quietly to the tall man: "Is that one?"

"No," the tall man said, without looking at the other. He watched the newcomers, looking from face to face.

He spoke to the oldest of the three. "Morning," he said. "You run this field?"

"No," the newcomer said. "You want the secretary of the Fair Association. He's in town."

"Any charge to use it?"

"I don't know. I reckon they'll be glad to have you use it."

"Go on and pay them," the limping man said.

The three newcomers looked at the airplane with that blank, knowing, respectful air of groundlings. It reared on its muddy wheels, the propeller motionless, rigid, with a quality immobile and poised and dynamic. The nose was big with engine, the wings taut, the fuselage streaked with oil behind the rusting exhaust pipes. "Going to do some business here?" the oldest one said.

"Put you on a show," the tall man said.

"What kind of show?"

"Anything you want. Wing-walking; death-drag."

"What's that? Death-drag?"

"Drop a man onto the top of a car and drag him off again. Bigger the crowd, the more you'll get."

"You will get your money's worth," the limping man said.

The boys still watched him. "Were you in the war?" the first boy said.

The third stranger had not spoken up to this time. He now said: "Let's get on to town."

"Right," the tall man said. He said generally, in his flat, dead voice, the same voice which the three strangers all seemed to use, as though it were their common language: "Where can we get a taxi? Got one in town?"

"We'll take you to town," the men who had come up in the car said.

"We'll pay," the limping man said.

"Glad to do it," the driver of the car said. "I won't charge you anything. You want to go now?"

"Sure," the tall man said. The three strangers got into the back seat, the other three in front. Three of the boys followed them to the car.

"Lemme hang on to town, Mr. Black?" one of the boys said.

"Hang on," the driver said. The boys got onto the running boards. The car returned to town. The three in front could hear the three strangers talking in the back. They talked quietly, in low, dead voices, somehow quiet and urgent, discussing something among themselves, the tall man and the handsome one doing most of the talking. The three in front heard only one speech from the limping man: "I won't take less . . ."

"Sure," the tall man said. He leaned forward and raised his voice a little: "Where'll I find this Jones, this secretary?"

The driver told him.

"Is the newspaper or the printing shop near there? I want some handbills."

"I'll show you," the driver said. "I'll help you get fixed up."

"Fine," the tall man said. "Come out this afternoon and I'll give you a ride, if I have time."

The car stopped at the newspaper office. "You can get your handbills here," the driver said.

"Good," the tall man said. "Is Jones's office on this street?"

"I'll take you there, too," the driver said.

"You see about the editor," the tall man said. "I can find Jones, I guess." They got out of the car. "I'll come back here," the tall man said. He went on down the street, swiftly, in his dirty coverall and helmet. Two other men had joined the group before the newspaper office. They all entered, the limping man leading, followed by the three boys.

"I want some handbills," the limping man said. "Like this one." He took from his pocket a folded sheet of pink paper. He opened it; the editor, the boys, the five men, leaned to see it. The lettering was black and bold:

DEMON DUNCAN
DAREDEVIL OF THE AIR
DEATH DEFYING SHOW WILL BE GIVEN
UNDER THE AUSPICES OF . . . .
THIS P.M. AT TWO P.M.

COME ONE COME ALL AND SEE DEMON DUNCAN
DEFY DEATH IN DEATH DROP & DRAG OF DEATH

"I want them in one hour," the limping man said.

"What you want in this blank space?" the editor said.

"What you got in this town?"

"What we got?"

"What auspices? American Legion? Rotary Club? Chamber of Commerce?"

"We got all of them."

"I'll tell you which one in a minute, then," the limping man said. "When my partner gets back."

"You have to have a guarantee before you put on the show, do you?" the editor said.

"Why, sure. Do you think I should put on a daredevil without auspices? Do you think I should for a nickel maybe jump off the airplane?"

"Who's going to jump?" one of the later comers said; he was a taxi-driver.

The limping man looked at him. "Don't you worry about that," he said. "Your business is just to pay the money. We will do all the jumping you want, if you pay enough."

"I just asked which one of you all was the jumper."

"Do I ask you whether you pay me in silver or in greenbacks?" the limping man said. "Do I ask you?"

"No," the taxi-driver said.

"About these bills," the editor said. "You said you wanted them in an hour."

"Can't you begin on them, and leave that part out until my partner comes back?"

"Suppose he don't come before they are finished?"

"Well, that won't be my fault, will it?"

"All right," the editor said. "Just so you pay for them."

"You mean, I should pay without a auspices on the handbill?"

"I ain't in this business for fun," the editor said.

"We'll wait," the limping man said.

They waited.

"Were you a flyer in the war, Mister?" the boy said.

The limping man turned upon the boy his long, misshapen, tragic face. "The war? Why should I fly in a war?"

"I thought maybe because of your leg. Captain Warren limps, and he flew in the war. I reckon you just do it for fun?"

"For fun? What for fun? Fly? *Grüss Gott.* I hate it, I wish the man what invented them was here; I would put him into that machine yonder and I would print on his back, Do not do it, one thousand times."

"Why do you do it, then?" the man who had entered with the taxi-driver said.

"Because of that Republican Coolidge. I was in business, and that Coolidge ruined business; ruined it. That's why. For fun? *Grüss Gott.*"

They looked at the limping man. "I suppose you have a license?" the second late-comer said.

The limping man looked at him. "A license?"

"Don't you have to have a license to fly?"

"Oh; a license. For the airplane to fly; sure, I understand. Sure. We got one. You want to see it?"

"You're supposed to show it to anybody that wants to see it, aren't you?"

"Why, sure. You want to see it?"

"Where is it?"

"Where should it be? It's nailed to the airplane, where the government put it. Did you thought maybe it was nailed to me? Did you thought maybe I had a engine on me and maybe wings? It's on the airplane. Call a taxi and go to the airplane and look at it."

"I run a taxi," the driver said.

"Well, run it. Take this gentleman out to the field where he can look at the license on the airplane."

"It'll be a quarter," the driver said. But the limping man was not looking at the driver. He was leaning against the counter. They watched him take a stick of gum from his pocket and peel it. They watched him put the gum into his mouth. "I said it'll be a quarter, Mister," the driver said.

"Was you talking to me?" the limping man said.

"I thought you wanted a taxi out to the airport."

"Me? What for? What do I want to go out to the airport for? I just come from there. I ain't the one that wants to see that license. I have already seen it. I was there when the government nailed it onto the airplane."

I I

Captain Warren, the ex-army flyer, was coming out of the store, where he met the tall man in the dirty coverall. Captain Warren told about it in the barber shop that night, when the airplane was gone.

"I hadn't seen him in fourteen years, not since I left

England for the front in '17. 'So it was you that rolled out of that loop with two passengers and a twenty model Hisso smokepot?' I said.

"'Who else saw me?' he said. So he told me about it, standing there, looking over his shoulder every now and then. He was sick; a man stopped behind him to let a couple of ladies pass, and Jock whirled like he might have shot the man if he'd had a gun, and while we were in the café some one slammed a door at the back and I thought he would come out of his monkey suit. 'It's a little nervous trouble I've got,' he told me. 'I'm all right.' I had tried to get him to come out home with me for dinner, but he wouldn't. He said that he had to kind of jump himself and eat before he knew it, sort of. We had started down the street and we were passing the restaurant when he said: 'I'm going to eat,' and he turned and ducked in like a rabbit and sat down with his back to the wall and told Vernon to bring him the quickest thing he had. He drank three glasses of water and then Vernon brought him a milk bottle full and he drank most of that before the dinner came up from the kitchen. When he took off his helmet, I saw that his hair was pretty near white, and he is younger than I am. Or he was, up there when we were in Canada training. Then he told me what the name of his nervous trouble was. It was named Ginsfarb. The little one; the one that jumped off the ladder."

"What was the trouble?" we asked. "What were they afraid of?"

"They were afraid of inspectors," Warren said. "They had no licenses at all."

"There was one on the airplane."

"Yes. But it did not belong to that airplane. That one had been grounded by an inspector when Ginsfarb bought it. The license was for another airplane that had been wrecked, and some one had helped Ginsfarb compound another felony by selling the license to him. Jock had lost his license about two years ago when he crashed a big plane full of Fourth-of-July holidayers. Two of the engines quit, and he had to land. The airplane smashed up some and broke a gas line, but even then they would have been all right if a passenger hadn't got scared (it was about dusk) and struck a match. Jock was not so much to blame, but the passengers all burned to death, and the government is strict. So he couldn't get a license, and he couldn't make Ginsfarb even pay to take out a parachute rigger's license. So they had no license at all; if they were ever caught, they'd all go to the penitentiary."

"No wonder his hair was white," some one said.

"That wasn't what turned it white," Warren said. "I'll tell you about that. So they'd go to little towns like this one, fast, find out if there was anybody that might catch them, and if there wasn't, they'd put on the show and then clear out and go to another town, staying away from the cities. They'd come in and get handbills printed while Jock and the other one would try to get underwritten by some local organization. They wouldn't let Ginsfarb do this part, because he'd stick out for his price too long and they'd be afraid to risk it. So the other two would do this, get what they could, and if they could not get what Ginsfarb told them to, they'd take what they could and then try to keep Ginsfarb fooled until it was too late. Well, this time Ginsfarb kicked up. I guess they had done it too much on him.

"So I met Jock on the street. He looked bad; I offered him a drink, but he said he couldn't even smoke any more. All he could do was drink water; he said he usually drank about a gallon during the night, getting up for it.

" 'You look like you might have to jump yourself to sleep, too,' I said.

" 'No, I sleep fine. The trouble is, the nights aren't long enough. I'd like to live at the North Pole from September to April, and at the South Pole from April to September. That would just suit me.'

" 'You aren't going to last long enough to get there,' I said.

" 'I guess so. It's a good engine. I see to that.'

" 'I mean, you'll be in jail.'

"Then he said: 'Do you think so? Do you guess I could?'

"We went on to the café. He told me about the racket, and showed me one of those Demon Duncan handbills. 'Demon Duncan?' I said.

" 'Why not? Who would pay to see a man named Ginsfarb jump from a ship?'

" 'I'd pay to see that before I'd pay to see a man named Duncan do it,' I said.

"He hadn't thought of that. Then he began to drink water, and he told me that Ginsfarb had wanted a hundred dollars for the stunt, but that he and the other fellow only got sixty.

" 'What are you going to do about it?' I said.

" 'Try to keep him fooled and get this thing over and get to hell away from here,' he said.

" 'Which one is Ginsfarb?' I said. 'The little one that looks like a shark?'

"Then he began to drink water. He emptied my glass too at one shot and tapped it on the table. Vernon brought him another glass. 'You must be thirsty,' Vernon said.

" 'Have you got a pitcher of it?' Jock said.

" 'I could fill you a milk bottle.'

" 'Let's have it,' Jock said. 'And give me another glass

while I'm waiting.' Then he told me about Ginsfarb, why his hair had turned gray.

" 'How long have you been doing this?' I said.

" 'Ever since the 26th of August.'

" 'This is just January,' I said.

" 'What about it?'

" 'The 26th of August is not six months past.'

"He looked at me. Vernon brought the bottle of water. Jock poured a glass and drank it. He began to shake, sitting there, shaking and sweating, trying to fill the glass again. Then he told me about it, talking fast, filling the glass and drinking.

"Jake (the other one's name is Jake something; the good-looking one) drives the car, the rented car. Ginsfarb swaps onto the car from the ladder. Jock said he would have to fly the ship into position over a Ford or a Chevrolet running on three cylinders, trying to keep Ginsfarb from jumping from twenty or thirty feet away in order to save gasoline in the ship and in the rented car. Ginsfarb goes out on the bottom wing with his ladder, fastens the ladder onto a strut, hooks himself into the other end of the ladder, and drops off; everybody on the ground thinks that he has done what they all came to see: fallen off and killed himself. That's what he calls his death-drop. Then he swaps from the ladder onto the top of the car, and the ship comes back and he catches the ladder and is dragged off again. That's his death-drag.

"Well, up till the day when Jock's hair began to turn white, Ginsfarb, as a matter of economy, would do it all at once; he would get into position above the car and drop off on his ladder and then make contact with the car, and sometimes Jock said the ship would not be in the air three minutes. Well, on this day the rented car was a bum or something; anyway, Jock had to circle

the field four or five times while the car was getting into
position, and Ginsfarb, seeing his money being blown
out the exhaust pipes, finally refused to wait for Jock's
signal and dropped off anyway. It was all right, only
the distance between the ship and the car was not as
long as the rope ladder. So Ginsfarb hit on the car and
Jock had just enough soup to zoom and drag Ginsfarb,
still on the ladder, over a high-power electric line, and
he held the ship in that climb for twenty minutes while
Ginsfarb climbed back up the ladder with his leg
broken. He held the ship in a climb with his knees, with
the throttle wide open and the engine revving about
eleven hundred, while he reached back and opened that
cupboard behind the cockpit and dragged out a suitcase
and propped the stick so he could get out on the wing
and drag Ginsfarb back into the ship. He got Ginsfarb in
the ship and on the ground again and Ginsfarb says:
'How far did we go?' and Jock told him they had flown
with full throttle for thirty minutes and Ginsfarb says:
'Will you ruin me yet?' "

III

The rest of this is composite. It is what we (groundlings, dwellers in and backbone of a small town interchangeable with and duplicate of ten thousand little
dead clottings of human life about the land) saw, refined and clarified by the expert, the man who had
himself seen his own lonely and scudding shadow upon
the face of the puny and remote earth.

The three strangers arrived at the field, in the rented
car. When they got out of the car, they were arguing
in tense, dead voices, the pilot and the handsome man
against the man who limped. Captain Warren said they
were arguing about the money.

"I want to see it," Ginsfarb said. They stood close;

the handsome man took something from his pocket.

"There. There it is. See?" he said.

"Let me count it myself," Ginsfarb said.

"Come on, come on," the pilot hissed, in his dead, tense voice. "We tell you we got the money! Do you want an inspector to walk in and take the money and the ship too and put us in jail? Look at all these people waiting."

"You fooled me before," Ginsfarb said.

"All right," the pilot said. "Give it to him. Give him his ship too. And he can pay for the car when he gets back to town. We can get a ride in; there's a train out of here in fifteen minutes."

"You fooled me once before," Ginsfarb said.

"But we're not fooling you now. Come on. Look at all these people."

They moved toward the airplane, Ginsfarb limping terrifically, his back stubborn, his face tragic, outraged, cold. There was a good crowd: country people in overalls; the men a general dark clump against which the bright dresses of the women, the young girls, showed. The small boys and several men were already surrounding the airplane. We watched the limping man begin to take objects from the body of it: a parachute, a rope ladder. The handsome man went to the propeller. The pilot got into the back seat.

"Off!" he said, sudden and sharp. "Stand back, folks. We're going to wring the old bird's neck."

They tried three times to crank the engine.

"I got a mule, Mister," a countryman said. "How much'll you pay for a tow?"

The three strangers did not laugh. The limping man was busy attaching the rope ladder to one wing.

"You can't tell me," a countrywoman said. "Even he ain't that big a fool."

The engine started then. It seemed to lift bodily from the ground a small boy who stood behind it and blow him aside like a leaf. We watched it turn and trundle down the field.

"You can't tell me that thing's flying," the country-woman said. "I reckon the Lord give me eyes. I can see it ain't flying. You folks have been fooled."

"Wait," another voice said. "He's got to turn into the wind."

"Ain't there as much wind right there or right here as there is down yonder?" the woman said. But it did fly. It turned back toward us; the noise became deafening. When it came broadside on to us, it did not seem to be going fast, yet we could see daylight beneath the wheels and the earth. But it was not going fast; it appeared rather to hang gently just above the earth until we saw that, beyond and beneath it, trees and earth in panorama were fleeing backward at dizzy speed, and then it tilted and shot skyward with a noise like a circular saw going into a white oak log. "There ain't nobody in it!" the countrywoman said. "You can't tell me!"

The third man, the handsome one in the cap, had got into the rented car. We all knew it: a battered thing which the owner would rent to any one who would make a deposit of ten dollars. He drove to the end of the field, faced down the runway, and stopped. We looked back at the airplane. It was high, coming back toward us; some one cried suddenly, his voice puny and thin: "There! Out on the wing! See?"

"It ain't!" the countrywoman said. "I don't believe it!"

"You saw them get in it," some one said.

"I don't believe it!" the woman said.

Then we sighed; we said, "Aaahhhhhhh"; beneath the wing of the airplane there was a falling dot. We

knew it was a man. Some way we knew that that lonely,
puny, falling shape was that of a living man like ourselves. It fell. It seemed to fall for years, yet when it
checked suddenly up without visible rope or cord, it
was less far from the airplane than was the end of the
delicate pen-slash of the profiled wing.

"It ain't a man!" the woman shrieked.

"You know better," the man said. "You saw him get
in it."

"I don't care!" the woman cried. "It ain't a man!
You take me right home this minute!"

The rest is hard to tell. Not because we saw so little;
we saw everything that happened, but because we had
so little in experience to postulate it with. We saw that
battered rented car moving down the field, going faster,
jouncing in the broken January mud, then the sound of
the airplane blotted it, reduced it to immobility; we
saw the dangling ladder and the shark-faced man
swinging on it beneath the death-colored airplane. The
end of the ladder raked right across the top of the car,
from end to end, with the limping man on the ladder
and the capped head of the handsome man leaning out
of the car. And the end of the field was coming nearer,
and the airplane was travelling faster than the car,
passing it. And nothing happened. "Listen!" some one
cried. "They are talking to one another!"

Captain Warren told us what they were talking
about, the two Jews yelling back and forth at one another: the shark-faced man on the dangling ladder that
looked like a cobweb, the other one in the car; the
fence, the end of the field, coming closer.

"Come on!" the man in the car shouted.

"What did they pay?"

"Jump!"

"If they didn't pay that hundred, I won't do it."

Then the airplane zoomed, roaring, the dangling figure on the gossamer ladder swinging beneath it. It circled the field twice while the man got the car into position again. Again the car started down the field; again the airplane came down with its wild, circular-saw drone which died into a splutter as the ladder and the clinging man swung up to the car from behind; again we heard the two puny voices shrieking at one another with a quality at once ludicrous and horrible: the one coming out of the very air itself, shrieking about something sweated out of the earth and without value anywhere else:

"How much did you say?"

"Jump!"

"What? How much did they pay?"

"Nothing! Jump!"

"Nothing?" the man on the ladder wailed in a fading, outraged shriek. "Nothing?" Again the airplane was dragging the ladder irrevocably past the car, approaching the end of the field, the fences, the long barn with its rotting roof. Suddenly we saw Captain Warren beside us; he was using words we had never heard him use.

"He's got the stick between his knees," Captain Warren said. "Exalted suzerain of mankind; saccharine and sacred symbol of eternal rest." We had forgot about the pilot, the man still in the airplane. We saw the airplane, tilted upward, the pilot standing upright in the back seat, leaning over the side and shaking both hands at the man on the ladder. We could hear him yelling now as again the man on the ladder was dragged over the car and past it, shrieking:

"I won't do it! I won't do it!" He was still shrieking when the airplane zoomed; we saw him, a diminishing and shrieking spot against the sky above the long roof of the barn: "I won't do it! I won't do it!" Before, when the speck left the airplane, falling, to be snubbed up by the ladder, we knew that it was a living man; again, when the speck left the ladder, falling, we knew that it was a living man, and we knew that there was no ladder to snub him up now. We saw him falling against the cold, empty January sky until the silhouette of the barn absorbed him; even from here, his attitude froglike, outraged, implacable. From somewhere in the crowd a woman screamed, though the sound was blotted out by the sound of the airplane. It reared skyward with its wild, tearing noise, the empty ladder swept backward beneath it. The sound of the engine was like a groan, a groan of relief and despair.

IV

Captain Warren told us in the barber shop on that Saturday night.

"Did he really jump off, onto that barn?" we asked him.

"Yes. He jumped. He wasn't thinking about being killed, or even hurt. That's why he wasn't hurt. He was too mad, too in a hurry to receive justice. He couldn't wait to fly back down. Providence knew that he was too busy and that he deserved justice, so Providence put that barn there with the rotting roof. He wasn't even thinking about hitting the barn; if he'd tried to, let go of his belief in a cosmic balance to bother about landing, he would have missed the barn and killed himself."

It didn't hurt him at all, save for a long scratch on his face that bled a lot, and his overcoat was torn completely down the back, as though the tear down the back of the helmet had run on down the overcoat. He came out of the barn running before we got to it. He hobbled right among us, with his bloody face, his arms waving, his coat dangling from either shoulder.

"Where is that secretary?" he said.

"What secretary?"

"That American Legion secretary." He went on, limping fast, toward where a crowd stood about three women who had fainted. "You said you would pay a hundred dollars to see me swap to that car. We pay rent on the car and all, and now you would—"

"You got sixty dollars," some one said.

The man looked at him. "Sixty? I said one hundred. When you would let me believe it was one hundred and it was just sixty; you would see me risk my life for sixty dollars. . . ." The airplane was down; none of us were aware of it until the pilot sprang suddenly upon the man who limped. He jerked the man around and knocked him down before we could grasp the pilot. We held the pilot, struggling, crying, the tears streaking his dirty, unshaven face. Captain Warren was suddenly there, holding the pilot.

"Stop it!" he said. "Stop it!"

The pilot ceased. He stared at Captain Warren, then he slumped and sat on the ground in his thin, dirty garment, with his unshaven face, dirty, gaunt, with his sick eyes, crying. "Go away," Captain Warren said. "Let him alone for a minute."

We went away, back to the other man, the one who limped. They had lifted him and he drew the two halves of his overcoat forward and looked at them. Then he said: "I want some chewing gum."

Some one gave him a stick. Another offered him a cigarette. "Thanks," he said. "I don't burn up no money. I ain't got enough of it yet." He put the gum into his mouth. "You would take advantage of me. If you thought I would risk my life for sixty dollars, you fool yourself."

"Give him the rest of it," some one said. "Here's my share."

The limping man did not look around. "Make it up to a hundred, and I will swap to the car like on the handbill," he said.

Somewhere a woman screamed behind him. She began to laugh and to cry at the same time. "Don't . . ." she said, laughing and crying at the same time. "Don't let . . ." until they led her away. Still the limping man had not moved. He wiped his face on his cuff and he was looking at his bloody sleeve when Captain Warren came up.

"How much is he short?" Warren said. They told Warren. He took out some money and gave it to the limping man.

"You want I should swap to the car?" he said.

"No," Warren said. "You get that crate out of here quick as you can."

"Well, that's your business," the limping man said. "I got witnesses I offered to swap." He moved; we made way and watched him, in his severed and dangling overcoat, approach the airplane. It was on the runway, the engine running. The third man was already in the front seat. We watched the limping man crawl terrifically in beside him. They sat there, looking forward.

The pilot began to get up. Warren was standing beside him. "Ground it," Warren said. "You are coming home with me."

"I guess we'd better get on," the pilot said. He did not look at Warren. Then he put out his hand. "Well . . ." he said.

Warren did not take his hand. "You come on home with me," he said.

"Who'd take care of that bastard?"

"Who wants to?"

"I'll get him right, some day. Where I can beat hell out of him."

"Jock," Warren said.

"No," the other said.

"Have you got an overcoat?"

"Sure I have."

"You're a liar." Warren began to pull off his overcoat.

"No," the other said; "I don't need it." He went on toward the machine. "See you some time," he said over his shoulder. We watched him get in, heard the airplane come to life, come alive. It passed us, already off the ground. The pilot jerked his hand once, stiffly; the two heads in the front seat did not turn nor move. Then it was gone, the sound was gone.

Warren turned. "What about that car they rented?" he said.

"He give me a quarter to take it back to town," a boy said.

"Can you drive it?"

"Yes, sir. I drove it out here. I showed him where to rent it."

"The one that jumped?"

"Yes, sir." The boy looked a little aside. "Only I'm a little scared to take it back. I don't reckon you could come with me."

"Why, scared?" Warren said.

"That fellow never paid nothing down on it, like Mr. Harris wanted. He told Mr. Harris he might not use it, but if he did use it in his show, he would pay Mr. Harris twenty dollars for it instead of ten like Mr. Harris wanted. He told me to take it back and tell Mr. Harris he never used the car. And I don't know if Mr. Harris will like it. He might get mad."

1929. UNCLE BUD AND THE THREE MADAMS

THE tables had been moved to one end of the dance floor. On each one was a black table-cloth. The curtains were still drawn; a thick, salmon-colored light fell through them. Just beneath the orchestra platform the coffin sat. It was an expensive one: black, with silver fittings, the trestles hidden by a mass of flowers. In wreaths and crosses and other shapes of ceremonial mortality, the mass appeared to break in a symbolical wave over the bier and on upon the platform and the piano, the scent of them thickly oppressive.

The proprietor of the place moved about among the tables, speaking to the arrivals as they entered and found seats. The Negro waiters, in black shirts beneath their starched jackets, were already moving in and out with glasses and bottles of ginger ale. They moved with swaggering and decorous repression; already the scene was vivid, with a hushed, macabre air a little febrile.

The archway to the dice-room was draped in black. A black pall lay upon the crap-table, upon which the overflow of floral shapes was beginning to accumulate. People entered steadily, men in dark suits of decorous restraint, others in the light, bright shades of spring, increasing the atmosphere of macabre paradox. The women—the younger ones—wore bright colors also, in hats and scarves; the older ones in sober gray and black and navy blue, and glittering with diamonds:

matronly figures resembling housewives on a Sunday afternoon excursion.

The room began to hum with shrill, hushed talk. The waiters moved here and there with high, precarious trays, their white jackets and black shirts resembling photograph negatives. The proprietor went from table to table with his bald head, a huge diamond in his black cravat, followed by the bouncer, a thick, muscle-bound, bullet-headed man who appeared to be on the point of bursting out of his dinner-jacket through the rear, like a cocoon.

In a private dining-room, on a table draped in black, sat a huge bowl of punch floating with ice and sliced fruit. Beside it leaned a fat man in a shapeless greenish suit, from the sleeves of which dirty cuffs fell upon hands rimmed with black nails. The soiled collar was wilted about his neck in limp folds, knotted by a greasy black tie with an imitation ruby stud. His face gleamed with moisture and he adjured the throng about the bowl in a harsh voice:

"Come on, folks. It's on Gene. It don't cost you nothing. Step up and drink. There wasn't never a better boy walked than Red." They drank and fell back, replaced by others with extended cups. From time to time a waiter entered with ice and fruit and dumped them into the bowl; from a suitcase under the table Gene drew fresh bottles and decanted them into the bowl; then, proprietorial, adjurant, sweating, he resumed his harsh monologue, mopping his face on his sleeve. "Come on, folks. It's all on Gene. I ain't nothing but a boot-legger, but he never had a better friend than me. Step up and drink, folks. There's more where that come from."

From the dance hall came a strain of music. The people entered and found seats. On the platform was the orchestra from a downtown hotel, in dinner coats. The proprietor and a second man were conferring with the leader.

"Let them play jazz," the second man said. "Never nobody liked dancing no better than Red."

"No, no," the proprietor said. "Time Gene gets them all ginned up on free whiskey, they'll start dancing. It'll look bad."

"How about the 'Blue Danube'?" the leader said.

"No, no; don't play no blues, I tell you," the proprietor said. "There's a dead man in that bier."

"That's not blues," the leader said.

"What is it?" the second man said.

"A waltz. Strauss."

"A wop?" the second man said. "Like hell. Red was an American. You may not be, but he was. Don't you know anything American? Play 'I Can't Give You Anything but Love.' He always liked that."

"And get them all to dancing?" the proprietor said. He glanced back at the tables, where the women were beginning to talk a little shrilly. "You better start off with 'Nearer, My God, to Thee,'" he said, "and sober them up some. I told Gene it was risky about that punch, starting it so soon. My suggestion was to wait until we started back to town. But I might have knowed somebody'd have to turn it into a carnival. Better start off solemn and keep it up until I give you the sign."

"Red wouldn't like it solemn," the second man said. "And you know it."

"Let him go somewheres else, then," the proprietor said. "I just done this as an accommodation. I ain't running no funeral parlor."

The orchestra played "Nearer, My God, To Thee." The audience grew quiet. A woman in a red dress came in the door unsteadily. "Whoopee," she said, "so long,

Red. He'll be in hell before I could even reach Little
Rock."

"Shhhhhhhh!" voices said. She fell into a seat. Gene
came to the door and stood there until the music
stopped.

"Come on, folks," he shouted, jerking his arms in a
fat, sweeping gesture, "come and get it. It's on Gene. I
don't want a dry throat or eye in this place in ten minutes." Those at the rear moved toward the door. The
proprietor sprang to his feet and jerked his hand at the
orchestra. The cornetist rose and played "In That
Haven of Rest" in solo, but the crowd at the back of
the room continued to dwindle through the door where
Gene stood waving his arm. Two middle-aged women
were weeping quietly beneath flowered hats.

They surged and clamored about the diminishing
bowl. From the dance hall came the rich blare of the
cornet. Two soiled young men worked their way toward
the table, shouting, "Gangway. Gangway," monoto-
nously, carrying suitcases. They opened them and set
bottles on the table, while Gene, frankly weeping now,
opened them and decanted them into the bowl. "Come
up, folks. I couldn't a loved him no better if he'd a been
my own son," he shouted hoarsely, dragging his sleeve
across his face.

A waiter edged up to the table with a bowl of ice
and fruit and went to put them into the punch bowl.
"What the hell you doing?" Gene said, "putting that
slop in there? Get to hell away from here."

"Ra-a-a-a-y-y-y-y!" they shouted, clashing their cups,
drowning all save the pantomime as Gene knocked the
bowl of fruit from the waiter's hand and fell again to
dumping raw liquor into the bowl, sploshing it into and
upon the extended hands and cups. The two youths
opened bottles furiously.

As though swept there upon a brassy blare of music the proprietor appeared in the door, his face harried, waving his arms. "Come on, folks," he shouted, "let's finish the musical program. It's costing us money."

"Hell with it," they shouted.

"Costing who money?"

"Who cares?"

"Costing who money?"

"Who begrudges it? I'll pay it. By God, I'll buy him two funerals."

"Folks! Folks!" the proprietor shouted. "Don't you realize there's a bier in that room?"

"Costing who money?"

"Beer?" Gene said. "Beer?" he said in a broken voice. "Is anybody here trying to insult me by—"

"He begrudges Red the money."

"Who does?"

"Joe does, the cheap son of a bitch."

"Is somebody here trying to insult me—"

"Let's move the funeral, then. This is not the only place in town."

"Let's move Joe."

"Put the son of a bitch in a coffin. Let's have two funerals."

"Beer? Beer? Is somebody—"

"Put the son of a bitch in a coffin. See how he likes it."

"Put the son of a bitch in a coffin," the woman in red shrieked. They rushed toward the door, where the proprietor stood waving his hands above his head, his voice shrieking out of the uproar before he turned and fled.

In the main room a male quartet engaged from a vaudeville house was singing. They were singing mother songs in close harmony; they sang "Sonny Boy." The weeping was general among the older women. Waiters were now carrying cups of punch in to them and they sat holding the cups in their fat, ringed hands, crying.

The orchestra played again. The woman in red staggered into the room. "Come on, Joe," she shouted, "open the game. Get that damn stiff out of here and open the game." A man tried to hold her; she turned upon him with a burst of filthy language and went on to the shrouded crap table and hurled a wreath to the floor. The proprietor rushed toward her, followed by the bouncer. The proprietor grasped the woman as she lifted another floral piece. The man who had tried to hold her intervened, the woman cursing shrilly and striking at both of them impartially with the wreath. The bouncer caught the man's arm; he whirled and struck at the bouncer, who knocked him halfway across the room. Three more men entered. The fourth rose from the floor and all four of them rushed at the bouncer.

He felled the first and whirled and sprang with unbelievable celerity, into the main room. The orchestra was playing. It was immediately drowned in a sudden pandemonium of chairs and screams. The bouncer whirled again and met the rush of the four men. They mingled; a second man flew out and skittered along the floor on his back; the bouncer sprang free. Then he whirled and rushed them and in a whirling plunge they bore down upon the bier and crashed into it. The orchestra had ceased and were now climbing onto their chairs, with their instruments. The floral offerings flew; the coffin teetered. "Catch it!" a voice shouted. They sprang forward, but the coffin crashed heavily to the floor, coming open. The corpse tumbled slowly and sedately out and came to rest with its face in the center of a wreath.

"Play something!" the proprietor bawled, waving his arms; "Play! Play!"

When they raised the corpse the wreath came too, attached to him by a hidden end of a wire driven into his cheek. He had worn a cap which, tumbling off, exposed a small blue hole in the center of his forehead. It had been neatly plugged with wax and was painted, but the wax had been jarred out and lost. They couldn't find it, but by unfastening the snap in the peak, they could draw the cap down to his eyes.

As the cortège neared the downtown section more cars joined it. The hearse was followed by six Packard touring cars with the tops back, driven by liveried chauffeurs and filled with flowers. They looked exactly alike and were of the type rented by the hour by the better class agencies. Next came a nondescript line of taxis, roadsters, sedans, which increased as the procession moved slowly through the restricted district, where faces peered from beneath lowered shades, toward the main artery that led back out of town, toward the cemetery.

On the avenue the hearse increased its speed, the procession stretching out at swift intervals. Presently the private cars and the cabs began to drop out. At each intersection they would turn this way or that, until at last only the hearse and the six Packards were left, each carrying no occupant save the liveried driver. The street was broad and now infrequent, with a white line down the center that diminished on ahead into the smooth asphalt emptiness. Soon the hearse was making forty miles an hour and then forty-five and then fifty.

One of the cabs drew up at Miss Reba's door. She got out, followed by a thin woman in sober, severe clothes and gold nose-glasses, and a short plump woman in a plumed hat, her face hidden by a handkerchief, and a small bullet-headed boy of five or six. The woman with the handkerchief continued to sob in snuffy gasps as they went up the walk and entered the lattice. Beyond the house door the dogs set up a falsetto uproar. When Minnie opened the door they surged about Miss Reba's feet. She kicked them aside. Again they assailed her with snapping eagerness; again she flung them back against the wall in muted thuds.

"Come in, come in," she said, her hand to her breast. Once inside the house the woman with the handkerchief began to weep aloud.

"Didn't he look sweet?" she wailed. "Didn't he look sweet!"

"Now, now," Miss Reba said, leading the way to her room, "come in and have some beer. You'll feel better. Minnie!" They entered her room with its decorated dresser, its wall safe, its screen, its draped portrait of a meek-looking man with an enormous moustache. "Sit down, sit down," she panted, shoving the chairs forward. She lowered herself into one and stooped terrifically toward her feet.

"Uncle Bud, honey," the weeping woman said, dabbing at her eyes, "come and unlace Miss Reba's shoes."

The boy knelt and removed Miss Reba's shoes. "And if you'll just reach me them house slippers under the bed there, honey," Miss Reba said. The boy fetched the slippers. Minnie entered, followed by the dogs. They rushed at Miss Reba and began to worry the shoes she had just removed.

"Scat!" the boy said, striking at one of them with his hand. The dog's head snapped around, its teeth clicking, its half-hidden eyes bright and malevolent. The boy recoiled. "You bite me, you thon bitch," he said.

"Uncle Bud!" the fat woman said, her round face, rigid in fatty folds and streaked with tears, turned upon the boy in shocked surprise, the plumes nodding precariously above it. Uncle Bud's head was quite round, his nose bridged with freckles like splotches of huge summer rain on a sidewalk. The other woman sat primly erect, in gold nose-glasses on a gold chain and neat iron-gray hair. She looked like a school-teacher. "The very idea!" the fat woman said. "How in the world he can learn such words on an Arkansaw farm, I don't know."

"They'll learn meanness anywhere," Miss Reba said. Minnie leaned down a tray bearing three frosted tankards. Uncle Bud watched with round cornflower eyes as they took one each. The fat woman began to cry again.

"He looked so sweet!" she wailed.

"We all got to suffer it," Miss Reba said. "Well, may it be a long day," lifting her tankard. They drank, bowing formally to one another. The fat woman dried her eyes; the two guests wiped their lips with prim decorum. The thin one coughed delicately aside, behind her hand.

"Such good beer," she said.

"Ain't it?" the fat one said. "I always say it's the greatest pleasure I have to call on Miss Reba."

They began to talk politely, in decorous half-completed sentences, with little gasps of agreement. The boy had moved aimlessly to the window, peering beneath the lifted shade.

"How long's he going to be with you, Miss Myrtle?" Miss Reba said.

"Just till Sat'dy," the fat woman said. "Then he'll go back home. It makes a right nice little change for him, with me for a week or two. And I enjoy having him."

"Children are such a comfort to a body," the thin one said.

"Yes," Miss Myrtle said. "Is them two nice young fellows still with you, Miss Reba?"

"Yes," Miss Reba said. "I think I got to get shut of them, though. I ain't specially tender-hearted, but after all it ain't no use in helping young folks to learn this world's meanness until they have to. I already had to stop the girls running around the house without no clothes on, and they don't like it."

They drank again, decorously, handling the tankards delicately, save Miss Reba who grasped hers as though it were a weapon, her other hand lost in her breast. She set her tankard down empty. "I get so dry, seems like," she said. "Won't you ladies have another?" They murmured, ceremoniously. "Minnie!" Miss Reba shouted.

Minnie came and filled the tankards again. "Reely, I'm right ashamed," Miss Myrtle said. "But Miss Reba has such good beer. And then we've all had a kind of upsetting afternoon."

"I'm just surprised it wasn't upset no more," Miss Reba said. "Giving away all that free liquor like Gene done."

"It must have cost a good piece of jack," the thin woman said.

"I believe you," Miss Reba said. "And who got anything out of it? Tell me that. Except the privilege of having his place hell-full of folks not spending a cent." She had set her tankard on the table beside her chair. Suddenly she turned her head sharply and looked at it. Uncle Bud was now behind her chair, leaning against the table. "You ain't been into my beer, have you, boy?" she said.

"You, Uncle Bud," Miss Myrtle said. "Ain't you

ashamed? I declare, it's getting so I don't dare take him nowhere. I never see such a boy for snitching beer in my life. You come out here and play, now. Come on."

"Yessum," Uncle Bud said. He moved, in no particular direction. Miss Reba drank and set the tankard back on the table and rose.

"Since we all been kind of tore up," she said, "maybe I can prevail on you ladies to have a little sup of gin?"

"No; reely," Miss Myrtle said.

"Miss Reba's the perfect hostess," the thin one said. "How many times you heard me say that, Miss Myrtle?"

"I wouldn't undertake to say, dearie," Miss Myrtle said.

Miss Reba vanished behind the screen.

"Did you ever see it so warm for June, Miss Lorraine?" Miss Myrtle said.

"I never did," the thin woman said. Miss Myrtle's face began to crinkle again. Setting her tankard down she began to fumble for her handkerchief.

"It just comes over me like this," she said, "and them singing that 'Sonny Boy' and all. He looked so sweet," she wailed.

"Now, now," Miss Lorraine said. "Drink a little beer. You'll feel better. Miss Myrtle's took again," she said, raising her voice.

"I got too tender a heart," Miss Myrtle said. She snuffled behind the handkerchief, groping for her tankard. She groped for a moment, then it touched her hand. She looked quickly up. "You, Uncle Bud!" she said. "Didn't I tell you to come out from behind there and play? Would you believe it? The other afternoon when we left here I was so mortified I didn't know what to do. I was ashamed to be seen on the street with a drunk boy like you."

Miss Reba emerged from behind the screen with

three glasses of gin. "This'll put some heart into us," she said. "We're setting here like three old sick cats." They bowed formally and drank, patting their lips. Then they began to talk. They were all talking at once, again in half-completed sentences, but without pauses for agreement or affirmation.

"It's us girls," Miss Myrtle said. "Men just can't seem to take us and leave us for what we are. They make us what we are, then they expect us to be different. Expect us not to never look at another man, while they come and go as they please."

"A woman that wants to fool with more than one man at a time is a fool," Miss Reba said. "They're all trouble, and why do you want to double your trouble? And the woman that can't stay true to a good man when she gets him, a free-hearted spender that never give her a hour's uneasiness or a hard word . . ." looking at them, her eyes began to fill with a sad, unutterable expression, of baffled and patient despair.

"Now, now," Miss Myrtle said. She leaned forward and patted Miss Reba's huge hand. Miss Lorraine made a faint clucking sound with her tongue. "You'll get yourself started."

"He was such a good man," Miss Reba said. "We was like two doves. For eleven years we was like two doves."

"Now, dearie; now, dearie," Miss Myrtle said.

"It's when it comes over me like this," Miss Reba said. "Seeing that boy laying there under them flowers."

"He never had no more than Mr. Binford had," Miss Myrtle said. "Now, now. Drink a little beer."

Miss Reba brushed her sleeve across her eyes. She drank some beer.

"He ought to known better than to take a chance with Popeye's girl," Miss Lorraine said.

"Men don't never learn better than that, dearie," Miss Myrtle said. "Where you reckon they went, Miss Reba?"

"I don't know and I don't care," Miss Reba said. "And how soon they catch Popeye and burn him for killing that boy, I don't care neither. I don't care none."

"He goes all the way to Pensacola every summer to see his mother," Miss Myrtle said. "A man that'll do that can't be all bad."

"I don't know how bad you like them, then," Miss Reba said. "Me trying to run a respectable house, that's been running a shooting-gallery for twenty years, and him trying to turn it into a peep-show."

"It's us poor girls," Miss Myrtle said, "causes all the trouble and gets all the suffering."

"I heard two years ago Popeye wasn't no good that way," Miss Lorraine said.

"I knew it all the time," Miss Reba said. "A young man spending his money like water on girls and not never going to bed with one. It's against nature. All the girls thought it was because he had a little woman out in town somewhere, but I says, mark my words, there's something funny about him. There's a funny business somewhere."

"He was a free spender, all right," Miss Lorraine said.

"The clothes and jewelry that girl bought, it was a shame," Miss Reba said. "There was a Chinee robe she paid a hundred dollars for—imported, it was—and perfume at ten dollars an ounce; next morning when I went up there, they was all wadded in the corner and the perfume and rouge busted all over them like a cyclone. That's what she'd do when she got mad at him, when he'd beat her. After he shut her up and wouldn't let her leave the house. Having the front of my house watched like it was a . . ." She raised the tankard from the table to her lips. Then she halted it, blinking. "Where's my—"

"Uncle Bud!" Miss Myrtle said. She grasped the boy by the arm and snatched him out from behind Miss Reba's chair and shook him, his round head bobbing on his shoulders with an expression of equable idiocy. "Ain't you ashamed? Ain't you *ashamed?* Why can't you stay out of these ladies' beer? I'm a good mind to take that dollar back and make you buy Miss Reba a can of beer, I am for a fact. Now, you go over there by that window and stay there, you hear?"

"Nonsense," Miss Reba said. "There wasn't much of it left. You ladies are about ready too, ain't you? Minnie!"

Miss Lorraine touched her mouth with her handkerchief. Behind her glasses her eyes rolled aside in a veiled, secret look. She laid the other hand to her flat spinster's breast.

"We forgot about your heart, honey," Miss Myrtle said. "Don't you reckon you better take gin this time?"

"Reely, I—" Miss Lorraine said.

"Yes; do," Miss Reba said. She rose heavily and fetched three more glasses of gin from behind the screen. Minnie entered and refilled the tankards. They drank, patting their lips.

"That's what was going on, was it?" Miss Lorraine said.

"First I knowed was when Minnie told me there was something funny going on," Miss Reba said. "How he wasn't here hardly at all, gone about every other night, and that when he was here, there wasn't no signs at all the next morning when she cleaned up. She'd hear them quarrelling, and she said it was her wanting to get out and he wouldn't let her. With all them clothes he was buying her, mind, he didn't want her to leave the house, and she'd get mad and lock the door and wouldn't even let him in."

"Maybe he went off and got fixed up with one of these glands, these monkey glands, and it quit on him," Miss Myrtle said.

"Then one morning he come in with Red and took him up there. They stayed about an hour and left, and Popeye didn't show up again until next morning. Then him and Red come back and stayed up there about an hour. When they left, Minnie come and told me what was going on, so next day I waited for them. I called him in here and I says 'Look here, you sonofabuh—'" She ceased. For an instant the three of them sat motionless, a little forward. Then slowly their heads turned and they looked at the boy leaning against the table.

"Uncle Bud, honey," Miss Myrtle said, "don't you want to go and play in the yard with Reba and Mr. Binford?"

"Yessum," the boy said. He went toward the door. They watched him until the door closed upon him. Miss Lorraine drew her chair up; they leaned together.

"And that's what they was doing?" Miss Myrtle said.

"I says 'I been running a house for twenty years, but this is the first time I ever had anything like this going on in it. If you want to turn a stud in to your girl' I says 'go somewhere else to do it. I ain't going to have my house turned into no French joint.'"

"The son of a bitch," Miss Lorraine said.

"He'd ought to've had sense enough to got a old ugly man," Miss Myrtle said. "Tempting us poor girls like that."

"Men always expects us to resist temptation," Miss Lorraine said. She was sitting upright like a schoolteacher. "The lousy son of a bitch."

"Except what they offers themselves," Miss Reba said. "Then watch them. . . . Every morning for four days that was going on, then they didn't come back. For a week Popeye didn't show up at all, and that girl wild as a young mare. I thought he was out of town on business maybe, until Minnie told me he wasn't and that he give her five dollars a day not to let that girl out of the house nor use the telephone. And me trying to get word to him to come and take her out of my house because I didn't want nuttin like that going on in it. Yes, sir, Minnie said the two of them would be nekkid as two snakes, and Popeye hanging over the foot of the bed without even his hat took off, making a kind of whinnying sound."

"Maybe he was cheering for them," Miss Lorraine said. "The lousy son of a bitch."

Feet came up the hall; they could hear Minnie's voice lifted in adjuration. The door opened. She entered, holding Uncle Bud erect by one hand. Limp-kneed he dangled, his face fixed in an expression of glassy idiocy. "Miss Reba," Minnie said, "this boy done broke in the icebox and drunk a whole bottle of beer. You, boy!" she said, shaking him, "stan up!" Limply he dangled, his face rigid in a slobbering grin. Then upon it came an expression of concern, consternation; Minnie swung him sharply away from her as he began to vomit.

1930.   PERCY GRIMM

IN THE town of Jefferson lived a young man named Percy Grimm. He was about twenty-five and a captain in the State National Guard. He had been born in the town and had lived there all his life save for the periods of the summer encampments. He was too young to have been in the European War, though it was not until 1921 or '22 that he realized that he would never forgive his parents for that fact. His father, a hardware merchant, did not understand this. He thought that the boy was just lazy and in a fair way to become perfectly worthless, when in reality the boy was suffering the terrible tragedy of having been born not alone too late but not late enough to have escaped first-hand knowledge of the lost time when he should have been a man instead of a child. And now, with the hysteria passed away and the ones who had been loudest in the hysteria and even the ones, the heroes who had suffered and served, beginning to look at one another a little askance, he had no one to tell it, to open his heart to. In fact, his first serious fight was with an ex-soldier who made some remark to the effect that if he had to do it again, he would fight this time on the German side and against France. At once Grimm took him up. "Against America too?" he said.

"If America's fool enough to help France out again," the soldier said. Grimm struck him at once; he was smaller than the soldier, still in his teens. The result was foregone; even Grimm doubtless knew that. But he took his punishment until even the soldier begged the bystanders to hold the boy back. And he wore the scars of that battle as proudly as he was later to wear the uniform itself for which he had blindly fought.

It was the new civilian-military act which saved him. He was like a man who had been for a long time in a swamp, in the dark. It was as though he not only could see no path ahead of him, he knew that there was none. Then suddenly his life opened definite and clear. The wasted years in which he had shown no ability in school, in which he had been known as lazy, recalcitrant, without ambition, were behind him, forgotten. He could now see his life opening before him, uncomplex and inescapable as a barren corridor, completely freed now of ever again having to think or decide, the burden which he now assumed and carried as bright and weightless and martial as his insignatory brass: a sublime and implicit faith in physical courage and blind obedience, and a belief that the white race is superior to any and all other races and that the American is superior to all other white races and that the American uniform is superior to all men, and that all that would ever be required of him in payment for this belief, this privilege, would be his own life. On each national holiday that had any martial flavor whatever he dressed in his captain's uniform and came down town. And those who saw him remembered him again on the day of the fight with the ex-soldier as, glittering, with his marksman's badge (he was a fine shot) and his bars, grave, erect, he walked among the civilians with about him an air half belligerent and half the selfconscious pride of a boy.

He was not a member of the American Legion, but that was his parents' fault and not his. But when Joe Christmas, the mulatto, was fetched back from Motts-

town on that Saturday afternoon, accused of killing
Miss Joanna Burden, he had already been to the commander of the local Post. His idea, his words, were
quite simple and direct. "We got to preserve order,"
he said. "We must let the law take its course. The law,
the nation. It is the right of no civilian to sentence a
man to death. And we, the soldiers in Jefferson, are the
ones to see to that."

"How do you know that anybody is planning anything different?" the Legion commander said. "Have
you heard any talk?"

"I don't know. I haven't listened." He didn't lie. It
was as though he did not attach enough importance to
what might or might not have been said by the civilian
citizens to lie about it. "That's not the question. It's
whether or not we, as soldiers, that have worn the
uniform, are going to be the first to state where we
stand. To show these people right off just where the
government of the country stands on such things. That
there won't be any need for them even to talk." His
plan was quite simple. It was to form the Legion Post
into a platoon, with himself in command vide his active
commission. "But if they don't want me to command,
that's all right too. I'll be second, if they say. Or a
sergeant or a corporal." And he meant it. It was not
vain glory that he wanted. He was too sincere. So sincere, so humorless, that the Legion commander with-
held the flippant refusal he was about to make.

"I still don't think that there is any need of it. And if
there was, we would all have to act as civilians. I
couldn't use the Post like that. After all, we are not
soldiers now. I don't think I would, if I could."

Grimm looked at him, without anger, but rather as
if he were some kind of bug. "Yet you wore the uniform

once," he said, with a kind of patience. He said: "I suppose you won't use your authority to keep me from talking to them, will you? As individuals?"

"No. I haven't any authority to do that, anyway. But just as individuals, mind. You mustn't use my name at all."

Then Grimm gave him a shot on his own account. "I am not likely to do that," he said. Then he was gone. That was Saturday, about four o'clock. For the rest of that afternoon he circulated about the stores and offices where the Legion members worked, so that by nightfall he had enough of them also worked up to his own pitch to compose a fair platoon. He was indefatigable, restrained yet forceful; there was something about him irresistible and prophetlike. Yet the recruits were with the commander in one thing: the official designation of the legion must be kept out of it—whereupon and without deliberate intent, he had gained his original end: he was now in command. He got them all together just before suppertime and divided them into squads and appointed officers and a staff; the younger ones, the ones who had not gone to France, taking proper fire by now. He addressed them, briefly, coldly: ". . . order . . . course of justice . . . let the people see that we have worn the uniform of the United States . . . And one thing more." For the moment now he had descended to familiarity: the regimental commander who knows his men by their first names. "I'll leave this to you fellows. I'll do what you say. I thought it might be a good thing if I wear my uniform until this business is settled. So they can see that Uncle Sam is present in more than spirit."

"But he's not," one said quickly, immediately; he was of the same cut as the commander, who by the way was not present. "This is not government trouble yet. Kennedy might not like it. This is Jefferson's trouble, not Washington's."

"Make him like it," Grimm said. "What does your Legion stand for, if not for the protection of America and Americans?"

"No," the other said. "I reckon we better not make a parade out of this. We can do what we want without that. Better. Ain't that right, boys?"

"All right," Grimm said. "I'll do as you say. But every man will want a pistol. We'll have a small arms' inspection here in one hour. Every man will report here."

"What's Kennedy going to say about pistols?" one said.

"I'll see to that," Grimm said. "Report here in one hour exactly, with side arms." He dismissed them. He crossed the quiet square to the sheriff's office. The sheriff was at home, they told him. "At home?" he repeated. "Now? What's he doing at home now?"

"Eating, I reckon. A man as big as him has got to eat several times a day."

"At home," Grimm repeated. He did not glare; it was again that cold and detached expression with which he had looked at the Legion commander. "Eating," he said. He went out, already walking fast. He recrossed the empty square, the quiet square empty of people peacefully at suppertables about that peaceful town and that peaceful country. He went to the sheriff's home. The sheriff said No at once.

"Fifteen or twenty folks milling around the square with pistols in their pants? No, no. That won't do. I can't have that. That won't do. You let me run this."

For a moment longer Grimm looked at the sheriff. Then he turned, already walking fast again. "All right," he said. "If that's the way you want it. I don't interfere with you and you don't interfere with me, then." It didn't sound like a threat. It was too flat, too final, too without heat. He went on, rapidly. The sheriff watched him; then he called. Grimm turned.

"You leave yours at home, too," the sheriff said. "You hear me?" Grimm didn't answer. He went on. The sheriff watched him out of sight, frowning.

That evening after supper the sheriff went back downtown—something he had not done for years save when urgent and inescapable business called. He found a picket of Grimm's men at the jail, and another in the courthouse, and a third patrolling the square and the adjacent streets. The others, the relief, they told the sheriff, were in the cotton office where Grimm was employed, which they were using for an orderly room, a P.C. The sheriff met Grimm on the street, making a round of inspection. "Come here, boy," the sheriff said. Grimm halted. He did not approach; the sheriff went to him. He patted Grimm's hip with a fat hand. "I told you to leave that at home," he said. Grimm said nothing. He watched the sheriff levelly. The sheriff sighed. "Well, if you won't, I reckon I'll have to make you a special deputy. But you ain't to even show that gun unless I tell you to. You hear me?"

"Certainly not," Grimm said. "You certainly wouldn't want me to draw it if I didn't see any need to."

"I mean, not till I tell you to."

"Certainly," Grimm said, without heat, patiently, immediately. "That's what we both said. Don't you worry. I'll be there."

Later, as the town quieted for the night, as the picture show emptied and the drugstores closed one by one, Grimm's platoon began to drop off too. He did not protest, watching them coldly; they became a little sheepish, defensive. Again without knowing it he had played a trump card. Because of the fact that they felt sheepish, feeling that somehow they had fallen short of his own cold ardor, they would return tomorrow if just to show him. A few remained; it was Saturday night anyhow, and someone got more chairs from somewhere and they started a poker game. It ran all night, though from time to time Grimm (he was not in the game; neither would he permit his second in command, the only other there who held the equivalent of commissioned rank, to engage) sent a squad out to make a patrol of the square. By this time the night marshal was one of them, though he too did not take a hand in the game.

Sunday was quiet. The poker game ran quietly through that day, broken by the periodical patrols, while the quiet church bells rang and the congregations gathered in decorous clumps of summer colors. About the square it was already known that the special Grand Jury would meet tomorrow. Somehow the very sound of the two words with their evocation, secret and irrevocable and something of a hidden and unsleeping and omnipotent eye watching the doings of men, began to reassure Grimm's men in their own makebelieve. So quickly is man unwittingly and unpredictably moved that without knowing that they were thinking it, the town had suddenly accepted Grimm with respect and perhaps a little awe and a deal of actual faith and confidence, as though somehow his vision and patriotism and pride in the town, the occasion, had been quicker and truer than theirs. His men anyway assumed and accepted this; after the sleepless night, the tenseness, the holiday, the suttee of volition's surrender, they were almost at the pitch where they might die for him, if occasion rose. They now moved in a grave and slightly awe-inspiring reflected light which was almost as palpable as the khaki would have been which Grimm wished them to wear, wished that they wore, as though each time they returned to the orderly room they dressed themselves anew in suave and austerely splendid scraps of his dream.

This lasted through Sunday night. The poker game ran. The caution, the surreptitiousness, which had clothed it was now gone. There was something about it too assured and serenely confident to the braggadocio; tonight when they heard the marshal's feet on the stairs, one said, "Ware M.P.'s," and for an instant they glanced at one another with hard, bright, daredevil eyes; then one said, quite loud: "Throw the son of a bitch out," and another through pursed lips made the immemorial sound. And so the next morning, Monday, when the first country cars and wagons began to gather, the platoon was again intact. And they now wore uniforms. It was their faces. Most of them were of an age, a generation, an experience. But it was more than that. They now had a profound and bleak gravity as they stood where crowds milled, grave, austere, detached, looking with blank, bleak eyes at the slow throngs who, feeling, sensing without knowing, drifted before them, slowing, staring, so that they would be ringed with faces rapt and empty and immobile as the faces of cows, approaching and drifting on, to be replaced. And all morning the voices came and went, in quiet question and answer: "There he goes. That young fellow with the automatic pistol. He's the captain of them. Special officer sent by the governor. He's the head of the whole thing. Sheriff ain't got no say in it today."

Later, when it was too late, Grimm told the sheriff: "If you had just listened to me. Let me bring him out of that cell in a squad of men, instead of sending him across the square with one deputy and not even handcuffed to him, in all that crowd where that damned

Buford didn't dare shoot, even if he could hit a barn door."

"How did I know he aimed to break, would think of trying it right then and there?" the sheriff said. "When Stevens had done told me he would plead guilty and take a life sentence."

But it was too late then. It was all over then. It happened in the middle of the square, halfway between the sidewalk and the courthouse, in the midst of a throng of people thick as on Fair Day, though the first that Grimm knew of it was when he heard the deputy's pistol twice, fired into the air. He knew at once what had happened, though he was at the time inside the courthouse. His reaction was definite and immediate. He was already running toward the shots when he shouted back over his shoulder at the man who had tagged him now for almost forty-eight hours as half aide and half orderly: "Turn in the fire alarm!"

"The fire alarm?" the aide said. "What—"

"Turn in the fire alarm!" Grimm shouted back. "It don't matter what folks think, just so they know that something . . ." He did not finish; he was gone.

He ran among running people, overtaking and passing them, since he had an objective and they did not; they were just running, the black, blunt, huge automatic opening a way for him like a plow. They looked at his tense, hard, young face with faces blanched and gaped, with round, toothed orifices; they made one long sound like a murmuring sigh: "There . . . went that way . . ." But already Grimm had seen the deputy, running, his pistol aloft in his hand. Grimm glanced once about and sprang forward again; in the throng which had evidently been pacing the deputy and the prisoner across the square was the inevitable hulking youth in the uniform of the Western Union, leading his bicycle by the

horns like a docile cow. Grimm rammed the pistol back
into the holster and flung the boy aside and sprang onto
the bicycle, with never a break in motion.

The bicycle possessed neither horn nor bell. Yet they
sensed him somehow and made way; in this too he
seemed to be served by certitude, the blind and untroubled faith in the rightness and infallibility of his
actions. When he overtook the running deputy he
slowed the bicycle. The deputy turned upon him a face
sweating, gaped with shouting and running. "He
turned," the deputy screamed. "Into that alley by—"

"I know," Grimm said. "Was he handcuffed?"

"Yes!" the deputy said. The bicycle leaped on.

Then he can't run very fast, Grimm thought. *He'll
have to hole up soon. Get out of the open, anyway.* He
turned into the alley, fast. It ran back between two
houses, with a board fence on one side. At that moment
the fire siren sounded for the first time, beginning and
mounting to a slow and sustained scream that seemed
at last to pass beyond the realm of hearing, into that of
sense, like soundless vibration. Grimm wheeled on,
thinking swiftly, logically, with a kind of fierce and con-
strained joy. *The first thing he will want is to get out of
sight,* he thought, looking about. On one hand the lane
was open, on the other stood the board fence six feet
high. At the end it was cut short off by a wooden gate,
beyond which was a pasture and then a deep ditch
which was a town landmark. The tops of tall trees
which grew in it just showed above the rim; a regiment could hide and deploy in it. "Ah," he said, aloud.
Without stopping or slowing he swept the bicycle
around and pedalled back down the lane toward the
street which he had just quitted. The wail of the siren
was dying now, descending back into hearing again, and
as he slewed the bicycle into the street he saw briefly

the running people and a car bearing down upon him. For all his pedalling the car overtook him; its occupants leaned shouting toward his set, forwardlooking face. "Get in here!" they shouted. "In here!" He did not answer. He did not look at them. The car had overshot him, slowing; now he passed it at his swift, silent, steady pace; again the car speeded up and passed him, the men leaning out and looking ahead. He was going fast too, silent, with the delicate swiftness of an apparition, the implacable undeviation of Juggernaut or Fate. Behind him the siren began again its rising wail. When next the men in the car looked back for him, he had vanished completely.

He had turned full speed into another lane. His face was rocklike, calm, still bright with that expression of fulfillment, of grave and reckless joy. This lane was more rutted than the other, and deeper. It came out at last upon a barren knoll where, springing to earth while the bicycle shot on, falling, he could see the full span of the ravine along the edge of town, his view of it broken by two or three Negro cabins which lined the edge of it. He was quite motionless, still, alone, fateful, like a landmark almost. Again from the town behind him the scream of the siren began to fall.

Then he saw Christmas. He saw the man, small with distance, appear up out of the ditch, his hands close together. As Grimm watched he saw the fugitive's hands glint once like the flash of a heliograph as the sun struck the handcuffs, and it seemed to him that even from here he could hear the panting and desperate breath of the man who even now was not free. Then the tiny figure ran again and vanished beyond the nearest Negro cabin.

Grimm ran too now. He ran swiftly, yet there was no haste about him, no effort. There was nothing vengeful about him either, no fury, no outrage. Christmas saw that, himself. Because for an instant they looked at one another almost face to face. That was when Grimm, running, was in the act of passing beyond the corner of the cabin. At that instant Christmas leaped from the rear window of it, with an effect as of magic, his manacled hands high and now glinting as if they were on fire. For an instant they glared at one another, the one stopped in the act of crouching from the leap, the other in midstride of running, before Grimm's momentum carried him past the corner. In that instant he saw that Christmas now carried a heavy nickelplated pistol. Grimm whirled and turned and sprang back past the corner, drawing the automatic.

He was thinking swiftly, calmly, with that quiet joy: *He can do two things. He can try for the ditch again, or he can dodge around the house until one of us gets a shot. And the ditch is on his side of the house.* He reacted immediately. He ran at full speed around the corner which he had just turned. He did it as though under the protection of a magic or a providence, or as if he knew that Christmas would not be waiting there with the pistol. He ran on past the next corner without pausing.

He was beside the ditch now. He stopped, motionless in midstride. Above the blunt, cold rake of the automatic his face had that serene, unearthly luminousness of angels in church windows. He was moving again almost before he had stopped, with that lean, swift, blind obedience to whatever Player moved him on the Board. He ran to the ditch. But in the beginning of his plunge downward into the brush that choked the steep descent he turned, clawing. He saw now that the cabin sat some two feet above the earth. He had not noticed it before, in his haste. He knew now that he had lost a point. That Christmas had been watching his legs all the time beneath the house. He said, "Good man.

His plunge carried him some distance before he could stop himself and climb back out. He seemed indefatigable, not flesh and blood, as if the Player who moved him for pawn likewise found him breath. Without a pause, in the same surge that carried him up out of the ditch again, he was running again. He ran around the cabin in time to see Christmas fling himself over a fence three hundred yards away. He did not fire, because Christmas was now running through a small garden and straight toward a house. Running, he saw Christmas leap up the back steps and enter the house. "Hah," Grimm said. "The preacher's house. Hightower's house."

He did not slow, though he swerved and ran around the house and to the street. The car which had passed him and lost him and then returned was just where it should have been, just where the Player had desired it to be. It stopped without signal from him and three men got out. Without a word Grimm turned and ran across the yard and into the house where the old disgraced minister lived alone, and the three men followed, rushing into the hall, pausing, bringing with them into its stale and cloistral dimness something of the savage summer sunlight which they had just left.

It was upon them, of them: its shameless savageness. Out of it their faces seemed to glare with bodiless suspension as though from haloes as they stooped and raised Hightower, his face bleeding, from the floor where Christmas, running up the hall, his raised and armed and manacled hands full of glare and glitter like lightning bolts, so that he resembled a vengeful and furious god pronouncing a doom, had struck him down. They held the old man on his feet.

"Which room?" Grimm said, shaking him. "Which room, old man?"

"Gentlemen!" Hightower said. Then he said: "Men! Men!"

"Which room, old man?" Grimm shouted.

They held Hightower on his feet; in the gloomy hall, after the sunlight, he too with his bald head and his big pale face streaked with blood, was terrible. "Men!" he cried. "Listen to me. He was here that night. He was with me the night of the murder. I swear to God—"

"Jesus Christ!" Grimm cried, his young voice clear and outraged like that of a young priest. "Has every preacher and old maid in Jefferson taken their pants down to the yellowbellied son of a bitch?" He flung the old man aside and ran on.

It was as though he had been merely waiting for the Player to move him again, because with that unfailing certitude he ran straight to the kitchen and into the doorway, already firing, almost before he could have seen the table overturned and standing on its edge across the corner of the room, and the bright and glittering hands of the man who crouched behind it, resting upon the upper edge. Grimm emptied the automatic's magazine into the table; later someone covered all five shots with a folded handkerchief.

But the Player was not done yet. When the others reached the kitchen they saw the table flung aside now and Grimm stooping over the body. When they approached to see what he was about, they saw that the man was not dead yet, and when they saw what Grimm was doing one of the men gave a choked cry and stumbled back into the wall and began to vomit. Then Grimm too sprang back, flinging behind him the bloody butcher knife. "Now you'll let white women alone, even in hell," he said. But the man on the floor had not moved. He just lay there, with his eyes open and empty of everything save consciousness, and with something, a shadow, about his mouth. For a long moment he looked up at them with peaceful and unfathomable and unbearable eyes. Then his face, body, all, seemed to collapse, to fall in upon itself, and from out the slashed garments about his hips and loins the pent black blood seemed to rush like a released breath. It seemed to rush out of his pale body like the rush of sparks from a rising rocket; upon that black blast the man seemed to rise soaring into their memories forever and ever. They are not to lose it, in whatever peaceful valleys, beside whatever placid and reassuring streams of old age, in the mirroring faces of whatever children they will contemplate old disasters and newer hopes. It will be there, musing, quiet, steadfast, not fading and not particularly threatful, but of itself alone serene, of itself alone triumphant. Again from the town, deadened a little by the walls, the scream of the siren mounted toward its unbelievable crescendo, passing out of the realm of hearing.

1940. DELTA AUTUMN

SOON now they would enter the Delta. The sensation was familiar to old Isaac McCaslin. It had
been renewed like this each last week in November for
more than fifty years—the last hill, at the foot of which
the rich unbroken alluvial flatness began as the sea
began at the base of its cliffs, dissolving away beneath
the unhurried November rain as the sea itself would
dissolve away.

At first they had come in wagons: the guns, the bedding, the dogs, the food, the whiskey, the keen heart-
lifting anticipation of hunting; the young men who
could drive all night and all the following day in the
cold rain and pitch a camp in the rain and sleep in the
wet blankets and rise at daylight the next morning and
hunt. There had been bear then. A man shot a doe or a
fawn as quickly as he did a buck, and in the afternoons they shot wild turkey with pistols to test their
stalking skill and marksmanship, feeding all but the
breast to the dogs. But that time was gone now. Now
they went in cars, driving faster and faster each year
because the roads were better and they had farther and
farther to drive, the territory in which game still existed
drawing yearly inward as his life was drawing inward,
until now he was the last of those who had once made
the journey in wagons without feeling it and now those
who accompanied him were the sons and even grandsons
of the men who had ridden for twenty-four hours in the
rain or sleet behind the steaming mules. They called

him "Uncle Ike" now, and he no longer told anyone how near eighty he actually was because he knew as well as they did that he no longer had any business making such expeditions, even by car.

In fact, each time now, on that first night in camp, lying aching and sleepless in the harsh blankets, his blood only faintly warmed by the single thin whiskey-and-water which he allowed himself, he would tell himself that this would be his last. But he would stand that trip—he still shot almost as well as he ever had, still killed almost as much of the game he saw as he ever killed; he no longer even knew how many deer had fallen before his gun—and the fierce long heat of the next summer would renew him. Then November would come again, and again in the car with two of the sons of his old companions, whom he had taught not only how to distinguish between the prints left by a buck or a doe but between the sound they made in moving, he would look ahead past the jerking arc of the windshield wiper and see the land flatten suddenly and swoop, dissolving away beneath the rain as the sea itself would dissolve, and he would say, "Well, boys, there it is again."

This time though, he didn't have time to speak. The driver of the car stopped it, slamming it to a skidding halt on the greasy pavement without warning, actually flinging the two passengers forward until they caught themselves with their braced hands against the dash. "What the hell, Roth!" the man in the middle said. "Can't you whistle first when you do that? Hurt you, Uncle Ike?"

"No," the old man said. "What's the matter?" The driver didn't answer. Still leaning forward, the old man looked sharply past the face of the man between them, at the face of his kinsman. It was the youngest face of

them all, aquiline, saturnine, a little ruthless, the face of
his ancestor too, tempered a little, altered a little, staring sombrely through the streaming windshield across
which the twin wipers flicked and flicked.

"I didn't intend to come back in here this time," he
said suddenly and harshly.

"You said that back in Jefferson last week," the old
man said. "Then you changed your mind. Have you
changed it again? This ain't a very good time to——"

"Oh, Roth's coming," the man in the middle said.
His name was Legate. He seemed to be speaking to no
one, as he was looking at neither of them. "If it was just
a buck he was coming all this distance for, now. But he's
got a doe in here. Of course a old man like Uncle Ike
can't be interested in no doe, not one that walks on two
legs—when she's standing up, that is. Pretty light-
colored, too. The one he was after them nights last fall
when he said he was coon-hunting, Uncle Ike. The one
I figured maybe he was still running when he was gone
all that month last January. But of course a old man like
Uncle Ike ain't got no interest in nothing like that." He
chortled, still looking at no one, not completely jeering.

"What?" the old man said. "What's that?" But he
had not even so much as glanced at Legate. He was
still watching his kinsman's face. The eyes behind the
spectacles were the blurred eyes of an old man, but they
were quite sharp too; eyes which could still see a gun-
barrel and what ran beyond it as well as any of them
could. He was remembering himself now: how last year,
during the final stage by motor boat in to where they
camped, a box of food had been lost overboard and how
on the next day his kinsman had gone back to the
nearest town for supplies and had been gone overnight.
And when he did return, something had happened to
him. He would go into the woods with his rifle each

dawn when the others went, but the old man, watching him, knew that he was not hunting. "All right," he said. "Take me and Will on to shelter where we can wait for the truck, and you can go on back."

"I'm going in," the other said harshly. "Don't worry. Because this will be the last of it."

"The last of deer hunting, or of doe hunting?" Legate said. This time the old man paid no attention to him even by speech. He still watched the young man's savage and brooding face.

"Why?" he said.

"After Hitler gets through with it? Or Smith or Jones or Roosevelt or Willkie or whatever he will call himself in this country?"

"We'll stop him in this country," Legate said. "Even if he calls himself George Washington."

"How?" Edmonds said. "By singing 'God Bless America' in bars at midnight and wearing dime-store flags in our lapels?"

"So that's what's worrying you," the old man said. "I ain't noticed this country being short of defenders yet, when it needed them. You did some of it yourself twenty-odd years ago, before you were a grown man even. This country is a little mite stronger than any one man or group of men, outside of it or even inside of it either. I reckon, when the time comes and some of you have done got tired of hollering we are whipped if we don't go to war and some more are hollering we are whipped if we do, it will cope with one Austrian paper-hanger, no matter what he will be calling himself. My pappy and some other better men than any of them you named tried once to tear it in two with a war, and they failed."

"And what have you got left?" the other said. "Half the people without jobs and half the factories closed by strikes. Half the people on public dole that won't work and half that couldn't work even if they would. Too much cotton and corn and hogs, and not enough for people to eat and wear. The country full of people to tell a man how he can't raise his own cotton whether he will or won't, and Sally Rand with a sergeant's stripes and not even the fan couldn't fill the army rolls. Too much not-butter and not even the guns——"

"We got a deer camp—if we ever get to it," Legate said. "Not to mention does."

"It's a good time to mention does," the old man said. "Does and fawns both. The only fighting anywhere that ever had anything of God's blessing on it has been when men fought to protect does and fawns. If it's going to come to fighting, that's a good thing to mention and remember too."

"Haven't you discovered in—how many years more than seventy is it?—that women and children are one thing there's never any scarcity of?" Edmonds said.

"Maybe that's why all I am worrying about right now is that ten miles of river we still have got to run before we can make camp," the old man said. "So let's get on."

They went on. Soon they were going fast again, as Edmonds always drove, consulting neither of them about the speed just as he had given neither of them any warning when he slammed the car to stop. The old man relaxed again. He watched, as he did each recurrent November while more than sixty of them passed, the land which he had seen change. At first there had been only the old towns along the River and the old towns along the hills, from each of which the planters with their gangs of slaves and then of hired laborers had wrested from the impenetrable jungle of water-standing cane and cypress, gum and holly and oak and ash, cotton patches which, as the years passed, became fields and then plantations. The paths made by deer and bear became roads and then highways, with towns in turn springing up along them and along the rivers Tallahatchie and Sunflower which joined and became the Yazoo, the River of the Dead of the Choctaws—the thick, slow, black, unsunned streams almost without current, which once each year ceased to flow at all and then reversed, spreading, drowning the rich land and subsiding again, leaving it still richer.

Most of that was gone now. Now a man drove two hundred miles from Jefferson before he found wilderness to hunt in. Now the land lay open from the cradling hills on the east to the rampart of levee on the west, standing horseman-tall with cotton for the world's looms —the rich black land, imponderable and vast, fecund up to the very doorsteps of the Negroes who worked it and of the white men who owned it; which exhausted the hunting life of a dog in one year, the working life of a mule in five and of a man in twenty—the land in which neon flashed past them from the little countless towns, and countless shining this-year's automobiles sped past them on the broad plumb-ruled highways, yet in which the only permanent mark of man's occupation seemed to be the tremendous gins, constructed in sections of sheet iron and in a week's time though they were, since no man, millionaire though he be, would build more than a roof and walls to shelter the camping equipment he lived from, when he knew that once each ten years or so his house would be flooded to the second storey and all within it ruined;—the land across which there came now no scream of panther but instead the long hooting of locomotives: trains of incredible length and drawn by a single engine, since there was no gradient anywhere and no elevation save those raised by forgotten aboriginal hands as refuges

from the yearly water and used by their Indian successors to sepulchre their fathers' bones, and all that remained of that old time were the Indian names on the
little towns and usually pertaining to water—Aluschaskuna, Tillatoba, Homochitto, Yazoo.

By early afternoon, they were on water. At the last
little Indian-named town at the end of pavement they
waited until the other car and the two trucks—the one
carrying the bedding and tents and food, the other the
horses—overtook them. They left the concrete and,
after another mile or so, the gravel too. In caravan they
ground on through the ceaselessly dissolving afternoon, with skid-chains on the wheels now, lurching and
splashing and sliding among the ruts, until presently
it seemed to him that the retrograde of his remembering
had gained an inverse velocity from their own slow
progress, that the land had retreated not in minutes
from the last spread of gravel but in years, decades,
back toward what it had been when he first knew it:
the road they now followed once more the ancient path-
way of bear and deer, the diminishing fields they now
passed once more scooped punily and terrifically by
axe and saw and mule-drawn plow from the wilderness'
flank, out of the brooding and immemorial tangle, in
place of ruthless mile-wide parallelograms wrought by
ditching the dyking machinery.

They reached the river landing and unloaded, the
horses to go overland down stream to a point opposite
the camp and swim the river, themselves and the bedding and food and dogs and guns in the motor launch.
It was himself, though no horseman, no farmer, not even
a countryman save by his distant birth and boyhood,
who coaxed and soothed the two horses, drawing them
by his own single frail hand until, backing, filling, trembling a little, they surged, halted, then sprang scram-

bling down from the truck, possessing no affinity for
them as creatures, beasts, but being merely insulated by
his years and time from the corruption of steel and
oiled moving parts which tainted the others.

Then, his old hammer double gun which was only
twelve years younger than he standing between his
knees, he watched even the last puny marks of man—
cabin, clearing, the small and irregular fields which a
year ago were jungle and in which the skeleton stalks of
this year's cotton stood almost as tall and rank as the
old cane had stood, as if man had had to marry his
planting to the wilderness in order to conquer it—
fall away and vanish. The twin banks marched with
wilderness as he remembered it—the tangle of brier
and cane impenetrable even to sight twenty feet away,
the tall tremendous soaring of oak and gum and ash
and hickory which had rung to no axe save the hunter's,
had echoed to no machinery save the beat of old-time
steam boats traversing it or to the snarling of launches
like their own of people going into it to dwell for a week
or two weeks because it was still wilderness. There was
some of it left, although now it was two hundred miles
from Jefferson when once it had been thirty. He had
watched it, not being conquered, destroyed, so much
as retreating since its purpose was served now and its
time an outmoded time, retreating southward through
this inverted-apex, this ∇-shaped section of earth between hills and River until what was left of it seemed
now to be gathered and for the time arrested in one
tremendous density of brooding and inscrutable im-
penetrability at the ultimate funnelling tip.

They reached the site of their last-year's camp with
still two hours left of light. "You go on over under that
driest tree and set down," Legate told him. "—if you
can find it. Me and these other young boys will do this."

He did neither. He was not tired yet. That would come later. *Maybe it won't come at all this time,* he thought, as he had thought at this point each November for the last five or six of them. *Maybe I will go out on stand in the morning too;* knowing that he would not, not even if he took the advice and sat down under the driest shelter and did nothing until camp was made and supper cooked. Because it would not be the fatigue. It would be because he would not sleep tonight but would lie instead wakeful and peaceful on the cot amid the tent-filling snoring and the rain's whisper as he always did on the first night in camp; peaceful, without regret or fretting, telling himself that was all right too, who didn't have so many of them left as to waste one sleeping.

In his slicker he directed the unloading of the boat— the tents, the stove, the bedding, the food for themselves and the dogs until there should be meat in camp. He sent two of the Negroes to cut firewood; he had the cook-tent raised and the stove up and a fire going and supper cooking while the big tent was still being staked down. Then in the beginning of dusk he crossed in the boat to where the horses waited, backing and snorting at the water. He took the lead-ropes and with no more weight than that and his voice, he drew them down into the water and held them beside the boat with only their heads above the surface, as though they actually were suspended from his frail and strengthless old man's hands, while the boat recrossed and each horse in turn lay prone in the shallows, panting and trembling, its eyes rolling in the dusk, until the same weightless hand and unraised voice gathered it surging upward, splashing and thrashing up the bank.

Then the meal was ready. The last of light was gone

now save the thin stain of it snared somewhere between the river's surface and the rain. He had the single glass of thin whiskey-and-water, then, standing in the churned mud beneath the stretched tarpaulin, he said grace over the fried slabs of pork, the hot soft shapeless bread, the canned beans and molasses and coffee in iron plates and cups,—the town food, brought along with them—then covered himself again, the others following. "Eat," he said. "Eat it all up. I don't want a piece of town meat in camp after breakfast tomorrow. Then you boys will hunt. You'll have to. When I first started hunting in this bottom sixty years ago with old General Compson and Major de Spain and Roth's grandfather and Will Legate's too, Major de Spain wouldn't allow but two pieces of foreign grub in his camp. That was one side of pork and one ham of beef. And not to eat for the first supper and breakfast neither. It was to save until along toward the end of camp when everybody was so sick of bear meat and coon and venison that we couldn't even look at it."

"I thought Uncle Ike was going to say the pork and beef was for the dogs," Legate said, chewing. "But that's right; I remember. You just shot the dogs a mess of wild turkey every evening when they got tired of deer guts."

"Times are different now," another said. "There was game here then."

"Yes," the old man said quietly. "There was game here then."

"Besides, they shot does then too," Legate said. "As it is now, we ain't got but one doe-hunter in——"

"And better men hunted it," Edmonds said. He stood at the end of the rough plank table, eating rapidly and steadily as the others ate. But again the old man looked

sharply across at the sullen, handsome, brooding face
which appeared now darker and more sullen still in the
light of the smoky lantern. "Go on. Say it."

"I didn't say that," the old man said. "There are good
men everywhere, at all times. Most men are. Some are
just unlucky, because most men are a little better than
their circumstances give them a chance to be. And I've
known some that even the circumstances couldn't stop."

"Well, I wouldn't say—" Legate said.

"So you've lived almost eighty years," Edmonds said,
"and that's what you finally learned about the other
animals you lived among. I suppose the question to ask
you is, where have you been all the time you were
dead?"

There was a silence; for the instant even Legate's jaw
stopped chewing while he gaped at Edmonds. "Well,
by God, Roth—" the third speaker said. But it was the
old man who spoke, his voice still peaceful and untroubled and merely grave:

"Maybe so," he said. "But if being what you call
alive would have learned me any different, I reckon I'm
satisfied, wherever it was I've been."

"Well, I wouldn't say that Roth—" Legate said.

The third speaker was still leaning forward a little
over the table, looking at Edmonds. "Meaning that it's
only because folks happen to be watching him that a
man behaves at all," he said. "Is that it?"

"Yes," Edmonds said. "A man in a blue coat, with a
badge on it watching him. Maybe just the badge."

"I deny that," the old man said. "I don't——"

The other two paid no attention to him. Even Legate
was listening to them for the moment, his mouth still
full of food and still open a little, his knife with another
lump of something balanced on the tip of the blade
arrested halfway to his mouth. "I'm glad I don't have

your opinion of folks," the third speaker said. "I take it you include yourself."

"I see," Edmonds said. "You prefer Uncle Ike's opinion of circumstances. All right. Who makes the circumstances?"

"Luck," the third said. "Chance. Happen-so. I see what you are getting at. But that's just what Uncle Ike said: that now and then, maybe most of the time, man is a little better than the net result of his and his neighbors' doings, when he gets the chance to be."

This time Legate swallowed first. He was not to be stopped this time. "Well, I wouldn't say that Roth Edmonds can hunt one doe every day and night for two weeks and was a poor hunter or a unlucky one neither. A man that still have the same doe left to hunt on again next year——"

"Have some meat," the man next to him said.

"—ain't so unlucky— What?" Legate said.

"Have some meat." The other offered the dish.

"I got some," Legate said.

"Have some more," the third speaker said. "You and Roth Edmonds both. Have a heap of it. Clapping your jaws together that way with nothing to break the shock." Someone chortled. Then they all laughed, with relief, the tension broken. But the old man was speaking, even into the laughter, in that peaceful and still untroubled voice:

"I still believe. I see proof everywhere. I grant that man made a heap of his circumstances, him and his living neighbors between them. He even inherited some of them already made, already almost ruined even. A while ago Henry Wyatt there said how there used to be more game here. There was. So much that we even killed does. I seem to remember Will Legate mentioning that too—" Someone laughed, a single guffaw, still-born. It ceased and they all listened, gravely, looking down at their plates. Edmonds was drinking his coffee, sullen, brooding, inattentive.

"Some folks still kill does," Wyatt said. "There won't be just one buck hanging in this bottom tomorrow night without any head to fit it."

"I didn't say all men," the old man said. "I said most men. And not just because there is a man with a badge to watch us. We probably won't even see him unless maybe he will stop here about noon tomorrow and eat dinner with us and check our licenses——"

"We don't kill does because if we did kill does in a few years there wouldn't even be any bucks left to kill, Uncle Ike," Wyatt said.

"According to Roth yonder, that's one thing we won't never have to worry about," the old man said. "He said on the way here this morning that does and fawns—I believe he said women and children—are two things this world ain't ever lacked. But that ain't all of it," he said. "That's just the mind's reason a man has to give himself because the heart don't always have time to bother with thinking up words that fit together. God created man and He created the world for him to live in and I reckon He created the kind of world He would have wanted to live in if He had been a man—the ground to walk on, the big woods, the trees and the water, and the game to live in it. And maybe He didn't put the desire to hunt and kill game in man but I reckon He knew it was going to be there, that man was going to teach it to himself, since he wasn't quite God himself yet——"

"When will he be?" Wyatt said.

"I think that every man and woman, at the instant when it don't even matter whether they marry or not, I think that whether they marry then or afterward or don't never, at that instant the two of them together were God."

"Then there are some Gods in this world I wouldn't want to touch, and with a damn long stick," Edmonds said. He set his coffee cup down and looked at Wyatt. "And that includes myself, if that's what you want to know. I'm going to bed." He was gone. There was a general movement among the others. But it ceased and they stood again about the table, not looking at the old man, apparently held there yet by his quiet and peaceful voice as the heads of the swimming horses had been held above the water by his weightless hand. The three Negroes—the cook and his helper and old Isham—were sitting quietly in the entrance of the kitchen tent, listening too, the three faces dark and motionless and musing.

"He put them both here: man, and the game he would follow and kill, foreknowing it. I believe He said, 'So be it.' I reckon He even foreknew the end. But He said, 'I will give him his chance. I will give him warning and foreknowledge too, along with the desire to follow and the power to slay. The woods and fields he ravages and the game he devastates will be the consequence and signature of his crime and guilt, and his punishment.'— Bed time," he said. His voice and inflection did not change at all. "Breakfast at four o'clock, Isham. We want meat on the ground by sunup time."

There was a good fire in the sheet-iron heater; the tent was warm and was beginning to dry out, except for the mud underfoot. Edmonds was already rolled into his blankets, motionless, his face to the wall. Isham had made up his bed too—the strong, battered iron cot, the stained mattress which was not quite soft enough, the worn, often-washed blankets which as the years passed were less and less warm enough. But the tent was warm; presently, when the kitchen was cleaned up

and readied for breakfast, the young Negro would
come in to lie down before the heater, where he could
be roused to put fresh wood into it from time to time.
And then, he knew now he would not sleep tonight anyway; he no longer needed to tell himself that perhaps
he would. But it was all right now. The day was ended
now and night faced him, but alarmless, empty of fret.
Maybe I came for this, he thought: *Not to hunt, but
for this. I would come anyway, even if only to go back
home tomorrow.* Wearing only his bagging woolen
underwear, his spectacles folded away in the worn case
beneath the pillow where he could reach them readily
and his lean body fitted easily into the old worn groove
of mattress and blankets, he lay on his back, his hands
crossed on his breast and his eyes closed while the
others undressed and went to bed and the last of the
sporadic talking died into snoring. Then he opened his
eyes and lay peaceful and quiet as a child, looking up
at the motionless belly of rain-murmured canvas upon
which the glow of the heater was dying slowly away
and would fade still further until the young Negro, lying
on two planks before it, would sit up and stoke it and lie
back down again.

They had a house once. That was sixty years ago,
when the Big Bottom was only thirty miles from Jefferson and old Major de Spain, who had been his father's
cavalry commander in '61 and '2 and '3 and '4, and his
cousin (his older brother; his father too) had taken him
into the woods for the first time. Old Sam Fathers was
alive then, born in slavery, son of a Negro slave and a
Chickasaw chief, who had taught him how to shoot, not
only when to shoot but when not to; such a November
dawn as tomorrow would be and the old man led him
straight to the great cypress and he had known the buck
would pass exactly there because there was something

running in Sam Fathers' veins which ran in the veins of the buck too, and they stood there against the tremendous trunk, the old man of seventy and the boy of twelve, and there was nothing save the dawn until suddenly the buck was there, smoke-colored out of nothing, magnificent with speed: and Sam Fathers said, 'Now. Shoot quick and shoot slow:' and the gun levelled rapidly without haste and crashed and he walked to the buck lying still intact and still in the shape of that magnificent speed and bled it with Sam's knife and Sam dipped his hands into the hot blood and marked his face forever while he stood trying not to tremble, humbly and with pride too though the boy of twelve had been unable to phrase it then: *I slew you; my bearing must not shame your quitting life. My conduct forever onward must become your death;* marking him for that and for more than that: that day and himself and Mc-Caslin juxtaposed, not against the wilderness but against the tamed land, the old wrong and shame itself, in repudiation and denial at least of the land and the wrong and shame, even if he couldn't cure the wrong and eradicate the shame, who at fourteen when he learned of it had believed he could do both when he became competent, and when at twenty-one he became competent he knew that he could do neither but at least he could repudiate the wrong and shame, at least in principle, and at least the land itself in fact, for his son at least: and did, thought he had: then (married then) in a rented cubicle in a back-street stock-traders' boarding-house, the first and last time he ever saw her naked body, himself and his wife juxtaposed in their turn against that same land, that same wrong and shame from whose regret and grief he would at least save and free his son and, saving and freeing his son, lost him.

They had the house then. That roof, the two weeks of each November which they spent under it, had become his home. Although since that time they had lived during the two fall weeks in tents and not always in the same place two years in succession and now his companions were the sons and even the grandsons of them with whom he had lived in the house, and for almost fifty years now the house itself had not even existed, the conviction, the sense and feeling of home, had been merely transferred into the canvas. He owned a house in Jefferson, a good house though small, where he had had a wife and lived with her and lost her, ay, lost her even though he had lost her in the rented cubicle before he and his old clever dipsomaniac partner had finished the house for them to move into it: but lost her, because she loved him. But women hope for so much. They never live too long to still believe that anything within the scope of their passionate wanting is likewise within the range of their passionate hope: and it was still kept for him by his dead wife's widowed niece and her children, and he was comfortable in it, his wants and needs and even the small trying harmless crochets of an old man looked after by blood at least related to the blood which he had elected out of all the earth to cherish. But he spent the time within those walls waiting for November, because even this tent with its muddy floor and the bed which was not wide enough nor soft enough nor even warm enough, was his home and these men, some of whom he only saw during these two November weeks and not one of whom even bore any name he used to know—De Spain and Compson and Ewell and Hogganbeck—were more his kin than any. Because this was his land——

The shadow of the youngest Negro loomed. It soared, blotting the heater's dying glow from the ceiling, the wood billets thumping into the iron maw until the glow, the flame, leaped high and bright across the canvas. But the Negro's shadow still remained, by its length and breadth, standing, since it covered most of the ceiling, until after a moment he raised himself on one elbow to look. It was not the Negro, it was his kinsman; when he spoke the other turned sharp against the red firelight the sullen and ruthless profile.

"Nothing," Edmonds said. "Go on back to sleep."

"Since Will Legate mentioned it," McCaslin said, "I remember you had some trouble sleeping in here last fall too. Only you called it coon-hunting then. Or was it Will Legate called it that?" The other didn't answer. Then he turned and went back to his bed. McCaslin, still propped on his elbow, watched until the other's shadow sank down the wall and vanished, became one with the mass of sleeping shadows. "That's right," he said. "Try to get some sleep. We must have meat in camp tomorrow. You can do all the setting up you want to after that." He lay down again, his hands crossed again on his breast, watching the glow of the heater on the canvas ceiling. It was steady again now, the fresh wood accepted, being assimilated; soon it would begin to fade again, taking with it the last echo of that sudden upflare of a young man's passion and unrest. Let him lie awake for a little while, he thought; He will lie still some day for a long time without even dissatisfaction to disturb him. And lying awake here, in these surroundings, would soothe him if anything could, if anything could soothe a man just forty years old. Yes, he thought; Forty years old or thirty, or even the trembling and sleepless ardor of a boy; already the tent, the rain-murmured canvas globe, was once more filled with it. He lay on his back, his eyes closed, his breathing quiet and peaceful as a child's, listening to it—that silence which was never silence but was myriad. He could almost see it, tremendous, primeval, looming, musing downward upon this puny, evanescent clutter of human sojourn which after a single brief week would vanish and in another week would be completely healed, traceless in the unmarked solitude. Because it was his land, although he had never owned a foot of it. He had never wanted to, not even after he saw plain its ultimate doom, watching it retreat year by year before the onslaught of axe and saw and log-lines and then dynamite and tractor plows, because it belonged to no man. It belonged to all; they had only to use it well, humbly and with pride. Then suddenly he knew why he had never wanted to own any of it, arrest at least that much of what people called progress, measure his longevity at least against that much of its ultimate fate. It was because there was just exactly enough of it. He seemed to see the two of them—himself and the wilderness—as coevals, his own span as a hunter, a woodsman, not contemporary with his first breath but transmitted to him, assumed by him gladly, humbly, with joy and pride, from that old Major de Spain and that old Sam Fathers who had taught him to hunt, the two spans running out together, not toward oblivion, nothingness, but into a dimension free of both time and space, where once more the untreed land warped and wrung to mathematical squares of rank cotton for the frantic old-world people to turn into shells to shoot at one another, would find ample room for both—the names, the faces of the old men he had known and loved and for a little while outlived, moving again among the shades of tall unaxed trees and sightless brakes where the wild strong immortal game ran forever before the tireless belling immortal hounds, falling and rising phoenix-like to the soundless guns.

He had been asleep. The lantern was lighted now. Outside in the darkness the oldest Negro, Isham, was beating a spoon against the bottom of a tin pan and crying, "Raise up and get yo foa clock coffy. Raise up and get yo foa clock coffy," and the tent was full of low talk and of men dressing, and Legate's voice, repeating: "Get out of here now and let Uncle Ike sleep. If you wake him up, he'll go out with us. And he ain't got any business in the woods this morning."

So he didn't move. He lay with his eyes closed, his breathing gentle and peaceful, and heard them one by one leave the tent. He listened to the breakfast sounds from the table beneath the tarpaulin and heard them depart—the horses, the dogs, the last voice until it died away and there was only the sounds of the Negroes clearing breakfast away. After a while he might possibly even hear the first faint clear cry of the first hound ring through the wet woods from where the buck had bedded, then he would go back to sleep again— The tent-flap swung in and fell. Something jarred sharply against the end of the cot and a hand grasped his knee through the blanket before he could open his eyes. It was Edmonds, carrying a shotgun in place of his rifle. He spoke in a harsh, rapid voice:

"Sorry to wake you. There will be a——"

"I was awake," McCaslin said. "Are you going to shoot that shotgun today?"

"You just told me last night you want meat," Edmonds said. "There will be a——"

"Since when did you start having trouble getting meat with your rifle?"

"All right," the other said, with that harsh, restrained, furious impatience. Then McCaslin saw in his hand a thick oblong: an envelope. "There will be a message here some time this morning, looking for me. Maybe it won't come. If it does, give the messenger this and tell h— say I said No."

"A what?" McCaslin said. "Tell who?" He half rose onto his elbow as Edmonds jerked the envelope onto the blanket, already turning toward the entrance, the envelope striking solid and heavy and without noise and already sliding from the bed until McCaslin caught it, divining by feel through the paper as instantaneously and conclusively as if he had opened the envelope and looked, the thick sheaf of banknotes. "Wait," he said. "Wait:"—more than the blood kinsman, more even than the senior in years, so that the other paused, the canvas lifted, looking back, and McCaslin saw that outside it was already day. "Tell her No," he said. "Tell her." They stared at one another—the old face, wan, sleep-raddled above the tumbled bed, the dark and sullen younger one at once furious and cold. "Will Legate was right. This is what you called coon-hunting. And now this." He didn't raise the envelope. He made no motion, no gesture to indicate it. "What did you promise her that you haven't the courage to face her and retract?"

"Nothing!" the other said. "Nothing! This is all of it. Tell her I said No." He was gone. The tent flap lifted on an in-waft of faint light and the constant murmur of rain, and fell again, leaving the old man still half-raised onto one elbow, the envelope clutched in the other shaking hand. Afterward it seemed to him that he had begun to hear the approaching boat almost immediately, before the other could have got out of sight even. It seemed to him that there had been no interval whatever: the tent flap falling on the same out-waft of faint and rain-filled light like the suspiration and expiration of the same breath and then in the next second lifted again—the mounting snarl of the outboard engine, increasing, nearer and nearer and louder and louder then cut short off, ceasing with the absolute instantaneity of a blown-out candle, into the lap and plop of water under the bows as the skiff slid in to the bank, the youngest Negro, the youth, raising the tent flap beyond which for that instant he saw the boat—a small skiff with a Negro man sitting in the stern beside the up-slanted motor—then the woman entering, in a man's hat and a man's slicker and rubber boots, carrying the blanket-swaddled bundle on one arm and holding the edge of the unbuttoned raincoat over it with the other hand: and bringing something else, something intangible, an effluvium which he knew he would recognize in a moment because Isham had already told him, warned him, by sending the young Negro to the tent to announce the visitor instead of coming himself, the flap falling at last on the young Negro and they were alone —the face indistinct and as yet only young and with dark eyes, queerly colorless but not ill and not that of a country woman despite the garments she wore, looking down at him where he sat upright on the cot now, clutching the envelope, the soiled undergarment bagging about him and the twisted blankets huddled about his hips.

"Is that his?" he cried. "Don't lie to me!"

"Yes," she said. "He's gone."

"Yes. He's gone. You won't jump him here. Not this time. I don't reckon even you expected that. He left you this. Here." He fumbled at the envelope. It was not to pick it up, because it was still in his hand; he had never put it down. It was as if he had to fumble somehow to co-ordinate physically his heretofore obedient hand with what his brain was commanding of it, as if he had never performed such an action before, extending the envelope at last, saying again, "Here. Take it. Take

it:" until he became aware of her eyes, or not the eyes
so much as the look, the regard fixed now on his face
with that immersed contemplation, that bottomless and
intent candor, of a child. If she had ever seen either the
envelope or his movement to extend it, she did not show
it.

"You're Uncle Isaac," she said.

"Yes," he said. "But never mind that. Here. Take it.
He said to tell you No." She looked at the envelope, then
she took it. It was sealed and bore no superscription.
Nevertheless, even after she glanced at the front of it,
he watched her hold it in the one free hand and tear the
corner off with her teeth and manage to rip it open and
tilt the neat sheaf of bound notes onto the blanket without even glancing at them and look into the empty envelope and take the edge between her teeth and tear it
completely open before she crumpled and dropped it.

"That's just money," she said.

"What did you expect? What else did you expect?
You have known him long enough or at least often
enough to have got that child, and you don't know him
any better than that?"

"Not very often. Not very long. Just that week here
last fall, and in January he sent for me and we went
west, to New Mexico. We were there six weeks, where
I could at least sleep in the same apartment where I
cooked for him and looked after his clothes——"

"But not marriage," he said. "Not marriage. He didn't
promise you that. Don't lie to me. He didn't have to."

"No. He didn't have to. I didn't ask him to. I knew
what I was doing. I knew that to begin with, long before honor, I imagine he called it, told him the time had
come to tell me in so many words what his code, I suppose he would call it, would forbid him forever to do.
And we agreed. Then we agreed again before he left

New Mexico, to make sure. That that would be all of it.
I believed him. No, I don't mean that; I mean I believed
myself. I wasn't even listening to him any more by then
because by that time it had been a long time since he had
had anything else to tell me for me to have to hear. By
then I wasn't even listening enough to ask him to please
stop talking. I was listening to myself. And I believed
it. I must have believed it. I don't see how I could have
helped but believe it, because he was gone then as we
had agreed and he didn't write as we had agreed, just
the money came to the bank in Vicksburg in my name
but coming from nobody as we had agreed. So I must
have believed it. I even wrote him last month to make
sure again and the letter came back unopened and I was
sure. So I left the hospital and rented myself a room to
live in until the deer season opened so I could make sure
myself and I was waiting beside the road yesterday
when your car passed and he saw me and so I was sure."

"Then what do you want?" he said. "What do you
want? What do you expect?"

"Yes," she said. And while he glared at her, his white
hair awry from the pillow and his eyes, lacking the spectacles to focus them, blurred and irisless and apparently
pupilless, he saw again that grave, intent, speculative
and detached fixity like a child watching him. "His great
great— Wait a minute—great great *great* grandfather
was your grandfather. McCaslin. Only it got to be Edmonds. Only it got to be more than that. Your cousin
McCaslin was there that day when your father and
Uncle Buddy won Tennie from Mr. Beauchamp for the
one that had no name but Terrel so you called him
Tomey's Terrel, to marry. But after that it got to be
Edmonds." She regarded him, almost peacefully, with
that unwinking and heatless fixity—the dark, wide,
bottomless eyes in the face's dead and toneless pallor

which to the old man looked anything but dead, but young and incredibly and even ineradicably alive—as though she were not only not looking at anything, she was not even speaking to anyone but herself. "I would have made a man of him. He's not a man yet. You spoiled him. You, and Uncle Lucas and Aunt Mollie. But mostly you."

"Me?" he said. "Me?"

"Yes. When you gave to his grandfather that land which didn't belong to him, not even half of it, by will or even law."

"And never mind that too," he said. "Never mind that too. You," he said. "You sound like you have been to college even. You sound almost like a Northerner even, not like the draggle-tailed women of these Delta pecker-woods. Yet you meet a man on the street one afternoon just because a box of groceries happened to fall out of a boat. And a month later you go off with him and live with him until he got a child on you: and then, by your own statement, you sat there while he took his hat and said goodbye and walked out. Even a Delta peckerwood would look after even a draggle-tail better ⁺han that. Haven't you got any folks at all?"

"Yes," she said. "I was living with one of them. My aunt, in Vicksburg. I came to live with her two years ago when my father died; we lived in Indianapolis then. But I got a job, teaching school here in Aluschaskuna, because my aunt was a widow, with a big family, taking in washing to sup——"

"Took in what?" he said. "Took in washing?" He sprang, still seated even, flinging himself backward onto one arm, awry-haired, glaring. Now he understood what it was she had brought into the tent with her, what old Isham had already told him by sending the youth to bring her in to him—the pale lips, the skin pallid and

dead-looking yet not ill, the dark and tragic and foreknowing eyes. *Maybe in a thousand or two thousand
years in America,* he thought. *But not now! Not now!*
He cried, not loud, in a voice of amazement, pity, and
outrage: "You're a nigger!"

"Yes," she said. "James Beauchamp—you called him
Tennie's Jim though he had a name—was my grandfather. I said you were Uncle Isaac."

"And he knows?"

"No," she said. "What good would that have done?"

"But you did," he cried. "But you did. Then what do
you expect here?"

"Nothing."

"Then why did you come here? You said you were
waiting in Aluschaskuna yesterday and he saw you.
Why did you come this morning?"

"I'm going back North. Back home. My cousin
brought me up the day before yesterday in his boat.
He's going to take me on to Leland to get the train."

"Then go," he said. Then he cried again in that thin
not loud and grieving voice: "Get out of here! I can do
nothing for you! Can't nobody do nothing for you!" She
moved; she was not looking at him again, toward the
entrance. "Wait," he said. She paused again, obediently
still, turning. He took up the sheaf of banknotes and
laid it on the blanket at the foot of the cot and drew
his hand back beneath the blanket. "There," he said.

Now she looked at the money, for the first time, one
brief blank glance, then away again. "I don't need it.
He gave me money last winter. Besides the money he
sent to Vicksburg. Provided. Honor and code too. That
was all arranged."

"Take it," he said. His voice began to rise again, but
he stopped it. "Take it out of my tent." She came back
to the cot and took up the money; whereupon once

more he said, "Wait:" although she had not turned, still stooping, and he put out his hand. But, sitting, he could not complete the reach until she moved her hand, the single hand which held the money, until he touched it. He didn't grasp it, he merely touched it—the gnarled, bloodless, bone-light, bone-dry old man's fingers touching for a second the smooth young flesh where the strong old blood ran after its long lost journey back to home. "Tennie's Jim," he said. "Tennie's Jim." He drew the hand back beneath the blanket again: he said harshly now: "It's a boy, I reckon. They usually are, except that one that was its own mother too."

"Yes," she said. "It's a boy." She stood for a moment longer, looking at him. Just for an instant her free hand moved as though she were about to lift the edge of the raincoat away from the child's face. But she did not. She turned again when once more he said Wait and moved beneath the blanket.

"Turn your back," he said. "I am going to get up. I ain't got my pants on." Then he could not get up. He sat in the huddled blanket, shaking, while again she turned and looked down at him in dark interrogation. "There," he said harshly, in the thin and shaking old man's voice. "On the nail there. The tent-pole."

"What?" she said.

"The horn!" he said harshly. "The horn." She went and got it, thrust the money into the slicker's side pocket as if it were a rag, a soiled handkerchief, and lifted down the horn, the one which General Compson had left him in his will, covered with the unbroken skin from a buck's shank and bound with silver.

"What?" she said.

"It's his. Take it."

"Oh," she said. "Yes. Thank you."

"Yes," he said, harshly, rapidly, but not so harsh now

and soon not harsh at all but just rapid, urgent, until he
knew that his voice was running away with him and he
had neither intended it nor could stop it: "That's right.
Go back North. Marry: a man in your own race. That's
the only salvation for you—for a while yet, maybe a
long while yet. We will have to wait. Marry a black
man. You are young, handsome, almost white; you could
find a black man who would see in you what it was you
saw in him, who would ask nothing of you and expect
less and get even still less than that, if it's revenge you
want. Then you will forget all this, forget it ever happened, that he ever existed—" until he could stop it at
last and did, sitting there in his huddle of blankets during the instant when, without moving at all, she blazed
silently down at him. Then that was gone too. She
stood in the gleaming and still dripping slicker, looking
quietly down at him from under the sodden hat.

"Old man," she said, "have you lived so long and forgotten so much that you don't remember anything you
ever knew or felt or even heard about love?"

Then she was gone too. The waft of light and the
murmur of the constant rain flowed into the tent and
then out again as the flap fell. Lying back once more,
trembling, panting, the blanket huddled to his chin and
his hands crossed on his breast, he listened to the pop
and snarl, the mounting then fading whine of the motor
until it died away and once again the tent held only
silence and the sound of rain. And cold too: he lay
shaking faintly and steadily in it, rigid save for the
shaking. This Delta, he thought: This Delta. *This land
which man has deswamped and denuded and derivered
in two generations so that white men can own plantations and commute every night to Memphis and black
men own plantations and ride in Jim Crow cars to
Chicago to live in millionaires' mansions on Lake Shore*

Drive; where white men rent farms and live like nig-
gers and niggers crop on shares and live like animals;
where cotton is planted and grows man-tall in the very
cracks of the sidewalks, and usuary and mortgage and
bankruptcy and measureless wealth, Chinese and Afri-
can and Aryan and Jew, all breed and spawn together
until no man has time to say which one is which nor
cares. . . . No wonder the ruined woods I used to
know don't cry for retribution! he thought: *The people*
who have destroyed it will accomplish its revenge.

The tent flap jerked rapidly in and fell. He did not
move save to turn his head and open his eyes. It was
Legate. He went quickly to Edmonds' bed and stooped,
rummaging hurriedly among the still-tumbled blankets.

"What is it?" he said.

"Looking for Roth's knife," Legate said. "I come back
to get a horse. We got a deer on the ground." He rose,
the knife in his hand, and hurried toward the entrance.

"Who killed it?" McCaslin said. "Was it Roth?"

"Yes," Legate said, raising the flap.

"Wait," McCaslin said. He moved, suddenly, onto his
elbow. "What was it?" Legate paused for an instant
beneath the lifted flap. He did not look back.

"Just a deer, Uncle Ike," he said impatiently. "Nothing extra." He was gone; again the flap fell behind him,
wafting out of the tent again the faint light and the
constant and grieving rain. McCaslin lay back down,
the blanket once more drawn to his chin, his crossed
hands once more weightless on his breast in the empty
tent.

"It was a doe," he said.

Appendix

1699-1945   THE COMPSONS

IKKEMOTUBBE. A dispossessed American king. Called *l'Homme* (and sometimes *de l'Homme*) by his fosterbrother, a Chevalier of France, who, had he not been born too late, could have been among the brightest in that glittering galaxy of knightly blackguards who were Napoleon's marshals, who thus translated the Chickasaw title meaning "The Man"; which translation Ikkemotubbe, himself a man of wit and imagination as well as a shrewd judge of character, including his own, carried one step further and anglicized it to "Doom." Who granted out of his vast lost domain a solid square mile of virgin north Mississippi dirt as truely angled as the four corners of a cardtable top (forested then because these were the old days before 1833 when the stars fell and Jefferson, Mississippi, was one long rambling one-storey mudchinked log building housing the Chickasaw Agent and his trading-post store) to the grandson of a Scottish refugee who had lost his own birthright by casting his lot with a king who himself had been dispossessed. This in partial return for the right to proceed in peace, by whatever means he and his people saw fit, afoot or ahorse provided they were Chickasaw horses, to the wild western land presently to be called Oklahoma: not knowing then about the oil.

JACKSON. A Great White Father with a sword. (An old duellist, a brawling lean fierce mangy durable imperishable old lion who set the well-being of the nation above the White House, and the health of his new political party above either, and above them all set, not his wife's honor, but the principle that honor must be defended whether it was or not because defended it was whether or not.) Who patented, sealed, and countersigned the grant with his own hand in his gold tepee in Wassi Town, not knowing about the oil either: so that one day the homeless descendants of the dispossessed would ride supine with drink and splendidly comatose above the dusty allotted harborage of their bones in specially built scarlet-painted hearses and fire-engines.

These were Compsons:

QUENTIN MacLACHAN. Son of a Glasgow printer, orphaned and raised by his mother's people in the Perth highlands. Fled to Carolina from Culloden Moor with a claymore and the tartan he wore by day and slept under by night, and little else. At eighty, having fought once against an English king and lost, he would not make that mistake twice and so fled again one night in 1779, with his infant grandson and the tartan (the claymore had vanished, along with his son, the grandson's father, from one of Tarleton's regiments on a Georgia battlefield about a year ago) into Kentucky, where a neighbor named Boon or Boone had already established a settlement.

CHARLES STUART. Attainted and proscribed by name and grade in his British regiment. Left for dead in a Georgia swamp by his own retreating army and then by the advancing American one, both of which were wrong. He still had the claymore even when on his homemade wooden leg he finally overtook his father and son four years later at Harrodsburg, Kentucky, just in time to bury the father and enter upon a long period of being a split personality while still trying to be the schoolteacher which he believed he wanted to be, until he gave up at last and became the gambler he actually was and which no Compson seemed to realize they all were, provided the gambit was desperate and the odds long enough. Succeeded at last in risking not only his neck but the security of his family and the very integrity of the name he would leave behind him, by joining the confederation headed by an acquaintance named Wilkinson (a man of considerable talent and influence and intellect and power) in a plot to secede the whole Mississippi Valley from the United States and join it to Spain. Fled in his turn when the bubble burst (as anyone except a Compson schoolteacher should have known it would), himself unique in being the only one of the plotters who had to flee the country: this not from the vengeance and retribution of the government which he had attempted to dismember, but from the furious revulsion of his late confederates now frantic for their own safety. He was not expelled from the United States; he talked himself countryless, his expulsion due not to the treason but to his having been so vocal and vociferant in the conduct of it, burning each bridge vocally behind him before he had even reached the place to build the next one: so that it was no provost marshal nor even a civic agency but his late co-plotters themselves who put afoot the movement to evict him from Kentucky and the United States and, if they had caught him, probably from the world too. Fled by night, running true to family tradition, with his son and the old claymore and the tartan.

JASON LYCURGUS. Who, driven perhaps by the compulsion of the flamboyant name given him by the sardonic embittered woodenlegged indomitable father
who perhaps still believed with his heart that what he
wanted to be was a classicist schoolteacher, rode up the
Natchez Trace one day in 1820 with a pair of fine
pistols and one meagre saddlebag on a small light-
waisted but stronghocked mare which could do the first
two furlongs in definitely under the halfminute and the
next two in not appreciably more, though that was all.
But it was enough: who reached the Chickasaw Agency
at Okatoba (which in 1860 was still called Old Jefferson) and went no further. Who within six months was
the Agent's clerk and within twelve his partner, of-
ficially still the clerk though actually halfowner of
what was now a considerable store stocked with the
mare's winnings in races against the horses of Ikkemotubbe's young men which he, Compson, was always
careful to limit to a quarter or at most three furlongs;
and in the next year it was Ikkemotubbe who owned
the little mare and Compson owned the solid square
mile of land which some day would be almost in the
center of the town of Jefferson, forested then and still
forested twenty years later, though rather a park than
a forest by that time, with is slave quarters and stables
and kitchen gardens and the formal lawns and promenades and pavilions laid out by the same architect who
built the columned porticoed house furnished by steamboat from France and New Orleans, and still the square
intact mile in 1840 (with not only the little white village called Jefferson beginning to enclose it but an
entire white county about to surround it, because in a
few years now Ikkemotubbe's descendants and people
would be gone, those remaining living not as warriors

and hunters but as white men—as shiftless farmers or, here and there, the masters of what they too called plantations and the owners of shiftless slaves, a little dirtier than the white man, a little lazier, a little crueller —until at last even the wild blood itself would have vanished, to be seen only occasionally in the nose-shape of a Negro on a cottonwagon or a white sawmill hand or trapper or locomotive fireman); known as the Compson Domain then, since now it was fit to breed princes, statesmen and generals and bishops, to avenge the dispossessed Compsons from Culloden and Carolina and Kentucky; then known as the Governor's house because sure enough in time it did produce or at least spawn a governor—Quentin MacLachan again, after the Culloden grandfather—and still known as the Old Governor's even after it had spawned (1861) a general—(called so by predetermined accord and agreement by the whole town and county, as though they knew even then and beforehand that the old governor was the last Compson who would not fail at everything he touched save longevity or suicide)—the Brigadier Jason Lycurgus II who failed at Shiloh in '62 and failed again, though not so badly, at Resaca in '64, who put the first mortgage on the still intact square mile to a New England carpetbagger in '66, after the old town had been burned by the Federal General Smith and the new little town, in time to be populated mainly by the descendants not of Compsons but of Snopeses, had begun to encroach and then nibble at and into it as the failed brigadier spent the next forty years selling fragments of it off to keep up the mortgage on the remainder: until one day in 1900 he died quietly on an army cot in the hunting and fishing camp in the Tallahatchie River bottom where he passed most of the end of his days.

And even the old governor was forgotten now; what was left of the old square mile was now known merely as the Compson place—the weedchoked traces of the old ruined lawns and promenades, the house which had needed painting too long already, the scaling columns of the portico where Jason III (bred for a lawyer, and indeed he kept an office upstairs above the Square, where entombed in dusty filingcases some of the oldest names in the county—Holston and Sutpen, Grenier and Beauchamp and Coldfield—faded year by year among the bottomless labyrinths of chancery: and who knows what dream in the perennial heart of his father, now completing the third of his three avatars—the one as son of a brilliant and gallant statesman, the second as battleleader of brave and gallant men, the third as a sort of privileged pseudo Daniel Boone-Robinson Crusoe, who had not returned to juvenility because actually he had never left it—that that lawyer's office might again be the anteroom to the governor's mansion and the old splendor) sat all day long with a decanter of whiskey and a litter of dogeared Horaces and Livys and Catulluses, composing (it was said) caustic and satiric eulogies on both his dead and his living fellowtownsmen, who sold the last of the property, except that fragment containing the house and the kitchengarden and the collapsing stables and one servant's cabin in which Dilsey's family lived, to a golfclub for the ready money with which his daughter Candace could have her fine wedding in April and his son Quentin could finish one year at Harvard and commit suicide in the following June of 1910; already known as the Old Compson place even while Compsons were still living in it on that spring dusk in 1928 when the old governor's doomed lost nameless seventeen-year-old great-greatgranddaughter robbed her last remaining sane male relative (her uncle Jason IV) of his secret hoard of money and climbed down a pear tree and ran off with a pitchman in a travelling streetshow, and still known as the Old Compson place long after all traces of Compsons were gone from it: after the widowed mother died and Jason IV, no longer needing to fear Dilsey now, committed his idiot brother, Benjamin, to the State Asylum in Jackson and sold the house to a countryman who operated it as a boarding house for juries and horse- and muletraders; and still known as the Old Compson place even after the boardinghouse (and presently the golfcourse too) had vanished and the old square mile was even intact again in row after row of small crowded jerrybuilt individuallyowned demiurban bungalows.

And these:

QUENTIN III. Who loved not his sister's body but some concept of Compson honor precariously and (he knew well) only temporarily supported by the minute fragile membrane of her maidenhead as a miniature replica of all the whole vast globy earth may be poised on the nose of a trained seal. Who loved not the idea of the incest which he would not commit, but some presbyterian concept of its eternal punishment: he, not God, could by that means cast himself and his sister both into hell, where he could guard her forever and keep her forevermore intact amid the eternal fires. But who loved death above all, who loved only death, loved and lived in a deliberate and almost perverted anticipation of death, as a lover loves and deliberately refrains from the waiting willing friendly tender incredible body of his beloved, until he can no longer bear not the refraining but the restraint, and so flings, hurls himself, relinquishing, drowning. Committed suicide in Cambridge Massachusetts, June 1910, two months after his sister's wedding, waiting first to complete the current academic year and so get the full value of his paid-in-advance tuition, not because he had his old Culloden and Carolina and Kentucky grandfathers in him but because the remaining piece of the old Compson mile which had been sold to pay for his sister's wedding and his year at Harvard had been the one thing, excepting that same sister and the sight of an open fire, which his youngest brother, born an idiot, had loved.

CANDACE (CADDY). Doomed and knew it; accepted the doom without either seeking or fleeing it. Loved her brother despite him, loved not only him but loved in him that bitter prophet and inflexible corruptless judge of what he considered the family's honor and its doom, as he thought he loved, but really hated, in her what he considered the frail doomed vessel of its pride and the foul instrument of its disgrace; not only this, she loved him not only in spite of but because of the fact that he himself was incapable of love, accepting the fact that he must value above all not her but the virginity of which she was custodian and on which she placed no value whatever: the frail physical stricture which to her was no more than a hangnail would have been. Knew the brother loved death best of all and was not jealous, would have handed him (and perhaps in the calculation and deliberation of her marriage did hand him) the hypothetical hemlock. Was two months pregnant with another man's child, which regardless of what its sex would be she had already named Quentin after the brother whom they both (she and the brother) knew was already the same as dead, when she married (1910) an extremely eligible young Indianian she and her mother had met while vacationing at French Lick

the summer before. Divorced by him 1911. Married
1920 to a minor movingpicture magnate, Hollywood,
California. Divorced by mutual agreement, Mexico
1925. Vanished in Paris with the German occupation,
1940, still beautiful, and probably still wealthy too,
since she did not look within fifteen years of her actual
forty-eight, and was not heard of again. Except there
was a woman in Jefferson, the county librarian, a mouse-
sized and -colored woman who had never married, who
had passed through the city schools in the same class
with Candace Compson and then spent the rest of her
life trying to keep *Forever Amber,* in its orderly over-
lapping avatars, and *Jurgen* and *Tom Jones* out of the
hands of the highschool juniors and seniors who could
reach them down, without even having to tiptoe, from
the back shelves where she herself would have to stand
on a box to hide them. One day in 1943, after a week
of a distraction bordering on disintegration almost, during which those entering the library would find her
always in the act of hurriedly closing her desk drawer
and turning the key in it (so that the matrons, wives
of the bankers and doctors and lawyers, some of whom
had also been in that old highschool class, who came
and went in the afternoons with the copies of the
Forever Ambers and the volumes of Thorne Smith carefully wrapped from view in sheets of Memphis and
Jackson newspapers, believed she was on the verge of
illness or perhaps even loss of mind), she closed and
locked the library in the middle of the afternoon and
with her handbag clasped tightly under her arm and
two feverish spots of determination in her ordinarily
colorless cheeks, she entered the farmers' supply store
where Jason IV had started as a clerk and where he
now owned his own business as a buyer of and dealer
in cotton, striding on through that gloomy cavern which

only men ever entered—a cavern cluttered and walled and stalagmite-hung with plows and discs and loops of tracechain and singletrees and mulecollars and side-meat and cheap shoes and horse linament and flour and molasses, gloomy because the goods it contained were not shown but hidden rather since those who supplied Mississippi farmers, or at least Negro Mississippi farmers, for a share of the crop did not wish, until that crop was made and its value approximately computable, to show them what they could learn to want, but only to supply them on specific demand with what they could not help but need—and strode on back to Jason's particular domain in the rear: a railed enclosure cluttered with shelves and pigeonholes bearing spiked dust-and-lint-gathering gin receipts and ledgers and cotton samples and rank with the blended smell of cheese and kerosene and harness oil and the tremendous iron stove against which chewed tobacco had been spat for almost a hundred years, and up to the long high sloping counter behind which Jason stood, and, not looking again at the overalled men who had quietly stopped talking and even chewing when she entered, with a kind of fainting desperation she opened the handbag and fumbled something out of it and laid it open on the counter and stood trembling and breathing rapidly while Jason looked down at it—a picture, a photograph in color clipped obviously from a slick magazine—a picture filled with luxury and money and sunlight—a Riviera backdrop of mountains and palms and cypresses and the sea, an open powerful expensive chromium-trimmed sports car, the woman's face hatless between a rich scarf and a seal coat, ageless and beautiful, cold serene and damned; beside her a handsome lean man of middleage in the ribbons and tabs of a German staff-general—and the mouse-sized mouse-colored spinster trembling and aghast at her own temerity, staring across it at the childless bachelor in whom ended that long line of men who had had something in them of decency and pride, even after they had begun to fail at the integrity and the pride had become mostly vanity and selfpity: from the expatriate who had to flee his native land with little else except his life, yet who still refused to accept defeat, through the man who gambled his life and his good name twice and lost twice and declined to accept that either, and the one who with only a clever small quarterhorse for tool avenged his dispossessed father and grandfather and gained a principality, and the brilliant and gallant governor, and the general who, though he failed at leading in battle brave and gallant men, at least risked his own life too in the failing, to the cultured dipsomaniac who sold the last of his patrimony, not to buy drink but to give one of his descendants at least the best chance in life he could think of.

"It's Caddy!" the librarian whispered. "We must save her!"

"It's Cad, all right," Jason said. Then he began to laugh. He stood there laughing above the picture, above the cold beautiful face now creased and dogeared from its week's sojourn in the desk drawer and the handbag. And the librarian knew why he was laughing, who had not called him anything but Mr. Compson for thirty-two years now, ever since the day in 1911 when Candace, cast off by her husband, had brought her infant daughter home and left the child and departed by the next train, to return no more, and not only the Negro cook, Dilsey, but the librarian too, divined by simple instinct that Jason was somehow using the child's life and its illegitimacy to blackmail the mother not only into staying away from Jefferson for the rest of her life, but into appointing him sole unchallengeable trustee of the money she would send for the child's maintenance, and had refused to speak to him at all since that day in 1928 when the daughter climbed down the pear tree and ran away with the pitchman.

"Jason!" she cried. "We must save her! Jason! Jason!"—and still crying it even when he took up the picture between thumb and finger and threw it back across the counter toward her.

"That Candace?" he said. "Don't make me laugh. This bitch ain't thirty yet. The other one's fifty now."

And the library was still locked all the next day too when at three o'clock in the afternoon, footsore and spent yet still unflagging and still clasping the handbag tightly under her arm, she turned into a neat small yard in the Negro residence section of Memphis and mounted the steps of the neat small house and rang the bell and the door opened and a black woman of about her own age looked quietly out at her. "It's Frony, isn't it?" the librarian said. "Don't you remember me—Melissa Meek, from Jefferson—"

"Yes," the Negress said. "Come in. You want to see Mama." And she entered the room, the neat yet cluttered bedroom of an old Negro, rank with the smell of old people, old women, old Negroes, where the old woman herself sat in a rocker beside the hearth where even though it was June a fire smoldered—a big woman once, in faded clean calico and an immaculate turban wound round her head above the bleared and now apparently almost sightless eyes—and put the dogeared clipping into the black hands which, like those of the women of her race, were still as supple and delicately shaped as they had been when she was thirty or twenty or even seventeen.

"It's Caddy!" the librarian said. "It is! Dilsey! Dilsey!"

"What did he say?" the old Negress said. And the librarian knew whom she meant by "he"; nor did the librarian marvel, not only that the old Negress would know that she (the librarian) would know whom she meant by the "he," but that the old Negress would know at once that she had already shown the picture to Jason.

"Don't you know what he said?" she cried. "When he realized she was in danger, he said it was her, even if I hadn't even had a picture to show him. But as soon as he realized that somebody, anybody, even just me, wanted to save her, would try to save her, he said it wasn't. But it is! Look at it!"

"Look at my eyes," the old Negress said. "How can I see that picture?"

"Call Frony!" the librarian cried. "She will know her!" But already the old Negress was folding the clipping carefully back into its old creases, handing it back.

"My eyes ain't any good any more," she said. "I can't see it."

And that was all. At six o'clock she fought her way through the crowded bus terminal, the bag clutched under one arm and the return half of her roundtrip ticket in the other hand, and was swept out onto the roaring platform on the diurnal tide of a few middle-aged civilians, but mostly soldiers and sailors enroute either to leave or to death, and the homeless young women, their companions, who for two years now had lived from day to day in pullmans and hotels when they were lucky, and in daycoaches and busses and stations and lobbies and public restrooms when not, pausing only long enough to drop their foals in charity wards or policestations and then move on again, and fought her way into the bus, smaller than any other there so that her feet touched the floor only occasionally, until a shape (a man in khaki; she couldn't see him at all because she was already crying) rose and picked her up bodily and set her into a seat next the window, where still crying quietly she could look out upon the fleeing city as it streaked past and then was behind, and presently now she would be home again, safe in Jefferson, where life lived too with all its incomprehensible passion and turmoil and grief and fury and despair, but there at six o'clock you could close the covers on it and even the weightless hand of a child could put it back among its unfeatured kindred on the quiet eternal shelves and turn the key upon it for the whole and dreamless night. *Yes* she thought, crying quietly, *that was it; she didn't want to see it know whether it was Caddy or not because she knows Caddy doesn't want to be saved hasn't anything any more worth being saved for nothing worth being lost that she can lose.*

JASON IV. The first sane Compson since before Culloden and (a childless bachelor) hence the last. Logical, rational, contained and even a philosopher in the old stoic tradition: thinking nothing whatever of God one way or the other, and simply considering the police and so fearing and respecting only the Negro woman who cooked the food he ate, his sworn enemy since his birth and his mortal one since that day in 1911 when she too divined by simple clairvoyance that he was somehow using his infant niece's illegitimacy to blackmail her mother. Who not only fended off and held his own with Compsons, but competed and held his own with the Snopeses, who took over the little town following the turn of the century as the Compsons and Sartorises and their ilk faded from it (no Snopes, but Jason Compson himself, who as soon as his mother died—the niece had already climbed down the pear tree and

vanished, so Dilsey no longer had either of these clubs
to hold over him—committed his idiot younger brother
to the state and vacated the old house, first chopping
up the vast once splendid rooms into what he called
apartments and selling the whole thing to a countryman
who opened a boardinghouse in it), though this was
not difficult since to him all the rest of the town and the
world and the human race too except himself were
Compsons, inexplicable yet quite predictable in that
they were in no sense whatever to be trusted. Who, all
the money from the sale of the pasture having gone for
his sister's wedding and his brother's course at Harvard,
used his own niggard savings out of his meagre wages
as a storeclerk to send himself to a Memphis school
where he learned to class and grade cotton, and so
established his own business, with which, following his
dipsomaniac father's death, he assumed the entire burden of the rotting family in the rotting house, supporting his idiot brother because of their mother, sacri-
ficing what pleasures might have been the right and
just due and even the necessity of a thirty-year-old
bachelor, so that his mother's life might continue as
nearly as possible to what it had been; this not because
he loved her but (a sane man always) simply because
he was afraid of the Negro cook whom he could not
even force to leave, even when he tried to stop paying
her weekly wages; and who despite all this, still managed to save $2840.50 (three thousand, as he reported
it on the night his niece stole it) in niggard and agon-
ized dimes and quarters and halfdollars, which hoard
he kept in no bank because to him a banker too was
just one more Compson, but hid in a locked steel box
beneath a sawn plank in the floor of his locked clothes
closet in the bedroom whose bed he made each morning himself, since he kept the room's door locked all

the time save for a half hour each Sunday morning
when, himself present and watching, he permitted his
mother and Dilsey to come in long enough to change
the bedlinen and sweep the floor. Who, following a
fumbling abortive attempt by his idiot brother on a
passing female child, had himself appointed the idiot's
guardian without letting their mother know and so was
able to have the creature castrated before the mother
even knew it was out of the house, and who following
the mother's death in 1933 was able to free himself
forever not only from the idiot brother and the house
but from the Negro woman too, moving into a pair of
offices up a flight of stairs above the supplystore containing his cotton ledgers and samples, which he had
converted into a bedroom-kitchen-bath, in and out of
which on weekends there would be seen a big, plain,
friendly, brazenhaired pleasantfaced woman no longer
very young, in round picture hats and in its season an
imitation fur coat, the two of them, the middleaged
cottonbuyer and the woman whom the town called,
simply, his friend from Memphis, seen at the local picture show on Saturday night and on Sunday morning
mounting the apartment stairs with paper bags from
the grocer's containing loaves and eggs and oranges
and cans of soup, domestic, uxorious, connubial, until
the late afternoon bus carried her back to Memphis.
He was emancipated now. He was free. "In 1865," he
would say, "Abe Lincoln freed the niggers from the
Compsons. In 1933, Jason Compson freed the Compsons from the niggers."

BENJAMIN. Born Maury, after his mother's only
brother: a handsome flashing swaggering workless
bachelor who borrowed money from almost anyone,
even Dilsey although she was a Negro, explaining to

her as he withdrew his hand from his pocket that she was not only in his eyes the same as a member of his sister's family, she would be considered a born lady anywhere in any eyes. Who, when at last even his mother realized what he was and insisted weeping that his name must be changed, was rechristened Benjamin by his brother Quentin (Benjamin, our lastborn, sold into Egypt). Who loved three things: the pasture which was sold to pay for Candace's wedding and to send Quentin to Harvard, his sister Candace, firelight. Who lost none of them, because he could not remember his sister but only the loss of her, and firelight was the same bright shape as going to sleep, and the pasture was even better sold than before, because now he and Luster could not only follow timeless along the fence the motions which it did not even matter to him were human beings swinging golfsticks, Luster could lead them to clumps of grass or weeds where there would appear suddenly in Luster's hand, small white spherules which competed with and even conquered what he did not even know was gravity and all the immutable laws, when released from the hand toward plank floor of smokehouse wall or concrete sidewalk. Gelded 1913. Committed to the State Asylum, Jackson, 1933. Lost nothing then either because, as with his sister, he remembered not the pasture but only its loss, and firelight was still the same bright shape of sleep.

QUENTIN. The last. Candace's daughter. Fatherless nine months before her birth, nameless at birth and already doomed to be unwed from the instant the dividing egg determined its sex. Who at seventeen, on the one thousand eight hundred ninetyfifth anniversary of the day before the resurrection of Our Lord, swung herself by a rainpipe from her window to the locked window of her uncle's locked and empty bedroom and broke a pane and entered the window, and with the uncle's firepoker ripped off the locked hasp and staple of the closet door and prized up the sawn plank and got the steel box (and they never did know how she had broken the lock on it, how a seventeen-year-old girl could have broken that lock with anything, let alone a poker) and rifled it (and it was not $2840.50 or three thousand dollars either, it was almost seven thousand. And this was Jason's rage, the red unbearable fury which on that night and at intervals recurring with little or no diminishment for the next five years, made him seriously believe it would at some unwarned instant destroy him, kill him as instantaneously dead as a bullet or a lightningbolt: that although he had been robbed not of a mere petty three but of almost seven, he couldn't even report it; he could not only never receive justification— he did not want sympathy—from other men unlucky enough to have one bitch for a sister and another for a niece, he couldn't even demand help in recovering it. Because he had lost four thousand dollars which did not belong to him he couldn't even recover the three thousand which did, since those first four thousand dollars were not only the legal property of his niece as a part of the money supplied for her support and maintenance by her mother over the last sixteen years, they did not exist at all, having been officially recorded as expended and consumed in the annual reports he submitted to the district Chancellor, as required of him as guardian and trustee by his bondsmen: so that he had been robbed not only of his thievings but his savings too, and by his own victim; he had been robbed not only of the four thousand dollars which he had risked jail to acquire, but of the three thousand which he had hoarded at the price of sacrifice and denial, almost a nickel and a dime at a time, over a period of almost twenty years: and this not only by his own victim but by a child who did it at one blow, without premeditation or plan, not even knowing or even caring how much she would find when she broke the drawer open; and now he couldn't even go to the police for help: he who had considered the police always, never given them any trouble, had paid the taxes for years which supported them in parasitic and sadistic idleness; not only that, he didn't dare pursue the girl himself because he might catch her and she would talk, so that his only recourse was a vain dream which kept him tossing and sweating on nights two and three and even four years after the event, when he should have forgotten about it: of catching her without warning, springing on her out of the dark, before she had spent all the money, and murdering her before she had time to open her mouth) and climbed down the pear tree in the dusk and ran away with the pitchman who was already under sentence for bigamy. And so vanished; whatever occupation overtook her would have arrived in no chromium Mercedes; whatever snapshot would have contained no general of staff.

And that was all. These others were not Compsons. They were black:

TP. Who wore on Memphis' Beal Street the fine bright cheap intransigent clothes manufactured specifically for him by the owners of Chicago and New York sweatshops.

FRONY. Who married a pullman porter and went to Saint Louis to live and later moved back to Memphis to make a home for her mother since Dilsey refused to go further than that.

LUSTER. A man, aged 14. Who was not only capable
of the complete care and security of an idiot twice his
age and three times his size, but could keep him entertained.

DILSEY.

They endured.